The Complete Dr. Thorndyke

Volume VII:

Pontifex, Son, and Thorndyke
When Rogues Fall Out
Dr. Thorndyke Intervenes

The Complete Dr. Thorndyke

Volume VII:

Pontifex, Son, and Thorndyke
When Rogues Fall Out
Dr. Thorndyke Intervenes

by

R. Austin Freeman

Edited by
David Marcum

ISBN Hardback 978-1-78705-681-7
ISBN Paperback 978-1-78705-682-4
AUK ePub ISBN 978-1-78705-683-1
AUK PDF ISBN 978-1-78705-684-8

These works are in the Public Domain in Great Britain
Portrait of Dr. Thorndyke by H.M. Brock (1908)

Published in the UK by
MX Publishing
335 Princess Park Manor, Royal Drive,
London, N11 3GX
www.mxpublishing.co.uk

David Marcum can be reached at:
thepapersofsherlockholmes@gmail.com

Cover design by Brian Belanger
www.belangerbooks.com and *www.redbubble.com/people/zhahadun*

CONTENTS

Introductions

Adventures

Pontifex, Son, and Thorndyke

When Rogues Fall Out

Book I – *The Three Rogues*

Book II – *Inspector Badger, Deceased*

Book III – *The Three Rogues*

Dr. Thorndyke Intervenes

The
Complete
Dr. Thorndyke

Volume VII:

Pontifex, Son, and Thorndyke
When Rogues Fall Out
Dr. Thorndyke Intervenes

Dr. John Thorndyke

5A King's Bench Walk
in the late 1890's when
Thorndyke would have moved in

5A King's Bench Walk
Photographed by the Editor
during his
Sherlock Holmes Pilgrimage No. 3
(September 8th, 2016)

Meet Dr. Thorndyke
by R. Austin Freeman

My subject is Dr. John Thorndyke, the hero or central character of most of my detective stories. So I'll give you a short account of his real origin – of the way in which he did in fact come into existence.

To discover the origin of John Thorndyke I have to reach back into the past for at least fifty years, to the time when I was a medical student preparing for my final examination. For reasons which I need not go into I gave rather special attention to the legal aspects of medicine and the medical aspects of law. And as I read my text-books, and especially the illustrative cases, I was profoundly impressed by their dramatic quality. Medical jurisprudence deals with the human body in its relation to all kinds of legal problems. Thus its subject matter includes all sorts of crime against the person and all sorts of violent death and bodily injury: Hanging, drowning, poisons and their effects, problems of suicide and homicide, of personal identity and survivorship, and a host of other problems of the highest dramatic possibilities, though not always quite presentable for the purposes of fiction. And the reported cases which were given in illustration were often crime stories of the most thrilling interest. Cases of disputed identity such as the Tichbourne Case, famous poisoning cases such as the Rugeley Case and that of Madeline Smith, cases of mysterious disappearance or the detection of long-forgotten crimes such as that of Eugene Aram. All these, described and analysed with strict scientific accuracy, formed the matter of Medical Jurisprudence which thrilled me as I read and made an indelible impression.

But it produced no immediate results. I had to pass my examinations and get my diploma, and then look out for the means of earning my living. So all this curious lore was put away for the time being in the pigeon-holes of my mind – which Dr. Freud would call the *Unconscious* – not forgotten, but ready to come to the surface when the need for it should arise. And there it reposed for some twenty years, until failing health compelled me to abandon medical practice and take to literature as a profession.

It was then that my old studies recurred to my mind. A fellow doctor, Conan Doyle, had made a brilliant and well-deserved success by the creation of the immortal Sherlock Holmes. Considering that achievement, I asked myself whether it might not be possible to devise a detective story of a slightly different kind – one based on the science of Medical Jurisprudence, in which, by the sacrifice of a certain amount of dramatic effect, one could keep entirely within the facts of real life, with nothing fictitious excepting the persons and the events. I came to the conclusion that it was, and began to turn the idea over in my mind.

But I think that the influence which finally determined the character of my detective stories, and incidentally the character of John Thorndyke, operated when I was working at the Westminster Ophthalmic Hospital. There I used to take the patients into the dark room, examine their eyes with the ophthalmoscope, estimate the errors of refraction, and construct an experimental pair of spectacles to correct those errors. When a perfect correction had been arrived at, the formula for it was embodied in a prescription which was sent to the optician who made the permanent spectacles.

Now when I was writing those prescriptions it was borne in on me that in many cases, especially the more complex, the formula for the spectacles, and consequently the spectacles themselves, furnished an infallible record of personal identity. If, for instance, such a pair of spectacles should have been found in a railway carriage, and the maker of those spectacles could be found, there would be practically conclusive evidence that a particular person had travelled by that train. About that time I drafted out a story based on a pair of spectacles, which was published some years later under the title of *The Mystery of 31 New Inn*, and the construction of that story determined, as I have said, not only the general character of my future work but of the hero around whom the plots were to be woven. But that story remained for some years in cold storage. My first published detective novel was *The Red Thumb-mark*, and in that book we may consider that John Thorndyke was born. And in passing on to describe him I may as well explain how and why he came to be the kind of person that he is.

I may begin by saying that he was not modelled after any real person. He was deliberately created to play a certain part, and the idea that was in my mind was that he should be such a person as would be likely and suitable to occupy such a position in real life. As he was to be a medico-legal expert, he had to be a doctor and a fully trained lawyer. On the physical side I endowed him with every kind of natural advantage. He is exceptionally tall, strong, and athletic because those qualities are useful in his vocation. For the same reason he has acute eyesight and hearing and considerable general manual skill, as every doctor ought to have. In appearance he is handsome and of an imposing presence, with a symmetrical face of the classical type and a Grecian nose. And here I may remark that his distinguished appearance is not merely a concession to my personal taste but is also a protest against the monsters of ugliness whom some detective writers have evolved.

These are quite opposed to natural truth. In real life a first-class man of any kind usually tends to be a good-looking man.

Mentally, Thorndyke is quite normal. He has no gifts of intuition or other supernormal mental qualities. He is just a highly intellectual man of great and varied knowledge with exceptionally acute reasoning powers and endowed with that invaluable asset, a scientific imagination (by a scientific imagination I mean that special faculty which marks the born investigator, the capacity to perceive the essential nature of a problem before the detailed evidence comes into sight). But he arrives at his conclusions by ordinary reasoning, which the reader can follow when he has been supplied with the facts, though the intricacy of the train of reasoning may at times call for an exposition at the end of the investigation.

Thorndyke has no eccentricities or oddities which might detract from the dignity of an eminent professional man, unless one excepts an unnatural liking for Trichinopoly cheroots. In manner he is quiet, reserved and self-contained, and rather markedly secretive, but of a kindly nature, though not sentimental, and addicted to occasional touches of dry humour. That is how Thorndyke appears to me.

As to his age. When he made his first bow to the reading public from the doorway of Number 4 King's Bench Walk he was between thirty-five and forty. As that was thirty years ago, he should now be over sixty-five. But he isn't. If I have to let him *"grow old along with me"* I need not saddle him with the infirmities of age, and I can (in his case) put the brake on the passing years. Probably he is not more than fifty after all!

Now a few words as to how Thorndyke goes to work. His methods are rather different from those of the detectives of the Sherlock Holmes school. They are more technical and more specialized. He is an investigator of crime but he is not a detective. The technique of Scotland Yard would be neither suitable nor possible to him. He is a medico-legal expert, and his methods are those of medico-legal science. In the investigation of a crime there are two entirely different methods of approach. One consists in the careful and laborious examination of a vast mass of small and commonplace detail: Inquiring into the movements of suspected and other persons, interrogating witnesses and checking their statements particularly as to times and places, tracing missing persons, and so forth – the aim being to accumulate a great body of circumstantial evidence which will ultimately disclose the solution of the problem. It is an admirable method, as the success of our police proves, and it is used

3

with brilliant effect by at least one of our contemporary detective writers. But it is essentially a police method.

The other method consists in the search for some fact of high evidential value which can be demonstrated by physical methods and which constitutes conclusive proof of some important point. This method also is used by the police in suitable cases. Finger-prints are examples of this kind of evidence, and another instance is furnished by the Gutteridge murder. Here the microscopical examination of a cartridge-case proved conclusively that the murder had been committed with a particular revolver, a fact which incriminated the owner of that revolver and led to his conviction.

This is Thorndyke's procedure. It consists in the interrogation of things rather than persons, of the ascertainment of physical facts which can be made visible to eyes other than his own. And the facts which he seeks tend to be those which are apparent only to the trained eye of the medical practitioner.

I feel that I ought to say a few words about Thorndyke's two satellites, Jervis and Polton. As to the former, he is just the traditional narrator proper to this type of story. Some of my readers have complained that Dr. Jervis is rather slow in the uptake. But that is precisely his function. He is the expert misunderstander. His job is to observe and record all the facts, and to fail completely to perceive their significance. Thereby he gives the reader all the necessary information, and he affords Thorndyke the opportunity to expound its bearing on the case.

Polton is in a slightly different category. Although he is not drawn from any real person, he is associated in my mind with two actual individuals. One is a Mr. Pollard, who was the laboratory assistant in the hospital museum when I was a student, and who gave me many a valuable tip in matters of technique, and who, I hope, is still to the good. The other was a watch- and clock-maker of the name of Parsons – familiarly known as Uncle Parsons – who had premises in a basement near the Royal Exchange, and who was a man of boundless ingenuity and technical resource. Both of these I regard as collateral relatives, so to speak, of Nathaniel Polton. But his personality is not like either. His crinkly countenance is strictly his own copyright.

To return to Thorndyke, his rather technical methods have, for the purposes of fiction, advantages and disadvantages. The advantage is that his facts are demonstrably true, and often they are intrinsically interesting. The disadvantage is that they are frequently not matters of common knowledge, so that the reader may fail to recognize them or grasp their significance until they are explained. But this is the case with

4

all classes of fiction. There is no type of character or story that can be made sympathetic and acceptable to every kind of reader. The personal equation affects the reading as well as the writing of a story.

R. Austin Freeman
(1862-1943)

5A King's Bench Walk
in the early 1900's when
Thorndyke was in practice

Dr. Thorndyke: In the Footsteps
of Sherlock Holmes
by David Marcum

When Sherlock Holmes began his practice as a "Consulting Detective", his ideas of scientific criminal investigations caused the London police to look upon him as a mere "theorist". He was perceived as an amateur to be tolerated, often with amusement – until, that is, his assistance was required. Then they were more than willing to come knocking upon his door, asking for whatever help that they could receive. And usually this help took the form of brilliant solutions to bizarre and otherwise insoluble problems.

Holmes espoused methods and ideas that were considered ludicrous in the late 1800's. For instance, his frustration knew no bounds when a crime scene was disturbed. Holmes realized that so much could be determined from the physical evidence – footprints, fibers, and spatters. The police were happy to trod into and disturb the evidence as if they were herds of field beasts, with the equivalent level of intelligence.

However, Holmes's methods, and the science behind catching criminals, eventually won out and became so important that it's hard to now imagine the world without them. Many of the exact same techniques and methods that he advocated are now standard practice. From being an amateur with unusual ideas, Holmes is now recognized around the world as The Great Detective. In 2002, Holmes received a posthumous Honorary Fellowship from the British Royal Society of Chemistry, based on the fact that he was beyond his time in using chemistry and chemical sciences as a means of solving crimes.

And before that, in 1985, Scotland Yard introduced *HOLMES* (*Home Office Large Major Enquiry System*), an elaborate computer system designed to process the masses of information collected and evaluated during a criminal investigation, in order to ensure that no vital clues are overlooked. This system, providing total compatibility and consistency between all the police forces of England, Scotland, Wales, and Northern Ireland, as well as the Royal Military Police, has since been upgraded by the improved *HOLMES 2* – and like the first version, there is absolutely no doubt as to who is being honored and memorialized for his work in dragging criminology out of the dark ages.

Many famous Great Detectives followed in Holmes's footsteps – Nero Wolfe and Ellery Queen, Hercule Poirot and Solar Pons – each with their own methods and techniques, but before they began their careers, and while Holmes was still in practice in Baker Street, another London consultant – Dr. John Thorndyke – opened his doors, using the scientific methods developed and perfected by Holmes and taking them to a whole new level of brilliance.

Meet Dr. Thorndyke

Dr. John Evelyn Thorndyke was born on July 4th, 1870. We don't know about where he was raised, or if he has any family. At no point will we be introduced to a more brilliant brother who sometimes *is* the British Government. He was educated at the medical school of St. Margaret's Hospital in London, and while there, he met fellow student Christopher Jervis. They became friends but, after completing school in 1895, they lost touch with one another. Over the next six years, Thorndyke remained at St. Margaret's, taking on various jobs, hanging "about the chemical and physical laboratories, the museum and *post mortem* room," and learning what he could. He obtained his M.D. and his Doctor of Sciences, and then was called to the bar in 1896.

He'd prepared himself with the hope of obtaining a position as a coroner, but he learned of the unexpected retirement of one of St. Margaret's lecturers in medical jurisprudence. He applied for the position and, rather to his own surprise, it was awarded to him. (He would continue to maintain his association with the hospital, going on to become the Medical Registrar, Pathologist, Curator of the Museum, and then Professor of Medical Jurisprudence, all while maintaining his own private consulting practice.

It was when Thorndyke was named lecturer that he obtained his chambers at 5A King's Bench Walk, in the Inner Temple, that amazing and historic area between Fleet Street and the River. Founded over eight-hundred years ago by the Knights Templar, it is one of the four Inns of Court, (along with the Middle Temple, Lincoln's Inn, and Gray's Inn.) The buildings along King's Bench Walk, and particularly No.'s 4, 5, and 6, have a great deal of historical significance – and not just because Dr. John Thorndyke practiced at 5A for a number of years.

Thorndyke was quite fortunate to obtain a suite of rooms on multiple floors at this location, which leads to speculation about his influence and resources – a question which has no answer. In any case, it was there that he opened his practice and began to wait for clients and cases. He also made the acquaintance of elderly Nathaniel Polton, that man-of-all-work with the crinkly smile who ran the household, as well as Thorndyke's upstairs laboratory.

Like Sherlock Holmes during those early years in the 1870's when he had rooms in Montague Street next to the British Museum and spent his vast amounts of free time learning his craft, Thorndyke also found a way to make the empty hours more useful. He had the unique idea of imagining increasingly complex crimes – often a murder or series of them, for instance – and then, when he had planned every single aspect of the crime, he would turn around and work out the solution from the other side. While doing this, he made extensive notes of each of these theoretical exercises, and retained them for their later usefulness when encountering real-life crimes.

His first legal case was *Regina v Gummer* in 1897. Sadly, no further information about this affair is ever revealed to us, but we may be certain that Thorndyke used his considerable skills to bring it to a satisfactory conclusion, adding to his reputation as he did so.

In the meantime, Jervis had a more unfortunate story. As his time at school ended, his funds ran out rather unexpectedly, and after paying his various fees, he was left with earning his living as a medical assistant, or sometimes serving as a *locum tenens*, moving from one low-paying and temporary job to another, with no prospects of improvement.

Jervis is unemployed on the morning of March 22nd, 1901 when he encounters Thorndyke a few doors up from 5A King's Bench Walk. The two friends are happy to see one another, and before long, Jervis is involved in an investigation that will change his life in several ways, as recounted in *The Red Thumb Mark*.

But it should not be assumed that every Thorndyke adventure is narrated by Jervis in a typical Watsonian manner. In fact, the very next book, *The Eye of Osiris*, is instead told from the perspective of one of Thorndyke's students, Dr. Paul Berkeley. It is one of several that provide a look at Thorndyke – and Jervis – from a different perspective. But Jervis returns as narrator in the third novel, *The Mystery of 31 New Inn*, and we see Thorndyke through his eyes for a good many of both the novels and short stories.

Here a word might be mentioned about the Chronology of the Thorndyke stories. For some this is an irrelevant factor, but for others – like me – understanding the correct chronological placement of the stories is very important. Like the volumes that make up the Sherlock Holmes Canon, the Thorndyke stories aren't published in chronological order – a case set in 1907 (such as "Percival Bland's Proxy") might be collected before one that occurs in 1908, ("The Missing Mortgagee"), or it might not. For instance, *The Red Thumb Mark* (1907) is set in March and April 1901. (This chronological placement, by the way, is determined by noticing that a specific date is given three times in the book – in the British fashion of day before month – *9.3.01* – or *March 9th, 1901*. The dates for the events of the rest of the book can be carefully worked out from this fixed point.)

The next book, *The Eye of Osiris* (1911) is primarily set in the summer of 1904 (with Chapter 1, something of a prologue, taking place in late 1902.) Then, the next book to follow, *The Mystery of 31 New Inn* (1912), jumps back to the spring of 1902, about a year after the events of *The Red Thumb Mark*, and before *The Eye of Osiris*. And one of the short stories, "The Man With the Nailed Shoes" occurs in September and October 1901, between the first two books. Clearly, there is a great deal of material for the chronologicist in the Thorndyke Chronicles.

As Jervis becomes a part of Thorndyke's world, following their reacquaintance in March 1901, he meets others in Thorndyke's circle, including policemen such as Superintendent Miller and Inspector Badger, lawyers like Robert Anstey, Marchmont, and Brodribb, and other physicians like Dr. Paul Berkeley and Dr. Humphrey Jardine. He also has more opportunity to learn from his friend as he begins his own studies in order to become a similar specialist in the medico-legal practice – although he'll never be another Thorndyke.

Through Jervis's eyes – as well as others along the way – we build up our knowledge of Dr. Thorndyke. In appearance, he is tall and athletic, just under six feet in height, slender, and weighing around one-hundred-and-eighty pounds. He is exceptionally handsome – and has been called the handsomest detective in literature. He has no vices, except – perhaps – that he enjoys a Trichinopoly cigar upon occasion when he is feeling especially triumphant – although there is one time when the criminal's knowledge of this fact leads to a clever attempt at Thorndyke's murder . . . .

There are several instances where Thorndyke displays a marked resemblance to Sherlock Holmes – and not just in his scientific approach to crime. The two men sometimes say similar things – such as when Holmes says "*It is quite a pretty little problem,*" (in "A Scandal in Bohemia") or ". . . *there are some pretty little problems among them*" (in "The Musgrave Ritual"). Thorndyke mimics this in *Felo de Se?* ("*There, Jervis,*" said he, "*is quite a pretty little problem for you to excogitate*") or "*Ah, there is a very pretty little problem for you to consider*" (in *The Eye of Osiris*).

And who can forget the many instances when Holmes refers to *data*:

- *"It is a capital mistake to theorize before one has data. Insensibly one begins to twist facts to suit theories, instead of theories to suit facts."* – "A Scandal in Bohemia"
- *"I had,"* said he, *"come to an entirely erroneous conclusion which shows, my dear Watson, how dangerous it always is to reason from insufficient data."* – "The Speckled Band"
- *"No data yet,"* he answered. *"It is a capital mistake to theorize before you have all the evidence. It biases the judgment."* – *A Study in Scarlet*
- *"The temptation to form premature theories upon insufficient data is the bane of our profession."* – *The Valley of Fear*
- *"Still, it is an error to argue in front of your data."* – "Wisteria Lodge"

Thorndyke's version? *". . . believe me, it is a capital error to decide beforehand what data are to be sought for."* – from *The Mystery of 31 New Inn*. There are others.

Then there is Holmes's quote from "The Man With the Twisted Lip":

"You have a grand gift of silence, Watson," said he. *"It makes you quite invaluable as a companion."*

Here's the Thorndyke equivalent:

"It has just been borne in upon me, Jervis," said he, *"that you are the most companionable fellow in the world. You have the heaven-sent gift of silence."*

And then there is the time, in "The Anthropologist at Large", that a client – expecting a Holmes-like performance as based on "The Blue Carbuncle" – presents Thorndyke with an object for examination:

"I understand," said he, *"that by examining a hat it is possible to deduce from it, not only the bodily characteristics of the wearer, but also his mental and moral qualities, his state of health, his pecuniary position, his past history, and even his domestic relations and the peculiarities of his place of abode. Am I right in this supposition?"*
The ghost of a smile flitted across Thorndyke's face as he laid the hat upon the remains of the newspaper. "We must

not expect too much," he observed. "Hats, as you know, have a way of changing owners . . . ."

Another area of intersection between Holmes and Thorndyke is the assembly of information. Recall Holmes's *"ponderous commonplace books in which he placed his cuttings"* as mentioned in "The Engineer's Thumb". We find, also in "The Anthropologist at Large", that Thorndyke does the same thing:

> *[H]is method of dealing with [the morning newspaper] was characteristic. The paper was laid on the table after breakfast, together with a blue pencil and a pair of office shears. A preliminary glance through the sheets enabled him to mark with the pencil those paragraphs that were to be read, and these were presently cut out and looked through, after which they were either thrown away or set aside to be pasted in an indexed book.*

No doubt and examination of Thorndyke's lodgings at 5A King's Bench Walk would reveal – in addition to a series of indexed commonplace books filled with clippings – a number of other items and aspects that would remind one of 221b Baker Street.

Like many locations where the detective's residence is almost a character in and of itself – Sherlock Holmes's London address at 221 Baker Street, and the New York homes of Ellery Queen on West 87th Street and Nero Wolfe's Brownstone on West 35th Street – Thorndyke's rooms at 5A King's Bench Walk are a living and vibrant place – from the entry way, where a heavy door known as "The Oak" leads visitors into a most comfortable wood-paneled sitting room, located on the (British) first floor, one flight up from the ground floor. On the next floor up, Polton has his laboratory and workshop, containing everything that is needed (or what might be manufactured) in order to solve the case.

On the next floor, underneath the attic, are bedrooms belonging to Thorndyke, Jervis, and Polton. Even after Jervis has married – and now you know that he does get married! – he continues to reside a good deal of the time in King's Bench Walk. As he explains in *When Rogues Fall Out* (1932, with the U.S. title of *Dr. Thorndyke's Discovery*):

> *Here, perhaps, since my records of Thorndyke's practice have contained so little reference to my own personal affairs, I should say a few words concerning my domestic habits. As the circumstances of our practice often made it*

desirable for me to stay late at our chambers, I had retained there the bedroom that I had occupied before my marriage; and, as these circumstances could not always be foreseen, I had arranged with my wife the simple rule that the house closed at eleven o'clock. If I was unable to get home by that time, it was to be understood that I was staying at the Temple. It may sound like a rather undomestic arrangement, but it worked quite smoothly, and it was not without its advantages. For the brief absence gave to my homecomings a certain festive quality, and helped to keep alive the romantic element in my married life. It is possible for the most devoted husbands and wives to see too much of one another.

Thorndyke's Other Appearances

Through the years, Thorndyke's reputation continues to grow, as presented through a number of adventures. Surprisingly, in light of the tens of thousands of Post-Canonical Sherlock Holmes that have come to light over the years, as discovered by latter-day Literary Agents taking over Watson's first Literary Agent, Sir Arthur Conan Doyle, stopped literary-agenting, there have been almost no additional Thorndyke cases brought to the public's attention. The few exceptions to this statement are *Goodbye, Dr. Thorndyke* (1972) by Norman Donaldson, and *Dr. Thorndyke's Dilemma* (1974) by John H. Dirckx. Both narratives deal with Thorndyke and Jervis in their latter years, and each is written by an expert in the field of Thorndyke scholarship.

Donaldson also wrote what might be the final scholarly word on the subject, *In Search of Dr. Thorndyke* (1971). In fact, he had intended his pastiche, *Goodbye, Dr. Thorndyke*, to be published as the conclusion to this book, but it ended up appearing separately.

To my knowledge, "The Great Fathomer", as Thorndyke is sometimes known, has rarely appeared in other locations. He is mentioned in the Solar Pons tale "The Adventure of the Proper Comma" by August Derleth, which finds Dr. Parker returning "from Thorndyke & Polton with an analysis of the capsules Mrs. Buxton had carried with her . . . ."

In my own book of authorized Solar Pons stories, *The Papers of Solar Pons* (2017), Thorndyke makes two appearances. "The Adventure of the Additional Heirs" has Pons and Parker visiting King's Bench Walk:

At 5A, we learned that our friend Thorndyke, the medical juris-practitioner, was out on some investigation or other, but Pons handed the papers, sans photograph, into the care of Polton, his crinkly-faced laboratory technician, with a detailed explanation of what he wished to learn. The man nodded and smiled, and without any extraneous chit-chat, shut the door, freeing us to return to Fleet Street. We paused at the edge of the walk to look at the photograph, still in Pons's hand.

Later Thorndyke sends Pons a detailed report that helps toward the solution of the problem. And in "The Affair of the Distasteful Society", set in July 1921, Pons and Parker attend the first meeting of a group gathered to honor Sherlock Holmes, where the following conversation occurs:

"I see that you invited Thorndyke, and that little Belgian over on Farraway Street," said Rath.
"And Sexton Blake as well," replied Sir Amory.
"Sexton Blake is a fictional character, Sir Amory," said Pons with a smile.

In my story, "The Adventure of the Two Sisters", included in *The New Adventures of Solar Pons*, Dr. Parker writes:

Pons was not the only detective who offered his services to the London populace, although he might have been the most well-known. We were friends with several others, including the former Belgian policeman who lived in Farraway Street, and another rather mysterious fellow in nearby Bottle Street. And of course, Pons went way back with Thorndyke, whose chambers were across town. It wasn't unusual for Pons and the others to regularly confer on investigations, or simply to sit down and share a few drinks and professional anecdotes.

Thorndyke doesn't just appear in some of my Solar Pons adventures. He's also been referenced off-stage in a couple of Sherlock Holmes adventures that I've pulled from Watson's Tin Dispatch Box – and it's more than likely that others will follow. In "The "London Wheel", contained in *The MX Book of New Sherlock Holmes Stories –*

Part IV: 2016 Annual (2016), Holmes, looking through some documents, states:

> *"I believe," said Holmes, "that I have enough amateur legal training that I can get a sense of the implications of the clauses in question in both of these documents." He pulled the folded pages from his pocket. "I thought about sending a message to my* protégé *Thorndyke in King's Bench Walk for his opinion, as he could have been here very quickly, should he be at home at all and not out on his own business. However, I don't believe that will be necessary.*

Perhaps it is a point of interest that Thorndyke is referred to Holmes's protégé. Possibly more information will be forthcoming, such as that which is hinted in my story, "The Coombs Contrivance" (in *The Irregular Adventures of Sherlock Holmes!*). Set in 1889, when Thorndyke was nineteen years old, Holmes and Watson are discussing a precocious Baker Street Irregular:

> *[Holmes] pinched the bridge of his nose. "Do you trust Levi's judgment, Watson?"*
> *I considered. "For an eight-year-old, he's remarkably perceptive – as much as any of the other Irregulars who have assisted you. The Wiggins family, or the Peakes, or Thorndyke, before he went away to university."*

So was Thorndyke, perhaps, a gifted Irregular who learned from The Master, and then went on to create his own successful practice, taking what he learned to a next very successful level? Possibly. In my story "The Inner Temple Intruder", to be found in *Sherlock Holmes and the Great Detectives*, such an origin story is posited. As Robert Downey, Jr. succinctly stated when playing Holmes in 2009's *Sherlock Holmes*: "Food for thought!"

Thorndyke is also mentioned in Bob Byrne's Holmes story, "The Adventure of the Parson's Son" (*The MX Book of New Sherlock Holmes Stories – Part III: 1896-1929*), wherein Holmes, examining a piece of evidence, cries:

> *"Ha! I believe we have discredited the coat entirely. Though I wish I could get Thorndyke to examine it. Would that we were back in London."*

And it isn't just Thorndyke who has appeared elsewhere. His lawyer friend Marchmont has assisted Holmes and Watson in a small way a couple of my own: "The Coombs Contrivance" and the forthcoming adventure *Sherlock Holmes and The Eye of Heka.*

Although I have encouraged these Thorndyke cameos in my own stories or in Holmes and Pons books that I edit, his appearances elsewhere are much more fleeting. In the 2015 BBC radio series *The Rivals*, Inspector Lestrade, Holmes's most frequent associate at Scotland Yard, is placed into the events of the Thorndyke short story "The Moabite Cipher". And Thorndyke has only had a handful of other media appearances. In 1964, the BBC produced seven episodes (now lost) of *Thorndyke*, starring Peter Copley. The episodes were:

- "The Case of Oscar Brodski'
- "The Old Lag"
- "A Case of Premeditation"
- "The Mysterious Visitor"
- "The Case of Phyllis Annesley" – Adapted from "Phyllis Annesley's Peril"
- "Percival Bland's Brother" – Adapted from "Percival Bland's Proxy"
- "The Puzzle Lock"

From 1971 to 1973, Thames TV aired *The Rivals of Sherlock Holmes*, and two stories were adapted: "A Message from the Deep Sea" starring John Neville (who had also played Holmes in 1965's *A Study in Terror*), and "The Moabite Cipher" starring Barrie Ingram. Except for a 1963 BBC Radio adaption of *Mr. Pottermack's Oversight*, and a few on-air readings by a single performer, there have been no other Thorndyke adaptations – which is a terrible shame, as the stories certainly lend themselves to visual and audible interpretations. Perhaps a new generation will discover Thorndyke, Jervis, and the rest, and they will find popularity once again, as they did more than a century ago.

Copley, Neville, and Ingram as Thorndyke

A Few (Hundred) Words About R. Austin Freeman
Thorndyke's Chronicler

Richard Austin Freeman was born on April 11, 1862 in the Soho district of London. He was the son of a skilled tailor and the youngest of five children. As he grew, it was expected that he would become a tailor as well, but instead he had an interest in natural history and medicine, and so he obtained employment in a pharmacist's shop. While there, he qualified as an apothecary and could have gone on to manage the shop, but instead he began to study medicine at Middlesex Hospital.

Austin Freeman qualified as a physician in 1887, and in that same year he married. Faced with the twin facts of his new marital responsibilities and his very limited resources as a young doctor, he made the unusual decision to join the Colonial Service, spending the next seven years in Africa as an Assistant Colonial Surgeon. This continued until the early 1890's, when he contracted Blackwater Fever, an illness that eventually forced him to leave the service and return permanently to England.

For several years, he served as a *locum tenens* for various physicians, a bleak time in his life as he moved from job to job, his income low, and his health never quite recovered. (These experiences were reflected in the narratives of Doctors Jervis and Berkeley.) However, he supplemented his meager income and exercised his creativity during these years by beginning to write. His early publications included *Travels and Live in Ashanti and Jaman* (1898), recounting some of his African sojourns.

In 1900, Freeman obtained work as an assistant to Dr. John James Pitcairn (1860-1936) at Holloway Prison. Although he wasn't there for very long, the association between the two men was enough to turn Freeman's attention toward writing mysteries. Over the next few years, they co-wrote several under the pseudonym *Clifford Ashdown*, including *The Adventures of Romney Pringle* (1902), *The Further Adventures of Romney Pringle* (1903), *From a Surgeon's Diary* (1904-1905), and *The Queen's Treasure* (written around 1905-1906, and published posthumously in 1975.) The specifics of the two men's writing arrangement are unknown to the present day, although much research was carried out by Freeman scholar Percival Mason ("P.M.") Stone, who was actually able to confirm Pitcairn's involvement and influence. Following this association, which apparently helped to train Freeman to be a better writer and to focus on a recurring character, his luck changed, and he was able, within just a few years, to abandon the practice of medicine, which had never been successful, and become a professional author.

In approximately 1904, Freeman began developing a mystery novella based on a short job that he had held at the Western Ophthalmic Hospital. This effort, "31 New Inn", was published in 1905, and it is the true first Dr. Thorndyke story. In it, we meet narrator Dr. Christopher Jervis, working as a *locum tenens*, moving from practice to practice in the same bleak existence that Freeman had experienced. Jervis becomes involved with a patient that may or may not be in danger. Unsure what to do, he recalls his former classmate, the brilliant Dr. John Thorndyke.

Curiously, this novella, (included in Volume II of this newly reissued collection *The Complete Dr. Thorndyke*), has numerous references to the events of the first Thorndyke novel, *The Red Thumb Mark*, which would not be published until 1907. Much of Freeman's life is obscure and unknown, including his writing processes and milestones, but clearly, with so much already clearly defined in this novella about Thorndyke and Jervis, he had firmly established not only fixed aspects of their histories, but the plot of *The Red Thumb Mark* as well, several years before the book's publication. One wonders why he chose to first publish "31 New Inn", since it occurs chronologically a whole year *after* the events of *The Red Thumb Mark*.

Interestingly – at least to a chronologicist such as myself – the original novella of "31 New Inn" is specifically set in April 1900, as indicated internally. However, when it was later revised to become the third Thorndyke novel, *The Mystery of 31 New Inn*, (1912, and included in Volume I of *The Complete Dr. Thorndyke*), the narrative's date is changed to 1902 – which fits, since the events definitely occur after *The Red Thumb Mark*, which takes place in March and April 1901.

Like Rex Stout's Nero Wolfe, who seemed to have sprung fully formed from his creator's brow, Thorndyke and his world are well-defined and immediately real. Although certain characters are added to the circle through the years, the basic layout – with Thorndyke, Jervis, and Polton (the man-of-all-work crinkly-smiled assistant) are always at 5A, ready to spring into action when Jervis – or one of the other varied narrators who show up throughout the series – arrive with a curious problem.

Freeman had found his voice with the Thorndyke books and short stories, and he was able to make use of his lifelong interest in medicine and natural science – often conducting extensive experiments to work out exactly how the solutions in his stories could be discovered. And in Thorndyke's early days, Freeman was able to turn the literary form inside out with the creation of the "Inverted Mystery Story", wherein the criminal is known from the beginning – the motive is explained, the planning and execution of the crime are observed, and the miscreant is left to believe that all is well and that he'll never be caught. And then, in the second part of the story, Thorndyke enters to inexorably follow the trail that is completely invisible to everyone else, scraping away, layer by layer and point by point, until the truth is inevitably revealed.

As Freeman explained:

> *Some years ago I devised, as an experiment, an inverted detective story in two parts. The first part was a minute and detailed description of a crime, setting forth the antecedents, motives, and all attendant circumstances. The reader had seen the crime committed, knew all about the criminal, and was in possession of all the facts. It would have seemed that there was nothing left to tell. But I calculated that the reader would be so occupied with the crime that he would overlook the evidence. And so it turned out. The second part, which described the investigation of the crime, had to most readers the effect of new matter.*

This format went on to be used by a great many authors through the years. For example several of the Lord Peter Wimsey narratives come close to being this type of story, and television's *Columbo* used this type of story-telling as its basis.

While these volumes are an attempt to reintroduce the modern reader to Thorndyke, and are a celebration of him and his world, it must be discussed at some point that Freeman held views that are unacceptable. Unlike Sir Arthur Conan Doyle, who spent his last decades championing spiritualism but never allowed it to creep into the Sherlock Holmes stories, Freeman sometimes did let his own prejudices make their way into the Thorndyke tales. In his book *Social Decay and Regeneration* (1921), he expressed his rather nationalistic view that England had become an "homogenized, restless, unionized working class". Worse, he inexcusably and detestably supported the eugenics movement, arguing that people with "undesirable" traits should not be allowed to reproduce by means such as "segregation, marriage restriction, and sterilization". He referred to immigrants as "Sub-Man", and argued that society needed to be protected from "degenerates of the destructive type."

Some have attempted to excuse his beliefs as being a product of his times. For instance, it has been written that he had a distrust of Jews because of the competition that his father, a tailor, had faced when Freeman was a boy. Later, he served in the Colonial Service in Africa during some of the worst years in terms of treatment of natives by the British, and as an older man, he existed in the Great Britain between the two wars when great upheavals disrupted much of what he had known and expected.

Sadly, there are occasional racial stereotypes and references in the Thorndyke books. As I explain in the *Editor's Caveat*, some of these stereotypes had to be unfortunately maintained within the story in order to accurately reflect the plot and the characters of those times. However, there are some words or phrases that were used in the original stories – vile racial epithets that have no business being repeated or perpetuated anywhere – that I have cheerfully and happily removed. (There weren't many of them, but any are too many.)

These books are intended to bring Dr. Thorndyke and his adventures to a new generation – and not to be an untouchable and sacred literary artifact, with every nasty stain preserved and archived for the historical record. As I warn in the *Caveat*, if readers find that they want to experience the original versions as they were first written, with those hateful words included, then they would be advised to go and seek out the original books, because you won't find that filth here. These versions celebrate Dr. Thorndyke and Dr. Jervis – who do not use the awful stereotyped language, I'm glad to say! – and as such, I felt no need whatsoever to include and perpetuate the objectionable and offensive material

From Thorndyke's creation until 1914, Freeman wrote four novels and two volumes of short stories. Then, with the commencement of the First World War, he entered military service. In February 1915, at the age of fifty-two, he joined the Royal Army Medical Corps. Due to his health, which had never entirely recovered from his time in Africa, he spent the duration of the war involved with various aspects of the ambulance corps, having been promoted very early to the rank of Captain. He wrote nothing about Thorndyke during this period, but he did publish one book concerning the adventures of a scoundrel, *The Exploits of Danby Croker* (1916).

Following the war, he resumed his previous life, writing approximately one Thorndyke novel per year, as well as three more volumes of Thorndyke short stories and a number of other unrelated items, until his death on September 28th, 1943 – likely related to Parkinson's Disease, which had plagued him in later years.

Upon learning the news, *Chicago Tribune* columnist Vincent Starrett wrote:

> *When all the bright young things have performed their appointed task of flatting the complexes of neurotic semi-literates, and have gone their way to oblivion, the best of the Thorndyke stories will live on – minor classics on the shelf that holds the good books the world.*

Raymond Chandler wrote in his famous essay, which initially appeared in a couple of magazines and then was published in the book of the same name, *The Simple Art of Murder* (1950):

> *This man Austin Freeman is a wonderful performer. He has no equal in his genre, and he is also a much better writer than you might think, if you were superficially inclined, because in spite of the immense leisure of his writing, he accomplishes an even suspense which is quite unexpected . . . There is even a gaslight charm about his Victorian love affairs, and those wonderful walks across London.*

In the introduction to *Great Stories of Detection, Mystery, and Horror* (1928), Dorothy L. Sayers, Chronicler of Lord Peter Wimsey, stated:

> *Thorndyke will cheerfully show you all the facts. You will be none the wiser . . . .*

Discovering Dr. Thorndyke

I first encountered Dr. Thorndyke in a rather backwards way – in passing only – and it took several decades to correct that mistake. In approximately 1980, my dad gave me Otto Penzler's *The Private Lives of Private Eyes, Spies, Crime Fighters, and Other Good Guys* (1977). This wonderful oversized book has biographies of twenty-five well-known heroes, along with lists of the original books featuring each one.

My dad bought it for me because it had a chapter about Sherlock Holmes. There were a few others in there that I recognized or had already read about– Ellery Queen and Perry Mason – and soon I would become fanatical about a few more – Nero Wolfe and Hercule Poirot. Over the next few years I would also find the chapters on James Bond and Lew Archer indispensable, and later than that I would come to appreciate the entries about Philip Marlowe, Sam Spade, Miss Marple, Philo Vance, and Lord Peter Wimsey. But there were a few that, to this day, I've never bothered to read – such as Modesty Blaise or Mr. Moto – and a few others that I skimmed but otherwise ignored. And one of these was the biography of Dr. Thorndyke.

That fact was easily understandable, as throughout the entire time that I was growing up in eastern Tennessee – and in the years since as well – I've never come across a Thorndyke book for sale here in the wild, either in a new bookstore or in a used one. If I'd found one, I might have bought and read it, liked it, and then sought out others. Instead, I was bound to discover Thorndyke by way of Sherlock Holmes.

I've been collecting traditional Sherlock Holmes pastiches since the same time that I discovered the Sherlockian Canon, when I was ten years old in 1975. Since that time, I've collected, read, and chronologicized literally thousands of them. It never gets old, and I'm constantly looking for more – and that means checking Amazon to see what new releases are on the horizon.

In 2012, someone – and I've never determined who – began releasing a variety of Holmes stories for Kindle under the author name *Dr. John H. Watson.* This wasn't too unusual – there have been a number of pastiches that officially list Watson as the author, rather than putting the editor of Watson's papers first. Of course, after determining that these latest entries weren't going to be available as real books, I bought the e-versions, and then printed them on real paper. (I cannot stand e-books – ephemeral electronic blips that you lease instead of buy. I'll only buy those titles if they aren't going to be released as legitimate books – and in this case, it's a good thing that I did, as each of these Kindle stories that I found and paid for were soon withdrawn.)

As I read these latest "Holmes" stories, I noticed that each had a definite style that captured the writing from the late 1800's or early 1900's. (No matter how modern pasticheurs try to achieve that, they never quite pull it off.) But in one of the first two or three titles that I read, I caught a couple of mistakes. In one story, Holmes and Watson leave 221 Baker Street and are immediately in the area around The Temple and Fleet Street, rather than in Marylebone, where Baker Street is properly located. On another occasion, the story's policeman – who had been identified up to that point as Inspector Lestrade – was inexplicably named *Superintendent Miller* – but only in one instance. And in another place in one of the stories, Holmes's address was stated to be *5A King's Bench Walk.*

It was then that some vague memory triggered in my head, and I realized why these stories had captured the style of the late Victorian and early Edwardian eras: *It was because they had actually been written then*. I recalled – from reading Otto Penzler's book of biographies so long ago - that 5A King's Bench Walk belonged to Dr. Thorndyke, and not Sherlock Holmes. Someone was taking the original Thorndyke stories, which I had never before read, and simply changing names: Dr. Thorndyke, Dr. Jervis, and Superintendent Miller became Sherlock Holmes, Dr. Watson, and Inspector Lestrade, respectively.

Between 2012 and 2014, the anonymous author continued to load new Kindle editions on Amazon of Thorndyke-converted to-Holmes stories, and I continued to buy them. As soon as I had one, I would read it, and then try to figure out the original Thorndyke story from which it was taken. When I'd done so, I'd post a review, identifying what this editor was doing, from where he or she was taking the story, and urging that person, whoever it was, give credit to R. Austin Freeman instead of listing the author as Dr. John H. Watson.

Soon after each of my reviews would appear, the story would be withdrawn. I don't know if it was because the editor had made enough money from the initial sales, or if my reviews alerted him or her that they're game had been uncovered. In any case, I still have the printed copies of each of these converted stories – possibly the only copies that are still in existence.

For the record, over that two year period, this editor produced sixteen converted tales – four of the original Thorndyke novels, and twelve short stories. One of the original short stories, "The Mandarin's Pearl", was converted twice, with slight variations – initially published as "The Dragon Pearl", withdrawn, and later revised and reloaded as "The Oriental Pearl":

- "The Bloodied Thumbprint" – Originally the first Thorndyke novel, *The Red Thumb Mark*;
- "The Eye of Ra" – Originally the second Thorndyke novel, *The Eye of Osiris*;
- "The Cat's Eye Mystery" – Originally the sixth Thorndyke novel, *The Cat's Eye*;
- "The Julius Dalton Mystery" – Originally the ninth Thorndyke novel, *The D'Arblay Mystery*;
- "The Green Jacket Mystery" – Originally "The Green Check Jacket";
- "Mr. Crofton's Disappearance" – Originally "The Mysterious Visitor";
- "The Coded Lock" – Originally "The Puzzle Lock";

- "The Duplicated Letter" – Originally "The Stalking Horse";
- "The Bullion Robbery" – Originally "The Stolen Ingots";
- "The Talking Corpse" – Originally "The Contents of a Mare's Nest";
- "The Blue Diamond Mystery" – Originally "The Fisher of Men";
- "The Dragon Pearl" – Originally "The Mandarin's Pearl". (This story was also reworked and published again as a Holmes story under the title "The Oriental Pearl");
- "The Ingenious Murder" – Originally "The Aluminium Dagger";
- "The Bloodhound Superstition" – Originally "The Singing Bone"; *and*
- "The Magic Box" – Originally "The Magic Casket".

For quite a while, I was happy to have these as Holmes stories, and I even considered converting the rest of the Thorndyke adventures into additions to the extended Holmes Canon as well. (For at that time I cared nothing for Dr. Thorndyke.) It was partly with these converted stories in mind that I was motivated to go ahead and publish *Sherlock Holmes in Montague Street* (2014, 2016), which did the same thing to the Martin Hewitt stories, making them early adventures of Holmes before he met Watson and moved to Baker Street. I had long before decided to my own satisfaction that Martin Hewitt *was* a young Sherlock Holmes, with his identity changed through the preparations of a different literary agent than Sir Arthur Conan Doyle.

The taking of old public-domain stories featuring other detectives as the main protagonists and switching them so that Holmes is the main character has also been done by Alan Lance Andersen for his collection *The Affairs of Sherlock Holmes* (2015, 2016), wherein various non-series Sax Rohmer stories from nearly a hundred years ago were reworked as Holmes tales. Other non-Holmes authors have sometimes done the same thing. Raymond Chandler revised some of his early short stories so that the original characters' names were changed to Philip Marlowe. Ross MacDonald – (Kenneth Millar) also rewrote his old stories as well, making them into Lew Archer cases instead. More recently, the British

ITV series *Marple* has taken non-Miss Marple Agatha Christie stories and converted them into episodes featuring that character.

So I had no problems with this type of change – and still don't. In fact, in my foreword to *Sherlock Holmes of Montague Street*, I wrote that I would rather have these converted Thorndyke stories as Holmes adventures, because I would rather read about Holmes than Thorndyke. But gradually my mind began to change, and I became more curious about Thorndyke, as presented in the proper fashion.

In 2013, I was able to go to London, as well as other places in England and Scotland, on the first (of three so far) Holmes Pilgrimages. For the most part, if a location wasn't related to Holmes, I didn't visit it. There were a few exceptions – I did intentionally visit Solar Pons's house at 7B Praed Street, Hercule Poirot's two residences, James Bond's flat in Chelsea – but everything else was pretty much pure Holmes.

One day, during my Holmesian rambles, I was making my way east down Fleet Street, and I visited both of the possible locations of "Pope's Court" (as featured in "The Red-Headed League"), Poppin's Court and Mitre Court. (The latter is also one of the locations where Denis Nayland Smith and Dr. Petrie had quarters in some of the Fu Manchu books.) I decided that Mitre Court was certainly the original of "Pope's Court", and I passed through it to find myself unexpectedly in The Temple.

That's the amazing thing about a Holmes Pilgrimage to London – one travels to a site and finds two more very close by. I had planned to visit The Temple, but hadn't realized that I was so close. And now here I was – and more interesting was the fact that I was walking along King's Bench Walk, which runs downhill from the Miter Court passage. I recalled that Thorndyke had lived at 5A, so I made my way there – but without too much awe on that day, because I hadn't actually read any Thorndyke adventures yet – just some converted Holmes stories.

After I returned home, the thought of that side-trip to Thorndyke's front door stuck in my mind, and I sought out and read the first novel in the series, *The Red Thumb Mark*. I was so impressed that I kept going, and discovered a wonderful series of books and stories – fascinating characters and mysteries, and very evocative descriptions of both the London and the countryside of those times.

When I returned on my second Holmes Pilgrimage in 2015, I took the second Thorndyke book with me, reading it while there – while also reading Holmes stories too, of course! This one, *The Eye of Osiris*, has a great deal of London atmosphere, and I spent part of one late afternoon tracking down locations in this book – or what's now left of them – in the area around Fetter Lane to the north of Thorndyke's home in The Temple. It was truly unforgettable.

And of course I made an intentional stop at King's Bench Walk on that 2015 trip, and again on Holmes Pilgrimage No. 3 in 2016. By that point I was a Thorndyke fan, and I took the trouble to write to the current occupiers of 5A before I traveled to see if I could step inside and perhaps spend a moment in Thorndyke's old quarters. Sadly, they did not respond – either because it was simply beneath them to do so, or possibly because they get too many people like me who want to make a literary pilgrimage to what is a functioning and thriving business location.

While making photographs at Thorndyke's old doorway, I had several chances to go inside when someone else would enter or leave – My ever-present deerstalker and I could have simply been bold enough to slip in and then talk my way onward. It worked at other places on my Holmes Pilgrimages – the laboratory at Barts where Holmes and Watson met, for instance, and the site of the (former?) Diogenes Club at No. 78 Pall Mall, where they acted just oddly enough to make me think that the club is still there. But for some reason, barging into Thorndyke's old chambers without proper permission didn't feel quite right. But if or when I make Holmes Pilgrimage No. 4, I'll definitely make an even greater effort to see the doctor's former rooms.

The Editor and his Deerstalker at 5A King's Bench Walk
September 2016

With many thanks . . . .

These last few years have been an amazing ride, and I've been able to play in the Sherlockian sandbox more than I'd ever imagined. (And subsequently, the Solar Pons sandbox, and now Thorndyke, too! Along the way, I've been able to meet some incredible people, both in person and in the modern electronic way, and also I've been able to read several hundred new Holmes adventures, as well as to be able to share them with others.

Still, what is most important is my amazingly wonderful wife (of over thirty years!) Rebecca, and our truly awesome son and my friend, Dan. I love you both, and you are everything to me! I am the luckiest guy in the world.

I have all the gratitude in the world for everyone that I've encountered along the way – It's an undeniable fact that Sherlock Holmes authors are the *best* people! I'd like to thank those who offer support, encouragement, and friendship, sometimes patiently waiting on me to reply as my time is directed in many other directions. Many many thanks to (in alphabetical order): Brian Belanger, Derrick Belanger, Bob Byrne, Roger Johnson, Mark Mower, Denis Smith, Tom Turley, Dan Victor, and Marcia Wilson.

In particular, I'd also like to especially thank Steve Emecz, who is always supportive of every idea that I pitch. It's been my particular good fortune that he crossed my path – it changed my life in a way that would have never happened otherwise, and I'm grateful for every opportunity!

I hope that these books will provide pleasure to those discovering Dr. Thorndyke for the first time, and to others who have known him for a long time. As always, I approach these matters from a Sherlockian perspective, so of course these stories, to me, are a peripheral extension of Holmes's world, and as such they are just more tiny threads woven into the ongoing Great Holmes Tapestry. However, they are wonderful on their own, and however one reads them, I wish great joy upon the journey.

David Marcum
(Revised October 2020)

Questions, comments, and story submissions
may be addressed to David Marcum at
thepapersofsherlockholmes@gmail.com

27

5A King's Bench Walk
in the late 1890's when
Thorndyke was in residence

Editor's *Caveat*

These stories have been prepared using modern text-converting software, and as such, occasional deviations in punctuation have occurred. Those who absolutely must have the original version, down to each jot and dash, should understand that this version was created in order to present Dr. Thorndyke's adventures to a modern audience, and not to preserve an absolute pristine model for the historical archives.

Similarly, these stories were written in a time when racial prejudice and stereotypes were much more common than today. While some of these stereotypes must be unfortunately maintained within the story in order to accurately reflect the plot and the characters of those times, there are some words that were used in the original stories – vile racial epithets that have no business being repeated or perpetuated anywhere – that I have cheerfully removed. (There weren't many of them, but *any* are *too many*.)

If readers find that they want to experience the original versions as they were first written, with those hateful and ignorant words included, then they would be advised to seek out the original books. These versions celebrate Dr. Thorndyke and Dr. Jervis – who do *not* use the awful stereotyped language, I'm glad to say! – and as such, I felt no need whatsoever to include objectionable and offensive material simply for the sake of honoring or archiving the historical record.

David Marcum
Editor

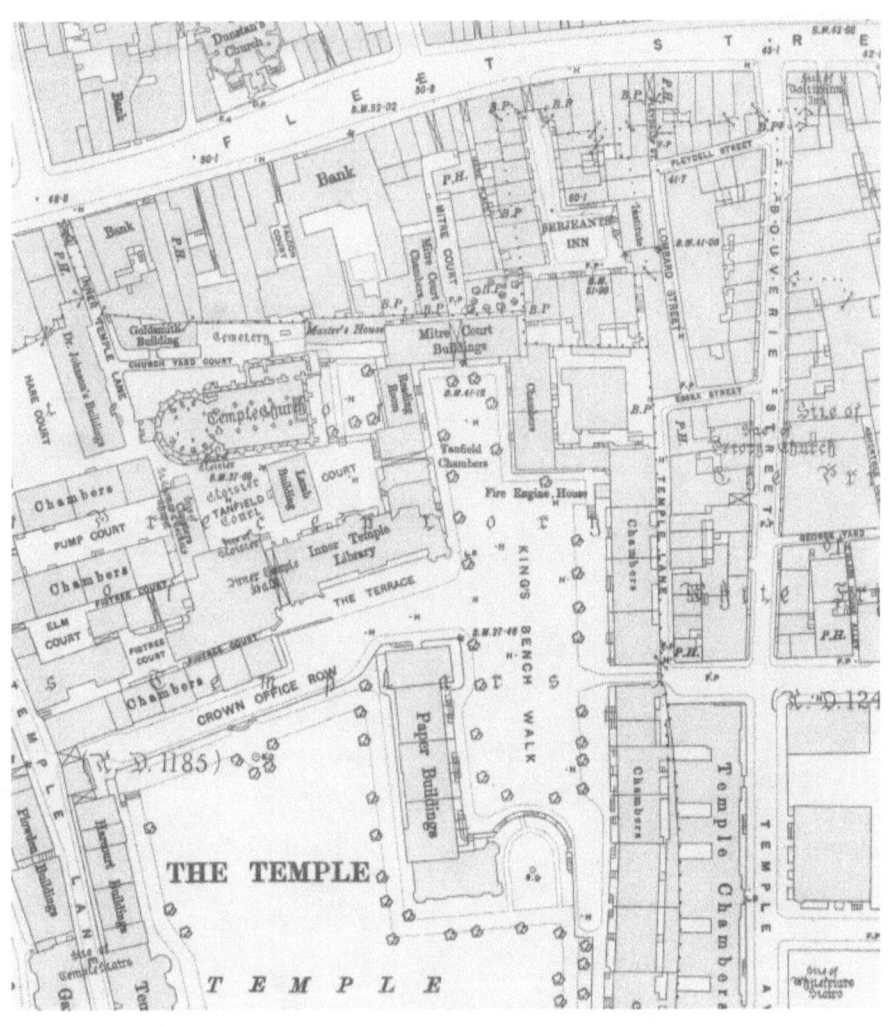

King's Bench Walk and the Temple, London
around 1900

33

PONTIFEX,
SON AND
THORNDYKE

*The Ace of
Detectives*

R.AUSTIN FREEMAN

1931 Hodder & Stoughton, London Cover

Chapter I
Destiny in an Egg-Chest
(Jasper Gray's Narrative)

A crab of mature age and experience is represented by an ancient writer as offering advice to his son somewhat in these terms: "My son, I have observed in you a most regrettable tendency to walk with ungraceful and unbecoming sidelong steps. Pray endeavour to conquer this pernicious habit and to adopt a straightforward and direct mode of progression."

Excellent advice! Though the gait of the existing generation of crabs leads one to fear that it failed to take effect.

The ancient parable was brought to my mind by the cigarette that I was lighting, for I had been the recipient of some most excellent paternal advice on the subject of cigarettes, coupled with the same on Irish whisky. My revered parent had, in fact, actually removed a choice Egyptian from his mouth the better to expound the subject, and, pointing to the accumulated ends on the hearth and the half-empty bottle on the mantelpiece, had explained with his admirable lucidity that these unsubstantial gauds were the inefficient substitutes for bacon for breakfast.

And yet I smoked. I did not consume Irish whisky, though I was perhaps restrained by reasons that were economic rather than ethical. But I smoked cigarettes, and recently I had started a pipe, having made the interesting discovery that the paternal cigarette ends were capable of reincarnation in a pipe-bowl.

I lit my cigarette and reflected on life and its problems. I was at the moment seated on a folded sack in an up-ended two-wheeled truck or hand-cart. In that truck, I had conveyed a heavy bale of stationery from my employers, Messrs. Sturt and Wopsall, to a customer at Mile End, after which I had drawn the empty truck into a quiet yard, up-ended it, and taken my seat in it as aforesaid. Since that day I have sat in many a more luxurious seat, in club divans, in hansom cabs. Yea! Even in the chariots of the mighty. But never have I found one quite equal to an up-ended truck with its floor turned to windward and a folded sack interposed between its tail and my own. There is much to be said for the simple life.

At this time I was just turned seventeen, and needless to say, I was quite poor. But poor boy as I was, there were many things for which I had to be thankful. In the first place, I enjoyed the supreme advantage of having escaped education – or rather, I should say, the particular brand that is supplied by the State. Other boys of like indigence were hauled off to Board Schools, where they contracted measles, chicken-pox, ringworm, and a most hideous accent, which would cling to them and, socially speaking, damn them hopelessly forever, even though they should subsequently rise – or sink – to millionaire-dom.

From this curse I was exempt. My accent was that of the upper middle-class, my vocabulary that of the man of culture, I could manage my *aitches* and express myself in standard speech. If the present was meagre, the future held untold potentialities, and this was the priceless gift of circumstance.

My father was a clergyman – or rather, I should say, he had *been* a clergyman. Why he had ceased to be a clergyman I never knew, though I associated the cessation of pastoral activities directly or indirectly with his complexion. When I knew him he was what he called a classical tutor and other people called a crammer, and the "crammees" being mostly of humble station, though ambitious, his income was meagre and precarious even at that.

But he was a wonderful man. He could construe the most difficult passages from the ancient authors and work out intricate problems in spherical trigonometry, when, from causes which I need not dwell upon, the functions of his legs were in temporary abeyance, on which occasions he would sit on the floor, for the excellent reason – as he lucidly explained – that "the direction of the force of gravity being geocentric, it was impossible to fall off". Yes, he was a remarkable man, and should surely have attained to distinction in the church. Not, to be sure, that you can conveniently sit on the floor to conduct morning service, but what I mean is that a man must be accounted more than ordinarily gifted in whom, once more to adopt his admirable phraseology, "the effect of alcoholic stimulation is merely to induce motor incoordination unaccompanied by psychical confusion".

I must not, however, allow mere family pride to lead me into digressions of unreasonable length. To return to the present incident: The cigarette had dwindled to about an inch-and-a-half, and I was beginning to consider the resumption of locomotive activities, when a man stopped at the entrance of the yard and then slowly advanced towards me. I thought he was going to order me to move on. But he did not. He sauntered down the yard, and, halting opposite the truck, surveyed me attentively until I became quite embarrassed and a little annoyed.

"Want a job, young feller?" he asked at length.

"No, thank you," I replied. "I've got one."

"So I see. Looks a pretty soft one, too. How much do they pay yer for sittin' in that truck?"

Of course it was no concern of his, but I was a civil youth and replied simply, "Ten shillings a week."

"And are they going to give yer a pension?"

"They may if I sit here long enough," I answered.

He pondered this statement thoughtfully and then resumed, "Sure yer don't want a job? Wouldn't care to earn five bob, for instance?"

Now this was a different matter. Five shillings was half my weekly wage. I was not pressed for time, for I had run all the way with the loaded truck and was entitled to loiter on the return journey.

"'What sort of job is it?" I asked, "and how long will it take?"

"It's to carry a case from Mansell Street to Byleses Wharf. Take yer about 'arf a hour."

"Very well," said I. "Five shillings is agreed upon, is it?"

"Five bob it is, to be paid on delivery. You cut along to Mansell Street, right 'and side next door to the 'bacca shop. I'll just mizzle on ahead and tell 'em you're coming."

He turned and left the yard at a much more sprightly pace than that at which he had entered, and immediately vanished from my sight. But he evidently discharged his mission, for, when I arrived at the house indicated, a seedy-looking man accosted me.

"Are you the bloke what's come for that case of eggs?"

"I've come for a case that's to go to Byles Wharf," I replied.

"That's right," said he. "And mind you're careful with that there case. J'ever hear about Humpty Dumpty what sat on a wall?"

I replied that I was quite familiar with the legend.

"Very well," said he. "There's two-thousand of 'em in that case, so you go slow and don't get a-joltin' 'em. We don't want 'em made into omlicks before their time. Now then, just hold that truck steady."

As he spoke, two men came out of the house carrying a large, oblong case on the top side, of which was pasted an enormous label inscribed, "*Fragile. This Side Up*". I steadied the truck by its pole and they slid the case into position with extraordinary care while the seedy person stood by to superintend and admonish. Having settled it securely, they wiped their hands on the backs of their trousers and retired into the house, when the seedy one administered a final caution.

"Remember what I told yer, young covey. Don't you go a-gallopin' that there case over the cobbles or a-bangin' it aginst lamp-posts, and you'd best take the back ways so as not to get run into by fire-ingines or sechlike. D'ye ogle?"

I assured him that I ogled perfectly and he then requested me to skedaddlle, which I did with the air and at the pace of one conducting a modest funeral.

But my circumspect manner and elaborate care seemed only to invite assaults from without. In Upper East Smithfield a van, attempting to pass me at a wobbling canter, caught the corner of the precious case a bang that was enough to have turned the whole consignment into "omlicks", and any that remained whole were like to have been addled by the van-driver's comments. Then in Pennington Street a man came running round a corner with a barrowful of empty casks, and I only escaped being capsized by turning quickly and receiving the impact of the collision on the back of the case. And, finally, an intoxicated Swedish seaman insisted on accompanying me down nearly the entire length of Old Gravel Lane, performing warlike music on the end of the case with a ship-wright's mallet.

As I turned into the gateway of Byles Wharf, I looked anxiously at my charge, rather expecting to find some oozing of yellow liquid from its joints. But no such traces of its stormy passage were visible, and I ventured to hope that the packing was better than I had been led to believe. Just inside the yard I encountered, somewhat to my surprise, the seedy stranger of Mansell Street, with another even seedier.

"Here you are then, young covey," said the former. "I hope you've been careful with them eggs."

I assured him that I had been most careful, but I did not think it necessary to mention that some other people had not. After all, you can't mend eggs, so the less said the better.

"Very well," said he, "you stay here a minute while I go and see if they're ready."

The two men went away and disappeared round the corner of a shed, leaving me holding the pole of the truck. Now the act of standing still and holding the pole of a truck soon becomes monotonous, especially to a youth of seventeen. Half-unconsciously I began, presently, to vary the monotony by working the pole up and down like a pump-handle. That couldn't hurt the eggs, and it produced a measured creak of the truck-springs that was interesting and pleasing.

Suddenly there smote on my ear a hoarse and muffled voice, which exclaimed fiercely, "Keep still, can't yer!"

I stopped instantly and looked around me. I had not noticed anyone near, and I didn't see anyone now. Could there be a ventriloquist hiding somewhere in the yard? The idea set my youthful curiosity aflame. I couldn't see him. But perhaps I could induce him to speak again and then I might locate the sound.

I renewed my application to the pump-handle with increased vigour, and the truck-springs squeaked joyously. The experiment was a perfect success. At the fourth or fifth squeak, a savage but muffled voice exclaimed, rather louder than before, "Keep still, I tell yer, yer young blighter!"

The mystery was solved. There was no doubt this time as to where the voice came from. It came from inside the case. Eggs indeed! And then I thought of the Swedish sailor and I am afraid I grinned.

The joy of a youth of my age at this romantic discovery may easily be imagined. Instantly my mind began to evolve speculations as to the identity of the imprisoned man. He seemed to take his incarceration in a philosophic spirit, though the Swedish mariner must have been a trial, to say nothing of the other incidents. But at this point my reflections were cut short by the reappearance of the two seedy strangers.

"Now, young shaver," said my original employer, "bring them eggs along this way."

He preceded me round the corner to the quay, alongside of which lay a barge with a hoisting tackle rigged from the end of a mast-derrick. There I was directed to halt and my two friends proceeded to lift the case tenderly out of the truck.

"Now you can mizzle," said the seedier of the two.

"I want my five shillings," said I.

The man put his hand in his pocket and produced a half-crown, which he presented to me. I examined it critically and held it out to him.

"This is no use," I said. "It's pewter. Besides, I was to have five shillings."

He was about to argue the point when the other man broke in impatiently, "Don't play the goat, Jim. Give the cove his dibs," on which the first man produced – from another pocket – five shillings of undoubtedly official origin. I pocketed them after careful scrutiny and offered him the "snide" half-crown. But he waved it aside magnanimously.

"You can keep that," said he. "'T'ain't no good to me if it's a wrong 'un. And now you can cut your lucky."

My "lucky" took me about a dozen yards along the quay, where I drew up behind a pile of bales to watch the progress of this stirring drama. The barge's tackle-rope had a sling hooked on the end, and this was now carefully passed round the case. The fall of the rope was put on the mast-winch, and, when all was ready, the word was given to "heave away". The men at the winch according hove away. The pawls clinked merrily, the rope tightened, the case rose clear of the ground and swung out like the bob of an enormous pendulum.

41

And then came the disaster. The barge was secured to two mooring-posts and was about ten feet away from the quay, so that the derrick had to be hauled over by guy-ropes. But the case had not been properly balanced in the sling, and no sooner had it swung clear of the edge of the quay than it began to slip through the rope loop.

"Look alive!" roared someone on the quay. "She's a-slippin'!"

One of the men left the winch and rushed for the guy-rope. But it was too late. Slowly, inexorably, the case slid through the loop and fell with a resounding plop! Into the water.

An agonised yell arose from the quay and a furious stampede among the onlookers. The bargees snatched up boat-hooks and setting-poles and scrambled along the deck. But, alas! A swift tide was running, and the case, gyrating and dancing like a cork in a mill race, was out of reach before the first boat-hook could be got over the side.

A barge's dinghy was made fast at the foot of a ladder hard by. Abandoning the truck, I slithered down the ladder, closely followed by a barge-boy, and we met in the boat with mutual recriminations. But there was no time to argue. The boy cast off the painter, and snatching up the paddle, dropped it in the transom-notch and began to scull furiously down stream. Ahead of us, we could see the case dancing along on the tide, turning round and round, vanishing and reappearing among the tiers of shipping. Presently, too, I saw another boat start in pursuit and recognised my two friends among its occupants.

But the case had got a flying start and pursuit was difficult among the crowded shipping. We were beginning to overhaul it when it disappeared behind a cargo steamer, and when we next saw it, it had been neatly snared by a couple of ropes and was being hoisted by hand through the gangway of a little Welsh schooner that was just hauling out of the tiers. The barge-boy and I approached the schooner on the off shore side and climbed on board unnoticed, for the other boat, containing my seedy acquaintances had just arrived on the in-shore side. My employer proceeded to state his claim. "Hi, Captain! That there's my case."

The captain leaned over the bulwark and regarded him with an affable smile.

"D'y'ear," my friend repeated. "That case belongs to me."

The captain's smile broadened. "Belonged," he corrected blandly.

"What d'yer mean?" demanded the seedy one. "You ain't going to try to stick to my property?"

The captain maintained his affable manner. "This is a case of salvage," said he.

"Git out," rejoined the other. "It's a case of eggs, and they're my eggs."

"Did you lay 'em yourself?" enquired the captain (a good deal nearer the mark than he thought). The question seemed to irritate my seedy friend, for he replied angrily, "Never you mind 'oo laid 'em. You just hand that case over."

At this moment there came a diversion. One of the sailors, who had been closely examining the case as it lay dribbling on the deck, suddenly started back, like a cat who has inadvertently smelt a hedgehog.

"Golly wores!" he exclaimed. "There's some-think alive inside!"

"Hey! What's that?" demanded the captain.

"There is, sir, swelp me! I 'eard it a-movin' about."

The captain looked sharply over the bulwark. "Here you, mister!" he sang out, "you haven't been sitting on those eggs, have you?"

"Sittin' on 'em? What d'yer mean?"

"Because they seem to have hatched themselves and the chickens are running about inside the case."

"Yes, and they're usin' the most shockin' langwidge, too," said an elderly seaman who had been pressing his ear to a crack in the case.

This report, reaching the occupants of the boat, caused very evident dismay. But my late employer made a last effort.

"Don't talk nonsense," he said, sulkily. "Pass that case over and I'll pay what's doo for salvage in reason."

"Not me," replied the captain. "I'm goin' to broach that case and see what's inside."

The effect of this decision was rather curious. The men in the boat consulted together hurriedly, then their craft was turned about and rowed away rapidly in the direction whence they had come.

Meanwhile the captain and his myrmidons proceeded to operate on the case. Producing one or two small crow-bars, they neatly prised up the lid and threw it back, when there rose from the case, somewhat after the fashion of the obsolete toy known as "Jack-in-the-Box", no less a person than the man who had originally chartered my truck. He stepped out sullenly and, confronting the group of grinning seamen, remarked in perhaps justifiably emphatic terms, that he had had enough of that mode of travelling for the present.

The captain looked at him attentively, and he looked at the captain, and then ensued a whispered conversation between them, which was interrupted by one of the crew remarking, "Looks like the police boat, don't it?"

The passenger turned and stared wildly in the direction indicated. A police gig was approaching slowly but doggedly over the strong tide, and besides the amphibious officials were two men in civilian garb who sat in the stern-sheets and kept their eyes ominously glued on the schooner.

The passenger bobbed down behind the high bulwark and gazed about him despairingly, and suddenly his eye lighted on me.

"Here, boy," he said, "get into that case."

"No thank you," said I.

He dived his hand frantically into his pocket and brought it out with a shining, yellow burden that clinked musically.

"Here, boy," he pleaded. "Here's five quid for you if you'll get into that case and let 'em nail it up."

Five sovereigns! It was a fortune to a lad in my position. And there really was no particular risk. I examined the coins – I was a fairly expert judge of money from my occupation, which often included "payment on delivery" – and found them genuine, and I succumbed. Stowing the money in an inside pocket, I stepped into the case and hunched myself up so as to occupy comfortably the rather limited accommodation.

"Don't you drop the case into the water again!" I said.

"Right-o, Sonny!" the captain answered. "We'll handle you carefully. Now there, look sharp!"

The lid was clapped on, a few smart but not noisy blows of a hammer drove home the nails, and I began to earn my magnificent wage. The interior of the case was unpleasantly damp and stuffy, though a sufficiency of air and a few streaks of light came through the chinks of the lid. Sounds from without also reached me freely and consisted, for the present, chiefly of suppressed laughter from the sailors and admonitions from the captain.

"Stow that chap down in the lazarette, Fred," said the latter, "and you men, don't stand about laughing like a lot o' fools. Get that tow-rope ready for the tug. Here comes the police boat."

There was a pause after this with some scuffling about the deck and a good deal of sniggering. Then I heard a sharp, official voice. "What's this case, Captain?"

"I don't know," was the reply. "Belongs to those men that you see running up them steps. They hooked it when they saw your boat coming."

"That's Jim Trout," said another voice, "and Tommy Bayste with him. What's in the case, Captain?"

"Can't say. Seems to be something alive in it."

"There!" said the first official. "What did I tell you, Smith. It's Powis right enough. We'd better get him out of the case and clap the darbies on him."

"Not on my ship, you won't," said the captain. "I can't have any criminals let loose here just as I'm hauling out to go to sea. You'd better take the case ashore and open it there."

"Gad!" exclaimed Smith, "the Captain's right, Sergeant. We'd better drop the case into the boat and take it ashore. Powis is an ugly customer to handle. He might capsize us all into the river."

"That's true," agreed the sergeant. "We'll take him as he is if the Captain will have the case let down into our boat."

The captain was most willing for certain private reasons not entirely unconnected with the lazarette. I heard and felt a rope sling passed round the case and my heart was brought into my mouth by the squeal of tackle-blocks. For a few seconds the case swung horribly in mid-air, then, to my unspeakable relief, I felt it subside on to the floor of the boat.

A good deal of laughter and facetious talk mingled with the measured sound of the oars as I was borne away. Suddenly the sergeant laughed out boisterously like a man who has had a funny idea. And apparently he had.

"I'll tell you what, Smith," he chuckled, "we won't open the case till we get to Holloway. We'll take it right into the reception ward. Ha! Ha!"

The joke was highly appreciated by Mr. Smith and his colleagues – a good deal more than it was by me, for I had had enough of my quarters already – and they were still in full enjoyment of it when another voice sang out, "Keep clear of that tug, West. She'll be right on top of us. Hi! Tug ahoy! Look out! Where the dev – "

Here there came an alarming bump and a confused chorus of shouts arose. The case canted over sharply, there was a fearful splash, and immediately, to my horror, water began to ooze in through the cracks between the boards. Two or three minutes of dreadful suspense followed. A loud churning noise sounded close at hand, waves seemed to be breaking over the case, and I had a sensation as if my residence were being dragged swiftly through the water.

It didn't last very long. Presently I felt the case run aground. Then it was lifted on to what I judged to be a barrow, which immediately began to move off over an abominably rough road at a pace which may have been necessary, but was excessively uncomfortable to me.

Hitherto very little had been said. A few muttered directions were all that I had been able to catch. But now a newcomer appeared to join our procession, and I began to gather a few particulars of the rescue.

"Any of the coppers drowned, d'ye think, Bill?"

"Not as I knows of. I see 'em all a-crawlin' up onto a dumb barge."

"Where's the tug now?"

"Islington, I should think. We left 'er on the mud with 'er propeller goin' round like blazes."

"What are you going to do with Powis, Bill?"

"We're going to shove the case into Ebbstein's crib and then nip off to Spitalfields with the barrer. And we've got to look slippery, or we'll have the coppers on our heels, to say nothin' of them tug blokes. They'll be wantin' our scalps, I reckon, when they find their craft on the mud."

This conversation was by no means reassuring. I was certainly out of the frying-pan but it remained to be seen what sort of fire I had dropped into.

Meanwhile I carefully stowed my treasure in a secret receptacle inside the back of my waistcoat and braced myself as well as I could to resist the violent jolting and bumping caused by the combined effects of speed, indifferent springs and an abominably rough road. It was during a readjustment of my position after a more than usually violent joggle that my hand, seeking a more secure purchase on the wet surface, came into contact with a small body which felt somewhat like a flat button. I took it between my fingers and tried by the sense of touch to determine what it was, but could make out no more than that it was hard and smooth, flat and oval in shape and about half-an-inch long. This did not tell me much, and indeed I was not acutely interested in the question as to what the thing might be, but eventually, on the bare chance that it might turn out to be something of value, I deposited it in my secret pocket for examination on some more favourable occasion. Then I wedged myself afresh and awaited further developments.

I had not long to wait. Presently the barrow stopped. I felt the case lifted off and carried away. The light ceased to filter in through the cracks of the lid and was replaced by a curious, sour smell. A muttered conversation with someone who spoke very imperfect English was followed by another brief journey and then the case came to rest on a wooden floor and the smell grew more intense. A confused jabbering in an uncouth foreign tongue seemed to pervade the foul air, but this was soon interrupted by the unmistakable English voice that I had heard before.

"I'll soon 'ave it open, Ebbstein, if you've got a jemmy. That's the ticket, mate. Look out, there, inside!"

The beak of the jemmy drove in under the top edge, one or two quick jerks dislodged the nails, the lid was lifted clear, and I popped up as the last occupant had done. A swift, comprehensive glance showed me an ill-lighted frowsy room with a coke fire on which a tailor's "goose" was heating, a large work-board on which were piled a quantity of unfinished clothing, and three wild-looking women, each holding a half-made garment and all motionless like arrested clockwork figures, with their eyes fixed on me. Besides these, and a barrel filled with herrings and cut cabbage floating in a clear liquid, were the two men who confronted me, of whom one was a common, stubbly-haired English East-Ender while the other was a pale, evil-looking foreigner, with high cheek-bones, black, up-standing hair, and a black beard that looked like a handful of horsehair stuffing.

"Blimey!" ejaculated the Englishman, as I rose into view, "'T'aint Powis at all! Who the blazes are you?"

"Who is he!" hissed the foreigner, glaring at me fiercely, "I will tell you. He is a bolice spy!" and his hand began to creep under his coat-skirt.

The Englishman held up his hand. "Now none o' that, Ebbstein," said he. "You foreigners are so bloomin' excitable. Tell us who you are, young un."

I told them all I knew, including the name of the schooner – the *Gladwys of Cardiff* – and I could see that Ebbstein rejected the whole story as a manifest fable. Not so the Englishman. After a moment's reflection, he asked sharply, "How much did he give you for getting into that case?"

"Five shillings and a duffer," I replied promptly, having anticipated the question.

"Where's the five bob?" he asked, and I indicated my left trouser's pocket. Instantly and with remarkable skill, he slipped his hand into the pocket and fished out the three coins.

"Right you are," said he, spreading them out on his palm, "one for you, Ebb, one for me, and one for yourself, young un." And here, with a sly grin, he returned me the pewter half-crown, which I pocketed.

"And now," he continued, "the question is what we're to do with this young toff. We can't let him run loose just now. He might mention our address." Ebbstein silently placed one finger under his beard, but the other man shook his head impatiently.

"That's the worst of you foreigners," said he. "You're so blooming unconstitootional. This ain't Russian Poland. Don't you understand that this boy was seen to get into that case and that the coppers'll be askin' for him presently? You'd look a pretty fine fool if they was to come here for him and you'd only got cold meat to offer 'em. Have you got a empty room?"

"Dere is der top room, vere Chonas vorks," said Ebbstein.

"Very well. Shove him in there and lock him in. And you take my tip, young feller, and don't give Mr. Ebbstein no trouble."

"Are you going away?" I asked anxiously.

"I'm going to see what's happened to my pal, but you'll see me back here some time to-night."

After a little further discussion, the pair hustled me up the grimy, ruinous stairs to the top of the house and introduced me to an extraordinarily filthy garret, where, after a brief inspection of the window, they left me, locking the door and removing the key.

The amazing folly of the ordinary criminal began to dawn on me when I proceeded to lighten the tedium of confinement by examining my prison. I was shut up here, presumably, because I knew too much, and behold! I was imprisoned in a room which contained incriminating objects connected with at least two different kinds of felony. An untidy litter of plaster moulds, iron ladles, battered pewter pots, and crude electrical appliances let me into the secret at once. For, young as I was, I had learned a good deal about the seamy side of London life, and I knew a coiner's outfit when I saw it. So, too, a collection of jemmies, braces, bits, and skeleton keys was quite intelligible. These premises were used by a coiner – presumably Mr. 'Chonas' – and a burglar, who was possibly Ebbstein himself.

I examined all the tools and appliances with boyish curiosity, and was quite interested for a time, especially when I discovered the plaster mould of a half-crown, very sharp and clear and coated with polished black lead, which seemed to correspond with the 'Duffer' in my pocket. The resemblance was so close that I brought forth the coin and compared it with the mould, and was positively thrilled when they proved to be one and the same coin.

Then it suddenly occurred to me that Ebbstein probably had forgotten about the moulds, and that if he should realise the position he would come up and secure his safety by those "unconstitootional" methods that he had hinted at. The idea was most alarming. No sooner had it occurred to me than I resolved to make myself scarce at all costs.

There was not much difficulty at the start. The window was fixed with screws, but there were tools with which to unscrew it, and outside was a parapet. I began by sticking the end of one jemmy in a crack in the floor and jamming the other end against the door, which was as effective as a bolt. Then I extracted the screws from the window with a turn-screw bit, softly slid up the bottom sash and looked out. Exactly opposite was the opening of a mews or stable yard, but it was unoccupied at the moment. The coast seemed quite clear, the house was not overlooked, and the parapet ran along the whole length of the street. Arming myself with a two-foot jemmy, I crawled out on to the broad gutter enclosed by the parapet, shut the window, and hesitated for a moment, considering whether I should turn to the right or the left. Providence guided me to the

48

left, and I began to crawl away along the gutter, keeping below the parapet as far as possible.

As I passed the dormer window of the next house, curiosity led me to peep in, but at the first glance my caution fled, and I rose boldly to press my face against the glass. I looked into an unfurnished room tenanted by one person only, a handsome – nay a beautiful – girl of about my own age. Her limbs were pinioned with thinnish rope, and she was further secured with the same rope to a heavy chair. A single glance told me that she was no East-End girl. She was obviously a young lady, and my premature knowledge of the seamy side of life enabled me to hazard a guess as to what she was doing here.

She had already seen me and turned her deathly pale face to me in mute appeal. In a moment I had my big clasp-knife out, and, thrusting it up between the sashes, pushed back the catch. I quietly pulled down the top sash and climbed over into the room. She looked at me with mingled hope and apprehension and exclaimed imploringly, "Oh! Take me away from this dreadful place – " but I cut her short.

"Don't speak," I whispered, "they might hear you. I'm going to take you away."

I was about to cut the rope when it occurred to me that it might be useful, as there seemed to be a considerable length of it. So I untied the knot and unwound the coils, recoiling the rope and throwing it round my neck. As the young lady rose stiffly and stretched herself, I silently carried the chair to the door, where I stuck its low back under the handle and jammed the back legs against the floor. No one could now get into the room without breaking the door off its hinges.

"Can you follow me along the parapet, Miss?" I asked with some misgiving.

"I will do anything you tell me," she answered, "if you will only take me away from this place."

"Then," I said, "follow me, Miss, if you please." And climbing back out of the window, I reached in and took her hands to haul her up after me. She was an active, plucky girl, and I had her out on the gutter behind the parapet in a twinkling. Then, having softly shut the window, in case it should be noticed from outside, I crouched down in the gutter and motioned to her to do the same.

In the gathering dusk, we began to crawl slowly away, I leading, but we had advanced only a few yards when I heard her utter a low cry, and at the same time felt her grasp the skirt of my jacket. Turning back, I saw her peering with an expression of terror through a hole in the parapet that opened into a rain-hopper, and, backing as best I could, I applied my eye to the hole, but failed to see anything more alarming than a woman on the opposite side of the street, who was looking at the houses on our side as if searching for a number. To be sure, she was not a pleasant-looking woman. Tall and gaunt, with dead black hair and a dead white face, and pale grey eyes that struck a discord with her hair, and were not quite a match in colour – for the left eye looked considerably darker than the right – she impressed me somehow as evil-looking and abnormal with a suggestion of disguise or make-up, a suggestion that was heightened by her dress, for she wore the uniform of a hospital nurse, and I found myself instinctively rejecting it as a masquerade.

Still, unprepossessing as she was, I could see nothing terrifying in her aspect until my companion whispered in my ear, "She is coming to fetch me." Then I vaguely understood and shared her alarm. But the greater the danger, the greater the need to escape as quickly as possible. Accordingly, with a few whispered words of encouragement, I started forward again, crawling as fast as the confined space permitted. I looked up at the windows as we passed, but did not venture to peep in, but near the end of the row, I made out on one the words "*To Let*", written with soap or whitewash, and on this, I raised my head and looked in. The appearance of the empty room with its open door confirmed the inscription, and I made bold, after a cautious look round, to slip back the catch with my knife, lower the top sash, and enter. A very brief inspection showed that the house was really empty, so I returned and, quickly helping my protégée in through the window, slid up the sash.

While we were exploring the empty house, the young lady told me her story. That very morning her governess had left her for a few minutes to call at an office, and while she was waiting in the Strand, the woman whom we had just seen had come to her to tell her that the governess had been run over and taken to the hospital. She was then hurried into a cab by the nurse and driven to the house in which I had found her.

There was no time, however, for detailed explanations. We were by no means out of the wood yet. All the outside doors, front and back, were locked, and though I could have broken out with the jemmy, it was not a very safe plan on account of the noise that I should make. But there was another plan that looked more feasible. This particular house had no back yard, but gave directly on a narrow court, into which it would be fairly easy to drop from the first-floor window by the aid of the rope.

No sooner had I conceived the idea than I proceeded to execute it. Raising the bottom sash of the back first-floor window, I passed the cord through the bars of the fireplace.

"Shall I go first, Miss?" I asked. "The rope is rather short, and I had better be there to catch you if you have to drop."

50

She agreed eagerly, and, after a careful look up and down the court, I took the doubled rope in my hand, climbed out of the window, and, slipping down easily until I was near the ends of the rope, let go and dropped on the pavement.

Looking up, I saw the young lady, without a moment's delay, seize the rope and climb out of the window. But instead of grasping the two parts of the rope together, she had taken one in each hand, which made the descent much less easy, and as she apparently held one part more tightly than the other, the more loosely-held part began to slip up as the "bight" ran through the bars of the grate above. Finally, she let go with one hand, when the released end flew up and she came down "by the run" holding on to the other. I stepped forward as she dropped the last few feet and caught her without difficulty, and as I set her on her feet, the rope came down by its own weight and fell in a confused coil on top of us. Half-unconsciously, I picked it up and flung it round my neck as I glanced about in search of the exit from the court.

At this moment a man came, treading softly, round a bend of the narrow passage – a foreigner, evidently, and so like Ebbstein that, for a moment, I really thought it was that villain himself. He stopped short and looked at me with scowling inquisitiveness. Then, suddenly, he seemed to recognise the young lady, for he uttered a sort of snarl and stepped forward. At the sound she turned and saw the man, and the low, trembling cry that she gave, and the incredulous horror that froze upon her face, will be fresh and vivid in my memory though I should live for a century.

"You shall come back with me now!" the wretch exclaimed, and rushed at her with his foul hands spread out like talons. My gorge rose at the brute. The blood surged noisily in my ears and my teeth clenched tightly. The jemmy in my hand seemed to whirl aloft of itself. I was dimly aware of a strong muscular effort and a dull-sounding blow, of a limp fall, and a motionless figure on the pavement. Perhaps the man was dead. I didn't know and I didn't particularly care. At any rate I did not stop to ascertain. Taking my companion by the hand, I drew her swiftly down the court, grasping the jemmy tightly, and quite ready to use it again if need be.

We were obviously in great danger. Even as David, when he went down into Ashdod, we walked in the midst of enemies. There were few people in the ill-lighted street into which we emerged, but those few eyed us with sinister glances and whispered together ominously. We walked on quickly but without appearing to hurry, and presently turned into a street that was quite deserted save for a hansom cab that had drawn up outside a small public house. I stepped forward joyfully, remembering the golden bribe that I could, and would willingly, offer for a safe passage, but my companion suddenly seized my arm and dragged me into a deep doorway.

"Don't let him see us!" she exclaimed breathlessly. "He is the man who brought me here, and he is one of them. I heard the nurse call him Louis."

We pressed back into the doorway and I watched the man putting on the horse's nose-bag. He certainly was a villainous-looking rascal – pale, black-eyed, with crisp, curly, black hair, the very opposite of the English horsey type. When he had secured the nose-bag, he turned and entered the public house, and at the same moment I made up my mind. Advancing quickly, I deliberately took off the horse's nose-bag and threw it down.

"Jump into the cab!" I said to my companion, flinging the coil of rope and the jemmy down on the foot-board, and she stepped in without a word. I led the horse forward a few paces clear of the house, and then I climbed quickly to the driver's seat and took the reins. My experience of driving was small, but I had driven our van once or twice under the carman's supervision, and knew how to handle the "ribbons". A gentle shake of them now started the horse at a walk and I had just plucked the whip out of its socket when there rose from the direction of the court a shout of alarm and a confused noise of many voices. I shook the whip and the horse broke into a trot. The voices drew nearer and, just as I turned the corner, a loud yell from behind us announced that the cabman had discovered his loss. I gave the horse a sharp cut and he broke into a canter.

On we rattled through one after another of the short and narrow slum streets, turning the sharp corners on one wheel and shaving the treacherous posts, and always the roar of angry voices seemed to pursue us, gathering in volume and seeming to draw nearer. The cab swayed, men leaped aside with curses, women and children sprang from the kennels screaming, windows were flung up, and people yelled at us from doorways. And still the roar from behind seemed to draw nearer, and still I sat with clenched teeth, grasping the reins convulsively and thinking only of the posts at the corners.

Presently we entered a longer street and I whipped up the horse afresh. At the end of this street we came out into a broad road and I took a deep breath. Now I knew where I was: Commercial Road East. Ashdod was behind us with the gibbering crowd of our enemies. I lashed the horse into a gallop and rattled gaily along the broad road, westward. The police might stop me if they pleased, I cared not a fig for them. My lady was safe from those vampires, and that was all that mattered.

As we approached Whitechapel High Street, I stopped and raised the trap to ask where I should drive my fare. The address she gave was 63 Dorchester Square and, having obtained this, I drove on once more. But I went more soberly now that the danger was over and avoided the main streams of traffic. Years of experience in the delivery of parcels had made me almost as familiar with London as a fully qualified cabman, and I threaded my way through quiet squares and by-streets with no difficulty beyond that of driving the cab straight and keeping clear of other traffic. In less than an hour I turned into Dorchester Square and, slowing down to read the numbers, at length drew up before a large house.

I climbed down quickly and, snatching off my cap, helped my fare to alight. She stood by the cab, still holding my hand and looking earnestly into my face, and her eyes filled.

"I want to thank you," she said with a little catch in her breath, "and I can't. But my mother will. I will send someone out to hold the horse in a minute."

She ran up the steps and rang the bell. The great door opened. It was opened by a tall footman who seemed to be prematurely grey – in fact his hair was perfectly white, though he looked quite young. He stared at the young lady for a second or two as if stupefied, then he let off a most undignified yell. "Miss Stella's come back!"

So her name was Stella. A pretty name and a fit one for a lovely young lady. But I liked not that footman. And the great house, with its unfamiliar pomp, cast a chill on me. I felt a sudden shyness, which may have been pride.

Why should I see her mother? There was nothing more to do. "Miss Stella had come back," and there was an end of it.

I led the horse a few yards farther on to a lamp-post and taking the reins, which had fallen down, I secured them to the post with what our packer calls a clove hitch. Thriftily, I gathered up the coil of rope from the footboard – the jemmy had jolted off – and then I walked away across the Square.

I looked in at Sturt and Wopsalls, though the premises were shut. But the foreman, who lived there, told me that my truck had been brought home by the police, and when he had heard my story he advised me to leave all explanations to him, which I did. Of course I said nothing about the young lady.

To my revered parent I was even more reticent. Experience had taught me to maintain a judicious silence about any pecuniary windfall until some periodical financial crisis called forth my savings. But he was singularly incurious about the details of my daily life. Even the coil of rope which I brought home on my arm drew from him no comment or question. And as the frugal supper was on the table and we were both pretty sharp set, conversation tended for a while to be spasmodic, with the result that the story of my adventures remained untold.

Chapter II
Treasure Trove
(Jasper Gray's Narrative)

It was not until I had retired to my room for the night and taken the unusual precaution of locking the door that I ventured to turn out the secret pocket at the back of my waistcoat and inspect the almost unbelievable wealth that the day's adventures had yielded. Indeed, so incredible did my good fortune appear that nothing short of a minute and critical examination of each coin separately would convince me that the windfall was a glorious reality.

But a reality it was, and as I laid out the shining coins on my dressing-table, my eyes travelled over them with something approaching awe. Five golden sovereigns! Wealth beyond my wildest dreams. As I recall the ecstasy with which I gazed at them, I can understand the joys of the old-fashioned miser. The paper vouchers which pass as money in these later, degenerate days hold no such thrills.

And what a fortunate inspiration that secret pocket had been! The sewing of it on had been but a mere boyish freak with no defined purpose, for nothing more valuable than an occasional stray silver coin had ever come into my possession. Yet, but for that invaluable pocket, the five sovereigns would have gone the way of the two half-crowns. And thus reflecting, I was reminded of the little object that I had picked up in the egg-chest and dipped my fingers into the recesses of the somewhat irregularly shaped pocket. The object, when I at last discovered it in a sunken corner, appeared to be a little oval glass plate, flat on one side and rounded on the other, and about half-an-inch in length. As it was coated with dirt, I carried it to the wash hand-basin and, having tenderly bathed and wiped it, brought it back to the candle. And then I received another thrill, for, holding it up to the light, I found it to be of a beautiful deep, clear green colour, whereupon I instantly decided that it must be an emerald. But more than this: As I looked through it with the rounded side towards me, there appeared, as if in its very substance, but actually engraved on the flat side, a little castle, such as one uses in playing chess, and above it the tiny head of some animal which seemed to combine the characteristics of a donkey and a crocodile, while, underneath the castle, in the tiniest of lettering, were the words,

"*Strong in Defence*". Evidently this emerald had dropped out of a seal or a signet ring.

I knew all about seals, for Sturt and Wopsalls were accustomed to secure small parcels for the post in this way, and occasionally the packer had allowed me to perform this interesting operation, having instructed me in the proper method and how to prevent the wax from sticking to the seal. But the warehouse seal was a big, clumsy, brass affair, quite different from this delicate little engraved gem. Hence it is needless to say that I was all agog to make a trial of my new treasure, and, failing any more suitable material, I made a number of experimental impressions on samples of wax from the candle before returning the gem to its secret hiding-place. Then, having bestowed my golden windfall at the bottom of a drawer filled with miscellaneous clothing – mostly outgrown – I went to bed, gloating happily over my sudden accession of wealth.

Throughout the following day – it was a Saturday, I remember – the consciousness of my new opulence never left me. I seemed to walk on air. For the first time in my life I was a capitalist. If I had chosen – only I was not such a mug – I could have gone quite extensively "on the bust" or brought something really expensive. It was a delightful sensation, and it cost nothing so long as I kept my capital intact.

But even more than my treasure of gold was the mysterious emerald, a source of joy to which the uncertainty as to its value contributed not a little. I had read somewhere that the emerald is the most precious of stones, even more precious than the diamond. And this was quite a good-sized stone. Why it might be worth a hundred pounds! I had heard of diamonds that were worth more than that. True, it was probably some other person's property, and the circumstances in which I had acquired it strongly suggested that it was stolen property. But what of that? I had not stolen it, and I was fully prepared to surrender it to the rightful owner if ever he should appear. Meanwhile it was mine to possess and enjoy, and I made the most of it, halting from time to time in unfrequented places to fish it out of its hiding-place and hold it up to the light, revelling in its gorgeous colour and the quaint little castle and the preposterous little donkey or crocodile or whatever he was, magnified by the lens-like convex back of the gem.

Presently I became possessed by an overwhelming desire to see those mystic figures embodied in wax – real wax, sealing-wax. A survey of my pockets, revealing the presence of several pennies, and my arrival opposite a small stationer's shop in Chichester Rents settled the matter. I went in and demanded a stick of sealing-wax. The presiding genius, a dry-looking elderly man, rummaged awhile among some shelves at the back of the shop, and at length produced a cardboard box which he laid on the counter and in which I perceived a number of sticks of black sealing-wax.

"I'd rather have red," said I.

"M'yes," said he, giving the box a sort of reproachful shake, "I seem to have run out of red for the moment. Won't black wax do?"

I was about to say "No," when I observed a portion of a broken stick in the box, and my habitual thrift suggested the chance of a "deal".

"How much for that broken piece?" I enquired.

He looked at the fragment disparagingly, picked it out with much deliberation, and laid it on the counter.

"Make you a present of that," said he, and taking up the box, turned his back on me as if to avoid my grateful acknowledgments.

I went forth gleefully from the shop with the little stump of funereal wax in my pocket and a growing urge to make a trial of it. But there are three factors to a sealing operation: The seal, the wax, and the document or letter. The first two I had, and even as I was searching my pockets, and searching in vain, for some letter or envelope which might form a plausible subject for an experiment, Providence, or Fate, in a playful mood, supplied the deficiency. Just as I was about to cross Fleet Street, a spectacled gentleman, who looked like a lawyer's clerk and carried in his hand a large sheaf of letters, blundered hastily out of Middle Temple Lane and collided with another hustler who was proceeding in the opposite direction. The shock of the impact dislodged one of the letters from his hand but, unaware of his loss, he hurried away eastward. I ran across the road and picked up the letter, but by the time I had secured it, he had disappeared into the crowd. However, there was no need to pursue him. The letter was stamped and obviously ready for posting. All I had to do was to walk down to the post office and drop it in the box.

With this intention I had turned eastward and was threading my way among the crowd when, happening to glance at the letter in my hand, I noticed that the flap of the envelope was very insecurely stuck down. The letter, as I had already observed, was addressed to a Mr. Brodribb, at New Square, Lincoln's Inn. Now, if Mr. Brodribb lived in Lincoln's Inn, he was probably a lawyer, especially as the letter had come from the Temple, and if he was a lawyer, the letter possibly contained important and confidential matter. It was highly improper that such a letter should be insecurely fastened. The least that I could do was to close the envelope as securely as was possible. And since mere gum had been tried in the balance and found wanting, the obvious proceeding was to seal it and make it absolutely safe.

No sooner had I conceived the idea than I set about its execution. Darting down Inner Temple Lane in search of a retired spot, I turned to the left beside the church and, passing Oliver Goldsmith's grave, came to a monument provided with a shelf which would serve the purpose to perfection. Here, with no one to observe my proceedings (though, indeed, they were innocent enough and even meritorious) I laid the envelope, the box of matches, the wax, and the seal. Very carefully and methodically I melted the wax until I was able to deposit a nearly circular patch on the flap of the envelope. Then, giving it a few moments for the excessive stickiness to subside, I laid the precious seal daintily in position and made steady pressure on it with my thumb.

The result was perfect, even to the microscopic markings on the castle, so perfect that I was loath to part with my work. Again and again I gloated over the beauty of its jet-like polish and the clean-cut device as I walked slowly down Fleet Street until I reached the post office, where, reluctantly I dropped the letter into the yawning mouth of the box. However, if I must needs part with the finished work, I retained the means of repeating it indefinitely – nor, to do myself justice, did I neglect my opportunities. Every parcel to which I could get access went forth enriched as to its exterior with a supplementary impression on the parcel wax, and a couple of ponderous rolls of cartoon paper which I conveyed in the truck to Studios in Ebury Street and at Chelsea, arrived at their destinations adorned with one or two black seals in addition.

It was late in the evening when I reached home – for Saturday was little different to me from other days, excepting that it held the promise of Sunday. I was rather tired and uncommonly hungry. But to a strong and healthy lad, mere fatigue is not unpleasant, especially with an immediate prospect of unrestricted rest, and my hunger was mitigated by the comfortable consciousness of a pound of streaky bacon in my pocket, the product of a trifling honorarium tendered by the Ebury Street artist. That bacon was dedicated to future breakfasts, but still at a pinch (and pinches were not infrequent in our household) it might be made to yield a highly acceptable supper.

However, as I toiled up the noble staircase that mocked our poverty with its faded, old-world magnificence, my nose informed me that the bacon could be reserved for its legitimate function. A savoury aroma on the second-floor landing, waxed in intensity as I mounted the "third pair", offering suggestions that I hardly dared to entertain. But when I opened the door of our sitting-room, my doubts were dispelled and my wildest hopes received glorious confirmation.

I recall very vividly the picture that greeted my eyes as I paused for a moment in the open doorway. Beside the fire, seated in the old

Windsor arm-chair and clad in his shabby dressing-gown, behold Pontifex (my revered parent – Pontifex Maximus on occasions of ceremony, shortened to Ponty in familiar conversation) delicately adjusting something that reposed in a frying-pan and murmured softly, exhaling a delicious fragrance. I sniffed and listened in ecstasy. More grateful than the odours of myrrh and frankincense was that delightful aroma, sweeter to my ears that soft, sibilant murmur than songs of Araby. For they conveyed, without the clumsy intermediary of speech, the entrancing idea of scallops, and lest any faintest misgiving might linger, there in the fender was ranged a goodly row of twelve empty scallop-shells.

As I entered, Pontifex looked up with a smile compounded of welcome, triumph, and congratulation. We were strangely different in many respects, but on one point our souls were tuned in perfect unison. We both had a gluttonous passion for scallops. It could not often be indulged, for the bare necessaries of life consumed the whole of our joint financial resources. Our ordinary diet – largely consisting of Irish stew – was supplied under a slightly ambiguous contract by the lady on the second-floor. But she was an indifferent culinary artist, and we did not trust her with such rare delicacies as scallops, or even with bacon. These called for more subtle treatment, and besides, the very process of cooking them was a feast in itself.

While Pontifex, with consummate artistry and an air of placid satisfaction, tended the scallops, I proceeded to cut the bread and butter in order that there might be no unnecessary delay. And as I thus busied myself, my mind became half-unconsciously occupied, in the intervals of conversation, with speculations on the train of circumstances that had produced this unlooked-for festivity. How came Pontifex to be able to buy these scallops? Only that morning funds had been so short that it had been doubtful whether they would run to butter. Could Ponty have received an unexpected payment? It might be so, but I doubted it. And as I weighed the probabilities – and found them wanting – a horrible suspicion began to steal into my mind.

Concerning my golden windfall I had, for sound economic reasons, kept my own counsel. But the "snide" half-crown I thought might be allowed to transpire, so to speak, in the form of a booby-trap for poor old Ponty, to which end I had that very morning planted it on the corner of the mantelpiece, experience having informed me of my respected parent's habit of snapping up any unconsidered trifles in the way of specie. It was a foolish joke, but I had taken it for granted that as soon as Ponty had the coin in his hand, he would see that it was a counterfeit. I had made no allowance for the difference between his eyesight and mine or our respective experiences of "snide" money. And now it looked as if my joke had failed disastrously. For I now remembered having noticed when passing a fishmonger's shop on my way home that scallops were marked two-shillings-and-sixpence-a-dozen. Of course, it might be only a coincidence. But a sensible man looks askance at coincidences, and the suspicious fact remained that a half-crown had disappeared and two-and-sixpence worth of scallops had unaccountably made their appearance.

However, I refrained from spoiling poor Ponty's enjoyment of the feast by raising the very awkward question, and I even managed to dismiss it from my own mind. So we had a banquet that a Lord Mayor might have envied. The scallops were cooked to perfection and served tastefully in their native shells, and when those shells had become once more empty and I had brewed myself a pot of tea while Pontifex mixed an uncommonly stiff jorum of grog and lit a cigarette, we experienced that sense of luxury and well-being that comes only to those who have to count their coppers and whose rare banquets are seasoned by habitual hard living.

But the question of the "snide" half-crown had to be disposed of, for if it had purchased those scallops, then the scallops had been virtually stolen, and if it had not, it must be lurking in Ponty's pocket, an element of potential danger. Thus, I reflected on the morrow as, in accordance with our Sunday morning routine, I shaved Pontifex, laid the table, fried the bacon, and made the tea. Accordingly, as soon as we were seated at table, I opened fire with a leading question, which Pontifex received with a waggish air of surprise.

"So that was your half-crown!" he exclaimed. "Now why did that very simple explanation not occur to me? I tried to remember how I came to put it there, but my memory was a complete blank. Naturally, as I realise now."

"So you annexed it and busted it on scallops."

Pontifex smiled blandly. "Your inference," he remarked, "illustrates the curious fact that it is sometimes possible to reach a correct conclusion by means of perfectly incorrect reasoning. The connection which you assumed between the Treasure Trove and the scallops, though false in logic, was true in fact. But as to your use of the colloquialism, 'busted', I would point out that even as omelettes cannot be made without the breaking of eggs, so scallops at two-shillings-and-sixpence-a-dozen cannot be eaten without the expenditure of half-crowns."

"Precisely. That was how I established the connection."

"Assumed, my son," he corrected. "You did not establish it. You will note that your middle term was not distributed."

"If the scallops were the middle term," I rejoined, flippantly, "they were distributed all right. We had six each."

"I mean," he said with a deprecating smile, "that you fell into the common confusion of the undistributed middle. You confused the generic half-crown with a particular half-crown."

"Oh, no I didn't." I retorted. "I wasn't born yesterday. I know that the generic half-crown is made of silver. But this particular half-crown was made of pewter."

Pontifex suddenly became serious. Laying down his knife and fork, he looked at me for several seconds in silent dismay. At length he exclaimed, "You don't mean, my son, that it was a base coin?"

"That is just what I do mean. Rank duffer. Made out of a pewter pot. Chappie probably prigged the pewter pot to make it."

Pontifex was too much overcome even to protest at my vulgarisms of speech. Still gazing at me in consternation, he exclaimed tragically, "But this is terrible, Jasper. I have actually committed a gross fraud on that most estimable fish monger! Unwittingly, it is true, but a fraud nevertheless." (It was characteristic of Pontifex that he refrained from any suggestion that my idiotic booby-trap was the cause of the disaster. No man was more sensible of his own faults or more oblivious of other people's.)

"Yes," I agreed, "you undoubtedly sold him a pup. Precious mug he must have been to let you. But I suppose, as it was Saturday night, he was pretty busy."

"He was. The shop was crowded with buyers. But, my son, we shall have to make restitution – though, really, in the present circumstances of – ah – financial stringency – "

He explored his various pockets, which appeared to be rich in truncated fragments of lead pencil, in addition to which they yielded a small bunch of keys, a pen knife with a broken blade, a sixpence and three half-pence. These treasures he regarded disconsolately and returned them whence they came. Then he turned an enquiring and appealing eye on me. He knew, of course, that I had received my wages on the previous day, but delicately refrained from explicit allusion to the fact. However, as the entire sum reposed untouched in my pocket, in the form of four half-crowns, and the fishmonger had to be paid, I produced the necessary coin and pushed it across the table. Usually, I was a little chary of handing money to Pontifex, preferring to pay our debts myself, for Ponty's ideas on the subject of *meum* and *tuum* were a trifle obscure – or perhaps I should say communistic – where my property was concerned, and the establishments of the tobacconist and the spirit merchant exercised a fatal fascination. But he was scrupulous enough in regard to strangers and I had no misgivings as to my present contribution safely reaching its proper destination. Accordingly, when I had furnished him with the means wherewith to make restitution to the defrauded fishmonger, I considered the incident of the "snide" half-crown as closed.

But it was not, as I discovered when I arrived home on Monday night. The fishmonger, it appeared, had communicated with the police, and the police were profoundly interested in the coin, which they recognised as one of a series which was being issued in considerable numbers by a coiner whom they had failed to locate or identify. In consequence, Pontifex had been requested to ascertain from me how the coin had come into my possession and to communicate the information to the fishmonger for transmission to the police.

Now, in my mind, there was little doubt as to the source of that half-crown. It had come from the work shop or studio of the mysterious artist who had been referred to as "Chonas". But my experiences under the too-hospitable roof of Mr. Ebbstein had begotten an unwillingness to be involved in any affair connected with that establishment. I am not peculiarly secretive, but I have a habit of keeping my own counsel. 'Chonas's' proceedings were no concern of mine, and I was not disposed to meddle with them. Wherefore, in reply to Ponty's not-very-eager enquiries, I stated simply and quite truthfully that I had received the coin from a man who was a total stranger to me. This answer satisfied Pontifex, who was not acutely interested in the matter, and once more I assumed that I had finished with that disreputable coin. And once more I was mistaken.

Chapter III
A Mystery and a Disappearance
(Dr. Jervis's Narrative)

There are some – and not a few, I fear – of the dwellers in, or frequenters of London to whom the inexhaustible charms of their environment are matters of no more concern than is the landscape which the rabbit surveys indifferently from the mouth of his burrow. For them the sermons in stones are preached in vain. Voices of the past, speaking their messages from many an ancient building or historic landmark, fall on deaf ears. London, to such as these, is but an assemblage of offices and shops, offering no more than a field for profitable activity.

Very different from these unreflective fauna of the town was my friend Thorndyke. Inveterate town-sparrow as he was, every link with the many-coloured past, even though it were no more than an ancient street-name, was familiar and beloved, never to be passed without at least a glance of friendly recognition. Hence it was natural that when, on a certain Tuesday morning, we crossed Chancery Lane to enter Lincoln's Inn by the spacious archway of the ancient gate-house, he should pause to glance round the picturesque little square of Old Buildings and cast his eyes up to the weathered carving above the archway which still exhibits the arms of the builder and the escutcheons of the ancient family whose title gave the inn its name.

We were just turning away, debating – not for the first time – the rather doubtful tradition that Ben Jonson had worked as a bricklayer on this gateway, when we became aware of a remarkably spruce-looking elderly gentleman who was approaching from the direction of New Square. He had already observed us and, as he was obviously bearing down on us with intent, we stepped forward to meet him.

"This meeting," said he, as we shook hands, "is what some people would describe as providential, if you know what that means. I don't. But the fact is that I was just coming to call on you. Now you had better walk back with me to my chambers – that is, if you are at liberty."

"May I take it," said Thorndyke, "that there is some matter that you wish to discuss?"

"You may, indeed. I have a poser for you, a mystery that I am going to present to you for solution. Oh, you needn't look like that. This is a genuine mystery. The real thing. I've never been able to stump you yet, but I think I'm going to do it now."

"Then I think we are at liberty. What do you say, Jervis?"

"If there is a chance of my seeing my revered senior stumped, I am prepared to stay out all night. But I doubt if you will bring it off, Brodribb."

Mr. Brodribb shook his head. "I should like to think you are right, Jervis," said he, "for I am absolutely stumped, myself, and I want the matter cleared up. But it is a regular twister. I can give you the facts as we walk along. They are simple enough, as facts. It is the explanation of them that presents the difficulty.

"I think you have heard me speak of my client, Sir Edward Hardcastle. I am the family solicitor. I acted for Sir Edward's father, Sir Julian, and my father acted for Sir Julian's father. So I know a good deal about the family. Now, yesterday morning I received a letter which was sealed on the outside with Sir Edward Hardcastle's seal. I opened the envelope and took out the letter, naturally assuming that it was from Sir Edward. Imagine my astonishment when I found that the letter was from Frank Middlewick, your neighbour in the Temple."

"It certainly was rather odd," Thorndyke admitted.

"Odd!" exclaimed Brodribb. "It was astounding. Here was Sir Edward's private seal – the impression of his signet ring – on the envelope of a man who, as far as I knew, was a perfect stranger to him. I was positively staggered. I could make no sense of it, and as it was obviously a matter that called aloud for explanation, I slipped the letter in my pocket and hopped off to the Temple without delay.

"But my interview with Middlewick only made confusion worse confounded. To begin with, he didn't know Sir Edward Hardcastle even by name. Never heard of him. And he was perfectly certain that the seal wasn't put on in his office. He had written the letter himself – I had already observed that it was in his own handwriting – but the envelope was addressed and the letter put in it by his clerk, Dickson, after the copy had been taken and the entry made in the index. Dickson states that he put the letter in one of the ordinary envelopes from the rack and he is quite certain that, when he closed it and stuck the stamp on, there was no seal on it. Of course, there couldn't have been. Then he took the letter, with a number of others, and posted it with his own hand at the post office in Fleet Street."

"Did he check the letters when he posted them?" Thorndyke asked.

"No, he didn't. He ought to have done so, of course. But it seems that he was in a deuce of a hurry, so he shot the whole lot of letters into the box at once. Careless, that was. A man has no business to be in such a hurry that he can't attend to what he is doing. However it doesn't matter, as it happens. The post-mark shows that the letter was actually posted there at the time stated. So there's no help in that direction."

"And what about your own premises? Who took the letter in?"

"I took it in myself. I was strolling round the square, having my morning pipe, when I saw the postman coming along towards my entry. So I waited and took my batch of letters from him, and looked them over as I strolled back to the house. This one with the seal on it was among the batch. That is the whole story. And now, what have you got to say about it?"

Thorndyke laughed softly. "It is a quaint problem," said he. "We seem to be able to take it as certain that the letter was unsealed when it left Middlewick's office. Apparently it was unsealed when it was dropped into the post office letter-box. It was certainly sealed when the postman delivered it. That leaves us the interval between the posting and the delivery. The suggestion is that somebody affixed the seal to the letter in the course of transit through the post."

"That seems quite incredible," said I. "The seal was the impression of a signet ring which couldn't possibly have been in the possession of any of the post office people – to say nothing of the general absurdity of the suggestion."

"Mere absurdity or improbability," replied Thorndyke, "can hardly be considered as excluding any particular explanation. The appearance of this seal in these circumstances is grotesquely improbable. It appears to be an impossibility. Yet there is the devastating fact that it has happened. We can hardly expect a probable or even plausible explanation of so abnormal a fact, but among the various improbable explanations, one must be true. All that we can do is to search for the one that is the least improbable, and I agree with you, Jervis, that the post office is not the most likely place in which the sealing could have occurred. It seems to me that the only point at which we make anything resembling a contact with probability is the interval between Dickson's leaving the office and the posting of the letters."

"I don't quite follow you," said Brodribb.

"What I mean is that at that point there is an element of uncertainty. Dickson believes that he posted the letter but, as he did not check the letters that he posted, it is just barely possible that this one may have in some way escaped from his custody."

"But," objected Brodribb, "it was certainly posted at the place and time stated. The post-mark proves that."

"True. But it might have been posted by another hand."

"And how does that suggestion help us?"

65

"Very little," Thorndyke admitted. "It merely allows us to suggest, in addition to the alternatives known to us – all of them wildly incredible and apparently impossible – a set of unknown circumstances in which the sealing might credibly have happened."

"That doesn't seem very satisfactory," I remarked.

"It is highly unsatisfactory," he replied, "since it is purely speculative. But you see my point. If we accept Dickson's statement we are presented with a choice of apparent impossibilities. Middlewick could not have sealed the letter. Dickson could not have sealed it. We agree that it appears impossible for the postal officials to have sealed it, and it is unimaginable that the postman sealed it. Yet it left Middlewick's hands unsealed and arrived in the postman's hands sealed. Thus the apparently impossible happened. On the other hand, if we assume that the letter passed out of Dickson's possession in some way without his knowledge, we are assuming something that is not inherently improbable. And if we further assume – as we must, since the letter was posted by somebody – that there was an interval during which it was in the possession of some unknown person, then we have something like a loop-hole of escape from our dilemma. For, since the assumed person is unknown to us, we cannot say that it was impossible, or even improbable, that he should have had the means of sealing the letter."

I laughed derisively. "This is all very well, Thorndyke," said I, "but you are getting right off the plane of reality. Your unknown person is a mere fiction. To escape from the difficulty, you invent an imaginary person who might have had possession of Sir Edward's ring, and might have had some motive for sealing with it a letter which was not his, and with which he had no concern. But there isn't a particle of evidence that such a person exists."

"There is not," Thorndyke agreed. "But I remind my learned friend that this perfectly incredible thing has undoubtedly happened and that we are trying to imagine some circumstances in which it might conceivably have happened. Obviously, there must be some such circumstances."

"But," I protested, "there is no use in merely inventing circumstances to fit the case."

"I don't quite agree with you, Jervis," Brodribb interposed. "As Thorndyke points out, since the thing happened, it must have been possible. But it does not appear to be possible in the circumstances known to us. Therefore, there must have been some other circumstances which are unknown to us. Now the suggestion that Dickson dropped the letter (which, I understand, is what Thorndyke means) is not at all improbable. We know that he was in a devil of a hurry, and I know that he is as blind as a bat. If he dropped the letter, somebody certainly picked it up and put it in the post, and I agree that that is probably what really occurred. I should think so on grounds of general probability, but I have a further reason.

"Just now I said that I had told you the whole story, but that was not strictly correct. There is a sequel. As soon as I left Middlewick, I sent off a reply-paid telegram to Sir Edward asking him if his signet ring was still in his possession and if he had sealed any strange letter with it. In reply, I got a telegram from his butler saying that Sir Edward was away from home and adding that a letter would follow. That letter arrived this morning, and gave me some news that I don't like at all. It appears that last Tuesday – this day week – Sir Edward left home with the expressed intention of spending a couple of days in Town and returning on Thursday afternoon. But he did not return on that day. On Friday, Weeks, the butler, telegraphed to him at the club, where he usually stayed when in town, asking him when he would be coming home. As no reply to this telegram was received, Weeks telegraphed next day – Saturday – to the secretary of the club enquiring if Sir Edward was still there. The secretary's answer informed him that Sir Edward had stayed at the club on Tuesday night, had gone out after breakfast on Wednesday morning and had not returned since, but that his suit-case and toilet fittings were still in his bedroom.

"This rather disturbed Weeks, for Sir Edward is a methodical man and regular in his habits. But he didn't like to make a fuss, so he decided to wait until Monday night, and then, if his master did not turn up, to communicate with me. As I have said, up to the time of his writing to me, Sir Edward had not returned, nor had he sent any message. So the position is that his whereabouts are unknown, and, seeing that he has left his kit at the club, the whole affair has a very unpleasant appearance."

"It has," Thorndyke agreed, gravely, "and in the light of this disappearance the seal incident takes on a new significance."

"Yes," I hastened to interpose, "and the assumed unknown person seems to rise at once to the plane of reality."

"That is what I feel," said Brodribb. "Taken with the disappearance, the incident of the seal has an ominous look. And there is another detail, which I haven't mentioned, but which I find not a little disturbing. The seal on this letter is impressed in black wax. It may mean nothing, but it conveys to me a distinctly sinister suggestion. Sir Edward, like most of us, always used red wax."

On this Thorndyke made no comment, but I could see that he was as much impressed as was our old friend and as I was, myself. Indeed, to me this funereal wax seemed to impart to the incident of the seal an entirely new character. From the region of the merely fantastic and whimsical, it passed to that of the tragic and portentous.

"There is just one point," said Thorndyke, "on which I should like to be quite clear. It is, I suppose, beyond doubt that this is really Sir Edward's seal – the actual impression of his signet ring?"

"You shall judge for yourself," replied Brodribb, and forthwith he started forward towards his entry. (Hitherto we had been pacing up and down the broad pavement of the square.) He preceded us to his private office where, having shut the door, he unlocked and opened a large deed box on the lid of which was painted in white lettering: "*Sir Edward Hardcastle, Bart*". From this he took out an envelope, apparently enclosing a letter and bearing on its flap a small seal in red wax. This he laid on the table, and then, extracting from his pocket wallet another envelope, bearing a similar seal in black wax, laid it down beside the other. Thorndyke picked them up and, holding them as near together as was possible, made a careful comparison. Then, through his pocket lens, he made a prolonged inspection, first of the red seal and then of the black. Finally, producing a small calliper gauge which he usually carried in his pocket, he measured the two diameters of each of the little oval spaces in which the device was enclosed.

"Yes," he said, handing the envelopes to me, "there is no doubt that they are impressions of the same seal. The possible fallacy is not worth considering."

"What fallacy do you mean?" asked Brodribb.

"I mean," he replied, "that if you would leave one of these impressions with me for twenty-four hours I could present you with an indistinguishable facsimile. It is quite easy to do. But, in the present case, the question of forgery doesn't seem to arise."

"No," agreed Brodribb, "I don't think it does. But the question that does arise, is, what is to be done? I suppose we ought to communicate with the police at once."

"I think," said Thorndyke, "that the first thing to be done is to call at the club and find out all that we can about Sir Edward's movements. Then, when we know all that is to be known, we can, if it still seems desirable, put the police in possession of the facts."

"Yes," Brodribb agreed, eagerly, "that will be much the better plan. We may be able to do without the police and avoid a public fuss. Can you come along now? It's an urgent case."

"It is," Thorndyke agreed. "Yes, we must let our other business wait for the moment. We had no actual appointment."

Thereupon, Brodribb drew the letters out of the envelopes and, having deposited the former in the deed box, which he closed and locked, bestowed the latter in his wallet.

"May want the seals to show to the police," he explained as he slipped the wallet into his pocket. "Now let us be off."

We made our way out of the square by the Carey Street gate and headed for the Strand by way of Bell Yard. At the stand by St. Clement's Church, we picked up an unoccupied growler and, when we had jammed ourselves into its interior, Brodribb communicated the destination to the cabman, who looked in on us as he closed the door. "Clarendon Club, Piccadilly."

The cabman thereupon climbed to his box and gave the reins a shake, and our conveyance started forward on its career towards the west.

"I take it," said Thorndyke, "that Sir Edward wears this ring on his finger?"

"Not as a rule," Brodribb replied. "It is an old ring – an heirloom, in fact – and it is rather a loose fit and apt to drop off. For that reason, and because he sets a good deal of value on it, Sir Edward usually carries it in his waistcoat pocket in a little wash-leather case."

"And what is the ring like? Is it of any considerable intrinsic value?

"As to its intrinsic value," replied Brodribb, "I can't tell you much, as I have not been told and don't know much about jewels. But I can tell you what it is like, and perhaps you can judge of its value from the description. The stone, I understand, is a green tourmaline of an unusually fine colour, flat on the front, which, of course bears the engraved device, and convex at the back. The ring itself is rather massive and ornamented with a certain amount of chased work, but the general effect is rather plain and simple. What should you say as to its value?"

"Principally artistic and sentimental," Thorndyke replied. "A tourmaline is a very beautiful stone, especially if it is cut so as to display the double colouring – which, apparently, this one was not, but it is not one of the very precious stones. On the other hand, a green tourmaline might easily be mistaken by a person who had no special knowledge for an emerald, which is, in certain cases, the most precious of all stones."

"In any case," said I, "it would be worth stealing, and certainly worth picking up if it happened to be dropped."

The discussion was interrupted by the stopping of the cab opposite the club. We all alighted and, as Thorndyke was paying the cabman, I followed Brodribb up the steps to the hall, where our friend presented his card to the porter and asked to see the secretary. Almost immediately, the messenger returned and ushered us to the private office where we found a small, grave-looking gentleman standing beside his desk to receive us.

"I am extremely relieved to see you, Mr. Brodribb," the secretary said when the necessary introductions had been made and the purpose of our visit stated. "I had the feeling that I ought to communicate with the police, but you understand the difficulty. The club members wouldn't like a public fuss or scandal, and then there is Sir Edward, himself. He would be annoyed if he should return to find himself the subject of a newspaper sensation. But now," he smiled deprecatingly, "I can transfer the burden of responsibility to your shoulders. Is there any information that I can give you?"

"If you have any," replied Brodribb. "I have seen your letter to Weeks, Sir Edward's butler."

"Then I think you know all that I have to tell. But perhaps there is something more that – " He broke off undecidedly and looked from Brodribb to Thorndyke with an air of vague enquiry.

"Could we have a look at the bedroom that Sir Edward occupied?" Thorndyke asked.

"Certainly," was the ready, almost eager response. "I will go and get the key."

He hurried away, evidently all agog to pass on his embarrassments to Brodribb and be clear of them. When he returned with the key in his hand, he invited us to follow him and preceded us along a corridor and up a back stairway to another corridor at a door in which he halted to insert and turn the key. As the door swung open, he stood aside to let us pass and, when we had entered, he followed and closed the door after him.

For a minute or more we all stood silently glancing around and taking in the general aspect of the room, and I could see that the distinctly uncomfortable impression that the appearance of the room produced on me was shared by my companions. Not that there was anything unusual or abnormal in its aspect. On the contrary, the room had precisely the appearance that one would expect to find in the bedroom of a gentleman who was in residence at his club. And that was, in the circumstances, the disquieting fact. For thus had the room been lying in a state of suspended animation, as one might say, for close upon a week, a fact which every object in it seemed to stress. The neatly-made bed with the folded pyjamas on the pillow, the brushes, nail scissors and other little toilet implements on the dressing-table, the tooth-brush, nail-brush, and sponge on the wash-stand, all offered the same sinister suggestion.

"I take it," said Thorndyke, voicing my own conclusion, "that Sir Edward wears a beard?"

"Yes," Brodribb replied.

"Then, since he had no razors, and all his travelling necessaries appear to be here, we may assume that he took nothing with him."

"Yes, that seems to be the case," Brodribb agreed, gloomily.

"Which implies," Thorndyke continued, "that, when he went away, he had the intention of returning here to sleep."

The implication was so obvious that Brodribb acknowledged it only with a nod and an inarticulate grunt. Then turning to the secretary, he asked, "Did he leave anything in your custody, Mr. Northbrook?"

"Nothing," was the reply. "Whatever he had with him and did not take away is in this room."

On this, Thorndyke stepped over to the dressing-chest and pulled out the drawers, one after another. Finding them all empty, he transferred his attention to a suit-case that rested on a trunk-stand. It proved to be locked, but the lock was an artless affair which soon yielded to a small key from Mr. Brodribb's voluminous bunch.

"Nothing much there," the latter commented as he held up the lid and glanced disparagingly at a few collars and a couple of shirts which seemed to form the sole contents of the case. He was about to lower the lid when Thorndyke, with characteristic thoroughness, took out the collars and lifted the shirts. The result drew from our friend an exclamation of surprise, for the removal of the shirts brought into view some objects that had been – perhaps intentionally – concealed by them: A large and handsome gold watch and guard, a bunch of keys, a tie-pin, set with a single large pearl, and one or two opened letters addressed to the missing man. The latter, Brodribb scanned eagerly and then replaced with an air of disappointment.

"Family letters," he explained. "Nothing in them that is of any use to us. But," he added, looking anxiously at Thorndyke, "this is a most extraordinary affair. Most alarming, too. It looks as if he had deliberately removed from his person everything of intrinsic value."

"Excepting the ring," Thorndyke interposed.

"True, excepting the ring. He may have forgotten that, unless he had intended to use it – to seal some document, for instance. But otherwise he seems to have jettisoned everything of value. I need not ask you what that suggests."

"No," Thorndyke replied, answering Brodribb's interrogative glance rather than his words. "Taking appearances at their face value, one would infer that he was intending to go to some place where personal property is not very secure. That is the obvious suggestion, but there are other possibilities."

"So there may be," said Brodribb, "but I shall adopt the obvious suggestion until I see reason to change my mind. Sir Edward went from here to some place where, as you say, personal chattels are not very safe. And where a man's property is not safe, his life is usually not safe either. What we have seen here, coupled with his disappearance, fills me with alarm, indeed with despair, for I fear that the danger, whatever it was, has already taken effect. This is the seventh day since he left here."

Thorndyke nodded gloomily. "I am afraid, Brodribb," he said, "that I can only agree with you. Still, whatever we may think or feel, there is only one thing to be done. We must go at once to Scotland Yard and put the authorities there in possession of all the facts that are known to us. This is essentially a police case. It involves the simultaneous search of a number of likely localities by men who know those localities and their inhabitants by heart."

Brodribb assented immediately to Thorndyke's suggestion, and when he had taken possession of the derelict valuables and given Mr. Northbrook a receipt for them, we shook hands with that gentleman and took our leave.

At Scotland Yard we had the rather unexpected good fortune to learn that our old friend, Superintendent Miller, was in the building and, after a brief parley, we were conducted to his office. On our entrance, he greeted us collectively and motioned to the messenger to place chairs for us. Then, regarding Thorndyke with a quizzical smile, he enquired, "Is this a deputation?"

"In a way," replied Thorndyke, "it is. My friend, here, Mr. Brodribb, whom you have met on some previous occasions, has come to ask for your assistance in regard to a client of his who is missing."

"Anyone I know?" enquired Miller.

"Sir Edward Hardcastle of Bradstow in Kent," Brodribb replied.

The Superintendent shook his head. "I don't think I have ever heard the name," said he. "However, we will see what can be done, if you will give us the necessary particulars."

He laid a sheet of paper on the desk before him, and, taking up his fountain pen, looked interrogatively at Brodribb.

"I think," said the latter, "you had better hear the whole story first and then take down the particulars. Or I could supply you with a full account in writing, which would save time just now."

"Yes," Miller agreed, "that would be the best plan." But nevertheless he held his pen in readiness and jotted down a note from time to time as Brodribb proceeded with his narrative. But he made no comments and asked no questions until that narrative was concluded, listening with the closest attention and obviously with the keenest professional interest.

"Well," he exclaimed, as Brodribb concluded, "that is a queer story, and the queerest part of it is that sealed letter. I can make nothing of that. It may be some odd chance or it may be a practical joke. But there is an unpleasant air of purpose about it. We can hardly believe that Sir Edward sealed the letter, and if he didn't, his ring was in someone else's possession. If it was, it may have been lost and picked up or it may have been stolen. There's an alarming lot of 'ifs' in this case. Do you know anything about Sir Edward's habits?"

"Not a great deal," replied Brodribb. "He is a quiet, studious man, rather solitary and reserved."

"Not in the habit of attending race meetings?"

"I should say not."

"Nor addicted to slumming?"

"No. I believe he spends most of his time at his place in Kent, and, apart from books, I think his principal interest is gardening."

"Ha!" said Miller. "Well, that leaves us pretty much in the dark. If a man was proposing to attend a race meeting, he might naturally leave his more valuable portable property at home, and the same if he was bound on some expedition into the slums, or if he expected to be in some sort of rough crowd. At any rate, the fact remains that he did turn out his pockets before starting from the club, so we can take it that he had in view the possibility of his getting into some shady company. We shall have to find out a bit more about his habits. What is this butler man, Weeks, like?"

"A most intelligent, conscientious, responsible man. He could probably tell you more about Sir Edward's habits than anyone. Would you like him to come and see you?"

"We've got to see him," Miller replied, "to fill in details, but I think it would be better for one of our men – unless I can manage it myself – to go down and see him at the house. You see, we shall want a full description of the missing man and at least one photograph, if we can get it. And we may want to go over his clothes and hats for private marks and Bertillon measurements."

"For Bertillon measurements!" exclaimed Brodribb. "But I thought you required the most minute accuracy for them."

"So you do if you can get it," replied Miller. "But, you see, the system depends on what we may call multiple agreements, like circumstantial evidence. It isn't a question of one or two accurate measurements but of the coincidence of a large number with no disagreements. If we should find an unrecognisable body with legs and forearms, thighs, and upper arms about the same length as Sir Edward's, and if the chest and waist measurements were about the same as his, and if the head would fit his hats, the hands would fit his gloves and the feet would fit his boots, and if there was no disagreement in any one measurement, then we should have established a very strong probability that the body was *his* body. It is surprising how much information an experienced man can get from clothes. Of course, I am speaking of clothes that have been worn and that have creases that mark the position of the joints. But even new clothes will tell you quite a lot."

"Will they really?" said Brodribb, in a slightly shocked tone – for, despite his expressed pessimism, he was hardly prepared to consider his client in the character of a body. "I can understand their use for comparison with those on the – er – person, but I should not have expected them to furnish measurements of scientific value. However, I think you have Weeks's address?"

"Yes, and I will just jot down one or two particulars – dates, for instance."

He did so, and when he had finished, as our business seemed to be concluded, we thanked him for his interest in the case and rose to depart. As we moved towards the door, Brodribb turned to make a last enquiry.

"Would it be admissible to ask if you think there is a reasonable chance of your being able to trace my missing client?"

Miller reflected awhile, assisting the process of cogitation by gently scratching the back of his head. "Well, Mr. Brodribb," he replied, at length, "I'm like the doctor, I'm not fond of guessing. The position is that this gentleman is either alive or dead. If he is dead, his body must be lying somewhere and it is pretty certain to come to light before very long. If he is alive, the matter is not so simple, for he must be keeping out of sight intentionally, and as he is not known to any of our people, he might be straying about a long time before he was recognised and reported. But I can promise you that everything that is possible shall be done. When we have got a good photograph and a description, they will be circulated among the police in all likely districts and instructions issued for a sharp look-out to be kept. That is about all that we can do. I suppose you would not care for us to publish the photograph and description?"

"I don't think it would be advisable," Brodribb replied. "If he should, after all, return to his club, it would be so extremely unpleasant for him – and for me. Later, it may be necessary, but for the present, the less fuss that we make, the better."

74

The Superintendent was disposed to agree with this view, and when Brodribb had once more promised to send full written particulars with a special impression of the missing seal, we finally took our departure.

Chapter IV
Mr. Brodribb's Perplexities
(Dr. Jervis's Narrative)

During the next few weeks we saw a good deal of Mr. Brodribb. Indeed, his visits to our chambers became so frequent, and he became so acutely conscious of their frequency, that he was reduced to the most abject apologies for thus constantly intruding on our privacy. But we always received him with the warmest of welcomes, not only for the sake of our long-standing friendship, but because we both realised that the warm-hearted old lawyer was passing through a period of heavy tribulation. For Mr. Brodribb took his responsibilities as a family solicitor very seriously. To him, the clients whose affairs he managed were as his own family, their welfare and their interests took precedence over every other consideration, and their property was as precious and sacred as if it had been his own.

Hence, as the time ran on and no tidings of the missing man came to hand, the usually jovial old fellow grew more and more worried and depressed. It was not only the suspense of waiting for news that kept his nerves on edge, but the foreboding that when the tidings should at last come, they would be tidings of tragedy and horror. Nor even was this all, for, presently, it began to transpire that there were further causes of anxiety.

From chance phrases of rather ambiguous import, we inferred that the baronet's disappearance bade fair to create a situation of some difficulty from the legal point of view, but as to the nature of the difficulties we were unable to judge until a certain evening when Brodribb at last unburdened himself of his anxieties and entered into explicit particulars. I do not think that he started with the intention of going into details, but the matter arose naturally in the course of conversation.

"I suppose," he began, "we could hardly expect to keep this horrible affair to ourselves, but I had rather hoped that we might have avoided scandal and gossip, at least until something of legitimate public interest occurred."

"And haven't we?" asked Thorndyke.

76

"No. There has been a leakage of information somewhere. Police, I suspect, unless it was someone at the club. It would hardly be Northwood, though, for he was more anxious than any of us to keep the affair dark. Anyhow, a notice of the disappearance has got into at least one newspaper."

"Which newspaper was it?"

"Ah, that is what I have been unable to ascertain. The way in which I became aware of it was this: A man – a relative of Sir Edward's and an interested party – called on me a day or two ago to make enquiries. He said that he had heard a rumour that Sir Edward was missing and wished to know if there was any truth in it. I asked him where he heard the rumour, and he said that he had seen some obscure reference to the matter in one of the evening papers, but he couldn't remember which paper it was. I pressed him to try to remember, for it struck me as most remarkable that he should have forgotten the name of the paper – he being, as I have said, an interested party. I should have expected him to preserve the paper, or at least have cut out the paragraph. But he persisted that he had no idea whatever as to what paper it was."

"It was, as you say, rather odd," commented Thorndyke. "If it isn't an indiscreet question, in what respect and to what extent was he an interested party?"

"In a very vital respect," replied Brodribb. "He thinks that he is the heir presumptive."

"And do I understand that you think otherwise?"

"No. I am afraid I am disposed to agree with him. But I am not going to commit myself. Meanwhile, he shows signs of being damned troublesome. He is not going to let the grass grow under his feet. He began to throw out hints of an application to the court for leave to presume death, which is preposterous at this stage."

"Quite," Thorndyke agreed. "But, of course, if Sir Edward doesn't presently turn up, alive or dead, that is what you will have to do, and having regard to the circumstances, the Court would probably be prepared to consider the application after a comparatively short period."

"So it might," Brodribb retorted, doggedly. "But he will have to make the application himself, and if he does, I shall contest it."

Here he suddenly shut himself up, dipping his fine old nose reflectively into his wineglass and fixing a thoughtful eye on the empty fireplace. But somehow, his abrupt silence conveyed to me in some subtle manner the impression that he would not be unwilling to be questioned further. Nor was I mistaken, for, after a pause, during which neither Thorndyke nor I had made any comment, he broke the silence with the remark, "But I've no business to come here boring you two fellows with a lot of shop talk – and my own private shop at that."

"Indeed!" said Thorndyke. "Are we then of no account? I rather thought that we were to some extent concerned in the case and that, to that extent, we might regard your shop as our shop."

"He knows that perfectly well, old humbug that he is," said I. "And he knows that nothing but our superlative good manners has restrained us from demanding full particulars."

Mr. Brodribb smiled genially and emptied his glass.

"Of course," said he, "if you are so polite as to express an actual interest in the civil aspects of the case, I shall take you at your word. It will be very helpful to me to talk matters over with you, though I really hardly know where to begin."

"You might begin," said Thorndyke, "by filling your glass. The decanter is on your side. Then you might tell us what your objections are to this claimant, whom you admit to be the heir presumptive."

"I don't admit anything of the kind," protested Brodribb as he filled his glass and pushed the decanter across the table. "I merely agree that his claim appears, at the moment, to be quite a good and well-founded one."

"I don't see much difference," said I, "between an heir presumptive and a claimant with a well-founded claim. But never mind. You object to the gentleman for some reason. Tell us why you object to him."

Brodribb considered the question for a while. At length he replied, "I think, if you are really interested in the state of affairs, it would be best for me to give you a short sketch of the family history and the relationships. Then you will understand my position and my point of view. I need not go back in detail beyond Sir Edward's father, Sir Julian Hardcastle.

"Sir Julian had two sons, Edward and Gervase. As the estate is settled *in tail male*, we can ignore the female members of the family. On Sir Julian's death, Edward, the elder, succeeded, and as he was already married and had one son, the succession was, for the time being, satisfactorily settled. The younger son, Gervase, married his cousin, Phillipa, a daughter of Sir Julian's brother William. There was a good deal of opposition to the marriage, but the young people were devoted to one another and in the end they made a run-away match of it."

"Was the opposition due to the near kinship of the parties?" I asked.

"Partly, no doubt. There is a very general prejudice against the marriage of first cousins. But the principal objection of the young lady's people was to Gervase, himself. It seems – for I never saw her – that Miss Phillipa was an extremely beautiful and attractive girl who might have been expected to make a brilliant marriage, whereas Gervase was a younger son with very little in the way of expectations. However, that might have passed. The real trouble was that Gervase had acquired some bad habits when he was up at Oxford and he hadn't shaken them off. Plenty of young fellows tend to overdo the libations to Bacchus during their undergraduate days. But it is usually mere youthful expansiveness which passes off safely when they come down from the 'Varsity and take up their adult responsibilities. Unfortunately, it was not so with Gervase. Conviviality passed into chronic intemperance. He became a confirmed drinker, though not an actual drunkard.

"I may as well finish with him, so far as his history is known to me, as that history complicates the present position. I may have given the impression that he was a waster, but he was not, by any means. He was a queer fellow in many respects, but, apart from his tippling habits, there was nothing against him. And he must have had considerable abilities, for I understand that he not only graduated with distinction, but was reputed the most brilliant classical scholar of his year. In fact he became a Fellow of his college, and after his marriage, I believe he took Orders, though he remained at Oxford in some teaching capacity. I don't know much of his affairs at this time. It wasn't my business, and Sir Edward did not talk much about him, but so far as I can gather, his career at the University came to a sudden and disastrous end. Something happened. I don't know what it was, but I suspect that he got drunk under circumstances that created a public scandal. At any rate, he was deprived of his Fellowship and had to leave Oxford, and from that time, with a single exception, all trace of him is lost – at least to me. But he must have felt his disgrace acutely, for it is clear that he cut himself off entirely from his family and went virtually into hiding on the continent."

"What about his wife?" I asked.

"She certainly went with him into exile, and though she never communicated with her family at this time, I think there is no doubt that, in spite of all his faults, she remained devoted to him. That appears plainly in connection with the single reappearance which I mentioned, of which I heard indirectly from Sir Edward. It seems that a friend of the family who had known Gervase at Oxford came across him by chance in Paris, and from his account of the meeting, it would seem that the poor fellow was in a very sad way. His appearance suggested abject poverty, and his manner was that of a man who had received some severe shock. He had a bewildered air and seemed to be only partially conscious of what was going on around him. He gave no account of himself in any respect save one, which was that he had lost his wife some time previously, but he did not say when or where she died. He did not seem

79

to have any distinct ideas as to place or time. The fact of his loss appeared to occupy his thoughts to the exclusion of everything else. In short, he was the mere wreck of a man.

"The friend – whose name I forget, if I ever knew it – had some idea of helping him and trying to get him into touch with his family, but before he could make any move, Gervase had disappeared. As he had given no hint as to his place of abode, no search for him was possible, and so this unfortunate man passes out of our ken. The only further news we got of him was contained in a notice in the obituary column of *The Times* some twelve months later which recorded his death at Brighton. No address was given, and, I am sorry to say, neither Sir Edward nor I made any enquiries at the time. I cut the notice out and put it with the papers relating to the estate, and there, for the time being the matter ended."

"There was no doubt that the notice really referred to him?" Thorndyke asked.

"No. He was described as '*The Reverend Gervase Hardcastle, M.A.* (so apparently he had taken orders), *formerly Fellow of Balliol College, Oxford*', and his age was correctly given. No, I think there can be no doubt that the notice referred to him. Of course, I ought to have looked into the matter and got all the particulars, but at the time Sir Edward's son and wife were both alive and well, so it looked as if there were no chance of any question arising with regard to the succession."

"It is not known, I suppose," said Thorndyke, "whether Gervase had any children?"

"No. There were no children up to the time when he left England. But it is possible that some may have been born abroad. But if so, since we have no knowledge whatever as to where he lived during his wanderings and don't even know in what country his wife died, we have no date on which to base any enquiries. As a matter of fact, both Sir Edward and I assumed that, at least, there was no son, for if there had been, we should almost certainly have received some communication from him after Gervase's death. That was what we assumed, but of course we ought not to have left it at that. But now we had better pursue the course of events.

"Gervase's death, as recorded in *The Times*, occurred sixteen years ago. Six years later, Sir Edward lost both his wife and his son – his only child – within a few days. A malignant form of influenza swept through the house and brought Sir Edward, himself, to the very verge of the grave. When he at length rose from his bed, it was to find himself a childless widower. This altered the position radically, and, of course, we ought to have made such enquiries as would have cleared up the question of the succession. But Sir Edward was, for the time, so broken by his bereavements that I hardly liked to trouble him about a matter which had ceased to be his personal concern, and on the few occasions when I raised the question, I found him quite uninterested. His view was that there was nothing to discuss, and assuming, as he did, that Gervase had died without issue (in which assumption I concurred) he was right. In that case, the heir presumptive was undoubtedly his cousin Paul, Phillipa's brother, and as Paul Hardcastle was an entirely eligible successor, Sir Edward made a fresh will bequeathing to him the bulk of his personal property.

"That was the position ten years ago. But four years ago Paul Hardcastle died, leaving only one child, a daughter some twelve years of age. Once more the position was altered, for, now, Sir Edward's near kin were exhausted and the new heir presumptive was a comparatively distant cousin – a grandson of Sir Julian's uncle, one David Hardcastle. On this, Sir Edward revoked his will and made another, by which about three-quarters of his personal property goes to Paul Hardcastle's daughter, in trust until she shall reach the age of twenty-one and thereupon absolutely. The remaining fourth, apart from certain legacies, goes to the heir of the estate – that is, to David Hardcastle."

"And supposing the young lady should die during her minority?" Thorndyke enquired.

"Then the property goes to the heir to the title and estate."

"Does the personal property amount to anything considerable?

"Yes, it is very considerable indeed. Sir Edward came into a comfortable sum when he succeeded, and his wife was a lady of some means, and he has been an excellent manager – almost unduly thrifty – so there have been substantial accumulations during his time. Roughly, the personalty will be not less than a hundred-thousand pounds."

"That," I remarked, "leaves some twenty-five-thousand for the heir to the title. He won't have much to complain of."

"No," growled Brodribb, "but I expect he will complain, all the same. In fact, he has complained already. He thinks that the whole of the money should have gone to the heir to enable him to support his position in suitable style."

"So," said I, "we may take it that the gentleman who called on you was Mr. David Hardcastle?"

"You may," replied Brodribb.

"And we may further take it that the said David is not exactly the apple of your eye."

"I am afraid you may. It is all wrong, I know, for me to allow my likes and dislikes to enter into the matter. But I have acted for Sir

81

Edward and for Sir Julian before him, and my father acted for Sir Julian and his father, Sir Henry, so that it is only natural that I should have a deep personal sentiment in regard to the family and the estate."

"Which," said I, "brings us back to the original question, What is the matter with David Hardcastle?"

Brodribb pondered the question, consciously controlling, as I suspect, his naturally peppery temper – but with no great success, for he, at length, burst out, "I can't trust myself to say what I feel about him. Everything is the matter. He is a changeling, a misfit, an outlander. He doesn't match the rest of the family at all. The Hardcastles, as I have known them, have been typical English landed gentry, straight-going, honourable men who lived within their income and paid their way and did their duty justly and even generously to their tenants.

"Now this man is a different type altogether. His appearance and manner suggest a flash bookmaker rather than a country gentleman. My gorge rose at him as soon as I clapped eyes on him, and I don't fancy I was any too civil. Which was a tactical mistake, under the circumstances."

"Is he a man of independent means," asked Thorndyke, "or does he do anything for a living?"

"I have never heard that he has any means," replied Brodribb, "and I do know that he is occasionally in pretty low water, for there are several loans from Sir Edward outstanding against him. As to his occupation, God knows what it is. I should say he is a sort of cosmopolitan adventurer, always on the move, prowling about the Continental watering-places, living on his wits, or the deficiency of other people's. A distinctly shady customer in my opinion. And there is another thing. In the course of his travels he has picked up a foreign wife, a Russian woman of some sort."

"What an inveterate old John Bull it is," chuckled Thorndyke. "But we mustn't be too insular, you know, Brodribb. There are plenty of most estimable and charming Russian ladies."

Brodribb grunted. "The Lady of Bradstow," said he, "should be an English lady. Besides, this person is not an estimable and charming lady, as you express it. She had to hop out of Russia mighty sharp in consequence of some political rumpus – and you know what that means in that part of the world. And a brother of hers was I believe, actually tried and convicted."

"Still," I urged, "political offences are not – "

"Are not what?" interrupted Brodribb. "I am surprised at you, Jervis, a member of the English Bar, condoning crime. A lawyer should revere the law above everything. No, sir, crime is crime. A man who would compass the death of a Tsar would murder anyone else if it served his purpose."

"At any rate," said Thorndyke, "we may sympathise with your distaste for the present claimant, but, as you say, your feeling as to his suitability or unsuitability for the position is beside the mark. The only question is as to the soundness of his claim. And that question is not urgent at the moment."

"No," agreed Brodribb, "not at this moment. But it may become urgent in twenty-four hours. And this fellow thinks that the question is settled already. As he talked to me in my office, his manner was that of the heir just waiting to step into possession."

"By the way," said Thorndyke, "I understand that he knows exactly how Sir Edward has disposed of the personal estate. How did he come by that knowledge?"

"Sir Edward gave him all the particulars as to the provisions of the will. He thought it the fair thing to do, though it seemed to me rather unnecessary."

"It was the kind thing to do," said I. "It will have saved him a rather severe disappointment. But what are you going to do if he shows signs of undue activity?"

"What the deuce can I do?" demanded Brodribb. "That is the question that is worrying me. I have no *locus standi*, and the beggar knows it. Practically told me so."

"But," I objected, "you are Sir Edward's man of business and his executor."

"I shall be the executor," Brodribb corrected, "when Sir Edward dies or his death is proved or presumed. So long as he remains alive, in a legal sense, my powers as an executor have not come into being. On the other hand, my position as his solicitor gives me no authority to act without his instructions. I hold no power of attorney. In his absence, I have really no *locus standi* at all. Of course, if he does not turn up, alive or dead, some arrangements will have to be made for administering the estate and carrying on generally. But the application for powers to do that will be made by the legally interested party – the heir presumptive."

"And supposing," said I, "Sir Edward should be proved to be dead – say by the finding of his body – your powers as the executor of the will would then come into being. In that capacity, would you accept David Hardcastle as the heir?"

Mr. Brodribb regarded me speculatively for some moments before replying. At length he said with quiet emphasis, and speaking very deliberately, "No, I should not – as matters stand at present." He paused, still with his eyes fixed on me, and then continued. "A very curious thing

83

has happened. After my interview with Mr. David, realising that the question of the succession might become acute at any moment, I did what I ought to have done long ago. I set to work to clear up the circumstances of Gervase's death and to try to settle the question as to whether there had been any issue of the marriage, and, if so, whether there could possibly be a son living. I began by looking up that cutting from *The Times* that I told you about. As I mentioned to you, no address was given. But there was the date, and with that I thought I should have no difficulty in getting a copy of the death certificate, on which, of course, the address would be stated, and at that address it might be possible to start some enquiries.

"Accordingly, off I went to Somerset House and proceeded to look up the register of deaths for that date. To my astonishment, the name was not there. Thinking that, perhaps, a wrong date had been given, I looked up and down the entries for a week or two before and after the given date. But there was no sign of the name of Gervase Hardcastle. Then I settled down to make a thorough search, beginning ten years before the date and going on ten years after. But still there was no sign of the name. I noted one or two other Hardcastles and got copies of the certificates corresponding to the entries, but the particulars showed them all to relate to strangers.

"Then I went down to Brighton and personally called upon the local registrars and got them to overhaul their records. But the result was the same in all the cases. There was no record of the death of Gervase Hardcastle. Now what do you make of that?"

"Mighty little," said Thorndyke. "Apparently, the notice in *The Times* was a false notice, but why it should have been inserted it is difficult to guess."

"Unless," I suggested, "he was living under an assumed name and that name was given to the registrar, the true name being published for the information of the family."

Thorndyke shook his head. "I don't think that will do, Jervis," said he. "The person who sent the notice to *The Times* knew his proper name, age, and description. There is no imaginable reason why a person having that knowledge should give a false name to the registrar, and there are the best of reasons why he should not."

"Is it possible," I suggested, "that he may have committed suicide and sent off the notice himself before completing the job?"

"It is possible, of course," replied Thorndyke, "but, in the absence of any positive fact indicating the probability of its having occurred, the mere possibility is not worth considering."

"No," agreed Brodribb, "it is of no use guessing. The important truth that emerges is that his death, which has been accepted all these years by the family as an established fact, has now become extremely doubtful. At any rate, there is no legal evidence that he is dead. No court would entertain a mere obituary notice unsupported by any corresponding entry in the register of deaths. Legally speaking, Gervase is presumably still living, and it is not at all improbable that he is actually alive."

"Then, in that case," said I, "why do you say that David has a good claim to be the heir?"

"Because he is here and visible – extremely visible – whereas the very existence of Gervase is problematical. David's claim is good unless it is contested by Gervase. In Gervase's absence, I think David would have no difficulty in taking possession. Who could oppose him? If I did, as executor (and I think I should have a try), the probability is that his claim would be admitted, subject to the chance that Gervase or his heir might come forward later and endeavour to oust him."

"And meanwhile?" asked Thorndyke.

"Meanwhile, I propose setting on foot some enquiries by which I hope to be able to pick up some trace of Gervase on the Continent. It isn't a very hopeful task, I must admit."

"I can't imagine any less hopeful task," said I, "than searching for a man who has been lost to sight for over sixteen years, who was probably living under an assumed name, and whose place of abode at any time is utterly unknown. I don't see how you are going to start."

"I am not very clear, myself," Brodribb admitted, and with this, as it was now growing late, he rose and, having gathered up his hat and stick, shook our hands despondently and took his departure.

Chapter V
Fine Feathers Make
Fine Birds
(Jasper Gray's Narrative)

The providence that doth shape our ends is apt to do so by methods so unobtrusive as entirely to escape our notice. Passively we float on the quiet stream of events with no suspicion as to whither we are being carried until at last we are thrown up high and dry on the shore of our destiny, the mere jetsam of unnoted circumstances.

When I drew up my truck at the shabby door of a studio in a mews near Fitzroy Square and pulled the bell-handle, no intelligible message was borne to me by the tintinnabulation from within, nor, when the door was opened by a pleasant-faced grey-haired woman in a blue overall, did I recognise the chief arbiter – or shall I say arbitress? – of my fate. I merely pulled off my cap and said, "A roll of paper, madam, from Sturt and Wopsalls."

"Oh, I'm glad you've come," she said. "Shall I help you to carry it in?"

"Thank you, madam," I replied, "but I think I can manage without troubling you."

It was an unwieldy roll of cartoon paper, six feet long and uncommonly heavy. But I was used to handling ponderous and unshapely packages, and I got the roll on my shoulder without difficulty. The lady preceded me down a passage and into a great, bare studio where, according to directions, I laid the roll down on the floor in a corner.

"You seem to be very strong," the lady remarked.

"I'm pretty strong, thank you, madam," I answered, adding that I got a good deal of exercise.

Here a second lady, rather younger than the first, turned from her easel to look at me.

"I wonder if he would help us to move that costume chest," she said.

I expressed my willingness to do anything that would be of service to them and, being shown the chest, a huge box-settle with an

86

upholstered top, I skilfully coaxed it along the bare floor to the place by the wall that had been cleared for it.

"Would you like a glass of lemonade?" the elder lady asked when she had thanked me.

I accepted gratefully, for it was a hot day, though, for that matter, I believe a healthy boy of seventeen would drink lemonade with pleasure at the North Pole. Accordingly a glass jug and a tumbler were placed on a little table by the settle and I was invited to sit down and refresh at my leisure, which I did, staring about me meanwhile with the lively curiosity proper to my age. It was a great barn of a place with rough, white-washed walls, which were, however, mostly covered with large paper cartoons on which life-size figure subjects were broadly sketched in charcoal. There were also a number of smaller studies of heads and limbs and some complete figures – complete, that is to say, excepting as to their clothing, and the strangely aboriginal state of these, even allowing for the heat of the weather, occasioned profound speculations on my part.

As I sat sipping the lemonade and gaping at the pictures with serene enjoyment, the two ladies conversed in low tones and disjointed scraps of their conversation reached my ears, though I tried not to listen.

"Yes – " (This was the elder lady.) " – and not only so handsome but so exactly the correct type. And a rare type, too. Even the colouring is absolutely perfect."

"Yes," agreed the other, "it is typical. So clean-cut, refined, and symmetrical. A little severe, but all the better for that, and really quite distinguished – quite distinguished."

Here I happened to glance at the ladies and was dismayed to find them both looking very attentively at me. I blushed furiously. Could they be talking about me? It seemed impossible. A Sturt and Wopsall's parcels-boy could hardly be described as a distinguished person. But it almost seemed as if they were, for the elder lady said with an engaging smile, "We want to see how you would look in a wig. Would you mind trying one on?"

This was a staggerer, but of course I didn't mind. It was rather a "lark" in fact. And when the lady produced from a cupboard a golden wig with long ringlets, I sniggered shyly and allowed her to put it on my head. The two women looked at me with their heads on one side and then at one another.

"It's the very thing, you know," said the younger lady.

The other nodded, and, addressing me, said, "Would you just frown a little and put on a rather haughty expression?"

Needless to say, I grinned like a Cheshire cat and, a heroic effort to control my features only ended in violent giggles. The two ladies smiled good-humouredly, and the elder said, in a wheedling tone, "I wonder if you would do me a very great favour."

"I would if I could," was my prompt and natural reply.

"It is this," she continued. "I am painting a picture of an incident in the French Revolution to be called *An Aristocrat at Bay*. I suppose you have heard of the French Revolution?"

I had. In fact I had read Carlyle's work on the subject – and didn't think much of it – and the *Tale of Two Cities,* which I had found greatly superior.

"Very well," my new friend went on, "then I will show you the sketch for the picture," and she led me to a great easel with a handle like that of a barrel-organ, on which was a large canvas with a sheet of cartoon paper pinned on it. The sketch, which was roughly put in with charcoal and tinted in parts with an occasional smear of pastel or wash of water-colour, showed a lady standing in a doorway at the top of a flight of steps around the foot of which surged a crowd of revolutionaries.

"My difficulty," the lady continued, "is this. I have got a model for the figure of the *Aristocrat*, but I can't get a suitable model for the head. Now you happen to suit perfectly and the question is, will you let me paint the head from you?"

"But it's a woman!" I protested.

That lady knew something about boys. "I know," she said, "but a man would do as well if he was clean-shaved and wore a wig. You will say yes, now, won't you? Of course it is a business arrangement. You will be paid for your time."

Eventually it was settled that I should sit from six to eight every morning – I wasn't due at the warehouse until half-past-eight – and breakfast in the studio afterwards. I didn't much like this latter arrangement, for Pontifex and I always breakfasted together and the old gentleman would miss me. My employer suggested that he should come to breakfast too, but this would not do. Poor old Ponty would have pawned my boots if the whisky had run short, but he took no favours from strangers. However, my salary was to be twelve shillings a week, Sunday sittings to be extra *pro rata*, and that would have to compensate. I agreed to the terms and the arrangement was fixed.

"Your hair is rather long," said my employer. "Would you mind having it cut short, so as to let the wig set more closely?"

Would I mind! For, twelve shillings a week I would have had my head shaved and painted in green-and-red stripes. As a matter of fact, I went that very evening to a barber and made him trim me until my head looked like a ball of brown plush – which must have made Providence wink the eye that was fixed on my destiny.

The sittings – or rather standings – began two days later, when I took up my pose on the model's throne, rigged out in the full costume of a royalist lady and an aristocrat, my first appearance in either character. After the sitting we all had breakfast in a corner of the studio, and the two ladies crammed me until I was ready to burst with nourishment and gratitude. They were dear women. I loved them both from the very beginning, with a slight preference, perhaps, for my employer, Miss Vernet, though, to be sure, the younger lady, Miss Brandon, was a lovable creature, too. But I must not linger on their perfections. Reluctantly I must leave them for a while to relate a most singular adventure that arose in part out of my employment by them.

It was, I think, on the day of my fourth sitting that I had a stroke of luck: A parcel – and not a very large one, either – to deliver to a bibliophile who kept a private press somewhere out Tottenham-way and close to the river Lea. It was virtually a day's holiday with a railway fare thrown in, and I set forth jubilantly with the parcel on my shoulder, whistling an operatic air as I went. The train bore me luxuriously to Black Horse Road Station. I found the house of the bibliophile, delivered my parcel, and then, free as air, struck out across the fields towards the river.

Along the shallow, winding stream that runs parallel to the Lea Navigation, I wandered with the ecstatic delight of the thoroughbred Londoner in rural scenes, be they never so homely. It was a day of wonders. I had hardly ever been in the country before and this mere suburb – though it was more rural then than now – gave to my urban eyes a veritable glimpse of Paradise. I looked into the few inches of running water and saw actual fish. I watched an angler and saw him land, with elaborate artifice, what looked like a piece of cheese. For the first time in my life I looked upon a living frog and chased it to its lair under the bank. And then I came on a group of urchins, disporting themselves, as naked as cherubim, in the shallows, and Providence closed its left eye firmly.

It was a roasting day. Those urchins were certainly naked and wet and probably cool. How delicious! And why not? There was no one about, and there was plenty of cover. Five minutes later, I had shed my garments beside a willow bush and was lying on my stomach in four inches of water making frantic efforts to swim.

I waded joyfully up the stream, sometimes almost knee-deep, and impersonated characters suitable to the scenery. Now I was some sort of Indian and impaled fish – which weren't there – with an imaginary barbed spear. There I discovered a curious lurking-place under a large pollard and between two clumps of willow-bush, and forthwith I tucked myself into it, becoming instantly – as I persuaded myself – invisible to mortal eyes. I was now an Indian no longer. My role had changed to that of some unclassified species of water-sprite, at least I think so, though I am not quite clear, for the fact is that, at this moment, a nursemaid with two children hove in sight on the bank facing me and, having sauntered along with exasperating slowness, finally sat down exactly opposite my hiding-place and produced a novelette which she began to read with much composure and satisfaction.

I watched her balefully, and I watched the children. Especially, I watched the children. And meanwhile I sat up to my hips in water, finding it delightfully cool and shady beneath the pollard.

The minutes wore on. It was still cool. Surprisingly so, considering the heat of the sun outside. In fact, my teeth presently began to chatter slightly and an urgent desire to sample the sunshine once more made itself felt. But there I was, and there I must stay until the young lady opposite moved on, for I was a modest youth with a rather exaggerated notion of the delicacy of young women. And, after all, the situation was of my own making.

At last, one of the children observed me and pointed me out with a yell of ecstasy. "Oh! Look, Nanny! What's that hiding in the water over there?

"It's nothing, dear," replied Nanny, without raising her eyes from her novelette, "Only a frog."

"But it looks like a man," the young viper protested.

"I know, dear. They do," and Nanny went on serenely with her reading.

The child was evidently dissatisfied and continued to stare at me with large, devouring eyes, and was presently joined by his fellow demon. But now a new object appeared, to divert their attention and mine. A man came along the bank just behind them, walking quickly and breaking now and again into a shambling trot. I watched him at first without special interest, but when he had passed, and a back view was presented, I found myself viewing him with suddenly-awakened curiosity. What first attracted my attention was a patch in the rear of his trousers. For my own trousers had a precisely similar patch – I had sewn it in myself, so I knew it thoroughly. It was an extraordinary coincidence. The two patches were identical in shape and colour, but more than this, the pattern of the man's trousers was absolutely the same as the pattern of mine. There could be no doubt about it. They were made from the same piece, or else – Yes! The horrible conviction forced itself on me – *they were my trousers!*

But that was not all. A glance at the coat, Yea! And even the cap, revealed familiar traits. The fellow was walking off in my clothes!

For a brief space, modesty, anger, and chilly horror struggled for mastery, and in that interval the man disappeared over a fence. Then modesty was "outed" and I stood up. The children howled with joy, the nursemaid bounced up and retreated, making audible references to a "disgusting creature", and I ran splashing through the shallows towards the spot where I had undressed, for it was fairly certain that the man had not come to this place unclothed. He must have left some sort of exuvium in place of mine. But if the exchange had been worth his while – Well! My expectations expressed themselves in a premonitory impulse to scratch myself, for whatever the clothes were like, I should have to put them on.

The reality turned out to be better and worse than my anticipations. The clothes were good enough, better than mine, in fact, though the colour – a dusty buff – was disagreeable. But it was the decoration that spoiled them. Some misguided person had covered them with a pattern that recalled the device on a bench mark. The broad arrow, to put it in a nutshell. My absent friend was a run-away convict.

I huddled the wretched garments on as quickly as I could, for I was chilled to the marrow, and as I stood up in that livery of shame, I was sensible of a subtle influence that exhaled from it, impelling me to skulk in unfrequented places and to sneak from cover to cover. Of course the mistake could be explained if I was arrested, but I didn't want to be arrested. I was safer at large. The better plan was to get home if possible, or make for Sturt and Wopsalls, where I was known. But how was I to get home? My return ticket was in the pocket of the vanished trousers in company with a clasp-knife and eighteen-pence, and miles of town lay between me and safety.

I crept stealthily round the meadows away from the river, keeping under the cover of hedges and fences and reviewing anxiously my chances of escape, which seemed hopelessly remote. Ahead of me, near the side of a meadow, were a couple of hayricks, like enormous loaves, and the narrow space between their ends looked a likely place in which to conceal myself while I thought over my plans. Accordingly I crept along under the hedge until I was opposite the ricks, when I dashed out across the open, darted into the space between the ricks, and nearly fell over a man who was lying there smoking a pipe.

"I beg your pardon," I stammered. "I didn't know you were here."

"Don't mention it," he replied suavely. "If I'd expected yer, I'd ha' told the footman to announce yer." He sat up, and, regarding me attentively, asked, "And how goes it? Doin' a bit of a skyboozle, I guess?" I assented vaguely, not being perfectly clear as to the nature of a skyboozle, and he then enquired, "How did yer git out o' the jug?"

"I didn't get out at all. I wasn't ever in."

"Lor!" he exclaimed. "Wasn't yer? Where did yer git them pretty clothes from?"

I described the disastrous circumstances of the exchange and he listened to my story with a foxy smile.

"Well I'm blowed!" was his comment. "What bloomin' impidence, to take and prig a young gentleman's clothes. I call it actially rude. And he seems to 'ave cut yer 'air, too. He oughtn't to 'a done that. He'll 'ave to be spoke to."

At this reference to my closely cropped hair, I started violently. That was an added danger that I had overlooked, and I was so much disturbed by it that I have no recollection of my friend's further remarks, only I know that they were few and brief, for he shortly rose and, knocking out his pipe (against the rick), looked at me with profound attention.

"Well," he said, at length, "I must be movin' on or I shall be late for lunch. You'd best lay down 'ere and 'ave a good rest, 'cos you may have to make a bolt for it any minute, and the fresher you are the quicker you'll be able to leg it. So long."

With these words of sage advice, he turned and sauntered away with funereal slowness, looking back once or twice to see if I had profited by his counsel. I sat down – not where he had been lying – and when he looked back again and observed this, he nodded approvingly and changed his direction slightly, so that he passed out of view. But the influence of that livery of dishonour had made me wary. After waiting a few seconds, I crept on all fours to the corner of the rick and peeped round, and behold! My friend's pace was funereal no longer, he was running across the meadow like a slip-shod, disreputable hare. And I had no difficulty in guessing at his destination.

I let him get well out of sight and then I followed his example in the opposite direction. Skirting the adjoining meadow, I came to a hedge that bordered a by-road, and here I lurked awhile, for a van was approaching, though it was still some distance away, and I was afraid to cross the road until it had passed. I watched the vehicle wistfully as it drew nearer. Through the opening of the tilt I could see that it was empty, or nearly so, and, from the conduct of the driver, who lolled in the corner of his seat and chanted a popular ballad, I judged that he had finished his delivery and was homeward bound.

Nearer and nearer drew the van at a steady jog-trot. Now I could see the driver's face and hear the words of his song. I could also make out the tops of one or two cases – probably empties – rising above the back

92

of his seat, and I crouched by a gap in the hedge, my heart thumping violently and my knees trembling. At last the van came rumbling by. I had a brief view of a familiar name and of the words "*Theobald's Road*" painted on the tilt, and it had passed.

I looked out of the gap. Besides the carter there was not a soul in sight. The tail-board of the van was up, its body was half empty, and the driver's back was towards me. In a moment, I was out through the gap and padding along swiftly in my soft prison shoes after the van. I had my hands on the tail-board, I gave a light spring, remained poised for a moment on the edge, and then stealthily crawling over, crept silently into the space between two empty cases. For the moment I was saved.

The van rattled along and the driver, all unconscious of his passenger, carolled blithely. From my retreat I could see out at the back by peeping round a case, and so ascertain our direction, and I was somewhat alarmed presently to observe that the road took a sharp turn towards the place where the tramp had disappeared. This made me so uneasy that I risked craning up to look out through the front of the van, and when I did so, I got a most terrible shock. Far away along the road, but coming towards us, was a small crowd of men, and, as we mutually approached, I could make out at least one constable in uniform among them. A little nearer and I was able to recognise the tramp, walking by the constable and evidently acting as guide. I broke out into a cold perspiration. Would that constable stop the van and search it? It was quite possible. It was even likely. And again I craned up and peeped at my enemies.

We were getting quite near when the tramp stopped and pointed at the ricks, no doubt. Then he climbed over the fence that bordered the road. The constable followed him and the others followed the constable, and so they passed out of view.

But they came into sight again shortly from the back of the van, and now I could see the ricks, too. The crowd had deployed out into a long, curved line and were advancing, in the highest style of strategy, under the direction of the tramp and the constable. It reminded me of the formation of the Spanish Armada, as that great fleet swept up-channel. I didn't see the end of it. The line was still deploying out to encircle the rick when the van turned sharply and rumbled over a bridge. I was sorry to miss the *denouement*, but perhaps it was better so. After all, my business was to get clear away.

The van rumbled on at its quiet jog-trot and all seemed plain sailing. Through the northern suburbs and gradually into the town by way of Stamford Hill and Stoke Newington. And still all went well until we came out of the Essex Road and drew nigh unto the Angel at Islington, when the Devil entered into the carman and caused him to draw up by a public house and inspect the interior of the van.

Of course he saw me at once, though I squeezed myself into the farthest corner between the cases, and with a sort of gruff reluctance, he ordered me to clear out. I begged to be allowed to travel with him as far as Theobald's Road, and began to tender explanations, but he shook his head decidedly.

"I'd be in chokee myself if I let you," said he, "and I can't afford that with a wife and family to keep."

There was nothing more to be said. Reluctantly and with deep misgivings, I bundled out and began to walk away briskly along the crowded pavement. But I didn't get far. Before I had gone a hundred yards, two tall men who were walking towards me suddenly roused and, darting at me, seized me by the arms.

"Have you got a pair of darbies about you, Sims?" one of them asked the other. Fortunately Mr. Sims had not, but suggested that "this young feller" did not look like giving trouble, whereupon, the two officers began to walk me along briskly in the direction of the Angel.

There was no lack of public recognition. I had already gathered quite a nice little following when I met the detectives, and my retinue increased so rapidly that before we reached the Angel we had become the centre of a hurrying hallooing crowd. At this point, my captors decided to cross the road.

Now the traffic about the crossroads by the Angel is usually pretty dense. On this occasion, I think it was denser than usual, and when our procession launched itself from the kerb, it reached a superlative degree of density. Vans, omnibuses, hansoms, all manner of vehicles slowed down that their drivers might get a better view of the man in motley. For the moment the roadway seemed to be completely choked with vehicles and foot-passengers, and from the closely-packed throng there arose a very babel of shouts and cheers. Thus we were standing in the roadway, jammed immovably, when above the universal uproar, rose a new sound, a thunderous rattle, jingling of small bells and a quick succession of shouts. The omnibuses, vans, and hansoms began to back hurriedly towards the pavements, their drivers cheering lustily and flourishing their whips, the mob surged to-and-fro, a cloud of smoke and sparks arose behind them, there was a vision of gleaming brass helmets and of galloping horses bearing down apparently straight on us, the rattling, jingling, and shouting swelled into a deafening roar, and the crowd surged away to the right and left.

"Look out, Sims!" yelled the other detective. "They'll be on top of us!" He thrust his shoulder into the crowd and dragged me out of the track of the oncoming engine. The horses dashed by within a few inches, the rushing wheels grazed our very toes, and still I kept a cool head. With eyes dazzled by the scarlet glare, the glitter of brass and the flying sparks, I watched for my chance and took it. As the shining boiler whizzed past, I made a quick snatch at the big brass rail that supports the foot-plate, and at the same moment, jumped forward. The sudden wrench nearly dislocated my arm, but it was a strong arm and I held on. The jerk whisked me clean out of the grasp of the two officers, I swung round behind the engine and, grabbing the engineer with my other hand, hauled myself on to the foot-plate. A single, instantaneous glance backward showed me two plain-clothes officers lying on their backs with their feet in the air. Of course, they could not have maintained that position permanently, but I saw them only for the fraction of a second and that was how they appeared.

The engine rattled on. The coachman and his two satellites had naturally seen nothing, and the four men who sat back to back on the body of the engine also appeared to be unaware of my arrival though, oddly enough, they were all on the broad grin and their "Hi, hies!" tended at times to be tremulous. Even the engineer, whom I clasped fondly by the waist, seemed to be oblivious of my presence and stolidly shovelled coal into the little furnace.

We swept round the corner at the Angel, and never shall I forget the way in which we thundered down Pentonville Hill with our brakes on and our horses at full gallop. I think I have never enjoyed anything so thoroughly. The engine skidded to-and-fro, the firemen yelled themselves purple, houses and lamp-posts flashed by, and far ahead, even unto King's Cross, an expectant crowd awaited us with welcoming bellows. We passed through the narrow strait at the foot of the hill like a royal procession, our arrival was respectfully anticipated at the crossing by the Great Northern, and we thundered down the Euston Road between ranks of waiting omnibuses like the leaders in a chariot race. We were approaching Tottenham Court Road when the engineer observed placidly, apparently addressing his remark to the pressure gauge, that "there was such things as telegraph wires and it might be as well to hop off." I accepted the friendly hint, and as we turned into the latter thoroughfare, I dropped from the foot-plate and made a bolt down Warren Street. The engine gave me a send-off, for it attracted so much attention that I was, at first, almost unnoticed. It was only when I had covered half the length of Warren Street that juvenile and other loafers, deciding that a convict in the hand is worth two fire engines in the bush, turned to follow my fortunes, or misfortunes, as the case might be.

What manner of crowd it was that howled at my heels, I cannot say, for I did not look back. I was on familiar ground and I now had a definite objective: Miss Vernet's studio backed on a mews, and there was a large window which was usually left open. That was my port of salvation. Swiftly I zigzagged up and down the narrow streets, keeping my pursuers at a respectable distance, and gradually drawing nearer to the vicinity of the mews. At length I shot round the last corner and, diving into the entrance of the mews, padded furiously over the rough cobbles. The place was fortunately empty, for it was now late afternoon, and halfway down, the open window yawned hospitably. Setting my foot on a brick plinth, I sprang up, grasped the window-sill and shot in through the opening like a harlequin.

My arrival on all-fours on the studio floor was hailed by startled shrieks from my two friends who were hard at work at their easels. But, of course, they recognised me at once, and a few words of breathless explanation enabled them to grasp the state of affairs.

"Get into the dressing-room instantly," said Miss Vernet, "and put on your costume."

"Yes, and throw us out those horrible clothes," added Miss Brandon.

I shot into the dressing-room and, peeling off the garb of infamy with the speed of a quick-change artist, threw the garments out and whisked the costume down from its pegs, and even as the roar of many voices from the mews outside announced the arrival of my pursuers, I dropped the gown over my head, secured the fastenings with trembling fingers, and clapped the ringlets on my stubbly pate. When I came out into the studio Miss Brandon had just closed the costume chest, on the lid of which she was piling palettes, paint-tubes, and sheafs of brushes, and Miss Vernet was standing at her easel.

"Now," she said briskly, "get on the throne and take up your pose, and pull your gloves on. They mustn't see your hands."

I had just struggled into my long gloves and taken up the pose when the murmur of voices announced the return of my pursuers from an unsuccessful quest at the end of the mews. There was a scrambling sound and a disreputable head and shoulders framed itself in the window, and the eyes appertaining thereto glared inquisitively into the studio. Then it disappeared with a suddenness suggestive of outside assistance, the scrambling sound was renewed and a helmeted head rose majestically in its place. The constable gazed in enquiringly, and had just opened his mouth as if about to speak, when he caught the stern and for bidding eye of Miss Vernet, which seemed to paralyse him completely.

"What are you doing at my window, sir?" the lady demanded acidly.

The constable's mouth opened once more and this time with more result.

"I beg your pardon, madam," said he, "but there is an escaped convict – " Here the constable disappeared with the same suddenness as the previous observer, his toes having apparently slipped off the brick coping. He did not reappear, but I heard a voice, which seemed to be his, enquiring irritably, "Where's the damn door?"

Somebody must have shown him the "damn door" for, after a brief pause, the studio bell rang and Miss Brandon, smothering her giggles, went out and returned accompanied by two constables and two elderly gentlemen. The latter came in in a state of hilarity that contrasted strongly with the solemnity of the officials.

"I hear you've got a convict hiding in here," said one of them, a fresh-faced farmer-like looking gentleman.

"What's that?" demanded Miss Vernet, whisking round from her easel.

"Yes, madam," said one of the constables, staring hard at the picture and then glaring at me. "A convict who has escaped from Pentonville is believed to have climbed in at your window."

"At my window!" shrieked Miss Vernet. "But what a frightful thing, and how disgraceful of you to let him. I call it a perfect scandal that a respectable householder, paying police rates, should be subjected to the annoyance and danger of having hordes of convicts and criminals swarming in at all the windows if they happen to be left open."

"Oh, droar it mild, madam," protested the constable. "It ain't as bad as that. There's only one of them."

"If there's one, there may be a dozen," Miss Vernet replied, rather illogically, I thought, "and I insist on your searching the premises and removing every one of them."

"Is that the window?" asked the gentleman who had spoken before. The constable admitted that it was. "But, my good man," the gentleman protested, "how could anyone have got in without being seen?"

The constable suggested that the ladies might have been looking the other way at the time, at which both the old gentlemen laughed aloud and shook their heads.

"At any rate," said Miss Vernet, laying down her palette, "I must insist on having the premises searched thoroughly." And thereupon she and Miss Brandon conducted the two constables out through the doorway that led to the kitchen and offices. As soon as they were gone, the two gentlemen settled themselves to examine the picture, and from the canvas they presently turned their attention to me with an intentness that made my flesh creep. The farmer-like gentleman seemed particularly interested, and having minutely compared me with the figure on the canvas, turned suddenly to his companion.

"This is a most extraordinary coincidence, Brodribb," said he, and as he spoke I was dimly aware of something familiar in the sound of the name.

The other gentleman – a fine, jovial-looking old cock with a complexion like that of a Dublin Bay prawn and hair like white silk – looked about him a little vaguely and then asked, "What is?

"That figure in the picture," his friend replied. "Doesn't it recall anything to your mind?"

Mr. Brodribb looked at the canvas with a frown of concentration and an air of slight perplexity, but apparently without the desired effect on his memory, for, after a prolonged stare, he shook his head and replied, "I can't say that it does."

"Come and stand here," said the other, stepping back a couple of paces, "and look carefully at the central figure only, taking the architrave of the doorway as the picture frame. Is there no portrait that you have ever seen that it reminds you of?"

Again Mr. Brodribb looked and again he shook his head.

"Dear, dear," exclaimed the farmer-like gentleman, "and to think how many dozens of times you must have looked on it! Don't you remember a portrait that hangs over the fireplace in the small drawing room at Bradstow? A portrait by Romney of, I think, a Miss Isabel Hardcastle."

Mr. Brodribb brightened up. "Yes, yes, of course," said he, "I remember the portrait that you mention. Not very well, though. But what about it?

"Why, my dear Brodribb, this figure is an almost exact replica. The dress is of the same character and the pose is similar, though that might easily be in an historical picture of the same period. But the most astonishing resemblance is in the face. This might be a copy."

Mr. Brodribb looked interested. "I remember the picture," said he, "and I recognise the general resemblance now you point it out, though I can't recall the face. I am not a portrait painter, you see, Sir Giles, so I haven't your memory for faces. But if the facial resemblance is as strong as you say it is in the two portraits, a very interesting fact seems to follow, for as this portrait is an excellent likeness of this young lady." (Here the old gentleman bowed to me deferentially, whereupon I grinned and turned as red as a lobster.) "She must be extremely like the subject of the other portrait, is it not so?"

Sir Giles laughed a fine, jolly, agricultural laugh. "*Q.E.D.*, hey, Brodribb. Very acutely argued. Discreetly, too, as we can't put the other lady in evidence. But, of course, you're right."

At this point the two ladies returned, accompanied by the constables, who were both looking into the interiors of their helmets and bore a subtle suggestion of having taken refreshment. They departed with thanks and apologies, and the two ladies and the gentlemen then engaged in a spirited discussion on the composition of the picture. I was glad when it came to an end and the two gentlemen took their leave – each with a valedictory bow to me, which I returned to the best of my ability – for I was tired and hungry and wanted to get home.

"Now, Jasper," said Miss Vernet, when she had shown them out, "the question is how we are to get you away from here. You can't wear the prison clothes, and you can't go home in your costume. What are we to do, Lucy?"

Miss Brandon reflected awhile and then suggested, "There's that widow's costume, you know. That would fit him."

"Yes, of course," agreed Miss Vernet, "it's the very thing. He shall put it on and I will walk home with him, myself."

And so the tragedy ended. Less than an hour later, a tall and gawky-looking widow might have been seen – but fortunately was not – sneaking up the stairs to the third floor of the house in Great Ormond Street. Pontifex was out shopping and came in later with a bottle under his arm, but by that time, my widowhood had come to an end. The resources of my wardrobe were slender, but they included two suits which I had outgrown before they had degenerated into mere scarecrow's costume, and into one of these I insinuated myself cautiously and with some misgivings as to its tensile strength. But, of course, it was impossible. Even Sturt and Wopsall's packer revolted at the sight of four inches of visible sock above my boots, and besides, I didn't dare to stoop. Miss Vernet had delicately hinted as we walked home at a desire to replace my lost garments, but, grateful as I was to her the thing was not to be thought of when I had five golden sovereigns hidden away. Accordingly the very next day, I disinterred two of them and, making my way to a shop of which I knew in the vicinity of Convent Garden, procured in exchange for them a most admirable second-hand suit, in which I came forth proudly with my outgrown exuvium under my arm. Never before had I been so well dressed. When I returned to the warehouse, the packer raised his brown-paper cap and made me a deep bow, and even Pontifex, who was not ordinarily acutely observant, eyed that suit in silence and with an evidently unsuccessful effort of memory.

But there was a fly in the ointment – or perhaps I should say that there was a fly – a butterfly – missing from the ointment. I hastened to sew in at the back of the waistcoat a commodious secret pocket. But alas! That pocket was empty. The miserable wretch who had absconded in my patched and threadbare clothes, had, all unconsciously, been the bearer of a priceless treasure. In the agitation of the moment, I had forgotten the emerald that reposed at the back of his – or rather my – waistcoat. Now, too late, the realisation of my loss was borne in on me and remained for weeks a deep and abiding sorrow.

Chapter VI
A Visit to Stratford Atte Bowe
(Dr. Jervis's Narrative)

The mystery surrounding the disappearance of Sir Edward Hardcastle was solved in a very startling and tragic manner, if, indeed, that can be called a solution which was even more mysterious than the problem which it solved. The news was brought to us late one afternoon by Mr. Brodribb, who burst into our chambers in a state of such extreme agitation that we were at once prepared for some tidings of disaster.

"Here is a terrible thing, Thorndyke!" he exclaimed, dropping into a chair and mopping his face with his handkerchief. "Sir Edward has made away with himself."

Thorndyke was evidently surprised at the news, as also was I, but he made no comment beyond a half-articulate "Ha," and Brodribb continued, "I have just had the information from the police. Superintendent Miller was kind enough to call on me and give me the report himself. He had no details but – to put the horrible affair in a nutshell – Sir Edward's body was found this morning hanging from a beam in an empty house at Stratford."

"At Stratford!" Thorndyke repeated, incredulously. For if the news of the suicide itself was surprising, the alleged circumstances were amazing.

"Yes," said Brodribb, "it is an astonishing affair. I can't imagine what can have taken him to Stratford. But I suppose that people in the state of mind that is associated with self-destruction are apt to behave in a rather unaccountable way. Perhaps some kind of explanation will be forthcoming at the inquest, which I understand from the Superintendent is to take place to-morrow. It appears that there are some circumstances that make it desirable to hold the inquiry as soon as possible."

We had no difficulty in guessing what those circumstances were, but neither of us made any comment.

"I shall have to go," Brodribb continued. "In fact the Superintendent warned me, but I should like you to be present to watch the proceedings, if you can manage it. Not that there is any real necessity, since there is no insurance question to raise and there seems unfortunately to be no doubt of the facts. But inquests are quite out of my province and I should feel more satisfied if I had your views on the affair."

"Very well," said Thorndyke. "I will attend the inquest on your instructions. But I think I had better be present at the *post mortem*, too. I should wish to have an opportunity of forming a direct judgement on the facts as well as hearing the evidence of the medical witness."

Brodribb nodded approvingly. "That is what I like about you, Thorndyke," said he. "You are so thorough – even beyond the necessities of the case. You take nothing on trust. But there is another matter. The Superintendent urged me – in fact, I may say that he ordered me – to go down to Stratford this evening and identify the body. He said that it was most important that the question of identity should be settled at once, and I suppose he is right. But it is frightfully unpleasant."

I suspected that it would be more unpleasant than he was aware of, but I kept my suspicions to myself, and he continued. "I don't see why the identification couldn't have been done by Weeks, Sir Edward's butler. They have summoned him by telegraph – I left his name and address with Miller, you remember – and I suppose he will have to see the body. However, the Superintendent insisted that I ought to go this evening, so there is no help for it. I suppose you couldn't come down with me?" he added, wistfully.

"Yes," Thorndyke replied, promptly, "I will come with you, and perhaps Jervis will keep us company."

He looked enquiringly at me, and, when I had assented – which I did readily enough – he resumed, "But there is one thing that must be done, at once, since there may not be time to-morrow. I must get a letter from the Home Office asking the coroner to give me the necessary facilities. Otherwise, I may be refused permission to be present at the *post mortem*."

"Would that matter?" asked Brodribb. "There can't be much question as to the cause of death."

"That is impossible to say," replied Thorndyke. "If I am to attend I may as well be in a position to check the medical evidence. That, in fact, is my proper function."

"But you won't find anybody at the Home Office now," Brodribb objected.

"I think I shall," said Thorndyke. "There is always some responsible person on late duty to attend to urgent business. I suggest that you two go on to Stratford and wait for me at the police station."

"No, we won't do that," said Brodribb. "We will wait for you at my office and then we can all go down together."

To this arrangement Thorndyke agreed and took his departure forth en route for Whitehall, while Brodribb and I, in more leisurely fashion, made our way out into Fleet Street and so, by way of Carey Street, to New Square. We did not, however, go into Brodribb's office, for our old friend was in a state of nervous unrest, and now that he was to have our company on his distasteful errand, was all impatience to start. Accordingly, we walked together up and down the pavement of the quiet square, exchanging now and again a few words but mostly occupied with our own thoughts.

What Brodribb's thoughts were I cannot guess, but my own were fully occupied by the communication that he had made to us. For, brief and sketchy as it was, it contained matter that certainly invited reflection. Thorndyke, I could see, was, if not actually suspicious, at least very definitely on his guard. His determination to check the official medical evidence by independent observation showed clearly that in his view there might be more in the case than might meet the eye of a routine investigator. And I found myself in complete agreement with him. The alleged facts carried a distinct suggestion of fishiness. As to the probability of Sir Edward's committing suicide I could form no opinion, but the circumstances in which the suicide had occurred called aloud for inquiry. I was, indeed, somewhat surprised at the easy-going fashion in which the usually astute Brodribb had accepted them. But perhaps I was doing him an injustice. Possibly he was purposely withholding his own doubts the better to test Thorndyke's attitude.

I had reached this point in my reflections when, on making a quarter-deck turn, I perceived my colleague advancing swiftly up the pavement from the Carey Street gate. We stepped out to meet him and, as he joined us, Brodribb greeted him with the comprehensive question: "Well, what news?"

"I have got a letter for the coroner asking for facilities, and a hansom waiting opposite the gate."

"Hmm," grunted Brodribb, "it will be a damned tight fit."

And I must admit that it was. Three large men, one of whom was distinctly of "a full habit", were more than the coach-builder had made allowance for. However, Thorndyke and I bore the brunt of the squeeze, and the journey was not a long one. In due course we unpacked ourselves at Liverpool Street Station and presently boarded a train bound for Bow and Stratford.

We travelled for the most part in silence, and what conversation passed was not connected with our present quest. There was, in fact, no opportunity for interchange of talk on confidential matters as our carriage contained, besides ourselves, three passengers, apparently businessmen

103

returning at the end of the day's work, not indeed to Stratford, but to some of the more savoury localities in the neighbourhood of Epping Forest. At length a strange and repulsive effluvium which began to filter in at the windows, suggestive of soap-boiling, glue-making and other odoriferous forms of industry, announced our approach to the classical neighbourhood of Stratford atte Bowe, and a minute or two later we disembarked, Brodribb snorting disgustedly and holding a large silk handkerchief to his nose. From the railway station we made our way to that of the police, to which Mr. Brodribb had been directed by Superintendent Miller, and presenting ourselves to the sergeant on duty in the outer office and stating our business, were duly conducted into the inner office and the presence of the Station Superintendent.

The latter turned out to be an eminently helpful officer. Possibly the Home Office letter (which, though it was addressed to the coroner, was shown to the Superintendent) requesting that Dr. Thorndyke should be given such facilities as he might reasonably require, might have influenced him, to say nothing of our virtual introduction by Superintendent Miller. But apart from this, he was a capable, businesslike man, quite free from any tendency to red tape officialism, and naturally inclined rather to help than to obstruct. Accordingly, when we had presented our credentials and explained our connection with the case, he proceeded to give us, without reserve, all the information that he possessed.

"The discovery," he began, "was made this morning about nine o'clock by a man named Holker, a retired ship's steward who owns a good deal of low-class weekly property about here – mostly small houses that he has picked up cheap and put in some sort of repair himself. He's what you'd call a handyman, able to do a job of bricklaying or plastering or joinery, so it doesn't cost him much to codge up these old derelicts that he buys. Now, some time ago he bought a row of half-a-dozen little houses that some fool had built on a bit of wasteland down by Abbey Creek. He got them for next to nothing as they had never been inhabited and were in a ruinous condition and stood by an unmade road that was often half under water. He meant to do them up and let them at low rents to some of the labourers at the works. In fact, he started work on one of them – Number Five – about a month ago, that is how we are able to fix the dates. The last time he was working there was Sunday, the twenty-first of June, and he is quite sure that nothing had happened then because he went all over the house. On Sunday night he was offered, and accepted, a temporary job on one of his old ships which traded to Marseilles, and on Monday morning he dropped in at the house to fetch away his tools. As he was in a hurry, he only went into the front room, where the tools had been left, but he could see that someone had been in the house by the fact that a glove was lying on the floor. He thought it queer, but, as I said, he was in a hurry and as it was an empty house with nothing in it to steal, he didn't trouble to look into the matter but just got his tools and came away.

"That was three weeks ago – this is the fourteenth. Now, Holker got back from his trip yesterday, and this morning he went round to get on with his work at the house. As soon as he got there he noticed the glove still lying on the floor. And then he noticed – well he noticed that there was something wrong about the house, so he went through to the kitchen and from there to the wash-house, and the first thing he saw when he opened the wash-house door was a man hanging from a tie-beam. There was no doubt that the man was dead and that he had been dead a pretty long time. Holker didn't stop to cut the body down. He just bolted out and came up here to report what he had seen. I happened to be here at the time, so I thought I had better go along and see into the affair, though the job didn't sound much of a catch from what Holker said. And I can tell you it wasn't. However, I needn't go into that. You can imagine what it was like for yourselves.

"Well, there was the body hanging from the beam and an old, broken-backed windsor chair capsized on the floor underneath. Evidently he had stood on the chair to tie the rope to the beam and when he had fixed the noose round his neck he had kicked the chair over and left himself dangling. It was all pretty obvious, fortunately, for one didn't want to spend a lot of time in that wash-house making observations. I just cut the rope when the constables had got the stretcher underneath and they lowered the body on to it, covered it up, and carried it away."

"Concerning the rope," said Thorndyke, as the Superintendent paused. "I presume the deceased found that on the premises?"

"No," the officer replied, "he must have brought the rope with him, for it wasn't Hiker's. It was a smallish, brown rope – looked like coir – and he'd brought more than he wanted, for there was a spare end about four feet long."

"And with regard to the glove that was mentioned – ?"

"Yes, I saw that in the front room. The fellow one was on the wash-house floor. I picked them both up and I've got them here."

"By the way," said Thorndyke. "How do you suppose the deceased man got into the house?"

"He must have got in by the window. He didn't get in by the front door, for Holker is sure he shut it when he left on Sunday and he found it shut when he went there on Monday morning. Of course, the lock is only a cheap builder's night-latch that anyone used to locks could open easily enough. But I don't suppose the deceased gentleman was accustomed to picking locks, and he didn't open it with a key, because he hadn't a key of any sort about him."

"I don't suppose," Thorndyke remarked, "that he was much accustomed to getting in at windows."

"Probably not," the officer agreed. "But, you see, sir, he got in somehow, and Holker found the sitting-room window unfastened on the Monday morning. So it would have been easy enough for anyone to get in. The window-sill is only about two-feet-six above the ground. And you remember that the one glove was lying on the sitting-room floor. As a matter of fact, it was just under the window."

There was silence for a few moments. Then Brodribb remarked, "The officer from Scotland Yard mentioned that the body had been identified by some letters that were found in the pockets. I suppose there were some other things?"

"Yes, but mighty few considering the man's position, and yet enough to show that the body had not been robbed. I've got the things here if you would like to see them."

He stepped over to a nest of drawers which stood on a massive shelf and, unlocking one of the drawers, drew it out bodily and brought it over to the table at which we were sitting. "There's the collection," said he. "It isn't quite what you'd expect to find on the person of a baronet. Look at that watch, for instance. Sort of thing that you could pick up at a cheap jeweller's for seven-and-six. What is rather odd, too, is that there are no keys. Not even a latch-key."

"He left his keys and his gold watch and some other valuables at his club," said Brodribb as he ran a gloomy eye over the contents of the drawer.

"Ah! Did he? Yes, very natural and very proper, too, having regard to what he intended to do. I'll make a note of that. It will be an important point for the coroner."

Brodribb was evidently sorry that he had spoken, but he did not lose his presence of mind. "Yes," he agreed. "The secretary of the club, Mr. Northbrook, will be able to tell you about it. I suppose you will have to summon him as a witness as Sir Edward was staying at the club."

"Yes, we shall want his evidence, and in fact, a summons has been served on him," the Superintendent replied, adding with a faint smile, "I take it that you'd rather not be called. But I'm afraid it can't be helped. You know more about his private and financial affairs than anybody else. The butler has been summoned, but he can't tell us what state the deceased's affairs were in, whereas you can give any information that is wanted. My sergeant, here, is the coroner's officer, and he will hand you the summons when he takes you over to the mortuary."

"Do you really think it necessary for me to go there?" Mr. Brodribb protested with evident discomfort. "The butler will be able to testify to the identity."

"Yes," the officer agreed, "that is so. But for our own information, now, we should like to know whether this is or is not Sir Edward's body. You had better run over and just take a glance at it."

Brodribb acquiesced with a faint groan and the Superintendent then reverted to the contents of the drawer. "Do you recognise any of these articles?" he asked.

Brodribb looked them over once again before replying. They comprised the watch, a pair of wash-leather gloves, a shabby leather cigar-case – empty – a small silver match-box, an old and well-worn pigskin purse, containing, as the officer demonstrated, three sovereigns, a handkerchief marked *E. H.*, a lead pencil, a fountain-pen, a small pocket-knife, some loose silver and coppers, and a letter-case, containing two five-pound notes and one or two letters in envelopes, addressed to "*Sir Edward Hardcastle, Bart., Bradstow, Kent*".

"No," Brodribb replied, at length. "I don't recognise any of these things. The handkerchief is marked with Sir Edward's initials, as you can see, and the envelopes bear his name and address, as you can also see. That is all. Would you like me to look through the letters?"

"There is no need," the officer replied. "The coroner will read them and he will ask you anything that he wants to know about them. And now you would like to step across to the mortuary? I will tell the sergeant to take you over."

He rose and, having replaced the drawer in its nest, passed through into an adjoining office and returned almost immediately accompanied by his subordinate, who bore in his hand a small blue paper.

"Here," said the Superintendent, "is your summons, Mr. Brodribb. Is there anything else that I can do for you?"

"There is one little matter, Superintendent," said Thorndyke. "I should like, if possible, to have an opportunity to inspect the house in which the body was found. I presume there is no objection?"

"None whatever," was the reply. "But you are not thinking of going there to-night? Better go to-morrow morning by daylight, before you attend at the *post mortem*. I'll see that there is someone to show you the place and let you in, and then we can tell you what time to turn up at the mortuary. But you'll waste your time at the house, for there is nothing to see but the end of a cut rope and an overturned chair."

107

"Well," said Thorndyke, "we will inspect them. It is a mere formality, but it is a good rule to see everything."

"So it is, sir," the Superintendent agreed, and with this he glanced at the sergeant, who forthwith opened the door and launched us into the street, the gathering darkness of which was tempered by the light of the lamp over the doorway.

"A pleasant night, gentlemen," he remarked as he led us across the road. "A trifle warm, perhaps, but that is seasonable, though for my part, I prefer rather cooler weather for mortuary jobs."

At this, Mr. Brodribb shuddered audibly and, as I observed that he had taken Thorndyke's arm, I suddenly realised that what was for me and my colleague a matter of mere daily routine was to our poor old friend a really distressing and horrible experience. Evidently Thorndyke had realised it too, for when the sergeant had unlocked a door at the bottom of a narrow alley and entered before us to light the gas, I heard him say in a low tone, "I'll go in first, Brodribb. You had better wait here till I call you."

The light from the large, shaded gas-lamps shone down brightly on the shrouded figure that lay on the central table and lit more dimly and fitfully the side benches, the great porcelain sink, and the white washed walls. Thorndyke and I, with the sergeant, advanced to the table and the latter drew back the sheet, exposing the head and shoulders of the corpse. It was not a pleasant spectacle, but, still, immeasurably less repulsive than I had expected from my experiences of the "found drowned" corpses that I had seen in riverside mortuaries, and what was more to the point, it appeared to be quite recognisable. For a few seconds we stood looking down at the shrunken, discoloured face. Then Thorndyke drew up the sheet and having arranged it so that the face alone was visible, called out to Brodribb, who thereupon entered, walking quickly and a little unsteadily, and stepped up to the table by Thorndyke's side.

A single horrified glance apparently disposed of any doubts or hopes that he may have entertained, for he turned away quickly, muttering, "Dear Lord! What an end!" and began to walk towards the door.

"Can you identify the body, sir?" the sergeant asked in matter-of-fact tones.

"I can," replied Brodribb, relapsing, despite his agitation, into legal precision. "The body is that of Sir Edward Hardcastle of Bradstow in Kent." And having made his statement, he walked out into the dark alley.

We followed almost immediately, for there was nothing to see that would not be better seen by daylight on the morrow. At the top of the alley we wished the sergeant "Good night," and while he hurried away in the direction of the office, we turned our steps towards the station.

During the short walk, hardly a word was spoken. Brodribb strode forward with his chin on his breast and his gaze bent on the ground, absorbed in gloomy reflections, while Thorndyke and I silently turned over in our minds the significance of what we had seen and heard. It was not until we were seated in a first-class carriage – of which we were the only occupants – that our friend came out of his "brown study". Then, as the train moved out of the station, he turned to my colleague and asked abruptly, "Well, Thorndyke, what do you think of it?"

Thorndyke considered a few moments before replying. "It is early," he said, at length, "to express, or even to form an opinion. At present, we have no technical data. All that we can do is to form a provisional opinion based on the facts now known to us. That you can do as well as Jervis and I can."

"Perhaps," said Brodribb. "All the same, I should like to hear what the facts convey to you."

"Then I may say," Thorndyke responded, "that they convey to me principally the urgent necessity of getting more facts. At present we are confronted by two sets of conflicting probabilities, and we await further facts to throw greater weight on the one or the other. For instance, the mode of death is markedly characteristic of suicide. When a man is found hanging, the probability is that he has hanged himself. The possible alternatives are accident and homicide. Accidental hanging is rare and is usually obvious on inspection. Homicidal hanging is extremely rare. So that the mode of death, in the absence of any elucidatory evidence, establishes a strong presumption of suicide. Evidence of motive or intention would turn that presumption into something approaching certainty. Absence of such motive would reduce the probability, but the presumption would remain. At present we have no evidence of motive or intention."

"You are not forgetting that he emptied his pockets of all valuables?" Brodribb objected.

"No, I am not. The exact significance of that proceeding is not obvious, but it does not appear to me to indicate an intention to commit suicide."

"Does it not? Do you not find a certain congruity between that action and the place and circumstances in which the body was found?"

"Undoubtedly I do," replied Thorndyke. "But the place and circumstances have no natural connection with suicide. That is what I mean by conflicting probabilities. If Sir Edward had been found hanging from a peg in his bedroom, the ordinary presumption of suicide would have existed, because suicides commonly act in that way. But here we have a man making preparations (as it appears to me) to go into some place where property on the person is not safe and being later found dead in a remote part of the town which we should suppose to be quite unknown to him. The circumstances are so abnormal and the conduct so strikingly unlike the usual conduct of suicides that the ordinary presumption based on the mode of death cannot be accepted."

"Then," said Brodribb, "what is it that you are suggesting?"

"At present, I am suggesting nothing excepting that I am not prepared to accept the Superintendent's account at its face value. Beyond that it is useless to go until we have heard what transpires at the inquest."

Brodribb nodded gravely. "Yes," he agreed. "Discussion at this stage is merely academic. But probably the evidence at the inquest will clear matters up. I suppose the *post mortem* will settle the question of suicide?"

"It may," Thorndyke replied, guardedly, "in a negative sense, by showing the absence of any alternative suggestion. But the conditions are not favourable for forming positive and definite opinions as to the exact circumstances in which death occurred."

"Well, you will be there, so, if it is possible to establish the fact of suicide – or to exclude it – by an examination of the body, we may say that the question will be decided to-morrow."

To this statement Thorndyke made no rejoinder, and as Brodribb relapsed into silent meditation and my colleague showed no inclination for further discussion, I followed their example and, as I smoked my pipe, turned the situation over in my mind.

In the colloquy to which I had listened, two things had impressed me rather forcibly. For the first time in my experience of him, Brodribb had appeared unprepared to defer to Thorndyke's judgement. It was evident that in his opinion the suicide of Sir Edward was virtually an established fact, and that in his view Thorndyke's scepticism was merely a manifestation of the specialist's tendency to see things through the medium of his own specialty. On the other hand it had struck me that Thorndyke had made little effort to influence his opinion. He had, it is true, fairly answered Brodribb's questions, but it was quite obvious to me that he had not put the case against suicide with nearly the force that was possible even with the few facts that we had. This might have been due to his habit of avoiding anything like premature conclusions, but I had the feeling that he was not unwilling that Brodribb should continue to take the case, as he had expressed it, at its face value.

At the terminus we separated, Brodribb setting forth alone in a hansom while Thorndyke and I decided to restore our circulations by a brisk walk homewards through the city streets on which the quiet and repose of evening had now descended. Having seen Brodribb fairly launched, we turned out of the station, and, crossing Liverpool Street, started at a swinging pace up New Broad Street. For a minute or two we walked on in silence while I debated inwardly whether or not I should propound my views to Thorndyke. Finally deciding in the affirmative, I began, cautiously, "Brodribb appears to me to have made up his mind definitely on this case. He seems quite convinced that Sir Edward hanged himself."

"Yes, that was what I gathered from his remarks on the case."

"I wonder why. He is a lawyer, and a pretty shrewd one, too."

"Yes, but not a criminal lawyer. His experience is all on the civil side and principally in relation to property. Still, he may have reasons for his views of the affair which he has not disclosed. He knew Sir Edward pretty intimately and he knows all about the family. There may be some highly pertinent facts connected with the dead man's personality and the family history which we know nothing about. I take it that you don't agree with Brodribb?"

"I do not, and neither, I suspect, do you."

"You are quite right, Jervis. I do not. But we must not allow ourselves to come to any sort of conclusion before we have seen and heard the evidence. We must try to approach to-morrow's investigation with a perfectly open mind, and I am not sure that we ought to be discussing it now."

"There is no harm," said I, "in just going over the ground – without prejudice."

"Perhaps not," he agreed, "and since my learned friend seems to have arrived at certain provisional conclusions, it would be interesting to hear his exposition of the case as it presents itself to him."

I reflected for a few moments, trying to arrange my ideas in an orderly sequence. At length I began. "Taking the points for and against the theory of suicide in this case, I know of only one in favour of it, the one that you mentioned – that unofficial hanging is usually suicidal. On the other hand, there are several reasons against it.

"First, there is the fact that he came to London. Why should he, if he had been intending to commit suicide? The natural thing, according to precedent, would have been to hang himself in his own bedroom or in a garret."

"There are precedents of the opposite kind, though," objected Thorndyke. "I recall a case of a lady who poisoned herself in a very secluded wood on a common or in a park near London and whose body was not discovered for some months. Still, I agree that the probabilities are with you. What is the next point?"

"It is the fact that he unloaded his pockets of all valuables before he set out from the club. Why did he do that? If it is suggested that it was to provide against the chance that his body might be robbed, the obvious answer is that he could have avoided that possibility by committing suicide on his own premises. And the way in which the things were hidden under his shirts strongly suggests an intention to return and recover them. By Brodribb this incident seems to have been accepted as proof of an intention to commit suicide, but to me it has quite the opposite significance. Your own suggestion, made at the time, that he was expecting to go to some place and among some people where he might expect to be robbed, seems to meet the case perfectly, and Brodribb's suggestion that where property on the person is not safe, the person is probably also in some danger seems to receive corroboration. You and Brodribb suggest in advance the possibility of his being exposed to danger of personal violence, and the next thing that happens is that he is found dead, having admittedly died a violent death."

Thorndyke nodded approvingly. "Yes," he admitted. "I think that is quite fairly argued."

"The next point," I continued, "is the place in which the body was found. It is an empty house in an obscure and remote part of a region which is quite unknown to the immense majority of Londoners, and almost certainly unknown to the deceased. How on earth did he get there and what could have been his object in going there? He could hardly have strayed thither by chance, for the place is difficult of access and right off the track to any more likely locality. On the other hand, the choice of this particular house suggests some local knowledge – knowledge of the existence of that desolate row of houses and of the fact that they were all uninhabited and likely to be left undisturbed and unexamined for months. The whole set of circumstances seems to me profoundly suspicious."

"There I am entirely with you," said Thorndyke. "That empty house on the edge of no-man's-land wants a deal of explaining."

"Then," I resumed, "there is that new, cheap watch, evidently bought as a substitute for the watch that he had left at the club. The purchase of that watch seems to me utterly to exclude the state of mind of a man intending immediately to commit suicide. Then, finally, there is a point which, strangely enough, seems to have been overlooked by Brodribb – the seal. That seems to me the most suspicious of all the elements in the case. The sealed letter was posted on the Saturday, but we have evidence that the hanging could not have occurred before

112

Sunday night at the earliest. Now, it is fair to assume that the letter was not sealed by Sir Edward."

"It is extremely unlikely," Thorndyke interposed, "but we can't say that it is impossible. And if we accept the hypothesis of suicide, it is not even very improbable. It might be suggested that Sir Edward adopted that method of announcing his death. But I may say that I agree with you in assuming that the letter was almost certainly sealed and posted by some other person."

"Then, in that case, Sir Edward's signet ring must have been in the possession of some other person at least twenty-four hours before the earliest moment at which he could have hanged himself in the empty house. That is a very remarkable and significant fact."

"Has it occurred to you, Jervis," Thorndyke asked, "that Sir Edward might have been wearing his ring that day, or some other day after he left the club, and that it might have slipped off his finger and been picked up by some chance stranger? We have been told that it was a very loose fit."

"That did occur to me," I replied, "but I think we must reject that explanation. You remember that Sir Edward usually carried the ring in a little leather case or bag in his pocket. Now, if he had lost the ring off his finger, the empty case would have been in his pocket. But apparently it was not. I looked for it carefully among the things in the drawer that the Superintendent showed us and it was not there. And it could hardly have been overlooked in a careful search of the pockets."

"No," Thorndyke agreed, "I think we may take it that the case was not there, though we shall have to verify its absence, since, as you say, the point is an important one and opens up some very curious possibilities. But here we are at our journey's end. Your masterly summing-up of the evidence has made the miles slip by unnoticed. I must compliment you on the completeness of your survey. And we shall be none the worse for having gone over the ground in advance, provided that we approach the actual investigation to-morrow without prejudice or any expectation as to what we are likely to discover."

As he concluded, we turned in at our entry and mounted the stairs to our landing. The door of our chambers was open, giving us a view of the lighted room, in which Polton was adding a few final touches to the supper table.

Chapter VII
Number Five Piper's Row
(Dr. Jervis's Narrative)

From my long association with Thorndyke, I was often able to deduce something of his state of mind and his intentions from observation of his actions. Particularly interesting was it to me to watch him (as unobtrusively as possible) packing his green canvas "research case" in preparation for some investigation for, by noting carefully the appliances and materials with which he provided himself, I could form a pretty clear idea as to the points that he thought it necessary to elucidate.

Thus, on the morning on which we were to set forth for our second visit to Stratford, I stood by with an attentive eye on his proceedings as he put into the case the various articles which he thought might be needed. I was specially interested on this occasion because, while I viewed the case with the deepest suspicion, I could think of no method of attack on the undoubtedly plausible *prima facie* appearances. Possibly Thorndyke was in the same position, but one thing became clear to me as I watched him. He was taking nothing for granted. As I observed him putting into the case the chemically clean bottles with stoppers prepared for sealing, I realised that he was prepared for signs that might call for an analysis. The little portable microscope and the box of blank-labelled slides, the insufflator, or powder-spray, the miniature camera and telescopic tripod, the surveyor's tape and small electric lamp, each indicated certain points which were to be subjected to exact tests and measurements, and the rubber gloves and case of *post mortem* instruments showed that he contemplated taking an active part in the actual necropsy if the opportunity should present itself. The whole outfit suggested his habitual state of mind. Nothing was to be taken on trust. The one undoubted fact was that Sir Edward Hardcastle was dead. Beyond that Thorndyke would accept no suggestion. He was going to begin at the beginning as if no cause of death had been hinted at.

One item of the outfit did certainly puzzle me considerably – a box of keys from Polton's rather doubtfully legal collection. The fact is that our worthy laboratory assistant held somewhat obscure views on certain aspects of the law, but on one subject he was perfectly clear: Whatever legal restrictions or obligations might apply to common persons, they had no application to "The Doctor". In his view, his revered employer was above the law. Thus, in the assumed interests of that employer, Polton had amassed a collection of keys that would have been enough to bring a "common person" within hail of penal servitude, and a portion of his illegal hoard I now saw going into the research case. I examined them with profoundly speculative eyes. The collection included a number of common latch-keys, a graded set of blanks – (How on earth had Polton managed to acquire those blanks, so strictly forbidden by the law?) – and a bunch of skeleton keys of the pipe variety, simple in construction but undeniably felonious in aspect.

I asked no questions concerning those keys, reserving to myself the prospective entertainment of seeing them produced and put to their mysterious use, as to which I could form no sort of surmise. They were certainly not to let us into the house, for we had already been promised free admittance. But it was useless to speculate. The explanation would come all in good time, and now the research case, having received its lading, was closed and fastened and we were due to start.

At Stratford, we found the Superintendent ready to receive us and in the same helpful spirit as on the preceding day.

"You are full early, gentlemen," he remarked, "as matters stand. The inquest opens, as you know, at four p.m., and the doctor has fixed two p.m. for the *post mortem*. So you'll have plenty of time to survey the 'scene of the tragedy', as the newspapers call it, though I don't fancy that you'll spend your time very profitably. However, that's your affair. You are acting for the executor, as I understand, so I suppose you have got to make a show of doing something."

"Exactly," Thorndyke agreed. "A specialist must make a demonstration of some kind. You gave my letter to the coroner?"

"Yes, sir. And it is just as well that you had it. Otherwise I don't fancy you'd have got many facilities. He's rather a touchy man and he seemed disposed to resent your coming here to hold what he calls 'an unofficial inquiry of your own'. However, it is all right. I am to let you see anything that you want to see, and the medical witness – he is the police surgeon's deputy – has got the same instructions. And now I expect you would like to start. I've got the key here, but I can't give it to you in case the coroner wants to inspect the place himself. Besides, you'll want someone to show you where it is."

He stepped to the door, and, looking into the adjoining office, called out, "Marshall, just take these two gentlemen down to Number Five Piper's Row. You needn't stay. Just let them into the house and bring the key back to me."

As he spoke, he produced from the nest of drawers a key with a wooden label attached to it which he handed to the constable, and I noticed that, as it passed from hand to hand, Thorndyke bestowed a quick glance on it, and I suspected that he was memorising its shape and size. It was, however, but a momentary glance, for the key disappeared immediately into the constabulary pocket and the officer, with a salute to his superior, turned and led the way out into the street.

The town of Stratford is not strikingly prepossessing in any part. There is nothing of the residential suburb about it. But the district to which we were conducted by Constable Marshall seemed to reach the very limit of what is attainable in the way of repulsive squalor by the most advanced developments of modern industry. Turning out of the High Street by Abbey Lane, we presently emerged from the inhabited areas on to a dreary expanse of marsh, on which a few anaemic weeds struggled to grow in the interstices of the rubbish that littered every open space. Gas works, chemical works, pumping stations, and various large buildings of the mill or factory type arose on all sides, each accompanied by its group of tall chimney-shafts, all belching forth smoke, and each diffusing the particular stench appropriate to the industry that it represented. A few rough roads, like urbanised cart tracks, flanked by drainage ditches, meandered across this region, and along one of these we picked our way until it brought us to the place where, as the Superintendent bluntly but justly expressed it, "some fool had built" Piper's Row.

"Not much to look at, are they, sir?" Constable Marshall remarked in comment on our disparaging glances at the unspeakably sordid, ruinous little hovels. "Mr. Holker bought them for a song, but I fancy he's going to lose his money all the same. This is the one."

He halted at a decaying door bearing the Number 5, fished the key out of his pocket, inserted it, gave it a turn, and pushed the door open. Then, as we entered, he withdrew the key, wished us "Good morning", closed the door and took his departure.

For some moments Thorndyke stood looking about the tiny room – for there was no hall, the sitting-room opening directly on the street – letting his eye travel over its scanty details, the rusty grate, the little cupboard in the recess, the small, low window, and especially the floor. He stepped across and tried the door of the cupboard, and, finding it locked, remarked that Holker had probably used it to stow away his tools.

"You notice, Jervis," he added, "that the appearance of the floor does not seem to support the theory that the house was entered by the window. There are foot-marks under the window, certainly, but they are

116

quite faint, whereas there are well-marked prints of muddy feet, two pairs at least, leading from the street door to the next room, which I suppose is the kitchen."

"Yes, I see that," I replied, "but as we don't know whose foot-prints they are or when they were made, the observation doesn't carry us very far."

"Still," he rejoined, "we note their existence and observe that they proceed, getting rapidly fainter, direct to the kitchen."

He passed through the open doorway, still narrowly examining the floor, and halted in the kitchen to look round. But, beyond the faint marks on the floor, there was nothing to attract notice and, after a brief inspection, we went on to the wash-house, which was what we had actually come to see.

Apparently the place had been left in the condition in which it had been found by Holker, for the decrepit Windsor chair still lay on its side, while almost directly above it a length of thinnish brown rope hung down from a short beam that connected the principal pair of rafters. At this Thorndyke, when he had finished his scrutiny of the floor, looked with an expression of interest that it hardly seemed to warrant.

"The Superintendent," he remarked, "spoke of a tie beam. It is only a matter of terminology, but this is rather what architects would call a collar beam. But the fact is of some interest. A tie beam, in a building of this size, would be within comfortable reach of a short man. But this beam is fully eight feet above the floor. Even with the aid of the chair, it is not so very accessible."

"No. But the rope could have been thrown over and pulled taut after the knot was tied. It is made fast with a fisherman's bend, which would run up close when the rope was hauled on."

"Yes," he agreed, "that is so. And, by the way, the character of the knot is worth noting. There is something rather distinctive about a fisherman's bend."

He stood looking up thoughtfully at the knot, from which a long end hung down beside the "standing part", which had been cut, as if the rope had been longer than was necessary for the purpose. Then he took the cut end in his hand and examined it minutely, first with the naked eye and then with the aid of a pocket lens. Finally, slipping on a glove, he picked up the chair, and, mounting on it, began deliberately to untie the knot.

"Is that quite in order, Thorndyke?" I protested. "We had permission to inspect the premises, but I don't think we were expected to disturb anything."

"We are not going to disturb anything in any essential sense," he replied. "When we have finished, we shall re-tie the knot and put the

117

chair as we found it. That will be good enough for the coroner's jury. You might give me the tape out of the case."

I opened the case and took out the long tape, which I handed to him and watched him as he carefully measured the rope and entered the length in his note book. It seemed an unaccountable proceeding, but I made no comment until he had re-fastened the rope and stepped down from the chair. Then I ventured to remark, "I should like to know why you measured that rope, Thorndyke. It seems to me that its length can have no possible bearing on anything connected with the case that we are investigating. Evidently I am wrong."

"When we are collecting facts," he replied, "especially when we are absolutely in the dark, we are not bound to consider their relevancy in advance. The length of this rope is a fact and that fact might acquire later some relevancy which it does not appear to have now. There is no harm in noting irrelevant facts, but a great deal of harm in leaving any fact unnoted. That is a general rule. But in this case there is a reason for ascertaining and recording the length of this piece of rope. Look at it attentively and see what information it yields."

I glared at the rope with concentrated attention, but all the information that it yielded to me was that it was a piece of rope.

"I am looking at it attentively," I said, doggedly, "and what I see is a length – about a fathom-and-a-half – of thinnish coir rope, the thinnest coir rope, I think, that I have ever seen. It is made fast at the end with a fisherman's bend and the other part has been cut."

"Why 'the other part'? I mean what is the distinction?"

"It is obvious," I replied. "The end proper has got the whipping on it."

"Exactly," said Thorndyke. "That is the point. Incidentally, it is not a coir rope. It is a hemp rope dyed, apparently with cutch. But that is a detail, though a significant one. The chief point is that the end is whipped. A rope with cut ends is a rope of no determinate length. It is simply a piece of rope. But a rope with whipped ends has a determinate length. It is a definite entity. It may be a boat's painter, a sheet, a halyard, a waterman's towing-rope – in any case it is a thing, not a part of a thing. Here we have a piece of rope with a whipping at one end. We haven't seen the other part, but we know that when it was complete it was whipped at both ends. And we know that, somewhere, there is a counterpart to this fragment and that the two together make up a known length."

"Yes," I agreed, "there is no denying the truth of what you have said, but it is a mere exposition of theory. Undoubtedly there does exist a piece of rope which is the complement to this piece. But as we have no

118

idea where it is and there is not the remotest chance that we shall ever meet with it, or that we should recognise it if we did, your measurement is a mere demonstration of a principle without any utility whatever."

"Our chance of meeting with that complementary portion is small enough, I must admit," said Thorndyke, "but it is not so infinitesimal as you think. There are some points which you have overlooked, and I think you have not fully taken in the immense importance of tracing the origin of this rope. But we must not waste time in discussion. This chair is the next subject for investigation. On the hypothesis that Sir Edward hanged himself, there should be prints of his fingers on some part of it, and if he did not, then there should be prints of the fingers of some other person."

"I think we can take it that there will be plenty of finger-prints on it," said I, "if they are not too old to develop. The latest must be at least three weeks old."

"Yes, it is rather a poor chance, but we will try our luck."

He opened the research case and brought out the insufflator with one of the powder containers which was filled with a pure white powder. Having fitted the container to the spray-producer, he placed the chair where the light fell on the front aspect of it and began to work the bellows, keeping at some distance from the chair, so that the cloud of white powder met the surface quite gently. Very soon the whole of the front of the chair became covered with a thin, uniform coating of the impalpably fine white dust. Then the chair was turned about by pushing and pulling the lower parts of the legs and the other aspect coated with powder. When this process was completed Thorndyke proceeded to tap each of the legs very lightly and quickly with the handle of a large pocket-knife. At once, in response to the faint jarring strokes, the white dust began to creep down the perpendicular surfaces, and in a few seconds there came into view a number of rounded, smeary shapes on the broad, flat top rail of the chair-back. Still, as the light, quick tapping went on, the powder continued to creep down, leaving the shapes more and more conspicuous and distinct. Finally, Thorndyke transferred his operations to the top of the chair-back, gradually increasing the force of his blows until practically the whole of the powder had been jarred off, leaving the shapes – now unmistakable finger-prints – standing out strongly against the dingy, varnished surface.

"Not a very promising lot," Thorndyke commented, after a preliminary inspection. "Several hopeless smears and several more super-imposed. Those won't be much use even to the experts."

With the aid of his pocket lens, he made a more critical survey of the one side while I examined the other, reinforcing the feeble light with the electric lamp.

"They are a very confused lot," I remarked. "The trouble is that there are too many of them on top of one another. Still, there are several that show a distinguishable pattern. I should think the finger-print experts will be able to make something of them."

"Yes," Thorndyke agreed, "I think so. It is surprising to see what shockingly bad prints they manage to decipher. At any rate, we will give them a chance."

Between us, we got out the little camera, mounted it on its tripod, and placed it in position by means of its wire sighting frame. Having measured the distance with the tape and set the focusing-scale, Thorndyke stopped the lens down to *F. 16*, and, taking out his watch, gave the long exposure that was demanded by the weak light and the small stop. Then, when, as a measure of safety, he had made a second exposure, we turned the chair round and repeated the operation on the opposite side.

"Are you going to leave the powder on the chair?" I asked as we re-packed the camera.

"No," he replied. "The police have had their opportunity. Perhaps they have taken it. At any rate it will be best for us to keep our own counsel as to our private investigations. And the photographs will be available if they are wanted."

With this he carefully dusted away all traces of the powder and when he had laid the chair in the place and position in which we had found it, he picked up the research case and we went back to the front room.

"Well," I said, moving towards the door, "I think we have seen everything here and we have picked up one or two crumbs – pretty small ones as far as I am concerned. But perhaps there is something else that you want to see?"

"Yes," he replied, "there are two more points that we ought to consider before we go. First there are those wheel-ruts. You noticed them, I suppose?

"I observed some ruts in the road as we came along. Deuced uncomfortable they were to a man with thin shoes. But what about them?"

"Apparently you did not notice them," said he, "excepting as a source of physical discomfort. Come out now and take a careful look at them."

He opened the street door and we stepped out on to the strip of rough ground that served as the footpath or "side-walk". The unmade road that passed the houses was bumpy with obscure impressions of feet that had trodden it when the surface was moist and there were faint suggestions of old ruts. But in addition to these was a pair of deep, sharply-defined ruts with clear hoof-marks between, which I now remembered having seen as we came out of Abbey Lane.

"I can't quite make up my mind as to the class of vehicle," he said. "What do you make of it?"

"A two-wheeled cart of some kind," I suggested. "A largish one, to judge by the space between the ruts."

"Yes, it is rather wide for a light cart. My provisional diagnosis was a good-sized gig or dog-cart – more probably a gig. It was evidently a light, high vehicle, as we can tell by the narrowness of the rims and the large diameter of the wheels."

"I can see that the rims were narrow, but I don't see how you arrive at the diameter of the wheels."

"It happens," he explained, "to be quite easy in this case. There is a notch in the edge of the near tyre, rather a surprising feature if you consider the strength of an iron tyre. It must have been caused by striking a sharp angle of granite or iron at some corner."

"I should have thought," said I, "that a blow that would notch the tyre would have broken the wheel."

"So should I." he agreed. "However, there it is, and it leaves a small, triangular projection at the side of the rut, and of course, the distance between two such projections is the circumference of the wheel. We may as well measure that distance, and the width between the two tracks and the width of the rims. Fortunately, there is no one here to spy on us."

I looked round as I unfastened the research case and handed out the tape. There was not a human creature in sight. Piper's Row might as well have been in the midst of the Sahara.

Taking advantage of the solitude, we went out on to the road and made the three measurements at our ease, and as I held one end of the tape while Thorndyke stretched it and took the reading, I speculated vaguely as to the object of the proceeding.

"The tyres are one-inch-and-a-half wide," he reported as he put away his note-book. "The width between the outside edges of the tyre-marks is fifty-seven inches, and the circumference of the wheels is thirteen-feet-ten-inches. That makes the diameter about four-feet-seven-and-a-half – that is, fifty-five-and-a-half inches.

"Yes," I agreed without much enthusiasm, "that will be about right. But why are we taking all this trouble? Is there anything particularly interesting about this cart?

"The interest attaching to this cart," he replied, "lies in the fact that it stopped at Number Five Piper's Row."

"The deuce it did!" I exclaimed. "That is rather remarkable, seeing that Number Five is an empty house."

"Very remarkable," he agreed. "It was quite a short halt," he continued, "unless the horse was more than usually patient. But there is no doubt about it. You can see where the tracks swerve in slightly towards the house. Then there is the spot where the ruts lose their regularity and broaden out somewhat, and there is quite plainly the re-duplication of the hoof-marks where the horse has trodden two or three times in nearly the same place. That could have happened only when the cart was stationary."

I was still looking down at the impressions to verify his statements when I was aroused by the slamming of a door. I looked up quickly and saw that a gust of wind had caught the door of Number Five and shut us out.

"Well, Thorndyke," I remarked with a faint grin, "that seems to put the stopper on that further point that you were going to elucidate."

"Not at all," he retorted. "I would say rather that it introduces it in a particularly opportune way. Do you mind opening the research case?"

I did so, and when he had replaced the tape in its compartment, he took out the box of keys which had so stimulated my curiosity. Opening it, he extracted the bunch of skeleton keys, and, glancing from them to the keyhole, he deliberately selected one and inserted it. It entered quite easily and when he gave it a turn and a slight push, the door opened and we walked in.

"You see, Jervis," he said, withdrawing it from the keyhole and holding it out to me, "here is a perfectly elementary skeleton key, made by simply cutting away the whole of the bit excepting the top and the bolt edge. I selected it with Constable Marshall's key in my mind."

"That was a ward key, I think?"

"Yes, it had three vertical slits in the bit, which ostensibly corresponded to three concentric wards in the lock."

"Why 'ostensibly'?"

"Because I suspect that they are not there. But in selecting the skeleton key I assumed that they were there, and you saw the result. Also you see the weakness of a ward lock. The wards are obstructions placed in the path of the key. The key which fits a particular lock has slits corresponding to the wards, so that it can turn and let the wards pass through. But it isn't necessary for the slits to fit the wards. All that is necessary is a hole in the key-bit large enough to let it pass the wards. The simplest plan is, as in this key, to cut out the whole of the bit excepting the distal edge – which enters the notch, or 'talon' of the bolt

122

and moves it – and the top edge which joins it to the key stem. I am speaking, of course, of comparatively simple locks."

"And you think that this lock hasn't any wards at all?"

"It is a mere guess based on the generally shoddy appearance of the fittings. But we can easily settle the question."

Once more he opened the key box and this time took out a locksmith's 'blank', which he compared with the skeleton key. Finding their bits about the same width, he tried the blank in the lock. It entered as easily as the skeleton had, and when he turned it, it made its circuit in the same manner and duly drew in the bolt.

"That," said Thorndyke, "makes it perfectly clear. This blank could not possibly have passed a ward. It follows that this lock contains nothing but a spring bolt. Consequently it could be opened by practically any key that would enter the keyhole and that was long enough in the bit to reach the notch of the bolt."

"By the way," said I, "if there are no wards, what is the function of those slits that you described in the key?"

"Their function, I take it, is purely commercial – a matter of salesmanship, to produce a certain moral effect on the purchaser. He sees a somewhat intricate key and naturally infers a corresponding intricacy in the lock. The ethics of commerce are sometimes a little difficult for the uncommercial mind to follow."

"Yes, by Jove," said I. "That dummy key does seem uncommonly like a fraud. But with regard to this lock – it is all very curious and interesting, but I don't quite see the purpose of these experiments. Obviously they have some bearing since you took the trouble to bring that collection of keys."

"Yes," he replied as he returned the box to the green canvas case and fastened the latter, "they have a bearing. We can discuss it as we walk back to the town, and I propose that we follow the tracks of the cart and see where it went to. It is bound to go our way, as this area of marsh is enclosed on the other three sides by the creeks."

We went out of the dismal little house, slamming the door behind us, and set forth along the rough footway in the direction in which the cart had gone. We walked a short distance in silence, then Thorndyke returned to my question.

"The bearing of what we have ascertained about that lock is this: We are invited to believe that entrance was effected into the house by the window because the door was shut and locked. But the fact, which we have established, that the lock is one which can be opened with almost any key – or even with a piece of stiff wire – makes any such supposition unnecessary. The house was accessible to anybody by way of the door."

"As far as Sir Edward was concerned," said I, "you remember that he had no keys on him at all."

"Yes. And that fact may have influenced the Superintendent. But it doesn't influence us. If Sir Edward went into that house of his own free will, it is of no concern to us whether he got in at the window or climbed down the chimney. But if we assume – as I take it we both do, without prejudice as to what may transpire at the inquest – that he was taken into that house forcibly, or in a state of unconsciousness, or actually dead, then the facility of access becomes a material fact, for the proceedings would necessarily be hurried. There would be no time for the manipulation of windows or picking of locks. Entry would have to be effected at once."

"That means," said I, "that the person or persons who entered knew what sort of lock was on the door."

"Undoubtedly," he agreed. "The house must have been known to at least one of the parties, and would, presumably, have been visited and explored. The plan must have been arranged and prepared in advance to enable it to be carried out quickly."

"What do you suppose to have been the actual *modus operandi*?" I asked.

"From what we have seen, I should reconstruct events somewhat thus: First, a scout would come to the place, try the lock, and ascertain that a particular key would open it, explore the house, and select the place where the victim could be most conveniently hanged. Then, at the appointed time, the victim – who must almost necessarily have been either dead or insensible – would be put in the cart and covered up, the three men – possibly two, but much more probably three – would mount to the seat and the cart would be driven to the house pretty late at night, so as to secure complete darkness.

"On arriving at Number Five, one man would jump down and open the door. The victim and the rope would then be handed down and carried in and the door shut. The cart would then be driven off, possibly to wait at some rendezvous outside the immediate neighbourhood. The two men, having concluded the business, would come out and walk to the rendezvous, and the whole party would then return whence they came."

"Yes," I said, "that sounds very complete and consistent. But aren't we taking rather a lot for granted? I admit that the stopping of that cart opposite Number Five is a highly suspicious circumstance – and here we are, back at Abbey Lane and here are the cart-tracks back with us. So the cart must have made the round expressly to call at Number Five, which strongly supports your theory. But still, we are assuming that the cart made that very suspicious call on that particular night. Of course, it is extremely probable that it did, and if it did, it almost certainly conveyed Sir Edward, alive or dead. The fatal flaw in the evidence is that we can't fix the date on which the cart called at the house."

"But I think we can, Jervis. One doesn't like to use the word certainty, but I think I can fix the date with the very highest degree of probability."

"Then," said I, "if you can do that, I accept your hypothetical reconstruction as almost certainly representing what actually happened. But I should like to hear the evidence."

"The evidence," he replied, "is based on two factors: One is the state of the road when the tracks were made. The other is the time at which the road could have been in that particular state. Let us consider factor one.

"You saw the ruts and the hoof-prints. They were deep and sharp but by no means dead sharp. There was a slight blurring of the edges of the impressions. The soil of the road was an impure clayey loam. Now, since the impressions were deep, the road must have been quite soft, but since the impressions were fairly sharp, the mud could not have been liquid or diffluent, for liquid or semi-liquid mud does not retain impressions. It could not have been raining when the impressions were made, for in the soft state of the road, rain would have largely obliterated them. For the same reason, no appreciable rain could have fallen after they were made.

"On the other hand, the road could not have dried enough to become plastic or semi-solid, or – on soil of this kind – the impressions would have been dead sharp. So it comes to this: The ruts were made after heavy rain – heavy enough to swamp the road. But there was an interval after the rain, long enough to allow the semi-liquid stage to pass off but not long enough to allow the mud to pass into the plastic or semi-solid stage.

"Now let us take the second factor – the time factor. I need not remind you of the long drought that has prevailed this summer. It began, as you probably remember, at the very end of May, and it still continues. In that drought there has been up to the present only a single break – a single, dramatic break. On Sunday, the twenty-first June, a tremendous storm burst over the London area, and for more than an hour the rain fell in torrents. The storm clouds came up quite suddenly about half-past-four in the afternoon and the rain ceased and the clouds rolled away with almost equal suddenness about six o'clock. And forthwith the drought resumed its sway. A hot, dry easterly wind followed the storm and the pavements dried up as if the water on them had been spirit.

"Now, during that heavy rain, these roads across the marshes must have been flooded. For the time being, their surfaces must have been just liquid mud. But we must remember that under that liquid mud, only a few inches down, was soil baked dry by weeks of drought. Before midnight the surface water would have soaked in, bringing the soil to the consistency shown by these ruts. By the following morning, or at least by noon, the plastic stage would have been reached, while by evening, after a day's hot sunshine and dry wind, the surface would have become too firm to yield deep impressions like these with their surrounding ridges. As I say, one doesn't like to use the word certainty, but I submit that we are justified in assuming with considerable confidence that these ruts were made on the night of Sunday, the twenty-first of June, probably after ten o'clock."

"More probably in the small hours of the morning," I suggested.

"The state of the road would admit of that view," he replied, "but other considerations suggest an earlier hour – say from eleven to half-past. A party of men with a dead or insensible man in a cart would not wish to attract notice or run the risk of being stopped and questioned. Up to midnight they would be pretty safe, but in the small hours a cart prowling round an unfrequented neighbourhood or travelling along a road that leads nowhere might excite the curiosity of an alert and enterprising policeman. However, that is mere surmise and not at present of special interest to us. The important point is the date and the approximate time."

"By the way, Thorndyke," I asked, "how do you manage to remember all these details? I recollect the storm, of course, and now that you mention it, I think I can corroborate the date and the time. But it is a mystery to me how you keep these dates and times in your memory, ready to be produced at a moment's notice."

"The solution of that mystery," he replied, "is quite simple. I don't. I keep a diary, a highly condensed affair, but I note in it everything that may need to be recalled. And I always enter the state of the weather, having learned from experience that it is often a vitally important means of fixing the time of other happenings, as in the present case. I looked it up last night, principally in connection with the possibility of finding muddy foot-prints in the house."

"After reading me a lecture on the impropriety of discussing the case in advance," I said with a grin, "and now you have built up a complete reconstruction of the events before we have even seen what the *post mortem* has to tell, to say nothing of the inquest."

He smiled deprecatingly. "We had no choice, Jervis. We could only observe the facts in the order in which they were presented. But, still, I

126

hope we shall approach the inquest without prejudice, and it is possible that we may get a surprise from the evidence of Brodribb or Weeks – but especially Brodribb. I suspect that he has something in his mind that he has not disclosed to us."

"The deuce!" I exclaimed. "You think there may have been reasons for anticipating the possibility of suicide? It will be a bit of an anti-climax if evidence of that kind is given, for it will knock the bottom out of your elaborate reconstruction."

"Not necessarily," he replied, "opinions and expectations are no answer to observed facts, and you must not forget, Jervis, that a known intention or tendency to commit suicide makes things uncommonly easy for a murderer. But it is time that we turned our attention to the subject of food. We are due at the mortuary at two o'clock, and it will not be amiss if we get there a few minutes before our time. How will this place do?"

He halted opposite a restaurant of somewhat fly-blown aspect, the fascia of which bore an Italian name. In the window, a "set piece" (consisting of two glass dishes of tomatoes flanking the head of a calf, who appeared from his complexion to have died of pernicious *anaemia*) was exhibited to whet the appetites of passers-by, while through the open doorway an unctuous odour suggestive of thick soup stole forth to mingle with the aroma from an adjacent soap-boiler's.

"Well," I said, "the soup inside smells better than the soap outside. Let us go in." Accordingly we went in.

Chapter VIII
Sir Edward Hardcastle, Bart., Deceased
(Dr. Jervis's Narrative)

Thorndyke's reasons for wishing to arrive at the mortuary a few minutes before the appointed time were not difficult to guess at. But they became crystal clear as soon as the constable, deputed by the Superintendent, had admitted us and retired. As soon as the door shut behind the officer, he stepped quickly across to the long shelf on which the clothing had been deposited and, picking up the shoes, turned them over, took a single glance at the soles, and then, without comment, held them out for my inspection.

No comment was needed. The soles were, relatively speaking, perfectly clean. There was not a trace of mud or any sign whatever of their having been damp. On the contrary, there still clung to them a certain amount of light dust, and this was still more evident on the welts and uppers. The condition of those shoes proved with absolute certainty that however and whenever Sir Edward Hardcastle had got into that empty house, he had not walked there on the night of Sunday, the twenty-first of June.

There was no time, however, to dwell on this striking confirmation of our previous conclusions. Thorndyke already had the research case open and had taken out the little finger-print box and produced from it the ready-inked copper plate, a piece of soft rag, and a couple of smooth cards. The latter he handed to me, and together we moved over to the great table and uncovered the hands of the corpse.

"We shan't get normal prints," he remarked, as he wiped the finger-tips one after the other and then touched them with the inked plate, "but they will be clear enough to compare with our photographs of those of the chair-back."

They were certainly not normal prints, for the finger-tips were shrunken and almost mummified. But, distorted as they were, the ridge-patterns were fairly distinct and quite decipherable, as I could see by the quick glance that I took at each print after pressing the inked finger-tip on the card.

"Yes," I agreed, "there will be no difficulty about these. I only wish the photographs were half as clear."

I handed them to him and he immediately slipped them into the grooved receptacle with which the box was provided. Then he closed the latter and replaced it in the research case.

"I am glad we were able to get that done unobserved," said he. "Now we can make our observations at our ease."

He took out of the research case a pair of rubber gloves and a case of *post mortem* instruments which he placed on a vacant spot on the great table. Then he brought out the tape and carefully measured the length of the corpse.

"Sixty-five inches," he reported. "Five-feet-five. You remember the height of that beam. Now we will have another look at those shoes."

He took them up once more and turned them over slowly to bring each part into view. Adhering to one heel was a small flat mass of some material which had apparently been trodden on, and which Thorndyke detached with his pocket-knife and deposited in an envelope from the research case.

"Looks like a small piece of soap," he remarked as he wrote "*Heel of Right Shoe*" on it and put it back in the case, "but we may as well see what it is. You notice several rubbed places on these shoes, but especially on the backs, as if the deceased had been dragged along a fairly smooth surface. Perhaps the back of his coat may tell us something more."

He laid the shoes down and, taking up the neatly folded coat, carefully unfolded it and held it up.

"I think you are right, Thorndyke," said I. "The coat is pretty dirty all over, but the back is noticeably more dusty than the other parts. It looks as if it had been dragged along a dirty floor, and those two bits of cotton sticking to it suggest indoor rather than outdoor dirt. And the same is true of the trousers," I added, holding them up for inspection. "There is a definitely dusty area at the back, and here is another piece of cotton sticking to the cloth."

"Yes, I think that point is clear," he said, "and it is an important point. The cotton is, as you say, definitely suggestive of a floor rather than an out-of-door surface." He picked off the three fragments, and, as he bestowed them with the other "specimens", remarked, "There is nothing very distinctive about cotton, but we may as well take them for reference. I wish we had time to go over the clothing thoroughly, but we had better not show too conspicuous an interest."

Nevertheless, he looked over each garment, quickly, but with intense scrutiny, passing each to me before taking up the next. Over one

129

object only – the collar – did he seem disposed to linger, and certainly its appearance invited notice, for not only was it extremely dirty and crumpled, but it seemed to be uniformly stained as if with weak tea. Moreover, as I held it in my hands, it gave me the impression of a sort of harsh stiffness unaccounted for by the material, for it was a collar of the kind known as "semi-stiff" which usually becomes quite limp after a day's wear. But now Thorndyke had passed on to an examination of the rope noose and I laid down the collar to join him.

"Evidently," said he, "as they were able to remove it without cutting it, the knot must have slipped open pretty easily. And you can see why. The noose was made with a running bowline, a rather unsuitable and unusual knot for the purpose. We will venture to untie it and measure its length, to add to our other measurement. You notice that both ends are cut, so that the whole length is only a part of the complete rope, whatever it was."

He rapidly unfastened the knot and measured the length of the piece, and when he had made a note of the measurement, he produced his pocket-knife and cut off a portion about eight inches long which he dropped into the research case. Meanwhile, I carefully re-tied the bowline and had just replaced it where we had found it when the door opened somewhat abruptly and a stout, well-dressed, middle-aged man bustled in and deposited a hand-bag on a side bench.

"I must really apologise to you, gentlemen," he said, civilly, "for keeping you waiting, but you know how difficult it is for a G.P. to keep appointments punctually. Inquests are the bane of my life."

He hung his hat on a peg by the door, and then, as he turned, his glance lighted on Thorndyke's rubber gloves and instrument case.

"Those your tools?" he asked, and when Thorndyke admitted the ownership, he enquired with evident interest, "Were you thinking of taking a hand in this job?"

"I came prepared to offer any assistance that might be acceptable," Thorndyke replied.

"That is very good of you – my name is Ross, by the way. Of course I know yours – very good of you, indeed. I don't mind confiding to you that I hate *post mortems*, and really, they are not very suitable jobs for a man who is going in and out of sick-rooms and examining living people."

"I quite agree with you," said Thorndyke. "Medicine and pathology do not mix kindly, and as I am a pathologist and not in medical practice, perhaps you would like me to carry out the actual dissection?"

"I should, very much," Dr. Ross replied. "You are an experienced pathologist and I am not. But do you think it would be in order?

"Why not?" Thorndyke asked. "You are instructed to make a *post mortem* inspection. You can do that without performing the dissection. The observations and inferences on which you will give evidence will be your own observations and inferences."

"Yes, that is true," agreed Ross. "But perhaps I had better make, say, the first incision. If I do that, I can say truthfully that I made the *post mortem* with your assistance. That is, if I am asked. The whole affair is a mere formality."

"Very well," said Thorndyke, "we will make the autopsy jointly." And with this he took off his coat, rolled up his shirt sleeves, drew on the rubber gloves, opened his instrument case, and removed the sheet with which the body had been covered.

I was somewhat amused at our colleague's casuistry and also at the subtlety of Thorndyke's tactics. The sort of examination that our friend would have made, on the assumption that the cause of death was obvious and the autopsy "a mere formality", would not have served Thorndyke's purpose. Now he would conduct the investigation in accordance with what was in his own mind.

Dr. Ross ran his eye quickly over the corpse. "It is not an attractive body," he remarked, "but it might easily have been worse after three weeks. Still, all those *post mortem* stains are a trifle confusing. You don't see anything abnormal about the general appearance, do you?

"Nothing very definite," replied Thorndyke. "Those transverse stains on the outer sides of the arms might be pressure marks, or they might not."

"Precisely," said Ross. "I should say they are just *post mortem* stains. They are certainly not bruises. What do you think of the groove?"

"Well," replied Thorndyke, "as we know that the body was hanging for three weeks, we can hardly expect to learn much from it. You notice that the knot was at the back and that it was a rather bulky knot."

"Yes," said Ross. "Wrong place, of course, and wrong sort of knot. But perhaps he hadn't had much practice in hanging himself. Shall I make the incision now?"

Thorndyke handed him a scalpel and he made an incision – a very tentative one. Then he retired to the open window and lit his pipe.

"You don't want to supervise?" Thorndyke enquired with a faint smile.

"What is the use? You are an expert and I am not. If you will tell me what you find, that will satisfy me. I accept your facts without question, though I shall form my own conclusions."

"You don't consider an expert's conclusions as convincing as his facts?" I suggested.

"Oh, I wouldn't say that," he replied. "But, you see, a medico-legal expert tends to approach an inquiry with a certain bias in favour of the abnormal. Take this present case. Here is an unfortunate gentleman who is found hanging in an empty house. A melancholy affair, but that is all that there is to it. Yet here are you two experts, with an enthusiasm that I admire and respect, voluntarily and cheerfully undertaking a most unpleasant investigation in search of something that pretty certainly is not there. And why? Because you utterly refuse to accept the obvious."

"It isn't exactly the function of a medico-legal expert to accept the obvious," I ventured to remind him.

"Precisely," he agreed. "That is my point. Your function is to look out for the abnormal and find it if you possibly can. To you, a normal case is just a failure, a case in which you have drawn a blank."

I was on the point of suggesting that his own function in this case was, in effect, the same as ours. But then, as I realised that his easy-going acceptance of surface appearances was making things easy for Thorndyke, I refrained and proceeded to "make conversation" along other lines.

"Your work as police surgeon must give you a good deal of medico-legal experience," I remarked.

"I'm not the police surgeon," he replied, "at least only by acting rank. The genuine artist is away on leave and I don't care how soon he comes back. This job is a hideous interruption of one's ordinary routine. But I see that the pathologist has made a discovery. What is the specimen that you are collecting?" he added as Thorndyke replaced the stopper in a bottle and stood the latter on a side bench.

"It is some fluid from the stomach," Thorndyke replied. "There was only an ounce or so, but I am surprised to find any in a half-mummified body like this."

"And you are preserving it for analysis, I suppose?" said Ross.

"Yes, just a rough analysis as a matter of routine. Would you write the label, Jervis?"

"Any particular reason for preserving that fluid?" asked Ross. "Any signs or suggestions of poison, for instance?

"No," replied Thorndyke. "But it will be just as well to exclude it definitely. The stomach is better preserved than I should have expected and less red."

"You don't suspect arsenic?"

"No, certainly not as a cause of death – nor, in fact, any other poison. The routine analysis is just an extra precaution."

"Well, I expect you are right, from your point of view," said Ross. "And, of course, poison is a possibility. The ways of suicides are so

132

unaccountable, I heard of a man who took a dose of oxalic acid, then cut his throat, ineffectually, and finally hanged himself. So this man may have taken a dose and failed to produce the desired effect, but he undoubtedly finished himself off with the rope, and that is all that matters to the coroner's jury."

"There are a number of small bodies which look like fish-scales sticking to the walls of the stomach," Thorndyke reported. "No other contents excepting the fluid."

"Well," Ross protested, "there is nothing very abnormal about fish-scales in the stomach. The reasonable inference is that he had been eating fish. What do you mean to suggest?"

"I am not suggesting anything," replied Thorndyke. "I am merely reporting the facts as I observe them. The lungs seem slightly cedematous and there is just a trace of fluid in them – only a trace."

"Oh, come," Ross expostulated, "you are not going to hint that he was drowned! Because he wasn't. I've seen some drowned bodies and I can say quite positively that this is not one. Besides, let us keep the facts in mind. This man was found hanging from a beam in a house."

"Once more," Thorndyke replied, a little wearily, "let me repeat that I am offering no suggestions or inferences. As we agreed, I report the facts and you form your own conclusions. There are one or two of these little bodies – fish-scales or whatever they are – in the air-passages. Perhaps you would like to look at them."

Dr. Ross walked over to the table and looked down as Thorndyke demonstrated the little whitish specks sticking to the sides of the bronchial tubes, and for the moment he seemed somewhat impressed. But only for a moment. Unlike the medico-legal expert, as his fancy painted him, Dr. Ross evidently approached an inquiry with a strong bias in favour of the normal.

"Yes," he said, as he returned to the window, "it is queer how they can have got into the lung. Still, we know he had been eating fish, and there must have been particles in the mouth. Perhaps he had an attack of coughing and got some of them drawn down his trachea. Anyhow there they are. But if you will excuse me for saying so, these curious and no doubt interesting little details are just a trifle beside the mark. The object of this examination is to ascertain the cause of death – if it isn't obvious enough from the circumstances. Now, what do you say? You have made a pretty complete examination – and uncommonly quick you have been over it. I couldn't have done it in twice the time. But what is the result? The alleged fact is that this man hanged himself. If he did, he presumably died of asphyxia. Is the appearance of the body consistent with death from asphyxia? That is the question that I shall be asked at the inquest, and I have got to answer it. What do you say?

"One doesn't like to dogmatise," Thorndyke answered, cautiously. "You see the state of the body. Most of the characteristic signs are absent owing to the drying and the other changes. But making all the necessary allowances, I think the appearances are suggestive of death from asphyxia. At any rate, there are no signs inconsistent with that cause of death, and there is nothing to suggest any other."

"That is what I wanted to know," said Ross, "and if you can give me one or two details, I will run off and put my notes in order so that I can give my evidence clearly and answer any questions."

Thorndyke dictated a brief description of the state of the various organs which Ross took down verbatim in his note-book. Then he put it away, got his hat from the peg, and picked up his hand-bag.

"I am infinitely obliged to you two gentlemen," he said. "You have saved me from a task that I hate and you have done the job immeasurably better than I could have done it and in half the time. I only hope that I haven't victimised you too much."

"You haven't victimised us at all," said Thorndyke. "It has been a matter of mutual accommodation."

"Very good of you to say so," said Ross, and having thanked us once more, he bustled away.

"I hope that you have not misled that good gentleman," I remarked as Thorndyke proceeded to restore, as far as possible, the *status quo ante* and render the corpse presentable to the coroner's jury.

"I have not misled him intentionally," he replied. "I gave him all the observed facts. His interpretation of them is his own affair. Perhaps, while I am finishing, you would complete the labels. That corked tube filled with water contains the fish-scales, as I assume them to be."

"Shall I write '*Fish-Scales*' on the label?"

"No, just write '*From Lungs, Mouth, and Stomach*', and perhaps you might look through the beard and the hair and see if you can find any more."

"The hair!" I exclaimed. "How on earth could they get into the hair?"

"Perhaps they did not," he replied. "But you may as well look. We are not adopting Ross's interpretation, you know."

I took a pair of dissecting forceps and searched among the rather short hair of the scalp, speculating curiously as to what Thorndyke could have in his mind. But whatever it was, it evidently agreed with the facts for my search brought to light no less than six of the little, white, lustrous objects.

134

"You had better put them in a separate tube," said Thorndyke, when I reported the find, "in case they are not the same as the others. And now it would be as well to have another look at the coat."

He had drawn the sheet over the whole of the body excepting the head and neck and now proceeded to clean and dry his rubber gloves and instruments. While he was thus occupied, I took up the coat and made a fresh and more detailed inspection.

"It is extraordinarily dirty at the back," I reported, "and there seems to be a slight stain on the collar and shoulders as if it had been wetted with dirty water."

"Yes, I noticed that," he said. "You don't see any foreign particles sticking to it or to any of the other garments?"

I looked the coat over inside and out but could find nothing excepting a tiny fragment of what looked like black silk thread, which had stuck to the flap of a pocket. I picked it off and put it in the envelope with the ends of cotton. Then I turned my attention to the other garments. From the trousers nothing fresh was to be learned, nor from the waistcoat – the pockets of which I searched to make sure that the little leather ring-case had not been overlooked – excepting that, like the coat, it showed signs on its collar of having been wetted, as also did the blue-and-white striped cotton shirt. I was examining the latter when Thorndyke, having finished "tidying up", came and looked over my shoulder.

"That stain," he remarked, "hardly looks like water, even dirty water, though it is surprising how distinct and conspicuous a stain perfectly clean water will sometimes make on linen which has been worn and exposed to dust."

He took the garment from me and examined the stained part intently, felt it critically with finger and thumb, and finally held it to his nose and sniffed at it. Then he laid it down and picked up the collar, which he examined in the same manner, by sight, touch and smell, turning it over and opening the fold to inspect the inside.

"I think," he said, "we ought to find out, if possible, whether this was water or some other fluid. We don't know what light the knowledge might throw on this extraordinarily obscure case."

He was still standing, as if undecided, with the collar in his hand when the sound of footsteps approaching down the alley became audible, whereupon he turned quickly, and, dropping the collar into the research case, closed the latter and took his hat down from the peg. The next moment the door opened and the sergeant looked in.

"Jury coming to view the body, gentlemen," he announced, and with a critical look towards the table, he added, "I thought I had better come on ahead and see that they shouldn't get too bad a shock. Juries are

135

sometimes a bit squeamish, but I see that the doctor has left everything tidy and decent. You know where the inquest is to be held, I suppose?"

"We don't," replied Thorndyke, "but if we lurk outside and follow the jury we shan't go far wrong."

We walked up to the top of the alley, where we met a party of rather apprehensive-looking men who were being personally conducted by a constable. We waited for them to return, which they did with remarkable promptitude and looking not at all refreshed by their visit, and we turned and followed in their wake, the sergeant, as coroner's officer, hurrying past us to anticipate their arrival at the place where the inquiry was to be held.

"It seems almost a waste of time for us to sit out the proceedings," I remarked as we walked along in the rear of the procession. "We have got all the material facts."

"We think we have," replied Thorndyke, "and it is not likely that we shall hear anything that will alter our views of the case. But, still, we don't know that something vital may not turn up in the evidence."

"I can't imagine anything that could account for the state of the dead man's shoes," said I.

"No," he agreed, "that seems conclusive, and I think it is. Nevertheless, if it should transpire in evidence that Sir Edward was seen in the neighbourhood before the rain started, the absence of mud on his shoes would cease to have any special significance. But here we are at the court. I expect Brodribb is there already and it will probably be best for him and for us if we select seats that are not too near his. He will want to give his whole attention to his own evidence and that of the other witnesses."

We watched the last of the jurymen enter the municipal office in which the proceedings were to take place, then we went in and took possession of a couple of chairs in a corner, commanding a view of the table and the place in which the witnesses would stand or sit to give their evidence.

Chapter IX
The Crowner's Quest
(Dr. Jervis's Narrative)

During the brief preliminary period, while the jury-men were taking their places and the court was pervaded by the hum of conversation and the rustle of movement, I looked about me to see who was present and if possible to identify the prospective witnesses. Brodribb was seated near the coroner's chair, and, by his rather unhappy, preoccupied look, I judged that Thorndyke, with his usual tact, had pretty accurately gauged his mental state. He caught my eye once and acknowledged my silent greeting with a grave nod, but immediately relapsed into his previous gloomy and meditative condition.

Seated next to him was an elderly – or perhaps I should say an *old* – man, for he looked well over sixty, who was, in appearance, such a typical example of the old-fashioned better gentleman's servant that I instantly placed him, correctly, as it turned out, as Mr. Weeks, Sir Edward's butler. Behind the coroner's chair was our friend the Superintendent, who was carrying on a whispered conversation with Dr. Ross. Our colleague struck me as looking a little nervous and sheepish and I noticed that he held a paper in his hand and glanced at it from time to time, from which I inferred that he was conning over his notes with a view to the prompt and confident delivery of his evidence.

At this point my observations were brought to an end by a premonitory cough on the part of the coroner, which had somewhat the effect of the warning rattle of a striking clock, as giving the company to understand that he was about to begin his address. Thereupon, silence fell on the assembly and the proceedings opened. Quite briefly and in general terms, he indicated the nature of the case which was the subject of the inquiry and, having sketchily recited the leading facts, proceeded to call the witnesses.

"It is the common practice," he said in conclusion, "to begin with the medical evidence, as the state of the body is usually the principal means of determining the cause of death and of answering the questions, How, When, and Where that death was brought about. But in the present case the circumstances surrounding the discovery of the body have so

137

important a bearing that I think it better to take the evidence on that point first. The first witness will be James Holker."

In response to the implied summons, a well-dressed, capable-looking man rose and approached the table. Having been sworn, he deposed that his name was James Holker, that he was by calling a ship's steward but now retired and living chiefly on the proceeds of certain house property that he owned. Among other such property was a row of houses known as Piper's Row, and it was in one of these houses, Number Five, to wit, that he made the discovery.

"On what date was that?" the coroner asked.

"On Tuesday, the fourteenth of July. Yesterday morning, in fact."

"Tell us exactly what happened on that occasion."

"I went round to Number Five to go on with some repairs that I had begun. I went straight into the front room – that is the living-room – and then I noticed a glove lying on the floor under the window. I remembered having seen that glove before. But now I noticed something very unpleasant about the air of the place and there seemed to be an unusual number of flies and blue-bottles about. So I went through to the kitchen and it was worse there. Then I opened the door of the wash-house and looked in, and there I saw a man hanging from a roof-beam. I didn't stop to examine him. I just bolted straight out of the house and ran up to the police station to report what had happened."

"You had no doubt that the man was dead?"

"None whatever. I could see at a glance that he had been dead a week or two. And it wasn't a matter of eyesight only – "

"No. Quite so. Now, have you any means of judging how long he had been hanging there?"

"Yes. I judge that he had been hanging there a little over three weeks."

"Tell us how you are able to arrive at that time."

"Well, sir, it was this way. On Sunday, the twenty-first of June, I put in a fairly full day's work at the repairs on Number Five, and nothing could have happened on that day, because I went all over the house. I worked on there all the afternoon up to getting on for five, and then, as I saw that it was coming on wet, I stowed my tools in a cupboard in the front room and ran off home as hard as I could go through the rain.

"That night, the captain of an old ship of mine, the *Esmeralda*, called to ask me to take a trip with him to Marseilles, as his steward had to go into hospital. I thought I'd like the trip, and I was glad to oblige the captain, so I said 'Yes' and set to work to pack my kit. Next morning, Monday, I ran round to Number Five to fetch my tools away. As I was in a hurry, I only went into the front room, where my tools were. But I could see that someone had been in the house, because there was a glove lying on the floor just under the window, and I noticed that the window was unfastened and slightly open. If I had had time I would have had a look round the house, but, as I was in a hurry to get on to the docks, and there was nothing in the house that anyone could take, I just took up my tools and came away."

"Did you pick up the glove?"

"No. I left it as it was, and when I went to the house yesterday, it was lying in the same place."

"Is there anything else that you can tell us about the case?"

"No, sir. That's all I know about it."

The coroner glanced at the jury. "Are there any questions that you wish to ask the witness, gentlemen?" he enquired. "If not, we will next take the evidence of Superintendent Thompson."

The Superintendent marched briskly up to the table and, having disposed with business-like brevity of the preliminary formalities, gave his evidence with a conciseness born of long experience.

"At ten-fifteen yesterday morning – that is Tuesday, the fourteenth of July – the previous witness, James Holker, came to the police station and reported to me that a dead man was hanging in a house of his, Number Five Piper's Row. I gave instructions for a wheeled stretcher to be sent there and then proceeded forthwith to the house in company with Holker and Constable Marshall.

"On entering, I went straight through to the wash-house, where I saw the dead body of a man hanging by a rope from a roof-beam. Nearly underneath the body but a little to one side was an overturned chair, and close to the chair a wash-leather glove was lying on the floor, and a little farther off a soft felt hat. A walking-stick was standing in the corner by the door. The deceased had no collar on, but I found the collar, afterwards, in his pocket, very dirty and crumpled. The rope by which the body was hanging was a small coir rope, a trifle thinner than my little finger. It was tied very securely to the beam above and the noose had a rather large knot, which was at the back of the neck."

"Could you form any idea as to how long the body had been hanging?" the coroner asked.

"I could only form a rough estimate. Judging by the advanced state of decomposition I concluded that it must have been hanging at least a fortnight, and I thought it probable that Holker's account, making it three weeks, was correct."

"Did there appear to be anything unusual in the method used by the deceased?"

139

"No. The way in which the suicide was carried out seemed quite simple and ordinary. Apparently, when he came into the wash-house, he stood his stick in the corner, threw down his hat and glove, took off his collar and put it in his pocket. Then he probably made the noose, stood on the chair and tied the rope to the beam, put the noose round his neck, pulled it fairly tight, drew up his legs and kicked the chair over so that he was left swinging free. That was what it looked like."

"Is there any evidence as to how the deceased got into the house?"

"I think there is no doubt that he got in by the front room window. He couldn't have got in by the street door, because it was locked – at least, so I am informed by Holker, who is quite sure that he shut it when he left the house on Sunday evening, the twenty-first of June – and the deceased had no keys on him. But there is positive evidence that he got in by the window, for when I went into the front room, I found the window unfastened and open a couple of inches, and just underneath it I found a wash-leather glove on the floor, which was evidently the fellow of the glove that was lying on the wash-house floor under the body."

"And with regard to the rope. Did the deceased find that on the premises?"

"No. He must have brought it with him. I questioned Holker about it and he informed me that it was not his, that he had never seen it before and that there was no rope of any kind in the house."

"Were there any signs that the body had been robbed?"

"No, and I think I can say definitely that it had not. There was not much in the pockets, considering the deceased gentleman's position, but there were things in them that no thief would have left. For instance, there was a purse containing three sovereigns and a letter wallet with two five-pound notes in it. And the small value of the contents of the pockets seems to be satisfactorily accounted for, as Mr. Brodribb has informed me that the deceased had emptied his pockets of most of his valuables, including his gold watch, before he left the club."

"Ah," said the coroner, "that is a significant fact. We must get the details from Mr. Brodribb. Are there any further facts known to you that ought to be communicated to the jury?"

"I think I ought to mention that the deceased's clothing was extraordinarily dirty and tumbled. The collar was excessively dirty and seemed to have been wetted, and so did the shirt at the neck, and the coat and trousers were very dusty at the back, as if the deceased had been lying on a dirty floor."

"What do you suggest as to the significance of those facts?"

"Taken with the fact that the deceased left the club (as I am informed) on Wednesday, the seventeenth of June, and could not have entered the empty house before Sunday night, the twenty-first of June, the state of his clothes suggests to me that he had been wandering about in the interval, perhaps spending the nights in common lodging-houses or sleeping in the open, and that he had washed himself at pumps or taps and got his head and neck wet. Of course, that is only a guess."

"Quite so. But it seems probable and certainly agrees with the known circumstances. Is there any thing more that you have to tell the jury?"

"No, sir. That is all the information that I have to give."

"Any questions, gentlemen?" the coroner asked, glancing at the jury. "No questions. Thank you, Superintendent. Perhaps, before we hear the next witness we had better recall Mr. Holker in order that he may confirm on oath those of his statements which have been quoted by the Superintendent."

Holker was accordingly recalled and formally confirmed those passages of the officer's evidence (referring to the door and the rope) when they had been read out by the coroner from the depositions. This formality having been disposed of, the coroner glanced through his notes and then announced, "We will take the medical evidence next so that the doctor may be able to get away to his patients. Dr. Ross."

Our colleague approached the table with less obvious self-possession than the experienced officer who had preceded him, but he was quite a good witness. He had made up his mind as to what he was going to say and he said it with a confident, authoritative air that carried conviction to the jury.

"You have made a thorough examination of the body of the deceased?" the coroner said, when the witness had been sworn and the other preliminaries despatched.

"I have," was the reply.

"And what was the result of your examination? You understand, Doctor, that the jury don't want you to go into technical details. They just want the conclusions that you arrived at. To begin with, how long should you say the deceased had been dead?"

"I should say that he had been dead not less than three weeks."

"Were you able to ascertain the cause of death?"

"I was able to form a very definite opinion. The condition of the body was so very unfavourable for examination that I hardly like to go beyond that."

"Quite so. The jury have seen the body and I am sure they fully realise its condition. But you were able to form a decided opinion?"

"Yes. I found distinct signs of death from asphyxia and I found nothing whatever to suggest any other cause of death."

141

"Well," said the coroner, "that seems to be sufficient for our purpose. Was there anything to account for the asphyxia?

"There was a deep groove encircling the neck, marking the position of the rope by which the deceased had been suspended."

Here the foreman of the jury interposed with the request that the witness would explain exactly what he meant by asphyxia.

"Asphyxia," the doctor explained, "is the condition which is produced when a person is prevented from breathing. If the breathing is completely stopped, death occurs in about two minutes."

"And how may the breathing become stopped?" the foreman asked.

"In various ways. By hanging, by strangling, by covering the mouth and nose with a pillow or other soft object, by drowning, or by immersion in a gas such as carbonic acid."

"What do you say was the cause of the asphyxia in this case?"

"As hanging causes asphyxia and the deceased was undoubtedly hanged, the asphyxia was presumably due to the hanging."

"That seems fairly obvious," said the coroner, "but," he added, looking a little severely at the foreman, "we mustn't ask the doctor to provide us with a verdict. He is giving evidence as to the facts observed by himself. It is for you to decide on the significance of those facts. He tells us that he observed signs of death from asphyxia. We have heard from other witnesses that the deceased was found hanging, the connection of those facts is a question for the jury. Is there anything else that you have to tell us, Doctor?"

"No, I observed nothing else that is relevant to the inquiry."

"Does any gentleman wish to ask the doctor any further questions?" the coroner asked, glancing at the jury, and as no one expressed any such desire, he continued, "Then I think we need not detain the doctor any longer. The next witness will be Herbert Weeks."

On hearing his name pronounced, Mr. Weeks rose and took his place at the table. Having been sworn, he stated that he had been butler to the deceased, whose father, Sir Julian, he had served in the same capacity. He had known the deceased practically all his (the deceased's) life and they were on very intimate and confidential terms.

"Had you ever any reason to expect that the deceased might make away with himself?" the coroner asked.

"No," was the reply. "Such a thing never occurred to me."

"Have you noticed anything of late in his manner or his apparent state of mind that might account for, or explain his having made away with himself? Has he, for instance, seemed worried or depressed about anything?"

Mr. Weeks hesitated. At length he replied, with an air of weighing his words carefully, "I don't think he was worried about anything. So far as I know, there was nothing for him to worry about. And I should hardly describe him as being depressed, though I must admit that he had not very good spirits. He had never really recovered from the shock of losing his wife and his son – his only child."

"When did that happen?"

"About ten years ago. They were both carried off by influenza within a few days, and Sir Edward himself nearly died of the same complaint. When he began to get better, we had to break it to him and I thought it would have killed him, and though he did at last recover, he was never the same man again."

"In what respect was he changed?"

"He seemed to have lost interest in life. When her ladyship and the young gentleman were alive, he was always cheerful and gay and full of schemes and projects for the future. He was constantly planning improvements in the estate and riding about the property with his son to discuss them. He was very devoted to his wife and son, as they were to him, a most affectionate and united family. When they died, it seemed as if he had lost everything that he cared for. He took no further interest in his property but just left it to the bailiff to manage and turned his business affairs over to Mr. Brodribb."

"And you say that he was changed in manner?"

"Yes. All his old high spirits went, though he was just as kind and thoughtful for others as he had always been. But he became grave and quiet in his manner and seemed rather dull and aimless, as if there was nothing that he cared about in particular."

The coroner reflected for a few moments on these statements. Then abandoning this line of enquiry, he asked, "When did the deceased leave home?"

"On Tuesday, the sixteenth of June."

"Did he inform you what his intended movements were?"

"Yes. He said that he was going to spend a couple of days in London and that he expected to return home on Thursday afternoon. He told me that he intended to stay at his club as he usually did when visiting London."

"Did you notice anything unusual in his manner on that occasion?"

"I thought that he seemed rather preoccupied, as if he had some business on hand that he was giving a good deal of thought to."

"He did not strike you as unusually depressed or anxious?"

"No, only that he gave me the impression that he was thinking out something that he did not quite understand."

"Was that the last time that you saw him alive?"

"Yes. I stood at the main door and watched him walk away down the drive, followed by one of the gardeners carrying his suit-case. I never saw him again until this morning, when I saw him in the mortuary."

Mr. Weeks delivered these statements in quiet, even tones, but it was easy to see that he was controlling his emotion with some difficulty. Observing this, the coroner turned from the witness to the jury.

"I think," he said, "Mr. Weeks has given us all the material facts known to him, so, if there are no questions, we need not prolong what is, no doubt, a very painful ordeal for him." He paused, and then, as no question was asked, he thanked the witness and dismissed him. A brief pause followed during which the coroner glanced quickly through his notes. Then Mr. Brodribb's name was called, and, bearing Thorndyke's prediction in mind, I gave his evidence my very special attention.

"What was the exact nature of your relations with the deceased?" the coroner asked, when the introductory matter had been disposed of.

"I was his solicitor. But in addition to my purely legal functions, I acted as his adviser in respect of the general business connected with the management of his property. I am also the executor of his will."

"Then you can tell us if there were any embarrassments or difficulties connected with his property that were causing him anxiety."

"I can. There were no embarrassments or difficulties whatever. His financial affairs were not only completely in order but in a highly favourable state. I may say that his estate was flourishing and his income considerably in excess of his expenditure. He certainly had no financial anxieties."

"Had he any anxieties of any kind, so far as you know?"

"So far as I know, he had none."

"You heard Mr. Weeks's description of the change in his manner and habits caused by his bereavement. Do you confirm that?"

"Yes, the loss of his wife and son left him a broken man."

"You attribute the change in him to the grief due to his bereavement?

"Principally. The loss of those so dear to him left an abiding grief. But there was a further effect. Sir Edward's lively interest in his estate and his ambition to improve it and increase its value were based on the consideration that it would in due course pass to his son, and probably to his son's son. Like most English landowners, he had a strong sense of continuity. But the continuity of succession was destroyed by his son's death. The present heir-presumptive is a distant relative who was almost a stranger to Sir Edward. Thus the deceased had come to feel that he was no more than a life-tenant of the estate, that, at his death, it would pass

144

out of the possession of his own family into the hands of strangers and there was no knowing what might happen to it. As a result he, not unnaturally, lost all interest in the future of the estate. But since, hitherto, this had been the predominant purpose of his life, its failure left him without any strong interest or aim in life."

The coroner nodded, as one who appreciates a material point of evidence.

"Yes," he said, "this loss of interest in life seems to have an important bearing on our inquiry. But beyond this general state of mind, did you ever notice any more particular manifestation. In short, did you ever observe anything that caused you to entertain the possibility that the deceased might make away with himself?"

Mr. Brodribb hesitated. "I can't say," he replied, after a pause, "that the possibility of suicide ever entered my mind."

"That, Mr. Brodribb, seems a rather qualified answer, as if you had something further in your mind. Am I right?"

Apparently the coroner was right, for Mr. Brodribb, after a few moments' rather uneasy reflection, replied with obvious unwillingness, "I certainly never considered the possibility of suicide, but, looking back, I am not sure that there were not some suggestions that were at least susceptible of such an interpretation. I now recall, for instance, a remark which the deceased made to me some months ago. We were, I think, discussing the almost universal repugnance to the idea of death when the deceased said (as nearly as I can remember), 'I often feel, Brodribb, that there is something rather restful in the thought of death. That it would be quite pleasant and peaceful to feel oneself sinking into sleep with the certain knowledge that one was never going to wake up.' I attached no weight to that remark at the time, but now, looking at it in the light of what has happened, it seems rather significant."

"I agree with you," the coroner said, emphatically. "It seems very significant indeed. And that suggests another question. I presume that you are pretty well acquainted with the affairs of the deceased's family?"

"Very well indeed. I have been connected with the Hardcastle estate during the whole of my professional life, and so was my father before me."

"Then you can tell us whether any instances of suicide have occurred among any of the deceased's relatives."

Once more Mr. Brodribb hesitated with a slightly puzzled and reluctant air. At length, he replied, cautiously, "I can only say that no instance of suicide in the family is known to me, or even suspected by me. But it seems proper that I should acquaint you with the rather mysterious and highly eccentric conduct of the deceased's brother,

Gervase. This gentleman became, unfortunately, rather intemperate in his habits, with the regrettable result – among others – that he was deprived of a fellowship that he held at Oxford. Thereafter, he disappeared and ceased to communicate with his family, and all that is known of him is that he was, for a time, living in poverty, and apparently in something like squalor, in Paris and other foreign towns."

"Had his family cast him off?"

"Not at all. Sir Edward's feelings towards him were quite friendly and brotherly. He would willingly have provided the means for his brother to live comfortably and in a manner suitable to his station. The self-imposed ostracism on Gervase's part was sheer perversity."

"And what became of this brother? Is he still living?"

"His death was announced in the obituary column of *The Times* about sixteen years ago without any address other than Brighton. Of the circumstances of his death, nothing whatever is known."

"Have you any reason to suppose that he made away with himself?"

"I have not. I mentioned his case merely as an instance of voluntary disappearance and generally eccentric behaviour."

"Exactly, as furnishing a parallel to the voluntary disappearance of the deceased. That is quite an important point. And now, as a final question, I should like to ask you to confirm what the Superintendent told us as to the deceased having emptied his pockets of things of value before leaving the club."

"The Superintendent's statement is, in the main, correct. When examining his bedroom at the club, I found in a locked suit-case – which I was able to unlock – a gold watch and chain, a valuable pearl tie pin, a bunch of keys, and a few private letters, which I glanced through and which threw no light on his disappearance."

"Ah," said the coroner, "a very significant proceeding. No doubt it struck you so?"

"It did, coupled with the fact that the owner was missing, and I communicated the facts at once to the police."

"Yes. Very proper. And that, I think, is all that we wish to ask you, unless there is anything else that occurs to you or unless the jury desire to put any questions."

Mr. Brodribb intimated that he had nothing further to communicate, and, as the jury made no sign, the witness was allowed to retire to his seat.

The next name called was that of Mr. Northbrook, the secretary of the club, but as his evidence for the most part merely confirmed and amplified that of the preceding witnesses, I need not record it in detail.

One new fact, however, emerged, though it did not seem to me, at the time, to have any particular significance.

"You say," said the coroner, "that you saw the deceased leave the club?"

"Yes. I was in the porter's office at the time, and, as the deceased passed the open door, I wished him 'Good morning', but apparently he did not hear me, for he passed out without taking any notice."

"And that, I take it, was actually the last time he is known to have been seen alive?

"Not absolutely the last time. He was seen a few minutes later by one of the club waiters, getting into a hansom cab. I have brought the waiter with me in case you wished to hear his account first hand."

"That was very thoughtful of you," said the coroner, "and I am glad you did. We should certainly wish to have the evidence of the last person who saw the deceased alive."

The waiter was accordingly called and sworn, when it transpired that his name was Joseph Wood and that he had mighty little to tell. That little may as well, however, be given in his own words.

"I was coming along Piccadilly from the west when I caught sight of Sir Edward Hardcastle, coming towards me. He was a good distance off, but I recognised him at once. I wait at the table that he always used, so I knew him very well by sight. While I was looking at him, a hansom drew up by the pavement and he got in, and then the hansom drove away. I didn't see him hail it, but he may have done. I couldn't see if there was anyone else in the cab, because its back was towards me, and as soon as he got in it drove away. I didn't see him say anything to the cabman, but he may have spoken up through the trap. The cab drove off in an easterly direction – towards the Circus. I did not notice the number of the cab. There was no reason why I should."

This was the sum of his evidence, and it was not clear to me why he had been brought so far to tell so little, for the trivial circumstance that he deposed to appeared to have no bearing whatever on the case, and I was not a little surprised to observe that Thorndyke took down his statements, apparently verbatim, in short-hand, a proceeding that I could account for only by bearing in mind his invariable rule that nothing could be considered irrelevant until all the facts were known.

The waiter, Joseph Wood, was the last of the witnesses, and, when he had concluded his evidence, the coroner, having announced that all the known facts were now in the jury's possession, made a brief inspection of his notes with a view to his summing-up. At length he began, "It is not necessary, gentlemen, that I should address you at great length. We have given to this painful case an exhaustive consideration which was called for rather by reason of the deceased gentleman's position and the interests involved than by any inherent difficulties. The case is, in fact, quite a simple one. All the material circumstances are known to us, and there is not the slightest conflict of evidence. On the contrary, all the witnesses are in complete agreement and the evidence of each confirms that of the others.

"The time at which this sad affair occurred is fixed beyond any possible doubt by Mr. Holker's evidence. The deceased must have entered the house, in which his body was subsequently found, during the evening or night of Sunday, the twenty-first of June, and this date is confirmed by the medical evidence. Thus, the questions When and Where are answered conclusively. Mr. Holker and the Superintendent both saw the dead body suspended from a beam, and the medical witness found signs of death from asphyxia, as would be expected in the case of a man who had died by hanging.

"The question of motive seems to be solved as completely as we could expect by the evidence of Mr. Weeks and especially by that of Mr. Brodribb. The terrible bereavement which the deceased suffered, the shipwreck of all his hopes and ambitions and the desolate state in which he was left, if they could not be properly regarded as conditions predisposing to suicide, furnish a reasonable explanation of it after the event.

"There is one feature in the case which did, at first, appear very strange and difficult to explain, and which, I may admit, occasioned this very rigorous inquiry. That feature is the extraordinary surroundings in which the body was discovered. How, one asked oneself, is it possible to account for the appearance of a man in the deceased's position in an empty house in the purlieus of Stratford? It seemed an insoluble mystery. Then came the evidence of the Superintendent and Mr. Brodribb. The one finds traces that, to the expert eye, tell of ramblings in sordid neighbourhoods and waste places, of nights spent in doss-houses or in the open. The other tells us of a relative – actually a brother of the deceased – who, in a strangely similar manner, had disappeared from his usual places of resort, cut himself off from family and friends and, by deliberate choice, had lived – and perhaps died – in surroundings of sordid poverty. I will not say that this evidence explains the proceedings of the deceased. Probably they will never be completely explained. But I do say that our knowledge of the brother's conduct makes that of the deceased perfectly credible.

"I will add only one further observation. If you find that the deceased made away with himself, as the evidence seems to prove, I think you will agree with me that, at the time and for some days

148

previously, he was not in his right mind. If that is your view, I will ask you to embody it in your verdict."

At the conclusion of the coroner's address, the jury consulted together. But their consultation occupied only a minute or two. Apparently they had already made up their minds, as they might well have done, taking the evidence at its face value. When the whispered conference came to an end, the foreman announced that they had agreed on their verdict and the coroner then put the formal question, "And what is your decision, gentlemen?

"We find," was the reply, "that the deceased committed suicide by hanging himself while temporarily insane."

"Yes," said the coroner, "I am in entire agreement with you, and I must thank you for the care and attention with which you have considered the evidence."

As the proceedings came to an end, Thorndyke and I rose and made our way out, leaving Brodribb in conversation with the coroner and the Superintendent.

"Well," I said as we halted outside to wait for our friend, "it has been quite entertaining, but I don't see that we have got much for our attendance."

"We have got one fact, at least," replied Thorndyke, "that was worth coming for. We now know that Holker was in the house until after the rain had begun to fall. That clears away any uncertainties on a point of vital importance. But we had better not discuss the case now. And I think – though it seems rather scurvy treatment of our old friend – but I think we had better keep our own counsel. Brodribb accepts the suicide as an established fact, and perhaps it is as well that he should. If we are going to work at this case, it will be all to the good that we hold the monopoly of the real facts. It will be a difficult and obscure case, but the difficulty will be materially reduced if we can watch the development of events quietly, without anyone suspecting that we are watching. This was no crime of sudden impulse. It was premeditated and arranged. Obviously there was, behind it, some perfectly definite motive. We have, among other things, to discover what that motive was. The criminals at present believe themselves to be entirely unsuspected. If they maintain that belief, they will feel at liberty to pursue their purpose without any special precautions, and we – also unsuspected – may get our chance. But here comes Brodribb."

I must confess that Thorndyke's observations appeared to me so cryptic as to convey no meaning whatever. That, I recognised, was owing to my own 'slowness in the uptake'. However, there was no opportunity to seek elucidation, for Brodribb had seen us and was now bearing down on us. He replied to our greeting with something less than his usual vivacity, and we set forth on our way to the station in almost uninterrupted silence.

Chapter X
A Summary of the Evidence
(Dr. Jervis's Narrative)

Mr. Brodribb's taciturn mood persisted even after we had taken possession of an empty first-class smoking compartment and lit our pipes. Evidently his recent experiences had depressed him profoundly, which, after all, was no matter for surprise. An inquest is not a jovial function under the most favourable conditions, and the conditions in the recent inquiry had been far from favourable for the friends of the deceased.

"It was a ghoulish business," he remarked in semi-apologetic explanation of his low spirits, "but, of course, it had to be, and the coroner managed it as decently as possible. Still, I had rather that he had managed without me."

"If he had," said I, "he would have missed what he regarded as most important evidence."

"Yes, I know," replied Brodribb. "That was what I felt, though I hated giving that evidence. The affair had to be cleared up, and I have no doubt that the jury were right in their verdict. I know you don't agree with me, Thorndyke, but I think your special experience has misled you for once."

"There is always the possibility," Thorndyke admitted, "that professional bias may influence one. In any case, our divergence of views does not affect the position in practice. The death of Sir Edward is an established fact and the ambiguity of your legal status is at an end."

"Yes," Brodribb agreed, "there is that very unsatisfactory compensation. I am now the executor and can act as I think best. I could only wish that the best course of action were a little more easy to decide on."

With this, he relapsed into silent reflection, possibly connected with the difficulties suggested by his last sentence, and as Thorndyke and I were unable to discuss before him the matters that were occupying our thoughts, we followed his example and devoted ourselves to the consideration of our own affairs.

Suddenly Brodribb sat up with a start and began to rummage in his inside breast-pocket. "Bless my soul!" he exclaimed. "What a fool I am! Clean forgot this. Ought to have mentioned it in my evidence."

Here he brought out a letter wallet, and, taking from it an envelope, opened the latter and tipped some small object out on to his palm.

"There!" he said, holding out his open hand to Thorndyke. "What do you think of that?"

Thorndyke picked up the object, and, having examined it, held it up to the light, when I saw that it was a little oval plate of a bright transparent green bearing an engraved device which I recognised instantly.

"The missing seal!" I exclaimed, taking it from Thorndyke to inspect it more closely. "Then we may assume that the great mystery is solved."

"Indeed, you may assume nothing of the kind," said Brodribb. "On the contrary, the mystery is more profound than ever and the chance of a solution more remote. I will tell you all about it – all that I know, that is to say. It is a queer story. Your friend, Superintendent Miller, brought it to me yesterday afternoon to compare with my seals and for formal identification by me (which I thought very kind and courteous of him), and this is the account he gave of its discovery.

"It seems that, about a week ago, a man escaped from Pentonville Gaol. I understand that he got away in the evening, and in some miraculous fashion – you know where the prison is, right in the middle of a populous neighbourhood – he kept out of sight until it was dark, which wouldn't have been much before eleven at this time of year. Then, with the same miraculous luck, he managed to slip away through the streets, right across the northern suburbs to the neighbourhood of Temple Mills by the River Lea.

"There he was lurking the next afternoon when he had another stroke of luck. Some devotee of the simple life had elected to take a bath in the river, and he must have strayed away some distance from his clothes, for our Pentonville sportsman found them unguarded. Possibly he may have watched the other sportsman taking them off. At any rate, he seized the opportunity, slipped off the prison clothes, and popped on the others. Then he nipped off across the meadows in the direction of Tottenham. And there it was that his luck deserted him for, by the merest chance, a plain clothes officer who knew him by sight, happened to meet him, and, as the hue-and-cry was out, he collared him forthwith.

"And now comes one of the quaint features of the story. At Tottenham Police Station they went through his pockets – they were really the other fellow's, of course – with mighty little result. The next day they took him back to Pentonville, and once more he was put into uniform. The clothes that were taken off him were put aside until they could be disposed of in some way. But a couple of days ago it occurred to one of the officers to go over them carefully to see if he could find out the lawful owner. And then he made a discovery. Apparently, the owner of those clothes was a pickpocket, for there was a secret receptacle in the back of the waistcoat, which had been overlooked at the first search, and in that secret pocket the officer found this stone."

"And what happened to the other man?" I asked.

"Ah!" chuckled Brodribb, quite recovering his natural spirits for the time being, "that's the cream of the joke. He found the gaol-bird's discarded garments in place of his own clothes and of course he had to put 'em on, since he couldn't go about naked. It was a lovely situation, almost as if he had walked into prison and locked himself in. However, as soon as he was dressed in his proper character, he made a bolt for it, and he had even better luck than the other fellow. In some perfectly incredible manner, he made his way, in broad daylight, right across North London and came to the surface at the Angel, of all unlikely places."

"At the Angel!" I repeated, incredulously.

"At the Angel," Brodribb reiterated, joyously. "Just picture to yourselves an escaped convict in full uniform, elbowing his way through the crowd at the Angel! Well, of course, it couldn't go on. A couple of plain-clothes men saw him and pounced on him in an instant. It looked as if his luck had given out. But apparently his wits were as nimble as his heels, for he got just a dog's chance and he took it. At the moment when the two constables were taking him across the road, a fire-engine came thundering along and they had to scuttle back out of the way. But as it flew past, our friend made a grab at the rail of the foot-plate and held on. The momentum of the engine whisked him out of the clutches of his captors and sent them sprawling, and when they got up, their prisoner was standing on the foot-plate and fading in the distance before their eyes. Of course, it is no use shouting after a fire-engine.

"Now the odd thing is," Mr. Brodribb continued in a slightly shaky voice, "that none of the fire-men on the engine seem to have noticed him, and the constables couldn't telephone a warning until they had found out where the fire was. So our friend stuck on the engine until it turned down Tottenham Court Road, when he hopped off and made a bolt down Warren Street. Naturally, he soon picked up some followers, but he kept ahead of them, flying up one street and down another until he arrived at Cleveland Mews with half the town at his heels. He turned into the mews, still well ahead, and shot down it like a rocket. And that was the last that was seen of him. The crowd and the police surged in after him, and as the mews is a blind alley, they were quite cocksure that they'd got him. But when they came to the blind end, there was not a sign of him. He had vanished into thin air. And he had vanished for good, you observe. For, as nobody knew who he was, nobody could identify him when once he had changed his clothes."

"No," I agreed, "he has got clear away, and I must admit that I think he deserved to."

"I am afraid that I agree with you," said Brodribb. "Very improper for a lawyer, but even lawyers are human. But the police were very puzzled, not only as to how he had managed to escape, but, when the real convict was captured, they couldn't make out why he ran away. Of course, when the seal was found in the pocket, they understood."

"I wonder how he did get away," said I.

"So do I," said Brodribb. "It was a remarkable exploit. I examined the place myself and could see no apparent way of escape."

"You examined the place?" I exclaimed in surprise.

"Yes. I forgot to mention that, by a remarkable coincidence, I happened to be there at the very time. I took Sir Giles Farnaby to see a client of mine who has a studio that fronts on the mews. When we arrived the police were actually searching the studio. They thought the fugitive might have got in at the open window, unnoticed by the two ladies who were at work there. So they went all over the premises. Just as well for our friend that they did, for while they were searching the studio premises he had time to make his little arrangements at the bottom of the mews. And now we shall never know how he came by that seal, though, as he seems to have been a pickpocket, we can make a pretty likely guess."

"Yes," Thorndyke agreed a little dryly, "it is always possible to guess. But guesses are not very valuable evidential assets. The police guessed that this man was a pickpocket, and we can guess that, being a pickpocket, he obtained the seal in the practice of his art. That guess is supported by the fact that the ring is the only article known to be missing from his person, and that the leather case in which it was usually carried, is also missing. On the other hand, it is not in agreement with the fact that the stone had been dismounted from the ring and that the ring was not found with it. The pickpocket usually takes his booty to the receiver as he finds it. It is the receiver who extracts the stones and melts down the metal. That is the usual procedure – but, naturally, there are exceptions."

"At any rate," said Brodribb, "what matters to us is that the man has vanished and no one knows who he is."

On this conclusion neither Thorndyke nor I made any comment, and the discussion was brought to an end by our arrival at Liverpool Street, where we saw Mr. Brodribb into a hansom and then embarked in another for the Temple.

During the meal which we found awaiting us at our chambers, I endeavoured to extract from Thorndyke some elucidation of the statement that had seemed to me so obscure. But he was not willing to enter into details at present.

"The position at the moment, Jervis," said he, "is this: We have no doubt whatever that Sir Edward Hardcastle was murdered. We have evidence that the murder was premeditated and the methods planned in advance with considerable care and some ingenuity. It was carried out by more than one, and probably several persons. It was, in fact, of the nature of a conspiracy. The purpose of the murder was not robbery from the person. The perpetrators, or at least some of them, were apparently of a low class, socially, and the victim seems to have walked, not entirely unsuspecting, into some sort of ambush.

"That is all that we know at present, and it doesn't carry us far. What we have to discover, if we can, is the identity of the murderers. If we can do that, the motive will disclose itself. If, on the other hand, we can uncover the motive, that will probably point to the murderers. We must proceed along both lines if we can. We must endeavour cautiously to ascertain whether Sir Edward had any enemies who might conceivably have been capable of a crime of revenge, and we must watch the consequences of his death and note who benefits by them."

"It is evident," said I, "that someone is going to benefit to the extent of a title and an uncommonly valuable estate."

"Yes, and we shall bear that in mind. But we mustn't attach undue weight to it. Whenever a well-to-do person is murdered, the heirs benefit, but that fact – though it furnishes a conceivable motive – does not cast suspicion on them in the absence of any other evidence. In practice, as you know, I like to leave the question of motive until I have got a lead in some definite direction. It is much safer. The premature consideration of motive may be very misleading, whereas its use as corroboration may be invaluable."

"Yes, I realise that," said I, "but in this case I don't see how you are going to get a lead. The murderers left plenty of traces of a kind, but they were the wrong kind. There was nothing personal about them – unless the finger-prints can be identified, and I doubt if they can. They were very confused and obscure. And even if they could be made out, they would be of no use unless they were the prints of criminals known to the police and recorded at the register."

155

Thorndyke laughed grimly. "My learned friend," he remarked, "is not disposed to be encouraging. But never mind. We have made many a worse start and yet reached our goal. Presently we will examine our material and see what it has to tell us. Perhaps we may get a lead in some direction from an unexpected source."

At the actual examination I was not present, for our expeditions to Stratford had left me with one or two unfulfilled engagements. Accordingly, as soon as we had finished our supper (or dinner – the exact status of our evening meal was not clearly defined), I went forth to despatch one of them, my regret tempered by the consideration that I should miss nothing but the mere manipulations, most of which were now fairly familiar to me, and that on my return I should find most of the work done and the results available.

And so it turned out. Re-entering our chambers about half-past-ten and finding the sitting-room untenanted, I made my way up to the laboratory where a glance around told me that the final stage of the investigation had been reached. On one bench was a microscope and a row of slides, each bearing a temporary or permanent label. On the chemical bench a sand-bath stood over a bunsen burner and bore a small glass evaporating dish, and one or two large watch-glasses containing fluid with a crystalline margin had apparently had their turn on the bath. Beside them in a beaker of fluid – presumably water – was the collar that had been abstracted from the mortuary by Thorndyke, who was at the moment gently prodding it with a glass rod, while his familiar demon, Polton, was engaged in vigorously wringing out the end of rope in a basin of hot liquid which exhaled the unmistakable aroma of soft soap.

"We have nearly finished," said Thorndyke, "and we haven't done so badly, considering that this is only the beginning of our investigation. Have a look at the specimens and see if you agree with the findings."

I went over to the microscope bench and ran my eye over the exhibits. As I did so, I was once more impressed by the wonderfully simple, orderly, and efficient plan on which my colleague worked. For years past – indeed, from the very earliest days of his practice – it had been his habit to collect impartially examples of every kind of natural and artificial material and to make, wherever it was practicable, permanent microscopic preparations of each. The result was an immense and carefully classified collection of minute objects of all kinds – hairs, feathers, insect scales, diatoms, pollen, seeds, powders, starches, textiles, threads, fibres – any one of which could be found in a moment and used for comparison with any new "find", the nature of which had to be determined. Thus he was, to a great extent, independent of books of reference and had the great advantage of being able to submit both the

156

new specimen and the "standard" to any kind of test with the micrometer or polariscope or otherwise.

In the present case, the specimens were laid out in pairs, the new, unknown specimen with a "*Certified*" example from the collection, and an eye-piece micrometer was in position for comparing dimensions. I took up one slide, labelled "*E. H. decd. 15. 7. 03. From Rt. Bronchus*", and placed it on the stage of the microscope. Instantly the nature of the object became obvious. It was a fish-scale – but, of course, I could not say what fish. Then I laid on the stage the companion slide from the collection, labelled "*Scale of Herring*", and made a rough comparison. In the shape of the margins, the concentric and radiating markings and all other characters, the two specimens appeared to be identical. I did not make an exhaustive examination, assuming that this had been done by Thorndyke, but went on to the other specimens. All the fish-scales were alike, as might have been expected, and I gave them only a passing glance. Then I picked up a slide labelled "*From Trachea*" and placed it on the stage. The specimen appeared to be a small piece of a leaf of some kind, a rather large leaf, as I judged by the absence of any indication of form, and by its thickness, and I observed that it seemed to have one cut edge.

Taking up the "*Reference*" slide, I read, "*Cuticle of Cabbage*".

"I don't remember this scrap of leaf, Thorndyke," said I.

"No," he replied. "I did not draw Ross's attention to it. It was wearisome to keep pointing out facts to a man who had already made up his mind. It seems to be a fragment of cabbage leaf, but it is of no special importance. The fish-scales prove the entrance of water to the lungs, which is the really significant fact."

"And this little melted fragment from the heel of the boot? It doesn't look like soap."

"It isn't. It is beeswax. I put that fragment on the slide to observe the melting-point."

The other two specimens were the scraps of cotton and silk thread that we had picked off the clothes. The silk thread was clearly shown, by comparison with the "*Reference Specimen*" to be a fragment of "*Buttonhole Twist*". The white cotton corresponded exactly with a reference specimen of basting cotton, but here the identification was less certain owing to the less distinctive character of the thread.

"Yes," Thorndyke agreed when I remarked upon this, "white cotton threads are a good deal alike, but I haven't much doubt that this is basting cotton. Still, I shall take the specimens to a trimmings-dealer and get an expert opinion."

"Have you made any analysis of the fluids from the stomach and lungs?" I asked.

"No," he replied, "only a preliminary test. But I think that has given us the essential facts, though as a measure of safety, I shall have a complete examination made. What I find is that both fluids contain a considerable amount of sodium chloride. They appear to be, and I have no doubt are, just simply salt water. We can't tell how salt the water was when it was swallowed and drawn into the lungs owing to the drying that had occurred in the body. But the salt is there, and that is the important point."

"You haven't yet tested the water in which you have soaked the collar?"

"No. We will do that now."

He poured a little of the water from the beaker in which the collar had been soaking through a filter into a test-tube. Then, with a pipette, he dipped up a small quantity of a solution of silver nitrate from a bottle and let it fall, drop by drop, into the test-tube. As each drop fell into the clear liquid it gave rise to a little milky cloud, which became denser with each succeeding drop.

"Chloride of some kind," I observed.

"Yes," said he, "and we may take it, provisionally, that it is sodium chloride. And that finishes our preliminary examination of our material. Have you got that rope clean, Polton?"

"Yes, sir," replied Polton, producing the end of rope from a towel in which he had been squeezing the last remains of moisture from it. "It is quite clean, but a good deal of the colour has come out. I think you are right, sir. It looks like cutch."

He exhibited the discoloured water in the basin and handed the piece of rope to Thorndyke, who passed it to me.

"Yes," I said, "I see now that it is a hemp rope. But it is odd that they should have been at the trouble of dyeing it to imitate coir, which is an inferior rope to hemp."

He made no reply, but seemed to look at me attentively as I turned the rope over in my hand, and finally took it from me without remark. I had the feeling that he had expected me to make some observation, and I wondered vaguely what it might have been. Also, I wondered a little at his interest in the physical characters of this rope, which really seemed to have no bearing on our inquiry, and even as I wondered, I had an uneasy suspicion that I had missed some significant point.

"How have the photographs come out?" I asked.

"I haven't seen them yet," he replied. "They are in Polton's province. What do you say, Polton? Is it possible to inspect them?"

"The enlargements are now washing," Polton replied. "I'll fetch them in for you to see."

He went through into the dark room and presently returned with four porcelain dishes, each containing a half-plate bromide print, which he laid down on the bench under the shaded light. All the four prints were enlargements to the same scale – about three times the natural linear size.

"Well," I remarked, as we looked them over together, "Sir Edward's finger-prints are clear enough, though they look a little odd, but the chair-back groups are a most unholy muddle. Most of the prints are just undecipherable smears."

"Yes," Thorndyke admitted regretfully, "they are a poor lot and too many superimposed and obliterating one another. But, still, I have some hopes. Our expert friends are wonderfully clever at sorting out imperfect prints, and some of these seem to me to have enough visible detail for identification. At any rate, one important negative fact can, I think, be established. I see no print that seems to resemble any of Sir Edward's."

"Neither do I, and, of course, if they were there, they would be more distinct than any of the others, being the most recent. But it would be a facer if the experts should find them there. That would fairly knock the bottom out of the entire case."

"It would, certainly," Thorndyke agreed. "But the probability is so negligibly remote that it is not worth considering. What is of much more interest is the chance of their being able to identify some of the prints as those of known criminals."

"Supposing they can?" said I. "What then?"

"In that case," he replied, "I think we should have to take Miller into our confidence. You see, Jervis, that our present difficulty is that we are dealing with a crime in the abstract, so to speak. The perpetrators are unknown to us. We have – at the moment – no clue whatever to their identity. But give us a name, turn our unknown criminals into actual, known persons, and I think we have enough evidence to secure a conviction. At any rate, a very little corroboration by police investigation would make the case complete."

"The deuce it would!" I exclaimed, completely taken aback. "I had no idea that the case had advanced as far as that. I thought it was rather a matter of strong suspicion than of definite evidence. But evidently your examination of the material has brought some new facts to light. Is it not so?"

"We have elicited a few new facts – nothing very startling, however. But the evidence emerges when we put together, in their proper order, the facts that we already knew with the new ones added. Shall we go over the evidence together and see what we really know about the case?"

I assented with enthusiasm and, having filled my pipe, disposed myself in the rather ascetic laboratory chair in a posture of attention and receptivity, and I noticed that Polton had unobtrusively drawn a stool up to the opposite bench, and, having stuck a watchmaker's glass into his eye, was making a shameless pretence of exploring the "innards" of an invalid carriage clock.

"Let us begin," said Thorndyke, "by taking the evidence in order without going into much detail. In the first place, we have established that Sir Edward Hardcastle was drowned in salt water in which considerable numbers of herring-scales were suspended."

"You think there is no doubt about the drowning?"

"I think it is practically certain," he replied. "The presence in the lungs of salt water and herring-scales, together with the presence of similar salt-water and herring-scales in the stomach, is nearly conclusive. That the herring-scales were water-borne and not the remains of food eaten is proved by our finding them in the hair. Add to this the fairly definite signs of asphyxia and no signs of any other cause of death, and the fact that the deceased's head and neck had been immersed in salt water containing suspended herring-scales, as proved by the scales which you found in the hair, by the stains on the neck of his shirt and on his collar, and by the salt which I extracted from that collar, and I think we have very complete and conclusive evidence of drowning."

"I agree," said I. "Excuse my interrupting."

"Not at all," he replied. "I want you to challenge the evidence if you do not find it convincing. To proceed, we find that Sir Edward's body, dead or alive, had been lying on, and apparently dragged along, the dirty floor of a room. Among the litter on that floor were short pieces of basting-cotton and button-hole twist and a fragment of beeswax. These materials suggest a room in which garments were being made – probably a tailor's work-room, though other people besides tailors use these materials.

"Next we find that the body was conveyed in a two-wheeled vehicle, which may have been a cart or gig, or perhaps a hansom cab – "

"Surely not a hansom, Thorndyke," I interrupted. "It had iron tyres."

"That doesn't absolutely exclude it," said he. "You occasionally meet with iron-tired hansoms even to this day. I saw one at Fenchurch Street Station only a few weeks ago – a shabby old crock with the old-fashioned, round-backed dickey, probably driven by the owner. The reason that I incline to the hansom is that the dimensions of this vehicle coincide exactly with those of a hansom. I looked them up in my notes

160

on the dimensions of various vehicles. The wheels of a hansom are fifty-five-and-a-half inches in diameter. The tyres, when of iron, are one-and-a-half inches wide, on a rim which is slightly thicker and which widens inwards towards the spokes. The track, or distance between the wheels, measured at the ground level from the outer edge of one tyre to the outer edge of the other, is fifty-seven inches. Now, these are exactly the dimensions that we noted in our measurements of the track of the unknown vehicle. It isn't by any means conclusive, but we are bound to take note of the coincidence."

"Yes, indeed," I assented. "It is a decidedly striking coincidence, a sort of Bertillon measurement, at least so it appears, though I don't know to what extent the dimensions of vehicles are standardised."

"At any rate," said he, "we note the possibility that this vehicle may have been a hansom cab, and whatever it was, it served to convey the body of Sir Edward to Five Piper's Row on Sunday, the twenty-first of June, at some time in the evening or night, but most probably between eleven and twelve. The body was carried into the house by at least two persons, one of whom appears to have been a waterside or sea-faring person."

"Is it clearly established that there was more than one person?" I asked.

"Yes. There were at least two sets of muddy foot-marks – and apparently only two – on the floor leading from the front door to the kitchen. They were not Holker's, for he arrived with dry feet. They were certainly not Sir Edward's, as we know from the state of his shoes, apart from the ascertained fact that he was dead when he was taken into the house. There were undoubtedly two men, and we can take it that neither of them was the driver of the vehicle since that made merely a pause at the house and not a prolonged stay.

"The body, then, was carried into the house by these two persons, one of whom – probably the nautical person – had brought with him a piece of rope which had been cut off a longer complete rope and which bears visible evidence of having been stolen."

"What do you mean by visible evidence?" I demanded. "Surely a rope which has been stolen is not visibly different from any other rope! The act of stealing a rope does not impress on it any new distinguishable properties."

"That is true," he admitted, "and yet it may be possible to recognise a stolen rope by its visible properties. Did you ever hear of a 'rogue's' yarn?

"Not to my knowledge."

161

"It is a device that used formerly to be employed in the Navy to check the stealing of cordage. Every rope that was made in the Royal Dockyards had one yarn in one of the strands which was different from all the others. It was twisted in reverse, and, if the rope was a white rope, the rogue's yarn was tarred, while in a tarred rope the tell-tale yarn was left white. Later, the special yarn was replaced by a single coloured worsted thread, which was spun into the middle of a yarn and so was not visible externally, but only at the cut end. This was a better device, as each dockyard had its own colour, so that when a stolen rope was discovered it could be seen at once which dockyard it belonged to.

"But the plan of marking rope in this way is not confined to the Navy. Many public, and even private bodies which use rope, have it made up with some distinctive mark – usually a coloured thread in one of the yarns. And that happens to be the case with this particular rope. It is a marked rope, evidently the property of some public or private body." He took the washed "specimen" from the bench and, handing it to me, continued. "You see this is a four-strand rope, and in two of the strands is a yarn in which has been twisted a coloured cotton thread, a red thread in the one and a green thread in the other."

I examined the little length of rope closely and, now that I had been told, the coloured threads were easy enough to see, though only at the cut ends. Now, too, I understood Thorndyke's intense interest in the rope. But there was another thing that I did not understand at all.

"I suppose," said I, "that it was these coloured threads that made you give so much attention to this rope?"

"Undoubtedly," he replied, "and you must admit that they were calculated to attract attention."

"Certainly, I do. But what puzzles me is how you came to see them at all. They are extremely inconspicuous, and must have been still more so before the rope was cleaned."

"There is no mystery about that," said he. "I saw them because I looked for them. You remember that you – like the Superintendent – took this rope for a coir rope. So did I, at first. Then I saw that the texture did not agree with the colour, that it was really a hempen rope dyed to imitate coir. Then I asked myself the question that you asked just now: Why should anyone dye a hemp rope to imitate the less valuable coir? The natural suggestion was that the rope had been disguised to cover unlawful possession. It was probably a stolen rope. This idea suggested the possibility that it might be a marked rope. Accordingly I carefully examined the cut end, and behold! The two coloured threads – very inconspicuous, as you inferred, but visible enough when looked for."

"But this is a very important fact, Thorndyke," said I.

162

"It is," he agreed. "It is by far the most valuable clue that we hold. In fact, if the finger-prints fail us, it is the only clue that leads away from generalities to a definite place and set of surroundings. We shall almost certainly be able to trace this rope to the place from which it was stolen, and that alone will tell us something of the person who stole it."

"Mighty little," said I.

"Probably. But if we are able to add only a little to what we know, that little may be very illuminating."

"What do we know about these men?" I asked.

"Perhaps I should have said 'infer' rather than 'know', but our inferences are fairly safe. First, we find a person evidently accustomed to handling cordage, and probably a seaman or waterside character – a person, probably the same, who has a stolen rope in his possession, a person who is in some way connected with a tailor's work-room or some similar establishment, and a person who uses, drives, and probably owns some two-wheeled vehicle, either a gig, a light cart, or possibly a hansom cab, and if the latter, an old cab, probably in poor condition and distinguished by the unusual character of iron tyres. Then there is the choice of Piper's Row. The selection of this particular house could hardly have been made by a complete stranger. It suggests a person with some knowledge of the place and of its usually undisturbed condition. Assuming the object to be the disposal of the body in some place where it would not be discovered until all traces of the crime – of the actual method of the murder – had disappeared, the hiding-place was extraordinarily well chosen. But for the mere accident of Holker's picking out this house for repairs, the body might have remained undiscovered for months and the plan have succeeded perfectly."

"It has succeeded pretty perfectly as it is," said I, "so far as the coroner and the police are concerned."

"Yes. But in another month the cause of death would have been completely unascertainable. But you notice that however long the interval might have been, the body would still have been identifiable by the contents of the pockets and the marking of the clothes. That seems to be worth noting."

"You mean that the intention was that the body should ultimately be identified?"

"I mean that there was no attempt to conceal the identity. The significance of that – such as it is – lies in the fact that in an ordinary murder the safety of the murderers is much greater if the identity of the murdered person is unknown, since, in that case, the police usually have nothing to indicate the identity of the murderer. But I doubt if there is

163

much in it. The intention evidently was, in this case, that the death should not be recognised as a murder at all."

"Yes, and they were very near to bringing it off. In fact, they have brought it off so far. They are still very decidedly birds in the bush. And the inquest was an absolute walk-over for them. All the evidence seemed to point to suicide, and that of Weeks and Brodribb must have been most convincing to people who already had a bias in that direction. By the way, did you pick up anything from the evidence besides that statement of Holker's?

"Nothing very definite," he replied. "There were certain hints and suggestions in the evidence of Weeks and in that of Joseph Wood, the waiter. Weeks, you remember, had evidently had the feeling that there was something unusual in the air when Sir Edward started from home that morning, and Wood seemed to me to have the impression that there was someone in the cab which drew up for Sir Edward to enter. He didn't say so – in fact he said that he did not know – but he mentioned pointedly that he did not see Sir Edward hail the cab or give any directions to the driver. Taking what was implied rather than stated by these two witnesses, there seems to be a suggestion that one, at least, of the murderers was known to Sir Edward, and the fact that he went away in a hansom, whether alone or with some other person, is certainly significant as pointing to a definite destination. It is quite inconsistent with the Superintendent's suggestion of aimless wandering.

"But we are straying away into a consideration of the general aspects of the case. To come back to the question that we were discussing, you see now what our position is at the moment. If Miller can give us the name of a person who has handled that chair at Piper's Row, we can give him sufficient information to enable him to put that person on trial for murder. Of course he would not do so off-hand. Before he moved, he would fill in detail and seek corroborative evidence. But there would be very little doubt of the result.

"On the other hand, if Miller cannot produce a known person, we shall be left with a very complete case of murder against some persons unknown. Then it will be our task to convert those unknown persons into known persons, and to do that we shall need to acquire some further facts."

There were some other points that I should have liked to raise. But Thorndyke's very definite conclusion seemed to put an end to the discussion, so much so that Polton threw off all pretence, and, removing the eyeglass from his eye, deliberately carried the clock to a cupboard and there deposited it as a thing that had served its purpose.

Chapter XI
Ashdod Revisited
(Jasper Gray's Narrative)

A good old proverb assures us that we may be sure our sins will find us out. I will not make the customary facetious commentary on this proposition. That joke has now worn rather thin. But the idiotic booby-trap that I set for poor old Ponty, rebounding on me again and again like a self-acting, perpetual-motion boomerang, illustrated the proverb admirably, while the encounter on my very doorstep with a dry-faced, plain-clothes policeman illustrated the joke. Most inopportunely, my sins had found me at home.

He must have had a description of me for he addressed me tentatively by name. I acknowledged my identity and he then explained his business.

"It's about that counterfeit half-crown that your father passed by mistake. I want to know, as well as you can remember, how it came into your possession."

Now, of course I ought to have told him all I knew. I realised that. But my recollections of Mr. Ebbstein's establishment were so exceedingly unpleasant that I boggled at the idea of being any further mixed up with it. And then there was Miss Stella. I couldn't endure the thought of having her name dragged into a disreputable affair of this sort. Wherefore I temporised and evaded.

"The man who gave it to me was a complete stranger," said I.

"Naturally," said the officer. "You didn't hear his name by any chance?"

"I heard another man call him 'Jim'."

"Well, that's something, though it doesn't carry us very far. But how came he to give it to you? Was it payment?"

I described the transaction with literal truth up to the point of the delivery of the coin but said nothing of the subsequent events. I think he must have been a rather inexperienced officer, for he assumed that the payment concluded the business and that I then came away. I didn't say so.

"You took the case up in Mansell Street. Do you remember what number?"

"No, but I remember the house. It was on the right-hand side, going from the High Street, just past a tobacconist's shop – next door, in fact. The shop had a figure of a Red Indian on a bracket outside."

He entered this statement in a large, black-covered note-book and then asked, "You took the case to Byles's Wharf, you say. Whereabouts is that? Isn't it somewhere down Wapping way?"

"Yes, this end of Wapping."

"And do you think you would know the man again?"

"I am sure I should."

He noted this down and reflected awhile. But having missed all the really relevant questions, he didn't seem able to think of any others. Accordingly, after a spell of profound thought, he put his note-book away and closed the proceedings.

I went on my way greatly relieved at having, as I hoped, at last shaken myself free of that accursed make-believe, but yet by no means satisfied with my conduct of the affair. I knew that, as a good citizen, I ought to have told him about "Chonas", and my default rankled in my bosom and again illustrated the proverb by haunting me in all my comings and goings. But the oddest effect of the working of my conscience was to develop in me a most inconsistent hankering to make my incriminating knowledge more complete. I became possessed by an unreasonable urge to revisit the scene of my adventure, to go down again into Ashdod, and turn my confused recollections into definite knowledge.

The opportunity came unexpectedly. I had to deliver a parcel of stationery at an office appertaining to a large warehouse in Commercial Road East. It was a heavy parcel, but not heavy enough to demand the use of the truck. I carried it on my shoulder, and when I had at length dumped it down in the outer office and taken my receipt for it, I was free and unencumbered. And the weight of the parcel seemed to justify me in taking a little time off to spend on my own affairs.

As I strolled back along Commercial Road East, I kept a sharp look-out for landmarks of that memorable journey with the hansom. Presently I came to the corner of Sidney Street, which I remembered having passed on that occasion, and which gave me what mariners call a "departure". I turned back, eastward, and, taking the first turning on the right (southerly), left the broad thoroughfare behind, and entered a maze of small streets. They were rather bewildering, but it is difficult thoroughly to bewilder a seasoned Londoner who is accustomed to wandering about the town on foot. (People who ride in conveyances don't count. They never become real Londoners). Presently I came to a corner which was marked at the kerb by an angular granite corner-stone. I remembered that stone. I had reason to (and so had the owner of the cab). Taking a fresh departure from it, I soon arrived at a little street at the end of which was a seedy-looking public-house distinguished by the sign of a lion and an inscription in Hebrew characters which suggested that the royal beast aforesaid was none other than the Lion of Judah.

I now had my bearings. This was the place where I had found and purloined the hansom. Just round the corner was the empty house from which Miss Stella and I had dropped down into the court. That was the last house in the street which I had come to identify, the street which was made illustrious by the residence therein of Mr. Ebbstein and his tenant, the ingenious "Chonas", to say nothing of the old villain whom I had knocked on the head.

I sauntered round the corner, keeping my eyes skinned (as our packer would have expressed it), but carefully avoiding any outward manifestation of interest. The illustrious street I learned from a half-illegible name-plate rejoiced in the romantic name of *Pentecost Grove*. Strolling along it, I took in the numbers – where there were any – with the tail of my eye, keeping account of them, since so many were missing, until I arrived exactly opposite the mews, or stable-yard, which I had seen from the window of my prison. Thereby I learned that Mr. Ebbstein resided at Number Forty-nine, and the person whose cranium I had damaged was to be found – if still extant – at Number Fifty.

If I had been content with this enlargement of my knowledge and taken myself off, all would have been well. But at this point, my intelligent interest over powered my caution. The stable-yard opposite, bearing the superscription *"Zion Place"*, yawned invitingly and offered an alluring glimpse of a hansom cab, horseless and apparently in dry dock. I couldn't resist that hansom cab. Without doubt, it was the identical hansom with which I had scattered the howling and blaspheming denizens of Ashdod. Of course, it didn't matter a "snide" half-crown whether it was or not. But I was sensible of an idiotic impulse to examine it and try to verify its identity. Accordingly I crossed the street and sauntered idly into Zion Place, gradually edging towards the object of my curiosity.

It was an extraordinarily shabby old vehicle and seemed to be dropping to pieces from sheer senile decay. But it wasn't really. The actual robustness of its old age was demonstrated by the near wheel, which memory impelled me to inspect narrowly. On the rim including the tyre was a deep, angular notch, corresponding, as I grinningly realised, with that sharp granite corner-stone and recalling the terrific lurch that had nearly jerked me from my perch. The notch was an honourable scar on which the builder and wheel wright might have looked with pardonable pride.

I had just reached this conclusion when I became aware of a face protruded round a stable door and a pair of beady eyes fixed very attentively on me. Then the face emerged, accompanied by a suitable torso and a pair of thin, bandy legs, the entire outfit representing the Jehu whom I remembered as bearing the style and title of Louis. He advanced towards me crab-wise and demanded, suspiciously, "Vell. Vat you vant in here?"

I replied that I was just having a look round.

"Ah," said he, "zen you shall take your look outside."

I expressed the hope that I had not intruded and, turning about, strolled up the yard and out into the street. He followed closely at my heels, not only up the yard, but along the street. Finding him still clinging to me, I quickened my pace, deciding now to get clear of the neighbourhood without delay. Heading towards The Lion, I was approaching the corner when two men came round it. One of them, whose head was bound with a dirty rag, instantly riveted my attention and stirred the chords of memory. Apparently my appearance affected him in a like manner, for, as soon as he saw me he stopped, and, after regarding me for a moment with an astonished glare, flung up his arms and uttered a loud cry which sounded to me like "Hoya!" At the same moment, his companion started forward as if to intercept me.

That uncanny, Oriental alarm-cry, repeated now and echoed by the other two men, instantly warned me of my danger. I remembered its effect last time – indeed, the aid of memory was needless, for already a dozen windows were thrown up and a dozen shaggy heads thrust out, with open mouths repeating that ill-omened word, whatever it might be. Pocketing my dignity, I evaded the attempt to head me off and broke into a run with the cab-driver and the other man yelling at my heels.

Past the Lion of Judah I bolted and along the street beyond for some fifty yards, but now my imperfect recollection of the neighbourhood played me false. For, coming to a narrow turning on my right, I assumed it to be the one by which I had come, and did not discover my error until I had covered more than half its length, when a sharp turn revealed a blind end. But the discovery came too late. Already the place was humming like an overturned hive, and, when I spun about to retrace my steps, behold! The end of the little street was blocked by a yelling crowd.

There was nothing for it but to go back, which I did at a brisk walk, and when the mob came forward to meet me with the obvious intention of obstructing my retreat, I charged valiantly enough. But, of course, it was hopeless. A score of dirty hands grabbed at me as I strove to push my way through and in a few moments I was brought to a stand with both my arms immovably held, and then began to be slowly pushed and dragged forward, and all around me were those strange, pale alien faces, all jabbering vociferously in an uncouth, alien tongue. Suddenly, out of this incomprehensible babel issued the welcome sound of some thing resembling English speech.

"Wot's the good of makin' all this rumpus? Give the bloke a clout on the 'ed and let 'im go."

I looked round at the speaker and instantly recognised the man who had given me the "snide" half-crown at Byles's Wharf, and even in my bewilderment, I could see that he was obviously nervous and uneasy.

"Let 'im go!" exclaimed a flat-faced, hairy alien who was hanging on to my arm. "You do not know zat he have try to kill poor Mr. Gomorrah!"

"I know," said the other. "'E 'it 'im on the 'ed. And wot I says is, 'it 'im on the 'ed and let 'im 'ook it. Wot's the good of raisin' a stink and bringin' the coppers round?"

"He shall pay for vot he 'ave done, Mr. Trout," the other replied, doggedly, and at this moment, my acquaintance with the bandaged head pushed his way through the crowd and stood for a few moments gloating over me with an expression of concentrated vindictiveness, and certainly the presence of the bandage after all these weeks suggested that he had some excuse for feeling annoyed with me. I thought that he was about to take "consideration for value received" forthwith, but then he altered his mind and, with a savage grin, directed his friends (as I gathered) to bring me along to some more convenient place.

"Don't be a fool, Gomorrah," urged my friend – whose name appeared to be Trout. "You'll get yourself and the rest of us into the soup if you ain't careful. This 'ere is England, and don't you forget it."

His warnings, however, had no effect and, once more an effort was made to propel me in the desired direction. It was clear to me that I was being led to the slaughter – not, however, like a lamb (whose policy I have always considered a mistaken one), for I proceeded to make things as uncomfortable as possible for the men who were holding me who, to do them justice, retaliated effectively in kind. The proceedings became distinctly boisterous with considerable wear and tear of my clothing and person, and our progress was neither dignified nor rapid. Suddenly, the man who was clinging to my right wrist, breathlessly addressed the still-protesting Trout.

"Here come Mr. Zichlinsky. Now ye shall see."

I looked anxiously at the new-comer who was thrusting through the crowd, and, as he came into view, I had two instantaneous impressions.

First, in spite of his shabby, ill-fitting clothes, he was obviously of a totally different social class from the others. Secondly, though he was certainly a stranger, his face seemed to awaken some dim and vague reminiscence. It was a villainous face – dead white with a pair of strangely colourless eyes of the palest grey, and the pallor of eyes and skin was intensified by a brush of jet-black hair that stood straight up on his hatless head. Though not actually uncomely, his appearance and expression were evil to the point of repulsiveness.

These were but momentary impressions of which I was but half-aware, for there was matter enough of another kind to keep my attention fully occupied. As soon as Mr. Zichlinsky had worked his way through to me, he introduced himself by slapping my face and remarking, with a sort of wild-cat grin, "So you haf come to see us again. Zis time you shall haf a brober velcome."

With this he slapped my face again, and then grabbing a handful of flesh and clothing together, helped the others to drag me along. Mr. Trout made yet one more appeal.

"For Gawd's sake, Mr. Zichlinsky, don't go and do nothing stoopid. This ain't Russia, yer know – "

Zichlinsky turned on him as if he would have bitten him. "Have I ask for you to tell me vot I shall do? Keep your hands out of my business!"

But there was yet another protestor. I could not see him, and, though I could hear his voice – speaking in barbarous French – I could make out only a word or two. But of those words, two – "*la pucelle*" – conveyed to me the gist of the matter.

Zichlinsky answered him less savagely and in excellent French, "It is not only revenge, though this beast has robbed me of a fortune. But he knows too much, and you can see for yourself he is a spy."

Here he refreshed himself again by slapping my face, and then, apparently goaded to fury by the recollection of his wrongs, snarled and bared his teeth like a dog, and, seizing my ear, began to pull and twist it with the ferocity of a madman. The pain and consequent anger scattered the last remains of my patience and caution. Wrenching my left hand free, I shot out my fist with the full strength of an uncommonly strong arm.

My knuckles impinged on his countenance exactly between his eyes, and the weight of the blow flung him backward like a capsized ninepin. If there had been room, he would have measured his length on the ground. As it was, some of his friends caught him, and he leaned against them motionless for a few seconds apparently dazed, while from the crowd a deafening yell of execration arose. Then he recovered

170

himself, and, with a horrid, womanish shriek, came at me with all his teeth exposed. And now I could see that he held a long, pointed knife in his hand.

I suppose that, until my time comes, I shall never be so near death as I was at that moment. The man was within a foot of me and his arm was swung out to strike. The nearest wretches in the crowd glared at me with gloating, fascinated eyes while my own followed the outward swing of the knife.

And then, in an instant, the fateful thing happened: A pair of strong hands – I think they were Trout's – seized and held the outswung arm. The din of triumphant yells died down suddenly, giving place to a strange silence. The hands which gripped my arms relaxed their hold so that I could shake myself free. I cast a bewildered glance around, and then I saw the cause of this singular change. Above the heads of the crowd appeared two constabulary helmets, and in another moment two stalwart policemen – the police patrol in pairs in neighbourhoods of this type – pushed their way to the centre of the throng. Zichlinsky hurriedly put away his knife – but not before one of the policemen had observed it – and was in the act of withdrawing when a stern official voice commanded him to stay.

"Now," said the constable who had noticed the knife, "what's going on here?"

Mr. Trout hastened to explain. "It's a parcel of foolery, Constable, that's what it is. A silly mistake. They took this young man for somebody else and they was going to wallop 'im."

"Seem to have done a fair amount of walloping already," the constable remarked apropos of my rather dishevelled condition. "And one of them," he added, fixing an accusing eye on Zichlinsky, "was going to do the walloping with a knife. I saw you putting it away. Now what might your name be?"

The question was evidently anticipated for Zichlinsky replied, promptly, "Jacob Silberstein."

"And where do you live?"

"I lodge with Mr. Gomorrah."

"Oh," said the constable, "you live with old Solomon Gomorrah, do you? That isn't much of a testimonial."

He produced a large, black-covered note-book in which he entered the particulars while the other constable peered curiously over his shoulder.

"What's that?" the latter asked. "Did he say he lived at Sodom and Gomorrah?"

"No," his colleague explained. "Solomon Gomorrah is a man – one of these cag-mag tailors. Makes shoddy trousers. What they call in Whitechapel a kickseys builder. You'll know all about Solomon when you've been a little longer on this beat." He ran an expert eye over the remaining bystanders (the production of the note-book had occasioned a rapid dwindling of the assembly, though curiosity still held the less cautious) and demanded, "But what was it all about? What did they want to wallop this young fellow for?"

Mr. Trout would have essayed to explain, but he was forestalled by an elderly woman who looked as if she might have been "collected" from the Assyrian room at the British Museum. "He is a vicked man! He have try to kill poor Mr. Gomorrah."

"Nothing of the sort!" said Trout. "T'wasn't this bloke at all. They thought 'e was 'im, but it wasn't. It was another cove altogether. 'E 'it 'im on the 'ed."

The constable's unsympathetic comment on this slightly confused explanation was that it probably served him right. "But," he asked, "where is Gomorrah?"

"Seems to have hooked it," said Trout, looking round vaguely, and I then observed that Zichlinsky had also taken the opportunity to fade away. The constable turned to me somewhat wearily and asked, "What is your name, sonny, and where do you live?"

"My name," I replied, "is Jasper Gray, and I live at 165 Great Ormond Street."

"Quite a treat to hear a Christian-like name," said the officer, writing it down. "So you don't belong to this select residential neighbourhood, and if you will take my tip, you'll clear out of it as quickly as possible. Better walk with us up to Commercial Road East."

I accepted the invitation gladly enough, and we turned away together from the now silent and rapidly emptying street, and as we went, the senior constable put a few judicious questions. "Do you know what the rumpus was about? Why did that man Silberstein want to knife you?"

"He said I had robbed him of a fortune. I don't know what he meant. I have never seen him before, to my knowledge. But his name is not Silberstein. It is Zichlinsky. I heard them call him by that name."

"Oh, Zichlinsky, is it?" said my friend, fishing out the note-book again. "Probably a 'wanted' name, as he gave a false one. We must see who he is. And now, here we are in Commercial Road East. You'd better have a penn'orth on a bus. Safer than walking. Got any coppers?"

He was slipping his hand into his trousers pocket, but I assured him that I was solvent to the extent of twopence, whereupon, waving away my thanks, he hailed a west-bound Blackwall omnibus and stood by to see me safely on board.

I was not sorry to sink down restfully on a cushioned seat (the constable had directed me to travel inside) for I had had a strenuous finish to a rather fatiguing morning. And as the omnibus rumbled along west ward I reflected on my late experiences, and once more the voice of conscience made itself heard. Evidently, Pentecost Grove was a veritable nest of criminals of the most dangerous type. Of those criminals I knew enough to enable the police to lay hands, at least on some and probably on all. Hitherto I had, for purely selfish reasons, kept my knowledge to myself. Now it was time for me to consider my duties as a citizen.

So I reflected as the leisurely omnibus jogged on along the familiar highway, and the sordid east gradually gave place to the busy west. When I dropped off opposite Great Turnstile my mind was made up. I would seek out the guardians of the law and tell them my story.

But once more Fate intervened. The guardians of the law forestalled my intentions, and the ears into which my story was delivered were not those of the mere official police.

Chapter XII
Of a Hansom Cab and
a Black Eagle
(Dr. Jervis's Narrative)

When I came down to breakfast on the day after the inquest, I found the table laid for one, a phenomenon which Polton explained by informing me that "The Doctor" had gone out early. "In a hansom," he added with a crinkly and cunning smile. "I fancy he's got something on. I saw him copying a lot of names out of the directory."

I followed his knowing glance to a side table, whereon lay a copy of *The Post Office Directory*, and had no doubt that he was right. *The Post Office Directory* was one of Thorndyke's most potent instruments of research. In his hands, and used with imagination and analytical feeling, it was capable of throwing the most surprising amount and kind of illumination on obscure cases. In the present instance, its function, I had no doubt, was quite simple, and so, on examination, it turned out to be. Although closed, the volume had two places conspicuously marked by slips of paper, one at the page devoted to rope manufacturers and the other at the list of ship chandlers, and a number of light pencil marks opposite names in the two lists showed that a definite itinerary had been made out.

"The Doctor said I was to show you this," said Polton, laying an open envelope beside my plate.

I drew out the enclosed letter, which I found to be a short and civil note from Mr. Northbrook, inviting us informally to lunch at the Clarendon Club. The invitation was for the current day, and the note was endorsed by Thorndyke: "*I have accepted, and shall be at the club at one o'clock. Come if you can.*"

I was a little surprised, for Thorndyke was evidently full of business, and I suspected that Northbrook merely wanted to extract comments on the inquest, but it was quite convenient for me to go, and, as Thorndyke clearly wished me to – quite possibly for some definite reason – I strolled forth in good time and made my way to the rendezvous by the pleasant way of St. James's and the Green Park.

Northbrook's intentions were as I had supposed, and I have no doubt that, in the course of a very pleasant lunch, he may have elicited some interesting comments on the previous day's proceedings. But Thorndyke was an extremely difficult man to pump, the more so as he had the manner of discussing affairs without any appearance of reservation. But I noted that no inkling was conveyed to Northbrook of any dissent from the finding of the jury.

I found myself speculating from time to time on Thorndyke's object in wasting rather valuable time on this leisurely and apparently purposeless conversation. But towards the end of the meal I received a sudden enlightenment. "This," he said, "I take to be the table at which Sir Edward usually took his meals?"

"Yes," replied Northbrook, "and a very pleasant table it is, looking out right across the Green Park. You judged, no doubt, by the fact that Joseph Wood is waiting on us?"

"You are quite right," said Thorndyke, "and that reminds me that I should like to have a word or two with Joseph Wood, presently."

"But certainly, my dear sir. You shall have an opportunity of interviewing him in the strictest privacy."

"Oh, that is not necessary at all," said Thorndyke. "There are no secrets. I merely wanted him to amplify one of the points in his evidence. Perhaps I may ask him now, as I see he is coming with the coffee."

"Do so, do so, by all means," said Northbrook, evidently delighted at the chance of hearing the "amplification".

Thus invited, Thorndyke addressed the waiter as he placed the coffee on the table.

"I wanted to ask you one or two questions about your evidence at the inquest concerning the hansom in which Sir Edward drove away."

"Yessir," said Wood, standing stiffly at attention.

"It seemed to me that you had an impression that there was someone in it when it drew up for him to get in."

"Yessir. I had. I didn't say so at the inquest, because I was there to tell what I saw, not what I thought."

"You were perfectly right," said Thorndyke. "It was for the coroner to ask for your opinions if he wanted them. But you did think so?"

"Yessir. I didn't see Sir Edward hail the cab, and I don't think he did. He just stopped and the cab drew up. Then he got in and the cab drove away. I didn't see him speak to the cabman, and I don't believe he did, for the man started off and whipped up his horse as if he knew where he had to go."

"You said you didn't notice the number of the cab. Of course, you would not."

"No, sir. I hadn't no occasion to."

"Did you notice what the cab was like – whether there was anything unusual in its appearance?

"Yessir, I did notice that. You couldn't help noticing it. That cab," he continued solemnly, "must have been the great-grandfather of all the cabs in London. You never see such a shabby old rattle-trap. Got an old round dickey with a sheet-iron back, like I remember when I was a boy, and, if you will believe me, sir, iron tyres! Iron tyres in this twentieth century! Why that cab must have been fifty years old if it was a day."

"Why didn't you say that in your evidence, Wood?" Northbrook demanded.

"Nobody asked me, sir," was the very reasonable reply.

"No. And, after all, I suppose it didn't very much matter what the cab was like. Do you think so, Doctor?

"It would have been helpful if we could have identified the cab and ascertained if anyone was in it and where it went to. That might have enabled us to fill in the picture. However, we can't, but, all the same, I must thank you, Wood, for telling me what you noticed."

After this little episode, I was not surprised when Thorndyke became suddenly conscious of the passage of time.

"Dear me!" he exclaimed with a glance at his watch, "how the minutes slip away in pleasant society! We shall have to get on the road, Jervis, and let Mr. Northbrook retire to his office. It was most kind of you to invite us, Mr. Northbrook, and we have both enjoyed a very agreeable interlude in the day's work."

He finished his coffee and we both stood up, and after a few more exchanges of compliments, we took our departure. As we descended the steps, a disengaged hansom approached and drew up in response to Thorndyke's hail. I stepped in, and, as my colleague followed, I heard him give the destination: "New Scotland Yard, Whitehall Gate."

"That waiter man's information was rather startling – at least, it was to me," I remarked as the cab horse padded away to the accompaniment of his softly tinkling bell.

"It is a very valuable addition to our small stock of facts," Thorndyke replied. "And how extraordinarily opportune Northbrook's invitation was. I was casting about for some way of getting a talk with Wood without making a fuss, and behold! Northbrook solves the difficulty in the simplest fashion. What did you think of the other point, the possible presence of some other person in the cab?

"I think it is more than merely possible. I should say it is very highly probable, especially in view of the peculiarity of the cab. And, of course, this new information confirms very strongly your suspicion that the Stratford vehicle was really a hansom."

"It does," he agreed. "In fact, I am assuming as a working hypothesis that the cab which bore Sir Edward away from the club conveyed his body to Piper's Row. On that assumption I am now going to Scotland Yard to find out what facilities there are for tracing a cab the number of which is unknown. I should like to see Miller in the first place if we are lucky enough to catch him."

By this time our "gondola" was turning from Trafalgar Square into Whitehall, and I was noting how strikingly it contrasted with the "rattle-trap" that Wood had described. This was a typical West End hansom, as smart and clean as a private carriage, furnished with gay silken blinds and at each side with a little mirror and a flower-holder containing a bunch of violets, and it slid along as smoothly as a sleigh, without a sound beyond the gentle and musical tinkle-tinkle of the bell on the horse's collar.

"If you want to catch Miller," said I, as we approached the main gateway of the Police Headquarters, "you are just in time. I see him coming out across the courtyard."

In effect, the Superintendent emerged into Whitehall just as we got out of the hansom, and, observing us, stopped to wait for us.

"Were you wanting to see me?" he asked with an inflection that subtly conveyed the earnest hope that we were not.

Thorndyke evidently caught that faint overtone, for he replied, "Only for a moment. Which way are you going?"

"Westminster Station – Underground."

"So are we, so we can talk as we go. What I want to know is this: There are still in London a few old hansom cabs with unconverted iron tyres. Now, could your people produce a list of those cabs?"

Miller shook his head. "No," he replied. "The register doesn't give particulars of the furnishing of particular cabs. Of course, we could find out by means of what they call an *ad hoc* investigation, but it would be a troublesome business. Possibly Inspector Radcliffe might be able to give you some information. He is our principal specialist in public vehicles."

He paused and seemed to reflect for a few moments. Then, suddenly, he emitted a soft laugh as if he had remembered something amusing. Which, in fact, turned out to be the case, for he resumed, "Talking of iron-tired cabs, Radcliffe told me a rather quaint story some time ago. Nothing much in it, but your question brought it to mind. It seems that a certain constable whose beat included Dorchester Square was going his round rather late one evening when he noticed a hansom cab drawn up about the middle of the south side of the square. There was no sign of the driver, and no one minding the horse, and as this was not quite according to Cocker, it naturally attracted his attention. But what specially tickled him was the way the horse was secured. The reins were made fast to a lamp-post with a clove hitch, just as a waterman makes fast his boat's painter to a railing or a thin iron post. The constable was a Margate man and familiar with the ways of boatmen, so it struck him as rather funny to see a cab moored to the lamp-post like a boat.

"However, he didn't take any notice but went off on his beat. When he came round the square the next time, the cab was still there and there was still no sign of the driver. He began to think it a bit queer, but he didn't want to make a fuss unnecessarily. But when he came round the third time and found the cab still there, he began to look into things. First he noticed that the cab was a most shocking old ramshackle – battered old round-backed dickey and iron tires – sort of cab that Queen Elizabeth might have driven about in. Then he looked at the horse and saw that it looked ready to drop with exhaustion. Just then as the sergeant happened to come round, the constable drew his attention to the cab, and the sergeant detailed another constable to take it round to a livery stable. There they gave the poor old horse a drink and a feed, and they say that he went for the oats as if he'd never tasted any before and nearly swallowed the nose-bag.

"Next morning, having found out from the register that the cab came from a little private yard down Mile End way, one of our men took it there and interviewed the owner, who drove it himself. It was a queer affair. The owner was a Polish Jew, about as unlike a horsey man as you can imagine. But what struck our man principally was that the fellow seemed to be in a blue funk. His story was that he had gone into a pub to get a drink, leaving the cab in charge of a man who happened to be loafing outside, and when he'd had his drink and come out, the cab was gone. Asked why he hadn't given information to the police, he said he hadn't thought of it, he was so upset. And that was all our man could get out of him. But as it was obvious that there was something behind the affair, our man took the fellow's name – though it was on the register – and reported the incident to Radcliffe.

"That's the story. I don't know whether it is of any interest to you, but if it is, I will tell Radcliffe to let you have particulars if you care to look him up. And he might be able to tell you about some other cabs with iron tyres."

Thorndyke thanked the Superintendent and said that he would certainly avail himself of the assistance thus kindly offered. Then, as the train began to slow down he rose. (I have not interrupted Miller's narrative to describe our movements but I may explain that, at

178

Westminster, we had all taken tickets, Miller's being for Bishopsgate and ours for the Monument, and that we had all boarded the same east-bound train.) When the train stopped we shook hands with the Superintendent and got out, leaving him to pursue his journey.

"That Polish gentleman sounds suspiciously like one of our friends," I remarked as we made our way out of the station.

"He does," Thorndyke agreed. "The man and the cab seem to fit the circumstances. It remains to be seen whether the date will. But I shall take an early opportunity of calling on Inspector Radcliffe and getting more precise details."

"Where are we going now?" I asked, having noted that our course seemed to be riverward.

"The Old Swan Pier," he replied, "whence we shall embark for a short voyage. The object of that voyage will, I hope, appear later."

As Thorndyke's answer, while withholding the explanation, did not deprecate speculation on my part, I gave the possibilities due consideration by the light of our further proceedings. From the Old Swan Pier we boarded one of the excellent and convenient river steamers which plied on the Thames in those days, by which we were borne eastward beneath the Tower Bridge and down the busy Pool. Cherry Gardens Pier was reached and left behind without supplying any hint, nor was I any the wiser when, as the boat headed in towards The Tunnel Pier, Wapping, my colleague rose and moved towards the gangway.

From the head of the pier, Thorndyke turned west ward along High Street, Wapping, commenting on our surroundings as he went.

"A queer, romantic old neighbourhood, this, Jervis, dull and squalid to look at now but rich in memories of those more stirring and eventful days which we think of fondly with the advantage of not having had to live in them. We are now passing Execution Dock – still, I believe, so called though it is now a mere work-a-day wharf. But a century or so ago you could have stood here and looked on a row of pirates hanging in chains."

"I shouldn't mind if you could now," I remarked, "if I could have the choosing of the pirates."

Thorndyke chuckled. "Yes," he said, "there was no nonsense about legal procedure in those days. If the intermediate stages were not all that could be desired, the final ones had the merit of conclusiveness. Here we approach The Town of Ramsgate Inn and Wapping Old Stairs, the latter a little disappointing to look at. The art of seasoning squalor with picturesqueness seems to have been lost. This is the goal of our pilgrimage."

As he spoke, he turned in at the gateway of a small dock and began to walk at a reduced pace along the quay. I looked around in search of some object that might be of interest to us but my glance met nothing beyond the craft in the basin – mostly lighters and Thames barges – the dreary dock buildings, the massive mooring-posts and bollards, and here and there a life-buoy stand. Suddenly, however, I became aware that these last, which my eye had passed almost without notice, were not viewed with the same indifference by Thorndyke, for he walked straight up to the nearest one and halted before it with an air of obvious interest. And then, in a moment, I saw what we had come for.

The lifebuoy stand was in the form of a screen supported on two stanchions. In the middle of the screen, under a little pent-house, was a massive wooden hook on which was hung the life-buoy and a coil of smallish rope. Neither the buoy nor the rope was secured in any way, but either or both could be freely lifted off the hook. I thought at first that Thorndyke was about to lift off the coil, but he merely sought one of the ends of the rope, and, having found it, looked at it for a few moments with close attention. Then, having spread out with his thumb the little brush of fibres that projected beyond the whipping, he made a more minute examination with the aid of his pocket lens. Finally, without comment, he handed the end of the rope and the lens to me.

A moment's careful inspection through the glass was sufficient.

"Yes," I said, "there is no doubt about it. I can see the red and the green threads plainly enough through the lens, though they are mighty hard to see with the naked eye. Which is unkind to the thief as giving him a false sense of security."

"It is for the thief, like the rest of us, to know his job," said Thorndyke, producing from his pocket the invaluable calliper gauge. He took the rope from me, and having measured the diameter, continued, "The agreement is perfect. This is a four-strand rope three-eighths-of-an-inch in diameter and having the two 'rogues' threads' of the same colour and similarly placed. So we may say that the place of origin of the Piper's Row rope is established beyond doubt."

At this moment an amphibious-looking person in a peaked cap who had been approaching slowly and with a somewhat stealthy manner made his presence known.

"What's the game?" he enquired, and then, by way of elucidation, "What are yer up to with that rope?"

Thorndyke faced him genially.

"You, I take it, are the dock keeper?"

"I ham," was the concise reply. "And what abaat it?"

"I should like, if you would not mind," said Thorndyke, "to ask you one or two questions. I may explain that I am a lawyer and am, at the moment, rather interested in the subject of rope-stealing. These life-lines look to me very exposed and easy to steal."

"So they are," our friend replied in a slightly truculent tone, "but what else can you do? Make 'em fast with a padlock, I suppose! And then you'd be in a pretty fine 'ole if a bloke went overboard and nobody hadn't got the key."

"Very true," said Thorndyke. "They must be free to lift off at a moment's notice. I see that. But I expect you find one missing now and again."

"Now and again!" repeated the dock-keeper. "I tell you, the way them ropes used to disappear was somethink chronic."

"That was before you took to marking them, I suppose?"

"How did you know we marked 'em?" our friend enquired suspiciously, and as Thorndyke silently held up the free end, he continued, "If you spotted them marks, you won't be much good to the spectacle trade. But you are quite right. Before we took to marking 'em, they used to go one after the other. Couldn't keep one no how. And we lost one or two – three altogether – after we took to the marks. But we got back two of 'em and dropped on the coves that pinched one of 'em, and now they've ogled that there's something wrong with our ropes and they leaves 'em alone – leastways they have for the last week or two."

Here he paused, but neither of us made any comment. Guided by long experience, we waited for the inevitable story to emerge, and sure enough, after a brief interval, our friend resumed, "Three ropes we lost after the marks was put in, and we got back two. The first one I found in a junk shop in Shadwell 'Igh Street. The bloke said he bought it of a stranger, and p'raps he did. Nobody could say he didn't, so there was no use in makin' a rumpus. I just collared the rope and told him to keep a sharper look out in future. The second rope I spotted laying in a boat alongside Hermitage Stairs. Nearly missed it, I did, too, for the artful blighters had gone and dyed it with cutch. Made it look just like a ky-ar rope. But I looks at it a bit hard and I thinks it looks uncommon like our rope, barrin' the colour, four strands, same size, looked about the same length as ours – ten fathoms, that is, to a inch – and it seemed to be laying spare in the boat. So I jumps down – there wasn't nobody in the boat at the time – and I has a look at the cut end. And there was our marks quite plain in spite of the cutch.

"Now it happened that while I was overhauling that rope, a bobby came out on the head of the stairs and stood there a-twiggin' of me.

"'That your boat?' he says.

"'No,' I says, 'it ain't.'

"'Then,' he says, 'what are you doin' with that rope?' he says.

"So I nips up the stairs with the rope in my hand and tells him how things is and who I am.

"'Well,' says he, 'are you goin' to charge this man with stealin' the rope?'

"'No,' I says, 'I ain't,' I says. 'I'm a-goin' to pinch this rope,' I says, 'and you've caught me in the very act, and you're goin' to run me in, and you're goin' to bring this bloke along to make the charge and to swear to his property.'

"The copper grins at this. 'You seem to be a pretty fly old bird,' he says, 'but it's a sound wheeze. You'll catch him on the hop if he swears to the rope.'

"Just then two blokes come down to the stairs. They take a long squint at me and the copper and then down they goes to the boat. One of 'em was a regler Thames water-rat and the other was one of them foreigners – hair down on his shoulders and a beard what looked as if he'd pinched it out of a horse-hair mattress. The copper grabs hold of my wrist and runs me down after them.

"'Here,' he says to the water-rat, 'is this your boat?'

"Water-rat didn't seem quite sure whether it was or not, but at last he said he supposed it was.

"'Well,' says the copper, 'I've just caught this man stealing rope out of your boat, and I'm going to take him along to the station, and you two have got to come along with me to identify your property.'

"Then I saw that my wheeze wasn't going to work. Water-rat bloke had rumbled me – seen me at the dock, I expect.

"'Wot property are yer talkin' about,' says he, beginning to cast off his painter from the ring. 'That there rope don't belong to me. Someone must have dropped it into the boat while we was up at the pub.'

"The copper reaches out and grabs the painter so that they couldn't hike off and he says, 'Well, it's somebody's rope and it's been pinched, and you've got to come along to the station to tell us about it.'

"I thought those coves was going to give trouble, but just then a Thames Police gig came along and the copper beckoned to 'em. So they pulls in and one of the water police helped us to take the two blokes to the station. I went along quite quiet, myself. When we got there, the inspector asks the water-rat what his name was. Water-rat didn't seem quite sure about it but at last he says, 'Frederick Walker,' he says, 'is my name,' he says.

182

"'No, it isn't,' says the inspector. 'Think again,' he says. 'Last time you was James Trout and you lived in King David Lane, Shadwell. Live there still?'

"'Yus,' says Trout. 'If you knowed, what did you ask me for?'

"'We don't want any of your sauce,' says the inspector, and then he turns to the other. 'What's your name and address?' he says.

"He shakes his head like as if he was trundling a mop. 'No speak Anglish,' says he.

"'Oh, rats!' says the inspector, 'you can't have forgot the English language in a couple of months. Last time you was Solomon Gomorrah and you lived in Pentecost Grove and was a tailor by trade. Any change?'

"'No,' says Solomon. 'It vas chust ze same.'

"'Well,' says the inspector, 'you'll have to stay here while I send a man round to see that the addresses are correct. Sure you don't want to make any change?'

"They said no, so I left the rope with the inspector and came away."

"And what was the end of it?" Thorndyke asked.

"That was," our friend replied. He expectorated scornfully and continued, "Both of 'em swore before the beak that it wasn't their rope, and we couldn't prove that it was, so he dismissed the case and told 'em to be more careful in future."

"And with regard to the third rope that you lost?"

"Ah," said the dock-keeper, regretfully, "I'm afraid that's a goner. Now that they know it's got a secret mark, they'll most likely have traded it away with some foreigner."

"You haven't done so badly," said Thorndyke. "I must compliment you on the smart way in which you found the lost sheep. And we needn't despair of the third rope. If you can give me the exact dates and the names and addresses, I may be able to help you, and you will certainly help me. I want to get a list of these rope thieves."

Our friend hereupon produced from his pocket a portentous note-book, the leaves of which he turned over rapidly. Having at last found the entry of the transaction, he read out the particulars, which Thorndyke duly entered in his own note-book.

"The length of these ropes, you say, is ten fathoms?"

"Ten fathoms exactly to a inch. I cut 'em off the coil myself and put on the whippings at the ends."

"I should have thought you would want them longer than ten fathoms," Thorndyke remarked.

"Why?" our friend demanded. "It's long enough for a man overboard. Of course, if he was going for a channel swim that would be a different matter. We haven't provided for that."

"Naturally," said Thorndyke. "And now, perhaps I had better make a note of your name and address in case I have any information to give you."

"My name," said the dock-keeper, "is Stephen Waters, and any letters addressed to me at the office here – Black Eagle Dock, Wapping – will find me. And I may as well have your name and address, if you don't mind."

Thorndyke produced a card from his case and handed it to Waters with the remark, "Better not mention to anyone that you have been in communication with me. The less we tell other people, the more we are likely to learn."

Mr. Waters warmly agreed with these sentiments (though his own practice had not been strikingly illustrative of them), and when we had thanked him for having so far taken us into his confidence, we bade him *adieu* and made our way out of the dock premises.

"Well," I exclaimed as we turned out into the High Street, "this has been a regular windfall. But how did you discover the place?"

"Oh, that was simple enough," replied Thorndyke. "I just took a list of rope-merchants and ship chandlers from *The Post Office Directory* and started systematically to call on them. One was bound, sooner or later, to strike the right one. But I was lucky from the beginning, for the second rope-merchant whom I called on gave me the name of a rope-maker who made a speciality of private ropes of unusual construction and particularly of marked ropes. So I went straight off to that maker and gave him the description of our rope, when it turned out that it was one of his own make. He had a big coil of it actually in stock and was good enough to give me a sample (when I had given him my card) as well as a direction to Black Eagle Dock. That was a stroke of luck, for I obtained, after a couple of hours' search, information that I had been prepared to spend a week on. But this meeting with Waters is a much bigger stroke of luck. We could, and should, have discovered eventually all that he has told us, but it would have involved a long and tedious investigation. This has been an excellent day's work."

"By Jove, it has!" I exclaimed. "With the Polish-Hebrew cab-driver and Mr. William Trout and the venerable Sodom-and-Gomorrah, we seem to have gathered up the whole party."

"We mustn't let our conclusions get ahead of our facts," Thorndyke protested. "We are doing extremely well. Our great need was to give to certain unknown persons 'a local habitation and a name'. We seem to have done that, but we have to make sure that it is the right habitation and the right name. Possibly the finger-prints may dispose of that question definitely."

Unfortunately, however, they did not. As we entered the Temple by the Tudor Street gate, we perceived Superintendent Miller advancing towards us from the direction of the Mitre Court entrance. He quickened his pace on seeing us and we met almost on our own threshold.

"Well, Doctor," he said as we turned into the entry together, "I thought I would come along and give you the news, though it isn't very good news. I'm afraid you've drawn a blank."

"Finger-prints unknown or undecipherable?" asked Thorndyke.

"Both," replied Miller. "Most of the marks are just smears, no visible pattern at all. There are two prints that Singleton says he could identify if they were in the records. But they are not. They are strangers, so that cat won't jump. Then there is a print – or rather part of a print, and bad at that – which Singleton thought, at first, that he could spot. But he decided afterwards that it was only a resemblance. You do get general resemblances in finger-prints, of course, but they don't stand systematic checking, character by character."

"And this one failed to pass the test?" asked Thorndyke.

"Well, it wasn't that so much," replied Miller. "It was a bad print and the identification was very uncertain, and when we came to look up the records, it didn't seem possible that the identification could be right. The print in the register that it resembled was taken from a man named Maurice Zichlinsky who was tried under extradition procedure for conspiracy to murder. The alleged crime was committed at St. Petersburg and, as the extradition court convicted him, he was handed over to the Russian police, and a note on the record says that he was tried in Russia and sentenced to imprisonment for life. Consequently, as he is presumably in a Russian prison at this moment, it seems to be physically impossible that this print can be his. That is, if these are recent finger-prints."

"They are," said Thorndyke. "So I am afraid it is an absolute blank. Can you show me which are the possible prints?"

"Yes," replied Miller. "Singleton marked them on the photograph and wrote the particulars on the back. Here they are," he continued, laying the photograph on the table, "these are the two possibles and this one, numbered 'three', is the one that might have been the Russian's."

"And with regard to the second photograph?"

"Ah," said Miller, producing it from his pocket, "Singleton was rather interested in that. Thought the prints looked as if they had been taken from a dead body."

"He was quite right," said Thorndyke. "They were, and the question was whether there was any trace of them on the other photograph."

185

"There was not," said Miller. "Of course, negative evidence is not conclusive, but Singleton couldn't find the least sign of them and he is pretty sure that they are not there. You see, even a smear may give you a hint if you know what you are looking for."

"Then," said Thorndyke, "we have not drawn an utter blank. We can take it that our known prints are not among the group, and that is something gained."

I now inducted the Superintendent into an easy chair while Thorndyke placed by his side a decanter of whisky, a siphon, and a box of cigars. It has sometimes struck me that my learned colleague would have made an excellent innkeeper, judging by the sympathetic attention that he gave to the tastes of his visitors in the matter of refreshments. Brodribb delighted in a particular kind of dry and ancient port and Thorndyke kept a special bin for his exclusive gratification. Miller's more modern tastes inclined to an aged and mellow type of Scotch whisky and a particular brand of obese and rather full-flavoured cigar, and his fancy also received due consideration.

"I was going to ask you," said Thorndyke, when the Superintendent's cigar was well alight, "at what time Radcliffe is usually to be found in his office."

"You needn't find him at all," replied Miller. "I thought you would probably want particulars of that hansom I told you about, so I got them for you when I saw him this afternoon."

"That was very thoughtful of you, Miller," said Thorndyke, watching with lively interest the extraction of a large pocket-book from the Millerian pocket.

"Not a bit," was the reply. "You are always ready to give me a bit of help. The driver's name, which is also that of the owner, as they are one and the same person, is Louis Shemrofsky and he keeps his blooming antique at a stable yard in Pentecost Grove, that is one of those little back streets somewhere between Commercial Road East and Shadwell – a pretty crummy neighbourhood, if you ask me – full of foreign crooks and refugees."

"I suppose," said Thorndyke, "you didn't happen to note the date on which the cab was found in Dorchester Square?"

"Oh, didn't I?" replied Miller. "Do you suppose I don't appreciate the importance of dates? The cab was found in the Square on Friday, the nineteenth of June, at about ten-fifteen p.m."

Thorndyke probably experienced the faint sense of disappointment of which I was myself aware. For, of course, it was the wrong date. Meanwhile, Miller watched him narrowly, and, after a short interval, was fain to let the cloven hoof come plainly into view.

"That interest you particularly?" he asked with suppressed eagerness.

Thorndyke looked at him thoughtfully for a few moments before replying. At length he answered, "Yes, Miller, it does. Jervis and I have a case in hand – a queer, intricate case with very important issues, and I think that this man, Shemrofsky, comes into the picture. We have quite a lot of evidence, but that evidence is in isolated patches with wide spaces between."

"Why not let me try to fill up some of the spaces," said Miller, eagerly, evidently smelling a case with possibilities of glory.

"I am going to ask for your collaboration presently," Thorndyke replied. "But just at the moment, the case is more suitable to my methods than to yours. And there is no urgency. Our activities are entirely unsuspected."

The Superintendent grinned. "I know," said he. "I've seen you do it before. Just work away out of sight until you are ready and then pounce. Well, Doctor, when you want me you know where to find me, and meanwhile, I'll do anything you want done without troubling you with inconvenient questions."

When the Superintendent had gone, I ventured to raise a question that had arisen in my mind during the conversation.

"Aren't you a little over-critical, Thorndyke? You spoke of spaces between patches of evidence but it seems to me that the case comes together very completely."

"No, Jervis," he replied. "It does not. We are getting on admirably, but we have not made out a coherent case. We have facts and we have probabilities. But the facts and the probabilities do not make complete contact."

"I do not quite follow you," said I.

"Let us look at our evidence critically," he replied. "The vehicle which went to Piper's Row was probably a hansom. Very probably but not certainly. That probable hansom was probably Shemrofsky's hansom and probably driven by Shemrofsky. We have to turn those probabilities into certainties. Again, the rope which was used to hang Sir Edward was stolen from Black Eagle Dock. We may treat that as a fact. It was dyed with cutch. That again is a fact. The rope found in the possession of Trout and Gomorrah was stolen from Black Eagle Dock and it was dyed with cutch. That is a fact. That it was stolen by, and was the temporary property of, one or both of them is highly probable but cannot be proved. The magistrate dismissed it as unproved. Gomorrah lives in Pentecost Grove. Shemrofsky's cab is kept in Pentecost Grove. Those are facts. The inference that Gomorrah and Trout and Shemrofsky were concerned in conveying that dyed rope (together with the body) to Piper's Row is very highly probable, but it cannot be certainly connected with the known facts.

"Again, the murder of Sir Edward we may regard as a known fact. He was probably murdered in a house in which is a tailor's work-room. Therefore he was probably murdered in Gomorrah's house. Still it is only a probability. And here there is a considerable space in our evidence. For Sir Edward was murdered by being drowned in salt water in which numerous herring-scales were suspended. Now, we have not traced that salt water or those herring-scales."

"No, we have not, and I can't even make a guess at what they may have been. Have you formed any theory on the subject?"

"Yes, I have a very definite opinion. But that is of no use. We have an abundance of excellent inferences. What we want is some new facts."

"But surely, Thorndyke," I protested, "a body of facts such as you have here, affording a series of probabilities all pointing in the same direction, is virtually equivalent to proof?"

"I don't think so," he answered. "I distrust a case that rests entirely on circumstantial evidence. A learned judge has told us that circumstantial evidence, if there is enough of it, is not only as good as but better than direct evidence, because direct evidence may be false. I do not agree with him. In the first place, direct evidence which may possibly be false is not evidence at all. But the evil of circumstantial evidence is that it may yield false inferences, as it has often done, and then the whole scheme is illusory. My feeling is that circumstantial evidence requires at least one point of direct evidence to establish a real connection of its parts with the question that is to be proved.

"For instance, if we could prove directly that Shemrofsky's cab was actually at Piper's Row on that Sunday night, we should link up all the other facts. Or again, if we could establish the fact of personal contact between Sir Edward and any of these suspected persons, that would connect the other facts with the murder. Or again, if we could prove by direct evidence that the remainder of that rope was or had been in the possession of Gomorrah or Trout or Shemrofsky, the other facts, and our inferences from them, would immediately become of high evidential value.

"And that is what we have got to do. We have to obtain at least one undeniable fact which will establish incontestably the actual connection of one or more of these persons with Sir Edward or with Number Five Piper's Row."

"Yes," I admitted, "I suppose you are right. It is an obscure case, after all. And there is one curious feature in it that puzzles me. I can't understand what object these men could have had in murdering Sir Edward. Nor can I imagine how he came to be in any way mixed up with a parcel of ragamuffins like these."

"Exactly, Jervis," said he. "You have struck the heart of the mystery. How came Sir Edward to be in this neighbourhood at all? We infer that he came voluntarily in Shemrofsky's cab to Pentecost Grove, probably with some other person. But why? And who was that other person? When we ask ourselves those questions, we cannot but feel that there is something behind this murder that we have not yet got a glimpse of."

"This seems to have been a conspiracy carried out by a gang of East End criminals of the lowest class. Legally speaking, they are no doubt the principals in the crime. But I have the feeling – the very strong feeling – that behind them was some person – or some persons – of a very different social class, who were pulling the strings. The motive of this crime has not yet come into sight. Probably if we can secure the actual murderer or murderers, the motive will be revealed. But until it is, our work will not be completed. To lay hands on the criminal puppets will not be enough. We have to secure the master criminal who has furnished at once the directing and the driving force."

Chapter XIII
Mr. Brodribb's Discovery
(Dr. Jervis's Narrative)

I am not quite clear how the matter arose. We had, I remember, been discussing with Mr. Brodribb some of the cases in which a contact occurs between legal and scientific theory, and eventually the conversation drifted towards the subject of personal identity in connection with blood relationship and heredity. Mr. Brodribb quoted a novel, the title of which has escaped me, and asked for an opinion on the problem in heredity that the story presented.

"I have rather forgotten the book," he said, "but, so far as my memory serves me, the story turns upon the appearance in a certain noble or royal family of a man who is completely identical in appearance and outward characteristics with a more or less remote ancestor – so completely identical that he can be passed off as a survival or re-incarnation of that very person. Now, I should like to know whether such a thing can be, in a scientific sense, admitted as possible."

"So should I, and so would a good many other people," I interposed. "But I don't think you will get Thorndyke to commit himself to a statement as to the possibility or impossibility of any particular form of inheritance."

"No," Thorndyke agreed. "A scientist is chary of declaring anything to be absolutely impossible. It is better to express it in terms or probability. Evidently a probability of one-to-a-thousand-millions is in practice equivalent to impossibility. The probability is negligible. But the statement keeps within the limits of what is known and can be proved."

"Hmm," grunted Brodribb. "Seems rather a hair-splitting distinction. But what is the answer to my question in terms of probability?"

"It is not at all simple," replied Thorndyke. "There are quite a number of different lines of probability to follow. First there is the multiplication of ancestors. A man has two parents, to both of whom he is equally related, four grandparents, eight great-grandparents, and so on by a geometrical progression. The eighth ancestral generation contains two-hundred-and-fifty-six ancestors, to all of whom he is equally related. Then the first question is, what is the probability of his completely resembling one of these two-hundred-and-fifty-six and bearing no resemblance to the other two-hundred-and-fifty-five?"

"Of course," said Brodribb, "the probability is negligible. And since *de minimis non curat lex* we may say that it doesn't exist."

"So it would seem," Thorndyke agreed. "But it is not quite so simple as that. Have you given any attention to the subject of Mendelism?

"Mendelism?" repeated Brodribb, suspiciously. "What's that? Sounds like some sort of political claptrap."

"It is a mode of inheritance," Thorndyke explained, "by which certain definite characteristics are transmitted unchanged and undiminished from generation to generation. Let us take the case of one such characteristic – colour-blindness, for instance. If a colour-blind man marries a normal woman, his children will be apparently normal. His sons will be really normal but of his daughters some will be carriers of colour-blindness. A proportion of their sons will be colour-blind. If these sons marry, the process will be repeated, normal sons, daughters who are carriers and whose sons may be colour-blind. Tracing the condition down the generations, we find, first a generation of colour-blind men, followed by a generation of normal men, followed by a generation of colour-blind men, and so on forever. The defect doesn't die out, but it appears only in alternate generations. Now see how this affects your question. Supposing that, of my two-hundred-and-fifty-six ancestors of the eighth generation, one had been colour-blind. That could not affect me, because I am of the odd generation. But my father – who would have been of the even generation – might have been colour-blind, and if I had had married sisters, I might have had colour-blind nephews."

"Yes, I see," said Brodribb, in a slightly depressed tone.

"And you will also see," pursued Thorndyke, "that this instance will not fit your imaginary case. The inheritance is masked by continued change of family name. Colour-blind Jones has normal sons, and colour blind grandsons. But those grandsons are not named Jones. They are his daughter's sons. Suppose his daughter has married a Smith. Then the defect has apparently moved out of the Jones family into the Smith family. And so on at each reappearance. It always appears associated with a new family name. But this will not do for the novelist. For his purpose, inheritance must usually be *in tail male* to agree with the devolution of property and titles.

"But even now we have not opened up the whole problem. We have to consider what characteristics go to the making of a visibly distinguishable personality and how those characteristics are transmitted from generation to generation."

"Yes," Brodribb admitted, wearily, "it is damned complicated. But there is another question, which I was discussing the other day with Middlewick. How far is a so-called family likeness to be considered as evidence of actual relationship? What do you say to that?"

"If the likeness were real and would bear detailed comparison," replied Thorndyke, "I should attach great importance to it."

"What do you mean by a real likeness?" asked Brodribb.

"I mean, first, that subtle resemblance of facial character that one finds in families. Then special resemblance in particular features, as the nose and ears – especially the ears – the hands and particularly the finger-nails. The nails are nearly as distinctive as the ears. If, added to these resemblances, there were similarities of voice and intonation and of gait and characteristic bodily movements, I should think that these agreements as a whole established a strong probability of blood relationship."

"That was Middlewick's view, though he did not present it in so much detail. I have always had rather strong doubts as to the significance of apparent personal likeness and I have recently met with a very striking case that serves to justify my rather sceptical attitude. I told Middlewick about it, but, of course he was not convinced, as I could not produce my example for his inspection."

"We aren't as unbelieving as Middlewick," said I. "Tell us about your case."

Brodribb fortified himself with a sip from his glass and smiled reminiscently. "It was an odd experience," said he, "and quite romantic in a small way. You remember my telling you about a visit that I paid with Sir Giles Farnaby to the studio of my friend and client, Miss Vernet?

"I remember. It was in connection with the adventure of the disappearing pickpocket in the convict suit."

"Yes, that was the occasion. Well, while Miss Vernet was assisting the police to search the premises, Sir Giles and I examined the picture that she was at work on. It was a large subject picture, called '*An Aristocrat at Bay*', showing a French noblewoman of the Revolution period standing in a doorway at the top of a flight of steps around which a hostile mob had gathered. Miss Vernet was apparently then working at the principal figure, for she had a model posed on the studio throne in the correct costume.

"Now, as soon as Sir Giles clapped eyes on the picture, he uttered an exclamation of surprise, and then he drew my attention to what he declared to be a most extraordinary coincidence. It seemed that the picture of the French lady was an exact counterpart of a portrait by

192

Romney that hangs in the small drawing-room at Bradstow, the architrave of the doorway representing the frame of the portrait. It was not only that the costume was similar and the pose nearly the same – there would have been nothing very astonishing in that, but he declared that the facial resemblance was so perfect that the figure in the picture might have been copied from the portrait. I wasn't able to confirm this statement at the time for, although I remembered the portrait and recognised the general resemblance, I hadn't his expert eye or his memory for faces. But what I could see was that the figure that Miss Vernet was painting was a most excellent likeness of the very handsome young lady who was posing on the throne.

"A few days later, however, I had to go down to Bradstow to see the bailiff and I then took the opportunity to have a good look at the portrait – which represented a Miss Isabel Hardcastle – and I assure you that Sir Giles's statement was absolutely correct. The figure in Miss Vernet's picture might have been a portrait of Isabel Hardcastle. But that figure, as I have said, was a perfectly admirable portrait of the young lady who was acting as the model."

"That is very interesting, Brodribb," said I. "Quite a picturesque incident as you say. But what is it supposed to prove?"

Brodribb looked at me fiercely. "The testimony of a reputable eye-witness," said he, "is good enough for a court of law. But apparently you won't accept anything short of the production in evidence of the actual things, the portrait, the picture, and the model. Must see them with your own eyes."

"Not at all," I protested. "I am not contesting your facts. It is your logic that I object to, unless I have misunderstood you. I ask again, what is your instance supposed to prove?"

"It proves," Brodribb replied severely, "that your theory – and Thorndyke's and Middlewick's – that personal resemblance is evidence of blood-relationship, is not supported by observed facts. Here is a portrait of Isabel Hardcastle, by a famous painter and presumably like her, and here is a young lady, the model, a perfect stranger, who is exactly like that portrait, and therefore, presumably, exactly like Isabel Hardcastle."

"But," I objected, "you have only proved half of your case. What evidence have you that this young lady – Miss Vernet's model – is not a blood-relation of Isabel Hardcastle?"

Brodribb turned as red as a lobster (boiled) and began to gobble like a turkey. Then, suddenly, he stopped and gazed at me with his mouth slightly open.

"Yes," he said, "I suppose you are right, Jervis. Of course I was taking that for granted."

With this he let the argument drop and seemed to lose interest in the subject, for he sat sipping his wine with a profoundly reflective air but speaking no word. After sitting thus for some time, he roused himself by a visible effort and, having emptied his glass, rose to take his leave. But even as he shook our hands and moved towards the door, I had the impression that he was still deep in thought, and I seemed to detect in his bearing a certain something suggestive of a settled purpose.

"I am afraid, Jervis," said Thorndyke, as our friend's footsteps died away on the stairs, "you have given Brodribb a sleepless night and perhaps sent him off to explore a mare's nest. I hope he has not taken you too seriously."

"If you come to that," I retorted, "you are the real offender. It was you who tried to prove that ancestral characteristics might reappear after several generations – and you didn't do it."

"No," he admitted, "the argument came to a premature end. Mendelian factors were too much for Brodribb. But it is an interesting problem, I mean the question as to the number of factors that go to the making of a recognisable personality and the possibilities of their transmission. The idea of a more-or-less complete re-incarnation is attractive and romantic, though I am afraid that the laws of chance don't offer much encouragement. But to return to Brodribb, I deeply suspect that you have sent him off in search of a re-incarnated Isabel Hardcastle. I only hope that he won't be too seriously disappointed."

"I hope so, too. When I saw how he took my objection, I was sorry I had spoken, for poor old Brodribb would give his eyes to discover some hitherto unknown Hardcastle whose claim he could set up against that of the present heir presumptive, though I don't see that a young lady would help him, seeing that the settlement is *in tail male*."

"No, but he is probably looking farther afield. We may safely assume the existence of at least one male relative, alive or dead."

"Yes, she certainly must have, or have had, a father. But there again one doesn't see any loophole for Brodribb. There can't be any unknown members of the family nearer to Sir Edward than David Hardcastle, unless he is thinking of the elusive Gervase. Perhaps he is."

"I have no doubt that he is," said Thorndyke, "and I wish him luck, though it doesn't look like a very hopeful quest. But time will show."

In effect, time did show and the time was not very long. Our suspicions as to Brodribb's activities were fully justified. He had "gone a-angling", but the fish that he landed was as great a surprise to himself as to us.

The news reached us four days after the conversation which I have recorded. It was brought by him in person, and even before he spoke, we knew by the way in which he danced into the room, fairly effervescing with excitement, that something of more than common import had happened.

"Congratulate me, gentlemen!" he exclaimed. "I have made a discovery, thanks to Jervis's confounded leg-pulling."

He flopped down in a chair and, when we had made suitable demonstrations of curiosity, he continued, "I have been making enquiries about the young lady who was posing as the Aristocrat for Miss Vernet."

"Ah!" I exclaimed. "And who is she?"

"That I can't say exactly at the moment. But, to begin with, *she* is a *he*. The young lady turns out to be a boy."

"Ha!" said I, "we smell a mystery."

"You smell the solution of a mystery," he corrected. "The young lady is not only *a* boy. She is *the* boy."

"The boy?" Thorndyke repeated enquiringly.

"Yes, *the* boy. The disappearing pickpocket. The gentleman in the convict suit. The police were quite right, after all. He had popped in through the open studio window. But I had better begin the story at the beginning.

"It appears that this lad – Jasper Gray by name – is employed by a firm of wholesale stationers, Sturt and Wopsalls, to deliver parcels. He seems to be a highly respectable youth – "

"With a secret pocket in the back of his waistcoat," I murmured.

"Yes, that is a queer feature, I must admit," said Brodribb. "But both the ladies seem to have the highest opinion of his character."

"Plausible young rascal, I expect," I said. "Naturally, he would be able to bamboozle a pair of innocent spinsters."

"That is quite possible," Brodribb admitted, "and he is certainly most unusually good-looking. I saw that, for myself, though the wig and the costume may have helped. But to continue, he came to the studio to deliver a roll of paper, and Miss Vernet was so struck with his appearance that she persuaded him to pose for the principal figure in her picture. It was a regular arrangement. He came and took up the pose every morning before going to work.

"Now you see how the escape was managed: When he found himself in the Tottenham Court Road in a prison suit, he simply made a bee-line for the studio. He knew about the open window and made straight for it and sprang in. Then the two women bundled him into the dressing-room where he made a quick change into his costume. They hid the prison clothes and he took up his pose on the throne. By the time the police arrived he had become transformed into a lady of the old noblesse. It was a delightful comedy. Now I can appreciate the solemn way in which Miss Vernet conducted the two unsuspecting constables over the premises to search for the missing convict."

"Can you?" said I, with mock severity. "I am surprised at you, Brodribb, a respectable solicitor, chortling over a manifest conspiracy to defeat the ends of justice. You are not forgetting that secret pocket or the fact that Sir Edward Hardcastle's seal was found in it?"

"Of course I am not," he replied. "That is the importance of the discovery. I expect he picked the seal up, though as you say, there is the secret pocket to be accounted for. But we shall soon know all about it. Miss Vernet has arranged for him to meet me at the studio the day after to-morrow. He was quite willing and he is prepared to tell me anything I want to know. I suggested that you might come with me and there was no objection to that, so I hope you will be able to come. It ought to be quite interesting to us all. What do you say?"

There was no doubt in my mind as to what Thorndyke would say, for, evidently, this young scallywag was one of the indispensable missing links.

"I will come with you with the greatest pleasure," he replied, "and no doubt Jervis will come too and add to the gaiety of the proceedings."

"Good," said Brodribb. "I will let Miss Vernet know." And with this he took his departure with an appearance of satisfaction that seemed to me to be somewhat disproportionate to the results of his embassy, for, whereas to us the tracing of the seal held untold potentialities of enlightenment, to Brodribb it could appear no more than a matter of curious and trivial interest.

"Yes," Thorndyke agreed when I commented on Brodribb's remarkable self-complacency. "I had the same impression. Believing as he does that Sir Edward made away with himself, he can have no reason for attaching any special significance to the fact that the seal was in the lad's possession. But he is obviously extremely pleased with himself, and I suspect we shall find that he has not disclosed to us the whole of his discovery. But we shall see."

And in due course we did see.

Chapter XIV
New Light on the Problem
(Jasper Gray's Narrative)

It was while I was carrying out some improvements on the studio skylight that Miss Vernet made her momentous communication. Of course, she didn't know that it was momentous. Neither did I. You never do. Providence has a way of keeping these little surprises up its sleeve and letting them fly at you when you are looking the other way.

But it was not only her communication that held such unsuspected potentialities. My very occupation, trivial and commonplace as it appeared, was fraught with a hidden significance which it was presently to develop together with that of other seemingly trifling actions.

At the moment, I was standing on the top of a rickety pair of steps which Miss Vernet was anxiously steadying while I fastened a rope to a swinging fan light. Hitherto that fan-light had been clumsily adjusted from below with the aid of a sort of boat-hook. Now, by means of the rope and a cleat on the wall, it could be conveniently set at any angle and securely fixed.

As I came down the steps, having completed the job, Miss Vernet murmured her thanks, mingled with expressions of admiration at the ingenuity of the arrangement. Then, after a pause, she said a little hesitatingly, "I have a confession to make, Jasper. I hope you won't be angry, but I have to a certain extent broken your confidence."

I looked at her in surprise but made no comment. There was nothing to say until I knew what she meant, so I waited for her to continue.

"Do you remember Mr. Brodribb?" she asked.

"I think so," I replied. "Isn't he the gentleman with beautiful silky white hair who came with Sir Giles to look at your picture?"

"Yes," she said eagerly. "I am glad you remember him. Well, for some reason, he is greatly interested in you. He came here yesterday on purpose to ask me about you. He put quite a lot of questions, which, of course, I couldn't answer, but I did let out about your coming here in those prison clothes."

"Is that all?" I exclaimed. "What does it matter? I don't mind his knowing. I don't care who knows now that the affair is over and we have sent the clothes back." (I had addressed the parcel myself to the Governor of Pentonville Prison and delivered it in person at the gate.)

She was obviously relieved at my attitude, but I could see that there was something more to come.

"I don't know why he is so concerned about you," she continued, "but he assures me that his interest is a proper and legitimate interest and not mere curiosity. He would very much like to meet you and ask you one or two questions. He thinks that you might be able to give him some information that would be very valuable and helpful to him. Do you think you would mind meeting him here one day?"

"Of course I shouldn't. Why should I? But I think he must be mistaken if he thinks I could tell him anything that would matter to him."

"Well, that is his affair," said she, "and naturally you won't tell him anything that you don't want to. I am sure, when you meet him, you will like him very much. Everybody does."

Accordingly we proceeded to arrange the date of the meeting which was fixed for the ensuing Thursday afternoon, subject to my obtaining leave of absence from Sturt and Wopsalls, and then, as an afterthought, Miss Vernet mentioned that Mr. Brodribb would like to bring a friend and fellow lawyer with him. This sounded rather portentous, but I made no objection, and when I went away (having secured the rope on its cleat) I left Miss Vernet happy in having success fully carried out the negotiations on Mr. Brodribb's behalf.

Sturt and Wopsalls raised no difficulties about the afternoon off, it being the first time that I had ever made such a request. I cleared up most of the deliveries in a strenuous morning, and, having made myself as presentable as the resources of my wardrobe permitted, presented myself at the studio punctually at three o'clock in the afternoon. I was the first arrival and thereby was enabled to assist the two ladies in setting out a tea-table that made my mouth water, and I was amused to observe that, of the three, I was the only one who was not in a most almighty twitter.

But even my self-possession sustained a slight jar when the visitors arrived, for Mr. Brodribb had gone beyond the contract and brought two friends with him – both, as I assumed, lawyers. But it appeared that I was mistaken, for it turned out that they were doctors. And yet, later, it seemed as if they were lawyers. It was rather confusing. However, they were all very agreeable gentlemen and they all addressed me as "Mr. Gray", which caused me to swell with secret pride and induced in Miss Brandon a tendency to giggles.

One thing which astonished me was their indifference to the delicacies with which the table was loaded. I had seen such things in pastry cooks' windows and had wondered sometimes if they tasted as well as they looked. Now I knew. The answer was in the affirmative. But these gentlemen trifled negligently with those incredible cakes and pastries as if they had been common "tommy", and as for Mr. Brodribb he positively ate nothing at all. However, the delicacies weren't wasted. Miss Vernet knew my capacity for disposing of nourishment and kept a supply moving in my direction.

Of course, there were no questions asked while we were having tea. The gentlemen mostly talked with the ladies about pictures and painting and models, and very entertaining their conversation was, only I found myself wishing that Mr. Brodribb had taken something to eat to distract his attention from me. For whenever I glanced at him, I met his bright blue eye fixed on me with an intensity of interest that would have destroyed my appetite if the food had not been so unusually alluring. Not that he was the only observer. I was distinctly conscious that his two friends, Dr. Jervis and Dr. Thorndyke, were "taking stock of me", as our packer would express it, but they didn't devour me with their eyes as Mr. Brodribb did.

As the closing phases of the meal set in, the conversation turned from the subject of pictures and models in general to Miss Vernet's picture and her model in particular, and while the two ladies were clearing away, I was persuaded to go to the dressing-room and put on my costume for the visitors' entertainment. When I came forth and took up my pose on the throne, my appearance was greeted with murmurs of applause by all, but especially by Mr. Brodribb.

"It is perfectly amazing," he exclaimed. "I assure you Thorndyke, that the resemblance is positively photographic."

"Do you think," Dr. Thorndyke asked, "that you are making full allowance for the costume and the pose?

"I think so," Mr. Brodribb answered. "To me the facial resemblance seems most striking. I should like you to see the portrait for yourself. Nothing short of that I know will convince you."

"At any rate," said Dr. Thorndyke, "we can understand how those unfortunate constables were deluded. I am all agog to hear Mr. Gray's account of that comedy of errors."

On this hint I retired once more to shed my gorgeous plumage and when I returned to the studio, I found half-a-dozen chairs arranged and the audience in waiting.

"Now, Jasper," said Miss Vernet, "you understand that Mr. Brodribb wants you to tell us the story in full detail. You are not to leave anything out."

199

I grinned a little uncomfortably and felt my face growing hot and red. "There isn't much to tell," I mumbled, "I expect Miss Vernet has told you all there is."

"Never mind," said Mr. Brodribb, "we want the whole story. To begin with, what took you to the River Lea?"

I explained about the parcel and the railway journey, and having thus broken the ice, and got fairly started, I went on to recount the successive events of that day of mingled joy and terror, gradually warming to my task under the influence of the genuine interest and amusement that my audience manifested. So great was their appreciation that – my shyness being now quite dissipated – I was quite sorry when I had brought my adventures down to the moment when I changed into my costume and took up my pose. For that was the end of my story – at least I thought it was. But my legal friends soon undeceived me. The end of the story was the beginning of the cross-examination.

Mr. Brodribb started the ball. "When that convict ran off with your clothes, did he take anything of value with them? Anything in the pockets, I mean."

"Yes," I answered. "There was my return ticket in the trousers' pocket and an emerald in a secret pocket at the back of the waistcoat."

"An emerald?" said Mr. Brodribb.

"Well, it was a green stone of some kind and it must have come out of a signet ring, because it had a seal engraved on it, a little castle with a motto underneath – "*Strong in Defence*" – and above it the head of some sort of animal that looked rather like a crocodile."

"What is known in heraldry as a Wyvern, I think. Now would you recognise an impression of that seal?"

I assured him that I most certainly should, where upon he carefully extracted from a pocket letter-case an envelope on which was a black seal.

"Now," said he, handing it to me, "just look at that seal and tell me if you think it was made with the stone that you had."

I looked at the seal and glanced at the address on the envelope, and then I grinned.

"I am quite sure it was," I answered, "because I made it myself."

"The deuce you did!" exclaimed Mr. Brodribb. "How was that?"

I described the incident of the dropped letter and was rather surprised at the amount of amusement it created, for I didn't see anything particularly funny in it. But they did, especially Dr. Jervis, who laughed until he had to wipe his eyes.

"Excuse me, gentlemen," said he, "but the recollection of the great pow-wow in New Square was too much for me. Mr. Gray had us all guessing that time."

"Yes," chuckled Mr. Brodribb, "we were a trifle out of our depth, though I would remind you that Thorndyke gave us practically the correct solution. But now, I wonder if you would mind, Mr. Gray, telling us how that seal stone came into your possession?"

I had been expecting this question, and obviously it had got to be answered. For the seal had probably been stolen and I had to make it clear that it had not been stolen by me. It would not be enough merely to say that I had found it.

"I have no objection at all," said I, "but it is rather a long story."

"So much the better," said Dr. Jervis, "if it is as amusing as the last. But tell us the whole of it."

"Yes," urged Dr. Thorndyke, "begin at the beginning and don't be afraid of going into detail. We want to know all about that seal."

My recent experience in Pentecost Grove had completely cured me of any tendency to reticence. Here was an opportunity to expose that nest of criminals and I resolved to take it. Accordingly, in obedience to Dr. Thorndyke's directions, I began with the incident of the truck and the egg-chest and recounted in full detail all the adventures and perils of that unforgettable day.

"Bless the boy!" exclaimed Miss Vernet, as I described my entry into the egg-chest on the schooner's deck, "he is a regular Sinbad the Sailor! But don't let me interrupt."

She did interrupt, nevertheless, from time to time, with ejaculations of astonishment and horror. But what interested me especially was the effect of my story on the three men. They all listened with rapt attention, especially Dr. Thorndyke, and I had the feeling that they were comparing what I was telling them with something that they already knew. For instance, when I described Ebbstein's house and the work-room with the goose on the fire and the sour smell and the big tub of herrings and cabbage, Dr. Jervis seemed to start, and then he turned to Dr. Thorndyke, and looked at him in a most singular way. And Dr. Thorndyke caught his eye and nodded as if he understood that look.

When I came to my escape from Ebbstein's house I hesitated for a moment, being, for some reason, a little unwilling to tell them about Miss Stella. But I had promised to give them the whole story and I felt that perhaps this part, too, might mean more to them than it did to me. So I described the rescue in detail and related how we had escaped together. And very glad I was that I had not held anything back. For I could see at once by Dr. Jervis's manner and expression that there was more in my story than I had understood.

"I hope," Miss Vernet interrupted as I was describing the escape from the empty house, "that you didn't kill that unfortunate wretch. It would really have served him right, but still – "

"Oh, it's all right," I reassured her. "I didn't kill him. I've seen him since."

This statement Dr. Thorndyke noted in a book which he had produced from his pocket and in which I had observed him jotting down short notes from time to time with a view, as I discovered later, to cross-examination, and to avoid interrupting my narrative. He was evidently deeply interested – much more so, I noticed, than Mr. Brodribb, who, in fact, listened with an air of rather detached amusement.

I now went on to describe our meeting with the hansom, and at the mention of that vehicle and the driver's name, Louis, Dr. Jervis uttered an exclamation of surprise or excitement. But the climax, for me, came when I brought my story to a close with our arrival at Miss Stella's house. Then, in an instant, Mr. Brodribb's detached interest gave place to the most intense excitement. He sat up with a jerk and, having stared at me in astonished silence for a few moments, demanded, "Dorchester Square, you say? You don't remember the number, I suppose?"

"It was Number Sixty-three," I replied.

"Ha!" he exclaimed, and then, "You didn't happen to learn the young lady's name?"

"I heard the footman refer to her as Miss Stella."

"Ha!" said Mr. Brodribb again. Then he turned to Dr. Thorndyke and said in a low, deeply impressive tone, "Stella Hardcastle. Paul's daughter, you know."

Dr. Thorndyke nodded. I think he had already guessed who she was – and for a little while no one spoke. It was Mr. Brodribb who broke the silence. "I've been a fool, Thorndyke. For the first – and last – time, I have set my judgement against yours. And I was wrong. I see it plainly enough now. I only hope that my folly has not caused a fatal hindrance."

Dr. Thorndyke looked at him with an extraordinarily pleasant smile as he replied, "We assumed that you would alter your mind when some of the facts emerged, and we have been working on that assumption." Then, turning to me, he said, "I have quite a number of questions to ask you, Mr. Gray. First of all, about that rope. You mentioned that you threw it on the foot board of the cab. Did you leave it there?"

Now, I had already noticed Dr. Thorndyke looking rather hard, now and again, at the rope that hung from the skylight, so I wasn't surprised at his question. But what followed did surprise me most uncommonly.

"No," I answered. "I brought it away with me."

"And what has become of it?"

I grinned (for I was pretty sure that he had "ogled" it, as our packer would say), and pointed to the rope. "That is it," said I.

"The deuce it is!" exclaimed Dr. Jervis. "And a brown rope, too. This looks like another windfall, Thorndyke."

"It does," the latter agreed, and rising, he stepped over to the cleat and taking the two ends of the rope in his hands, looked at them closely. Then he brought a magnifying-glass out of his pocket and had a look at them through that.

"Were both of these ends whipped when you found the rope?" he asked as Dr. Jervis took the glass from him and examined the ends through it.

"No," I answered. "Only one end was whipped. I did the other end myself – the one with the white whipping."

He nodded and glanced at Dr. Jervis, who also nodded. Then he asked, "Do you think, Miss Vernet, that we might have this rope down to examine a little more completely?"

"But, of course," she replied. "Jasper will – "

I didn't hear the finish, for I was off, hot-foot for the steps. Evidently there was mystery in the air and it was a mystery that I was concerned with. I had the rope down in a twinkling and handed it to Dr. Thorndyke, who had just taken possession of the studio yard measure, which he now passed to Dr. Jervis.

"Measure the rope carefully, Jervis, and don't pull it out too taut."

I helped Dr. Jervis to take the measurement, laying the rope on the table and pulling it just taut but not stretching it, while Mr. Brodribb and the two ladies looked on, mightily interested and a good deal puzzled by the proceedings. When we had made the measurement, Dr. Jervis wrote the length down on a scrap of paper and then did the measurement over again with practically the same result. Then he laid the yard measure down and asked, "What do you say the length is, Thorndyke?"

"If the whole remainder is there," was the reply, "it should be forty-six feet, four-and-a-half inches."

"It is forty-six feet, five inches," said Dr. Jervis, "which we may take as complete agreement."

"Yes," said Dr. Thorndyke, "the difference is negligible. We may take it as certain that this is the remainder."

"The remainder of what?" demanded Mr. Brodribb. "I see that you have identified this rope. What does that identification tell you?"

"It tells us," Dr. Thorndyke replied, "that this rope was stolen from Black Eagle Dock, Wapping, when it was sixty feet long, that a piece thirteen feet, seven inches long was cut off it, that that piece was taken in a two-wheeled vehicle – probably a hansom cab – on the night of Sunday, the twenty-first of June, to Number Five, Piper's Row, Stratford. Those facts emerge from the identification of this rope, from Mr. Gray's story and from certain other data that we have accumulated."

"Good God!" exclaimed Mr. Brodribb. "Then this was the very rope! Horrible, horrible! But, my dear Thorndyke, you seem to have the whole of the case cut and dried! Can you give the villain a name?"

"We shall not mention names prematurely," he replied. "But we haven't finished with Mr. Gray yet. I think he has something more to tell us. Isn't it so? You said just now that you had seen the man whom you knocked on the head on some later occasion. Would you mind telling us about that?"

I didn't mind at all. On the contrary, I was only too delighted to put my new knowledge into such obviously capable hands. Therefore I embarked joyfully on a detailed narrative of my journey of exploration, to which Dr. Thorndyke listened with the closest attention, jotting down notes as I proceeded but never interrupting. Others, however, were less restrained, particularly Mr. Brodribb, who, when I had described the murderous attempt of the man with the knife, broke in excitedly, "You say that this man spoke in French to the other."

"Yes, and quite good French, too."

"Then we may take it that you understand French?"

"Yes, I speak French pretty fluently. You see, I was born in France or Belgium – I am not quite sure which – and we lived in France until I was nearly four. So French was the first language that I learnt. And my father speaks it perfectly, and we often converse in French to keep up our knowledge of the language."

He nodded as if the matter were quite important. Then he asked, "You say that this man accused you of having robbed him of a fortune?"

"Yes," and here I repeated the exact words that the man had used.

"Have you any idea what he meant?"

"Not the least. So far as I know, I had never seen him before."

"You didn't by any chance hear what his name was?"

"Yes, I did. He gave the name of Jacob Silberstein to the policeman. But that was not his name. I heard two of the people call him Mr. Zichlinsky."

At this Mr. Brodribb fairly exploded. I have never seen a man so excited. He spluttered two or three times as if he was going to speak, and then, whisking an envelope out of his pocket, scrawled something on it, and, apologising to the rest of us, passed it to Dr. Thorndyke, who glanced at it and handed it to Dr. Jervis, remarking, "This is extremely

204

valuable confirmation of what we had inferred. It seems definitely to establish the fact that Maurice Zichlinsky is in England – assuming this to be Maurice, of which I have little doubt."

Mr. Brodribb stared at him in astonishment. "How did you know that his name was Maurice?" he demanded.

"We have been looking into matters, you know," said Dr. Thorndyke. "But we mustn't interrupt Mr. Gray or he may overlook something important."

I had not, however, much more to tell, and when that little was told, I waited for the inevitable cross-examination.

"There are one or two points that I should like to have cleared up," said Dr. Thorndyke, glancing at his notes. "First, as to the cab that you saw in the yard. You seem to have had a good look at it. I wonder if you noticed anything unusual about the near wheel?"

"I noticed one thing," said I, "because I looked for it. There was a deep notch on the edge of the tyre. I fancy I made that notch when I bumped the cab over a sharp corner-stone. The tyre was worn very thin. I wonder that the jolt didn't break the wheel."

"It is a mercy that it didn't," said he. "However, the notch was what we wanted to know about. And now, as to the names and addresses of these people. Can you give us those?"

"The street that I went to is Pentecost Grove. Ebbstein, and Jonas, the coiner, live at Number Forty-nine. Gomorrah lives next door, Number Fifty, the house in which I found Miss Stella. Zichlinsky lives there, too. He lodges with Gomorrah. The cab-yard turns out of Pentecost Grove just opposite Ebbstein's house. It is called Zion Place. I don't know where Trout lives."

"He lives in Shadwell," said Dr. Thorndyke. "We have his address." On hearing which, Mr. Brodribb chuckled and shook his head. I think he found the doctor as astonishing as I did. He seemed to know everything. However, this seemed to finish the cross-examination, for Dr. Thorndyke now rose to depart and took leave of the ladies with polite acknowledgments of their hospitality. As he shook hands with me, he gave me a few directions concerning the rope.

"You had better put it away in a safe place," said he, "and remember that it is of the greatest value, as it will be produced in evidence in an important case. When the police take possession of it, which they will probably do very shortly, they will want you to certify to its identity. I will send you a rope to replace it for the skylight."

Finally, he took down my address in case he might have to write to me, and then he turned to Mr. Brodribb.

"You are not coming with us, are you?" he asked.

"No," replied Mr. Brodribb. "I want to have a few words with Mr. Gray on another matter. Perhaps, if he is going homeward, I may walk part of the way with him."

On this hint, I, too, made preparations for departure, and we issued forth together in the wake of the two doctors.

"I want you to understand," said Mr. Brodribb as we walked up the mews, "that I am not poking my nose into your affairs from mere curiosity. If I seem to ask impertinent questions, believe me I have very good reasons."

"I quite understand that, sir," said I, wondering what the deuce was coming next. Nothing came for a little while, but at length he opened fire.

"You mentioned just now that you lived abroad in your early childhood. Have you any recollection of how and where you lived?"

"Very little. I was quite a small child when we came to England. I remember seeing dogs harnessed in carts and I have a dim recollection of an old woman in a big white cap who used to look after us. I expect we were very poor, but a little child doesn't notice that."

"No," said Mr. Brodribb with a sigh. "There are many advantages in being young. You don't remember your mother?"

"No. She died when I was quite an infant. But she must have been a very good woman, for my father once said to me that she had been a saint on earth and was now an angel in heaven. I think he was very devoted to her."

Rather to my surprise, Mr. Brodribb appeared to be deeply moved by my reply. For some time he walked on in silence, but at length, he asked, "Did you ever hear what your mother's name was?"

"Yes. Her Christian name was Phillipa."

"Ha!" said Mr. Brodribb in a tone of deep significance, and I wondered why. But I was quite prepared for his next question. "Your father, I take it, is a man of considerable education?"

"Oh, yes, sir. He is quite a learned man. He is a classical tutor – crams fellows for examinations in classics and mathematics."

"Do you happen to know if he was always a tutor, or if he ever had any other vocation?"

"I have an idea," said I, "that he was at one time a clergyman."

"Yes. Probably. Clergymen often do become tutors. You haven't any idea, I suppose, why he abandoned his vocation as a clergyman?"

I hesitated. I didn't like the thought of disclosing poor old Ponty's failings, but I remembered what Mr. Brodribb had said. And, obviously, there was something behind these questions.

"I suppose, sir," I said, at length, "there is no harm in my confiding in you. The fact is that my father is not very careful in the matter of stimulants. He doesn't ever get intoxicated, you know, but he sometimes takes a little more than would be quite good for a clergyman. I expect it is due to the rather dull, lonely life that he leads."

"No doubt, no doubt," said Mr. Brodribb, speaking with a singular gentleness. "I have noticed that classical tutors frequently seem to feel the need of stimulants. And it is, as you say, a dull life for a man of culture."

He paused, and seemed to be in a little difficulty, for after an interval he resumed in a slightly hesitating manner, "I have a sort of idea – rather vague and indefinite – but I have the feeling that I may have been slightly acquainted with your father many years ago, and I should very much like, if it could be managed, to see whether my memory is or is not playing me false. I don't suppose your father cares much for encounters with strangers?"

"No, he does not. He is extremely reserved and solitary."

"Exactly. Now if I could get an opportunity of seeing him without making any formal occasion – just a casual inspection, you know, even by passing him in the street – "

"I think you might have a chance now, sir," said I. "He has a teaching appointment from four to six on Thursdays and usually comes straight home. It is now a few minutes to six, so if we step out, we shall probably meet him. If we do, I will point him out to you and then you would like me to leave you, I expect."

"If you don't mind, I think it would be better," said he, "and if I may make a suggestion, it would be as well, for the present, if you made no mention of this conversation or of your having met me."

I had already reached this conclusion and said so, and for a while we walked on at a slightly quickened pace in silence. As we crossed the top of Queen Square by the ancient pump that stands in the middle of the crossing, I began to keep a sharp look-out, for Ponty was now due, and we had hardly crossed to the corner of Great Ormond Street when I saw the familiar figure turn in from Lamb's Conduit Street and come creeping along the pavement towards us.

"That is my father, sir," said I, "that old gentleman with the stoop and the walking-stick."

"I see," said Mr. Brodribb. "He has something under his arm."

"Yes," I answered, and there being no use in blinking the fact, I added, "I expect it is a bottle. Good evening, sir."

He shook my hand warmly and I ran on ahead and dived into our entry. But I didn't run up the stairs. A reasonable and natural curiosity impelled me to linger and see what came of this meeting. For some thing told me that Mr. Brodribb could, if he chose, enlighten the mystery of my father's past on which I had often vaguely speculated, and that these present proceedings might not be without some significance for me.

From the entry I watched the two men approach one another and I thought they were going to pass. But they did not. Mr. Brodribb halted and accosted Ponty, apparently to ask for some direction, for I saw my father point with his stick. Then, instead of going on his way, Mr. Brodribb lingered as if to ask some further questions. A short conversation followed – a very short one. Then the two old gentlemen bowed to one another ceremoniously and separated. Mr. Brodribb strode away down the street and Pontifex came creeping homeward more slowly than ever with his chin on his breast and something rather dejected in his manner.

He made no reference to the meeting when he entered the room, whither I had preceded him, but silently placed the bottle on the mantelpiece. He was very thoughtful and quiet that evening, and the matter of his thoughts did not appear to be exhilarating. Indeed he seemed to be in such low spirits that I found myself wishing that Mr. Brodribb had taken less interest in our affairs. And yet, as I watched poor old Pontifex despondently broaching the new bottle, my thoughts kept drifting back to that meeting and those few words of conversation, and again the suspicion would creep into my mind that perhaps the shadows of coming events were already falling upon me.

Chapter XV
Thorndyke's Plan of Attack
(Dr. Jervis's Narrative)

"A most astonishing experience, Thorndyke," I commented as we walked away from Miss Vernet's studio after our meeting with Jasper Gray (recorded above in his own words).

"Yes," he agreed, "and not the least astonishing part of it was the boy himself. A truly Olympian errand boy. I have never seen anything like him."

"Nor have I. As an advertisement of democracy, he would be worth his weight in gold to a propagandist. If he could be seen strolling across the quadrangle of an Oxford College, old-fashioned persons would point him out as a type of the young British aristocrat. Yet the amazing fact is that he is just a stationer's errand boy."

Thorndyke chuckled. "I am afraid, Jervis," said he, "that as a demonstration of the essential equality of men he would fail, as demonstrations of that kind are apt to do on going into particulars. Our young friend's vocabulary and accent and his manners and bearing, while they fit his personal appearance well enough, are quite out of character with his ostensible social status. There is some mystery in his background. But we needn't concern ourselves with it, for I can see that Brodribb's curiosity is at white heat. We can safely leave the private enquiries to him."

"Yes. And I suspect that he is pursuing them at this moment. But speaking of Brodribb, I think you rather took his breath away. He was positively staggered at the amount of knowledge that you disclosed. And I don't wonder. He was hardly exaggerating when he said that you had the whole case cut and dried."

"I wouldn't put it so high as that," said Thorndyke. "We can now be confident that we shall lay our hands on the murderer – but we haven't done it yet. We have advanced our investigations another stage and I think the end is in sight. But we have yet another stage before us."

"It is surprising," I remarked, "how our knowledge of the case has advanced step by step, almost imperceptibly."

"It is," he agreed, "and an intensely interesting experience it has been, to watch it closing in from the vaguest generalities to the most complete particularity. We began with a purely speculative probability of murder. Then the murder became an established fact and its methods and procedure ascertained. But the perpetrators remained totally unknown to us and even unguessed at. Then, as you say, step by step, our knowledge advanced. One figure after another came into view, first as mere contacts with the known circumstances, then as possible suspects, until at last we seem to have the whole group in view and can begin to assign to each his place in the conspiracy."

"It seems to me," said I, "that Jasper Gray's information should help us to do that off-hand."

"It is extremely valuable," he replied. "But the enormous importance of what he has told us is really tactical. He has placed an invaluable weapon in our hands."

"What weapon do you mean?" I asked.

"I mean the power to make an arrest whenever we please. And that, when the moment comes, will be the very keystone of our tactics."

"I don't quite see either point – how we have the power or what special value it is. You wouldn't suggest an arrest before you are prepared to prove the murder charge against a definite person."

"But that, I suspect, is precisely what we shall have to do. Let me explain. The abduction of Miss Hardcastle is a new fact. It is very illuminating to us, but we can't prove that it was connected with the murder of Sir Edward. Nevertheless, it is a crime, and we actually know two of the guilty parties, Shemrofsky and Gomorrah. With Gray's assistance, we could lay a sworn information now, and on his and Miss Stella's evidence, we could secure a conviction. Of course, we shall not do anything of the kind. We have got to make sure of the woman who lured the girl away. Brodribb evidently suspects that she is Mrs. David Hardcastle – at least that is what I gathered when he wrote down her maiden name, Marie Zichlinsky, for our information – and I think he is probably right. You remember that she had a brother who was convicted in Russia of a conspiracy to murder. He also thinks that the Zichlinsky who tried to murder Gray is that brother. And again I suspect that he is right.

"But these are only suspicions, and we cannot rush into action on suspicions. We have to prove them right or wrong. If we can turn our suspicions into demonstrable truths, we shall have our whole case complete and can act at once and with confidence."

"Then what do you propose to do?"

"First, I propose to settle the question, if I can, as to whether the Zichlinsky of Pentecost Grove is the Maurice Zichlinsky whose finger-prints are in the records at Scotland Yard. If he is the same man, I shall then try to ascertain if the convict, Maurice Zichlinsky, is Mrs. David Hardcastle's brother."

"But I understood Brodribb to say that he was."

"So did I," said Thorndyke. "But I must get a categorical statement with particulars as to the date of the extradition proceedings. If Brodribb can confirm his implied statement, then I shall have to test our suspicion that the woman who managed the abduction of Miss Stella was Marie Zichlinsky, alias Mrs. David Hardcastle."

"You will have your work cut out," I remarked. "I don't see how you are going to prove either proposition."

"There are no insuperable difficulties in identifying the woman," he replied, "though I have not yet made a definite plan. As to Zichlinsky, I shall ask Singleton to re-examine our finger-print."

"But he has already said that he can't identify it."

"That was not quite what I understood. I gathered that he recognised the print, but then rejected his identification on extrinsic evidence. He realised that a man who is in a Russian prison cannot make a finger-print in London. But if I re-submit the print with the information that the man is believed to be in London and that there are circumstances which make it probable that the print was made by him, we may get an entirely different report, especially if I have previously communicated the facts to Miller."

I laughed with malicious glee. "Really, Thorndyke," I chuckled, "I am surprised at you! Actually, you are going to set Miller on to ginger-up Singleton and induce him to swear to a doubtful finger-print. And this after all your professions of scepticism regarding finger-print evidence!"

"My dear Jervis," he replied with an indulgent smile, "let us be reasonable. If this finger-print conforms in pattern to the one at the Record Office, it is Zichlinsky's finger-print. There is no question of forgery. It is obviously a real finger-print. The only problem is its identity of pattern. And we are not proposing to ask for a conviction on it. We shall use it merely to enable us to secure the person of Zichlinsky and charge him with the crime. Nor need you be uneasy about Singleton. He won't swear to the print unless he is prepared to prove its identity in court, factor by factor, on an enlarged photograph."

"No, I suppose he won't. But what plan of action is in your mind? Assuming that all our suspicions are confirmed, including the finger-print, what do you propose to do?"

"I propose to make arrangements with Miller that the whereabouts of each of the parties shall be ascertained and an overwhelming force kept ready for action at a moment's notice. Then, at the appointed time, we shall swoop down on the whole crowd simultaneously – Mrs. David,

211

Zichlinsky, Gomorrah, Shemrofsky, Ebbstein, and, if it seems practicable, James Trout."

"But," I protested, "you could never charge all these people with the murder. The magistrate would insist on your making out a *prima facie* case, and you couldn't do it."

"No," he replied. "But that is where Jasper Gray's information is so invaluable. We don't need a prima facie case for the charge of murder against any of these persons, excepting Zichlinsky. And in his case, the finger-print, which we are assuming to be provable, will be enough. In all the other cases, we shall proceed on different charges, on which we can make out a *prima facie* case. Mrs. David, Gomorrah and Shemrofsky will be charged with the abduction. Ebbstein – against whom we have nothing but deep suspicion – will be roped in as an accessory of the felonious proceedings of his lodger, Mr. Jonas, the ingenious manufacturer of half-crowns. As to Trout, I am not sure whether we can get him on suspicion of having stolen the rope. I should like to. He would be extremely useful. I must see what Miller thinks about it."

"But when you have got all these people by the heels? What then?"

"Ah, then we shall allow the subject of the murder to leak out, and it will be remarkable if, among this gang of rascals, there is not at least one who will be prepared to volunteer a statement. Take the case of Shemrofsky – he was probably a principal in the second degree as to the murder. It is unlikely that he took part in the actual killing, and if he did not, he will probably be very willing to clear himself of the major charge by giving evidence as to who actually committed the murder. Again there is Trout. He probably selected the house at Stratford. He probably stole the rope, and the fisherman's bend and the running bowline look like his work. He is an associate of Gomorrah's, but it is very unlikely that he had a hand in the murder. If he could be charged, he would almost certainly make for safety by putting the onus on the shoulders of the actual murderers."

"It seems a rather unsatisfactory method," I objected. "You are going to depend very largely on bluff."

"It is unsatisfactory," Thorndyke admitted, "but what else can we do? We know that these people conspired together to commit the murder. One or more of them *did* actually commit the murder. The rest are principals in the second degree. The only proceeding open to us is to charge them all and let them sort themselves out."

"But supposing they don't sort themselves out? What can you prove independently?"

"Let us see," he answered, "what sort of case we could make out. I am assuming that Singleton can identify the finger-print and that Stella and Gray can identify Mrs. David, because without that evidence we should not proceed at all. We should require further investigation. But, assuming those identifications, we shall proceed somewhat thus:

"First, we charge Mrs. David, Shemrofsky, and Gomorrah with the abduction, and observe that we here bring into evidence the motive – the elimination of the principal beneficiary under Sir Edward's will, with reversion to the husband of Mrs. David. That charge we can prove conclusively.

"We then charge the whole group with conspiracy to commit murder. Here, again, the motive comes into view. The murder of Sir Edward leaves – or is believed to leave – the succession to the property and title open to the husband of Mrs. David."

"What about David, himself?"

"At present he doesn't seem to come into the picture, though naturally he lies under suspicion of complicity. We have no direct evidence against him. But to continue. The abduction, with its apparent motive, connects itself with the murder, of which the motive is similar. Mrs. David stands to gain by the success of both crimes. But we have proved her to be guilty of one of the crimes. This is presumptive evidence of her guilt in respect of the other crime, since the two crimes appear to be parts of the same transaction. Then the evidence against Zichlinsky operates against her since he is her brother and has no motive excepting that of benefiting her.

"Gomorrah is implicated by the facts that the rope used to hang the deceased is known to have been in his possession, that Zichlinsky was his lodger, that he is proved to have been concerned in the abduction, and was therefore a confederate of Mrs. David.

"Shemrofsky was concerned in the abduction and is thus implicated in the conspiracy. We can bring weighty evidence to prove that he was at Piper's Row on the night of Sunday, the twenty-first of June, and that he assisted to convey the body of the victim to that house.

"Zichlinsky is proved, by his finger-print, to have been in the Stratford house and to have handled the chair. He is Mrs. David's brother and so stands to benefit, indirectly, by the deaths of Stella and Sir Edward. His statement, overheard by Jasper Gray, would be admitted as evidence of his being an interested party.

"As to Trout, all that is actually against him is his connection with the rope. But, if the police could definitely connect him with the neighbourhood at Stratford, that would be a material point. The importance of getting him charged is that, although he was almost certainly an accessory, it is most improbable that he had any hand in the murder, and from what Gray has told us as to his efforts to restrain

Zichlinsky and Gomorrah, we may suspect that he disapproved of their violent proceedings and would not be prepared to take any risk in shielding them. He is really an outsider of the gang."

"Well," I said, "you have a better case than I thought, though it isn't up to your usual standard."

"No," he admitted, "but it is the best that we can do. And probably we shall get some further detail. We have not yet ascertained how much Miss Stella will be able to enlarge our knowledge. But, in any event, we have a substantial case to start with. We can prove the fact of the murder and the conveyance of the body to the house at Stratford, and by means of the rope, we can definitely connect this group of persons with the crime. Moreover, we can prove that one, at least, of those persons had a very strong motive for committing the murder and was known to have committed another crime – the abduction – apparently with the same motive."

"To say nothing," said I, "of the fact that the circumstances of the abduction strongly suggest an intention to commit another murder."

"Exactly," he agreed. "Zichlinsky's remark that he had been robbed of a fortune makes that fairly clear."

"I suppose," said I, after a pause, "that you now have a tolerably complete picture in your mind as to the actual course of events?"

"Yes," he replied. "Of course, it is largely inferential, but I think I can reconstruct the whole crime in outline with considerable confidence that my reconstruction is broadly correct. Perhaps it would be helpful to go over it and see exactly what we shall have to prove."

"It would be extremely helpful to me," I said, "seeing that it is, in effect, the case for the prosecution."

"Then," said he, "we will begin quite at the beginning and adopt the narrative style to save words. First some communication was made to Sir Edward, probably verbally and probably by some confidential envoy of Mrs. David's, begging him to grant an interview to some person who was unable to come to him. This person may have been her brother, who, being a fugitive from Russia, might naturally be in hiding and might be living in an otherwise unlikely neighbourhood. Sir Edward consented, with some misgivings, as we may judge from Weeks's description of his preoccupied state when he left home. It was arranged that Mrs. David should meet him with a hansom at an appointed place near his club and convey him to the place where the person was living. The approximate whereabouts of this person's place of abode was mentioned, as suggested by Sir Edward's precautions in leaving his valuables at the club, which also suggests that he was not without suspicions as to the nature of the transaction.

"On his arrival at Pentecost Grove, in Shemrofsky's cab, he was introduced to Zichlinsky and, probably almost at once, the attack was made on him. I am disposed to think that the original intention was to hang him, but that, suddenly during the struggle, it became necessary to silence him. A knock on the head was not practicable as it would have produced a recognisable injury, and made the pretence of suicide untenable. The alternative, adopted on the spur of the moment, was to thrust his head into the brine tub, and this having been done, he was held there until he was dead."

"They must have been savage brutes!" I exclaimed. "But their savagery was their undoing. If they had hanged him, it would have been difficult to prove the murder, if not impossible."

"Hardly impossible, Jervis," said he. "You will remember that we had virtually decided against suicide before we saw the body. And then there were the shoes and the wheel-tracks. Still, the drowning made the case much more conclusive."

"By the way," said I. "You mentioned that you had a hypothetical explanation of the salt and the herring scales. Was it a brine tub that was in your mind?"

"It occurred to me as a possibility, and the only one I could think of. I happened to know that it is the habit of low-class East European aliens to keep in their living or working rooms a tub of brine containing herrings and cut cabbage. The crime seemed to be associated with that part of London in which colonies of these people are settled, and it had a certain crude atrocity that was unlike English crime. Then the appearances agreed with this supposition and with no other. The man had been drowned, but only his head and neck had been wetted. He might have been held over the side of a boat or a landing-stage, but that theory would not account for the salt and the herring scales. But a receptacle containing salt water and herrings met the conditions exactly. And that little shred of cabbage gave strong confirmation. Still, it was only a hypothesis, and even now it is but an inference. It remains to be proved."

"I don't think there is much doubt of it," said I, "though it had never occurred to me. Of course, when Jasper Gray mentioned the tub of herrings and cabbage floating in brine, the explanation came in a flash. But go on with your reconstruction."

"There isn't much more to say. The body was kept at Gomorrah's house – or Ebbstein's, whichever it was. Ebbstein's house fits the conditions perfectly but Gomorrah's is probably exactly similar – until Sunday night, perhaps because then there would be fewer people about down by the creeks. Then one man – probably Trout – was sent on ahead to get the house open and see that all was clear. The body was put into

215

Shemrofsky's cab – probably it was placed upright, sitting on the seat – and accompanied by one of the murderers, who was almost certainly Zichlinsky. Then, as it had been a wet evening, the glass front could be let down without appearing remarkable, and the two occupants, the living and the dead, would thus be practically invisible from the outside.

"On the arrival of the cab at the house, the advance man – call him Trout – would give the signal 'all clear' and the body and the rope would then be quickly carried in by him and Zichlinsky. Probably Trout made the rope fast to the beam and prepared the noose while Zichlinsky held up the body. As soon as it was suspended, they would turn the chair over and make the other arrangements. Then they would go into the front room, open the window, and drop the glove under it. Finally, they would look out to see that there was no one about and then come away and make for the rendezvous where Shemrofsky would be waiting for them with his cab. Or he may have driven straight home, leaving them to follow on foot or in an omnibus.

"That is how I think the plan was carried out, and that is the account that I shall give to Miller as the basis of enquiries and of such questions as he may think fit to put to the prisoners."

"And what do you propose to do at the moment?"

"My first proceeding," he replied, "will be to see Miller and try to get the finger-print question settled. Then I shall consult with Brodribb as to the best way of ascertaining whether the woman who captured Miss Stella was or was not Mrs. David Hardcastle. I have a plan in my mind, but as it involves Brodribb's co-operation, I can't decide on it until I have secured his agreement."

"My impression is," said I, "that Brodribb will agree gladly to anything that you may suggest."

"That is my impression, too," said Thorndyke. And subsequent events proved that we were both right.

Chapter XVI
Mrs. David Hardcastle
(Jasper Gray's Narrative)

My premonitions of some impending change in the conditions of my life, dimly associated with Mr. Brodribb, were revived some days later when I saw that gentleman coming out of our office in earnest conversation with Mr. Wopsall. The apparition caused me some surprise, and when Mr. Wopsall beckoned to me, I came forward with alacrity, bubbling over with curiosity.

"You are going off duty for a day or two, Gray," said Mr. Wopsall. "Mr. Brodribb wants you to attend at his office to-morrow and perhaps afterwards. He will give you your instructions, and you will understand that they have my full concurrence, and I need hardly suggest that you smarten yourself up a bit and try to do us credit."

With this he shook hands with Mr. Brodribb and retired to his office, leaving us together, and we drifted out into the street to pursue our business. However, he had not much to say. In effect, he wished me to present myself at his abode in New Square, Lincoln's Inn, punctually at ten o'clock on the following morning, when he would give me more detailed instructions, and having delivered himself of this request and satisfied himself of my ability to find my way to his office, he shook my hand warmly and went his way with an air of deep satisfaction.

As he had given me no hint as to the nature of the business on hand, it was natural that I should spend the remainder of the day in speculating with the most intense curiosity on the circumstances that called for my presence in a place so remote from the scene of my customary activities, and it was equally natural that I should make my appearance in the place of assignation with more than common punctuality. Indeed, the word "punctuality" understates the case for, although I had spent a full hour operating on my clothes with a sponge, a nail-brush, and a flat iron, I strolled into the Square from Chancery Lane at the moment when the hands of the big clock showed a quarter-past-nine. (I say "the hands" advisedly, for the joker who put up that clock had omitted the figures on the dial, substituting for them a dozen exactly similar marks.)

I stood for some time inspecting that eccentric clock-face with mildly surprised interest. Then I transferred my attention to a fine peartree that some rural-minded lawyer had trained up the side of his house, and I was still contemplating this phenomenon when I became aware of a somewhat chubby gentleman in a broad-brimmed straw hat and slippers who was sauntering up the pavement smoking a very large pipe. At the moment, his head was inclined forward so that the hat-brim concealed his face, but as we approached, he raised his head, and, the hat ascending with it, disclosed the countenance of Mr. Brodribb.

"Ha!" he exclaimed as he caught sight of me, "You are a little before your time, which is a good fault, if that is not a contradiction of terms. The early bird catches the worm, as the rather ambiguous proverb has it – ambiguous, I mean, as to the moral to be conveyed. For while the early rising is obviously advantageous to the bird, it is obviously disadvantageous to the worm. He had better have stayed in bed a little longer. However, here you are, and it will be all to the good if we get our arrangements completed in advance."

He pulled out a prosperous-looking gold watch (apparently, he didn't trust the clock) and having looked at it thoughtfully, continued, "I shall want you to sit at a desk in my outer office, and you are to try to look as if you'd been there all your life. You are supposed to be one of my clerks. Do you understand?"

I assured him (but not in those words) that I "rumbled him", as our packer would say, and he went on, "I am expecting some visitors presently. They will come to the outer office and you will take down their names on a slip of paper and then come into my office and announce them. And while you are taking down their names, I should like you to have a good look at them so that you will be able to recognise them if you should see them again."

This sounded agreeably mysterious, and once more, I assured him – in suitable terms – that I "ogled" perfectly.

"If anyone asks you any questions," he continued, "be as evasive as you can. Don't give any information."

I remarked that I hadn't much to give, to which he replied that perhaps I had more than I realised. "But in any case," said he, "keep your own counsel. If they should ask you who you are, say you are my clerk."

"That won't be quite correct, sir," I ventured to remind him.

"Bless the boy!" he chuckled, "we aren't as particular as that in the law. But, in fact, you are my clerk. I appoint you to the post this very instant. Will that satisfy your scruples?"

I agreed that it would, though the appointment was obviously a legal fiction, and, the preliminaries being thus arranged, I was presently inducted into the outer office, of which I seemed to be the sole occupant, and installed at a handsome mahogany desk, furnished with blotting-pad, an inkstand with three ink bottles – black, green and red – a pile of paper slips, and a number of quill pens.

At ten o'clock precisely, Mr. Brodribb entered his private office and shut the door, and there descended on the premises a profound silence, through which I could hear faintly the sound of movement in the inner office with an occasional squeak of a quill pen, by which I judged that the communicating door was by no means sound-proof. But I discovered later that there was a second, baize-covered door which could be shut when required to ensure privacy.

The minutes ran on. Soon the novelty of the situation exhausted itself. I began to be bored by the continued occupancy of the leather-seated stool and to be sensible of a faint yearning for a parcel to deliver. Sitting still was well enough when one was tired, but it was no sort of occupation for an active youth at ten o'clock in the morning. However, it had to be, so failing any opportunity for physical exercise, I directed my attention to the quill pens and the three bottles of ink. I had never used a quill pen and had no considerable experience of coloured inks. Now I proceeded to make a few experiments and was greatly pleased with the results. Beginning with a spirited portrait of Mr. Gomorrah, I discovered the surprising potentialities of a polychromatic medium. The green ink enabled me to do full justice to his complexion, while the red ink imparted a convincing surgical quality to his bandaged head.

I was adding the finishing touches to this masterpiece of portraiture when I became aware of sounds penetrating the door – not Mr. Brodribb's door, but another which apparently gave access to an adjoining room. The sounds conveyed the impression of several persons moving about on an oil-clothed floor and were accompanied by the dragging of chairs. But after a short time these sounds died away, and I had just returned to my polychrome portrait when the crescendo music of a pair of creaky boots informed me that someone was approaching the outer door. A moment later, that door was flung open and a largish gentleman with a puffy face, not unadorned with pimples, stamped into the room, and having bestowed on me a disparaging stare, demanded, "Is Mr. Brodribb disengaged?"

I sprang up from my stool and spluttered at him ambiguously. Meanwhile he stood, holding the door open and looking out into the lobby.

"Come along!" he exclaimed impatiently addressing some person outside, whereupon the person addressed came along, and in a moment completed my confusion.

I recognised her instantly, which was the more remarkable since she was strikingly changed since I had last seen her, changed as to her

219

habiliments and even in her person, for then her hair had been jet black whereas now it was of a glaring red. But I knew her all the same. Hers was a face that no make-up could disguise. And if her hair had changed, her eyes had not, and now I saw why they had appeared different in colour. The pupil of the left eye, instead of being a round black spot, was drawn out to the shape of a key hole. Nor did her handsome clothing make any essential change in her appearance. From the moment when my glance fell on her as she entered the room, I never had the shadow of a doubt that she was the ill-omened nurse at whom I had peered through the gutter-hole in Pentecost Grove.

I suppose I must have gone even beyond Mr. Brodribb's instructions to "have a good look at" the visitors, for the odd silence was broken by her voice demanding angrily and with a faint foreign accent, "Well! What are you staring at me like that for?"

I mumbled a semi-articulate apology which she ignored, continuing, "Go at once to Mr. Brodribb and tell him that Mr. and Mrs. Hardcastle wish to see him."

I pulled myself together rapidly, but incompletely, and, dimly recalling Mr. Brodribb's directions concerning the slips of paper, I grabbed up the portrait of Gomorrah, and, blundering into his private office without knocking, slapped it down on his writing-table. He regarded it for a moment with a stupefied stare and then exclaimed, "What the dev – "

But at this point his eye caught the two visitors, who, waiving ceremony, now appeared in the doorway. He rose to receive them, and I hastily made my escape, leaving the door open, an omission the enormity of which I realised when I saw – and heard – Mr. Hardcastle ostentatiously slam it.

I crept back to my stool and drew a deep breath, conscious that I had made rather a hash of the business, so far. Well, every man to his trade. One couldn't expect the practice of parcels delivery to produce expertness in the duties of a lawyer's clerk. Still, I must manage the next visitors better, and having formed this resolution, I fell, naturally enough, into deep reflection on the astonishing thing that had just happened.

So this woman's name was Hardcastle. But Miss Stella's name was Hardcastle too. Very odd, this. They must be relatives, but yet they had seemed to be strangers, for Miss Stella had referred to her simply as "a woman." But at this point my train of thought was interrupted by Mr. Hardcastle's voice, penetrating the door. He was speaking in a loud, excited tone – not to say shouting – and I could hear quite distinctly what he was saying.

"But, damn it, Brodribb, the man is dead! Been dead a matter of fifteen years or more. You know that as well as I do."

There followed a sudden silence, and then I heard the thud of a closing door which I judged to be the baize inner door of Mr. Brodribb's office, a conclusion that was confirmed by the fact that, thereafter, Mr. Hardcastle's rather raucous voice percolated through only in a state of extreme attenuation. Even this I tried to ignore, and I had just resumed my speculations on the possible relationship of Mrs. Hardcastle and Miss Stella when I was rendered positively speechless by a new and even more astonishing arrival. For, without any warning of premonitory footfalls, the outer door opened softly and gave entrance to none other than Miss Stella herself.

She was not alone. Closely following her was a very pleasant-looking lady whom I judged, from a recognisable resemblance, to be her mother, and who asked me if Mr. Brodribb was at liberty. Before I could collect my wits to reply, Miss Stella uttered a little cry of surprise and ran to me holding out her hand.

"You haven't forgotten me, have you?" she asked, as I took her hand rather shyly.

"No, indeed, miss," I answered emphatically. "I shouldn't be likely to forget you."

"This is fortunate!" she exclaimed. "I was afraid that I should never see you again and never be able to thank you."

Here she turned to the other lady, who was gazing at us in evident astonishment, and explained, "This is the gentleman who rescued me and brought me home that night. Let me introduce my knight-errant to my mother."

On this, the elder lady darted forward and seized both my hands. I thought she was going to kiss me, and shouldn't have minded if she had. What she was about to say I shall never know, though it is not difficult to guess, for at this moment the door of Mr. Brodribb's office flew open and Mr. Hardcastle's voice, raised to an infuriated shout, was heard proclaiming, "It's a damned conspiracy! You are setting up this impostor for your own ends. But you had better have a care, my friend. You may find it a dangerous game."

He stamped out, purple and gibbering with wrath, and close behind him came his wife. Her ghastly white face was indescribable in its concentrated malice and fury, but as soon as I caught sight of it, I knew why Zichlinsky's face had stirred my memory. She might have been his sister. But this recognition came only in a half-conscious flash, for the sight of her strung me up to readiness for the inevitable clash. And the next moment it came. Mr. Hardcastle had pushed roughly past the two

221

ladies and his wife was following, when, just as they came abreast, Miss Stella turned her head and looked at the woman. As their eyes met, she uttered a cry of terror and shrank back, seizing my arm and making as if she would have taken shelter behind me.

For a moment there was a strange effect of arrested movement in the room, all the figures standing motionless as in a tableau. Mr. Hardcastle had turned and was staring in angry astonishment, his wife stood glaring at the terrified girl, and Mr. Brodribb looked on with frowning curiosity from the doorway of his office. It was he who broke the silence. "What is it, Miss Stella?"

"The woman," she gasped, pointing at Mrs. Hardcastle. "The nurse who took me to that dreadful house."

"What the devil does she mean?" demanded Mr. Hardcastle, looking in bewilderment from Miss Stella to his wife.

"How should I know?" the latter snarled. "The girl is an idiot. Let us get away from this den of swindlers and lunatics."

She moved towards the door with an assumed air of unconcern, though I could see that she was mightily shaken by the encounter. Mr. Hardcastle preceded her and wrenched the door open. Then he stood for a moment with the open door in his hand looking out.

"Don't block up the door like that, man," he said, irritably. "Come in or get out of the way."

The unseen person elected to come in, and having come in, he promptly shut the door and turned the key. Mr. Hardcastle looked at him fiercely and demanded, "What the devil is the meaning of this, sir?

"I take it," replied the newcomer, "that you are Mr. David Hardcastle?"

"And supposing I am. What then?"

"And this lady is Mrs. David Hardcastle, formerly Marie Zichlinsky?"

Mrs. Hardcastle glared at him with an expression that reminded me of a frightened cat. But she made no reply. The answer came from Mr. Brodribb.

"Yes, Superintendent, she is Mrs. David Hardcastle, and she has been identified by Miss Stella Hardcastle, who is here."

The woman turned on him furiously. "So," she exclaimed, "this is a trap that you had set for us, you sly old devil! Well, Superintendent, what do you want with Mrs. David Hardcastle?"

The Superintendent looked at Miss Stella and asked, "What do you say, Miss Hardcastle? Do you recognise this lady, and if so, what do you know about her?"

"She is the woman who was dressed as a nurse and who enticed me by false pretences to a house where I was imprisoned and bound with rope and from which this gentleman rescued me."

If a look could have killed, "this gentleman" would have been a dead gentleman. As it was, he was only a deeply interested gentleman.

"This," exclaimed Mrs. David, "is a parcel of foolery. The girl is mistaking me for some other person if she isn't merely lying."

"We can't go into that here," said the Superintendent. "We are not trying the case. I am a police officer and I arrest you for having abducted and forcibly detained Miss Stella Hardcastle, and I caution you that anything that you say will be taken down and may be used in evidence against you."

Mrs. Hardcastle was obviously terrified but she maintained a certain air of defiance, demanding angrily, "What right have you got to arrest me? Where is your warrant?"

"No warrant is necessary in a case of abduction," the Superintendent explained civilly.

"But you have only a bare statement. You cannot arrest without an information given on oath."

The lady struck me as being remarkably well informed in the matter of police procedure. But the Superintendent knew a thing or two for he replied, still in the same patient and courteous manner, "Miss Hardcastle has already laid a sworn information as to the facts. I assure you that the arrest is perfectly regular and the less difficulties you make, the less unpleasant it will be for us all."

During these proceedings Mr. Hardcastle had looked on with an air of stupefaction. All the bluster had gone out of his manner and his puffy face had suddenly turned white and haggard. He now broke in with the bewildered enquiry, "What is this all about? I don't understand. What are they talking about, Marie?"

She gave him a single wild, despairing look, and then she made a sudden dash for the door of communication. In a moment she had wrenched it open, only to reveal the presence of two massive plain-clothes officers standing just inside. For one moment she stood gazing at them in dismay, then she turned back and faced the Superintendent. "Very well," she said, sullenly. "I will come with you if I must."

"I am afraid you must," said he, "and, if you take my advice, you will not make a disagreeable business worse by any sort of resistance."

He glanced at the two officers and asked, "Have you got a cab waiting?" and on receiving an affirmative reply, he said, addressing the older of them, "Then you will take charge of this lady, and of course, you will avoid any appearance of having her in custody, provided she accompanies you quietly. You know where to go."

As the two officers entered the room and shut the door Mr. Hardcastle turned to the Superintendent. "Is it possible for me to accompany my wife?" he asked.

The Superintendent shook his head. "I am afraid that is quite impossible," said he, "but you can attend at the police court and apply for her to be admitted to bail. I will give you the necessary directions presently."

Here the senior of the two officers indicated to Mrs. Hardcastle that he was ready to start, whereupon her husband stepped towards her, and, laying his hands on her shoulders, kissed her livid cheek. She pushed him away gently without looking at him and, with a set face and a firm step, followed the first officer out of the room and was in turn followed by the other.

As soon as they were gone, Mr. Hardcastle looked at my employer, gloomily, but with none of his former bluster. "Is this your doing, Brodribb?" he asked.

Mr. Brodribb, who looked considerably upset by what had just happened, replied gently, "There was no choice, Mr. Hardcastle. If there had been, you would have been spared the distress of witnessing this catastrophe."

"Yes," said the Superintendent, who had taken possession of my desk and was writing on one of the paper slips. "We are all very sorry that this trouble has fallen on you. But the trouble was not of our making. Now, here are the particulars that you will want and the directions as to what you had better do. But I must warn you that the magistrate may refuse bail. Still, that is his affair and yours. The police can't accept bail in a case of this kind."

He handed the paper to Mr. Hardcastle, who glanced through it, put it in his pocket, and, without another word, walked dejectedly to the door and passed out of our sight. And with his disappearance there seemed to come a general relaxation of tension. Mr. Brodribb especially appeared to feel the relief, for, as the door closed, he drew a deep breath and murmured, "Thank God that's over!"

"Yes," said Miss Stella's mother, "it was a dreadful experience, though it is difficult to feel any sort of sympathy except for her unfortunate husband. May I take it, Mr. Brodribb, that this was the business that required my presence here and Stella's?"

"Yes," was the reply. "There were some other matters, but they will have to wait. But I shall hope to do myself the honour of calling on you in the course of the next day or two."

"Then our business here is finished for to-day?"

Mr. Brodribb glanced at the Superintendent, who replied, "I shall want Miss Hardcastle to identify one or two of the persons who will be charged with the abduction, but it is not urgent, as we have Mr. Gray here and enough evidence of other kinds to cover the arrests. So we need not detain these two ladies any longer."

The two ladies accordingly made their *adieux* to Mr. Brodribb and then bade me a very cordial farewell. As she shook my hand, the elder lady said with a smile, "We have found you at last, Mr. Gray, and we are not going to lose sight of you again. We shall hold Mr. Brodribb responsible for you."

With this and a gracious bow to the Superintendent, she passed out of the door which I held open for her, her arm linked in Miss Stella's, and both acknowledged my bow with a valedictory smile.

"Now," said the Superintendent, glancing at his watch, "it is time for us to be moving, Mr. Brodribb. I told Dr. Thorndyke that we should be there by half-past-eleven, and it's nearly that now."

Mr. Brodribb went into his office where, besides securing his hat and stick, he apparently rang a bell, for a dry-looking gentleman – a genuine clerk – made his appearance from a communicating door and looked at his employer enquiringly.

"I am going now, Bateman," said Mr. Brodribb. "Did you order the cab?"

"The cab is now at the door, sir," replied Mr. Bateman, on which the Superintendent went out and Mr. Brodribb followed, pushing me in front of him. I was naturally somewhat curious as to our destination, but, as I had only to wait until our arrival to satisfy my curiosity, I wasted no effort on speculation, but gave my attention to my fellow passengers' conversation – from which, however, I did not gather very much.

"I don't know why you want me to come," Mr. Brodribb remarked. "I don't know anything but what Dr. Thorndyke has told me."

The Superintendent chuckled. "You are in much the same position as the rest of us," said he. "But you may as well see how far we can confirm his information. We've got most of these birds in the hand now, and it remains to be seen how much we shall get out of them."

"But you can't interrogate prisoners concerning the crimes that they are charged with."

"No, certainly not. But we can let them talk after they have been cautioned, and we can let them make statements if they want to."

"Do you think they will want to?" asked Mr. Brodribb.

"I shall be very surprised if some of them don't. You see, out of this batch, one or two, or perhaps three, are the actual principals. The rest are accessories. But an accessory, when he sees the rope dangling before his nose, is going to take uncommon care that he isn't mistaken for a principal in the first degree. He'll probably lie like Ananias, but it is tolerably easy to sort out the lies and separate the facts."

At this point the cab, which had been rumbling down Whitehall, turned in at a large gateway and drew up at the entrance to a building which I decided to be the police headquarters, judging by the constabulary appearance of all the visible occupants. Here we disembarked and made our way to a barely furnished room containing a large table, furnished with writing materials and a few chairs. Seated at the table with their backs to the windows were Dr. Thorndyke, Dr. Jervis, and a gentleman whom I did not know. Exactly opposite the table was a door, at each side of which a police officer in uniform stood stiffly on guard, which led me to surmise that "the birds in hand" were not very far away.

"Now," said the Superintendent when the brief greetings had been exchanged, "the first thing will be for Mr. Gray to identify the various parties. It is a mere formality, but it is necessary to connect his statements with actual persons. You will just look at the prisoners, Mr. Gray, and if you recognise any of them, you will tell us who they are and what you know about them."

With this, he led me to the door, which was then thrown open by one of the guardians.

Chapter XVII
Some Statements and
a Tragedy
(Jasper Gray's Narrative)

As I stood for a moment in the open doorway and looked through into the large room beyond, I was sensible of an uncomfortable thrill. The grim spectacle on which I looked was an impressive illustration of the omnipotence of the law and its inexorable purpose when once set in motion. The room was as bare as the other, containing only a central table and a number of chairs ranged along the walls, on six of which, spaced at wide intervals, the prisoners were seated, each guarded by two constables. A single comprehensive glance took them all in, and then my eyes wandered back to Mrs. Hardcastle, and I hoped that Mr. Brodribb had not seen her.

She sat, rigid and ghastly, a very image of despair. The misery and deadly fear that her haggard face expressed wrung my heart in spite of my knowledge of her wickedness, though to be sure, the whole extent of her wickedness was not then known to me. But even if it had been, her dreadful condition would still have shocked me.

"I recognise this lady," I said huskily in answer to the Superintendent's question. "I saw her in Pentecost Grove the day I escaped with Miss Stella Hardcastle. She was then dressed as a nurse."

"It is a lie!" she exclaimed, casting a tigerish glance at me. "This young fool has mistaken me for some stranger."

The Superintendent made no comment and we passed on to the next chair.

"This is James Trout," said I. "All I know about him is that he gave me a bad half-crown and that he tried to prevent the other man from stabbing me."

"Have you ever seen this man before?" the Superintendent asked when we came to the next prisoner. The man looked at me wolfishly, and as I answered in the affirmative, he uttered a sort of snarl. And again I was struck by his resemblance to Mrs. Hardcastle.

"He gave the name of Jacob Silberstein to the policeman," said I, "but I heard some of the people address him as Mr. Zichlinsky."

227

The three remaining prisoners were Ebbstein, Gomorrah, and the cab-driver, Louis, and when I had identified them we went back to the other room and once more the door was shut. The Superintendent took his seat at the table between Dr. Thorndyke and Mr. Brodribb, the strange gentleman laid a large note-book on the table before him and uncapped a fountain-pen, and I was given a chair next to Mr. Brodribb and provided with a blotting-pad, paper and pens, and ink.

"You will listen to any statements that are made, Mr. Gray," said the Superintendent, "and if any of them appear to you to be incorrect you will make no remark but write down the correction for our information later. And I need not say that you are to regard anything that you may hear as strictly secret and confidential."

I signified that I clearly understood this, and the Superintendent then addressed Dr. Thorndyke.

"I think we had better begin with Trout. He is the most likely subject."

As Dr. Thorndyke agreed, the Superintendent gave the name to one of the constables on guard, who then opened the door, and, entering the large room, presently returned accompanied by Trout, who was given a chair opposite the middle of the table and facing the Superintendent. The latter looked at him doubtfully for a moment or two as if considering how he should begin, but Trout solved the problem by opening the proceedings himself.

"You are makin' a rare to-do about that bit of rope, sir," he complained. "I don't see why I've been brought here along o' them foreign crooks. Suppose I did pinch that rope – which I didn't. But suppose I did. It's nothin' to make all this fuss about."

"You are quite right, Trout," said the Superintendent. "The mere stealing of the rope is no great matter. We could let the dock company deal with that. It is a much more serious matter that we are concerned with, and the way the rope question comes into it is this: A piece cut off that rope – how long did you say that piece was, Doctor?"

"Thirteen feet," Dr. Thorndyke replied.

"A piece thirteen feet long was cut off that rope, and this piece was taken to a house at Stratford – Number Five, Piper's Row."

He paused and looked steadily at Trout, who in his turn gazed at the Superintendent with an expression of astonishment and unmistakable alarm.

"The persons who took that piece of rope to that place," the Superintendent continued, "also conveyed there the body of a man who had been murdered and they used the rope to hang that body from a beam."

228

"But," protested Trout, "that man hadn't been murdered. The inquest found that he hung himself."

"Yes, but we have since ascertained that he was murdered – drowned in a very unusual way. Now wait a moment, Trout. Before you say anything I must caution you that whatever you say will be taken down in writing and may be used in evidence against you at your trial."

"My trial!" gasped Trout, now evidently terrified. "What do you mean, sir? Why are you cautioning me like this?"

"Because I now charge you with the murder of this man, Sir Edward Hardcastle, whose body was found in that house."

"Me!" shrieked Trout, turning as pale as a bladder of lard. "You charge me! Why I don't know nothin' about it!"

"You are charged," the Superintendent continued in calm, even tones, "together with Maurice Zichlinsky, Solomon Gomorrah, Louis Shemrofsky, and Marie Hardcastle, with a conspiracy to murder the person I have named. Now, remember my caution. You are not bound to say anything and you had better think carefully before you do say anything. If you wish to make a statement you can do so, and it will be taken down in writing and you will be required to sign it. But there is no need for you to say anything at all."

Trout reflected with an alarmed eye on the officer. Evidently he was thunderstruck by the turn of events and mightily puzzled how to act. At length, he said cautiously, "Supposing I was prepared to make a statement – though I don't know nothin' about the affair, mind you – "

"If you don't know anything, your statement wouldn't help us much," the Superintendent remarked dryly.

"Well, if I was able to tell you anything at all, would you drop this charge against me?"

"No," was the prompt reply. "I can make no promise or bargain with you. But if you are innocent, it will clearly be to your advantage that the true facts should be known. But don't decide hastily. You had better go into the other room and think it over, and while you are considering whether you would like to make a statement, we will have Shemrofsky in."

"Don't you take no notice of what Shemrofsky says," Trout implored with obvious apprehension. "He's the biggest liar as ever drove a cab."

"Very likely," said the Superintendent. "But we shall have to listen to him if he wants to say anything. And if he chooses to tell lies, that is his look-out."

Here the Superintendent nodded to Trout's custodian and uttered the single word, "Shemrofsky," whereupon the officer conducted his charge back to the other room and shut the door. There followed a short interval, during which we all sat looking at the closed door, awaiting the emergence of the other prisoner. Suddenly, a murmur of voices and a confused sound of movement was audible from within. Then the door flew open and a constable rushed out.

"The woman prisoner, sir!" he exclaimed in a dismayed tone. "There's something the matter – "

Before he could finish, the Superintendent and the two doctors had sprung to their feet and darted in through the open doorway. From where I sat I got a glimpse of a row of prisoners and constables craning forward with horrified faces, and opposite to them Mrs. Hardcastle supported by two officers. When I first saw her, she was sitting bent forward with her head nearly on her knees, but then the officers raised her until she leaned back in her chair, when her arms fell down at her side, her head fell back and her chin dropped, leaving her mouth wide open. That was the last that I saw of her, for at that moment the door closed, and when, after a considerable interval, it opened again, her chair was empty.

As the Superintendent and the two doctors returned to their places Mr. Brodribb looked at them enquiringly.

"Too late," said the Superintendent. "She was dead when the doctor got to her."

"Dear, dear!" Mr. Brodribb murmured in a shocked tone. "Poor creature! I suppose her death was not – er – "

"Natural?" said Dr. Thorndyke. "No. It was apparently cyanide poisoning. She must have kept a little supply concealed on her person in case of an emergency. Probably one or two tablets."

"Yes," growled the Superintendent, "and we might have expected it. Ought to have had her searched. However, it's too late to think of that now."

But in spite of these expressed regrets, I had the feeling that he was less disturbed by the tragedy than I should have expected. And so with the others. Even the sensitive, soft-hearted Mr. Brodribb took the catastrophe with singularly calm resignation. Indeed, it was he who gave voice to what was probably the general view.

"A shocking affair. Shocking. And yet, perhaps, in view of what might have been – "

He did not finish the sentence, but I gathered that he was rather more relieved than shocked by what had happened. And later, I understood why.

After a decent pause, the business was resumed. Once more the door opened and now the cabman, Louis, was led out by an officer and brought up to the table, and a glance at him told me that, on him, at least, the recent tragedy had fallen with shattering effect. His face was blanched to a tallowy white and damp with sweat, his eyes stared, and his thin, bandy legs trembled visibly.

The Superintendent regarded him with a critical eye and addressed him in passionless but not unfriendly tones.

"Sit down, Shemrofsky. The officer who arrested you has cautioned you that anything that you say may be used in evidence against you. Now, bear that caution in mind."

"Yes," replied Shemrofsky, "I shall remember. But zere is noding against me. I drive a cab. Zere is no harm to drive a cab."

Mr. Miller nodded but made no comment, and Shemrofsky continued, "Zey say I take avay ze young lady, but zat is not true. Ze young lady get into ze cab by herself. Madame tell me vere to drive and I drive zere. Ze young lady get out of ze cab and go into ze house. I do not make her go. Madame could tell you I know noding of vot she do. But now Madame is dead and zere is nobody to speak for me."

"Very well," said the Superintendent. "We will let that pass. But there is another charge, and I caution you again that anything you say may be used in evidence against you. Don't forget that."

Shemrofsky turned, if possible, paler and stared apprehensively at the officer. "Anozer charge!" he exclaimed.

"Yes. It refers to a gentleman who was brought from Piccadilly, near Dover Street, to Number Fifty Pentecost Grove. In that house he was murdered, and his body was taken to Number Five Piper's Row, Stratford. The murder was committed by Maurice Zichlinsky, Solomon Gomorrah, and certain other persons, and I charge you with being one of those other persons. Now, remember my caution."

For a few moments Shemrofsky gazed at the Superintendent in speechless consternation. Then he broke out, passionately, "You charge me zat I help to kill zat chentleman! I tell you I haf noding to do vid zat. I did not know zat anybody kill him. Somebody tell you lies about me. If Madame vas here, she vould tell you zat I chust drive ze cab vere I am told. Zat is all. I know noding of vot zey do."

The Superintendent wrote down these statements, though the gentleman at the end of the table was apparently the official scribe. But he made no remark, and presently Shemrofsky continued, "Somebody have tried to put ze blame on me. But I shall tell you all zat I know. Zen you vill see zat I haf noding to do vid killing zis chentleman."

"Do you mean," said the Superintendent, with ill-concealed satisfaction, "that you wish to make a statement? You are not bound to say anything, you know. But if you wish to make a statement, you may, and it will be taken down in writing and, when you have read it and find it correct, you will be required to sign it. But do exactly as you think best."

"I shall tell you all vot I know," said Shemrofsky, whereupon the Superintendent glanced at the recording officer – who took a fresh sheet of paper – and advised the prisoner to stick to the truth and begin at the beginning.

"You had better start," said he, "by telling us what you know as to how this gentleman came to Pentecost Grove."

"He came in my cab." said Shemrofsky. "I vill tell you how it vos. Vun morning – it vas a Vednesday – Madame say to me zat a friend is coming to see Mr. Zichlinsky – zat vas her broder – and as he vould not know ze vay she vould fetch him in my cab. So she get in ze cab and tell me to drive to Dover Street, Piccadilly. Ven ve get zere, I valk ze horse slowly. Zen ze chentleman come. Madame push up ze trap vid her umbrella and I stop. Ze chentleman get into ze cab and I drive to Pentecost Grove as I haf been told. Madame and ze chentleman get out and go into Mr. Ebbstein's house."

"Ebbstein's!" exclaimed the Superintendent. "I understood it was Gomorrah's."

"No, it vos Ebbstein's. Vel, zey go in and I take my cab to ze yard. I see ze chentleman no more and I hear noding about him. Zen, on Sunday, Gomorrah come to me and say zat Mr. Zichlinsky want me to take ze chentleman to Stratford. He tell me to come for him at night a liddle before eleven. Ven I come to ze house – Mr. Ebbstein's – Gomorrah tell me ze chentleman haf got drunk. He vos very drunk, so Gomorrah and Ebbstein haf to help him out to ze cab."

"What do you mean by 'help him out'?" asked the Superintendent. "Was he able to walk?"

"No, he vos too drunk. Zey haf to carry him out. Zey sit him in ze cab and zen Mr. Zichlinsky get in and sit by his side. Zey tell me to let down ze glass front, so I let it down and zen I drive to Stratford. Zey tell me to go up Stratford High Street, and ven I get zere I pull up ze trap and Mr. Zichlinsky tell me vich vay to go. Presently ve come to a row of houses vich seem to be empty, all but vun, vere I see a man standing at an open door. He make a sign to me and I stop and pull up ze glass front. Zen ze man get in and help Mr. Zichlinsky to take ze chentleman out of ze cab and carry him into ze house. Zey shut ze door and I drive avay and go home."

"Was there any light in the house?" the Superintendent asked.

"Zere vos a lantern on ze floor chust inside."

"With regard to this man," said Mr. Miller. "Was he anyone that you knew?"

"It vos very dark," Shemrofsky replied, evasively. "I could not see him plainly."

"Still," said the Superintendent, "he was quite close to you when he got into the cab. I don't want to press you, but if you know who he was you had much better say so."

"Vell," Shemrofsky replied, reluctantly, "it vos very dark. I could not see vell, but ze man seem to look a liddle like Mr. Trout."

"Ha! And what happened after that?"

"Noding. I go home and zat is all I know." The Superintendent reflected awhile. Then he held out his hand to the scribe, who passed him the written statement. When he had glanced through it he read it slowly aloud, including the questions.

"Now, Shemrofsky," he said, "is that all you know? Or would you like to add anything to it?"

"Zat is all I know," was the reply, whereupon "the deponent" was provided with a pen, an instrument with which he seemed unfamiliar, but with which he contrived to make some sort of mark, which the Superintendent countersigned as witness. Then Shemrofsky was conducted back to the other room, whence Trout was brought forth to take his place.

"Well, Trout," the Superintendent said, genially. "Have you thought it over?"

"Yus," was the reply, "and I am going to make a statement. I ain't going to lump in with them foreign crooks. I don't 'old with their ways and I've told 'em so over and over again."

"Then I take it that you are going to tell us all that you know about this affair and that you are going to make a true statement."

"I am," replied Trout, "though, mind you, I don't know anything but what I've been told."

"What you have been told," said the Superintendent, "is not evidence. Still, it is your statement, so you can say what you please. You had better begin at the beginning and take the events in their proper order."

"The beginning of the affair, as I understand," said Trout, "was when this gent came to Ebbstein's house. He came in Shemrofsky's cab with Madame – she was Zichlinsky's sister, I believe. They went in together, but Madame came out again almost at once and went into Gomorrah's house. Shemrofsky told me this. The rest of the story I had from Gomorrah.

"It seems that Madame took the gent into Ebbstein's work-room. There was no work being done there that day, so the women what worked for him had been given a day off. There was three men there:

233

Zichlinsky, Ebbstein, and Gomorrah, and as soon as Madame was gone, the whole three set about the gent. But he gave 'em more trouble than they had bargained for. They had meant to hang him and they'd got the rope ready, but they couldn't manage him, and all the time, he was fairly raising Cain – hollering 'Murder!' fit to fetch the roof off. Just then a woman runs in and says there was two coppers coming up the street. Ebbstein wanted to knife the gent straight away, but Zichlinsky wouldn't let him, but as they was close to the pickle tub, they got him bent down and Zichlinsky shoved his head down into the brine and held it there while the other two lifted his legs. They held on like that until the coppers had passed out of the street, and when they took his head out of the brine he was dead."

"You had better say what you mean by 'the pickle tub'," said the Superintendent.

"It is a big tub of brine what they pickles their herrings and cabbage in. There wasn't much in it but brine just then. They filled it up with fish and cabbage the next day."

"And about this rope that you say they had ready. What do you know about that?"

"It was a bit about a couple of fathoms long that was cut off a rope that belonged to Gomorrah. I don't know where he got it. But I know the rope because he brought the piece to me and asked me to show him how to make a noose in it. That was the day before they did the gent in. Of course, I didn't know what he wanted it for, so I made a running bowline in the end just to show him."

"I see," said the Superintendent (and no doubt he did). "What happened next?"

"Well," replied Trout, "when they'd done him in, they'd got to dispose of the body. For the time being they stowed it away in the cellar, and a rare fright they got while it was there, for some coves brought an egg-chest to the house in a mighty hurry. They thought Powis was inside it, but when they opened it a strange young man popped out. I fancy it was this young gentleman," he added, indicating me, "and a pretty narrow squeak he had, for Ebbstein thought he was a spy and, being in a blue funk about the body that he'd got in his cellar, he wanted to do the young man in to make things safe. But the bloke what had brought the case wasn't going to be mixed up with any throat slitting – of course, he didn't know anything about the body downstairs – so they locked the young man up in Jonas Markovitch's room, and he got out of the window and hiked off.

"However, that's another story. To come back to this job: The night they did the gent in, Gomorrah comes to me and says that him and

234

Ebbstein is in difficulties. He says the gent was took ill – had a stroke, or somethink – and died suddenly, and they don't know what to do with the body. He asks me if I know of any safe place where they could plant it, where it wouldn't be found for a little while. Of course, he didn't say anything about the murder at that time. If he had, I wouldn't have had anything to do with the business. But as it seemed to be just an accident, I didn't see no harm in giving 'em a bit of advice.

"Now, I happened to know Stratford pretty well. Got a married sister what lives there. And I knowed about those empty houses in Piper's Row, so I told Gomorrah about them and he thought they'd suit to a 'T'. So he asked me to take Zichlinsky and Shemrofsky down to the place and show 'em the way, and he gave me a bunch of skeleton keys and some tools to get in. But I didn't want 'em, for when I went down there that night with Zichlinsky and Shemrofsky and picked out a likely-looking house, I found I could open the door with my own latch-key. So I told Zichlinsky that I would lend him the latch-key when he wanted to get into the house. And I did. I lent him the key on the Sunday afternoon and he give it me back the next morning."

"You didn't go with him to Stratford when he took the body there?"

"Me! Not much. He wanted me to, but I wasn't going to be mixed up in the business."

"Do you know who did go with him?"

"No. I don't know as anybody did. Anyhow, it wasn't me."

"When did you first hear about the murder?"

"Not until after the body was found. When I heard about it being found hanging in the wash'us, I smelt a rat. So I asked Gomorrah about it and then he let on by degrees. He wasn't quite himself just then on account of a knock on the head that he got from this young gentleman. First he put it all on to Zichlinsky, but afterwards I got the whole story out of him."

The Superintendent waited for some further observations, but as none were forthcoming, he asked, "Is that all you've got to tell us?"

"That's the lot, sir," Trout replied with cheerful finality, adding, "and quite enough too."

"Not quite enough, Trout," the Superintendent corrected. "There's one other little matter that we want some information about. Have you got that small object about you, Mr. Brodribb?"

Mr. Brodribb had, and presently produced it from an envelope which he took out of his letter case. As he laid it down on the clean, white blotting pad, I recognised with something of a thrill my long-lost and deeply lamented emerald.

Mr. Trout regarded it stolidly and, when the Superintendent asked him what he could tell us about it, he promptly replied, "Nothing."

"That isn't much," the officer remarked. "Perhaps if I tell you something about it you'll remember something more. You probably know that Powis is in detention awaiting his trial. Now, this stone was in his possession, and he says that you sold it to him."

"Well," protested Trout, "supposing I did. It ain't got nothin' to do with this other business."

"But it has a great deal," said the Superintendent. "This stone was in a ring which is known to have been on the person of the gentleman who was murdered. This is the ring that it came from – " (Here the Superintendent took from his pocket and laid on the blotting pad a rather massive gold ring in which was an empty oval space.) " – and this ring was found in the possession of Jonas Markovitch, who says that he bought it from you."

"He's a liar!" exclaimed Trout, indignantly. "He sold me the stone, himself. He took it out of the ring because it wasn't no good to him, as he was going to melt down the metal. I gave him a bob for it and I sold it to Powis for five bob. Markovitch told me he found the ring on the work-room floor."

"Well, why didn't you say so at first, Trout?" said the Superintendent in a tone of mild reproach.

"I forgot," replied Trout, adding irrelevantly. "Besides, I couldn't see that it mattered."

As it appeared that he had nothing further to communicate, his statement was read over to him, and, when he had suggested one or two trifling alterations, he signed it with considerable effort and the addition of two good-sized blots which he endeavoured to lick up. The addition of the Superintendent's signature completed the formalities and the prisoner was then conducted back to the other room. As the door closed behind him, the Superintendent uttered a grunt of satisfaction.

"Not so bad," said he. "With your evidence, Doctor, and Mr. Gray's and these two statements, we may say that we have a complete case."

"You think these two men will be willing to go into the witness box?" asked Mr. Brodribb.

"Oh, they will be willing enough," replied the Superintendent, "seeing that their evidence tends to clear them of being directly concerned in the murder."

"What about Singleton?" Dr. Thorndyke asked. "Will he swear to Zichlinsky's finger-print?

"Yes," the Superintendent answered. "He would have sworn to it before, only that it seemed impossible, and that he has such a holy terror

236

of you since that Hornby case. But now he is ready to swear to it and give details as to the agreement of the separate features. So we have got a strong case even without these statements. But, Lord! Doctor, you haven't left us much glory. Here is your information – " (He took a paper from his pocket and opened it before him.) " – describing the whole crime in close detail, and here are these two statements, and, making allowance for a few obvious lies, they are identical. The only weak spot was the murder charge against 'Madame', as they call her, and she has solved that difficulty by throwing in her hand. Her suicide almost amounts to a confession – for although she hadn't been charged with the murder, she must have seen that she was going to be – and it will have put the fear of God into the others."

"Speaking of the others," said Dr. Thorndyke, "do you propose to offer the three principals the opportunity to make voluntary statements?"

"Of course, they can if they like," the Superintendent replied, "but I have advised them to say nothing until they have consulted their Rabbi or a lawyer. As they will be on trial for their lives, it would not be proper to encourage them to talk at this stage. No doubt they will elect to give evidence at their trial, and each of them will try to clear himself by incriminating the others. But that is their look-out."

"With regard to David Hardcastle," said Mr. Brodribb, "I assume that you take the same view as I do: That he had no hand in the affair at all."

"That is so," was the reply. "We have nothing against him. He seems to be right outside the picture. He would be, you know. This is not an English type of crime. It is pretty certain that Madame kept him entirely in the dark about the whole affair. And now, gentlemen, I think we have finished for the present and I am very much obliged to you for your help. You will be kept informed as to any further developments."

With this, the meeting broke up, and as it seemed that my valuable services were no longer in demand at Mr. Brodribb's office, I was released (with a substantial fee for my attendance), after a cordial hand-shake with the four gentlemen, and went forth to view the neighbourhood of Westminster and to reflect upon the surprising circumstances in which I had become involved.

Chapter XVIII
The Wheel of Fortune
(Jasper Gray's Narrative)

To most of us, a retrospect of life presents a picture of a succession of events each of which is visibly connected with those that have gone before. Times change indeed and we change with them, but the changes are gradual, progressive, evolutionary. The child grows up to manhood and in so doing reacts on his environment in such a way as to set up in it responsive changes. But he remains the same person and his environment remains substantially the same environment. Though both alter insensibly from day to day and from year to year, there is no point at which the connection of the present with the past is definitely broken.

This is the common experience, to which my own offers a striking exception. For into my life there came a break with the past so sudden and complete that in a few moments I not only passed into a totally new environment, but even seemed, in a sense, to have acquired a new personality.

The break came on the third day after my attendance at the police headquarters. I can recall the circumstances with the most intense vividness, as well I may, for, with the material gain was linked an irreparable loss that has left a blank in my life even unto this day. I was still on leave from Sturt and Wopsalls, 'standing by' at Mr. Brodribb's request, for possible, and unknown, duties, and having nothing to do on this particular morning had taken up my position in a reasonably comfortable chair to listen while Pontifex expounded the Latin language to one of his pupils.

How clearly the picture rises before me as I write! The shabby room, ill-furnished and none too clean, the deal table – its excessive dealiness partially cloaked by a threadbare cover – invitingly furnished with one or two books and a little pile of scribbling paper, and the two figures that faced one another across the table – Pontifex, sitting limply in his Windsor elbow-chair and looking strangely old and frail, and the stolid pupil with eyes sullenly downcast at his book. I watched them both, but especially Pontifex, noting uneasily how he seemed to have aged and withered within the last week or two and wondering how much of the change was attributable respectively to Mr. Brodribb or Johnny

Walker, and noting, further, that the latter was conspicuously in abeyance at the moment.

Mr. Cohen, the present recipient of instruction, was not a promising pupil. It was not that he was a fool. By no means. I had seen him conducting the business of the paternal pawnbroker's shop and could certify as to his being most completely on the spot, so much so that my mission (as Ponty's agent) turned out a financial failure. But Mr. Cohen's genius was exclusively commercial. As a classical scholar he was hopeless. Poor Ponty groaned at the sound of his footsteps on the stair.

This morning the subject of study was Virgil's *Georgics*, Book Four, of which the opening paragraph had been dealt with, painfully and incompletely, in the previous lesson.

"Now, Mr. Cohen," said Pontifex, with a cheerful and encouraging air, "we begin with verse eight, which introduces the subject of the poem. *Principio sedes apibus statioque petenda*. Let us hear how you render that into English."

Mr. Cohen glared sulkily at his book, but rendering there was none beyond certain inward mutterings which had a suspiciously expletive quality. Pontifex waited patiently awhile, and then, as no further sound was forthcoming, he made a fresh start.

"Perhaps we shall simplify matters if we attack the translation word by word. Let us take the first word, *Principio*. How shall we translate *Principio*, Mr. Cohen?"

Mr. Cohen reflected and at length pronounced the word "Principal," possibly influenced unconsciously by some reminiscence of the three golden balls.

"No," said Pontifex, "that will hardly do. Possibly, if you recall the opening sentence of *The Gospel of St. John in the Vulgate. In principio erat verbum* – ahem – " Here Ponty pulled up short, suddenly realising that Mr. Cohen was probably not familiar with *The Gospel of St. John in the Vulgate* or any other form. After a short pause he continued, "Shall we say '*to begin with*' or '*in the first place*'?"

"Yes," Mr. Cohen agreed promptly, "that's all right."

"Very well," said Ponty. "Now take the next word, *sedes*."

"Seeds," suggested Mr. Cohen.

"Not seeds," Ponty corrected mildly. "We must not allow ourselves to be misled by analogies of sound. Think of the word sedentary. What is the distinguishing characteristic of a sedentary person, Mr. Cohen?"

"Doesn't take enough exercise," was the reply.

"Very true," Ponty admitted, "and for the reason that he usually occupies a seat. '*Seats*' is the word we want, not '*seeds*'. '*In the first place seats*' *statioque* – seats and a – and a what, Mr. Cohen?"

"Station," was the confident answer.

"Excellent!" exclaimed Ponty. "Perfectly correct. Seats and a station *petenda*," he paused for a moment and then, despairing of Cohen's grammar, translated, "must be procured, or more correctly, sought. In the first place, seats and a station must be sought *apibus* the – for the what, Mr. Cohen?"

"*Apes*," replied Cohen, promptly.

"No, no," protested Ponty. "Not *apes*. Similarities of sound are misleading us again. Think of the English word, *apiary*. You know what an apiary is, Mr. Cohen?"

Mr. Cohen said that he did, and I didn't believe him. "Well now," said Ponty, persuasively, "what does one keep in an apiary?"

"Apes," was the dogged answer.

What the end of it would have been I shall never know, for at this point footsteps became audible, ascending the stairs. Pontifex listened uneasily and laid down his book as they reached the landing. There was a short pause, and then a soft, apologetic tapping at the door. I sprang up, and, crossing the room, threw the door open, thereby disclosing the astonishing apparition of Mr. Brodribb and Miss Stella's mother.

For a moment, I was so disconcerted that I could only stand, holding the door open and staring vacantly at our visitors. Not so Pontifex. At the first glance he had risen and now came forward to receive them with a dignified and rather stiff bow, and having placed chairs for them excused himself and turned to his gaping and inquisitive pupil.

"I am afraid, Mr. Cohen," said he, "that we shall have to suspend our studies for this morning."

"Right you are," replied Cohen, rising with unscholarly alacrity. Gleefully he snatched up his book and was off like a lamplighter. As his boots clattered down the stairs, Pontifex faced Mr. Brodribb with an air of polite and rather frosty enquiry, and the latter, who had not seated himself, showed less than his usual self-possession.

"I feel, sir," he began hesitatingly, "that I should apologize for what must appear like an intrusion, especially after your clearly expressed desire to be left untroubled by visitors."

"You need have no such feeling," replied Pontifex, "since I have no doubt that I am indebted for the honour of this visit to some unusual and sufficient circumstances."

"You are quite right, sir," rejoined Mr. Brodribb. "Circumstances have arisen which have made it imperative that I should communicate with you. I should have hinted at them when I had the pleasure of meeting you the other day, but your reception of me was not encouraging. Now, I have no choice, and I have ventured to ask Mrs. Paul Hardcastle to accompany me in the hope that her presence may – ha – lessen the force of the impact."

Pontifex bowed to the lady and smiled a frosty smile. I looked at him in astonishment. The familiar Ponty seemed to have suffered some strange transformation. This cool, dignified, starchy old gentleman was a new phenomenon. But Mrs. Paul would have none of his starch. Starting up from her chair, she ran to him impulsively and took both his hands.

"Why are you so cold to us, Sir Gervase?" she exclaimed. "Why do you hold us at arm's length in this way? Are we not old friends? It is true that the years have drifted in between us. But we were friends when we were young, and nothing has ever befallen to weaken our friendship. We both loved dear Phillipa and we both treasure her memory. For her dear sake, if for no other, let us be friends still."

Pontifex softened visibly. "It is true, Constance," he said, gently, "that my heart should warm to you for the sake of that sweet saint, of whose devotion I was so unworthy. Pardon a crabbed old man who has made the world his enemy. One does not gather gratefully the harvest of one's own folly. Forgive me, cousin, and let us hear about your mission."

"It is not my mission, Sir Gervase," she replied. "I came because Mr. Brodribb thought that my presence might make things easier for you."

"That was most kind of you," said he. "But why do you call me Sir Gervase?"

"The answer to that question," interposed Mr. Brodribb, "explains the occasion of this visit. I have to inform you with deep regret that your brother, Sir Edward, died some weeks ago. If I had then known your whereabouts, I should, of course, have communicated with you – not only as his brother but as his heir."

Pontifex looked at Mr. Brodribb in a queer, bewildered fashion and then seemed to fall into a sort of half-conscious dreamy state.

"Dear, dear," he muttered, "so brother Edward is gone – and I am left. My old playmate gone and no word of farewell spoken."

Suddenly he came out of his reverie and addressed Mr. Brodribb sharply. "But you spoke of me as his heir. How can that be? He had children."

"He had one child," said Mr. Brodribb, "a son. That son died some ten years ago. Consequently, the title and the settled estate devolve on you. I may say, have devolved, since there is no question as to the succession."

241

Pontifex listened to him attentively, but with the same curiously bewildered air. He seemed thunderstruck. After a moment or two he dropped into his chair and sat slowly shaking his head and muttering. Presently he looked up at Mr. Brodribb, and said in a weak, shaky voice, "No, no, Mr. Brodribb. It is too late. This is not for me."

I stood somewhat in the background, watching Pontifex with growing anxiety. Like him, I was astounded by Mr. Brodribb's news. But in that matter I did not feel deeply concerned at the moment. My entire attention was concentrated on the change which had come over my father. It had begun in the very instant when our visitors had appeared in the open doorway. In spite of his cool, stiff bearing, I could see by his sudden change of colour, and the trembling of his hands, that he was intensely agitated. And now, Mr. Brodribb's announcement had inflicted a further shock. It was evident to me that the sudden accession to rank and fortune, so far from giving him pleasure or satisfaction, was profoundly repugnant. And dear Mrs. Paul, with the kindest intentions, did but make matters worse and intensify the shock.

"It is not too late, cousin," said she. "How can it be when there are years of prosperity and ease before you? Think, dear Sir Gervase, think of the bright future which begins from to-day. You will leave all this –" She glanced round the shabby room. " – the poverty and ill-paid labour and the struggle for mere daily bread, and go to live in modest affluence in your own fine house with your park and woodlands around you and your servants to minister to your comfort. And you will come back to take your place among your own people in the station of life which properly belongs to you. Think, too, of this dear boy – Phillipa's own boy, and so like her – who, in his turn, shall carry on the honourable traditions of our family. And think of her, who loved you and him and would have been so rejoiced to see you both come back to the inheritance of your fathers."

Pontifex listened to her gravely, and, as she concluded, he looked at me with one of his rare, affectionate smiles.

"Yes, Constance," he said weakly, "you are right. He is Phillipa's own boy. Faithful and loving and good like his mother."

Once more, he lapsed into reverie and I stood gazing at him in dismay with a growing terror at my heart. For a horrible pallor was spreading over his face and even his poor old nose had faded to a sickly mauve. I think my alarm began to be shared by the others, for an uneasy silence settled on the room. And even as we looked at him he seemed to shrink and subside limply into his chair with his chin upon his breast, and so sat for a few moments. Then he rose slowly to his feet, his face turned upward and his trembling hands thrust out before him as one groping in the dark. I heard him murmur, "*Domine non sum dignus!*" and sprang forward to catch him in my arms as he fell.

How shall I write of that time of sorrow and desolation? Of the emptiness that came upon my little world now that my earliest and dearest companion – almost, as he had sometimes seemed, my child – was gone from me forever? But need I write of it at all? My tale is told, the tale of the destiny that came to me, all unsuspected, in the egg-chest. My father's death wrote *Finis* to one volume of my life. With that the old things passed away and all things became new. Jasper Gray was dead, and Sir Jasper Hardcastle had stepped into his shoes.

Yet must I not make my exit too abruptly. The world which I had left lived on, and the drama in which I had played my part still claimed me as a *dramatis persona*. I pass over the quiet funeral and the solemn procession to the great vault in the shadow of the flint-built tower of the village church at Bradstow, my translation to the house at Dorchester Square, where the white-headed footman (whose deceptive powder I now detected) shattered my nerves by addressing me as "Sir Jasper," and where my cousin, Stella, openly worshipped me as her incomparable Galahad. It was all encompassed by an atmosphere of unreality through which I wandered as one in a dream.

More real was the scene at the Old Bailey – the grimly sordid old Sessions House that is now swept away – where I gave my evidence amidst a breathless silence and afterwards, as the representative of the deceased, sat with Mr. Brodribb at the solicitors' table and listened to Dr. Thorndyke as, with deadly clarity, he set forth the crushing tale of incriminating facts. Quite unmoved, I remember, by any qualm of pity, I heard those five wretches frantically striving to cast the guilt on one another and each but hurrying himself to his own doom. Clearly, but still without a qualm, I recall the pusillanimous shrieks for mercy as the black-capped judge consigned the three murderers to the gallows, and the blubberings of Shemrofsky and the sullen protests of Trout as their terms of penal servitude were pronounced.

It was a memorable experience, and it affected me with a curious, impersonal interest. As I sat at the table, I found myself again and again reflecting on the irony of it all, on the singular futility of this crime. For it was the means of defeating, finally and completely, its original object. The wretched woman who, in her greed and impatience to possess, had planned and directed it, had extinguished her husband's claim for ever. If she had but held her hand, poor Pontifex would have lived and died in his hiding-place, his very existence unsuspected, and she would in due course have become the Lady of Bradstow. It was the murder of my uncle Edward that brought my father into view.

The years have rolled away since these events befell. They have been prosperous years of sober happiness, as they must needs have been, for a man can hardly fail to achieve happiness who is a hero in his wife's eyes. And such is my lot, though undeserved. To this day I am Stella's incomparable Galahad.

Yet, though I would not under-value the gifts of Fortune, I am fain often to reflect on the inconsiderable part that mere material possessions play in the creation of human happiness. As I survey the fine old mansion, the shady park, and the wide domain which is all my own, I find them good to look upon and to possess. But, nevertheless, there are times when I feel that I would gladly give much of them to look once more on dear old Ponty, sitting in his shabby dressing-gown, delicately tending the frizzling scallops. How little it cost to give us pleasure in those days! Mr. Weeks's salary would have made us rich, and we could have had scallops every night. But perhaps the habitual scallop would not have had the same flavour.

THE END

1932 Hodder & Stoughton, London Cover
U.S. Title: Dr. Thorndyke's Discovery

To My Friend
Lady Adams

For Auld Lang Syne

Book I: The Three Rogues

Chapter I
The Backsliding of
Mr. Didbury Toke

There is nothing so deceptive as a half-truth. The half that is true has a certain suggestive power that lends to the other half a plausibility and a credibility that it does not possess in its own right. This interesting psychological fact was realized, at least subconsciously, by Mr. Didbury Toke. For Mr. Toke was a collector of antique and other works of art, a connoisseur and a dealer. He really was. It was not a pose or a pretence. He was a bona fide collector, and a connoisseur who had that genuine love of fine and beautiful works that is the indispensable condition of real connoisseurship. But Mr. Toke was also a fence. And that was where the illusory element came in. Any person who, not being a known collector and a recognized dealer, should have been seen, as he frequently was, in the company of definitely shady characters, would inevitably have attracted the attention of the guardians of the law. But everyone knows that the really enthusiastic collector must needs seek his quarry where it is most likely to be found, and there is no need to watch him, for no crook or fence would be so foolish as to sell doubtful merchandise to a collector who is going to expose it forthwith in his show-cases, or a dealer who is going to offer it in the open market. So Mr. Didbury Toke went about his lawful occasions unmolested and unsuspected and, under the cover of them, did a little unlawful business if it happened to come his way.

It came his way pretty often in these latter days.

But this was a comparatively new development. For many years he had carried on his activities in the most scrupulously correct manner. And so he might have continued to the end, but for some exceptional circumstance. We are all, indeed, the creatures of circumstance. But circumstances are not entirely beyond human control. Their control is, however, largely proportionate to our control of ourselves. And that was where Mr. Toke had failed. At a critical moment he found himself unable to resist a sudden temptation. But let us have done with generalities and consider the circumstances in detail.

The descent to Avernus is proverbially easy and, in practice, it is usually somewhat gradual. But there are exceptions, and the case of Mr. Didbury Toke furnishes an example. For his start upon that famous decline was the result of an incident quite unforeseen and, to a certain extent, beyond his control. At any rate, the determining cause – or perhaps we should say the predisposing cause – was a convulsion of nature for which he certainly could not be held responsible – being, in fact, no less than a thunderstorm. Mr. Toke did not like thunderstorms. Few of us do, especially when they come on us in the open country, in which the only refuge visible is the illusory shelter offered by scattered hedgerow elms.

At the moment Mr. Toke was pursuing his way along the rather unfrequented road that led from the village in which his house was situated to the neighbouring market town of Packington. As he walked at an easy pace on the grass verge of the road, his thoughts were pleasantly occupied by reflections on a little windfall that he had recently picked up at a country auction, so much so that his immediate surroundings received but the vaguest attention. Suddenly, he was aroused from his meditations by a low rumble from the far distance behind him and, turning sharply, became aware of an obvious inkiness of the sky and, low down, an arched edge of blackness surmounting a pale area in which, even as he looked, jagged streaks of light shot up from the dim horizon.

Mr. Toke looked about him uneasily. He had passed no habitation, so far as he could remember, for the last mile, and Packington lay some two miles farther on. But, clearly, it was useless to think of turning back. His only chance of shelter, apart from the treacherous elms, was in some possible inn or cottage that might lurk unseen by the roadside ahead. Accordingly, he resumed his progress in that direction, mending his pace appreciably as his ears were smitten by a sound as if a Brobdingnagian tea-tray had been kicked by a Titanic foot.

Swiftly Mr. Toke padded along the solitary, inhospitable road while the leaves of the elm trees shivered audibly and elemental bangings from behind announced the approach of the storm. And then, just as the first big drops began to fall with an audible plop on the earth, a slight turn of the road revealed a cottage, hitherto hidden by a clump of trees. It was but a humble labourer's dwelling, timber-built and roofed with thatch, but to Mr. Toke's eagerly searching eyes it was more grateful than a baronial mansion. As a resounding crash from behind mingled with the hiss of a sudden deluge, he frantically unfastened the button of the gate and darted up the path to the small porch that sheltered the door. Nor did he come as a mere suppliant doubtful of his welcome, for, on the jamb of the door hung a small board bearing the single word "*Teas*". It was a laconic announcement, but brevity is the soul of wit, and to Mr. Toke it was as a charter of freedom conferring the right to enter unquestioned.

The door was opened in response to his rather urgent thumps by an elderly labourer, who looked first at Mr. Toke and then at the sky, as if he suspected the former of some responsibility for the unfavourable state of the weather. But he uttered no word and, as the rain was playing freely on Mr. Toke's back, that gentleman proceeded bluntly to state his wants.

"Can I have some tea?" asked Mr. Toke.

The man seemed surprised at the request. "Tea, you wants," said he. He took another critical survey of the landscape, and then replied cautiously, "I'll ask the old woman."

As "the old woman" was plainly in view, sitting by the fire and obviously attentive to the conversation, the precaution seemed hardly necessary. In fact, she anticipated the question.

"Why, certainly, Tom. I can get the gentleman a cup of tea if he wants one." She rose stiffly from her chair and cast an enquiring glance at the kettle which reposed in unpromising silence on the hob.

"You have a notice by your door that you supply teas," Mr. Toke ventured to remark.

"Yes," the master of the house admitted. "That there board was put up by my darter. She's gone and got married, so we don't do much in that line nowadays. Never did, in fact. Oo's coming out 'ere for tea?"

Mr. Toke agreed that the road was not actually congested and, meanwhile, under the guidance of his host, squeezed himself past an obstructive table towards a Windsor arm-chair which he distinguished with some difficulty in the pervading gloom. For, now that the door was closed, the room was almost in darkness, the small window, obscured by dirt and invading creepers, admitting only a fraction of the feeble light from the inky sky.

"Seems as if we was going to have a bit of rain," the host remarked, by way of making conversation. Mr. Toke agreed that there was a suggestion of moisture in the air, and ventured to express the hope that it would do the country good.

"Ay," said his host, "a bit of rain is allers useful at this time o' year. In reason, mind yer. Yer don't want it a-comin' down like brickbats, a-flattenin' down the crops. A nice, soft, steady rain is what ye wants for the land. Keeps it miste, d'ye see."

Mr. Toke assimilated this lucid explanation as he watched the old woman coaxing the unresponsive kettle with sticks of firewood. By degrees, his eyes were becoming accustomed to the obscurity. Already, he had converted the sound of harsh, metallic ticking into the visual impression of a drum clock, perched on the mantelshelf, and now as let his glance wander questingly round the dim interior, it was not an idle glance. By no means. Not, it is true, that he was ordinarily much concerned with the simple domestic antique. But all is fish that comes to a collector's net, and experience had taught him that if "Honesty lives in a poor house, like your fair pearl in your foul oyster," so was it occasionally with the treasures that the past has bequeathed to the present. So Mr. Toke had made it a rule of life to "keep his weather eyelid lifting" even in the most unlikely surroundings.

"Main lucky for you, it is," remarked his host, as a resounding crash shook the door and made the window-frames rattle, "that you struck this house in time. There ain't another this side of The Rose and Crown, and that's a good mile-and-a-half further on down the road. You'd a-caught it proper if you'd a-been out in it now."

"Yes, indeed," said Mr. Toke. "Holy water in a dry house is better than this rain-water out of doors."

His host did not, apparently, recognize the quotation, for he looked at him suspiciously, and replied in a somewhat surly tone, "There ain't no holy water in this house. We're Baptisses, we are."

"Ha!" said Mr. Toke. "I was merely repeating an old saying. And there is some truth in it, you know."

"So there may be," was the grudging reply. "I don't hold with none of them there superstitions. Lord! Look at that!"

"That" was a blinding flash that flooded the room with violet light, and was instantly followed by a shattering crash directly overhead, as if some aerial three-decker had fired a broadside straight down the chimney. The instantaneous flash, followed by what seemed to the dazzled eye a period of total darkness, left Mr. Toke with a strangely vivid impression of the cottage interior, in which all its details were clearly visible: The seated figure of his host, the old woman, standing by the fire, the tea-pot poised in her hand, the little dresser with its modest crockery set out in an orderly array, and one or two pictures on the wall. But all these things lay, as it were, on the margin of his field of vision, seen, indeed, but only half-consciously perceived. For it happened that, at the moment of the flash, Mr. Toke's eyes had been fixed upon a dim square patch of paleness that was just barely discernible in the darkest corner of the room, and he had been speculating on the nature of the object to which it appertained. The flash solved that problem. The pale, square patch was the dial of a long-case clock. Anyone could have seen that much. But Mr. Toke saw a good deal more. It is true that the object was seen only for an infinitesimal fraction of a second (plus a further sixteenth-of-a-second for what the physiologists call "the persistence of visual impressions"), and that in that instant of time it had revealed little more than a dark silhouette. But a silhouette may be highly significant. It was to Mr. Toke. The square-headed hood, flanked by twisted pillars, the slender body, the low plinth, taken together, suggested a date before the time of good Queen Anne. There were, indeed, two hands – pointing to an impossible hour and clearly indicating that the clock was not a "going concern" – but there was nothing incongruous in this, for two-handed clocks and even eight-day movements, were made before the dawn of the eighteenth century.

But what really did worry Mr. Toke was the appearance of the dial. It was obviously white. Now the seventeenth-century clock-maker had a soul above a painted dial. If this dial was painted, as it appeared to be, there were two possibilities: Either the old dial had been barbarously covered with paint or, at some time, the clock had fallen into the hands of a Philistine and had its original movement replaced by a new one.

It was a momentous question, and Mr. Toke debated it anxiously as he stirred his tea and kept up a rambling conversation with his host. Of course, it was none of his business – at least one would have said so. But one would have been wrong. Mr. Toke intended to make it his business. There are, indeed, some who maintain that to strike a keen bargain with an ignorant man who happens to possess some valuable object is a base act almost tantamount to robbery. This was not Mr. Toke's view. He held most emphatically that the expert was fully entitled to the usufruct of his knowledge. And there is something to be said for this point of view. A man does not become a connoisseur without the expenditure of time, effort, and money, and as to the person who, by chance inheritance, happens to possess a Rembrandt or a Leonardo and elects to use it as a tea-tray or to cover up a damp place on the wall, it is not easy to grow sentimental over his rights. After all, the base collector rescues the treasure from imminent destruction, and preserves it for the benefit of mankind at large.

At any rate, Mr. Toke, recalling the fugitive vision of that elegant silhouette, kept an acquisitive eye on the dim, pale square, which, like the grin of the Cheshire cat, persisted when all else had vanished, and cast about for some mode of strategic approach to the subject. Presently his host, all unconsciously, gave him an opening.

"You takes your tea early," he remarked (it had just turned half-past-three).

Mr. Toke pulled out his watch and glanced at the drum clock on the mantelshelf.

"Is your clock right?" he asked.

"Ay – leastways as near as I can tell. I sets him by the carrier's cart. He go past every morning at nine o'clock, sharp."

255

"Ha," said Mr. Toke, "and does it keep good time – the clock, I mean?"

"Ay, he do that. Wunnerful good time he keeps. And I only give three shillings for him, brand noo."

"Really," said Mr. Toke. "It's surprising how cheap clocks are nowadays."

"Ay," agreed the host, "times has changed. It's what they calls progress. Now, that old clock in the corner, he wasn't never bought for three shillings. No, nor for three pund."

Mr. Toke stared into the dark corner indicated, as if he had not noticed the clock before. But the corner was less dark now, for, with the last crash, the storm seemed to have spent its wrath, and now a gleam of sunshine stole in at the window and so brightened up the room that the shape of the clock became distinctly visible.

"No," Mr. Toke concurred, "there were no three-shilling clocks in the days when that was made. Have you had it long?"

"Had him from my old woman's grandfather. And he had him from the squire what he was coachman to. So he wasn't made yesterday. He's like my old woman and me – he's one of the has-beens."

"Does it keep good time?" Mr. Toke asked, regardless of the wildly erroneous position of the hands.

His host chuckled. "Don't keep no time at all. Won't go. My darter's husband has a tinker at him now and again – he's a plumber and gas-fitter by trade – but it ain't no use. The' old clock's wore out. Takin' up room to no purpose. Chap offered me five shillin' for him, and I'd a-took it. But my old woman said no. So we kep' him."

"It wasn't a very liberal offer," Mr. Toke remarked.

"That's what I thought," said the old woman. "'Twasn't enough for a good old clock, even if it won't go. I said so to Tom at the time."

"Well," growled Thomas, "who's a-going for to pay good money for a clock what won't even tick?"

Mr. Toke decided that the time had come to open negotiations.

"There are such people," said he. "I have a friend who has quite a fancy for old clocks. He would probably be willing to give you a couple of pounds for it."

"Then," said Thomas, "I be glad if you'd send him along this way. What d'you say, Susan?"

"Two pounds 'ud be very useful," replied the old woman. "But I doubt if he'd give it when he see the clock. It be terrible old."

Mr. Toke rose and strolled across to the corner. The light was now quite good, and at close quarters it was possible to make out the details. And at some of those details Mr. Toke's gorge rose, and he half regretted the liberality of his offer. The venerable time-piece had received the most shocking treatment from some Vandal. The case was encrusted with varnish, apparently applied with a tar brush, and the brass dial had received a thick coat of white paint. Yet, through the treacly depths of the varnish and the layer of paint, other details were faintly discernible which he noted with deep satisfaction.

The clock had been an aristocrat in its day. The dark wood of the case was richly ornamented with marquetry, and a framed panel seemed to enclose some initials and a date, though Mr. Toke could not actually decipher them. But their presence hinted at a possibly traceable history, which would greatly enhance the value of the piece. A glance at the dial showed it to be undoubtedly the original one. The corner ornaments – simple cherubs' heads – were quite characteristic of the period, as were the hour and minute figures, where they were distinguishable, and the hands, though their form was obscured by a thick coat of black enamel paint, showed the simple elegance that marks the work of the earlier makers. Mr. Toke, seeking in vain to decipher the maker's name, was reassured. Perhaps, after all, the plumber's contribution did not go beyond the paint and the varnish.

"Do you happen to remember the name of the squire who originally owned the clock?" Mr. Toke enquired.

"His name was Hawkwood," the old woman replied. "Sir John Hawkwood."

Mr. Toke made a mental note of the name and announced, "I am inclined to think that my friend would be willing to give a couple of pounds for this clock, if you are prepared to sell it."

Thomas was undoubtedly prepared to sell, and said so with some emphasis, and the old lady opined that two pounds would be more useful than the clock.

"Very well," said Mr. Toke, "then we will consider the matter settled. How am I to get the clock to my house?"

"Where is your house?" the practical-minded Thomas demanded.

"I live at Hartsden Manor, just outside the village."

"I knows him," said Thomas. "A tumbledown old house just alongside the old church what is shut up. 'Tain't fur from here. A couple of mile. I could run th' old clock down in my barrer."

"When?" asked Mr. Toke.

"Now, if yer like. I suppose yer pays on delivery?"

"Certainly. When I receive the clock, you'll receive the money."

With this stimulus, Thomas awoke to strenuous activity. The clock was hauled out of its corner and, while Mr. Toke detached the pendulum and secured the weights in a packing of spare garments, old Susan went in search of a blanket, and Thomas retired to fetch the "barrer." In a few minutes all was ready. The clock, decently swathed in the blanket, and faintly suggesting an impending inquest, was tied firmly on the barrow and Thomas signified that the procession was ready to start.

The journey to Hartsden was, for the most part, uneventful. One or two wayfarers on the road greeted the barrow and its burden with surprised grins and, at the entrance to the village, a group of schoolboys, just released from bondage, formed up into an orderly procession and followed the barrow, two by two, with bare and bowed beads and unseemly giggles, a proceeding that attracted unnecessary attention, and added appreciably to the gaiety of the neighbourhood for the time being.

"Passel o' grinnin' fules," said Thomas, casting a resentful and contemptuous glance at the little party of smiling bystanders as he drew up at the gate of the house while Mr. Toke unfastened it to admit him to the short drive. As the gate swung open, he stooped to grasp the handles of the barrow at the moment when one of the juvenile mourners advanced, with his handkerchief held to his eyes, to drop a dandelion on the shrouded clock.

The business was soon concluded to mutual satisfaction. The clock was conveyed to a disused room at the back of the house and deposited on a rough table. Then Mr. Toke wrote out a receipt in such terms as amounted to a formal conveyance of the property and, when the vendor had subscribed his sign manual, two sovereigns were laid on the table.

"Thank ye, sir," said Thomas, transferring them to his pocket. "I hopes the clock will suit your friend. I shouldn't like to think of it being left on your hands."

"He'll have to take it now that I have paid for it," replied Mr. Toke. "But you needn't worry. He'll be quite satisfied."

In point of fact, the "friend" was more than satisfied. A rapid inspection showed that the case was in excellent condition under the crust of varnish, and through the latter, it was now possible to see that the dark walnut was adorned with marquetry of a richness unusual in such early work. For, in the strong light, the date was clearly legible as well as the initials, grouped in a triangle around a heart – J. H. M. 1692, the H being uppermost and, as Mr. Toke reasonably surmised, representing the name, Hawkwood. The dial and hands, too, were of appropriate style and of the same excellent workmanship, and on the former could now be deciphered, through the paint: "Robert Cooke, Londini, fecit."

From this general, preliminary inspection Mr. Toke proceeded to the consideration of details. He had already noticed that the case was closed at the bottom. Now, on opening the door, he observed a partition closing the interior space at an appreciably higher level. This was rather

258

remarkable, for the position of this upper partition was such as possibly to interfere with the proper fall of the weights. But what was still more remarkable was the way in which it was secured. There were four screws, but, though the wood of the partition appeared to be old, the screws certainly did not. Their bright, clean heads seemed to shout, "Nettlefold!"

Mr. Toke was quite interested. Between those two partitions there must be a space. That space might be an ancient hiding-place. But the screws hardly supported that view. At any rate, the question could soon be set at rest. And the first turn of the screwdriver settled it. The readiness with which the screw turned suggested a touch of tallow, and a greasy stain on the wood around the hole was clear confirmation. The other three screws followed with the same ease, and then, by inserting a bradawl into one of the holes, it was possible to prise up the loose partition.

Now, whether this had or had not been an ancient hiding-place, it was quite clear that the contents were modern, consisting of a parcel wrapped in undeniable newspaper. Mr. Toke lifted it out and, having cut the string, carefully opened it. And then he got the surprise of his life. There were several layers of paper, the innermost being of clean tissue paper and, when the last of these was turned back, there was revealed to Mr. Toke's astonished gaze a magnificent diamond necklace and a still more magnificent pendant.

For some moments he stood staring at the gorgeous bauble, lost in amazement. Then a slow grin stole over his face. Now he understood how it was that the "tinkerings" of the plumber and gas-fitter had failed to make the clock go. "My darter's husband" had had other fish to fry. But that estimable artisan seemed to have taken unnecessary risks, for the door had a lock. Apparently it was not in working order, and the key was missing (perhaps in the plumber's possession). Common prudence would have suggested a repair to the lock. But, possibly, it had been left for fear of attracting attention. Thomas was not, it had seemed, gifted with a peculiarly enquiring mind. Perhaps the plumber had adopted the more prudent course.

But the obvious question arose: What was to be done? Mr. Toke believed that he recognized the necklace. He thought that he recalled a daring daylight robbery at a great London house when the thief had entered a bedroom by way of a stack-pipe while the family were at dinner and got away unseen with a diamond necklace – presumably this very one – said to be worth £20,000. There would therefore be no difficulty in discovering the owner. Indeed, there was no need for him to do anything of the kind. All that was necessary was to report the discovery to the police. And this was what occurred to Mr. Toke as the obvious thing to do.

But was it so very obvious, after all? Mr. Toke looked at the necklace, and somehow the obviousness of that course of action seemed to grow less. In the course of his rather varied life, Mr. Toke had been connected for a year or two with the diamond and gem trade. That tended strongly to influence his point of view. It was not that he was a great judge of gems. He was not, though, of course, he could price a stone approximately. But the vital fact, in regard to the present transaction, was that he knew the ropes. The man who had stolen this jewel had been reduced to the necessity of hiding it until such time as he should find a "fence" who would take the incriminating treasure off his hand and ask no questions. And what would that fence pay him for it? No more than a paltry fraction of its real value. Now he, Mr. Toke, could dispose of it at something like its market price.

He looked at it with a calculating eye. It was a fine necklace. Probably the report had not greatly over-estimated its value. Every stone in it was a valuable stone. But there was no one of those fine brilliants that was of spectacular value. Not one of them was of a size that would involve questions or possibly lead to identification. He could safely deal with any of them in the ordinary market.

And, after all, why not? He had not stolen the necklace. So far as he was concerned, it was a case of treasure trove, pure and simple. So he told himself, casuistically trying to smother his not very lively scruples. Of course, he knew quite well that he was contemplating a theft. But although, up to this time, he had been a least conventionally honest, he was, if not actually avaricious, highly acquisitive by nature, as is apt to be the case with collectors. He had the passion to possess and, even if he had been unable to dispose of these diamonds, he would still have been reluctant to give them up.

The conflict in his mind was not a long one. There were the diamonds – ten thousand pounds' worth of them, at a moderate estimate – staring him in the face and inviting him to accept the gifts of Fortune. There was absolutely no danger. The transaction was as simple and safe as an ordinary commercial deal. Suppose the plumber should denounce him to the police. It was wildly improbable, but suppose he did? Well, who was going to prove that the diamonds were ever there? The plumber's unsupported testimony would go for nothing, and apart from him, there was, presumably, no one who had any knowledge of their whereabouts – unless it was "my darter", but neither of these was in a position to swear that the diamonds were in the clock-case when it was

260

removed from its late owner's custody. Mr. Toke's position was impregnable. He simply knew nothing about the matter.

But he was not going to leave it at that. No sooner had he taken the fateful resolution to treat this gorgeous derelict as treasure trove than the inevitable psychological effect began to manifest itself. The contemplation of a criminal act immediately began to generate the criminal mentality. Safe as the enterprise was, he was going to make it safer. The tracks, already confused, must be further confounded. His intention had been to clean the case himself. He was a fairly expert french polisher. Not that he had contemplated french polishing this old case. On the contrary, his intention had been to un-french-polish it. But now he realized the inexpediency of meddling with it at all. It should go, just as it was, for treatment to some third party. Thus would the issues be further confused.

Having made his decision, he acted promptly. The very next day he conveyed the clock to a roomy closed car that he had lately adopted, and bore it up to town. There he deposited the movement at the premises of a reliable "chamber worker" in Clerkenwell for a careful overhaul, and then carried the case to Curtain Road and handed it to a skilful cabinet-maker with the instruction that it was to be cleaned and wax-polished, but left structurally intact, with the exception of any trifling repairs that might be unavoidable. The lock was to be repaired and fitted with a key of the correct pattern according to the date on the panel.

When he had done this, Mr. Toke felt that he had made his position unassailable. He allowed himself to hope that he would be left in undisputed possession of his treasure trove. But his hopes were tempered by a suspicion that he had not heard the last of the worthy Thomas's too-ingenious son-in-law. And subsequent events justified his suspicions.

261

Chapter II
Enter Mr. Hughes

It was a little over a week after his acquisition of the clock that Mr. Toke's forebodings began to be realized. On that day, about eleven in the forenoon, his housekeeper, Mrs. Gibbins, came to him as he sat in his study writing letters, and announced with something of an air of mystery that a man wished to see him.

"A man?" Mr. Toke repeated. "Do you mean a gentleman?"

Mrs. Gibbins made it extremely clear that she did not.

"Did he say what his business was?"

"No, sir. I asked him, but he said he wanted to see you on private business. He wouldn't say what it was. He is waiting in the hall. I told Margaret to keep an eye on him." (Margaret was Mrs. Gibbins's niece and functioned as housemaid.)

"Well," said Mr. Toke, "I suppose you had better bring him in here. But I can't imagine who he can be," which was not perfectly candid on Mr. Toke's part. He had a strong suspicion that the visitor would turn out to be an exponent of the plumbing and gas-fitting arts. And even so it befell. When Mrs. Gibbins returned, she was accompanied by a somewhat seedy stranger of truculent aspect, whose appearance suggested a Labour agitator or a working man of strongly political leanings.

"Well," said Mr. Toke, when the housekeeper had retired, "what is it that you want to see me about?"

His visitor crept towards him with an air of mystery and secrecy, and replied impressively, "It's about a clock what you bought off of my father-in-law, Mr. Hobson."

"Yes," said Mr. Toke, "I remember. An old clock, a good deal out of repair. Yes. What about it?"

"Well, you see, Mr. Hobson hadn't got no right for to sell you that clock. 'Twasn't his for to sell. That clock belongs to my wife. It was give to her as a wedding present."

Mr. Toke reflected rapidly. It would be perfectly practicable to restore the clock, since its contents were now securely concealed in an undiscoverable hiding-place. The clock, itself, valuable as it was, had become, by comparisons negligible. Nevertheless, Mr. Toke's strongly acquisitive temperament made him reluctant to disgorge. Besides, to what purpose should he restore the clock? Its return, empty, would not dispose of the business. It was not the clock but the necklace that this worthy craftsman was seeking. And then there was the practical certainty that his statement was a barefaced untruth. No, there was nothing to be gained by an attempt to compromise.

"This is very unfortunate," said Mr. Toke, "but I am afraid you will have to settle the matter with Mr. Hobson. He has the money. I have no doubt that, if you put it to him, he will hand it over to you."

"But my wife don't want to sell the clock, nor more don't I."

"Ha," said Mr. Toke, "that is a pity, because, you see, the clock has been sold. I bought it in a perfectly regular manner, and I have Mr. Hobson's receipt for the price of it."

"But don't I keep telling yer that old Hobson hadn't no right for to sell it?"

Mr. Toke admitted that the matter had been mentioned. "But," he continued, "that is really not my concern. You must settle the affair with your father-in-law."

"Ho, must I? Fat lot of good it 'ud be talking to him. No, Mister, I'm going to settle with you, I am. You've got my clock, and you're going to hand it over. I've got the barrer outside."

Mr. Toke complimented him on his providence, but declined to consider the demand.

"Look here," the stranger exclaimed in a threatening tone, "if you don't want any trouble, you just hand that clock over. I'm going to have it, you know. I'm going to make you hand it over. See? You think I can't, but I tell you I can."

"I am sure you can," Mr. Toke agreed. "That is just my point. If the clock is yours, you can compel me to return it. All you have to do is to go to your solicitor, give him proof of your title to the property, and instruct him to recover it in the ordinary way. He will make no trouble about it."

"Gawd!" exclaimed the other. "I don't want all that trouble and fuss. And I don't want no solicitors. I shall just inform the police."

"Yes," said Mr. Toke, "you could do that. If your father-in-law did actually sell a clock that was not his property, he undoubtedly was guilty of a criminal act. You might prosecute him. So might I, for obtaining money from me by false pretences. But you would have to prove that the clock was yours, in any case. It would be less trouble to instruct a solicitor, and you would avoid the scandal."

Mr. Toke's calm, detached attitude seemed rather to nonplus his visitor, for the latter stood for some time gazing at him, breathing hard but uttering no word. At length he resumed, in a milder, even pacific tone, "I don't want to make no trouble for old Hobson, seeing as he is my wife's father. And I don't want no truck with solicitors. I'll tell you what I'll do. You hand me back that clock, and I'll give you the two quid what you paid for it. I can't say no fairer than that."

But Mr. Toke shook his head regretfully. "I am sorry, Mr. – I didn't quite catch your name – "

"My name is Dobey. Charles Dobey, if you want to know."

"Thank you. I was saying that I am extremely sorry that I can't accept your offer. But, to begin with, the clock is not here, and as I have already spent a substantial sum of money on it, I should not be prepared to sell it at the price that I gave for it."

"What do you mean about spending money on it?" Mr. Dobey asked with evident uneasiness.

"Well, you see," said Mr. Toke, "in the first place, I had to send the case to a cabinet-maker's – "

"What!" gasped Dobey. Then, controlling himself, he demanded, huskily, "What was the cabinet maker going to do to it? There wasn't nothing the matter with the case."

"Nothing structural," Mr. Toke agreed. "But it wanted a clean up. I told him to clean off all the old varnish and put on a slight wax polish. That was all. And I have had the movement put in order. So you see, the clock is now worth a good deal more than I gave for it."

"And where is it now?" Mr. Dobey asked, gloomily.

"I have sent it to Messrs. Moore and Burgess, the eminent auctioneers, and I understand that it will be put up for sale next Thursday – a week from to-day."

Mr. Dobey reflected on this statement with an expression compounded of dejection and bewilderment. And, meanwhile, Mr. Toke looked him over, critically. He was not much to look at. He presented none of those interesting "stigmata" that distinguish the criminal countenance in the plates of Lombroso's treatises. He was just a common "low-grade" man of the type that may be seen by the dozen, taking the air in the exercise yard of any local prison, with darkish red hair and – not unusually – a nose to match, hands suggestive of deficient washing rather than excessive labour, and a noticeably shifty and furtive cast of countenance.

At length be pulled himself together for a final effort.

"This is all very well, you know, Mister, but I can't allow you to put up my clock to auction just as if it was your own. You'll have to get it back, and I'll make you an allowance for what you've spent on it."

"I'm afraid I can't agree to that." said Mr. Toke. "You seem to be forgetting that, at present, I am the legal owner of that clock. The receipt that I hold establishes my ownership, and if you claim that the clock is yours, it is for you to produce evidence of ownership. You haven't done that, you know and, if you haven't any papers to prove that it was given to your wife, I don't think you would be able to do it."

"I could swear a affidavit," said Mr. Dobey.

"M'yes," agreed Mr. Toke. "But you have to be a bit careful about affidavits. There is such a thing as perjury, you know. I shouldn't recommend an affidavit."

Mr. Dobey received this advice with a bewildered stare. He could make nothing of it. Mr. Toke's bland, impersonal attitude left him, for the moment, speechless. At length, he asked, lamely, "Well, what am I to do? I ought to be able to get my own clock back – leastways, my wife's clock."

"So you are," said Mr. Toke. "There's nothing to prevent you from going to the auction and bidding."

For some moments Mr. Dobey was too much over come to be capable of any reply. At last, he exclaimed, hoarsely, "Well, I am blowed, I reely am. You've got the blinkin' sauce to tell me to go to the blinkin' auction and buy in my own clock. And you to take the money. I never heard the likes of it!"

"I merely threw out the suggestion," said Mr. Toke. "I thought you were anxious to get the clock. You could always sell it and get your money back, you know."

Futile as the suggestion seemed, it was craftily conceived, and Mr. Toke, furtively watching his visitor, saw that it had taken effect. The aggressive expression faded out of Mr. Dobey's countenance and gave place to one indicative of reflection.

"Where do these auction blokes hang out?" he asked after a longish pause.

Mr. Toke took out from his letter case a card on which was inscribed, "*Mr. Didbury Toke, 151 Queen Square, Bloomsbury, Tuesday and Friday, 11 to 5 or by Appointment*" On the back of this he wrote the address of the auctioneers, and handed it to Mr. Dobey, who, having read what was written, turned the card over and studied the printed inscription.

"I'll have to think over this," he remarked gloomily, and then, as if a new idea had struck him, he demanded, "What is the name of the cabinet-maker what did the clock up?"

"His name," said Mr. Toke, writing on a slip of paper as he spoke, "is Levy, Maurice Levy, and his place is in Curtain Road."

"Sounds like a sheeny," Dobey remarked, disparagingly.

"He is, as you have guessed, of the Jewish faith," Mr. Toke admitted. "A most excellent workman and a thoroughly honest man."

"Ho," said Mr. Dobey, in a tone of obvious scepticism. But he seemed to get some comfort from the description, nevertheless. He gazed reflectively at the slip of paper for a while, and then, slowly and reluctantly, rose.

"Well," he remarked in an aggrieved tone, "this ain't what I expected, but I suppose there's no use staying here chin-waggin' to no purpose."

He moved dejectedly towards the door, and Mr. Toke piloted him to the hall and launched him with a suave "Good morning" from the front door, watching him with a faint smile as he slouched down the short drive. He was not dissatisfied with the result of the interview. His subtle hint had evidently taken effect. And though there would certainly be trouble if Dobey really bought the clock, it would be better so than that some other purchaser should have his house burgled, with the possibility of a capture and awkward explanations.

On the following Wednesday, the day before the sale, Mr. Toke arrived betimes at the rooms of Messrs. Moore and Burgess to watch the company of dealers and connoisseurs who had gathered to view the goods that were to be sold on the following day. There were two large rooms, connected by a wide doorway and, immediately opposite the doorway, the clock was standing, ticking solemnly in proof of its perfectly restored health. Mr. Toke halted before it and surveyed it with not unpardonable pride. By the joint efforts of Mr. Levy and the Clerkenwell artist, the shabby outcast that had cumbered the floor of Thomas Hobson's cottage had been restored to its rightful status as an aristocrat among clocks. The fine, dark walnut case with its rich marquetry had emerged from the crust of varnish as a butterfly comes forth from its pupa-shell, the brass dial with its cherub-heads and its silver hour-circle had been cleansed of the paint, and yet not cleansed too much, and the hands once more showed the fine, simple workmanship of their period.

Mr. Toke stood and let his eyes travel over its revived beauties with the genuine pleasure of the connoisseur, congratulating himself on having been the means of rescuing it from its unworthy surroundings and the risk of destruction. But, even as he gloated, he kept a watchful eye on the entrance through which new-corners were constantly pouring in, and it was, perhaps, just as well that he did, for, even as he held the narrow door of the clock open and peered in to see that the partition had not been tampered with, the countenance of Mr. Dobey came into view among the little crowd of new arrivals.

Now there was really no reason why Mr. Toke should have made any secret of his presence in the rooms. As a collector, it was quite natural that he should be there. But recent transactions had engendered in him a new furtiveness and secrecy. He didn't want Dobey to see him, and he did want to keep an eye on Dobey. Accordingly, having shut the clock-case, he made his way, as well as the crowded state of the rooms would let him, through the doorway into the other room, and looked about for some means of concealment. A large French armoire seemed to offer the best cover for, from the shadow behind it, he could get a good view of the adjoining room in a large mirror.

Here, then, he established himself, and soon the bereaved artisan came into view. He was quite respectably dressed, and would have been unnoticeable but for the self-consciousness which caused him to move stealthily and suspiciously among the crowd. Very soon he spied the clock and crept up to it with ill-assumed unconcern. Mr. Toke watched him with grim amusement. Evidently, the changed appearance of the clock puzzled him considerably. The distinctive characteristics, now so striking, had been hidden by the varnish, and were unfamiliar to him, He stared at the clock, and then gazed about in search of another. But this was the only clock in the room. Finally, after a furtive glance to right and left, he ventured to open the door of the case and peer in. Then, evidently, some chord of memory was struck. No doubt the four Nettlefold screws were old friends. At any rate, he closed the door with an air of decision, and once more began to look about him furtively and uneasily, while Mr. Toke watched expectantly to see what his next move would be.

For some time Dobey crept to and fro rather aimlessly, gazing at the exhibits, but keeping in the neighbourhood of the clock, and Mr. Toke had the feeling that he was waiting for someone. And so it turned out, presently. The meeting was singularly unostentatious but Mr. Toke, watching narrowly, noted the mutual recognition. The new-corner was a well-dressed man, obviously of a superior class to Mr. Dobey, who walked in confidently and, having looked round, glanced at the catalogue that he held and then walked straight up to the clock. He stood before it and surveyed it critically, point by point: Tried the lock, opened the door of the case, gazed into the interior and reclosed it. And it was at this moment that the meeting took place. There was no sign of recognition, but, as the stranger stood inspecting the clock, Dobey sidled up and for a moment stood by his side. Nothing appeared to be said, but the stranger made an entry in his catalogue. Then Dobey moved away and, after a few vague glances at some of the exhibits, faded away towards the entry and vanished into the outer world.

With the disappearance of Mr. Dobey, concealment became no longer necessary. Mr. Toke emerged boldly, and made his way into the other room with the purpose of getting a closer look at Mr. Dobey's friend. The circumstances were favourable for getting, at least, an unobserved back view, and the observant Mr. Toke, beginning with a minute inspection from the rear, arrived at the decision that the unknown wore a wig. It was an exceedingly good wig – so good and well-fitting as to suggest a bald or shaved head underneath. Having made this interesting observation, Mr. Toke contrived to obtain a view of the stranger's face. It impressed him as a rather curious face, but he presently realized that the peculiarity of expression was due to the absence of eyebrows. Either they were naturally deficient or they had been shaved off. The presence of the wig suggested the former, but the meeting with Mr. Dobey made the latter possibility quite conceivable. At any rate, the dark-brown wig, with eyes to match, and the curiously blank forehead, rendered the stranger easy to recognize, which was satisfactory, as Mr. Toke intended to keep an eye on him, if, as seemed likely, he should turn up at the sale on the following day.

And turn up he did. Mr. Toke, keeping a bright look-out, saw him come in, catalogue in hand, and select a seat well in view of the auctioneer. Mr. Toke saw him fairly seated and then found a place for himself, where he could command an uninterrupted view of the stranger without making himself conspicuous. As he was not going to bid, he had no need to be in a position to catch the auctioneer's eye.

His vigil was not unduly prolonged, for the clock came early in the list. As the number approached, he watched the wigged stranger, but his queer blank face showed no sign of uneasiness. He watched the proceedings stolidly, and did not even glance at his catalogue. Evidently, he was not a jumpy man.

At length the fateful number was reached. The auctioneer cleared his throat and announced, not without gusto, "Long-case clock by Robert Cooke of London, dated 1692, in a case of fine walnut wood, enriched with elaborate marquetry. A most exceptional lot, this, gentlemen. It is really a museum piece. I have never seen a clock of this early period in such perfect condition. It is virtually untouched. With the exception of a modern partition in the bottom of the case, there are no restorations or repairs. It is in the very condition in which the maker turned it out. And I understand that an authentic history accompanies it. The initials on the case are those of Sir John Hawkwood and the Lady Margaret, his wife. Now, gentlemen, what shall we say for this unique clock?"

Almost before he had finished speaking, a voice answered, "Fifty pounds."

Mr. Toke grinned. This was, in effect, an ultimatum. The speaker meant to have the clock, and made no secret of his intention. But he was not the only pebble on the beach, as the vulgar saying has it. His challenge was immediately taken up by another enthusiast.

"Fifty-five."

"Sixty."

"Sixty-five."

The bids followed one another with hardly a moment's interval, and the price hopped up by fives until it reached a hundred and ninety. Then there was a slight slackening, but still the bidding went on, at at a reduced pace. And all the time the gentleman in the wig sat gazing stolidly before him and uttering not a word. Mr. Toke began to be uneasy. Was he not going to bid, after all? Had he merely come to get the name of the purchaser with a view to a subsequent burglary? That was an unpleasant position. Not that it mattered very much, but, still, Mr. Toke didn't want a burglary. No one could say what disagreeable results might follow. But at this point his anxieties were dissipated by a sudden activity on the part of the wigged gentleman. The price had reached two hundred and five and, after the last bid, a somewhat lengthy pause occurred. The auctioneer repeated the bid, solemnly, and his hand stole towards his hammer. But at this moment, the wigged stranger looked at the auctioneer and nodded.

"Two hundred and ten," the latter chanted, and repeated the refrain three times with increasing emphasis. But now there was no answer. The appearance of a new competitor at the eleventh hour was too much for the others. After a long and anxious pause, the hammer came down with a sharp rap and Mr. Toke drew a deep breath.

The name of the wigged gentleman, it transpired, was Hughes. As soon as he had communicated this fact, he rose and walked over to the clock and stood for a while surveying it with apparent satisfaction. Then he turned the key in the lock, put it in his pocket and sauntered out of the room and, as the purchase of the clock left Mr. Toke with no further interest in the proceedings, he also presently rose and left the premises. And, as he wended his way to his office, he speculated, not without a shade of anxiety, on the probabilities of the immediate future. Messrs Hughes and Dobey were going to suffer a somewhat severe disappointment. It was not likely that they would suffer in silence. He had a strong presentiment that he had not heard the last of that necklace or of its quondam owners. As to Dobey, he was a negligible ass. But Mr. Hughes was in a rather different class. His conduct at the auction showed considerable judgment and self-restraint. He was clearly a gentleman who knew his own mind. A man of courage and resolution.

Mr. Toke was rather sorry that Mr. Hughes had come into the affair.

Chapter III
An Unholy Alliance

Lovers of paradox assure us that it is the unexpected that happens. Perhaps they are right. But the unexpected holds no monopoly. Sometimes the expected happens. It did, for instance, on a certain Friday afternoon – the very day, in fact, after the auction. On that day, in accordance with the announcement on his cards, Mr. Toke was in attendance at his professional premises. At the moment he was seated at the writing-table in the inner room – it was hardly an office – writing one or two letters. He was quite alone, for he had no clerk or secretary. He had no use for one, since his business was entirely personal and his transactions few, though the amounts involved were usually substantial. So there he sat, writing his letters, but by no means engrossed with the matter thereof.

To tell the literal truth, Mr. Toke was just a shade nervous. The auction had not gone quite according to plan. He had reckoned on Mr. Dobey, whereas he now had to deal with Mr. Hughes, which was a slightly different proposition. Accordingly, he sat, making shift to write, but with an attentive ear on the outer door.

It was within a few minutes of five o'clock, and he was preparing for a scrupulously punctual departure, when the expected happened. The outer door opened and, through the slight opening of the door communicating with the outer room, he saw a man enter. He rose and, stepping out into the other room found himself confronting Mr. Hughes. The visitor looked at him critically and affirmed, "I wish to see Mr. Didbury Toke."

"Fortunate man!" said Mr. Toke. "Your wish is realized even as you utter it. In what way can I be of service to you?"

"I should like to have a few words with you in private," was the reply.

"Again," said Mr. Toke, with genial facetiousness, by way of keeping up his spirits, "you are favoured. For here we are, *solus cum solo*, with none to supervise, as the poet expresses it. You can say anything you like and no one will be the wiser."

He led the way into the inner room and, shutting the communicating door, indicated a chair adjoining the writing-table, resumed his seat at the table, and looked expectantly at his visitor.

"I have come to see you on behalf of Mr. Charles Dobey," said the latter. "My own name is Hughes."

"I hope Mr. Dobey is not unwell," said Mr. Toke.

"He is not," was the reply, "but he wished me to act on his behalf, as being more experienced in business affairs. The matter is this: A short time ago you purchased from a certain Thomas Hobson an antique clock. Dobey states that the clock was actually his property, but I am not going into that. The point is, that there was certain property, which certainly was Dobey's, concealed in that clock. He had been in the habit of using it as a safe."

"What an extraordinarily stupid thing to do!" exclaimed Mr. Toke.

"I agree," said Mr. Hughes. "But he did. He stowed this property in a cavity between two partitions, the upper of which was secured with screws."

"Was this property of any considerable value?" Mr. Toke asked.

"I understand that it was."

"Dear me!" exclaimed Mr. Toke, "I wish I had known. May I ask what was its nature?"

"I understand that it consisted of jewellery," replied Mr. Hughes. "But the point is, that it has disappeared. Acting on Dobey's instructions, I bought the clock, and Dobey removed the partition in my presence. The cavity underneath was empty."

"Dear me," said Mr. Toke. "Was it, indeed? Now, I wonder how it can have disappeared."

"Dobey assumes that you removed it, and it seems a reasonable supposition. I have come to ask you what you propose to do about it."

Mr. Toke leaned back in his chair and, placing his finger-tips together, looked steadily at Mr. Hughes. He had, indeed, been looking at him throughout the interview and, as the light from the window fell full on the queer, rather sinister face, he had been able to study it advantageously. I use the word "study" advisedly, for at the first glance he had been aware of a faint stirring of memory. Mr. Toke had an exceedingly good memory for faces and, although this face was strange to him, yet, as he looked, it seemed to set some chord of memory vibrating.

"May I ask what leads you to suppose that I removed this property?" he asked, without any sign of resentment.

"It is obvious enough," Hughes replied. "The property was there when the clock came into your possession, and it isn't there now."

"But," protested Toke, "you seem to be over-looking the number of hands through which the clock has passed. There is the cabinet-maker,

271

the clock-maker who fitted the movement to the case, and various unknown persons who had access to it at the auction rooms."

"And there is yourself, the only one of the lot who happens to have the means of disposing of valuable jewellery."

"That is quite true," Mr. Toke agreed. "If Dobey had offered me the jewellery, I could certainly have disposed of it to advantage. Unfortunately, he did not. And you must see that my professional standing has no bearing on the question as to who found the jewellery, assuming it to have been really there. The fact is that I, of course, saw the partition, and I saw that it had no business to be there. But I make it a rule, when I buy a piece with the intention of selling it, to leave it exactly as I find it. And I instructed the cabinet-maker to make no structural changes in the case – otherwise, he would, no doubt, have removed the partition, as it might be thought to stand in the way of the weights. Still, it might be worthwhile to ask him if he did remove it."

"I have," said Mr. Hughes, "and he states very positively that he did not. And I believe him."

"So do I," said Mr. Toke. "He is a most respectable man, and would, I am sure, have reported to me if he had made any discovery. And so, I think, would the clock-maker. If the property was really there, it must have been abstracted by someone after it was delivered at the auction rooms."

Mr. Hughes received this statement in gloomy silence, but with a lowering of the brows – or, at least, of the region where the brows should have been – that plainly expressed his unbelief. But he did not leave it at mere facial expression. After a somewhat lengthy pause, he said, in low, emphatic tones, "Look here, Mr. Toke, all this evasion is no good. You have got those jewels. It is of no use your telling me that you haven't. I am perfectly sure that you have."

"Very well," Mr. Toke replied calmly, "then there is no more to be said. You have your legal remedy, you know."

"You know that we have nothing of the sort," replied Hughes. "I realize that you can stick to them if you like. The question is, do you intend to hold on to them, or are you willing to make some sort of arrangement with Dobey?"

Mr. Toke reflected. Once before, when he had discovered the jewels, he had stood at the cross-roads, and he had taken the wrong turning. Now he stood at the cross-roads again. Should he share the loot with these two rascals, or should he accept the gifts of Fortune and snap his fingers at them?

It was a momentous question – more momentous than he knew. If he could have looked into the future and seen the consequences that hung on his decision, that decision might have been very different. But Mr. Toke was like the rest of us. He could be wise enough after the event. But the future was a matter of guess work. And it is always possible to guess wrong. Probably Mr. Toke guessed wrong on this occasion. At any rate, he made the fateful decision, and the future was to show that it was the wrong one.

"I cannot be committed to any opinions that you may have formed," said he. "As to these jewels, I feel no conviction that they were ever there. Mr. Dobey is a plumber and gas-fitter. Now, what has a gas-fitter to do with valuable jewels?"

"We need not go into that," Mr. Hughes said, brusquely.

"Very true. We need not," Mr. Toke agreed. "There is certainly a particular kind of gas-fitter who comes into the possession of valuable jewels. But he is not an honest kind of gas-fitter, whose word could be accepted without proof. I am very doubtful about those jewels."

"Then I take it that you don't mean to make any kind of arrangement?"

"I am willing to make one concession," Mr. Toke replied. "As I assume that you bought the clock for the purpose of recovering the jewels, I am ready to take it back at the price that you paid, subject to its being in the same condition as when it was sold."

"Well," said Hughes, "I suppose we must be thankful for small mercies. We don't want to drop a couple of hundred on an empty shell. I will accept your offer. The clock shall be delivered here in good condition next Tuesday, if that will suit you."

"It will suit me perfectly," replied Mr. Toke. "And as to payment? Will a crossed cheque do?"

"Certainly," Hughes replied and, for the first time, his rather unprepossessing countenance was illuminated by the ghost of a smile.

Mr. Toke was secretly surprised, but he concealed the fact and rejoined, "One naturally prefers to draw crossed cheques. Shall I give the cheque to the person who delivers the clock?

"No," replied Hughes. "I will come with it, or soon after."

Mr. Toke nodded and, as the other rose to depart, said facetiously, and perhaps a little untactfully, "I am sorry that things have turned out so unsatisfactorily for Mr. Dobey, but if he had brought his heirlooms to me, instead of hiding them in a clock in someone else's house, we might have made some mutually satisfactory arrangement – that is, if he wished to dispose of them. You might mention the fact to him for his future guidance."

It was not a tactful thing to say, under the circumstances and, for a moment, Mr. Hughes looked decidedly vicious. But, if he was an angry man, he was also a politic man. He was not going to let temper stand in the way of self-interest. Just as the great difficulty of the murderer is the disposal of the body, so the great difficulty of those who acquire unlawful goods is the disposal of the loot. Now Mr. Toke undoubtedly had the means of disposing of valuable property. Mr. Hughes had not. For though, like Mr. Toke, he knew the ropes, there were circumstances that hindered his appearance in the places where precious things were bought and sold. Therefore, to Mr. Toke's surprise, instead of resenting the advice, he replied dryly, "He will be grateful for the tip. Shall I tell him that you are prepared to waive the question of title deeds?"

Mr. Toke smiled blandly. "When I am offered property for purchase," he said, "I assume that the vendor is the owner. It is a reasonable assumption."

"Quite," agreed Hughes. "But suppose there seems to be a flaw in the title. How would that affect the transaction? I suppose it would be a case of a knock-down price, at any rate?"

"My dear sir," said Mr. Toke, "you know very well that property which is hampered by conditions that hinder its sale in the open market is of less value than property not so hampered. That has to be allowed for in order to leave a reasonable profit to the purchaser. But the allowance need not be excessive."

Hughes reflected with a calculating eye on Mr. Toke. After a considerable pause, he said, rather suddenly, "Look here, Mr. Toke. I want to ask you a plain question. I don't know a great deal about Dobey's affairs, but I fancy that he sometimes comes by oddments of property – jewellery, for the most part – that are not quite negotiable in the regular markets. I don't know where he picks them up. It isn't my affair. Now the question is, in plain language, would you be prepared to take them off his hands and give him a fair price for them?"

"If I bought them, I should give a fair price, allowing for difficulties of disposal. But I couldn't have Dobey coming here, you know, or at my private house."

"I realize that," said Hughes. "But that could be arranged. May I take it that you would be willing to buy the goods and ask no questions?"

Mr. Toke was a little staggered by the bluntness of the phrase, but he answered with belated caution, "My business, hitherto, has been of a strictly legitimate kind. My reputation in the trade is spotless. Still, if the affair could be arranged with absolute discretion, I might be prepared to consider a deal of the kind that you propose."

"Very well," said Hughes, "I will tell Dobey. And, if he should happen to pick up any chance trifles, we must consider how the negotiations could be carried out."

With this Mr. Hughes took his leave and departed with very mixed feelings. On the one hand, he was possessed by a murderous hatred of Mr. Toke. That the latter had the diamonds – that he had quietly annexed the product of an almost unique coup – he had no doubt. But he was equally sure that Mr. Toke's position was impregnable. By no means that he could think of could that discreet gentleman be made to disgorge. On the other hand, much to his surprise, Toke seemed quite willing to act as a receiver of stolen property. That was all to the good, for Toke would probably pay better prices than the wretched pittances offered by the regular "fences." And he would be much safer to deal with, provided the transactions were kept on the discreet lines that both of them desired. So Mr. Hughes was not displeased, especially as the arrangement promised, sooner or later, to give him a chance to settle accounts with Mr. Toke.

The latter gentleman, left alone in his office, was also a little surprised at himself. After years of blameless dealing, he had suddenly proposed to embark on the perilous activities of the "receiver". Why this sudden change of outlook? He was a little puzzled, though he dimly perceived the explanation, which was, in reality, fairly simple. He had dismounted the diamonds from their settings, and had made an estimate of their marketable value. The amount that he could safely reckon on pocketing by their sale came out at the highly satisfactory figure of seven-thousand pounds. Now, seven-thousand pounds takes a great deal of earning by legitimate industry. Naturally he was impressed by this "easy money" – the immemorial lure that has drawn so many on to the broad road that leadeth to destruction. But the really potent influence was the fact that he was already in actual possession of stolen property, and making preparations to dispose of it. The first step had been taken and, in taking it, he had made a curious discovery. He had discovered that, apart from the attraction of easily won wealth, there was a certain element of excitement and adventure in the acquirement and sale of illicit property that was only feebly present in lawful dealing.

On the following Tuesday the clock was duly delivered, and Mr. Toke was in the act of winding it when Mr. Hughes arrived. His greeting was not effusive, nor was it in any way hostile. He merely stated that he had come for the cheque.

"A crossed cheque, you said, drawn to your own name, I suppose?"

"Yes. Arthur Hughes."

Mr. Toke wrote out the cheque and handed it to Hughes with the remark, "Well, you've got your money back, at any rate."

"Some of it," responded Hughes, adding, "Are you sure you won't reconsider the other little matter?"

But Mr. Toke's heart was hardened. Already, in effect, he had his hand on that seven-thousand pounds.

"If you mean the problem of the alleged lost property in the clock," said he, "I can only repeat that I know nothing about it, and that I am profoundly sceptical as to its having been there – at any rate when the clock came into my possession."

"Very well," said Hughes, "then we must leave it at that. And now as to the other matter – the question of your negotiating some of Dobey's unconsidered trifles. Have you considered the question of procedure?"

"In a general way," replied Mr. Toke. "In the interests of us both, we must avoid jeopardizing my position as a reputable dealer. You realize that?"

Hughes realized it perfectly. Not that he was in the least tender about Mr. Toke's reputation in the abstract, but he saw clearly that a reputable dealer could obtain, and pay, better prices than a common fence. He said so, and Mr. Toke continued, "To that end, there must be as little contact as possible. I can't have Dobey coming here, and the less you come here, yourself, the better. We must avoid leaving tracks."

"Certainly," Hughes agreed, "if you can see how to avoid leaving them."

"I think I can. We will go into that presently. But there is another point. We shall simplify matters a great deal if we try to treat one another quite fairly and honestly."

Mr. Hughes's thoughts turned, inevitably, towards the despoiled clock, and he grinned openly and undisguisedly. Nevertheless, he assented to the proposition. Mr. Toke observed and interpreted the grin, but continued unabashed, "What I mean is, that if the vendor and purchaser are each content with actual, realizable values, contacts, even by post, will be reduced to a minimum."

Hughes nodded with the air of one waiting for further details, and Toke continued, "Supposing, for instance, Dobey submits a parcel of goods with a specified price. Now, if that price is a fair one it can be paid, and there is the end of the matter. But if he makes an excessive claim, the goods must be returned, or there must be a course of bargaining, involving, in either case, an undesirable number of contacts. Or, if he should submit a parcel for an offer, and I make such an offer as, in my judgment, is the best that is practicable. If he accepts that offer without haggling, again contacts are reduced to a minimum. You see my point?"

"Yes, and I agree in principle. One can't do more until one sees how things work out in practice. How do you suggest that samples should be submitted? You don't want them left by hand, and the post is not very safe – an accident is always possible. Have you any plan?"

"A simple method occurs to me," said Mr. Toke "It is this. On receiving notice in some prearranged manner that a sample is to be delivered, I draw my car up at night in a quiet place, opposite a blank wall, with the doors locked, but the rear window open. I then leave it for a few minutes unattended. It would be quite easy for a passer-by to drop a small parcel in at the window unobserved and pass on. A few suitable localities could be designated by numbers for greater safety in making arrangements."

Mr. Hughes considered this proposal and, on the whole, approved.

"It would work all right," said he, "provided both parties keep to the principle of a square deal. Otherwise, the party who dropped his goods into the other man's window would take a biggish risk."

"Quite so," agreed Mr. Toke. "That is why I emphasized the necessity for scrupulous fair dealing on both sides."

They spent some time in settling a few details and in arranging a simple code for use in unavoidable letters. Then Hughes rose as if to depart. But, as he was turning away from the table, he paused and then sat down again.

"There is one little affair that we might settle as I am here," said he. He unbuttoned his coat and from an inner pocket produced a little wash-leather bag. From this he extracted a ring set with a single large emerald and laid it down on the table.

"Any offers?" he asked.

Mr. Toke took it up and examined it.

"A fine stone," he remarked, approvingly, "a very fine stone. Well cut, too. These step-cut stones often have the table too large. I can offer you thirty pounds for this ring."

"It is worth a good deal more than that," said Hughes.

"It is," agreed Mr. Toke. "It might fetch sixty at a suitable auction. I will give you forty-five if I may sell it publicly and say where I got it. Is that possible?"

"No," replied Hughes. "I am selling it on commission, and I don't know where the vendor got it."

"Then," said Toke, "thirty is the outside price. You see, this is an important stone. Someone is sure to have the particulars of it – the measurements and weight – so it could be identified. If I take it, I shall either have to have it re-cut or put it into store for a year or two. Still, you might get a better price from someone else."

Hughes, however, knew that he certainly would not, having tried a fence, who offered him ten pounds. But he did not mention this fact. He merely replied, "Very well. I suppose you know best. I'll take thirty, if you can't offer any more."

Accordingly the amount was paid – in cash – and Mr. Hughes took his leave.

We need not pursue the details of the subsequent transactions. The visible parties to those transactions were Toke and Hughes and, as both of them were reasonable men, the necessary conditions were loyally observed and everything went fairly smoothly. Toke made it a rule to give the best prices that were economically possible, and these were so much better than those obtainable from the regular fences that Hughes found it practicable to purchase illicit goods from certain practitioners other than Dobey, with the result that Mr. Toke was almost embarrassed by the magnitude of the transactions. Yet it was all to the good. For the increased amount of capital at his disposal enabled him not only to make more important purchases in his own legitimate line, but to indulge in the luxury, dear to the true collector's heart, of keeping specially choice pieces which he would otherwise have had to sell.

But it had another effect, and a very queer effect it was. There was a side to Mr. Toke's character which we have not had occasion to mention, because, in the ordinary affairs of life, it did not show itself. But the fact is, that there was in Mr. Toke's mental make-up a very definite streak of the miser. It was very strange. In his daily business of life, and even in his domestic affairs, he was a perfectly normal man, with a banking account and investments, an ordered financial system, and a completely rational sense of values. Yet, behind it all was that queer mental twist and, when it showed itself, Mr. Didbury Toke was a miser – a genuine miser, too, of the real "Blackberry Jones" brand.

But perhaps it was not so very strange, after all. For Mr. Toke was a born collector, and what is a miser but a collector of a rather irrational kind? A collector whose joy is in mere possession, regardless of the qualities – other than intrinsic value – of the things possessed? At any rate, there it was, and it must be mentioned because certain consequences, directly traceable to it, have to be recorded hereafter. And, for the same reason, it is necessary to describe briefly the ways in which this queer trait manifested itself.

In the good old days before the war, Mr. Toke was accustomed to keep, in one of the rooms adjoining the gallery at the Manor House in which his collection was lodged, a drawer filled with sovereigns. It was a secret hoard, not provided for current use, but like the rest of the collection, a treasure to be enjoyed by mere gloating and contemplation. At night, when the gallery door was locked, he would bring it out and set it on the table. Then, in the genuine "Blackberry Jones" manner, he

278

would sit himself down to gloat over its glittering contents, taking up handfuls of the shining coins or spreading them out on the table in rows or geometrical patterns.

Perhaps there was something to be said for this rather odd pursuit. The Sovereign was a handsome coin, particularly as to the reverse, which displayed Pistrucci's magnificent St. George. But though Mr. Toke was far from unappreciative of Pistrucci's masterpiece, it was not that work of art which endeared the coins to his heart, as subsequent events proved. For in the days that followed the war, he was compelled to make inroads on his treasure to carry out some of his foreign deals, and to furnish himself for his journeys abroad. Gradually, the golden contents of the drawer dwindled, until only a hundred or so of the coins were left.

It was at this point that the inflow of ill-gotten wealth came to his relief. The parcels of jewellery that Mr. Hughes dropped periodically in through the window of his car consisted principally of "trade" articles, which, however valuable intrinsically, were of no artistic merit. Mr. Toke's procedure was to pick out the stones and dispose of them through the ordinary trade channels. Their sale yielded him a modest profit, and with this he was content, at least for a time. But presently the gold mountings began to accumulate. If the transactions had been lawful ones, be would simply have taken these mountings to a bullion dealer and realized the value of the gold. But the gold mounts were precisely the most recognizable parts of the "swag." It was quite impracticable to dispose of them in the state in which they came to him.

Then he decided to melt them down and, to this end, he provided himself with a small crucible furnace that burned coke or charcoal – there was no gas at the Manor House – and was fitted with a foot bellows. He also obtained a few crucibles, one or two jewellers ingot moulds, and the necessary tongs and other implements, and with these appliances he set to work to reduce the miscellaneous collection of stoneless jewellery to neat little ingots, each of which he carefully marked with a punch to show its "fineness" in carats.

But even this did not quite solve the difficulty. For, as we have seen, Mr. Toke was an eminently cautious gentleman, and it was borne in on him that the sale of gold ingots on a somewhat considerable scale was a proceeding that might, in the course of time, lead to inconvenient enquiries. He was known as a dealer in stones. But gold ingots were things that needed to be accounted for. He decided, at least for the present, not to run the risk.

So, by degrees, the ingots accumulated. But Mr. Toke was not disturbed. On the contrary, the larger his stock grew – and it grew apace – the less desirous did he become to dispose of it. For a curious change

279

had come over him. Gradually, the affection that he had felt for the sovereigns transferred itself to the growing pile of ingots, and at nights, when he had turned out the surviving remnants of coins from the drawer, he would bring forth the ingots from the cupboard where they were secreted and lay them out on the table or build them up into little stacks. And as the stacks grew steadily in size and number, he would think of his partners and their mysterious activities with pleasant anticipations of yet further additions to his hoard, which was rapidly becoming more real to him than the less visible wealth that was represented by the figures in his bank books and his lists of investments.

Occasionally he found himself speculating on the part that Mr. Hughes played in this curious, unlawful business. Was he a receiver, pure and simple, or was he an actual operator? On the rare occasions when they met, Hughes maintained the most profound reticence. Mr. Toke's view was that Hughes and Dobey formed a small firm to which Hughes contributed the brains and power of contrivance, and Dobey the manual skill and executive ability.

Possibly he was right. At any rate, as we have said, all went well and smoothly, and Dobey, more fortunate than most of his fellow practitioners, continued to keep out of the clutches of the law.

Chapter IV
Mr. Toke's Indiscretion

In a remote corridor at the top of a large building in Holborn, the rather infrequent visitors might have seen a door, glazed with opaque glass, on which was painted the name of Mr. Arthur Hughes. No further information was vouchsafed, but if the directory had been consulted it would have been ascertained that Mr. Hughes was a patent agent. His practice was not extensive, but still, on certain rare occasions, stray members of that peculiarly optimistic class, prospective patentees, discovered his existence by means of the directory aforesaid, and subjected him to a mild surprise by appearing in his office.

Their visits were not unwelcome for, though the business that they brought was of little enough value, they rendered possible the keeping of books which could be produced in evidence of a bona fide industry.

The visitor, however, who appeared on a certain afternoon was not one of these clients, nor was he connected with the patent industry – being, in fact, none other than Mr. Didbury Toke. Mr. Toke was a good deal out of breath, having climbed the long staircase as a matter of precaution, and now sat panting across the table behind which Mr. Hughes was seated, regarding him with undisguised impatience.

"It's a devil of a way up," said Mr. Toke.

"It is if you are fool enough to walk," was the ungracious reply. "Why the deuce don't you use the lift?"

"Well," Mr. Toke explained, "one is apt to meet people in a lift, or at least be seen and possibly remembered, by the lift girl, at any rate. It is better to avoid contacts as far as possible."

"You're mighty careful," said Hughes, sourly. "You're glad enough to mop up the profits of our little enterprises, but you don't mean to take any of the risks."

"Not if I can help it," Toke admitted. "Why should I? And what good would it be if I did?"

The question was so obviously reasonable (since the safety of each member of the firm was essential to the well-being of the others) that Hughes was reduced to a non-committal snort, and might have left it at that had not Toke rather untactfully added, "And I am not aware that you are in the habit of exposing yourself unnecessarily."

Mr. Hughes was apparently in a somewhat irritable state of mind, for he took needless umbrage at this remark.

281

"Oh," he exclaimed, "so you think so, too, do you?"

"Too?" repeated Toke, interrogatively.

"Yes. You are taking up the same position as that infernal Dobey."

"I hope not," said Mr. Toke. "But what is Dobey's position?

"In effect the same as yours. He says that he takes all the risks while we take most of the profits."

"I did not say that," Mr. Toke protested. "I admit that I keep out of harm's way to the best of my ability. And, really, I suppose, as a matter of fact, Dobey does take more risks than we do."

"Do you?" snarled Hughes. "How do you know what risks I take?"

Mr. Toke had to admit that he knew very little about the matter. "But," he continued, "there is no use in mutual fault-finding. We each have our respective parts to play, and each of us is indispensable to the others."

"That isn't Dobey's view," said Hughes. "I have discovered that he has been doing some jobs on his own, and what is worse, he has found some other market for the swag. He is a slippery devil. Thanks to me, he has been able to work in safety, and do uncommonly well. Now he thinks he knows all there is to know, and he is going to work on his own and stick to all the stuff that he collects – the ungrateful bounder!"

Mr. Toke expressed his profound disgust at this base conduct of the unappreciative gas-fitter. "But, after all," he added optimistically, "I suppose he is not the only pebble on the beach."

"No," Hughes admitted, "but he is a pretty big pebble, from our point of view. We can't afford to lose his little contributions. But it is not only that. Now that he seems to have gone off on his own, and knows that I have spotted him, he may give us trouble, especially if he should get into a tight place. As I said before, he is a slippery devil. But he had better look out. If I see any signs of his making trouble, I shall make things most unpleasantly lively for him. However, he hasn't starved us out yet. I have got quite a nice little collection from another artist. Got it here, too. I don't usually bring stuff to this place, but I had to, on this occasion. So here it is, all ready for you to take away when we have settled preliminaries."

"Oh, dear!" exclaimed Mr. Toke, "how very unfortunate! I can't possibly take it now. I called to tell you that I am just starting on a longish tour on the Continent."

"Well, you'll just have to put off the start for a day. I can't have the stuff here, and I certainly can't store it while you are browsing about the Continent."

"But," protested Mr. Toke, "I have made all my arrangements. I have shut up the wing of my house where I keep my collection and sealed the doors, and I have notified my solicitor that I have started."

"I suppose you can alter your arrangements if you please. You are your own master."

Mr. Toke shook his head, and was about to add some confirmatory remarks when Hughes suddenly lost what little patience he had and broke out, angrily. "Look here, Toke, you are going to take that stuff. You have got to. I am not going to keep it in store for months. Besides, I want the money for it. There is a hundred-and-fifty pounds' worth in this parcel. You can look at it now and, if you are afraid to take it away with you, I will plant it in your car later."

"But," pleaded Toke, "I haven't got my car. I took it to the garage this morning to be overhauled and taken care of while I am away. I should have to go by train with the confounded stuff in a hand-bag."

Mr. Hughes was on the point of demanding what the occasion of the train journey might be, seeing that the "stuff" was presumably to be deposited either at Mr. Toke's bank or in his safe-deposit. That was how he had always understood that Mr. Toke secured his valuables. But the reference to the train journey seemed to offer a rather curious suggestion. And, Mr. Hughes being a decidedly reticent, not to say secretive, gentleman, refrained from either comment or question. But he stuck to his point, and continued to insist that the property must be transferred. If he had done so in a polite and tactful manner, all might have been well. Unfortunately, he adopted a bullying, hectoring tone that jarred heavily on Mr. Toke's already ruffled feelings. As a result, his customary suavity gave place to a slightly forbidding manner.

"I think," he said stiffly, "you misunderstand the nature of our relations. I purchase from you at my convenience. You are addressing me as if I were some sort of subordinate, as you might address Dobey – who, by the way, doesn't seem to have found your manners endearing."

"He will find them a good deal less endearing if he doesn't take care, and so will you. Don't you come here with your damned superior airs. You are one of the firm, and I am the boss of the firm, and you have got to understand that."

"And suppose I don't accept that relationship? Suppose I retire from the firm, as you call it, and wash my hands of you? Would that suit you?"

"It wouldn't suit you if the police got to know that the eminently respectable Mr. Didbury Toke had been doing a roaring trade in stolen gems."

Mr. Toke's face hardened. "It is a great mistake to utter threats," he said in a warning tone. And then, in total disregard of the admirable principle that he had just laid down, he continued, "And, in fact, it would not suit you particularly well if the police should be induced to take an interest in you."

"But they couldn't," retorted Hughes. "You couldn't prove anything against me. I've made it my business to see to that. In regard to this swag, the man who collected it is at one end and the man who marketed it – that's you – is at the other. I don't appear in it at all."

Mr. Toke smiled sourly. "I see," he said, quietly, "that you don't remember me. But my memory is better."

"What the devil do you mean?" Hughes demanded angrily, but with a startled expression which he failed to control.

"Of course," Mr. Toke continued, calmly, "I am a good deal changed. So are you since the days when you used to have a sandy moustache and a bushy head of hair. But, all the same, I recognized you at the first glance." (Which was not quite correct. It had taken him some three months to convert a vague sense of familiarity into a definite identification.) "The sight of you carried me back to the time when I used to have connections with the assaying industry, and when a good deal was heard about a certain famous thumb-print."

He stopped rather abruptly – and wished that he had stopped sooner, as he noted the effect of his foolish speech. Hughes did not trouble to contest the statement, but sat gazing fixedly at the speaker, and the concentrated malignity that expressed itself in that look brought Mr. Toke suddenly to his senses. The gentle art of making enemies is an art that is practised only by fools. But Mr. Toke was not a fool, and he certainly did not want to make an enemy of Mr. Hughes. He saw clearly that reconciliation was the necessary policy, and proceeded forthwith to swallow his pride.

"This won't do, Hughes," he said in a conciliatory tone. "We are behaving like a couple of fools. Of course we sink or swim together. I understand that. I was annoyed at having my arrangements upset and lost my temper. Let us have a look at that stuff."

Without a word, Hughes rose and walked across to a small safe which he unlocked and threw open. From some inner recess in it he produced a parcel which he laid on the table. Then he stepped over to the door and, having slipped the catch of the lock, came back and began methodically to untie the string of the parcel. When the various wrappings were loosened, there was exposed to view a miscellaneous collection of jewellery which Mr. Toke diagnosed as probably the pooled swag from several different robberies. He looked it over with tepid

284

interest, being anxious chiefly to get the business over and bring the rather unpleasant interview to an end.

"Well," he said, "there's nothing sensational about it. You say you want a hundred-and-fifty for this lot. It's quite enough, but it isn't worthwhile to haggle over a trifle. I'll give you what you ask. I suppose a cheque won't do for you?"

"No," Hughes replied gruffly, "of course it won't."

"It's infernally inconvenient," Toke grumbled. "This will eat up the greater part of the cash that I had provided for travelling."

He produced a fat wallet from his pocket and sorted out its contents, a process that was watched by Hughes with a curious, avid interest as he retied the string of the parcel.

"Fifteen tens," said Toke. "Will that do? I would rather keep the fives for use on the road."

As Hughes made no reply, but silently held out his hand, Toke placed in the latter the sheaf of crisp, rustling notes, and closed his wallet, fastening it and returning it to his pocket.

"Now, Hughes," he said as he dropped the parcel into his handbag and put on his hat, "let us forget the nonsense that we talked just now and bury the hatchet. We shan't see each other again for a month or two. Don't let us carry away unpleasant memories."

He held out his hand genially, and Hughes, relaxing with an effort the grimness of his expression, took it and gave it a formal shake.

"I suppose," said he, "you will spend the night at Hartsden?"

"No," replied Toke, "I can't do that. I want to catch the night – or rather early morning – train to Dover."

"You will have some trouble in making the various connections," Hughes remarked. "There aren't so very many trains to and from Hartsden. It is a pity that you didn't keep your car for another hour or two."

"Yes," Toke agreed reflectively. "I think you are right. The trains will be an awkward complication. I rather think that I will just get the car out again or borrow another. That will make me independent of trains."

"But what will you do with the car?" asked Hughes, who was beginning to take an interest in Toke's movements.

"I dare say I shall be able to run it down to the garage. Or perhaps I shall be able to get a taxi driver to run it round from the station. It will only take him a few minutes."

"Yes," Hughes agreed, "that will be quite simple. And the car will enable you to take your own time. Much better than the suburban trains. Well, so long. I hope you will have a pleasant and profitable trip."

He gave a sort of valedictory grin – the nearest that he could get to the semblance of a friendly smile – and accompanied Toke out into the corridor where he stood, watching the retreating figure of his associate in iniquity. And, even as he looked, the grin faded from his features and was replaced by a scowl of the most intense malice.

He went back into his office, still scowling forbiddingly, and with the air of one wrapped in profound thought. Which was, in fact, his condition. For Mr. Toke's indiscreet outburst had furnished him with the matter for anxious cogitation. That Toke could or would "blow on" the little transactions that took place between them had never occurred to him. Nor did it now. He had made his position at least as safe as that of Mr. Toke himself. Neither of them could effectively blow on the other. But now it appeared that Mr. Toke could, by merely uttering a few words in the proper quarter, send him, Mr. Hughes, to a term of penal servitude. This was quite a different affair. The sudden appearance of Mr. Toke as a potential accuser was, to put it very mildly, an extremely disagreeable surprise. Up to this time, Hughes had believed that one person only in the whole world had penetrated the very effective disguise with which a natural affliction had furnished him as a free gift. For Mr. Hughes's wig was, in any case, a necessity. An attack of the complaint known as *Alopecia areata* had produced large bald patches which had to be covered up by a wig, and this, together with the loss of his eyebrows, and aided by the removal of his beard and moustache, had so metamorphosed him that, though he avoided all old haunts and old acquaintances, he was almost completely secure from recognition. But as we have said, there was one person who had appeared, at least, to suspect his identity, and whose existence kept him in a state of constant watchfulness and anxiety. And now there was another.

Mr. Hughes was not a scrupulous man, and if he was a cautious man, he was ready to take a present risk for the sake of future safety. In the very moment when Mr. Toke had foolishly proclaimed his power, he had made a decision. He was not going to walk abroad with this everlasting menace at his elbow. One dangerous enemy was more than enough. Two were more than could be borne. The plain fact was that Mr. Toke knew too much, and that fact pointed to the obvious remedy. So much Hughes had decided even while Toke was speaking. The rest was only a question of ways and means.

Apparently this question also was in course of being settled, for Mr. Hughes, after pacing up and down the office for a few minutes, began, in a leisurely and deliberate fashion, to make certain changes in his visible characteristics that suggested a definite purpose. It is one of the compensations of being compelled to wear a wig that one can choose one's wig and even, on occasion, change it. Of this privilege Mr. Hughes proceeded to avail himself. From a locked drawer in a locked cupboard he took out a wig of a pronounced red and of a fluffy, rather ragged texture, strikingly different from the sleek, dark brown one that he was wearing. Having locked the door, he put on the new wig, and then produced from the drawer a reddish moustache, a small bunch of hair of the same colour, and a bottle of spirit gum. With some of the latter, he anointed the base of the moustache (which was not one of those artless devices used by the amateur actor, but a workmanlike affair, made by a regular theatrical wig-maker) and carefully affixed it to his upper lip with the aid of a small mirror.

When he had fixed it securely in position he cut off some wisps of hair from the bundle and, having stuck them along the upper margin of the moustache, combed them over the latter and finally trimmed them off with scissors. The effect was extremely realistic, and when, in the same way, a pair of darkish eyebrows had been attached, the transformation was complete.

But Mr. Hughes was too old a hand to trust a make up, no matter how excellent, farther than was unavoidable. The afternoon was already merging into evening. Another half-hour and the dusk would have fallen. Then not even close inspection would penetrate the disguise. So Mr. Hughes proceeded with caution. Having tidied up the office, he put away the bottle and the other materials and appliances which he had been using, and was in the act of locking the cupboard when he seemed to remember something that he had forgotten, and hastily reopened the door. Then that something was searched for and found in another locked drawer, revealing itself as a sheath-knife of the kind used by old-fashioned sailors (and commonly known as a "Green river knife"), furnished with a narrow waist-strap. Having slipped the knife inside the waistband of his trousers, he secured it in place by means of the strap. Then he took a glance at a time table and jotted down a few figures on a slip of paper which he put in his pocket, after which he walked over to the window and stood for a while, looking down into the fast-emptying street.

Already the daylight was beginning to fade, and the quiet of evening was settling down on the city. Judging that the time had come, he emerged cautiously into the dim corridor, locked the door behind him and set forth. Emulating Mr. Toke's discretion, he avoided the lift, taking his way down the unfrequented staircase from the bottom of which he hurried along the lower corridors, and so out into the street. Even there he preserved his attitude of caution, threading his way through the quieter back thoroughfares, and maintaining that incessant watchfulness that has to be habitual with those who are on unsatisfactory terms with the law.

By the time that he reached the station the daylight was visibly weakening. He walked confidently to the booking-office, where he took a first-class single ticket to Hartsden Junction, which, as he knew, was some three-quarters of a mile from the hamlet which gave it its name. He was by no means unacquainted with the locality, for, if the truth must be told, he and Dobey had reconnoitred the neighbourhood with the idea of a possible nocturnal visit to Mr. Toke's premises on some occasion when that gentleman was absent on one of his periodical excursions abroad. That visit had never been made, for the reason that Mr. Toke had let it be very clearly understood that he kept on those premises nothing but the "pieces" that formed his collection – porcelain figures, bronzes, and other objects, valuable enough in themselves, but of no use to merchants of the class to which Hughes and Dobey belonged. All negotiable property, he had explained, was kept securely in the strong room of his bank or in the safe that he rented at the safe-deposit establishment, and this had seemed such an obvious precaution that both rascals had accepted the statement and abandoned the idea of the nocturnal raid.

But now, by the light of the admission that Mr. Toke had so incautiously made, that he was proposing to convey this parcel of stolen property to his house, evidently with the intention of leaving it there during his absence abroad, Mr. Hughes began to reconsider the situation. The main object of his journey was not irreconcilable with certain other transactions and, as he was borne by the fast express to the neighbourhood of Mr. Toke's residence, he turned over quite a number of interesting possibilities.

The night had definitely fallen when Mr. Hughes approached the hamlet of Hartsden by the road from the Junction. He looked about him with his habitual wariness, but there was little need, for, as he passed through the single street, not a soul was to be seen and, but for the lighted windows, the place might have been uninhabited. Beyond the hamlet the old manor house stood in dignified isolation, and adjoining it was the disused churchyard, enclosing the ruinous church – now also disused and replaced by a new building at the other end of the village.

It was towards the churchyard that Hughes directed his steps, making for the gateway without hesitation as if by a considered plan. On arriving there, he paused for a moment to glance down the road – of which the gateway commanded a clear view. Then he pushed open the rickety gate and entered. Slowly he walked along the narrow path that led to the church, looking back from time to time to see that he still had an uninterrupted view of the road. Presently the path turned slightly to the right and, passing into the shadow of a great yew tree, was encompassed by darkness so complete that Hughes was able only with the greatest difficulty to grope his way along it. Here, by the side of a large sarcophagus tomb which stood between the yew tree and the wall, he stopped and looked about him. Finding that the road was now no longer in sight, he slowly retraced his steps until he was, able once more to look out through the gateway along the road that formed the only approach to the village. And here he selected a spot where he could keep a look-out, secure from the observation of any chance wayfarer who might pass along from the village.

He was prepared for a long vigil, for it was possible that Toke might be delayed and, in any case, the car would take considerably longer to cover the distance than the fast train by which Hughes had travelled. To beguile the time, he produced his cigarette-case and took out a cigarette. But his habitual caution warned him not to light it in view of the road. Accordingly, he retired past the yew tree into the darkest corner of the churchyard, behind the great tomb, and there, crouching low against the plinth of the tomb, he struck a match, held it for a moment to the cigarette and blew it out. But even then he held the cigarette shrouded in his hand, and when he returned to his look-out, he was careful to ensconce himself behind the tall headstone that he had selected as cover so that the glow of the cigarette should not be visible from outside.

But it was a tedious business, waiting in the gloom of the darkening churchyard for the coming of the man who could send him to penal servitude. And it was rendered none the more pleasant by a somewhat acute anxiety. For, though he had a perfectly clear purpose, the carrying into effect of that purpose could not be planned in exact detail. The precise method of procedure must be determined by Mr. Toke's actions, and these could not be foreseen.

Time ran on. One by one, the lights in the windows of the few houses that were visible from the churchyard went out, and the chime of the clock in the new church at the end of the village, borne faintly on the night air, told out quarter after quarter. It was just striking the hour of ten when Hughes, having lighted his sixth cigarette, came out from behind the sarcophagus tomb and crept back to his look-out, and at that moment the lights of a car came into sight far away down the road.

Hughes was not a nervous man. But the message that those glimmering lights conveyed to him set his heart thumping and his hands trembling so that the cigarette dropped unheeded from his fingers. It is one thing to contemplate an atrocious deed from afar, but quite another to feel the irrevocable moment of action drawing nigh. With a feeling of shuddering dread, but yet never for an instant abandoning his dreadful intent, he watched the lights gradually wax brighter until the approaching car was actually entering the village. Apparently it was fitted with a powerful but silent engine, for no throb or hum of mechanism was borne to his ears.

Suddenly the lights went out, and for a few moments the car was perceptible neither to eye nor ear. Then it became faintly visible as a dim spot of deeper darkness. Nearer and nearer it came, now growing into a defined shape, and recognizable as a large, closed car. Hughes craned out from behind the headstone to watch it as it passed the gate. But it did not pass the gate. Just as it reached the farther wall of the churchyard, it slowed down suddenly and turned off to the left and was instantly lost to view.

To Hughes, in his state of extreme nervous tension, this unexpected behaviour was highly disconcerting. He had assumed that Mr. Toke would drive up to his gate, get out, and open it, and then run the car up the drive to the door of the house. Much puzzled and somewhat alarmed, he crept out from behind the headstone and began to steal softly and cautiously down the path towards the gate. But he had gone only a few steps when he was startled by the sudden appearance of Mr. Toke within a few paces of the gate and walking briskly towards it with the evident intention of entering the churchyard.

Sweating and trembling from the sudden shock, Hughes staggered back to the headstone and crouched down behind it, cursing silently and for the moment overcome by terror. A step or two more and he must have been seen, and who could say what would have happened then? Toke could hardly have failed to grasp the situation, and Toke was no weakling. It had been a near thing.

From his lurking-place he saw Mr. Toke, hand-bag in hand, walk up the path with the assured manner of a man who is making for a definite destination. When he had passed the headstone Hughes craned out to watch the retreating figure and, as it disappeared into the darkness under the yew tree, he rose and followed stealthily, crouching low to keep out of sight among the crowded tombstones. Presently he halted just at the edge of the patch of shadow and watched from the shelter of a crumbling tomb that was enclosed by an ivy-covered railing. From the impenetrable darkness under the yew tree there came a faint grinding or creaking sound. It lasted but a few moments, but, after a brief interval it was repeated. After yet another short interval, Hughes rose and came out from behind the railed tomb. Then he, too, disappeared into the darkness under the yew tree.

The minutes passed, but no sound came from that eerie corner of the churchyard over which the yew tree cast its sinister shadow. The clock of the distant church told out a quarter and then another. The reverberations of the bell had just died away when the silence was broken once more by that curious faint grinding or creaking sound. It was followed, almost immediately, by what sounded like a muffled cry. Again there was a brief space of silence. Then the grinding sound was repeated. And, after that, again silence.

The time ran on. Save for the murmur of the trees, as the leaves were gently stirred by the soft breeze, and the faint, indefinite voices of the night, not a sound disturbed the stillness that brooded over the churchyard. Away in the distance, the clock of the new church made its announcements to the sleeping village of the passage of the minutes that perish for us and are reckoned. But among the grey headstones and under the solemn yew tree, nothing stirred and no sound broke in to disturb the peace of the dead.

So the time passed, measured out impassively, quarter by quarter, by the distant chimes. More than an hour had slipped away since those two figures had been swallowed up in the dark cavernous depths under the yew tree, when the silence of the night was at last broken by the faint grinding creak. After the lapse of a few seconds, it was repeated. Then a figure appeared creeping stealthily out of the shadow and down the path towards the gate, which, as it emerged into the dim light, revealed itself as that of Mr. Hughes.

There was something curiously secret and furtive in his demeanour. He walked slowly, setting down his foot at each step with evident care to make no sound, and every few seconds he paused to listen and look about him. Thus he crept down to the gate, where again he halted and stood, listening intently and gazing into the darkness, first up the village street, and then across at the old manor house, sleeping among its trees. But it seemed that in the whole village there was no living creature besides himself waking and moving.

From the gate he turned to the right and, in the same silent, furtive manner, stole along the wall of the churchyard towards the place into which the car had seemed to disappear. Short as the distance was, it seemed interminable in the agony of suspense that possessed him. For the car was indispensable. It had been the keystone of his plan – the appointed means of safety and escape. But suppose it had been seen, or, still worse, taken away! The fearful possibility brought the sweat afresh to his already clammy brow, and set his trembling limbs shaking so that he staggered like a drunken man.

At length he reached the corner of the wall. Beside the churchyard ran a narrow, leafy lane, enclosed between the high wall and a tall hedgerow, and as dark as a cellar. He peered desperately into the dense obscurity, but at first could see nothing. With throbbing heart he stole up the lane as quickly as he dared, still craning eagerly forward into the darkness, yet still careful not to trip on the rough ground. Suddenly he gave a gasp of relief, for, out of the darkness ahead, a shape of deeper darkness emerged and, as he hurried forward, he recognized the big covered car with which he had had so many dealings in the past.

Shaken as he was, he still had all his wits about him, and he realized that there must be no false start. Once he was on the move, he must get straight away from the neighbourhood. It would never do to be held up on the road by any failure of the engine or other occasion of delay. Accordingly, he went over all the working parts with the aid of a small electric lamp that he produced from his pocket and satisfied himself that all was in order. Then he threw the light back along the lane to see that the way was clear for steering out in reverse. That was the immediate difficulty. There seemed to be no room to turn round. He would have to back out, and to back out at the first attempt.

At length he prepared for the actual start. Getting into the driver's seat, he switched on the lights and the ignition and pressed the electric starter. Instantly, the silence was shattered by a roar that seemed fit to rouse the whole countryside, and brought the sweat streaming down his face. Still, though the hand that held the steering wheel shook as if with a palsy, he kept his wits under control. The lane was practically straight and the car had been run straight in. By the dim light of the rear lamp he could see through the rear window well enough to back the car down the lane to the road.

At last, he was out in the open, as he could see by the light from the front lamps shining on the corner of the churchyard wail. He put the steering-wheel over and started forward, now quite noiselessly, through the village street and so out on to the London road.

It was getting on for two o'clock when he drove into the small car-park attached to the garage.

"Late, ain't you?" said the night watchman. "They told me Mr. Toke was going to bring her back by half-past eleven. Did he miss his train?"

"No," replied Hughes. "He caught his train all right. It was my fault. I had to go somewhere else and couldn't bring her along any sooner."

"Well," was the philosophical response, "better late than never."

"Very much better," Hughes agreed. "Good night – or rather, good morning."

He paused for a moment to light a cigarette, and then walked out into the street and was lost to sight.

Book II: Inspector Badger Deceased

Chapter V
The Tragedy in the Tunnel

Mr. Superintendent Miller was by no means an emotional man. He had his moments of excitement or irritation, but in general he was a person of a calm exterior, and gave the impression of one not easily ruffled. That was my view of him, born of years of intimacy. But the Superintendent Miller whom I admitted to our chambers in response to a somewhat peremptory knock was a new phenomenon. His flushed, angry face and lowering brow told us at once that something quite out of the ordinary had occurred, and we looked at him expectantly without question or remark. Nor was there any occasion for either for, without seating himself or even taking off his hat, he came instantly to the point.

"I want you two gentlemen to come with me at once, if you can. I've got a car waiting. And I want you to bring all your wits and knowledge to bear on this case as you never brought them before."

Thorndyke looked at him in surprise. "What is it, Miller?" he asked.

The Superintendent frowned at him fiercely, and replied in a voice husky with passion, "It is Badger. He has been murdered. And I look to you two gentlemen as officers of the law to strain every nerve in helping us to bring the crime home to the villain who committed it."

We were profoundly shocked, and we could easily understand – and indeed share – his wrathful determination to lay hands on the murderer. It is true that Inspector Badger had been no favourite with any of the three of us. His personal qualities had not been endearing. But now this was forgotten. He had been, in a sense, an old friend, if at times he had seemed a little like an enemy. But especially he was a police officer, and to a normally constituted Englishman, a police officer's life is something even more sacred than the life of an ordinary man. For the police are the guardians of the safety of us all. The risks that they accept with quiet matter-of-fact courage are undertaken that we may walk abroad in security and rest at night in peace and confidence. Well may we feel, as we do, that the murder of a police officer is at once an outrage on the community and on every member of it.

"You may take it, Miller," said Thorndyke, "that we are at your command, heart and soul. Where do you want us to go?"

293

"Greenhithe. That is where the body is lying and where the murder must have been committed. There is a fairly good train in a quarter-of-an-hour, and the car will get us to the station in five minutes. Can you come?"

"We must," was the reply, and without another word Thorndyke rose and ran up to the laboratory to notify our assistant, Polton, of our sudden departure. In less than a minute he returned with his "research case" in his hand, and announced that he was ready to start, and as I had already made the few preparations which were necessary, we went down to the car.

During our brief journey to the station nothing was said. As we arrived at the platform from the booking office, the train came alongside, and the passengers poured out. We took up our position opposite a first-class coach and, when the fresh passengers had all bestowed themselves and the train was on the point of starting, we entered an empty compartment and shut ourselves in.

"It is very good of you gentlemen," said Miller, as the train gathered speed, "to come off like this at a moment's notice, especially as I have not given you any inkling of the case. But there will be plenty of time for me to tell you all I know – which isn't very much at present. Probably we shall pick up some fresh details at Greenhithe. My present information is limited to what we have heard over the telephone from there and from Maidstone. This is what it amounts to.

"Yesterday morning poor Badger went down to Maidstone to look over a batch of prisoners for the Assizes and see if there were any old acquaintances lurking under an alias. But principally his object was to inspect a man who had given the name of Frederick Smith, but whom he suspected of being a certain crook whose real name was unknown to us. We were a good deal interested in this man. For various reasons we associated him with a number of burglaries of a rather clever type – one-man jobs, which are always the most difficult to deal with if they are efficiently carried out. And we had something to go on in one case, for Badger saw the man making off. However, he got away, and neither he nor the stuff was ever traced. So our position was that here was a man whom we suspected of quite an important series of crimes, but who was, so to speak, in the air. He was not even a name. He was just a 'person unknown.' Whether we had his finger-prints under some name we couldn't guess, because nobody knew him by sight excepting Badger, and his opinion was that the man had never been in custody, and couldn't be identified – excepting by himself."

"But," said I, "surely Badger could have put a description of him on record."

"M'yes," replied Miller. "But you know what Badger was like. So beastly secretive. One doesn't like to say it now, but he really didn't play the game. If he got a bit of information, instead of passing it round for the benefit of the force and the public, he would keep it to himself in the hope of bringing off a striking coup and getting some kudos out of it. And he did bring it off once or twice, and got more credit than he deserved. But to come back to this Maidstone business. Badger gleaned something from the reports concerning the prisoners there that made him suspect that this man, Smith, might be the much-wanted burglar. So down he went, all agog to see if Smith was the man he had once got a glimpse of."

"I shouldn't think a recognition of that kind, based on a mere passing glance, would have much value as evidence," I objected.

"Not in court," Miller admitted. "But it would have had considerable weight with us. Badger had a devil of a memory for faces, and we knew it. That was his strong point. He was like a snapshot camera. A single glance at a face and it was fixed on his memory forever."

"Do you know if he recognized the man?" Thorndyke asked.

"He didn't," replied Miller, "for the man wasn't there. In some way he had managed to do a bolt, and up to the present, so far as I know, they have not been able to find him. It is quite likely that he has got clean away for, as he was wearing his own clothes, he won't be very easy to track. However, Badger seems to have satisfied himself that the man was really the one he was looking for – probably he thought he recognized the photographs – and this morning he started for Town with the papers – the personal description, photographs, and finger-prints – for examination and comparison at the Criminal Record Office. But he never arrived, and about eleven o'clock his body was found near the middle of the Greenhithe Tunnel. The engine driver of an up-train saw it lying across the rails on the down-side, and reported as soon as he got into Greenhithe. But it seemed that at least one train had been over it by then. I gather that – but there! I don't like to think of it. Poor old Badger!"

"No," Thorndyke agreed sympathetically. "It is too horrible to think of. But still, as we have to investigate and ascertain what really happened, we must put aside our personal feelings and face the facts, terrible as they are. You spoke of his having been murdered. Do you know if there were any signs, apart from the mutilation caused by the train passing over him, that he had met a violent death? Is it clear that it was not an accident?

"Quite clear, I think," replied Miller. "I know nothing about the condition of the body, but I know that there was no open door on the off-side of the train that he travelled by."

"That would seem to be conclusive," said Thorndyke, "if the fact can be established. But it isn't always easy to prove a negative. A passenger, getting into an empty compartment and finding the door open, would naturally shut it and might not report the circumstance. The point will have to be enquired into."

"Yes," Miller agreed, "but I don't think there is much doubt. You must remember that the train passed through Greenhithe Station and past the signal boxes both there and at Dartford. An open door on the off-side would be very noticeable from the down platforms. Still, as you say, the point will have to be settled definitely. Probably it has been by now. We shall hear what they have to say when we get to Greenhithe. But for my part I have no doubt at all, door or no door. Badger was not the sort of fool who leans out of the window of a moving train without seeing that the door is fastened. It is a case of murder, and the murderer has got to be found and dealt with."

If the Superintendent may have seemed to have formed a very definite opinion on rather slender evidence, that opinion received strong confirmation when we reached Greenhithe. Awaiting us on the platform were a detective sergeant and one of the senior officers from Maidstone Prison. They had travelled up from Maidstone together, apparently comparing notes and making enquiries by the way.

"Well, sir," said the sergeant, "I think we can exclude the suggestion of accident, positively and certainly. It was unlikely on the face of it. But we have got some definite facts that put it out altogether. This officer, Chief Officer Cummings, whose duties include all matters relating to descriptions and records, handed to Inspector Badger the papers relating to the prisoner, Frederick Smith – finger-prints, description, and photographs – and saw him put them into his letter wallet. Now, I have been through that wallet with the greatest care, and there is not a trace of any of those papers in the wallet or in any of his pockets."

"Ha!" exclaimed Miller in a tone of grim satisfaction, "that settles it. I take it, Cummings, that there is no possible doubt that the Inspector had those papers in his pocket when he started from Maidstone?"

"Not a shadow of doubt, sir," replied Cummings. "I gave him the papers, carefully folded, and saw him put them into his wallet – just into the open wallet, as they were too large to go into the pockets without further folding. He stowed the wallet away in his inside breast pocket and buttoned his coat. And I can swear that it was in his pocket when he started, for I walked with him to the station and actually saw him into the

296

train. He asked me to walk down with him, as there were various questions that he wanted to put to me respecting the prisoners – especially this man, Smith."

"Yes," said Miller, "we shall have to have a talk about Mr. Smith presently. But the fact that the Inspector had those papers on his person when he got into the train, and that they were not on the body, makes it certain that he was not alone in the carriage."

"It does, sir," the sergeant agreed. "But apart from that, we have got direct evidence that he was not. The station-master at Strood gave us the particulars. The Inspector's train stopped there, and he had to get out and wait a few minutes for the London train. The station-master saw him standing on the platform and, as they knew each other, he went up to him, and they had a few words together. While they were chatting the London train came in and drew up at the platform. Inspector Badger was just moving off to find a compartment when a man came along from the entrance. As soon as the Inspector saw this man, he stopped short and stood watching him. The man walked rather quickly along the train, looking in at the windows, and got into an empty first-class smoking compartment. But the station-master noticed that, before he got in, he looked into each of the adjoining compartments, which were both empty. As soon as he had got in and shut the door after him, the Inspector wished the station-master 'Good morning,' and began to saunter slowly towards the compartment that the stranger had got into. A few paces away from it he stopped and waited until the guard blew his whistle. Then he walked forward quickly and got into the compartment where the strange man was."

"Could the station-master give you any description of the man?"

"No, sir. No description that would be of any use. He said he was a middle-aged man of about medium height, not noticeably stout or thin, moderately well-dressed in a darkish suit, and wearing a soft felt hat. He thought that the man had darkish red hair and rather a red nose. But that isn't very distinctive. And he thought he was clean-shaved."

"Did you ask him if he would know the man again if he saw him?"

"I did, sir, and he said that he might or he might not, but he didn't think he would, and he certainly wouldn't swear to him."

The Superintendent emitted a growl of dissatisfaction and, turning to the Chief Officer, asked, "What do you say, Cummings? Does the description suggest anything to you?"

The officer smiled deprecatingly. "I suppose, sir, you are thinking of Frederick Smith, and it does seem likely. Smith certainly has darkish red hair and a reddish nose. And he is about that age and about that height and he hasn't got a beard, and when I last saw him he was wearing a darkish suit and a soft felt hat. So it might have been Smith. But as the description would apply to a good many men that you might meet, it isn't much good for identification."

"No," growled Miller, "not enough details. And now that the finger-prints and detailed description are gone, it might be difficult to prove his identity even if we should get hold of him."

"It isn't as bad as that, sir," said Cummings. "As it happens, luckily, we have a duplicate of the finger-prints, at least of some of them. The officer who took the finger-prints made rather a mess of one of the rolled impressions. So he had to waste that form and start over again. Fortunately, the spoiled form wasn't destroyed. So we've got that, and of course we've got the negatives of the photographs, and the officer who took the description can remember most of the items. There will be no difficulty in proving the identity if we can get hold of the man. And that ought not to be so very difficult, either. There are several of us who have seen him and could recognize him."

The Superintendent nodded. "That's all to the good," said he, "but before we can recognize him, we've got to find him. The train didn't stop here, I understand."

"No, sir," the sergeant replied. "The first stop after Strood was Dartford. We've been over there, but we had no luck. There were a lot of people waiting for the train, so the platform was pretty crowded, and it was not easy to see who got out of the train. None of the porters noticed any first-class passengers getting out, though there must have been one, for a first-class ticket was collected – from Maidstone."

"Maidstone!" exclaimed Miller. "Well, that couldn't have been our man. He came onto the Strood platform from the entrance."

"So the station-master says. But the booking-office clerk there doesn't remember issuing any first-class ticket, or any ticket at all to Dartford."

"Hmm," grunted Miller. "Looks rather as if he didn't get out at Dartford. May have chanced it and gone on to London. We must have all the tickets checked. Did you make any enquiries from the ticket collector?"

"Yes, sir. But it was no go. He hadn't noticed any of the passengers particularly. Two or three of the men who passed out answered the station-master's description more or less. Of course they would. But he didn't really remember what any of them was like, and he couldn't say whether either of them was a first-class passenger. I suppose he just looked at the tickets and didn't see anything else."

"Yes," Miller agreed. "But we will go into this matter presently. We mustn't keep these gentlemen waiting." He turned to Thorndyke and

298

asked, "What would you like to do first, Doctor? I suppose you will want to inspect the tunnel, and I should like you to take a look at the body."

"The body has been examined, sir," said the sergeant, "by one of the local doctors. He was rather cautious in his opinions, but I understood that he found no marks of violence – no wounds or injuries excepting the accidental ones."

"Where is the body?" the Superintendent asked.

"In an empty store, sir, down below. They put it there out of sight until it could be moved to the mortuary."

Miller looked at us enquiringly, and Thorndyke reflected for a few moments.

"I think we had better take the tunnel first and see if we can pick up any traces from which we can gather a hint. It isn't very likely. The inside of the carriage, if we could have identified and examined it, would have been more hopeful as a source of information. However, the carriage is not available and the tunnel is. Will it be safe to explore it now?"

As he asked the question he glanced at the station-master, who took out his watch and consulted it.

"There is a down-train due in a couple of minutes," said he. "We had better let that go through. Then the line will be clear for a full hour on the down-side."

"You have pretty long intervals," Miller remarked.

"We have," the station-master admitted, "but they will be a good deal shorter when the electrification is completed. At present only the steam trains come on from Dartford. There goes the signal."

We waited until the train had drawn up at the platform, discharged its two or three passengers and proceeded on its way. Then we walked on to the end of the platform, descended to the permanent way and, marching in a procession headed by the station-master, along the rough side-path, presently entered the mouth of the tunnel, advancing along the space between the down-side rails and the smoke-blackened wall.

There is always something rather eerie about a tunnel, even a comparatively short and straight one like that at Greenhithe, in which the light is never completely lost. It is not the obscurity only or the strange reverberating quality that the vaulted roof imparts to the voice. The whole atmosphere is weird and uncanny, there is a sense of remoteness from the haunts of living men, heightened by the ghostly, whispering sounds which pervade the air, confused and indistinguishable echoes from the far-away world of light and life.

The light from the entrance followed us quite a long way, throwing our indefinitely elongated shadows into the twilight before us until they were lost in the deeper gloom ahead. Gradually, the warm glow of the station-master's lantern and the whiter circles of light from the electric lamps carried by Thorndyke and the Superintendent replaced the dwindling daylight and told us we were approaching the middle of the tunnel. The combined lights of the three lamps illuminated the ground with a brilliancy that was accentuated by the encompassing darkness, lighting up the rails and sleepers and the stones of the ballast, and bringing into view all the little odds and ends of litter that had been jettisoned from passing trains: Scraps of newspaper, match-boxes, spent matches, cigarette-ends – trivial by-products of civilized human life, insignificant and worthless, but each scanned attentively by six pairs of eyes.

It was in the heart of the tunnel that Miller remarked, in a hollow voice with an accompaniment of chattering echoes:

"Someone has chucked away a pretty good cigar. Shocking waste. He hasn't smoked a quarter of it."

He spoke feelingly, for it was just the type of cigar that he favoured: A big, dark-coloured cigar of the Corona shape. Thorndyke let the light from his inspection lamp fall on it for an instant, but he made no reply, and we continued our slow progress. But, a few moments later, I suddenly missed the light from his lamp (we were marching in single file and he brought up the rear of the procession)and, looking round, I saw that he had gone back and was in the act of picking up the cigar with his gloved left hand. As he evidently did not wish his proceedings to be noticed by the others, I continued to walk on at a slightly reduced pace until he overtook me, when I observed that he had carefully enclosed the cigar in two of the seed envelopes that he invariably carried, and was now tenderly wrapping it in his handkerchief before disposing of it in his breast pocket.

"Any special significance in that cigar?" I asked.

"It is impossible to say," he replied. "A half-smoked cigar must have some significance. It is for us to see whether it has any significance for us."

The answer was a little cryptic and left me with the suspicion that it did not really disclose the motive for his evidently considered act. To one unacquainted with Thorndyke and his methods of research, the salving of this scrap of jetsam must have appeared entirely foolish, for there seemed no more reason for taking and preserving this cigar than for collecting the various empty match-boxes and cigarettes that lay strewn around.

But I knew Thorndyke and his ways as no one else knew him. I knew that it was his principle to examine everything. But the word "everything" has to be construed reasonably. There was always some

300

selection in the objects that he examined, and I had the feeling that this cigar had presented to him something more than its mere face value.

So I reflected as we walked on slowly, scanning the ballast by the light of our lamps. But no other object came into view to engage our attention until we reached the spot where the tragedy had occurred. Here we halted with one accord and stood looking down in silence at the gruesome traces of the disaster. Miller was the first to break the silence.

"There seems to have been a lot of blood. Doesn't that suggest that he was alive when the train went over him?"

"Yes," replied Thorndyke, "in a general way, it does. But we shall be able to judge better from an examination of the body." Then, turning to the station-master, he asked, "How long could he have been lying on the line when the down-train came along?"

"Not more than a minute," was the reply. "Perhaps not that. The two trains passed in the tunnel."

"And how was the body lying? You came with the search party, I think?"

"Yes, I directed the search party. The body was lying across the rails slantwise with the feet towards the Greenhithe end. It was lying nearly on its back. But, of course, the train passing over it may have changed its position. Still, it is rather curious that the feet should have been pointing that way. If a man steps out of a moving train, his feet come to the ground and catch, and he flies forward head first. The position of the body almost seemed to suggest that he fell out head downwards."

"Yes," agreed Thorndyke. "But there isn't much in it, for he certainly did not step out. And a man who falls out by the unexpected opening of the door may fall in almost any position. Have you had any detailed report from the driver of the down-train?"

"Yes. I had a talk with him when he brought the train back from New Brompton. But he had very little to tell. He never saw the body at all, and he wouldn't have known of the accident if it hadn't been for the chance that the fireman happened to look over the near side of the foot-plate and caught just a passing glimpse of a pair of feet sticking out from under the engine. He shouted out as soon as he saw them, but of course there was nothing to be done. It was a fast train, and it couldn't have been pulled up in its own length, even if that would have been any good."

"And where did he pass the up-train?"

"He was just passing the rear of it when the fireman shouted."

"Did he notice any open door?"

"No. But that is not to say that there was *not* an open door. He didn't really see the other train at all. They had just opened the furnace

301

door and the light from that must have dazzled him. It was the light from the furnace reflected from the roof and walls of the tunnel that enabled the fireman to see the body."

"It is unnecessary to ask in what part of the train Badger was travelling," said Thorndyke. "He must have been near the front unless it was a very long train."

"It was rather a long train," said the sergeant. "The station-master at Strood told us that, though he couldn't say exactly how many coaches there were. Of course, we can easily find out, and we shall have to. But he was able to tell us where Inspector Badger's compartment was. It was right up in front, in the second coach – rather an unusual position for a first class compartment."

While this interrogation was proceeding, we had been walking on slowly towards the east end of the tunnel, scrutinizing the ground as we went but without any further result. We now came out into the open in a cutting and, on the station-master's advice, continued our examination of the permanent way as far as Swanscombe Halt, but nothing came into view that threw any light on the tragedy. At the halt we waited a few minutes for an up-train that was then due, in which we travelled back to Greenhithe – an arrangement that not only saved time and effort, but gave Thorndyke the opportunity of observing, with his head out of the window, the conditions of light prevailing in the tunnel and the visibility of one part of the train from the others.

As we came out on to the platform at Greenhithe, Miller looked wistfully at my colleague.

"Did you think of having a look at the body, Doctor?" he asked, adding, "I should feel more satisfied if you would. A local doctor hasn't had the experience of criminal cases that you and Dr. Jervis have."

"I don't suppose that the local doctor would have missed any signs that bore on the cause of death," said Thorndyke. "But still, an additional examination is at least an extra precaution. Perhaps the station-master will direct someone to show us the way."

The station-master elected to show us the way himself, and preceded us down the stairs. Reluctantly, I followed Thorndyke, leaving the others on the platform and, as I descended the stairs, I was, for the first time in my professional life conscious of a shrinking repugnance to the atmosphere of tragedy and death. After all, a doctor has his human feelings. It is impossible to look on the mutilated corpse of an old acquaintance as the mere "subject" of an investigation. But, as a matter of fact, I took no part in the actual examination. I saw that the body still lay on the tarpaulin-covered stretcher and that part of the clothing had been removed, but I stood aloof by the door, leaving the inspection to

Thorndyke, who evidently realized my state of mind, for he made his examination in silence and with no suggestion that I should join him.

One thing, however, I did observe, and with considerable surprise. When he had completed his examination of the body, he opened his research case and took from it the portable finger-print outfit that formed part of its permanent equipment. Taking out the ready-inked copper plate and a couple of cards, he proceeded, in his neat, methodical way, to make a set of ten prints, one of each digit.

"Why are you taking his finger-prints?" I asked. "Does anything hinge on them?"

"Not at present," he replied. "But it is possible that some finger-prints may be found and, if they may be, it might be very important to be able to say if they were or were not Badger's. So I am securing the means of comparison while they are available."

Thus stated, the motive for the proceeding seemed reasonable enough, but yet the explanation left me wondering if there was not something more definite in Thorndyke's mind. And this vague suspicion was strengthened when, as I helped him to repack the research case, I saw him deposit in it, and pack with extreme care, the derelict cigar which be had picked up in the tunnel. But I made no comment, and as the gruesome business was now completed, I took up the research case and led the way out of the store.

"Apparently," he said as we ascended the stairs, "the local practitioner was right. There are no signs of any injuries that might have been inflicted before he fell on the line. But one thing is clear. He was certainly alive when the train ran over him and for at least a few seconds after."

"Then," said I, "it might really have been an accident."

"So far as the appearances and condition of the body are concerned, it might. But if there was another person in the compartment and that person has not reported an accident, the probabilities are overwhelmingly in favour of either a crime, or what we may call an 'incriminating misadventure'."

"What do you mean by an 'incriminating misadventure'?" I asked.

"I mean a misadventure which would probably not have been accepted as such. Miller believes that the other passenger was the escaped prisoner, Frederick Smith. Suppose that Miller is right. Suppose that Badger recognized the man and tried to arrest him. That the man resisted and a struggle occurred. I don't see why it should unless Badger had handcuffs with him and tried to put them on. But suppose a struggle to have occurred, in the course of which the door became unfastened and Badger fell out. That would have been a pure misadventure. But it is not

303

likely that the man would have reported it, for he would realize the improbability of his statement being believed. He would trust rather to the probability of his presence in the carriage being unknown."

"I have no doubt that he would," I agreed, "and wisely, too. For no one would believe his statement. He would be charged with murder and most probably convicted. But you don't entertain the possibility of a misadventure, do you?

"As a bare possibility, yes. But it is wildly improbable, and still more so if those documents were really in Badger's pocket and have really disappeared. That is a crucial point. For, if it is certain that they were removed from the wallet, that is not only evidence of a conflict having taken place, but suggests in the strongest possible way that Badger had been rendered unconscious or helpless. But that suggestion at once raises the question: How was he rendered unconscious or helpless? The state of the body seems to exclude physical violence such as throttling or a knock on the head. Yet it is difficult to think of any other means."

"Very difficult," I agreed, "particularly in the alleged circumstances – the casual and unexpected meeting of two men in a railway carriage, and if one of those men was, as the theft of the documents seems to imply, a man just escaped from prison, the difficulty is still greater. Such a man would presumably be unprovided with anything but his fists. Indeed, the mystery is how he could have procured his ticket."

"Yes," Thorndyke assented, "that calls for explanation. But we must not mix up hypothesis and fact. Miller assumes that the man was the prisoner, Smith, and it is possible that he was. But we must not let that possibility influence us. We have to approach the inquiry with a perfectly open mind."

As he concluded, we came out on to the platform, where we found our friends awaiting us. In a few words Thorndyke communicated to them the results of his inspection, at which Miller was visibly disappointed.

"It is an extraordinary thing," said he. "Badger was a pretty hefty fellow and a skilled wrestler and boxer. I can't imagine even a strong man putting him out through the door unless he had disabled him first. And, in any case, you would expect to find some signs of a scrap. Did you propose to make any further examination?"

"It doesn't seem very necessary," Thorndyke replied. "But perhaps you might like me to be present when the local doctor does the *post mortem*. There are other possibilities besides gross physical injury."

"That is what I was thinking," said Miller, "and I should be glad if you could be present at the *post mortem*. Then I could feel satisfied that nothing had been overlooked. I understand that the inquest is to be held to-morrow afternoon at four o'clock and the *post mortem* at two. Can you manage that?"

"I shall have to, if you think it important," was the reply.

As Miller was making grateful acknowledgments, the station-master approached to convey to us the welcome tidings that a fast train to London was due in a few minutes.

"Are you coming back with us, Superintendent?" Thorndyke asked.

"I may as well," Miller replied. "The sergeant will carry on with the case, and I must set some inquiries going at the London end. And, by the way, Cummings, are you returning to Maidstone to-day?"

"Yes, sir," answered the Chief Officer. "I shall take the next train back."

"Then," said Miller, "you had better have those finger-prints of Smith's photographed and send either the photographs or the original up to Headquarters with the portrait photographs and the personal description. See to it at once, for we may want the information at any moment. In fact, we want it now."

"Very well, sir," replied Cummings. "I expect the photographs have been done already, but in any case, I will see that you get them some time to-morrow."

The short remaining interval was occupied by Miller in the delivery of detailed instructions to the sergeant. Then the train came hissing into the station, and Thorndyke, Miller, and I took our places in a compartment to which we were escorted by our three coadjutors.

Chapter VI
Thorndyke Examines
his Material

On the way up to town little was said on the subject of our investigation, and that little was mainly contributed by Miller. Thorndyke, unwilling as he always was to go far beyond the ascertained facts, maintained a tactful reticence, tempered by a sympathetic interest in the Superintendent's comments and suggestions.

"What I can't understand," said Miller, "is how that fellow managed to get Badger out of the door. It wouldn't be easy in the case of an ordinary man, but in the case of a man like Badger – a trained police officer and a pretty hefty one at that – it seems incredible."

"It would seem," I suggested, with little conviction, "that he must have been taken unawares."

"But how could he?" retorted Miller. "He knew that he was shut in with an escaped prisoner and that the other man probably knew that he knew it. You can take it that Badger would have watched him like a cat with a mouse. And the other fellow would have had to get the door open. That's rather a noticeable proceeding. No, when you think of the circumstances, it seems impossible that Badger could have been caught off his guard, and in a tunnel, too, of all places. What do you say, Doctor?"

"I agree with you," replied Thorndyke, "that it seems impossible that Badger could have been put out by mere physical violence."

"Are you quite sure that there were no signs of any injury? No bullet wound or marks of a life-preserver or sand-bag, or anything of that sort?"

"I think I can say positively," Thorndyke answered, "that there was no bullet wound and no bruises on the head, though I shall examine the body more minutely to-morrow when I attend at the *post mortem*. As to a sand-bag, that would probably leave no external marks. But it is an infinitely unlikely weapon to be used in a railway carriage, even in a tunnel. The carriage was presumably lighted like this one, and although that lamp gives a mere glimmer, hardly visible in daylight, the carriage would not be dark enough to make the use of a sand-bag practicable."

"No," Miller agreed, "it wouldn't. I was just feeling around for some sort of explanation. What about chloroform? Have you considered that?"

"Yes," replied Thorndyke, "and I think we can exclude it. At any rate I could discover no trace of it. But, as a matter of fact, it is really not practicable to administer chloroform forcibly to a strong man. The whiff from a handkerchief, producing instant unconsciousness, appertains to fiction. In practice, the forcible use of chloroform involves a rather prolonged struggle, and results in very characteristic marks on the skin around the mouth and nose. There were no such marks in this case, nor any other signs whatever."

"Then," Miller rejoined disconsolately, "I'm done. There must be some sort of explanation, but I'm hanged if I can think of one. Does anything occur to either of you gentlemen?"

For my part, I was as much in the dark as the Superintendent and had to admit it, and Thorndyke, as I expected, refused to commit himself to any speculative opinions.

"There isn't much use in theorizing at this stage," said he. "We want more facts, and we want confirmation of the assumptions that we have been treating as facts. For instance, the identity of the man who was seen to get into the carriage at Strood."

"M'yes," Miller agreed reluctantly. "I don't think there's much doubt, but, as you say, a little direct proof would be more satisfactory. Probably we shall get some more details in the course of a day or two. Meanwhile, I'm afraid I've taken up a lot of your time to very little purpose. We don't know much more than we did when we started."

"Apparently we do not," Thorndyke admitted. "But I don't regret the expedition. It was desirable for our own satisfaction to go over the ground at once and make sure that we had not missed anything."

"I'm glad you take that view, Doctor," said Miller, "but, all the same, you've got mighty little for your pains – nothing, in fact, excepting what you have gleaned from your examination of the body, and that doesn't seem to help us much."

"It doesn't," Thorndyke agreed. "But we must not forget that negative evidence has its value. The exclusion of one possibility after another leaves us eventually with the one that has to be accepted."

Miller received this rather academic observation without enthusiasm, remarking, truly enough, that the early stages of that sort of investigation were apt to be a little discouraging. "Possibly," he added, "something new may come out at the inquest, though it isn't likely. And it is just possible that, when we get those finger-prints from Maidstone, we may find that we are dealing with a known criminal. But even that would not prove the fact of the murder."

"As to that," said I, "if it can be proved, as apparently it can, that this man was alone with Badger in the compartment when the disaster occurred, that will create a pretty strong presumption of murder."

"No doubt," agreed Miller. "But presumption is a different thing from proof. If he should give a plausible account of an accident – such as leaning out of the window of an unfastened door – we shouldn't believe him, but we couldn't disprove his statement, and you might find it hard to get a jury to convict. If there is any doubt, the accused is entitled to the benefit of it. What we want is something in the way of positive evidence, and all that we have got is that certain documents have apparently been taken from the person of the deceased."

"I should call that pretty weighty positive evidence," said I, "especially as the documents included the suspect's finger-prints and description. What do you think, Thorndyke?"

"I think," he replied, "that we shall be in a better position to form opinions after the inquest, when we shall know what facts are really available. And speaking of the inquest, Miller, what is to be done with regard to notes of the evidence? Are you employing a shorthand reporter, or shall I bring or send my own man?"

"I don't see that either is necessary," replied Miller. "We can get a copy of the depositions if we want one."

"That may meet your requirements," said Thorndyke, "but it may not suit me so well. I think I will send a reporter of my own, and you can have a copy of the notes if you have any use for them."

The Superintendent accepted this offer with suitable acknowledgments, and the subject dropped for the time. As the train moved out of London Bridge Station, however, I ventured to raise another subject of more immediate interest, at least to me.

"What are we going to do in the matter of food, Thorndyke?" I asked. "Does Polton know when to expect us?"

"Obviously not," was the reply, "as we did not know ourselves. I told him that we should get some food on the way, and I suggest that the Coffee Room at the Charing Cross Hotel will be the best place to stoke up. Perhaps the Superintendent will join us."

"Very good of you, Doctor," said Miller, "but I think I must get on to my office to finish up one or two odds and ends. Possibly we shall travel down together to-morrow, but if not, we shall meet at the inquest. By that time I shall probably have seen those finger-prints from Maidstone."

Accordingly, we separated at Charing Cross, Miller striding away towards the entrance while Thorndyke and I made our way to the Hotel Coffee Room, where, with one accord, we demanded whatever might be ready at the moment. The long fast that our various activities had entailed had disposed us both to find a better use for our jaws than conversation. But as the entrée dish emptied and the level in the claret bottle sank, my interest in our quest revived and I began cautiously to put out feelers. It had been evident to me that Thorndyke was not prepared to accept Miller's interpretation of the facts, and the question that I asked myself – and by implication put to him – was: Had he any alternative theory? But my feelers felt nothing but a steady, passive resistance to discussion, which, however, was not entirely unilluminating, for long experience of Thorndyke had taught me that when he was more than usually uncommunicative, he had something up his sleeve.

Now, could he have anything up his sleeve on the present occasion? Was there something that he had seen and the rest of us had overlooked? Naturally I could not be sure, but there had been so little to see that it seemed hardly possible. His examination of the body could not have yielded any fact that he had net disclosed. It was quite unlike him to withhold any observed fact when he made a report. As I turned over the events of the day, I could recall only two that seemed to involve any obscurity or uncertainty. Thorndyke had taken the dead man's finger-prints. I did not see why. But it was a simple and reasonable proceeding and Thorndyke's explanation had seemed adequate. But was it possible that he had something more definite in his mind?

Again, he had picked up a half-smoked cigar in the tunnel. That I could make nothing of. I could imagine no possible bearing that it could have on the case. The subsequent taking of the finger-prints suggested a suspicion that the cigar had been smoked by Badger. But supposing it had? What light could that fact conceivably throw on the crime? I could perceive no relevancy at all. Nevertheless, the more I reflected on these two incidents, the more strongly did I suspect that they were connected with something definite in Thorndyke's mind – something connected with Badger's finger-prints, or even with those of the other man – which would, indeed, furnish highly relevant and important evidence.

That suspicion deepened when, on our arrival at our chambers, he made his way straight up to the laboratory with an air of evident purpose. There we found our laboratory assistant, Polton, apparently engaged in a *post mortem* examination of the dismembered remains of a clock. He greeted us with a crinkly smile of welcome and, scenting some more alluring activity, abandoned the autopsy and slipped off his stool.

"Is there anything that you are wanting, sir?" he asked, as Thorndyke ran a seeking eye along the shelves.

"Haven't we a holder for objects that are to be photographed?" Thorndyke enquired.

"Yes, sir. The stand forceps," was the reply and, opening a cupboard, Polton produced an appliance somewhat like an enlarged edition of the stage forceps of a naturalist's microscope – a spring holder supported on a heavy foot and furnished with a universal joint. As Polton set the appliance down on the bench, Thorndyke opened his research case and, taking from it the envelope containing the cigar, extracted the latter with a pair of forceps and fixed it in the jaws of the holder, which grasped it near the pointed end. Anticipating the next move, I repaired to the cupboard and brought forth an insufflator, or powder spray, and a wide-mouthed bottle filled with a fine, white powder, both of which I placed on the bench without remark. Thorndyke acknowledged the attention with a smile, enquiring, "What are the odds that we draw a blank?"

"You are gambling on the chance of finding Badger's finger-prints?" I suggested.

"It is hardly a gamble, as we don't stand to lose anything," he replied. "But I thought it worthwhile to try. There is at least a possibility."

"Undoubtedly," I agreed. "And the probability is not so very remote. What I don't see is the relevancy of their presence or absence. Does it matter to us or to anybody else whether Badger was or was not smoking a cigar when he met his death?"

"That question," he replied, "we may leave until we see what luck we have. The might-have-beens certainly do not concern us."

As he was speaking, he filled the container of the spray with the white powder and, starting the bellows, blew a jet of powder on to the cigar, turning the latter round by degrees until every part of it was covered with a white film. Then, swinging up the arm of the holder until the cigar was upright, he took a little box-wood mallet that Polton had picked out of a rack and handed to him, and began rapidly and lightly to tap the foot of the holder. As the slight concussions were transmitted to the cigar, the film of powder on its surface crept gradually downward, uncovering the dark body by degrees, but leaving a number of light-coloured patches where the powder had adhered more closely. Slowly, as the tapping continued, the loose powder became detached until only the lightest dusting remained, and meanwhile the light patches grew more distinct and defined, and began to show faintly the characteristic linear patterns of finger-prints. Finally, Thorndyke blew gently on the cigar, rotating it as before by means of the universal joint. And now, as the last vestiges of the loose powder were blown away, the finger-prints – or at least some of them – grew suddenly quite clear and distinct.

Polton and I pored eagerly over the curious markings (though it had been almost a foregone conclusion that some finger-prints must appear, since somebody had held the cigar in his fingers) while Thorndyke once more opened his research case and took from it a couple of cards, each bearing five finger-prints and each scribed with the name of Inspector Badger. Laying the two cards on the bench beside the holder, he took a magnifying glass down from a nail on the wall and carefully scanned through it first the prints on the card and then those on the cigar. After several prolonged comparisons he seemed to have reached a conclusion, though he made no remark but silently handed me the glass.

I began with a thorough inspection of the prints on the cards. They were beautifully distinct, having been skilfully executed with finger-print ink, and showed, with the sharpness of an engraving, not only the ridge-pattern but the rows of tiny white dots on the black lines which represented the mouths of the sweat glands. When I had to some extent memorized the patterns, I turned my attention to the cigar, selecting first a rather large print which looked like that of a thumb. It was slightly blurred as if the thumb had been damp, but it was quite legible, and when I compared it with the two thumb prints on the card, I recognized it pretty confidently as that of the left hand.

Having reached a positive result, I felt no further examination was worthwhile. But before giving my decision, I handed the glass to Polton, who took it from me with a crinkle of satisfaction and bent eagerly over the cards. But I think he had already made his observations with the naked eye, for, after a very brief inspection, he delivered his verdict.

"It's a true bill, sir." He pointed at the large print with a pencil and added, "That is Mr. Badger's left thumb."

"That was my opinion, too," I said in confirmation.

"Yes," Thorndyke agreed, "I think there is no doubt of it, though it will have to be verified by a detailed comparison of the separate characters. But it establishes a *prima facie* case. There are a number of other, less distinct prints, but we need not examine them now. The important thing is to secure a permanent record which can be safely handled. How many photographs shall we want, Polton?"

"You will want to show every part of every finger-print free from distortion," said Polton, stating the problem and slowly rotating the cigar as he spoke. "Six photographs would do it at a pinch, but if it is important, I should do twelve and make it safe. That would give you about four views of each finger-print."

"Very well, Polton," said Thorndyke, "we will make twelve exposures. And if you have the plates ready, we will get them done at once."

As the making of twelve exposures promised to be a tedious business and my assistance was not required, I took one or two sheets of paper from the rack and, laying them on the work-bench, proceeded to occupy myself usefully in drawing up a summary of the day's experiences and the facts, such as they were, which had transpired during our investigations. But they were few and apparently not very significant, so that I was not long in coming to the end of my summary when I laid down my pen and transferred my attention to Thorndyke's proceedings.

It was evident that the discovery of Badger's thumb-print had not exhausted his interest in the derelict cigar for, as each negative was developed and washed, he brought it to the bench and, holding it over a sheet of white paper under the lamp, scrutinized it through his lens and compared it with the prints on the cards. I did not quite understand the object of this detailed comparison, for the identification of the one print had established the fact that the cigar had been smoked by Badger, whatever the significance of that fact might be. The identification of further prints seemed rather like flogging a dead horse. Eventually I was moved to make a remark to that effect.

"That is true enough," said he, "but we have to get all the information that our material will yield. As a matter of fact, I am not looking for the remainder of Badger's prints. I am looking to see if there are any prints which are not his."

"And are there?"

"Yes, there is at least one and a problematical second one, but that is practically obliterated by the heat from the burnt end. The other is a fairly clear print, apparently a thumb, and it is certainly not either of Badger's thumbs."

"From which, I presume, you infer that the cigar was given to Badger by someone else?"

"That is the reasonable inference, and as he was alone with another man in the carriage, the further inference is admissible that the giver of the cigar was that other man. That, however, is only a probability which will have to be considered in relation to the other facts."

"Yes," I agreed. "It might have been given to him at Maidstone to smoke in the train. I don't see how you are to prove either view, or that you would be much forrarder if you did."

I was, in fact, rather puzzled by the intense interest that Thorndyke displayed in this cigar, for surely nothing could be less distinctive or more hopeless for purposes of identification than a commodity which is manufactured in thousands of identical replicas. But as Thorndyke must necessarily realize this, I could only suppose that there was some point the significance of which I had overlooked, and with this probability in

312

my mind, I followed my colleague's proceedings closely in the hope that the point which I had missed would presently emerge.

When the last of the negatives had been developed and examined, Thorndyke took the cigar out of the holder and wiped it clean of all traces of the powder.

"That," he remarked, "is the advantage of carrying out these investigations ourselves. If Miller had seen those finger-prints, he would have insisted on annexing the cigar to produce as an 'exhibit' at the trial – if there ever is one. Whereas our photographs, properly attested, are equally good evidence, and the cigar is at our disposal for further examination."

The advantage was not very obvious to me, but I discreetly abstained from comment, and he continued, "It is a rather unusual cigar, considerably above the ordinary dimensions. The part which remains is five-inches-and-an-eighth long. Judging by the thickness – a full three-quarters-of-an-inch – the complete cigar was probably well over six inches in length. How much over we can't say. There are some enormously long cigars made for civic banquets and similar functions."

"No doubt," said I, "a cigar merchant could identify the type and give us the actual dimensions."

"Probably," he agreed. "But it is enough for us to note that it was an exceptionally large cigar and pretty certainly an expensive one. And then, as if the size were not enough, there is the strength of the tobacco. The appearance of the leaf tells us that it is an uncommonly strong weed. Taking the size and the strength together, it would be rather more than enough for an ordinary smoker."

All of this was doubtless true, but it seemed to have no bearing on the question as to how Inspector Badger had met with his death. I was still puzzling over Thorndyke's apparently irrelevant proceedings when I received a sudden enlightenment. Having finished his examination of its exterior, Thorndyke laid the cigar on the bench and with a long thin knife, cut it cleanly lengthwise down the middle. The action set a chord of memory vibrating, and incidentally engendered in me a desire to kick myself. For, years ago, I had seen Thorndyke cut open another cigar.

"Ha!" I exclaimed. "You are thinking of that poisoned cheroot that Walter Hornby sent you."

"That we inferred to have been sent by him," Thorndyke corrected. "We were pretty certainly right, but we had no actual proof. Yes, it seemed possible that this might be a similar case."

I looked closely at the cut surfaces of the two halves. In the case of the cheroot, the section had shown a whitish patch where the alkaloid – it was aconitine, I remembered – had dried out of the solution. But nothing of the kind was visible in these sections.

"I don't see any signs of the cigar having been tampered with," said I. "There doesn't seem to be any trace of a hypodermic needle as there was in the cheroot, or any crystals or foreign matter of any kind."

"As to the needle," said Thorndyke, "the heat and the steam from the burning end would probably obliterate any traces. But I am not so sure of the absence of foreign matter. There is certainly no solid material, but the whole of the inside has a greasy, sodden appearance which doesn't seem quite natural, and the smell is not like that of a normal cigar."

I picked up one of the halves and cautiously sniffed at it.

"I don't make out anything abnormal," said I. "It is devilish strong and rather unpleasant, but I can't distinguish any smell other than that of virulently rank tobacco."

"Well," said Thorndyke, "there is no use in guessing. We had better ascertain definitely. And as the foreign matter, if there is any, appears to be a liquid, we will begin by making an attempt to isolate it."

He glanced at Polton, who, having put the negatives to drain, had now reappeared and was casting wistful glances at the divided cigar.

"Will you want any apparatus prepared, sir, or any reagents?" he asked.

"A fairly wide-mouthed ten-ounce stoppered bottle and some sulphuric ether will do for the start," replied Thorndyke, and as Polton went to the chemical side of the laboratory in search of these he laid a sheet of paper on the bench and, placing on it one of the halves of the cigar, proceeded to cut it up into fine shreds. I took possession of the other half and operated on it in a similar manner, and when the whole cigar had been reduced to a heap of dark-brown, clammy "fine-cut" tobacco, we shot it into the bottle, which Thorndyke then half-filled with ether.

"This is going to be a long job," I remarked, looking a little anxiously at my watch. "This stuff ought to macerate for two or three hours at least."

"We need not complete the examination to-night," Thorndyke replied, reassuringly, as he gave the bottle a shake. "If we can decide whether there is or is not any foreign substance present, that will be enough for our immediate purposes, and we ought to be able to settle that in half-an-hour."

Thorndyke's estimate seemed to me rather optimistic, unless – as I was disposed to suspect – he had already decided that some foreign substance was present and had formed some opinion as to its nature. But

I made no comment, contenting myself with an occasional turn at shaking the bottle or prodding the mass of sodden tobacco with a glass rod.

At the end of half-an-hour, Thorndyke decanted off the ether – now stained a brownish yellow – into a beaker which he stood in a pan of warm water to hasten the evaporation, while Polton opened the windows and door to let the vapour escape.

"It's an awful waste of material, sir," he remarked, disapprovingly. "We ought to have done this in a retort and recovered the ether."

"I suppose we ought," Thorndyke admitted, "but this is the quicker way, and time is more precious than ether. Dr. Jervis wants to get done and go to bed."

As he was speaking, we all watched the beaker, in which the liquid dwindled in bulk from minute to minute, growing darker in colour as it grew less in volume. At length it was reduced to a thin layer at the bottom of the beaker – less than half a teaspoonful – and as this remained unchanged in volume, and the odour of ether became rapidly less intense, it was evident that evaporation had now ceased. Thorndyke took up the beaker and, having smelled the contents, turned it from side to side to test the fluidity of the liquid, which flowed backwards and forwards some what sluggishly like a thinnish oil.

"What do you say it is, Jervis?" he asked, handing the beaker to me.

"Probably a mixture," I replied. "But it smells like nicotine and it looks like nicotine, excepting as to the colour, and as it has been extracted from a cigar, I should say that it is nicotine, stained with colouring matter."

"I think you are right," he said, "but we may as well confirm our opinions. The colour test will not answer very well owing to the staining, but it will probably work well enough to differentiate it from coniine, which it resembles in consistency, though not very much in smell. Can we have a white tile, Polton, or the cover of a porcelain capsule?"

From the inexhaustible cupboard Polton produced a small white, enamelled tile which he laid on the bench, while Thorndyke picked up a glass rod which he dipped into the liquid in the beaker and then touched the middle of the tile, leaving a drop on the white surface.

"I have rather forgotten this test," said I, leaning over the tile, "but it seems to me that this drop shows quite a distinct green tint in spite of the staining. Is that what you expected?"

"Yes," he replied. "The green tint is characteristic of nicotine. Coniine would have given a pink colour. But we had better try Roussin's Test and settle the question quite definitely. We shall want two test tubes and some iodine."

While Polton was supplying this requisition, Thorndyke took up a clean filter paper and laid it on the drop of liquid on the tile, which it immediately soaked up, producing an oily spot of a distinct green colour.

"That," said he, "further supports the suggestion of nicotine. But it is not conclusive in the way that a chemical test is."

Once more I had the feeling that he was flogging a dead horse, for there seemed to be no reason whatever for doubting that the liquid was nicotine. However, I kept this view to myself, taking the opportunity to refresh my memory as to the procedure of Roussin's Test, while Polton followed the experiment with breathless interest.

It was quite a simple test. Into one test tube Thorndyke dropped a few particles of iodine and poured on them a small quantity of ether. While the iodine was dissolving, he poured a little ether into the other test tube and, with a pipette, dropped into it a few minims of the liquid from the beaker. When the iodine was dissolved, he poured the solution into the other tube. Almost immediately a brownish-red precipitate separated out and began to settle at the bottom of the tube.

"Is that according to plan?" I asked.

"Yes," he replied. "The result is positive, so far, but we must wait a few minutes for the final answer to our question. If this liquid is nicotine, the precipitate will presently crystallize out in long, slender needles of a very characteristic colour – ruby red by transmitted light and dark blue by reflected light."

He stood the test tube in a stand and, seating himself on a high stool, proceeded to fill his pipe, while Polton stationed himself opposite the test tube stand and kept an expectant eye on the little mass of sediment. Presently I saw him pick up the magnifying glass and, having drawn down an adjustable lamp, make a closer inspection. For three or four minutes be continued to watch the test tube through the glass, assisting his observations by placing a sheet of white paper upright behind the stand. At length he reported progress.

"It is beginning to crystallize – long, thin blue crystals."

"Try it against the light," said Thorndyke.

Very slowly and carefully, to avoid disturbing the formation of the crystals, Polton lifted the tube from its stand and held it between the lamp and his eye.

"Now they are red," he reported, "like thin splinters of garnet."

I took the tube from his hand and examined the growing mass of fine, needle-like crystals, crimson against the light and deep blue when the light was behind me, and then passed it to Thorndyke.

"Yes," he said when he had verified our observations, "that is the characteristic reaction. So now our question is answered. The liquid that we extracted from the cigar is nicotine."

"Well," I remarked, "it has been a very interesting experiment, and I suppose it was worth doing, but the result is not exactly sensational. Nicotine is what one might expect to extract from a cigar, though I must say that the amount is greater than I should have expected, especially as we haven't got the whole of it."

Thorndyke regarded me with an indulgent smile.

"My learned friend," said he, "has allowed his toxicology to get a little rusty, and thereby has missed the point of this experiment. It is not a question of quantity – there ought not to have been any nicotine at all."

As I gazed at him in astonishment and was beginning to protest, he continued. "The nicotine that we dissolved out with the ether was free nicotine. But there is no free nicotine in a cigar. The alkaloid is combined with malic acid. If this had been a normal cigar, we should have got no free nicotine until we had treated the cigar – or a decoction of it – with a caustic alkali, preferably caustic potash."

"Then," I exclaimed, "this nicotine had been artificially introduced into the cigar."

"Exactly. It was a foreign substance, although it happened to be a natural constituent of a cigar. Probably it was injected into the open end with a hypodermic syringe. But at any rate there it was, and I think that its presence disposes of Miller's question as to how Inspector Badger was put out of the carriage on to the line."

"You think that he was suffering from nicotine poisoning?"

"I have no doubt of it. We have seen that he smoked at least an inch of this cigar. The cigar contained naturally anything up to eight-per-cent of combined nicotine, part of which would pass into the smoke. To this had been added not less than half a fluid drachm of free nicotine. Now, when we consider that the lethal dose of nicotine is not more than two or three drops, and that more than that amount must have been contained in the part that was burned, we are pretty safe in assuming that the smoker would have been reduced, at least, to a state of physical helplessness."

"You have no doubt that he was alive when the train went over him?"

"No. But though he was undoubtedly alive, I think it quite likely that he was moribund. He had apparently taken nearly, if not quite, the full lethal dose."

"It is a little surprising," I remarked, "that he went on smoking so long that he did not grow suspicious, seeing that he knew who his fellow passenger was, as apparently he did."

317

"I don't think it is very surprising," replied Thorndyke. "The procedure had been so well calculated to avert suspicion. Let us suppose – as probably happened – that the stranger produces a cigar-case. There are two cigars in it – one, no doubt, bearing a private mark. The stranger takes the marked cigar and holds out the case to Badger. Now Badger, as we know, usually smoked a pipe, but he was very partial to a cigar, and he preferred a strong one. He would certainly have taken the cigar and would have been impressed by its strength. Probably, owing to the presence of the free nicotine, the cigar would not have burned freely. He would have had to draw at it vigorously to keep it alight, and so would have drawn into his mouth a large amount of the vaporized nicotine.

"Presently he would begin to feel unwell, but at first he would feel nothing more than ordinary tobacco-sickness, and before he had time to become suspicious, he would be in a state of collapse. Nicotine, you will remember, is probably, with the exception of hydrocyanic acid, the most rapid of all poisons in its action."

"Yes, but if Badger was really in a moribund state, it would seem that it was a tactical mistake to throw him out on the line. If the murderer had simply sat him up in a corner and got out at the next station, no suspicion of any crime would have arisen. The body might not have been observed until the train reached London, and when it was discovered and examined, death would have appeared to have been due to natural causes, or to excessive smoking, if the nicotine poisoning had been detected."

"I don't think that would have done, Jervis," Thorndyke replied. "Your plan would have involved too many contingencies. The next stop was at Dartford – a fairly busy junction. Someone might quite probably have got in there and seen the murderer getting out. And again, Badger might have recovered. You can usually tell when a man is dead, but it is difficult even for an expert to be certain that an insensible man is dying. No, this man was taking no risks, or as few as possible. And he was a desperate man. Probably Badger was the only officer who knew him, and he was aware of the fact. His safety depended on his getting rid of Badger."

"I gather," said I, "that you don't accept Miller's view as to the identity of the other passenger. It struck me that he was rather jumping at conclusions."

"He was, indeed," Thorndyke agreed, "in a most surprising manner for so shrewd and experienced an officer. It was a positive obsession. I never entertained the idea for a moment for, apart from the total absence of evidence, it bristled with impossibilities. The man was a runaway prisoner. He was, it is true, wearing his own clothes, but he would

318

probably have no hat and his pockets would almost certainly be empty. How could such a man have got a first-class ticket? And how could he have got away from Maidstone to make his appearance so promptly at Strood? The thing is inconceivable.

"But we had better adjourn this discussion. It is past midnight, and Polton is yawning in a way that threatens us with the job of reducing a dislocation of the lower jaw. The rest of the nicotine extraction can wait till the morning, if it is necessary to pursue the question of quantity. The actual amount is of no great consequence. The presence of free nicotine is the essential fact, and we have established that."

"And thereby," said I, as the meeting broke up, "prepared quite a pleasant little surprise for Superintendent Miller."

Chapter VII
The Persistence of
Superintendent Miller

As I undressed, and for the short time that I lay awake, I revolved in my mind the amazing events of the evening, and in the morning, no sooner was I in possession of my waking senses than the question presented itself afresh for consideration. What was it that had impelled Thorndyke to secure and preserve that cigar? It had looked like a mere chance shot, but all my knowledge and experience of Thorndyke and his ways was against any such explanation. Thorndyke was not in the habit of making chance shots. Moreover, the act had been deliberate and considered. He had seen the cigar by the instantaneous flash of the lamp. He had walked on for a few paces, and then he had slipped on a glove and gone back to pick up the cigar and bestow it in his pocket with evident care. In those few instants of reflection, something must have occurred to him to suggest the incredible possibility that had been turned into ascertained fact in the laboratory. Now, what could that something have been?

When we met at the breakfast-table, I proceeded without delay to present my problem for solution.

"I have been wondering, Thorndyke," said I, "what made you pick up that cigar. Evidently, the results of the examination were not entirely unexpected."

I could see that my question, also, was not unexpected, but he did not reply immediately, and I continued. "That cigar was perfectly normal to look at. Yet it seems as if some intuition had suggested to you the possibility of its amazingly abnormal qualities. It is an utter mystery to me."

"I pray you, Jervis," he replied, smilingly, "not to accuse me of intuitions. I have always assumed that intuitions are for those who can't reason. But let us consider the circumstances surrounding that cigar. We will take first the *prima facie* appearances, disregarding, for the moment, our own personalities and our special knowledge and experience.

"Here was a cigar which had been lighted and thrown away, less than half-smoked. Now, its condition offered evidence, at a glance, of some sudden change in the state of mind of the smoker. That would be true even of a cigarette. Normally, a man either wants a smoke or he does not. If he does, he lights the cigarette and smokes it. If he does not, he

320

doesn't light it. But if he lights it and then throws it away, that act is evidence of a change of purpose, and that change is almost certainly determined by some change in his circumstances or surroundings.

"But what is true of a cigarette, which costs about a penny, is more emphatically true of a cigar of an expensive type, which must have cost at least half-a-crown. There must have been some definite reason for its having been thrown away. But within a few yards of the place where the cigar was lying, a man had been murdered. There had been two men in a smoking-compartment. If the deceased had been smoking a cigar, he would obviously not have finished it, and the same is almost certainly true of the other. Hence there was an appreciable probability that this cigar had some connection with the murder. But, since a cigar which has been smoked is practically certain to bear finger-prints, it would have been reasonable in any case to secure the cigar and see, if possible, whose finger-prints it bore.

"So much for the general aspects of the incident – which I should have thought would have been obvious to Miller. We, however, were not concerned only with the general aspects. We had special knowledge and special experience. I have told you how, in the early days of my practice, when I had little to do, I used to occupy myself in the invention of crimes of an unusual and ingenious kind and in devising methods of detection to counter them. It was time and effort well spent, for each crime that I invented – and circumvented – though it was imaginary, yet furnished actual experience which prepared me to deal with such a crime if I should encounter it in real life. Now, among the criminal methods which I devised was the use of a cigar as the means for administering poison."

"Yes," said I. "I remember, and very fortunate it was for you that you did. The fact that the possibility was in your mind probably saved your life when our friend, Hornby, sent you that poisoned cheroot."

"Exactly," he agreed. "The imaginary case had the effect of a real case, and when the real case occurred, it found me prepared. And now let us apply these facts to the present case. You heard Miller's sketch of the tragedy as he had heard it told through the telephone, and you will remember that he put his finger on the point that most needed explanation: How had Badger been put out of the carriage on to the line? According to the report, no gross injuries had been found. He had not been shot or stabbed or bludgeoned. He seemed simply to have been thrown out. Yet how could such a thing be possible? A Metropolitan police-officer is a formidable man, and Badger was a fine specimen of his class – big, powerful, courageous, and highly trained in the arts of offence and defence. He could not have been off his guard, for he knew that he was travelling with a criminal and must have been prepared for an attack. How then could he have been thrown out? That was Miller's difficulty, and it was a real one, assuming that the report had given the true facts.

"The train journey down gave us time to think it over. That time I employed in turning over every explanation that I could think of. Since direct violence seemed to be ruled out, the only reasonable supposition was that, in some way, Badger must have been rendered insensible or helpless. But in what way? You heard Miller's suggestions, and you could see that none of them was practicable. To me, it appeared that poison in some form was the most likely method. But how do you set to work to poison a man in a railway carriage?

"I considered the various methods that were physically possible. The most obvious was to offer a drink from a flask. That would be effective enough – but not with a detective inspector of the C.I.D. Badger would have refused to a certainty, and poisoned sweets would have been still more hopeless. Then the possibility of a poisoned cigar occurred to me. The idea seemed a little extravagant, but still, the method had actually been used within my own experience. And there was no denying that it would have met the case perfectly. The offer of a cigar would have appeared, even to a cautious police officer, a quite unsuspicious action. And we know that Badger liked a cigar and would almost certainly have accepted one. So, in spite of the fact that, as I have said, the suggestion seemed rather far-fetched, I made a mental note to keep the possibility in mind.

"At Greenhithe the absence of any traces of violence was confirmed. Then we went into the tunnel, and behold! Almost the first object that we notice is a half-smoked cigar. There was not much need for intuitions."

I admitted a little shamefacedly that there was not. It was the old story. An item of knowledge or experience that was once in Thorndyke's mind was there forever, and what is more, it was available for use at any moment, and in any set of circumstances. I had not this gift. My memory was good enough, but I had not his constructive imagination. I could only use my experiences when analogous circumstances recurred. The poisoned cheroot had come by post. Thereafter, I should have looked with suspicion on any cigar that arrived by post from an unknown source. But Thorndyke had the idea in his mind, ready to apply it to any new set of circumstances. It was a vital difference.

Having settled this question, I passed on to another that had exercised my mind a good deal.

"You seem," I said, "to have decided pretty clearly how the actual murder was carried out. Have you carried the matter any farther? Have you any theory of the general *modus operandi* of the crime?"

"Only in quite general terms," he replied. "I think we are forced to certain conclusions. For instance, the fact that the murderer had the poisoned cigar available compels us to assume that the crime was not only premeditated but very definitely planned. My impression is that poor Badger was under a delusion. He thought that he was stalking a criminal, whereas, in fact, the criminal was stalking him. I suspect that he knew what was going on at Maidstone, and that he kept Badger in sight. I believe that he saw him into the train at Maidstone and travelled with him in that train to Strood."

"There seem to be at least two objections to that theory," said I. "To begin with, he could hardly have avoided being seen at Maidstone. For leaving Badger out of the picture, there was Cummings, who certainly knew him by sight and would surely have spotted him at the station."

"I see," said Thorndyke, "that you are adopting Miller's view that the murderer was the man Smith. That view seems to me quite untenable. I have never entertained it for a moment."

"You are not forgetting the resemblance between the two men? That both men had red hair and a noticeably red nose? It would be a remarkable coincidence, if they were different men."

"Very true," he agreed. "But don't let us lose sight of the collateral circumstances. If we assume that this was a carefully planned murder, as it appears to have been, we have to be on the look-out for such ordinary precautions as a murderer would probably take. Now a red nose with red hair is a rather uncommon combination and, as you say, its occurrence in two men in these peculiar circumstances would be a remarkable coincidence. But there are such things as wigs and rouge and grease-paint, and these are just the circumstances in which we might look to see them used. The very simplest make-up would do. Consider how easy it would have been. Supposing a dark man with close-cropped hair gets into an empty carriage at Maidstone. Just before reaching Strood, he slips on a red wig and gives his nose an infinitesimal touch of rouge. On arriving at Strood, he hops out, and at once makes for the stairs leading to the subway. There, or elsewhere, he waits for the arrival of the London train and, when it comes in, he emerges, boldly, on to the platform, and lets himself be plainly seen."

"But don't you think Badger would have spotted the wig?" I objected.

"I feel pretty sure that he would," Thorndyke replied. "But why not? The stranger was there for the express purpose of being spotted. And you notice a further use that the make-up would have had. For, after the murder, he could have doffed the wig and cleaned off the rouge, and forthwith he would have been a different person. The description of him, as he had been seen at Strood, no longer applied to him. He could show himself boldly at Dartford and leave no trace. What is the second objection?"

"I was thinking of the fact – if it is a fact – that he took the risk of stealing Smith's finger-print papers from the body. It was a very serious risk. For if he had been stopped and searched and they had been found on his person, that would have convicted him of the murder beyond any question. And, moreover, the very fact that they were taken furnishes evidence of murder and effectually excludes the possibility of misadventure. The taking of such a risk points to a very strong motive. But they were Smith's finger-prints, and if he were not Smith, what strong motive could he have had for taking them?"

"Admirably argued," Thorndyke commented. "But perhaps we had better postpone the consideration of that point until we have actually ascertained that the papers were really taken from the body. The point is of importance in more than one respect. As you, very justly remark, the taking away of these papers converts what might have been accepted as a misadventure into an undeniable murder. And the man who took them – if he did take them – could not have failed to realize this. You are certainly right as to the strength of the motive. The question that remains to be solved is, What might have been the nature of that motive? But I think we shall have to adjourn this discussion."

As he spoke, I became aware of footsteps ascending the stairs, and growing rapidly more audible. Their cessation coincided with a knock at the door, which I instantly recognized as Miller's. I sprang up and threw the door open, whereupon the Superintendent entered and fixed a mock-reproachful eye on the uncleared breakfast-table.

"Well, gentlemen," he said, by way of greeting, "I thought I would just drop in and give you the news in case you were starting early. You needn't. The *post mortem* is fixed for two-thirty, and there is nothing else for you to do."

"Thank you, Miller," said Thorndyke. "It was good of you to come round. But, as a matter of fact, we are not going – at least, I am not, and I don't think Jervis is."

The Superintendent's jaw dropped. "I am sorry to hear that," said he in a tone of very real disappointment. "I was rather banking on your getting us something definite to go on. We haven't got much in the way of positive evidence."

"That," Thorndyke answered, "is why we are not going. We have got some positive evidence, and we think – and so will you – that we had better keep it to ourselves, at least for the present."

The Superintendent cast an astonished glance at my colleague.

"You have got some positive evidence!" he exclaimed. "Why – How the deuce? – But there, that doesn't matter. What have you discovered?"

Thorndyke opened a drawer and produced from it a pack of mounted photographs and the two cards bearing Badger's finger-prints, which he laid on the table.

"You may remember, Miller," he said, "pointing out to me in the tunnel that someone had thrown away a half-smoked cigar."

"I remember," the Superintendent replied. "An uncommon good weed it looked, too. I had half-a-mind to pick it up and finish it – in a holder, of course."

"It's just as well that you did not," Thorndyke chuckled. "However, I picked it up. I thought there might possibly be some finger-prints on it. And there were. Some of them were Badger's. But there were some others as well."

"How were you able to spot Badger's finger-prints?" Miller demanded in a tone of astonishment.

"I took the records from the body," Thorndyke replied, "on the chance that we might want them."

Miller stared at my colleague in silent amazement.

"You are a most extraordinary man, Doctor," he exclaimed, at length. "You seem to have the gift of second sight. What on earth could have made you – but there, it's no use asking you. Are these poor Badger's prints?"

"Yes," Thorndyke answered, "and these are the photographs of the cigar with the prints developed on it."

Miller pored eagerly over the photographs and compared them with the prints on the cards.

"Yes," said he, after a careful inspection, "they are clear enough. There is poor old Badger's thumb as plain as a pikestaff. And here is one – looks like a thumb, too – that certainly is not Badger's. Now we are going to see whose it is."

He spoke in a tone of triumph, and as he spoke, he whisked out of his pocket, with something of a flourish, a large leather wallet. From this he extracted a blue document and spread it out on the table. On it, among other matter, were four sets of finger-prints – the "tips" of the two hands, both sets complete, and the two sets of "rolled impressions," of which those of the right hand consisted only of two perfect impressions and a

325

smear. Miller confined his attention principally to the tips, glancing backward and forward from them to the photographs, which were spread out on the table. And, watching him, I was sensible of a gradual change in his demeanour. The triumphant air slowly faded away, giving place, first to doubt and bewilderment, and finally to quite definite disappointment.

"Nothing doing," he reported, handing the paper to Thorndyke. "They are not Smith's finger-prints. Pity. I'd hoped they would have been. If they had been, they would have fixed the murder on him beyond any doubt. Now we shall have to grub about for some other kind of evidence. At present, we've got nothing but the evidence of the station-master at Strood."

Thorndyke looked at him with slightly raised eyebrows.

"You seem," said he, "to be overlooking the importance of those other finger-prints. If they are not Smith's, they are somebody's, and the person who made them is the person who gave Badger that cigar."

"No doubt," Miller agreed. "But what about it? Does it matter who gave him the cigar?"

"As it happens," Thorndyke replied, "it matters a great deal. We have analysed that cigar and we found that it contained a very large dose of a deadly volatile poison."

Miller was thunderstruck. For some moments he stood, silently gazing at Thorndyke, literally open-mouthed. At length, he exclaimed in a low, almost awe-stricken tone, "Good God, Doctor. This is new evidence with a vengeance! Now we can understand how poor old Badger was got out on to the line. But how in the name of fortune came you to analyse the cigar?"

"There was just the bare possibility," Thorndyke replied. "We thought we might as well make the trial."

Miller shook his head. "It's second sight, Doctor. There's, no other name for it. It looks as if you had spotted the poison in the cigar as it lay on the ground in the tunnel. You are a most astonishing man. But the question is, how the deuce he got hold of that cigar."

"Who?" demanded Thorndyke. "You don't, surely, mean Smith?"

"Certainly I do," Miller replied, doggedly. "Who else?"

"But," Thorndyke protested with a shade of impatience, "you have just ascertained, beyond any reasonable doubt, that the cigar was given to Badger by some other person."

But the Superintendent was not to be moved from the conviction that apparently had possession of his mind. "Those other prints," he insisted, "must be the prints of the man from whom Smith got the cigar. We shall have to find out who he is, of course. But it is the murderer we

326

want. And the murderer is Frederick Smith, or whatever his real name is."

Thorndyke's sense of humour apparently got the better of his vexation, for he remarked with a low chuckle, "It seems odd for me to pose as the champion of finger-print evidence. But, really, Miller, you are flying in the face of all the visible facts and probabilities. There is absolutely nothing to connect the man Smith with that cigar."

"He may have worn gloves," suggested Miller.

"He may have worn a cocked hat," retorted Thorndyke. "But there is no reason to believe that he did. Why do you cling to the unfortunate Smith in this tenacious fashion?"

"Why," rejoined Miller, "look at the description on his paper and then recall what the station-master at Strood said."

Thorndyke took up the paper and read aloud: "'*Height: 67 inches. Weight: 158 pounds. Rather thick-set, muscular build. Hair, darkish red. Eyes, reddish brown. Complexion, fresh. Nose, straight, medium size, rather thick and distinctly red*.' Yes, that seems to agree with the station-master's description. I see that he gives no address, but describes himself as a plumber and gas-fitter."

"Probably that is right," said Miller. "A considerable proportion of the men who take to burglary started life as plumbers and gas-fitters. Their professional training gives them an advantage."

"It must," I remarked a little bitterly, recalling the ravages of a gas-fitter on my own premises. "There seems to be a natural connection between gas-fitting and house-breaking."

"At any rate," said Thorndyke, who was now inspecting the photographs – one profile and one full face – "the description fits the man's presumed avocation, without insisting on the gas-fitting. It is a coarse, common face. Not very characteristic. He might be a burglar or just simply a low-class working-man."

"Exactly," the Superintendent agreed. "It's the sort of mug that you can see by the dozen in the yard at Brixton or in any local prison. Just a common, low-grade man. But that hasn't much bearing on our little problem."

"I don't think I quite agree with you there, Miller," said Thorndyke. "The man's general type and make up seem to have a rather important bearing. We are dealing with a crime that is distinctly subtle and ingenious, and which seems to involve a good deal more knowledge than we should expect an ordinary working-man to possess. The face fits the assumed character of the man, but it does not fit the crime. Don't you agree with me?"

"I'll not deny," the Superintendent conceded, grudgingly, "that there is something in what you say. Probably we shall find that there was some man of a different class behind Smith."

"But why insist upon Smith at all? The poisoned cigar is the one solid fact that we have and can prove. And, as you have admitted, we have not a particle of evidence that connects him with it. On the contrary, the evidence of the finger-prints clearly connects it with someone else. Why not drop Smith, at least provisionally?"

Miller shook his head with an air of resolution that I recognised as hopeless.

"Theory is all very well, Doctor," he replied, "and I realise the force of what you have pointed out. But you remember the old story of the dog and the shadow. The dog who let go the piece of meat that he had in order to grab the other piece that he saw reflected in the water was a foolish dog. I'm not going to follow his example. This man, Smith, was seen to get into the carriage with Badger. He must have been in the carriage when Badger was killed, and no one else was there. If he didn't murder Badger, it's for him to explain how the thing happened. And I fancy he'll find the explanation a bit difficult."

Thorndyke seemed, for a moment, inclined to pursue the argument. But then he gave up the attempt to convince the Superintendent and changed the subject.

"What was the charge against Smith?" he asked.

"He was charged with uttering counterfeit paper money," Miller replied. "It was a silly affair, really. I can't think how the magistrate came to commit him. It seems that he went into a pub in Maidstone for a drink and tendered a ten-shilling note. The publican spotted it at once as a bad one and he gave Smith in charge. At the police station he was searched and two more notes were found on him. But they were both genuine and so was the rest of the money that he had about him. His statement was that the note had been given to him in change, and that he did not know that it was bad, which was probably true. At any rate, I feel pretty sure that the Grand Jury would have thrown out the bill. He was a mug to complicate matters by bolting."

"So, as an actual fact, there is no evidence that he was a criminal at all. He may have been a perfectly respectable working-man."

"That is so," Miller agreed rather reluctantly, "excepting that Badger seemed to have been satisfied that he was the crook that he had been on the look-out for."

"As he never saw the man," said Thorndyke, "that is not very conclusive. Do you know how the escape was managed?"

328

"Only in a general way," replied Miller. "It doesn't particularly concern me. I gather that it was one of those muddles that are apt to occur when prisoners are wearing their own clothes. Got himself mixed up with a gang of workmen. But he'd better have stayed where he was."

"Much better," Thorndyke agreed with some emphasis. "But to return to the case of the unknown man who prepared the poisoned cigar, I think you will agree with me that we had better keep our own counsel about the whole affair."

"I suppose so," answered Miller. "At any rate, I think you are right to keep away from the inquest. The coroner might ask you to give evidence, and then you'd have to tell all you know, and the story would be in every blessed newspaper in the country. I take it you are prepared to swear to the poison in that cigar?

"Certainly, and to produce the poison in evidence."

"And you are going to let me have a photograph of those finger-prints?"

"Of course. There is a set ready for you now, including two of Badger's. And, as to those from the cigar, it is just possible that you may find them to be those of some known person."

"It's possible," Miller admitted, "but I don't think it very likely."

"Nor do I," said Thorndyke, with a faint smile, by which I judged that he realized, as I did, that Miller's suspicions, even in the matter of the cigar, were still riveted on the elusive Smith.

"With regard to this paper of Smith's," said Thorndyke, as he handed Miller the set of photographs that had been reserved for him. "I should like to take a copy of it for reference. A photographic copy, I mean, of the portraits and the finger-prints."

Miller looked a little unhappy. "It wouldn't be quite in order," he objected. "An official document, you know, and a secret one at that. Is it of any importance?"

"It is impossible to say, in advance," replied Thorndyke. "But I shall be working at the case on your behalf and in collaboration with you. It might be important, on some occasion, to be able to recognize a face or a finger-print. Still, if it is not in order, I won't press the matter. The chances are that the copy will never be needed."

But Miller had reconsidered the question. He was not going to put any obstacles in Thorndyke's way.

"If you think a copy would be helpful," said he, "I'll take the responsibility of letting you have one. But I can't let the document go out of my possession. Can you take it now?"

"Yes," Thorndyke replied. "It will be only a matter of a minute or two to make one or two exposures."

Without more ado, he took the document and went off with it to the laboratory. As he disappeared, the Superintendent commented admiringly on the efficiency of our establishment.

"Yes," I replied, with some complacency (though the efficiency was none of my producing), "the copying camera is a great asset. There it is, always ready at a moment's notice to give us a perfect facsimile of any thing that is set before it – an infallible copy that will be accepted in any court of law, But you have quite as good an outfit at the Yard."

"Oh yes," Miller agreed, "our equipment and organization are good enough. But in a public department, you can't get the flexibility and adaptability of a private establishment like yours, where you make your own rules and use your own judgment as to obeying them. This can't be the Doctor already."

It was, however. Thorndyke had just made the exposures and left the development to be done later. He now returned the document to the Superintendent, who, having carefully bestowed it in his pocket with the photographs, rose to take his departure.

"I hope, Doctor," he said, as he shook hands with Thorndyke, "that I haven't seemed unappreciative of all that you have done. That discovery of yours was a most remarkable exploit – a positive stroke of genius. And it has given us the only piece of real evidence that we have. Please don't think that I'm not grateful."

"Tut, tut," said Thorndyke, "there is no question of gratitude. We all want to catch the villain who murdered our old friend. Are you going to the inquest?"

"No," replied Miller. "I am not wanted there and, now that you have given me this new information, I feel, like you, that I had better keep away, for fear of being compelled to let the cat out of the bag. You said you were sending a shorthand reporter down to take notes for you."

"Yes," said Thorndyke. "Polton has made all the arrangements, and has told our man to type the notes out in duplicate so that you can have a copy."

"Thanks, Doctor," said Miller. "I think they may be useful, after all – particularly the station-master's evidence concerning the man he saw at Strood."

"Yes," agreed Thorndyke. "It will be a great point if he can recognize the prison photograph – and an almost equally great one if he cannot."

I seemed to gather from the Superintendent's expression that he did not view the latter contingency with any great enthusiasm. But he made no rejoinder beyond again wishing us "Good morning," and at length took his departure, escorted to the landing by Thorndyke.

Chapter VIII
A Review of the Evidence

When Thorndyke re-entered the room, closing the oak door behind him, he appeared to be in a thoughtful and slightly puzzled frame of mind. For a minute or more, he stood before the fireplace filling his pipe in silence and apparently reflecting profoundly. Suddenly he looked up at me and asked, "Well, Jervis, what do you think of it all?"

"As to Miller? I think that he has his nose glued to the trail of Mr. Frederick Smith."

"Yes," said he. "The Smith idea almost amounts to an obsession, and that is a very dangerous state of mind for a detective superintendent. It may easily lead to a bad miscarriage of justice."

"Still," I said, "there is something to be said for Miller's point of view. The man who got into the train at Strood did certainly agree, at least superficially, with the official description of the man Smith."

"That is quite true," Thorndyke admitted. "The report of the evidence at the inquest will show what sort of description the station-master is prepared to swear to. But I don't feel at all happy as to Miller's attitude. We shall have to watch events closely, for we are deeply concerned in this investigation, and it will be just as well if we go over the facts that are known to us and consider what our own attitude must be."

He took up a pencil and a note-block and, dropping into an easy chair, lit his pipe and opened the discussion.

"I think, Jervis," he began, "we are justified in assuming that the man who got into the carriage at Strood is the man who murdered Badger."

"I think so," I agreed. "That is, if we assume that it was really a case of murder. Personally, I have no doubt on the subject."

"I am assuming that the document was really in Badger's pocket when he started, and that it was not there when his body was examined by the sergeant. The inquest notes will confirm or exclude those assumptions. At present, our information is to the effect that they are true. And if they are true, the document must have been taken from Badger's pocket, and that fact furnishes *prima facie* evidence of murder. But if Badger was murdered, the Strood man must be presumed to be the murderer, since no other possibility presents itself. Hence, the question that we have to settle, or at least to form a definite opinion on, is: Who was the Strood man?

"Now, our information is to the effect that he had red or reddish hair and a noticeably red nose. But the man Smith has dark-red hair and a noticeably red nose. Then it is possible that the Strood man may have been Smith. But mere coincidence in these two characteristics does not afford positive evidence that he was. For two men resembling one another in these respects might be otherwise very different."

"That is so," said I. "But you must admit that it is a rather remarkable coincidence. And you have often pointed out, with great justice, that coincidences call for very careful consideration."

"Precisely," said he. "And that is what I am going to insist on now. We have to note the coincidence and ask ourselves what its significance may be. It is, as you say, a quite remarkable coincidence. Neither of these peculiarities is at all common. If you were to examine any considerable collection of men – such, for example, as a battalion of infantry – how many men with dark-red hair would you find in it? Not more than one or two. Perhaps not one. But, of the one or two, or say half a dozen, that you found, how many would have noticeably red noses? Most probably none. Improbabilities become rapidly cumulative as you multiply the characteristics that are postulated us appearing coincidently.

"The position, then, in regard to the Strood man is this: In two salient personal characteristics, he resembled the man Smith. That resemblance can be accounted for by three hypotheses, one of which must be true:

"1. That the Strood man was Smith.

"2. That he was another man who happened to resemble Smith.

"3. That he was another man who had been purposely made up or disguised so as to resemble Smith.

"Those are the only possibilities and, as I said, one of them must be true. Let us take them in order and consider their respective probabilities. We begin with the first hypothesis, that the Strood man was Smith. Now, in order to judge of the probability of this, we have to consider what we know of the personality of Smith and of the Strood man respectively and to decide whether what we know of the one is compatible with what we know of the other.

"Now, what do we know of Smith? First, we have the fact that he described himself as a plumber and gas-fitter. As that description seems to have been accepted by the prison officials, we may assume that it fitted his appearance and manner, and we see that his face is of the type

332

characteristic of the lower-class of working-man. We know, further, that he had just escaped from prison, and that he was known and could have been recognized by several persons at the prison, including Chief Officer Cummings. It is probable that when he escaped, his pockets were empty and he may have been hatless.

"Now as to the Strood man. It is almost certain that he had a first-class ticket, that he travelled from Maidstone in Badger's train and – if so, he must have been on the platform at Maidstone at the same time as Badger and Cummings. He carried in his pocket a cigar which had been treated with a poison which is practically unprocurable commercially and which he must almost certainly have prepared himself. Now, Jervis, does it seem to you possible that those two descriptions could apply to one and the same person?"

"No," I replied, "it certainly does not, though you omitted to mention that Smith is probably a burglar."

"That is not known to us, though I admit that it is not improbable. But it really has no bearing. Even if we knew that he was a burglar, all the obvious discrepancies would remain. I submit that the hypothesis that the Strood man was the escaped prisoner, Smith, must be rejected as untenable.

"We pass on, then, to the next possibility, that the Strood man was *not* Smith, but was a man who happened to resemble Smith these two physical characteristics. In order to state the probabilities, it is necessary to note that the Strood man was apparently in this train with the premeditated purpose of murdering a police officer, and that a few hours previously a man with dark-red hair and a noticeably red nose had escaped from a Maidstone prison and was still at large. Bearing in mind the rarity of this combination of physical characters, what do you think of the probability of the coincidence?"

"Well," I replied, "obviously, the chances against are a good many thousands to one. But that is not quite the same thing as certainty."

"Very true, Jervis," he agreed, "and very necessary to remember. It is by no means safe to apply the laws of chance to individual cases. A prize of £30,000 in a lottery or sweepstake necessarily implies sixty-thousand ten-shilling tickets, of which all but one must be blanks, so that the chances against any ticket holder are fifty-nine-thousand-nine-hundred-and-ninety-nine to one. Nevertheless, in spite of that enormous adverse chance, someone does win the prize. You are quite right. Long odds against do not exclude a possibility. But, still, we have to bear the odds in mind and, if we do, we shall be very indisposed to accept this coincidence.

"We are left with the third hypothesis: that the Strood man was an unknown man, deliberately disguised or made up to resemble the escaped prisoner, Smith. This suggestion, though it has certain positive elements of probability, has also certain weighty objections, as I have no doubt you have noticed."

"I see one objection," said I, "that seems to exclude the suggestion altogether. If the Strood man had made up to resemble Smith, he must have had the means with him, provided in advance. He couldn't have gone about, habitually, with a red wig and a bottle of rouge in his pocket. But the escape of Smith was a contingency that couldn't have been foreseen. If we accept the idea of the make-up, we have to suppose that, after hearing of Smith's escape, this man was able to provide himself with the wig and the rouge. That seems to be quite incredible."

Thorndyke nodded, approvingly.

"Very true," said he. "My learned friend has made a palpable hit. It is a very serious objection and, as you say, it appears, at the first glance, to be insuperable – to render the hypothesis quite untenable. But if you consider the circumstances more thoroughly, you will see that it does not. The probability is that we are dealing with one of those combinations of chance and design that are always so puzzling and so misleading. Let us exercise our imaginations a little further and make one or two more hypotheses. Let us suppose that this man had already decided to avail himself of Smith's conspicuous peculiarities and to personate him to that extent – presumably for some unlawful purpose. He would then have had the wig and the rouge in readiness. Suppose that he is staying in Maidstone, perhaps keeping a watch on Smith. Smith, however, is in custody, with the certain result that his personal peculiarities will be noticed in detail and recorded.

"This will make him much better worth personating. If the stranger is keeping a watch on Smith, he will know about the prosecution, and he will know that there is a good chance of an acquittal. Suppose, now, at this point, two unforeseen events happen: Smith makes his escape, and then Badger turns up in Maidstone. The stranger has, as the murder pretty clearly proves, some strong reason for getting rid of Badger. But here is a set of unforeseen circumstances that creates a first-class opportunity. The apparent impossibility of the disguise is an additional favourable factor."

I was impressed by my colleague's ingenuity and said so, perhaps with some faint suggestion of irony in my tone.

"Of course," I hastened to add, "all that you suggest is quite possible. The trouble is that it is quite imaginary. There is not a particle of direct evidence to suggest that it is true – that what you postulate as having possibly happened, really did happen."

"No," Thorndyke admitted, "there is not. It is hypothesis, pure and simple. So far, I do not contest your objection. But I remind you of our position. We have three hypotheses which represent all the imaginable possibilities. One of the three must be the true one. But we have already excluded two as being quite untenable on the grounds of extreme improbability. The third is admittedly difficult to accept, but it is far less improbable than either of the other two. And you notice that, if we make the assumptions that I suggest, what follows presents a high degree of probability. I mean that a man, setting out to commit a murder, under circumstances in which he must be seen in the company of his prospective victim, would be taking a very ordinary precaution if he should so alter his appearance that a description of the murderer would not be a description of himself. And if he had the opportunity to make up so as to resemble some other person, and that other person an escaped prisoner, it would be very much to his advantage to take it. How great the advantage would be, we can see for ourselves by the attitude of our old friend, the Superintendent."

"Yes, by Jove!" said I. "The deception, if it is one, has operated most effectively on Miller. And, if your suggestion is correct, it will explain another rather incomprehensible thing – I mean the taking from the body of the prison record. That naturally suggested that the murderer was the man whose description was on the stolen document. In fact, my impression is that it is the document as much as the personal resemblance that is sticking in Miller's gullet."

"I think you are right," said Thorndyke. "At any rate, the combined effect of the two facts – the theft of the document and the personal characteristics – is undoubtedly responsible for his state of mind. But, to return to our discussion, I think that, out of the three hypotheses from which we have to choose, we are forced to adopt the third, at least provisionally: That the man who murdered Badger is not Smith, but is some unknown man who had deliberately made up to the end that he might be mistaken for Smith."

"Yes," I agreed. "I suppose we are, since the other two suppositions cannot be reasonably entertained. But I could wish that it were a little more easy to accept. It involves an uncomfortable amount of unproved assumptions."

"So it does," he admitted. "But there it is. All three hypotheses seem to be full of improbabilities. But, as one of them must be the true one, since there are no others, we have no choice but to adopt the one that presents the smallest number of improbabilities and the greatest number of probabilities. Still, as I have said, our acceptance is only provisional. We may have to revise our opinions when we have the evidence of the witnesses at the inquest before us."

In the event, however, we did not. On the contrary, when, late in the evening, our very expert stenographer delivered the copy of his notes – typed in duplicate – the report of the witnesses' evidence tended rather to confirm Thorndyke's conclusions. There was nothing very definite, it is true, but the few additional facts all pointed in the same direction.

There was, for instance, the station-master's evidence. It seemed that, in the interval, he had thought matters over, and his statements were now more decided. He was able, moreover, to amplify his description of the suspected stranger. The latter he described as a well-dressed man of about middle age, carrying a good-sized hand-bag of brown leather, but no stick or umbrella, and wearing a soft felt hat. The man had a rather conspicuously red nose. He had noticed that particularly – thought the gentleman looked as if he were in the habit of "taking a drop". And he was quite clear about the colour of the man's hair. He noticed it as the stranger was getting into the carriage and the sun shone on the back of his head. It was distinctly red – dark red or auburn – not bright red, and certainly not sandy. Probably in the sunlight, it may have looked rather redder than it really was. But it was definitely red hair.

"Do you think that you would recognise the man if you were to see him?" the coroner asked.

"I don't much think I should," was the cautious reply. "At any rate, I shouldn't be able to swear to him."

Here the coroner apparently produced the prison form with the two photographs and handed it to the witness.

"I want you to look at those two portraits," said he, "and tell us whether you recognize them."

The witness examined them and replied that he did not recognize them.

"Does the face that is shown in those photographs seem to you to resemble the face of the red-haired stranger?"

"I don't see any resemblance," the witness replied.

"Do you mean," the coroner pursued, "that you simply don't recognize the face, or that it seems to you to be a different face?"

"I should say that it is a different face. The man I saw looked more like a gentleman."

"You are definitely of opinion that these photographs are not portraits of the man that you saw. Is that so?"

"Well, sir, I shouldn't like to be positive, but these photos don't look to me like the man I saw on the platform."

That was all that was to be got out of the station-master and, so far, it tended to support Thorndyke's view, as also did the evidence of the ticket collector at Dartford, who was the next witness. He, like the station-master, seemed to have turned the matter over in his mind, though he was not able to give much more information. He did, however, remember collecting a first-class ticket, and recalled noticing that it was from Maidstone to London.

"That," said the coroner, "is a point of some significance. This passenger started from Maidstone with the intention of going to London, but at Dartford – the next station after Greenhithe – he suddenly changed his mind. It is a fact to be noted. Do you remember what this man was like?"

"I can't say that I remember him very clearly," the witness answered. "You see, sir, I was looking at the tickets. But I do remember that he was carrying a largish brown hand-bag."

"Do you remember anything peculiar in his appearance? You have heard the last witness's description of him. Can you say whether this passenger agreed with that description?"

"I wouldn't like to say positively whether he did or whether he didn't. I can only say that I didn't notice that he had a particularly red nose, and I didn't notice the colour of his hair. As far as I remember him, he seemed an ordinary, gentlemanly sort of man – the sort of man that you would expect to hand in a first-class ticket."

So much for the ticket collector. His evidence did not carry us very far. Nevertheless, such as it was, its tendency was to support Thorndyke's suggestion. There could be little doubt that the man who had given up the first-class ticket was the Strood man, and the fact – though it was only a negative fact and of little weight at that – that the special peculiarities of nose and hair had not been observed, seemed to lend a faint support to Thorndyke's further suggestion that, as soon as the murder had been committed, those special peculiarities would be eliminated.

There was little else in the evidence that was of interest to us. The engine-driver's evidence had practically no bearing, for poor Badger's body was unquestionably on the line, and the details as to how long it could have been there did not affect our enquiry. As to the body itself, the fact that no injuries could be discovered other than those inflicted by the train now caused us no surprise, though, to the coroner, it was naturally rather puzzling. Indeed, the problem that had so exercised the mind of Superintendent Miller was the problem that the coroner discussed at the greatest length and with complete failure to find any plausible solution. I read his very just and reasonable comments with

337

considerable sympathy, not without a twinge of compunction as I reflected on the way in which we had withheld from him the one conclusive and material fact.

"The greatest mystery in this strange case," he observed, "is the absence of any traces of injury. Here was a powerful, highly trained police-officer, flung out on the line by a man whom he had apparently intended to arrest. He had not been shot, or stabbed, or stunned by a blow on the head, or in any way disabled. He had been simply thrown out. It seemed incredible, but there were the facts. But for the known presence in that carriage of another person, and that person a suspected criminal, the condition of the body would have pointed to an accident of a quite ordinary kind. But the presence of that other man, and especially the fact – which has been quite conclusively proved by the evidence of Chief Officer Cummings – that a certain document was taken from the pocket of the deceased, puts accident entirely out of the question.

"But it adds enormously to the difficulty of understanding how this crime could have been committed. For obviously, the deceased would not have allowed this document to be taken from him without very energetic resistance. The great mystery is how any ordinary man could have taken this document forcibly from this powerful, capable officer and then opened the door and thrown him out on to the line. I must confess that I cannot understand it at all.

"However, our failure to unravel the mystery of the actual method employed by the murderer does not leave us in any doubt as to how the deceased met his death, which is the subject of our inquiry. The presence of that unknown man, his immediate disappearance at the very first opportunity, and the theft of that document, are facts that are too significant to allow of any but one interpretation.

"The next question presents much more difficulty – the question as to the identity of that man. If we think that we can give him a name, it is our duty to do so. But it is not the concern of a coroner's inquest to prove the guilt of any particular person. That is the office of a court of criminal jurisdiction. Unlike such a court, we have the choice of returning an open verdict – open, that is to say, as regards the identity of the criminal. And, if we have any doubt as to his identity, that is our proper course. Now you have heard the evidence relating to the identity of the man who shared the compartment with the deceased. You cannot have failed to notice the conflicting nature of that evidence, nor can you have failed to be impressed by the unlikeliness of an escaped prisoner showing himself openly on the platform of Maidstone Station. Still, if you are satisfied with such proof of his identity as has been given, your finding must be to that effect, but, if you have any doubts, you will be wiser to leave the investigation of that point to the police."

This eminently judicious advice the jury accepted, eventually returning a verdict of "Murder by some person unknown."

"Well," said Thorndyke, as I handed him back the copy of the notes, "has my learned friend any comments to make?"

"Only," I replied, "that the evidence, such as it is, seems rather to justify your choice of the third hypothesis."

"Yes," he agreed. "There is not much that is new. But there is one point that I dare say you noticed. The Strood man was carrying a fair-sized hand-bag. That supports the 'make-up' theory to this extent: That a hand-bag would be almost a necessity, seeing that a wig is a rather bulky article, and one that must not be too roughly treated, as it would be by being stuffed in the pocket. Then, the ticket collector's evidence, little as it was worth, leaned to our side. He did not notice that the passenger had either a red nose or red hair, which might mean either that those characters were not there to notice, or simply that he took no note of the man's appearance. There isn't much in it either way.

"But there is one other point that emerges – a slightly speculative point, but very important in its bearing if we accept it, though rather obvious. If we assume that this man was made up to pass, at least in a printed description, as Frederick Smith, that points to some kind of connection between him and Smith. He must, as you very justly observed, have made his preparations in advance. That is to say, he had decided, at least a few days previously, and probably more, to adopt Smith's peculiarities to cover some unlawful proceedings of his own. Now, it is highly improbable that he would have selected a complete stranger as the model for his disguise and, as a stranger, he could not have known that Smith was under suspicion of being a member of the habitual criminal class. But it was this suspicion that gave the disguise its special value. The evident probability is that he had some rather intimate knowledge of Smith."

"That does seem to be so," I agreed. "But if it is true, another interesting probability emerges. If he knew something about Smith, then there must have been something *to* know – that is to say, our friend Badger's suspicions of Smith were not without some real foundation. And again, the connection that you suggest might account for the theft of the finger-print document. It might not suit the murderer to have the finger-prints of his under-study – or over-study – at Scotland Yard."

"I think you are right," said Thorndyke, "as to the probable facts, though I am doubtful about your view of the motive. The theft of the document threw the suspicion at once on Smith, since they were his finger-prints and description. That would appear to have been the object of the theft as it was the object of the disguise."

"If it was," said I, "it was a diabolical scheme."

"Very true," Thorndyke agreed, "but murderers are not a peculiarly scrupulous class, and this specimen seems to have been even below the average in that respect. But to revert to your suggestion that Badger's suspicions probably had some foundation, you notice that the fact of Smith's having taken the chance to escape tends to confirm your view. Taking his position at its face value, that escape was really not worthwhile. He was apparently innocent of the offence with which he was charged, and pretty secure of an acquittal. His escape merely complicated the position. But if he was a regular criminal who ran the risk of being recognized by some visiting detective, it might well have appeared to him to be worthwhile to try the chance of getting away in the hope that he might keep away."

At this point our discussion was interrupted by the sound of a visitor approaching our landing. A moment later the identity of that visitor was disclosed by a characteristic knock at the door.

"I happened to be passing this way," said Miller, as I let him in, "so I thought I would just drop in and see if your shorthand notes were available. I have seen the newspaper reports of the inquest."

"Then you will have seen that the station-master did not recognise the prison photographs," said Thorndyke, as he handed the Superintendent his copy of the typed notes.

"Yes," growled Miller. "That's rather disappointing. But you can't expect an ordinary, unskilled person to spot a face after just one casual glance. Of course, Badger spotted him. But he was a genius in that way. It was a special gift."

"A rather dangerous one, as it turned out," I remarked.

"It was, under the circumstances," said Miller. "But what made it dangerous was poor Badger's secretiveness. He liked to hold the monopoly – to feel he was the only detective officer who could identify some man who was wanted but unknown. Even in cases that he was not really concerned in, he would keep a criminal's personal description up his sleeve, as it were. I remember, for instance, in that Hornby case – the Red Thumb Mark case, as they called it – how close he was."

"But he wasn't on that case, was he?" I asked.

"No. That was my case, and a pretty mess I made of it. But Badger was in court on another case, and it seems that, for some reason, he kept an eye on that man, Hornby – the one I had a warrant for, you know – while the experts were giving their evidence. Well, as you remember, Hornby slipped off, and I went after him and missed him, and when it came to making out a description of him, I had to apply to you for details. I doubt if I could have spotted him if I had met him in the street. But long afterwards, Badger told me that he had a perfectly clear mental picture of the man's face, and that he was certain that he could spot him at a glance if ever they should meet. And he was like that with quite a number of crooks of the more uncommon kind. He could recognize them when no one else could. It was a valuable gift – to him. Not so valuable to us. And, as you say, it has its dangers. If a really vicious crook got to know what the position was, he might show his teeth, as this man did in the train. Badger would have been wiser in several respects to have shared his information with his brother officers."

"Yes," said Thorndyke, "it is not very safe to be the sole repository of a secret that threatens another man's life or liberty. I have had reason to realize that more than once. By the way, have you had an opportunity of getting that strange finger-print examined – the one, I mean, that we found on the cigar?"

"Yes, and drawn another blank. I took it to the Finger-print Bureau, but they haven't got it in any of the files. So your poison-monger is a 'person unknown' at present. What you might expect. Probably sits in the background and supplies his infernal wares to crooks of a less subtle kind. However, your photo has been filed in the 'Scene of the Crime' series of single finger-prints. So we shall be able to place him, if we ever get him in custody. That will be quite a nice little surprise for him. But I mustn't stay here gossiping. I've got a lot to do before I knock off for the day. Among other things, I must go carefully through these notes that you have been so kind as to let me have, though I am afraid there is nothing very helpful in them."

As he retired down the stairs, Thorndyke stood looking after him with a faint smile.

"You observe," he remarked, "that our friend is still under the influence of the Smith obsession. I have never known Miller to be like this before. We have given him a piece of evidence of cardinal importance, and he treats it as something merely incidental. And that thumb-print, which is, almost beyond any doubt, the thumb-print of Badger's murderer, he files away as a thing that may possibly be of some slight interest on some unvisualized future occasion. It is an astonishing state of mind for an officer of his experience and real ability. We shall have to watch this case for his sake as well as our own. We must try to prevent him from making a false move, and we have got to find poor Badger's murderer, if any efforts of ours are equal to a task that looks so unpromising."

341

"It certainly looks unpromising enough," said I. "The man whom we have to find is a mere phantom, a disembodied finger-print, so to speak. We don't know his name. We don't even know what he is like, since the only description we have of him is the description of a disguise, not of a man. We can only assume that he has neither red hair nor a red nose. But that description applies to a good many other people."

Thorndyke smiled at my pessimism, but was fain to agree that I had not overstated the case. "Still," he continued, hopefully, "things might have been worse. After all, a finger-print is a tangible asset. We can identify the man if we are ever able to lay hands on him."

"No doubt," I agreed, less hopefully, "but the laying hands on him is the whole problem. And it seems to be a problem with no solution."

"Well," he rejoined, "what we have done before we can do again. We have had to deal with unknown quantities, and we have resolved them into known quantities. It is not the first time that we have been confronted with the uncompleted equation, '$X=?$'."

"No, indeed," said I. "You used that very formula, I remember, in the case of that man whom Miller was speaking of just now, Walter Hornby, and on the very occasion he referred to. I recall the incident very vividly. Don't you remember? When you passed me that slip of paper with the scribbled note on it, '$x=Walter\ Hornby$'?"

"I remember it very well," he replied. "And I have quite good hopes that we shall complete the equation in this case, too, if we are patient and watchful."

"Knowing you as I do," said I, "and remembering those other cases, I, also, am not without hope. But I cannot imagine how you are going to get a start. At present there is absolutely nothing to go on."

"We shall have to wait for some new facts," he rejoined, "and remember that the force of evidence is cumulative. At present, as you say, the whole case is in the air. But I have a strong feeling that we have not heard the last of Mr. Frederick Smith. Now that his finger-prints and description are extant, I think we may look for him to make another appearance, and when he does, I suspect that we shall make a step forward."

At the moment, I did not quite perceive the bearing or significance of this statement, but, later, as had so often happened, I looked back on this conversation and marvelled at my obtuseness.

Chapter IX
Thorndyke Discourses
on Finger-prints

Thorndyke's prediction was verified with a promptitude that neither of us expected, for little more than fortnight had elapsed after our conversation on the subject when the elusive figure of Mr. Frederick Smith once more flitted across our field of vision. It was but a fleeting and spectral appearance and disappearance – at least that was what we gathered from the news paper. Indeed, we might have missed it altogether had not Thorndyke's eye been attracted by the heading of the small and inconspicuous paragraph: *"Escaped Prisoner Breaks Into House."*

"What, already!" he exclaimed, and as I looked up enquiringly he proceeded to read out the brief account:

> *A daring robbery – or rather, attempted robbery – was committed yesterday in broad daylight by a man who escaped a short time ago from Maidstone Gaol. The scene of the attempt was a detached house in Sudbury Park, N.W., which had been left unoccupied owing to the owners having gone out for a day's motoring. Apparently the man was disturbed, for he was seen making off hurriedly, but, though he was immediately pursued, he disappeared and succeeded in making good his escape. However, he was seen distinctly by at least two persons, and the description that they were able to give to the police enabled the latter to identify him as the escaped prisoner.*

As he laid down the paper, Thorndyke looked at me with a faint smile.

"Well," he said, "what does that announcement convey to my learned friend?"

"Not very much," I replied, "excepting a red head with a red nose affixed to it. Obviously, the observers noted his trade-marks."

"Yes," he agreed. "And you observe that he elected to do this job in broad daylight. He must be a conceited fellow. He seems to be unduly proud of that nose and those auburn locks."

"Still," said I, "he had to enter the house when it was unoccupied, and that happened to be in the day time, when the owners were out in their car. Only, what strikes me is that the identification is not very satisfactory, even allowing for the rarity of red hair in combination with a red nose."

"Wait until you have heard Miller's account of the affair," he rejoined. "I am prepared to hear that the identification was more complete than one would gather from the paper. But we shall see."

We did see, a few days later and, as usual, Thorndyke was right. When, about eight o'clock at night, the Superintendent's well-known knock sounded on the door, I rose expectantly to admit him and, as he strode into the room, something of satisfaction and complacency in his manner suggested that he was the bearer of news that he was going to enjoy imparting to us. Accordingly, I hastened to dispose of the preliminaries – the whisky decanter, the siphon, and the inevitable box of cigars – and when he was comfortably settled in the arm-chair, I gave him the necessary "lead off".

"I am sorry to see that our friend, Freddy, has been naughty again."

He looked at me for a moment enquiringly, and then, as the vulgar phrase has it, he "rumbled" me.

"Ah," said he, "you mean Frederick Smith of Maidstone. Saw the paragraph in the evening paper, I suppose?"

"Yes. And we thought it uncommonly smart of your people to spot Mr. Frederick Smith from the casual description of one or two persons who caught a glimpse of him as he was making off."

Miller evidently felt himself to be in a position to ignore the hardly veiled sarcasm, for, without noticing it, he replied, "Ah, but it was a good deal more than that. Of course, when we heard the description, we pricked up our ears. But we soon got some clues that made us independent of the description. I've come in to tell you about it, since you are really interested parties.

"I dare say you know this place, Sudbury Park. It is one of the queer old London survivals – a row of detached houses, each standing in its own grounds, with gardens backing on the Regent's Canal, and little lanes here and there running up from the tow-path between the gardens to the road on which the houses front. The grounds that surround them are mostly pretty thickly wooded – sort of shrubberies – and they are enclosed by fairly high walls, the tops of which are guarded in the old-fashioned way by broken bottles and bits of glass set in cement.

"Now, it seems that our friend first drew attention to himself by breaking one of the back windows and making a good deal of noise in doing it. Then a couple of women, attracted by the noise, saw him trying to get in at the window. They were at a back window of one of the houses on the opposite side of the Canal. Naturally as soon as they saw what he was up to, they raised a philalloo and ran down to the garden to watch him over the wall. Their squawking brought a party of bargees along the tow-path, and when the bargees had been 'put wise' about the house-breaker, off they started, full gallop, towards a bridge that crosses the Canal two- or three-hundred yards farther down.

"Meanwhile, our honest tradesman, hearing the hullabaloo, concluded that the game was up, and came tumbling out through the window like a harlequin, and was in such a hurry that he left his cap inside, and so displayed his beautiful auburn hair to the best advantage. He had been working in his shirt-sleeves and, when he started to run, the reason was obvious. He wanted his coat – which he carried on his arm – to lay on the broken bottles on the top of the wall so that he could climb over without tearing his trousers. And that is what he did. He laid the coat over the party wall, and over he went into the next shrubbery. But, unfortunately for him, as he dropped down on the farther side, the coat slipped off the wall and dropped down into the garden that he had left. For a moment he seemed disposed to go back for it. But by that time the bargees were running across the bridge, bellowing like bulls of Bashan. So our friend thought better of it, and bolted away into the shrubbery and was lost to sight."

"Was he not seen by the occupants of that house?" Thorndyke asked.

"No – because there weren't any. It was an empty house. So all he had to do was to slip up by the side way and go out by the tradesmen's entrance. But it is odd that no one saw him in the road. You would think that a red-headed man in his shirt-sleeves, legging it up a quiet road, would attract some attention. But, apparently, no one saw him, so he got clear away – for the present, at any rate.

"But we shall have him, sooner or later. Sooner, I fancy, for I tell you we mean to have him. And the traces that he left will make him a valuable catch when we do get him. A capture will mean a conviction to a dead certainty."

"That is putting it rather strongly," I remarked.

"Not too strongly," he replied, confidently. "Let me tell you what we found. First there was the broken glass. We went through that carefully, and on one of the pieces we found a most beautiful impression of Mr Frederick Smith's right thumb. And thereby hangs a tale which I will tell you presently. Then there was the coat. That looked hopeful. But what it actually yielded was beyond our wildest hopes. Most of the contents of the pockets were of no particular interest. But there was one treasure of inestimable value – an empty envelope that had apparently been used to carry some hard object, for there were some sharp, rubbed marks on it. But they did not interest us. What set us all agog was the address – Mr. Charles Dobey, 103 Barnard's Buildings, Southwark.

"I need not tell you that we went off like record-breaking lamplighters to Barnard's Buildings. There, at the office, we learned that the tenant of Number 103, Mr. Dobey, was a gentleman with a red head and a nose to match. So up we went to Number 103. We had provided ourselves with a search warrant, and the officer who went with me took with him a little battery of skeleton keys. So we soon had the door open."

"What kind of key opened it?" asked Thorndyke.

"Oh, just a common pipe key with the bit filed away. The sort you generally use, I expect," Miller added with a grin. "It was only a common builder's latch. Well, when we got inside we had a look round, but at first there didn't seem to be much to see. It was just common, squalid sort of room with hardly any furniture in it. Looked as if it was not regularly lived in, which agreed with what the man in the office said – that he didn't very often see Mr. Dobey. However, presently we discovered, hidden under the bed, a good-sized oak box. It had a quite good lever lock which gave my colleague no end of trouble to open. But it was worth the trouble. When at last he got it open, we saw that we had struck it rich. It was a regular treasury of evidence.

"First there was a full outfit of good-class burglar's tools, and there were one or two little packets of jewellery which we have since been able to identify from our lists as part of the swag from a burglary at a jeweller's shop. Well, that was all to the good. But the real prize was at the bottom of the box. I wonder if you can guess what it was?"

He looked a little anxiously at Thorndyke, and did not seem particularly gratified when the latter suggested, "It did not chance to be a document?"

"That is just what it did chance to be," Miller admitted, adding, "You are a devil at guessing, Doctor. But you are quite right. It was the paper that was taken from poor Badger's pocket in that infernal tunnel at Greenhithe. So now we have got conclusive evidence as to who murdered Badger. Of course, we shall have to look into the meaning of that cigar of yours. But we shan't want to produce it in evidence or rely on it in any way for the purposes of the prosecution, which is as well, for it wouldn't have been particularly convincing to the jury. But there is one more point which makes this find extraordinarily complete. It is in connection with this finger – or rather, *thumb*-print. You probably know that we started, some time ago, a special collection of finger-prints – mostly single impressions – known as the '*Scene of the Crime Series*'.

346

They are either originals or photographs of prints that have been found at places where a crime has been committed, but where the criminal has got away without being recognized. Most of them are, naturally, the prints of known men. But there are a few prints that we cannot associate with any known criminal. We can't put a name to them.

"Now, in this collection we had three sets of prints which had been found on premises that had been broke into, evidently by a burglar of rather exceptional skill and ingenuity, who seemed to have worked alone, and whose technique we thought we recognized in several other jobs in which no finger-prints were found. For some reason, when we got Smith's finger-prints from Maidstone and found that they were not in the general collection, the officer in charge omitted to try them with the *'Scene of the Crime Series'*, but since then he has made the comparison, and it turns out that those three sets of prints are undoubtedly Mr. Charles Dobey's. So now we are able to identify him as that peculiarly talented burglar."

"Is there any special advantage in being able to do so?" Thorndyke asked. "I take it that you will proceed on the murder charge."

"Certainly we shall," Miller replied. "But there is the question of identification. We have got to make it quite clear that the man who got into the train at Strood was this same Charles Dobey. And then there is the question of motive. Badger was the only officer who knew Dobey by sight. He went down to Maidstone that very day for the express purpose of identifying him."

"You are not forgetting that you cannot produce any evidence that he ever did identify him?"

"No, I am not forgetting that. But he went down, having judged from the description that Frederick Smith was the man who had committed those various burglaries. And it now turns out that he was right. These finger-prints prove that Dobey was the man."

"It seems to me," said I, "that the fact that the stolen paper was found in his possession will be sufficient, unless it can be rebutted, to establish the case for the prosecution, without referring to the burglaries at all. You can't include them in the indictment – not in an indictment for murder – and if you attempt to introduce them, and if the court allows you to, you will have to prove them, which will complicate the issues."

The Superintendent admitted the truth of this, but said that he was not going to take any chances.

"And at any rate," he concluded, "you must agree that we have got a remarkably complete case."

Thorndyke did agree, and with so much emphasis that, once more, Miller looked at him with a shade of anxiety.

347

"I know what you are thinking, Doctor," said he. "You are thinking that it is too good to be true."

"Not at all," Thorndyke disclaimed with a smile, "though you must admit, Miller, that he has made things as easy for you as he could."

"He certainly behaved rather like a fool," Miller conceded. "That is often enough the way with crooks. You don't see any snags, do you?"

"No," replied Thorndyke. "It looks all perfectly plain sailing. All you have to do now is to catch your hare, and he doesn't seem to be a particularly easy hare to catch."

"I don't think we shall have very much difficulty about that," said Miller. "He is an easy man to describe, and we shall circulate his description all over the country. In fact, we have done so already."

"Yes," said Thorndyke, "that was what I meant. You had him placarded at all the police-stations throughout the land, and then you find him engaged in breaking and entering in the very heart of London."

Yet again, Miller glanced with a trace of uneasiness at Thorndyke, but he made no comment on what sounded a little like a rather cryptic hint, and shortly afterwards rose and took his departure.

When he had gone, I was disposed to continue the discussion, but my colleague showed no enthusiasm. Yet I could see that he was reflecting profoundly on what the Superintendent had told us, which encouraged me to make a last effort.

"After all," I said, "we can't ignore plain fact. This story of Miller's is difficult to reconcile with we know – with regard to that cigar, for instance – but it is a consistent body of evidence, each item of which can be proved beyond question. And the discovery of that paper in the man's possession seems conclusive as it is possible for evidence to be. In view of your very convincing argument, it does really appear as if the solution of your problem is $X = Charles\ Dobey$. Or is there some fallacy in Miller's case?

"There is no obvious fallacy," Thorndyke replied. "The case presents, as you say, a perfectly consistent body of evidence. Taken at its face value, Miller's case is conclusive. The real question is whether the completeness and consistency are the results of unaided chance or of an ingeniously devised plan. It is a question we are, at present, unable to decide. Perhaps, when Dobey is brought to trial, he may be able to produce some new facts that may help us to come to a conclusion."

As this seemed to close the discussion, I knocked out my pipe and glanced at my watch.

"Time for me to be moving on," said I, "if I am to get home within the permitted hours. I told Juliet that I should be home to-night. And by the way, I have a message for you. I am instructed to remind you that it is quite a long time since you paid your last visit."

"So it is," he admitted. "But we have not had many spare afternoons lately. However, to-morrow afternoon is free. Do you think it would be convenient to Juliet if I were to call and pay my respects then?"

"I happen to know that it will, as I took the precaution to ask what afternoons were unengaged. Then I will tell her to expect you, and you had better turn up as early as you can. She always looks for a long pow-wow when you come."

"Yes," he replied, "she is very patient of my garrulousness. Then I will come as early as possible, and prepare myself for a special conversational effort. But it is really very gracious of her to care for the friendship of an old curmudgeon like me."

"It is," I agreed. "Odd, too. I can't imagine why she does."

With this Parthian shot, and without waiting for a rejoinder, I took myself off en route for the Temple Station.

Here, perhaps, since my records of Thorndyke's practice have contained so little reference to my own personal affairs, I should say a few words concerning my domestic habits. As the circumstances of our practice often made it desirable for me to stay late at our chambers, I had retained there the bedroom that I had occupied before my marriage and, as these circumstances could not always be foreseen, I had arranged with my wife the simple rule that the house closed at eleven o'clock. If I was unable to get home by that time, it was to be understood that I was staying at the Temple. It may sound like a rather undomestic arrangement, but it worked quite smoothly, and it was not without its advantages. For the brief absence gave to my homecomings a certain festive quality, and helped to keep alive the romantic element in my married life. It is possible for the most devoted husbands and wives to see too much of one another.

Thorndyke redeemed his promise handsomely on the following afternoon, for he arrived shortly after three o'clock, having, I suspect, taken an early lunch to that end, for it presently transpired that he had come straight from Scotland Yard, where he had been conferring with the experts of the Finger-print Bureau.

"Was your pow-wow concerned with any particular case that we have in hand?" I ventured to enquire.

"No," he replied. "I went there to get some further information respecting the new system of dealing with single finger-prints that was devised by Chief Inspector Battley. I have been studying his book on his method of classification and making a few tentative trials. But I wanted to make sure that my application of the method yielded the same results

349

as were obtained by the experts. So I went to Scotland Yard and asked them to check my results."

"I suppose," my wife suggested, "you are still a good deal interested in finger-prints?"

"Yes," he replied, "almost necessarily, since they so constantly crop up in evidence. But apart from, that, they are curious and interesting things in a number of ways."

"Yes," she agreed, "interesting and curious and rather horrible – at least that is how they appear to me. I never hear of a finger-print but my thoughts go back to that awful trial, with Reuben in the dock and poor Aunt Arabella in the witness-box giving evidence about the Thumbograph. What a dreadful time it was!"

I am afraid I was disposed to grin at the recollection, for poor Mrs. Hornby had brought the proceedings as near to farce as is humanly possible in a criminal trial where an honourable gentleman stands indicted for a felony. But I controlled my features and, as to Thorndyke, he was, as usual, gravely sympathetic.

"Yes," he agreed, "it was an anxious time. I was not at all confident as to how my evidence would be received by the judge and the jury and, if they had failed to be properly impressed, Reuben would certainly have gone to penal servitude. By the way, we sent the Thumbograph back to Mrs. Hornby after the trial. Do you happen to know what she did with it?"

"She didn't do anything with it," Juliet replied, "because I annexed it."

"What for?" I asked – rather foolishly, perhaps.

"Can't you imagine?" she demanded, flushing slightly. "It was a little sentimental of me, I suppose, but I kept it as a souvenir. And why not? It had been a terrible experience, but it was over, and it had ended happily – for me, at any rate. I have something to thank the Thumbograph for."

"It is very nice of you to say that, Juliet," said I. "But why have you never shown it to me? I have at least as much to be thankful for, though, to tell the truth, I had overlooked the fact that it was the Thumbograph that introduced us to one another."

"Well," said Thorndyke, "suppose you produce this disreputable little matchmaker and let us revive our memories of those stirring times. I haven't seen a Thumbograph for years."

"I am not surprised," said Juliet. "The report of your evidence at the trial was enough to kill the demand for them forever. But I will go and fetch it."

She went away and returned in a minute or two with the souvenir, which she handed to Thorndyke, a little oblong volume, bound in red cloth with the name "*Thumbograph*" stamped in gold on the cover. I looked at it with a new interest as Thorndyke turned over the leaves reminiscently while Juliet looked over his shoulder.

"Doesn't it bring all those horrors back?" saic she, "and especially poor Mrs. Hornby's evidence. Here is Miss Colley's thumb-print, which Reuben was supposed to have smeared, and here is Aunt Arabella's, and here is mine, and there is that wretch Walter's."

"Characteristically, the best impression in the book," said Thorndyke. "He was a remarkably capable scoundrel. He did everything well."

"I wonder if we shall ever see him again?" I mused. "When he slipped away from the court, he seemed to vanish into thin air."

"Yes," said Thorndyke, "another instance of his capability. It is not so very easy for a man who is badly wanted by the police to disappear, once and for all, as he did."

He turned over the leaves once more until he came to the one which bore the print of Reuben Hornby's thumb. Underneath it Reuben's name was written in pencil and, below this, the signatures of the two witnesses, "*Arabella Hornby*" and "*Juliet Gibson*".

"Do you remember," said Juliet, "the night Aunt Arabella and I brought the Thumbograph to your chambers? It was a thrilling experience to me."

"And to Thorndyke too, I imagine," said I. "For it was then that he knew for certain that the Red Thumb Mark was a forgery. I saw him make the discovery, though I did not know at the time what the discovery was. Wasn't it so, Thorndyke?"

"It was," he replied. "And what was even more important, I thought I had found the means of convincing the court. You are quite right, Juliet. It was a memorable occasion for me."

As he continued to turn over the leaves and scrutinize the various thumb-prints, I reverted to our previous conversation.

"I don't quite understand what you were doing at the Yard to-day," said I. "The classification of finger-prints is interesting enough in its way. But it doesn't specially concern us."

"It doesn't concern us at all," he agreed. "But *identification* does. And that is where Battley's method is valuable to us. The beauty of it is that, apart from classification for index purposes, it affords a means of rapid identification, and moreover makes it possible to express the distinctive characters of a given finger-print in a formula. Now this is an immense convenience. We often have occasion to identify a finger-print with an original or a photograph in our possession. But we can't always carry the print or photograph about with us. But if we can express the characters of the print in a formula, we can enter that formula in our note-books, and have it ready for reference at any moment."

"But," I objected, "a formula would hardly be sufficiently definite for a reliable identification."

"Not, perhaps, for a final identification to swear to in evidence," he replied, "though you would be surprised at the accuracy that is possible. But that is not the purpose aimed at. The use of the method at the Bureau is principally to enable the searchers to find a given finger-print quickly among the thousands in the collections of single finger-prints. Our use of it will be to form an opinion rapidly on the identity of a print in which we happen to be interested. Remember, we don't have to give evidence. Finger-print evidence, proper, is exclusively the province of the regular experts. We have only to form an opinion for our own guidance. Come," he continued, "I have the apparatus in my bag, which is in the hall, and here is the Thumbograph with a selection of prints to operate on. Why shouldn't we have a demonstration of the method? You will find it quite amusing."

"It does sound rather thrilling," said Juliet and, thus encouraged by the vote of the predominant partner, Thorndyke went out to find his bag.

"Let me first explain the general principle of the method," said he, when he returned with a small leather bag in his hand. "Like all really efficient methods, it is essentially simple though extremely ingenious. This is the sole apparatus that is necessary."

As he spoke, he opened the bag and took out a magnifying glass, which was mounted on three legs, the feet of which were fixed into a brass ring which enclosed a plate of glass.

"This circular glass plate," he explained, "is the essential part of the instrument. If you look through the lens, you will see that the glass plate has engraved on it and coloured red a central dot surrounded by seven concentric circles. The first circle is three millimetres from the dot. The other circles are each two millimetres from the next. The central space is denoted by the letter A. The spaces between the other circles are denoted, successively, by the letters B, C, D, E, F, and G, and the space outside the outermost circle is denoted by H. The letters are, of course, not marked on the glass, but I have here a diagram which shows their position."

He laid on the table a card on which were described the seven circles, each marked with its appropriate letter, and then, taking up the Thumbograph, once more turned over the leaves.

"I think," said he, "we will select the estimable Walter's thumb-print as the *corpus vile* for our experiment. It is the best print in the book, and it has the further advantage of being a peculiarly distinctive type with a rather striking pattern. It has the general character of a whorl with a tendency towards that of a twinned loop – that is, a pair of loops folded into each other with the convexities turned in opposite directions. But we will call it a whorl, and treat it as such, merely noting the alternative character. You will see that the pattern is formed by a number of black lines, which are the impressions of the ridges on the thumb. In this print the centre of the patterns, or 'core', consists of a pair of little loops, from which the lines meander away in a rather irregular spiral. At a little distance from the core, these lines meet another set of lines at an angle, forming a Y-shaped figure known as a 'delta'. There will be another delta on the opposite side of the thumb, but it is too far round to appear in this print. It would be visible in a 'rolled impression' – that is, a print made by rolling the inked thumb over on a card or paper, but in this print, made by a single contact, only the right delta appears.

"And now as to the use of the instrument. We lay the glass plate on the print, so that the dot just touches the top of the upper loop. And now you see the masterly simplicity of the method. For, since a circle has no right or wrong way up, when once you have set the dot in the appointed place, all the other lines must be correctly placed. Without any further adjustment, they show with absolute accuracy the distance from the centre of any part of the pattern. And this distance can be expressed, quite unmistakably, by a single letter."

He placed the instrument on the thumb-print in the book and, having carefully adjusted it, drew out his note-book and looked at my wife.

"Now, Juliet," said he, "just look through the lens and tell me the letter that indicates the position of the delta – which is actually the right delta, though it is the only one visible."

Juliet peered through the magnifying glass and studied the print for a while. At length, she looked up a little doubtfully and announced, "It seems to me that the third line cuts right through it. So it lies half in the space 'C' and half in 'D'. Which of the two would you call it?"

"The rule," he replied, "is that if a character is cut by a line, it is reckoned as lying in the space outside that line."

"Then this delta lies in the space 'D'," she concluded.

"Quite right," said he. "We will mark it 'D' and, as the other delta is not in the print, we must mark it simply with a query. And now we proceed to the rest of the examination, the ridge-tracing and ridge-counting. We will take the tracing first. What you would have to do if both the deltas were visible would be to follow the ridge that runs from the left delta towards the right. Obviously, it must take one of three courses: It may pass below, or outside, the right delta, or below, or inside, or it may meet, or nearly meet, the corresponding ridge from the

353

right delta. Those are the three categories: Outside, inside, or meeting, by the initials *I, M, O.*"

"But," objected Juliet, "as the left delta is not visible, it is impossible to trace a ridge from it."

"That might be true in some cases," replied Thorndyke, "but it is not in this, for, if you look at the print, you will see that, wherever the left delta may have been, a ridge passing from it towards the right must have passed well outside the right delta."

Juliet examined the print again and agreed that it was so.

"Very well," said Thorndyke, "then we will mark it *O,* and proceed to the ridge-counting, which will complete the formula. You have to count the ridges between the centre of the core and the delta. Put aside the measuring glass and use my lens instead, and I will give you a point to help you to count the ridges."

He handed her his pocket lens, and produced from his bag what looked suspiciously like a dentist's excavator, with the sharp point of which he indicated the ridges that were to be counted. Then he laid a visiting-card on the print to give a straight line from the centre to the delta, and she proceeded to count along its edge with the point of the excavator. Having gone over the ground twice, she announced the result.

"I make it twelve. But I am not quite sure, as some of the ridges fork, and might be counted as one or two. Will you count them?"

Thorndyke took the excavator from her and rapidly checked her result.

"Yes," said he, "I agree with you. I think we may safely put it down as twelve, though the bifurcations do, as you say, create a slight ambiguity. If the other delta had been visible there would, of course, have been a second circle-reading and a second ridge-count, which would obviously have been an advantage for identification. Still, what we have done gives us the main distinctive characters of this print, and we can express them by a simple formula of a few letters and numbers. Thus, the type of pattern is a whorl, with something of the character of a twinned loop. Accordingly, we put down a *W* with *T.L.* in brackets. The core, or central character – the pair of little, loops – lies entirely in the circle *A.* Now, there are five kinds of '*A*' cores: The plain eye – just a tiny circle – the eye enclosing some smaller character, the left-hand spiral, the right-hand spiral, and any other '*A*' form of an unclassifiable type. Now, in this print, the core is a left-hand, or anti-clockwise spiral, and accordingly belongs to the category *A3.* The delta, we agreed, lies in the space *D.* The ridge-tracing was outside – *O* – and the ridge-count twelve. We can express all these facts in a formula, thus:

"*Walter Hornby. Right thumb. W (? T.L.), A3, ?, O, D, ?, 12.*"

"That is concise enough," I remarked. "But, after all, it gives you only a skeleton of the pattern. It would not enable you to identify a print with any approach to certainty."

"It does not aim at certainty," he replied, "but merely at such a degree of probability as would justify action or further research. But I think you hardly appreciate the degree of probability that this formula expresses. It records five different positive characters and one negative. Now, taking the five only, if we accept the very modest chance of four to one against each of these characters being present in a print which is not Walter Hornby's, the cumulative effect of the five together yields a chance of over a thousand-to-one against the print being that of some person other than Walter Hornby.

"But for our purposes, we are not obliged to stop at these five characters. We can add others, and we can locate those others either by the use of Battley's circles or by ridge-counting with a direction-line. For instance, in this print, to the left of the core and a little downwards, the seventh ridge shows one of those little loops known as 'lakes', the ninth bifurcates, and the eleventh has another, larger lake. To the right of the core the third ridge has a small lake, the fifth ridge bifurcates, the eighth has a free end, and the tenth bifurcates. There are seven additional characters which we can add to our formula, giving us twelve characters in all, the cumulative effect of which is a probability of over sixteen-millions to one against the print being the thumb-print of any person other than Walter Hornby, and that is near enough to certainty for our purpose. It would undoubtedly justify an arrest, and we could leave the final proof or disproof to the experts."

He added the extra characters to the formula in his note-book, and showed us the completed entry, which certainly afforded convincing testimony to the efficiency of the method. In fact, it impressed me – and my wife, too – so profoundly that, in an access of enthusiasm, we fell upon the Thumbograph forthwith, and with the aid of Chief Inspector Battley's ingenious instrument, proceeded to construct formulas to express the characters of the other thumb-prints in the book, while Thorndyke smoked his pipe regarded our activities with benevolent interest, seasoned by occasional advice and criticism of the results.

"It is quite an amusing game," Juliet remarked. "If only the inventors of the Thumbograph had known of it and printed directions in the book, it might have become a fashionable drawing-room pastime, and they would have made a fortune."

"Perhaps it is as well that they did not," said I. "The Thumbograph was a dangerous toy, as we discovered – or rather, as Thorndyke did."

"Yes," Thorndyke agreed, "it was a mischievous plaything. But don't forget that it acted both ways. If it supplied the false accusation, it also supplied the conclusive answer. Walter Hornby had more reason than any of us to regret that he ever set eyes on the Thumbograph. And it may be that he has not yet come to the end of those reasons. He has evaded justice so far. But the debt is still outstanding."

Book III – The Three Rogues

Chapter X
Mr. Woodburn's Story

Inventors are a much-misunderstood class. The common man, in his vanity and egotism, supposes that they exist to supply him with various commodities of which he dimly perceives the need. But this is an entirely mistaken view. The inventor produces his invention because, in the existing circumstances, it has become possible. It is true that he, himself, tends to confuse the issues by persuading himself optimistically that his invention has a real and important utility. His inventive mind goes so far as to create an imaginary consumer, so that he sees life in a somewhat false perspective. The genius who devised a family Bible which could be opened out to form a billiard table no doubt envisaged a pious type of player who had need of some means of combining the Canon of Scripture with a cannon off the red, while, to the inventor of a super magic-lantern which could throw pictures on the clouds, the night sky was no more than a suitable background on which to declare the glory of Blunt's Milky Toffee.

But this is mere self-delusion. In reality, the inventor is concerned with his invention. Its use is but a side issue which hovers vaguely on the periphery of his mental field of vision. I emphasise the fact, because it has a bearing on the events which I am recording. For our invaluable laboratory assistant, Polton, was an inveterate inventor and, being also an accomplished and versatile craftsman, was able to turn out his inventions in a completely realised form.

So it happened that a certain large cupboard in the laboratory was a veritable museum of the products of his inventive genius and manual skill, examples of ingenuity – sometimes fantastically misguided – the utility of which he would expound to Thorndyke and me with pathetic earnestness and appeals to "give them a trial". There were spectacles which enabled the wearer to see behind him. There was a periscope walking-stick with which you could see round a corner, a large pedometer with movable dials for metres and yards and a micrometer adjustment of impracticable accuracy, and all sorts of clockwork devices and appliances for out-of-the-way photographic operations. But optical instruments were his special passion, whence it followed that most of his inventions took an optical turn.

I am afraid that I did not treat these children of Polton's imagination with the respect that they deserved. Thorndyke, on the other hand, made a point of always examining even the wildest flights of the inventor's fancy with appreciative attention, realizing – and pointing out to me – that their apparent oddity was really due to the absence of appropriate circumstances, and that those circumstances might arise at any moment and give an unexpected value to what seemed to be a mere toy. And that was what happened on the present occasion. One of Polton's most eccentric productions suddenly revealed itself as an invaluable instrument of research. But perhaps I am beginning the story at the wrong end. I had better turn back and take the incidents in their proper order.

It was rather late one afternoon when there arrived at our chambers a dapper, well-dressed gentleman of distinctly horsey appearance, who gave the name of Woodburn, and who, rather to my surprise, turned out to be a solicitor. He presented Mr. Brobribb's card, on which were scribbled a few words of introduction.

"I have come to see you," he explained, "on the advice of my friend Brodribb. I came up to Town expressly to confer with him on a rather queer case that has turned up in my practice. We talked over the legal issues without coming to any very definite conclusion, but Brodribb thought that there were certain points in the case that were more in your line than in either his or mine. And I am certainly inclined to agree with him to the extent that I am decidedly out of my depth."

"And what about Mr. Brodribb?" Thorndyke asked. "He is a pretty acute lawyer."

"He is," Mr. Woodburn agreed, heartily. "But this is not altogether a question of law. There are some other points on which he thought you would be able to help us. I had better give you an outline of the case. But first, I had better explain that I am a country practitioner with my principal office at Packington in Kent, and that my clients are chiefly the farmers and country gentlemen of the surrounding district.

"Now, one of these clients is a gentleman named Mr. Didbury Toke. He is a sort of superior dealer in works of art and antiquities. He has an office in Town, but he resides at an ancient house called Hartsden Manor in the village of Hartsden and usually spends a good deal of his time there. But from time to time he has been in the habit of taking more or less prolonged trips to the Continent for the purpose of rooting about for antiques and works of art. On these occasions, it has been his custom to shut up that part of the house in which his collection is lodged, and seal all the doors and windows in any way giving access to it.

"Well, about two months ago, he set forth on one of these expeditions and, according to his usual custom, he locked up and sealed all the approaches to the rooms containing the collection and gave the keys into my custody."

"What happened to the seal?" asked Thorndyke.

"That I can't tell you," replied Mr. Woodburn. "He didn't give it to me, but I have an impression that he deposited it at his bank in London. I know that he did on a previous occasion. Still, he may have carried it on his person. I happen to know that it is a large, clumsy, antique ring, which he was certainly not in the habit of wearing.

"Well, as I said, he handed the keys to me, but at the same time, he gave me very definite instructions – in writing – that the rooms were not on any account to be entered or the seals tampered with in any way. You see that his instructions were quite explicit and, in fact, decidedly emphatic."

"Apparently," said Thorndyke, "he allowed you no discretion and provided for no contingencies. Is that not so?"

"That is so," replied Mr. Woodburn. "His instructions amounted to an absolute prohibition of any interference with the seals or any attempt to enter the enclosed rooms. That is the matter which I have be discussing with Mr. Brodribb, and which I want to discuss with you, because this prohibition has become highly inconvenient. Circumstances have arisen which seem to make it very desirable to enter those enclosed rooms. But before I go into those circumstances, I had better tell you a little more about the arrangements of the house and those particular rooms.

"The main part of the closed premises consists of a very large room – about forty feet long – called the great gallery, but adjoining this are three or four smaller rooms, some of which are used to house part of the collection, and some are kept as workrooms, in which Mr. Toke does his mending and other odd jobs connected with the collection. The great gallery and the rooms attached to it occupy the whole of a wing which runs at right angles to the rest of the house and, as there is only one door giving access to the gallery and its annexed rooms, the whole group of apartments is completely cut off and isolated.

"Now the circumstances to which I referred are these: Mr. Toke's household ordinarily consists of his housekeeper and her niece, who acts as housemaid, but when he is away from home, a nephew of the housekeeper usually comes to stay there, so that there may be a man on the premises. He is there now, so there are three persons living in the

359

house, and those three persons are agreed that, from time to time, they have heard sounds at night apparently coming from the great gallery. It sounds incredible, and I must admit that when they first reported the matter to me, I was disposed to be sceptical. I am not entirely unsceptical now. But they are extremely positive and, as I said, they are all agreed. So I thought it my duty to go over to the manor house and make an inspection, and the result of that inspection was only to make the whole affair still more incomprehensible. For the seals were all intact, and there was not a sign anywhere of anyone having broken into the place."

"You examined the windows, of course?" said Thorndyke.

"Yes. There are five large windows, and I examined them all from outside by means of a ladder. They certainly had not been opened, for I could see that the catches were all in their places. But I may say that the windows are all secured from inside with screws, and those screws are sealed. Mr. Toke leaves nothing to chance."

"Could you see into the room?" asked Thorndyke.

"No. The shutters were not closed, but the windows are covered by lace or net curtains, so that, although the gallery is quite light, it is impossible to see in from the outside."

"You have spoken of the collection," said Thorndyke. "Perhaps you had better tell us something about its nature and value."

"As to its value," said Mr. Woodburn, "I believe that is very considerable, but as it consists chiefly of pottery and porcelain, Bow and Chelsea figures, bronzes, and small statuary. It would be of no interest, to a burglar – at least, that is what I understood from Mr. Toke."

"I am not sure that I agree with Mr. Toke," said Thorndyke. "Of course, since you cannot melt down porcelain figures into unrecognizable ingots, they are not suitable for the common type of burglar. The ordinary 'fence' would not trade in them, and they could not be offered in the open market. But they are really valuable things and fairly portable, and they would not be so very difficult to dispose of. The ordinary collector is not always as scrupulous as he might be, but there is one kind of collector who is not scrupulous at all. One may take it that a millionaire who has made his millions by questionable transactions may be prepared to spend them in a like manner. The point is of some importance for, whereas the repeated occurrence of these sounds – assuming them to have occurred – is not consistent with the idea of an ordinary burglary, it does suggest the bare possibility of some enterprising persons quietly removing the more valuable parts of the collection piecemeal."

"You do, then, really entertain the possibility that these sounds are not merely imaginary?"

360

"I have an entirely open mind," replied Thorndyke. "But I understood you to say that you had gone into the question of fact on the spot, and that you were satisfied that the reports were sufficiently convincing to justify serious enquiry."

"That is so," said Mr. Woodburn. "But I may say that Brodribb scouted the idea. He was incredulous as to the sounds having been heard at all, seeing that the closed rooms are so completely isolated and so distant from the rest of the house, and he suggested that if there had been any sounds, they were probably due to rats. I don't agree with him as to the rats. Of course, I enquired whether that could be the explanation, but I think it can be excluded. The noises that rats make are pretty characteristic, and they don't at all agree with the description of the sounds that these people gave. And they tell me that there are no rats in the house, which seems to settle the question for, although rats will harbour in empty rooms, they don't stay there. They must come out for food. But Brodribb's other objection is more weighty. The great gallery is a good distance from the rest of the house. What do you really think of the probabilities?"

"Well," replied Thorndyke, "the answer to your question involves the statement of a rather bald truism. If there is no access to the closed rooms other than the door of which you spoke, and that door is still locked and the seal is still unbroken, evidently no one can possibly have entered those rooms. On the other hand, if sounds have been heard of such a nature as to make it certain that someone had entered those rooms, then it follows that there must be some means of access to those rooms other than those which are known to you. I apologize for the obviousness of the statement."

"You needn't," said Mr. Woodburn. "It puts the matter into a nutshell. I saw the dilemma myself. But what do you suggest?"

"In the first place," said Thorndyke, "may I ask if it is impossible to get into touch with Mr. Toke?"

"Ah," said Mr. Woodburn, "there you have raised another point, Apparently, it is impossible for me to get into touch with my client, and that is a matter that I am not entirely happy about. Mr. Toke is by no means a good correspondent. But when he is travelling, as a rule, he sends me a short note now and again, just to give me the chance of communicating with him if the occasion should arise. And he has been in the habit of sending me parcels – purchases that he has made – to put in my strong room or to deposit at his bank. But this time, I have had not a single line from him since he went away. It is really rather strange, for Mr. Toke is a methodical, business-like man, and he must realize that it is most undesirable that his solicitor and man of business should have no

361

means of communicating with him. It might be extremely awkward, even disastrous. It is extremely awkward now. If I could get into touch with him, he would pretty certainly authorize me to break the seals and see if his collection is all as it should be. As he can't, the question arises as to what I ought to do. Should I, for instance, take it that these exceptional circumstances absolve me from the obligation to abide literally by his instructions? Brodribb thought not. What is your view of the case?"

"I am disposed to agree with Brodribb. The difficulty seems to be that you have not established the exceptional circumstances. There is only a suspicion, and Mr. Toke might think, as Brodribb does, that the suspicion was not a reasonable one. You have said that Mr. Toke's instructions were very explicit and even emphatic. He was clearly most anxious that those rooms should not be entered or the seals broken. He has said so, and he has given quite definite instructions on the subject. This being so, we must assume that he had good and sufficient reasons for giving those instructions. We cannot judge what those reasons were, or how strong they were. But it is always safe to assume that a man means what he says, especially when he says it quite clearly and unmistakably.

"Suppose you 'interpret' his instructions and proceed to break the seals and enter the rooms. Suppose you find everything normal and, at the same time, find something that shows you that the rooms ought not to have been entered by anyone except Mr. Toke himself. That might create a very awkward situation."

Mr. Woodburn laughed. "You think it possible that Mr. Toke may have something hidden in those rooms that he wouldn't like anyone else, to see? Well, of course, it may be so. But I may mention that Mr. Didbury Toke is a most respectable gentleman."

"I am not suggesting the slightest reflection on Mr. Toke's moral character," said Thorndyke, laughing in his turn. "Probably, his motive was nothing more than extreme solicitude for his collection. Still, he may have things locked up in his gallery the existence of which, in that place, he might well wish to keep secret – things, for instance, of great intrinsic value which might invite the attentions of burglars."

"Yes," said Woodburn, "I suppose you are right. He always swore that there was nothing there that a burglar would look at. But that may have been a mere precaution. Which brings us back to the question, What is to be done?"

"I think the answer to that is fairly simple," said Thorndyke. "These statements certainly call for investigation. Two points require to be cleared up. First, is it certain that there is really no possibility of access to these rooms other than the door that you mentioned? And, second, assuming the first to be true, is it certain that access has not been obtained by means of that door?"

"But how could it have been?" Mr. Woodburn exclaimed. "The door is sealed. I examined it most carefully, and I can assure you that the seals are undoubtedly intact."

"That is not absolutely conclusive," Thorndyke replied with a faint smile. "Seals are not difficult to counterfeit. For instance, if, for any legitimate purpose you asked me to enter those rooms and replace the seals when I came out, I should find no difficulty in doing so."

"Really!" exclaimed Mr. Woodburn. Then, subsiding into a grin, he added, "You are a rather dangerous sort of person, but I am not surprised that Brodribb has so much confidence in you. Perhaps you can suggest some way in which I might set about testing the correctness of these statements – or better still, perhaps you would be willing to undertake the investigation yourself? I do feel that something ought to be done."

"So do I," said Thorndyke. "Incredible as the statements sound, what is stated is by no means impossible. And, if we should find that some persons either could have effected an entrance or had actually done so, the position would be entirely changed. You would then certainly be justified in breaking the seals and entering the rooms."

"And asking you to replace the seals after, eh?" suggested Woodburn, with a broad grin. Apparently, Thorndyke's accomplishments had made a profound impression on him.

Thorndyke smilingly dismissed the suggestion and enquired, "Is there no way, so far as you know, of getting a glimpse into the room from the outside?"

"No way at all," was the reply. "I tried peering in at the windows, but it was impossible to see any thing through the curtains. I even tried the keyhole. There is a monstrous great keyhole in the door. I myself should think the key must be quite a formidable weapon, though I have never seen it. The door is secured by a Chubb lock, of which I have the key. Well, I peered through that keyhole, but all I could see was a patch of wall on the side of the room opposite. Naturally, because the door opens into the room at the extreme end of one side."

"Could you give me a description of the room, or preferably a sketch?" Thorndyke asked.

"I have an architect's plan of the house in my bag," Woodburn replied. "I brought it up to show Brodribb, but he was not interested, as he did not believe the story. However, you are not so sceptical. I'll get it out."

He rummaged in his bag and presently produced a small roll of tracing-cloth, on which was a clearly drawn plan of the house and its immediate surroundings.

"The scale of the particular room," he remarked, "is not as large as we should like. But you can see the main features. This crooked corridor leads to the gallery wing, and you see that it ends in a turn at right angles. So, when the door is open, you look in across the end of the room. The door opens inwards, and there are three steps down to the floor level. You can see for yourself that a keyhole in that door is of no use for the purpose of inspection."

"Can you tell us anything about the furniture, or how the floor space is occupied?" Thorndyke asked.

"With the exception of a few chairs and a large table across the farther end of the room, there is practically no furniture excepting the wall-cases. There is range of them along each side wall between the windows, and the two doors that open into the four small rooms at the side of the gallery."

"There seems to be no access to those rooms excepting through the doors from the gallery."

"No, there is not. Those rooms seem to have been originally a corridor, which has been divided up by partitions. They all open into one another – at least, each opens into the next. Two of them have cabinets full of pottery and porcelain, and the other two are work-rooms in which Mr. Toke does jobs such as mending and cleaning the pieces."

"What is there above and below the gallery?" asked Thorndyke.

"Above, I suppose, are lofts. I don't know how you get to them, but I don't think they would help us. You couldn't see through the floor, and you couldn't bore holes in it, as the gallery has a fine seventeenth-century plaster ceiling. Under the gallery is a range of cellars, but they are not accessible, as they are all secured with good padlocks, and both the padlocks and the doors are sealed."

"Mr. Toke was certainly pretty thorough in his methods," Thorndyke remarked. "It would be a serious responsibility to break into his Bluebeard chambers."

"Yes, confound him," Woodburn agreed. "I wish to goodness it was possible to communicate with him and let him take the responsibility. I wonder why the deuce he has never sent me a line. I hope nothing has happened to him abroad. You can never be sure in these days of motors and sudden death."

"When did you say he went away?" Thorndyke asked.

"On the ninth of August," replied Woodburn, "at least that is the date he gave me. He came to my office on the eighth to give me the keys and his final instructions, and he then said that he intended to start for Paris on the following night."

"Do you know if he did actually start then?"

"Well, yes – indirectly. I happen to use the same garage to put up my car, when I come to town, as Mr. Toke uses. He recommended it to me, as a matter of fact. There I ascertained that he deposited his car on the morning of the ninth of August. But, oddly enough, he took it out again in the evening, and it was not returned until some time in the small hours of the following morning."

"Then," I said, "he couldn't have caught his train."

"I think he did. He did not return the car himself. It was brought in by a stranger, whom the night watchman described, picturesquely, as a 'ginger Lushington', and this person reported that Mr Toke had caught his train, and that the lateness of the delivery of the car was due to some fault of his own."

"I wonder what the watchman meant by a 'ginger Lushington'?" said I.

"Yes," said Woodburn, "it is a quaint expression. I asked him what it meant in common English. Apparently, it was a term of inference. The word 'ginger' referred to the colour of the man's hair and, as his nose was tinted to match, the watchman inferred the habitual use of stimulants. But apparently Toke caught his train all right."

As Mr. Woodburn interpreted the watchman's description, I caught Thorndyke's eyes for a single instant, and I saw that he had noted the significance of that description. It was probably the merest coincidence, but I knew that it would not pass without close scrutiny. And I could not but perceive that thereafter his interest in Mr. Woodburn's affairs became appreciably more acute.

"Do I understand," he asked, "that you feel an actual uneasiness about your client?"

"Well," was the reply, "I must admit that I am by no means happy about him. You see, this prolonged silence is a complete departure from his usual habit. And time is running on. This is the eleventh of October, and he has made no sign. All sorts of thing may happen to a man who is in a strange country and out of all touch with his friends. I don't like it at all. However, it was not about Mr. Toke that I came to consult you, though I may have to ask for your assistance later. It is about these queer happenings at the Manor House. Now, what do you suggest? I should like you, as an expert, to take up the inquiry yourself. Do you care to do that?"

"I am quite willing to make a preliminary investigation," Thorndyke replied. "That would involve personally interrogating the servants and making a careful survey of the premises. If it seems to be a mare's nest, we can let it drop. But if we discover some hitherto unsuspected means of access to the gallery, or find evidence that some persons have, in fact, entered the premises, we can consider what action is to be taken. Would that meet your views?"

"Perfectly," replied Woodburn. "When could you come down and take a look at the place?"

"I suggest the day after to-morrow, early in the afternoon, if that will suit you."

"It will do quite well," said Woodburn. "There is a good train from Charing Cross at two-thirty. If you can catch that, I will meet you at the station with my car and take you straight on to the house."

Thorndyke made a note of this arrangement, and Mr. Woodburn then took his leave, evidently very well pleased at having transferred some of his anxieties to more capable shoulders.

When he returned from the landing, having seen his visitor safely launched down the stairs, Thorndyke picked up the plan, which Mr. Woodburn had left on the table and, glancing at it, turned to me with a smile.

"A queer affair, Jervis," said he. "I wonder if there is anything in it?"

"Personally," I replied, "I should be disposed to suspect a mare's nest. There is something a little creepy about a big, old house, especially if a part of it is shut up and sealed. Those servants may easily have got a trifle jumpy and imagined that they heard sounds in the dead of the night."

"That is quite possible," he agreed. "But then we must not overlook the fact that the thing alleged is also quite possible. And it is not so very improbable. Precautions of the kind that Mr. Toke has taken may have a certain boomerang quality. The place is locked, bolted, barred, and sealed. That is all well enough so long as the precautions take their expected effect. But if they fail, they fail with a most horrid completeness. Here, for instance, is a collection of really valuable things. It is all nonsense to say that they are of no interest to burglars. It depends on the burglar. Fine pieces of porcelain and high-class bronzes are easily negotiable in the right markets. The burglar's real difficulty is in getting them away. Silver and gold can be carried away regardless of injury, as they are to be melted down, but these things are fragile, and their value depends on their being uninjured. Now, if it is only possible for a burglar to obtain access to Mr. Toke's gallery, everything else made easy for him. He can work at his leisure and take these things away one or two at a time in the most suitable manner. I think the affair is worth looking into, even on its own merits.

"But you notice that there is another aspect of the case that deserves attention. Woodburn is obviously anxious about Mr. Toke – and not without some reason. In a legal sense, Mr. Toke has disappeared. His whereabouts are unknown to the very man to whom they should be known. Now, suppose that some mishap has befallen him, and suppose that circumstance to be known to some person – some unscrupulous person – who also knows about the collection. That is a bare possibility that has to be considered. And then we have to note the fact that the only evidence that Toke did really catch his train is the statement of an unknown stranger."

"Who happens to have had red hair and a red nose," I remarked.

Thorndyke chuckled. "True," he admitted. "But we mustn't allow ourselves, like Miller, to be obsessed by a mere matter of complexion. Still, we will bear even that fact in mind. And there is one other fact, with a possible inference. Toke's instructions to Woodburn suggest something more than mere caution. They have a suggestion of secrecy – so much so that one asks oneself if it is possible that he may have some property concealed in the gallery of a different kind from the ostensible collection. I find it quite an attractive case, though, as you say, it may easily turn out to be a mare's nest."

"What do you propose to do when you go down to Hartsden?" I asked.

"I have no definite programme," he replied, "beyond making the best possible use of my eyes and ears. The obviously desirable thing would be to get a look at the interior of the gallery, and see if there are any signs of disturbance – whether, for instance, the cases have or have not been emptied."

"Yes," I agreed, "I realize that, but I don't see how you are going to manage it, as, apparently, it is impossible to see in either by the windows or the door."

"It doesn't sound promising, I must admit," said he. "But we shall see when we get there. Perhaps Polton may be able to help us."

"Polton!" I exclaimed. "How do you suppose that he may be able to help?"

"Don't be so scornful," he protested. "Is an inventor and mechanical genius worth nothing? I shall certainly put the problem to him as soon as I am clear about it myself."

In spite of the rather ambiguous phraseology, I suspected that Thorndyke had something quite definite in his mind. But I asked for no particulars. Long experience had taught me that he preferred to present his ideas in a mature and complete form rather than in that of a preliminary sketch. And, to tell the bald truth, my curiosity was not painfully acute. So I could wait patiently for enlightenment to come in due course.

Chapter XI
Hartsden Manor House

As the train moved out of the station, Thorndyke lifted his invaluable green canvas research case from the seat to the rack, and then, with the tenderest care, disposed similarly of a walking-stick of the most surpassing hideousness.

"That," I remarked, eyeing it with profound disfavour, "looks like one of Polton's contraptions."

"It is," he replied, "if the word 'contraption' can be accepted as the proper designation of an extremely efficient and ingenious optical instrument. He made it many years ago, but an instrument of virtually identical construction was produced during the war under the name of 'trench periscope.' It is really a modern version of the ancient device of parallel inclined mirrors, which you may see in any old book on physics – only the mirrors are replaced by total-reflection prisms."

"Have you ever used it before?" I asked.

"Yes, on one or two occasions, and found it to answer its purpose perfectly. I have brought it to-day on the chance that we may find some chink or hole through which we can poke it to get a view of the inside of the gallery."

"You won't get it through that keyhole that Woodburn spoke of, large as it is," said I.

"No," he agreed. "But, as to that, we are not at the end of our resources – or rather Polton's. He has devised an instrument for the express purpose of looking through awkwardly placed keyholes. I have it in my case."

He lifted the case down and, having opened it, produced from it a small cylindrical wooden case with a screw cap. The latter being removed, he was able to draw out what looked like a brass pencil holder.

"This," he explained, "is a little Galilean telescope, magnifying about one-and-a-half diameters. In front of the object glass is fixed a small, oblong mirror, which is pivoted so that it can be set at any angle by turning this milled ring at the eyepiece end. Of course, it has to be parallel to the tube when the instrument is passed into the keyhole." He handed it to me, and I put it to my eye, after setting the mirror at a suitable angle.

"It doesn't seem a very efficient affair," I remarked. "It has such a wretchedly small field."

"Yes," he admitted, "that is the trouble with keyholes. But this is only an experimental form. If it seems suitable in principle, we can easily devise something more efficient. What we have to ascertain first of all is whether we can see through the keyhole at all. Looking at the plan, there seems to be nothing structural in the way, but there may be some piece of furniture that will cut off the view of the room. If there is, the keyhole will be of no use to us."

I handed the little toy back to him with a shade of impatience. "But why," I asked, "all this fuss? Why go about a perfectly simple inquiry in this complicated, roundabout way? If there is good reason to believe that someone has entered the room, why not just walk in and investigate in a reasonable, straightforward manner? It seems to me that you and Brodribb are standing on rather pedantic legal scruples."

He shook his head.

"I don't think so, Jervis," said he. "When you get clear instructions, you ought to assume that the instructor means what he says. But there is another matter, which I could only hint at to Woodburn. This man, Toke, is extraordinarily secretive. He has not only fastened up every opening with locks and bolts and screws, and put seals on the fastenings, but he has forbidden his solicitor, in the most emphatic way, to enter those rooms. Now, seals furnish no security against burglars. Their security is against his own trusted man of business. You or I or any reasonable person would have left the seal with Woodburn and asked him to inspect the place from time to time to see that all was well. Why has he shut out Woodburn in this secretive fashion? We must assume that he has his reasons. But what can they be? It may be mere crankiness, or it may not. Mr. Toke may be, and probably is, a most respectable gentleman. But supposing he is not? Supposing that his activities as a dealer in works of art cover some other activities of a less reputable kind? And supposing that the products of those other activities should happen to be hidden in those sealed rooms? It is not impossible.

"But if Woodburn – or we, as his agents – should enter in the face of explicit instructions to the contrary, and discover something illicit, the position would be extremely awkward. Professional secrecy does not cover that kind of thing."

"Still," I objected, "you are prepared to enter if you find evidence that someone else has."

"Certainly," he replied. "We should have to enter or inform the police. But we should then have no choice, whereas we have at present. And that raises another question. If we break in and find traces of unlawful visitors, we shall probably spoil our chances of making a capture. We are not ready now, and our entry would almost certainly

370

leave some traces that would warn them not to reappear. Whereas, if we should discover evidences of visitors before we make our own entry, we should be able to make arrangements to catch them when they make their next visit."

I agreed without much enthusiasm, for it seemed to me that Thorndyke was taking a mere rumour much more seriously than the circumstances justified. In fact, I ventured a hint to that effect.

"That is quite true, Jervis," he admitted. "It is a mere report, at present. Yet I shall be a little surprised if we find a mare's nest. There is something distinctly abnormal about the whole affair. But we shall be better able to judge when we have got a statement from the servants."

"We have heard what they have to say," I replied, still extremely sceptical of the whole affair. "But, possibly, cross-examination may elicit something more definite. As you say, we shall see."

With this the discussion dropped, and we smoked our pipes in silence as we watched, from the window, the gradual transition from the grey and rather dreary suburbs to the fresh green of the country. At Hartsden Junction, Mr. Woodburn was waiting on the platform, looking more like a smart livery stable keeper than a lawyer, and evidently keenly interested in our arrival.

"I am glad to see you," he said, as we walked out to the approach, "for the more I think about this affair, the more do I suspect that there is something amiss. And I have been reflecting on what you said about the seals. I had no idea that it was possible to forge a seal."

"I don't think," said Thorndyke, "that you need attach much weight to the forgery question. It is merely a possibility that has to be borne in mind. In the present case, it is highly improbable, as an intruder would have to pass through the house to reach the sealed door."

"Still," objected Mr. Woodburn, "that door seems to be the only way in. Otherwise, why should Mr. Toke have sealed it?"

There was a fairly obvious reply to this, but Thorndyke made no rejoinder, and by this time we had reached the car, into which Mr. Woodburn ushered us and then took his place at the steering-wheel, looking as unsuitable for his post as if he had been at the tiller of a fishing smack.

As the car was of the saloon type, we saw little of our surroundings and nothing of the house until, entering through an open gate, we passed up a shady drive and stopped opposite a handsome stone porch. The door stood open and framed the figure of a pleasant-looking middle-aged woman.

"This," said Mr. Woodburn, introducing us, "is Mr. Toke's housekeeper, Mrs. Gibbins. I have told her about you, and she is as much interested in you as I am."

Mrs. Gibbins confirmed this by a smile and a curtsy. "I am sure, gentlemen," said she, "we shall all be very grateful to you if you can find out what these mysterious sounds are, and put a stop to them. It is very uncomfortable to feel that strangers – and dishonest strangers, too – are creeping about the house in the dead of the night."

"It must be," Thorndyke agreed, warmly. "But, before we start to find out what those sounds are, we want to be quite sure that they really exist."

"There is no doubt about their existing," Mrs. Gibbins rejoined, with intense conviction. "We have all heard them. And they certainly come from the gallery wing, for my nephew, Edward, got out of bed on two occasions and went part of the way down the corridor and listened, and he was quite sure that the sounds came from the gallery or the rooms that open out of it. And it wasn't rats. Everybody knows the kind of sound that rats make, scampering about an empty room. It wasn't like that at all. It was like someone moving about quietly and, now and again, moving things. But there is another thing that can't be explained away. This house is supplied with water from an Artesian well. The water is pumped up by a windmill into a tank, which is on the level of the top floor, and it runs from the tank into the pipes that supply the house. The tank being so high up, the pressure of the water is quite considerable, and whenever a tap is running in any part of the house, you can hear a distinct hum in the main pipe. Of course, you can hear it much more distinctly at night when every thing else is quiet.

"Now, I am a rather light sleeper, especially towards morning and, on several occasions – over and over again – I have heard the water humming in the pipe when all the household were in bed and asleep. And always about the same time – just before it begins to get light."

"That is very remarkable, Mrs. Gibbins," said Woodburn. "You did not tell me about the water. It is a most striking fact. Don't you think so, Doctor?"

"I do," replied Thorndyke, "especially when taken with the other sounds. I take it, Mrs. Gibbins, that there is water laid on in the gallery wing?"

"Yes, sir. There is a lavatory with a fixed basin and a cold-water tap over it, and there is also a peculiar sort of sink – Mr. Toke calls it a chemical sink, I believe – in the work-room."

"And you say that the sound of running water occurs always at the same time? Do you never hear it at other times?"

"Oh, yes," she replied, "we hear it occasionally at other times. Not very often, though. But it seems to occur always when we have heard the other sounds. It is just as if the person had been doing some job and had a wash before he went away."

Mr. Woodburn laughed cheerfully.

"Tidy fellow, this," said he. "I wonder what he does in there. It's a quaint situation. He'll be ringing for his breakfast next."

"Can you form any idea," Thorndyke asked, "how often these sounds occur?"

"I should say," replied Mrs. Gibbins, "that they happen pretty regularly twice a week – generally on Wednesdays and Fridays."

Mr. Woodburn laughed heartily. Thorndyke's appearance on the scene had evidently acted favourably on his spirits.

"Quite a methodical chap," he chuckled. "Keeps regular hours, and has a wash and brush up before he goes home."

"We mustn't take him too much for granted," Thorndyke reminded him. "We have got to establish his existence as a matter of undoubted fact, though I must admit that Mrs. Gibbins's account is extremely circumstantial and convincing. It establishes a case for a very thorough investigation and I think we had better begin by having a look at the door of the gallery. What will be about the height of that keyhole that you spoke of?"

Mr. Woodburn indicated the height by reference to a point on his own waistcoat. "But I am afraid the keyhole won't help you much," he added. "As I think I told you, I couldn't see anything through it, excepting a patch of the opposite wall."

"Perhaps we can manage to get a better view," said Thorndyke. "That is, if there is nothing in the way. Probably, Mrs. Gibbins can tell us about that. How was the furniture arranged when you were in there last?"

"There is very little furniture in there, at all," the housekeeper replied, "unless you call the wall-cases furniture. There is a large table across the end of the room, and there are three chairs, one arm-chair and two ordinary dining-room chairs. The arm-chair is behind the table, nearly in the middle, and the other two are at the ends of the table."

"You say they 'are'," Thorndyke remarked. "Do you mean that that is how they were placed when you were last in the room?"

"Yes, sir. But I think they must be like that still, because the last time I was in there was on the day when Mr. Toke went away. I helped him to shut up the room and seal the door. They couldn't very well have been moved after that."

"Apparently not," Thorndyke admitted. "Then, in that case, we may as well go and have a look at the door and see if it is possible to get a glimpse of the inside of the room. And perhaps we had better take a chair with us, as the keyhole is at a rather inconvenient height."

Mr. Woodburn picked up a chair and led the way out of the morning room in which we had been holding our conversation, across the hall and into a narrow passage, which became almost dark as a sharp turn cut off the light from the doorway by which we had entered.

"Queer old place," he remarked as the corridor took another turn. "All holes and corners. I am wondering how you are going to see into that room. I couldn't, but I suppose a man who can produce another man's seal out of a top hat won't make any difficulty about seeing round a corner."

"We have only undertaken to try," Thorndyke reminded him. "Don't let us take credit prematurely."

The disclaimer was not entirely unnecessary for, when the corridor took yet another abrupt turn and brought us to a blind end in which was a massive door it became clear to me, from the manner both of Mrs Gibbins and Mr. Woodburn, that there was an expectation of some sort of display of occult powers on Thorndyke's part. So much so that, for the first time, I felt quite grateful to Polton.

"There you are," said Mr. Woodburn, placing the chair in position and standing back expectantly to watch the proceedings, as if he had some hopes of seeing Thorndyke put his head through the keyhole, "Let us see how you do it."

My colleague seated himself with a deprecating smile and, laying the research case on the floor, unfastened the catch and raised the lid, whereupon Mr. Woodburn and Mrs. Gibbins craned forward to peer in, Having taken a preliminary peep through the keyhole, Thorndyke produced the little wooden case and drew out Polton's diminutive spy-glass, which he inserted easily enough into the roomy opening. As he applied his eye to the tiny eyepiece and turned the milled ring to adjust the mirror, the two observers watched him with bated breath – as, indeed, did I, and with no small anxiety. For apart from the importance of the result, a complete failure would have been a shocking anticlimax. Great, therefore, was my relief when Thorndyke announced, "Well, at any rate, there is no obstruction to the view, such as it is. But it is not easy to make out the arrangement and relative positions of things with such a very restricted field of vision. However, as far as I can see, there are no signs of any appreciable disturbance. I can see the wall-cases at the end of the room, and their shelves are filled with what look like Bow and Chelsea figures. So there has been no robbery there. The cases at the sides of the room are not so easy to see, but I think I can make out the contents, and they appear to contain their full complement. Evidently, so far as the collection is concerned, there has been no robbery on any considerable scale.

"Then the position of the furniture corresponds generally with Mrs. Gibbins's description. There is an arm-chair behind the table and an ordinary dining-chair at each end. I can also see what looks like a shallow box or case of some kind on the table."

"A box on the table?" exclaimed Mrs. Gibbins. "That is curious. I don't remember any box, or anything else, on the table."

"Perhaps Mr. Toke put it there after you left," suggested Mr. Woodburn.

"But he couldn't," Mrs. Gibbins objected. "I went out with him and helped him to seal up the door. He couldn't have gone back after that."

"No. That is obvious," Woodburn admitted. "So it looks as if someone had been in the room, after all."

"Do you say, positively, Mrs. Gibbins, that there was nothing on the table when you left the room with Mr. Toke?" Thorndyke asked.

"Well, sir," the housekeeper replied, "one doesn't like to be too positive, but I certainly thought that there was nothing on the table. In fact, I feel sure that there wasn't."

"That seems pretty conclusive," said Woodburn. "What do you think, Doctor?"

"It is conclusive enough to us," Thorndyke replied, diplomatically. "But as a lawyer, you will realize the difficulty of coming to a definite decision on negative evidence. To justify you in acting in direct opposition to your client's instructions, you ought to have undeniable positive evidence. We are not considering our own beliefs, but the legal position."

"Yes, that is true," Mr. Woodburn conceded, evidently interpreting Thorndyke's polite hint that ladies are sometimes apt to confuse the subjective with the objective aspects of certainty.

"Do you see any thing else?"

"No. I think that is the sum of my observations, But remember that the room is strange to me. Perhaps if you, who know the room, were to take a look through the instrument, you might detect some change that would not be apparent to me."

To say that Woodburn jumped at the offer would be to understate the case. In his eagerness to occupy the seat of observation, he nearly sat on Thorndyke's lap. But, apparently, Polton's "contraption" did not come up to his expectations, for, after peering in at the eyepiece for some seconds, he said in a tone of slight disappointment, "I don't seem to make much of it. I can only see a tiny bit at a time, and everything looks in its wrong place. The table seems to be right opposite this door instead of where I know it to be."

"You must disregard the positions of things," Thorndyke explained. "Remember that you are looking into a mirror."

"Oh, I hadn't realized that," said Woodburn, hastily. "Of course, that explains the odd appearance of the room." He reapplied his eye to the instrument, and now was able to manage it better, for he presently reported, "I think the cases look all right and everything else appears as usual. As to that box, of course, I can say nothing. I have never seen it before, and I can't quite make out what sort of box it is. It looks like metal."

"That was what I thought," said Thorndyke. "Perhaps Mrs. Gibbins may recognize it." The suggestion was evidently acceptable, for the housekeeper "outed" Mr. Woodburn with great promptness and, having seated herself, applied her eye to the instrument. But she was even less successful than her predecessor, for, after a prolonged stare through the eyepiece, she announced that she could see nothing but the carpet, which appeared, unreasonably, to have affixed itself to the opposite wall. However, Thorndyke came to her aid, and eventually enabled her to see the mysterious box on the table, concerning which she again asserted with deep conviction that, not only was she quite sure that it had not been there when she and Mr. Toke had vacated the room, but that she was equally certain that she had never seen the box before at all.

When she had finished her observations (which seemed to concern themselves principally with the floor and the ceiling), I came into the reversion of the chair, by way, ostensibly, of confirming the previous observations. And, when I came to look through the little instrument in the conditions for which it was designed, I was disposed to be apologetic to Polton. The field of view was, indeed, extremely small, but the little circular picture at which one looked was beautifully clear and bright, and the fine adjustment for moving the mirror enabled one to shift the field of vision gradually and preserve a continuity in the things seen that had, to some extent, the effect of a larger field.

"Well," said Woodburn, as I rose from the chair, "what have we arrived at? Or haven't we arrived at any conclusion?"

"I think," said Thorndyke, "that we must conclude that our observations tend to confirm the suspicion that someone had obtained access to this room. But I do not think that we have enough evidence to justify us in disregarding Mr. Toke's very definite instructions."

"Then," said Woodburn, "what do you suggest that we ought to do?"

"I suggest that we make a careful survey of the house to see if we can find any means of access to this room that the seals do not cover, and if, as I expect, we fail to find any such means, then we must make some more exact and continuous observations from this door."

"You don't suggest that we post someone at this keyhole to keep watch continuously, do you?" exclaimed Woodburn.

"No," replied Thorndyke. "That would be impracticable. But I think we could achieve the same result in another way. At any rate, I will take the preliminary measures before we go away from here, in case they may be needed."

He withdrew the "spy-glass" from the keyhole and, having put it away in the research case, produced from the latter a small cardboard box which, when the lid was removed, was seen to contain a number of little cylinders of hardwood about six inches long and of varying diameters, from a quarter-of-an-inch up to five-eighths.

"These," he explained, "are gauges that my assistant has made to obtain the exact dimensions of the keyhole, so that he can make a more efficient instrument."

"The instrument that you have got is efficient enough," said Woodburn. "The trouble will be to get someone to stay here to use it."

"Perhaps we can produce an instrument that will do its work without an attendant," replied Thorndyke. "But we will talk about that when we have made our survey. Now, I will just take these measurements."

He seated himself once more and proceeded to pass the larger cylinders one by one through the keyhole. All of them passed through fairly easily excepting the two largest, which were returned to the box.

"The internal diameter of the keyhole," said Thorndyke, "is nearly nine-sixteenths of an inch. Probably it has been a little enlarged by wear, but even so the key must have been an out-size. I shall call it half an inch."

He marked, with a pencil, the approved cylinder and, having returned it to the box, announced that he was ready to proceed to the next item in the programme.

"Perhaps," he suggested, "we had better take a glance at the lofts which are over the gallery."

Mr. Woodburn looked interrogatively at the housekeeper, who volunteered the information that the entrance to them was at the top of the back staircase, and that the key was on her bunch.

"The entrance to the lofts is not sealed, then?" Thorndyke remarked.

"Apparently not," said Woodburn. "Which suggests that we are not likely to find anything of interest in them. Still, we may as well have a look at them and satisfy ourselves."

We followed the housekeeper through a surprising labyrinth of passages and rooms, which seemed to be on all sorts of levels, with steps up and down, which made it necessary to approach all doors with caution to avoid being tripped up or stepping into empty air. Eventually, we came to an unlocked door which gave entrance to the back staircase, up which Mrs. Gibbins preceded us in a dim twilight. At each landing, open doors gave glimpses into dark and mysterious corridors which apparently burrowed among the bedrooms, and the top landing showed us, in addition, a locked door with an enormous keyhole, into which the housekeeper inserted a ponderous key. The door creaked open and revealed a flight of narrow, ladder-like stairs, up which we crawled painfully and cautiously, Thorndyke bringing up the rear, encumbered with his research case and the Poltonic walking-stick.

There was no door at the top of the stairs (which seemed a lost opportunity on the part of the architect), and only a pretence of a landing outside the narrow doorway which gave entrance to the lofts. Here we stood for a few moments, looking into the long range of well-lighted lofts that stretched away on either side. There was something a little weird and impressive in the aspect of those great, wide attics with their rough oaken floors, littered with the cast-off household gods of forgotten generations, stretching away into the distance among the massive and almost unhewn timber of the great roof. Each of the two ranges – for we stood at the angle of the body and the wing of the house – was lighted by a pair of dormer windows on each side, filled with little panes of greenish glass set in leaded casements, so that we were able to see the whole extent with the exception of a few dark corners at the extreme ends.

"Well," said Woodburn, looking a little distastefully at the littered floor, covered, as it seemed, with the dust of centuries, "is it worthwhile to go in? Looks a bit dusty," he added, with a glance at his brilliantly polished boots.

"I think I will just walk down the lofts," said Thorndyke, "as a matter of form, though it is pretty clear that there have been no recent visitors. But there is no need for you to come."

That it was but a mere formality became evident as soon as we had started, for, glancing back, I could see that we had left plain and conspicuous footprints in the impalpable dust that lay in an even coating on the bumpy floor. Evidently, we were the first visitors who had trodden that floor for, at least, some years.

"Still," said Thorndyke, when I made a remark to this effect, "we had to establish the fact. If there is some secret way into the gallery, our

378

only chance of discovering it will be by excluding, one by one, all the places in which it is not to be found. This is evidently one of them."

"Well," said Woodburn, as we emerged, "we can write off the lofts, I think. Dust has its uses, after all. What are we going to explore next?"

"I suppose," Thorndyke replied, "we had better examine the outside of the premises."

"Yes," Woodburn agreed, "that seems to be the reasonable thing to do, seeing that, if there have been any visitors, that is where they must have come from. But there is mighty little to see. I can tell you that much, for I have made a thorough inspection myself."

Mr. Woodburn was right. There was very little indeed to see. The gallery stood above a range of what were now cellars, but had formerly been rooms, as we gathered from the windows, some entirely bricked up, while others were reduced to small openings, glazed with ground glass and protected by stout iron bars. The only approach to them was from within the house, by a massive door at the bottom of a flight of stone steps, and that door was not only sealed, but also secured by a heavy padlock of the Yale type, of which the minute key-slit was covered by a sealed label.

From outside the house, there was no entrance of any kind to the gallery wing. The windows of the gallery itself looked on the garden at the back of the house, but an inspection of them by means of the ladder, which had been put there for our convenience, only served to confirm Woodburn's account of them. They were obviously untouched, and the lace curtains on the inside made it impossible to get the faintest glimpse into the room. The windows of the rooms which communicated with the gallery were equally impossible as a means of access. We examined them with the aid of the ladder from the narrow strip of garden that separated the side of the wing from the high wall that enclosed the whole domain. They, also, were evidently intact, and were guarded internally by massive shutters that effectually excluded the possibility of seeing in.

"That seems to be the lot," said Woodburn, as we put the ladder back where we had found it, "unless there is anything else that you would like to see."

Thorndyke looked up at the house, inquisitively, and then glanced along the wall down the garden. "I think," said he, "I understood you to say that there was a churchyard on the other side of that wall."

"Yes. Do you want to see it? I don't know why you should."

"We may as well take a look at it," was the reply. "Any visitors, entering the house at night, would probably come over that wall rather than through the front grounds, particularly if there is a churchyard to take off from. A country churchyard is pretty secluded at night. It would even be possible to use a portable ladder."

"So it would," agreed Woodburn. "And this is a disused churchyard. They have built a new church at the other end of the village, the Lord knows why. They had better have restored the old church. But any visitors to the old churchyard would have the place to themselves at night."

"Then let us go and inspect it," said Thorndyke. "If there have been repeated visits, there ought to be some traces of the visitors."

We went back through the house and out by way of the drive and the front gate. Turning to the right, we walked along the front of the Manor House grounds to the end of the enclosing wall where it was joined by the lower wall of the churchyard. Presently, we came to a dilapidated wooden gate which yawned wide open on its rickety hinges. Passing in through this, we took our way along an overgrown path, past a tall headstone and a decayed altar tomb, enclosed by rusty, ivy-grown railings. In front of us, a great yew tree cast a deep shadow across the path, and beyond, a smallish, ancient-looking church, with gaping windows from which the tracery had disappeared, huddled under a dense mantle of ivy, looking the very picture of desolation and decay. As we walked, Thorndyke looked about him critically, keeping an attentive eye on the ground beside the path, the high, neglected grass which everywhere sprang up between the graves being obviously favourable to a search for "traces."

So we advanced until we entered the gloomy shadow of the great yew tree. Here Thorndyke halted to look about him. "Somewhere in this neighbourhood," said he, "would be the most probable place for a nocturnal operator to make his arrangements. That is the Manor wall in front of us. I can see the roof of the gallery wing through the trees. That big sarcophagus tomb will be nearly opposite the end of the wing."

"Yes," I said. "It seems to mark the position that would be most convenient for negotiating the wall, and if you notice the grass, there seems to be a faint, rather wide track, as if it had been walked over by someone who had been careful not to tread it down all in one place."

"I think you are right," said Woodburn. "Now you mention it, I think I can make out the track quite plainly. It seems to lead towards that tomb."

"The grass has certainly been walked over," Thorndyke agreed, "and I see no signs of its having been trodden anywhere else. But don't let us confuse matters by walking over it ourselves. Let us strike across the graves and approach along the wall."

We followed this course, keeping close to the wall as we approached the great tomb. The latter stood about ten feet from the wall and, as we drew near, I was surprised to notice that the grass between the tomb and the wall appeared quite untrodden.

Thorndyke had also noticed this rather unexpected circumstance and, when we were within a yard or two of the tomb, he halted and looked curiously along the ground at the foot of the wall.

"There is certainly no sign of the use of any ladder," he remarked. "In fact, there is no indication of any one having approached close to the wall. The track, if it really is one, doesn't appear to go beyond the tomb."

"That is what it looks like to me," agreed Woodburn, "though I am hanged if I can see any reason why it should. They couldn't have jumped from the top of the tomb over the wall."

"It looks," I suggested, "as if this place had been used rather as a post of observation, or a lurking-place where the sportsman could keep out of sight until the coast was clear." We approached the tomb from the direction of the wall and sauntered round it, idly reading the inscriptions, which recorded briefly the life-histories of a whole dynasty of Greenlees, "*late of Hartsden Manor in this Parish*", beginning with one John Greenlees who died in 1611. At length he turned away and began to retrace his steps down the path towards the gate.

"They were a turbulent family, these Greenlees," said Woodburn. "Always in hot water. Bigoted Papists in early days and, of course, Jacobites after the Revolution. From what I have heard, Hartsden Manor House must have seen some stirring times."

While he was speaking, I was glancing through the inscriptions on the back of the tomb. Happening to look down, I noticed a match in the grass at my feet, and stooped to pick it up. As I did so, I observed another, on which I made a search and ultimately salved no less than six.

"What have you found, Jervis?" Thorndyke asked, as I rose.

I held out my hand with the six matches in it. "All from the same place at the back of the tomb," said I. "What do you make of that?"

"It might mean five failures on a windy day or night," he replied, "or six separate cigarettes, and the operator may have come here to get a 'lee side', or he may have got behind the tomb so that the light should not be seen from the road. But we must not let our imaginations run away with us. There is nothing to show that the person or persons who came to this tomb have any connection with our problem. We are looking for some means of access to the gallery and, up to the present, we have not found any. The fact, if it were one, that some persons had been lurking about here, waiting for a chance to enter, wouldn't help us. It would not tell us how they got in, which is what we want to know."

Nevertheless, he continued, for some time, to browse round the tomb, dividing his attention between the inscriptions and the grass that bordered the low plinth.

"Well," said Woodburn, "we seem to have exhausted the possibilities, unless there is anything else that you want to see."

"No," replied Thorndyke, "I don't think it is of any use to prolong our search. I suspect that there is some way into the house, but if there is, it is too well hidden to be discoverable without some guiding hint, which we haven't got. So the answer to our first question is negative, and we must concentrate on the second – does anyone, in fact, effect an entrance to the gallery?"

"And how do you propose to solve that problem?" enquired Woodburn.

"I propose to install an automatic recorder which will give us a series of photographs of the interior of the room."

"And catch 'em on the hop, eh?" said Woodburn. "But it doesn't seem possible. Why, you would have to take a photograph every few minutes, and then you wouldn't bring it off, because the beggars seem to come only at night."

"I am not expecting to get photographs of the visitors themselves," Thorndyke explained. "My idea is that, if any persons do frequent those rooms, they will almost certainly leave some traces of their visits. Even the moving of a chair would be conclusive evidence, if it could be proved, as it could be by the comparison of two photographs which showed it in different positions. I shall send my assistant, Mr. Polton, down to set up the apparatus, and perhaps you will give Mrs. Gibbins instructions to give him all necessary facilities, including the means of locking up the corridor when he has fixed the apparatus and set it going."

To this Mr. Woodburn agreed gleefully and, as a train was due in a quarter-of-an-hour, we embarked in his car without re-entering the house.

Chapter XII
The Unknown Coiner

From Charing Cross we walked home to the Temple, entering it by way of Pump Court and the Cloisters. As we were about to cross King's Bench Walk, I glanced up at the laboratory window and caught a momentary glimpse of Polton's head, which however vanished even as I looked and, when we arrived at our landing, the door of our chambers was open, and he was visible within, making a hypocritical pretence of laying the dinner-table, which had obviously been laid hours previously. But his pretended occupation did not conceal the fact that he was in a twitter of anxiety and impatience, which Thorndyke proceeded at once humanely to allay.

"It had to be a cold dinner, as I didn't know what time you would be home," Polton explained, but Thorndyke cut short his explanations and came to the essential matter.

"Never mind the dinner, Polton," said he. "The important point is that your automatic watcher will be wanted, and as soon as you can get it ready."

Polton beamed delightedly on his employer as he replied, "It is ready now, sir, all except the objective. You see, the clock and the camera were really made already. They only wanted a little adaptation. And I have made an experimental objective, and done some trial exposures with it. So I am ready to go ahead as soon as I have the dimensions of the keyhole."

"I can give you those at once," said Thorndyke, opening the research case and taking out the wooden cylinders. "The keyhole will take a half-inch tube fairly easily."

Polton slapped his thigh joyfully. "There's a stroke of luck!" he exclaimed. "You said it would be about half-an-inch, so I used a half-inch tube for my experimental objective. But I never dared to hope that it would be the exact size. As it is, all I have got to do is to fix it on to the camera. I can do that tonight and give it a final trial. Then it will be ready to set up in place to-morrow. Perhaps, sir, you will come up presently and see if you think it will do. I shall have got it fixed by the time you have finished dinner."

With this, having taken a last glance at the table, he retired in triumph, with the box of cylinders in his hand.

"What is this 'automatic watcher'?" I asked, as we sat down to our meal. "I assume that it is some sort of automatic camera. But what is its special peculiarity?"

"In its original form," replied Thorndyke, "it consisted of a clock of the kind known as an English Dial, with a magazine camera fixed inside it. There was a simplified striking movement which released the shutter at any intervals previously arranged. It also had an arrangement for recording the time at which each exposure was made. It was quite a valuable appliance for keeping a watch on any particular place. It could be set up, for instance, opposite the door of a strong room or in any similar position."

"But suppose the thief made his visit in the interval between two exposures?"

"That was provided for by a special attachment whereby the opening of the door was made to break an electric circuit and release the shutter, so that whenever the door was opened an exposure was made and the time recorded. But for our present purpose, although we have retained the principle, we have had to modify the details considerably. For instance, we have separated the clock from the camera, so that it can be fixed far enough away from the door to prevent its tick from being heard in the gallery. The releasing mechanism of the clock is connected with an electromagnet in the camera which actuates the shutter and the film roller. The lens is in a tube five inches long, with a reflecting prism at the farther end, which will, of course, be passed through the keyhole, and the camera screwed on to the door. That is a rough sketch of the apparatus. You will see the details of it when we go up to make our inspection."

"And how often do you propose to make an exposure?" I asked.

"One exposure every twenty-four hours would do for us," he replied, "as we merely want a daily record of the positions of the various objects in the room. But that does not satisfy Polton. He would like an exposure every hour. So we have arrived at a compromise. There will be an exposure every six hours. Of course, those made at night will show nothing, and both of those made in daylight, when the room will be unoccupied, will, presumably, be alike. But I can see that Polton will not be happy if there is not a good string of exposures."

"Supposing the exposures are all alike?" I suggested.

Thorndyke laughed grimly. "Don't be a wet blanket, Jervis," said he. "But I must admit that it would be something of an anticlimax and distinctly disappointing, though not entirely unexpected. For if there are really visitors, it is quite possible that they do not go to the gallery at all. Their business, whatever it may be, is, quite conceivably, carried on in one of the rooms that open out of the gallery. So a negative result with the camera would not prove that no one had entered the gallery wing."

It was my turn to smile, and I did so. "It is my belief, Thorndyke," said I, "that you don't mean anything to disprove it. You are not approaching the investigation with an open mind."

"Not very open," he admitted. "The housekeeper's statement, together with all the other circumstances of the case, make a very strong suggestion of something abnormal – so strong that, as you say, I am not prepared to be easily satisfied with a negative result. And now if we have finished, we had better go up to the laboratory and have a look at Polton's masterpiece."

We rose and were just moving towards the door when a firm tread became audible on the landing, and was followed by a familiar knock on the brass knocker of the inner door.

"Miller, by Jove!" I exclaimed. "How unfortunate! But I can entertain him while you go up to Polton."

"Let us hear what he has to say, first," replied Thorndyke, and he proceeded to throw open the door.

As the Superintendent entered, I was impressed by a certain curious mixture of jauntiness and anxiety in his manner. But the former predominated, especially as he made his triumphant announcement.

"Well, gentlemen, I thought you would be interested to hear that we have got our man."

"Dobey?" asked Thorndyke.

"Dobey it is," replied Miller. "We've got him, we've charged him, and he is committed for trial."

"Come and sit down," said Thorndyke, "and tell us all about it."

He deposited the Superintendent in a comfortable arm-chair, placed on the little table at his elbow the whisky decanter, the siphon, and the box of the specially favoured cigars, and while the tumbler was being charged and the cigar lighted, he filled his pipe and regarded his visitor with a slightly speculative eye.

"Where did you catch him?" he asked, when the preliminary formalities were disposed of.

Miller removed the cigar from his mouth in order the more conveniently to smile.

"It was a quaint affair," he chuckled. "We caught him in the act of picking the lock of his own front door. Rum position, wasn't it? Of course, the key was at the police station at Maidstone. We had been keeping a watch on the flat, but it happened that day that one of our sergeants was going there with a search warrant to have another look over the premises in case anything should have been missed at the first search. When he got up to the landing, there was my nabs, angling at the keyhole with a piece of wire. He was mightily surprised when the sergeant introduced himself, and still more so when he was told what he was charged with."

"Was he charged with the murder or the house-breaking?"

"Both. Of course, the usual caution was administered, but, Lord, you might as well have cautioned an oyster."

"Did he say nothing at all?"

"Oh, the usual thing. Expressed astonishment – that was real enough, beyond a doubt. Said he didn't know what we were talking about, but was perfectly sure that he didn't want to make any statement."

"I suppose he pleaded 'Not Guilty' at the police court?"

"Yes. But he wouldn't say anything in his defence, excepting that he knew nothing about the murder and had never heard of Inspector Badger, until he had got legal advice. So the magistrate adjourned the hearing for a couple of days, and Dobey got a lawyer to defend him – a chappie named Morris Coleman."

"Of Kennington Lane?"

"That's the man. Solicitor and advocate. Downy bird, too, but quite a good lawyer."

"Yes," said Thorndyke, "I have seen him in court. A cut above the ordinary police-court advocate. And what did he have to say?"

"Reserved his defence, of course. They always do if the case is going for trial. That's the worst of these police-court solicitors. But it usually means that they haven't got any defence, and of course that is what it means now, so it doesn't matter. But it is a time-wasting plan when they have got a defence, and the judge usually has something to say about it. Still, you can't cure them. They think they get an advantage by springing a defence on the court that nobody expected."

"You say you are proceeding on both the charges. Why are you bringing in the house-breaking?"

"Well, of course," replied Miller, "it is the murder that he will actually be tried for. But we shall have to prove the facts of the house-breaking to explain how the stolen paper came to be found."

As he gave this explanation, the Superintendent stole a slightly furtive glance at Thorndyke, which I understood when the latter remarked, dryly, "True. And the evidence of the witnesses to the house-breaking may serve to supply the deficiencies of the station-master at Strood. I take it that they will be able to identify Dobey."

"They have. Picked him out instantly from a crowd of thirty other men. And as to that station-master, it's just a silly excess of caution and over-conscientiousness. He didn't look at the man particularly, and so he won't swear to him. But, as his description of the man agrees with that of the witnesses to the house-breaking, and they are ready to swear to Dobey, it will, as you say, help matters a bit. But, of course, the finding of the paper in his possession is the really crucial piece of evidence."

"It is more than that," said Thorndyke. "It is the whole of the evidence in regard to the murder. Without it, your bill would never get past the Grand Jury. And as to the house-breaking, as it can't be included in the indictment, I doubt whether the court will allow any reference to it. That, however, remains to be seen."

"Well," rejoined Miller, "it doesn't matter a great deal. The paper fixes the crime on him."

With this, he dipped his nose into his glass and resumed his cigar with the air of having disposed of the subject, and I took the opportunity to raise another point.

"Did you say that Dobey was found picking his lock with a piece of wire?" I asked.

"Yes," he answered with a chuckle. "Quaint situation, wasn't it?"

"It strikes me as more than quaint," I replied. "It is most extraordinary that he should not have provided himself with a key of some sort."

"It is," Miller agreed. "But it was a simple latch, and I expect he was pretty handy with the wire. And I don't suppose he often went to the flat. Still, as you say, he must have been a fool not to get a key."

"He must," said I. "It is a striking example of the criminal mentality."

"Yes," agreed Miller. "They are not a very bright lot." He paused reflectively for a few moments, puffing at his cigar reflectively, and then resumed in a meditative tone. "And yet it doesn't do to rate them too low. We say to ourselves that they are all fools. So they are, or they wouldn't be crooks. Crime is never a really sound economic proposition. But there is one thing that we must bear in mind: There are two kinds of crooks – those that get caught, and those that don't. And a crook that doesn't get caught may never come into sight at all. If he manages well enough, his existence may never be even suspected. I have just heard of a case in which the existence of a man of this class has been disclosed by a mere chance. But we don't know who he is, and we are not very likely to find out. I'll tell you about the case. It's a queer affair.

"Just recently, one of our men who specializes in note forgeries and knows a good deal about money of all kinds had to spend a week or two on the Continent. When he was about to return, he changed his foreign money into English and got one or two sovereigns. Now, when he got home and had a look at those sovereigns, he thought there seemed to be something queer about one of them. So he got a chemist to weigh it, but the weight was apparently all right – it was only an ordinary shop scale, you know, but it weighed within a fraction of a grain. Then he measured it, but all the dimensions seemed to be correct. But still, to his expert eye, it didn't look right, and it didn't sound right when he rang it. So he took it to an assayist whom he knew, and the assayist tried its specific gravity and tested it so far as was possible without damaging the coin, and he reported that it was undoubtedly gold of about the correct fineness. But still our man wasn't satisfied. So he took it to the Mint, and showed it to one of the chief officials. And then the murder was out. It wasn't a milled coin at all. It was a casting. An uncommonly good casting and very neatly finished off at the edge, but an undoubted casting to the skilled eye. So they passed it on to the assay department and made a regular assay of it. The result was very quaint. It was gold right enough, and just about twenty-two carat, but it was not exactly the composition of a sovereign. There was a slight difference in the alloy. That was all. There was no fraud. The proper amount of gold was there. Yet it was a counterfeit coin. Now, what do you make of that?"

"Nothing," I answered, "unless it was a practical joke."

"Well, it wasn't. The Mint people asked us to look into the matter, and we did. The result was that we found one or two more specimens of this queer, unofficial money – you couldn't call it base coin – in France, Belgium, and Holland. Evidently, there is a regular manufacture."

"But what on earth can be the meaning of it?" I demanded.

Miller chuckled. "We can only guess," said he, "but we can take it that the sportsman who makes those sovereigns doesn't do it for fun. And if he makes a profit on them, he doesn't buy his gold from the bullion dealers, and he doesn't pay the market price for it. On the other hand, he probably sells it for export at considerably above its nominal value, now that gold is so difficult to get. So if he steals his gold, or gets it cheap from the thieves, and sells it at a premium, he doesn't do so badly. And he will be mighty hard to catch. For the coins are genuine golden sovereigns, and only a fairly expert person would be able to spot them. And experts are pretty rare nowadays. Once, every little shopkeeper was an expert, but now there are plenty of people who have never seen a sovereign."

"It is a clever dodge," I remarked, "if the gold is really stolen."

"Clever!" repeated Miller, enthusiastically. "It's a stroke of genius. You see, it avoids all the crook's ordinary difficulties. He can get rid of the stones pretty easily, as they can't be identified separately. But the gold is less easy to dispose of at a decent price. For if a bullion dealer is willing to buy it – which he probably isn't, if he is a respectable man –

the transaction is known, and the vendor has left dangerous tracks, and the ordinary fence will only give a knock-down price. He must make a big profit to set off the risk that he takes.

"But there is another case that has just come to light – probably the same man. You know that, for some time past, the Mint has been calling in all real silver money. Now, since this sovereign incident, it occurred to the people there to look over the silver coins that came in and, at the first cast, they came on a half-crown that turned out to be a casting. But it was silver. Further search brought one or two more to light. Someone was making silver half-crowns.

"Now, here was a paradoxical situation! The coiner was making good silver coin while the Mint was issuing base money. Of course, coining is illegal. But this coiner could not be charged with uttering base coin. It would be hard to prove to a jury that it was counterfeit.

"Here you see the difference between the stupid crook and the clever crook. The fool tries to grab the whole – and doesn't do it. He makes his coin of pewter and probably steals that. They generally used to. If he got half-a-crown for his pewter snide, it would be all profit. But he doesn't, because it is a duffer. So he has to sell it cheap to the snide man. And he gets caught. But this sportsman puts, say, a shilling's worth of silver into his half-crown, and he doesn't have to pay the snide man. He can pass it quite safely himself. And he doesn't get caught."

"He runs the risk of getting caught if he passes it himself," I objected.

"Not at all," said Miller. "How should he? What you're overlooking is that the coins are good coins. They pass freely, and they will bear assay. Only an expert can spot them, and then only after close examination. But he must make a big profit. He could easily get rid of a hundred a day. There's seven-pounds-ten-shillings profit, even if he buys the silver at the market price, which he probably does not. That silver is most likely burglars' loot – silver tea-pots and candlesticks melted down – stuff that he would have to sell to a fence at about the price of brass. I tell you, Dr. Jervis, that coiner is a brainy customer. He'll want a lot of salt sprinkled on his tail before he'll get caught."

"I think you are rather over-estimating his profits," said I. "He has not only to pass the coins. He has got to make them. Good workmanship like that means time and labour. And there is the gold. Most trade jewellery is made of a lower-grade gold than twenty-two-carat. He would either have to buy fine gold from the bullion dealers to bring his low-grade gold up to standard, or to do a good deal of conversion himself."

While Miller was considering this difficulty, the door opened and Polton's head became visible, his eyes riveted on the Superintendent's back with an expression of consternation. I think he would have withdrawn, but that Miller, in some occult manner, became aware of his presence and addressed him.

"Good evening, Mr. Polton. We were just discussing a little problem that is rather in your line. Perhaps you would give us your opinion on it."

On this, Polton advanced with a slightly suspicious eye on the Superintendent, and Miller proceeded to put his case.

"The problem is, how to make sovereigns – castings, you know – out of jewellery composed of low-grade gold. Supposing you had got a lot of rings, for instance, of eighteen-carat gold. Now, how would you go about turning them into twenty-two carat sovereigns?"

Polton crinkled at him reproachfully.

"I am surprised at you, Mr. Miller – an officer of the law, too – suggesting such a thing. Of course, I wouldn't do anything of the sort."

"No, no," chuckled Miller, "we know that. It's just a question of method that we want explained. Because somebody has done it, and we would like to know how he managed it."

"Well, sir," said Polton, "there is no particular difficulty about it. He would weigh up the eighteen-carat gold and take part of it, say a little more than half, flatten it out on the stake or in a rolling mill if he had one, break it up quite small, and boil it up in nitric acid. That would dissolve out the alloy – the copper and silver – and leave him pure gold. Then he would melt that down with the proper proportion of the eighteen-carat stuff, and that would give him twenty-two-carat gold."

"And as to making the coins? Would that be much of a job? How many do you think he could make in a day?"

"A man who knew his job," said Polton, "wouldn't make any trouble about it. He would make his mould in a casting flask that would cast, say, twenty at a time, and he would use a matrix that would dry hard and give a good many repeats. There would be a bit of finishing work to do on each coin – cutting off the sprue, where the metal ran in, and making good the edge. But that is not a big job. They make a special edge tool for the purpose."

"Oh, do they?" said Miller, with a sly grin. "You seem to know a good deal about it, Mr. Polton."

"Of course I do," was the indignant response, "seeing that I have been dealing with tool-makers in the metal trade since I was a boy. Not that the respectable makers in Clerkenwell have anything to do with burglars' and coiners' tools. But, naturally, they get to know what is made."

"Yes, I know," said Miller. "Our people get some useful tips from them, now and again. And I shall know where to send them if they want some more, eh, Mr. Polton? Technical tips, I mean, of course."

Polton crinkled indulgently at the Superintendent, and when the latter, having glanced at his watch, suddenly emptied his glass and rose, his expression became positively affectionate.

"I am afraid I have wasted a lot of your time with my gossip," said Miller, apologetically as he drew on his gloves, "but I thought you would like to have the news. Probably you will look in at the Old Bailey and see how the case goes. The sessions are just beginning now, and I expect the case will come on in the course of a few days."

"We shall certainly drop in if we can," said Thorndyke, "and see what comes of your efforts. Won't you throw away that stump and take a fresh cigar?" he added, holding out the box as the Superintendent essayed to strike a match.

"Seems a waste," replied Miller, turning a thrifty eye on the stump. But he succumbed, nevertheless, and when he had selected a fresh cigar and amputated its point with anxious care, he lit it (with a match that Polton had struck in readiness), shook hands, and took his leave.

As the door closed on the sound of his retiring footsteps, Polton fell to, in his noiseless, dexterous fashion, on the dismantling of the dinner-table and, as he prepared a tray for transport to the upper regions, he announced, "The camera is finished, sir, and all ready for inspection, if you have time to come up and have a look at it."

"Then let us go up at once," said Thorndyke, "and perhaps we can take some of the debris with us and save another journey."

He loaded a second tray and followed Polton up the stairs, while I brought up the rear with an empty claret jug and a couple of dish covers.

The "automatic watcher", which its creator exhibited with justifiable complacency, was a singularly ingenious appliance. The clock was enclosed in a small box, on the front of which was a miniature dial, and the almost inaudible tick was further muffled by a pad of felt between its back and the wall. The camera, to which it was connected by an insulated wire, was another small box, fitted with mirror plates to fasten it to the door. From its front projected a brass tube, five inches long, and half-an-inch thick, at the end of which was an enclosed prism with a circular opening facing at right angles to the axis of the tube.

"There are two film holders," Polton explained, "each taking six yards of kinematograph film, and each enclosed in a light-tight case with a dark-slide, so that it can be taken out and another put in its place, so I can go down and bring away one film for development and leave the other to carry on. I have set the clock to make an exposure every six hours, beginning at twelve o'clock, noon."

"And what about the shutter?" asked Thorndyke. "Does it make much of a click?"

"It doesn't make any sound at all," replied Polton, "because it moves quite slowly. It is just a disc with a hole in it. When the clock makes the circuit, the disc moves so that the hole is opposite the lens, and stays there until the circuit is broken. Then it moves round and closes the lens and, at the same time, the roller makes a turn and winds on a fresh piece of film. I'll make an exposure now."

He turned the hand of the clock until it came to six, while Thorndyke and I listened with our heads close to the camera. But no sound could be heard, and it was only by repeating the proceeding with our ears actually applied to the camera that it was possible to detect faint sounds of movement as the shutter-disc revolved.

"I suppose," said Thorndyke, "you focus on the film?"

"Yes," replied Polton, "there's plenty to spare, so I use a piece as a focusing screen and waste it. And the barrel of the lens can be turned so as to get the prism pointing at the right spot. I think it will do, sir."

"I am sure it will," Thorndyke agreed, heartily, "and I only hope that all your trouble and ingenuity and skill will not have been expended in vain."

"That can hardly be, sir," was the cheerful response. "The photographs are bound to show something, though it may not be exactly what you want. At any rate, it's ready and, with your permission, I will pop down with it to-morrow, as soon as I have finished with the breakfasts."

"Excellent!" said Thorndyke. "Then, if Mrs. Gibbins's belief is well founded, the 'watcher' will be installed in time for the Wednesday-night visit."

Chapter XIII
Rex v. Dobey

During the next day or two, I was sensible of a certain tension and unrest that seemed to affect the atmosphere of our chambers in King's Bench Walk. Polton, having successfully installed his apparatus in the corridor at Hartsden Manor House, was in a fever of impatience to harvest the results. I believe that he would have liked to sit down beside his camera and change the film after each exposure. As it was, he had fixed it on Tuesday morning and, as no result could be expected until Thursday, at the earliest, circumstances condemned him to two whole days of suspense.

But Polton was not the only sufferer. My long association with Thorndyke enabled me to detect changes in his emotional states that were hidden from the eye of the casual observer by his habitually calm and impassive exterior and, in these days, a certain gravity and preoccupation in his manner conveyed to me the impression that something was weighing on his mind. At first, I was disposed to connect his preoccupation with the affairs of Hartsden Manor, but I soon dismissed this idea. For in those affairs there was nothing that could reasonably cause him any anxiety. And Thorndyke was by no means addicted to fussing unnecessarily.

The explanation came on the Wednesday evening, when we had finished dinner and taken our armchairs, and were preparing the post-prandial pipes.

"I suppose," said he, pushing the tobacco jar to my side of the little table, "you will turn up at the Old Bailey to hear how Dobey fares?"

"When is the trial?" I asked.

"To-morrow," he replied. "I thought you knew."

"No," said I. "Miller didn't mention any date, and I have heard nothing since. I think it would be interesting to hear the evidence, though we know pretty well what it will be."

"Yes, we know the case for the prosecution. But we don't know what Dobey may have to say in reply. That is what interests me. I am not at all happy about the case. I don't much like the attitude of the prosecution – if Miller has represented it fairly – particularly the dragging in of the house affair."

"No," I agreed, "that seems quite irrelevant."

"It is," said be. "And it is a flagrant instance of the old forensic dodge of proving the wrong conclusion. The identification of Dobey by these women is evidently expected to convey to the jury in a vague sort of way that the station-master's refusal to swear to the identity of the Strood man is of no consequence."

"It is quite possible that the judge may refuse to allow the house affair to be introduced at all."

"Quite," he agreed, "especially if the defence objects. But still, I am not happy about the case. The intention of the prosecution to introduce this irrelevant matter to prejudice the jury and their suppression of the evidence regarding the poisoned cigar – which really is highly relevant – suggests a very determined effort to obtain a conviction."

"I take it that you do not entertain the possibility that Dobey may have committed the murder?"

"No, I don't think I do. As you say, we know the case for the prosecution and we know that it is a bad case. There is a total lack of positive evidence. But, still, there is the chance that they may get a conviction. That would be a disaster, and it would, at once, raise the question as to what we should have to do. Obviously, we couldn't let an innocent man go to the gallows. But it would be a very difficult position."

"What are the chances of a conviction, so far as you can see?"

"That depends on what Dobey has to say. The case for the prosecution rests on the finding of the stolen document in his flat. There is no denying that that is a highly incriminating circumstance and, if he can produce nothing more than a mere denial of having taken it, the chances will be decidedly against him."

"It is difficult to see what answer he can give," said I. "The document was certainly taken from Badger, before or after his death. It was certainly found in Dobey's flat, and apparently Dobey was the sole occupant of that flat. I don't see how he is going to escape from those facts."

"Neither do I," said Thorndyke. "But we shall hear what he has to say to-morrow, and if he is found guilty, we shall have to consider very seriously what our next move is to be."

With this, the subject dropped. But, at intervals during the evening, my thoughts went back to it, and I found myself wondering whether Thorndyke had not perhaps allowed himself to undervalue the evidence against Dobey. The finding of that document in his rooms would take a great deal of explaining.

My intention to hear the case from the beginning was frustrated by a troublesome solicitor who first failed to keep an appointment, and then detained me inordinately, so that when, at last, I arrived at the Central Criminal Court and, having hurriedly donned my wig and gown, slipped into the counsels' seats beside Thorndyke, the case for the prosecution was nearly concluded. But by the fact that the finger-print expert was then giving evidence, I knew that the prosecution had succeeded in introducing the house-breaking incident. As I listened to the evidence, I looked quickly round the court to identify the various *dramatis personae* and, naturally, looked first at the dock, where the prisoner stood "on his deliverance", listening with stolid calm to the apparently indestructible evidence of the expert.

As I looked him over critically, I was not surprised at the eagerness with which the police had fastened on his salient peculiarities. He was quite a striking figure. Dull and commonplace enough in face and feature, the combination of a rather untidy mop of dark-red hair with a noticeably red nose set in a large pale face made him an ideal subject for identification. From the prisoner I turned to his defending solicitor, Mr. Coleman, who sat at the solicitors' table, listening with sphinx-like impassiveness to the expert's authoritative pronouncements. Equally unmoved was the prisoner's counsel, a good-looking man named Lyon who specialized in criminal practice. The counsel for the prosecution, a Mr. Barnes, was on his feet at the moment, and his junior, Mr. Callow, was industriously taking notes of the evidence.

"Have the defence objected to this evidence?" I asked Thorndyke in a whisper, as the leader for the Crown put what seemed to be his final question.

"No," was the reply. "The judge questioned the relevance of it, but, as the defence did not seem interested, he gave no ruling."

It seemed to me that Mr. Dobey's case was being rather mismanaged, and I was confirmed in this opinion when his counsel rose to cross-examine.

"You have stated that the marks on this window glass are the prints of the prisoner's fingers. Are you quite certain that those marks were not made by the fingers of some other person?"

"The chances against their having been made by the fingers of any person other than the prisoner are several thousand-millions."

"But is it not possible that you may have made some mistake in the comparison? You don't, I suppose, claim to be infallible?"

"I claim that the method employed at the Bureau is infallible. It does not depend on personal judgment, but on comparison, detail by detail, of the questioned finger-print with the one which is known. I have made the comparison with the greatest care, and I am certain that I have made no mistake."

"And do you swear, positively, of your certain knowledge, that the marks on this window-glass were made by the fingers of the prisoner?

"I do," was the reply, whereupon, having thus unnecessarily piled up the evidence against his client, Mr. Lyon sat down with an air of calm satisfaction. I was astonished at the apparent stupidity of the proceeding. It is seldom worthwhile to cross-examine finger-print experts at all closely, for the more they are pressed, the more do they affirm their absolute certainty. And I noticed that my surprise seemed to be shared by the judge, who glanced with a sort of impatient perplexity from the counsel to the sphinx-like solicitor who was instructing him. It must be an exasperating experience for a judge – who knows all the ropes – to have to watch a counsel making a hopeless muddle of a case.

The next witness was a middle-aged woman who gave the name of Martha Bunsbury, and who was examined by Mr. Barnes in the plain, straightforward fashion proper to a prosecuting counsel.

"Kindly look at the prisoner and tell us whether you recognise him."

The witness bestowed a disdainful stare on the prisoner, and replied, promptly, "Yes. I picked him out of a whole crowd at Brixton Prison."

"Where and when had you seen him before that?"

"I saw him on the second of August, breaking into a house in Sudbury Park. I happened to be at the window at the back of my house when I heard the sound of glass being broken. So I looked out, and then I saw the prisoner getting into the back window of the house in Sudbury Park that is just opposite mine. So I opened the window and called out. Then I ran down to the garden and gave the alarm to two men who were coming along the towing-path of the canal."

"And what happened next?"

"The lady next door to me came out into her garden and she began to call out too. Then the two men started to run along the tow-path towards the bridge, but the prisoner, who had heard us giving the alarm, backed out of the window and ran across the garden with his coat on his arm. When he came to the wall, he laid the coat on the top of it, because the wall has broken glass all along the top, and climbed over. But, as he dropped down outside, the coat dropped down inside. He turned round, and was going to climb back to get it, but by that time, the two men were running over the bridge. So he left the coat and made off up a side lane between two houses. And that is the last I saw of him."

"Yes. A very excellent description," said Mr. Barnes. "But now I want you to be extremely careful. Look again at the prisoner, and see if you are quite certain that he is really the man whom you saw in the garden of that house. It is most important that there should be no possibility of a mistake."

"There isn't," was the immediate and confident reply. "I am perfectly certain that he is the man."

On this, Mr. Barnes sat down and Mr. Lyon rose to cross-examine.

"You have said that you saw the housebreaker from the back window of your house, breaking a back window of a house opposite. How far would that window be from yours?"

"I really couldn't say. A fair distance. Not so very far."

"You spoke of a canal. Is the opposite house on the same side of the canal as your house?"

"No, of course it isn't. How could it be? It is on the opposite side."

"And how long is your garden?"

"Oh, a moderate length. You know what London gardens are."

"Should I be right in saying that, at the time that you saw this man, you were separated from him by the length of two gardens and the width of the canal?"

"Yes. That is what I said."

"And you say that, having seen this total stranger at that very considerable distance, you are quite certain that you are able to recognize and remember him?"

"Yes, I am quite certain."

"Can you tell us how you are able to identify him with such certainty?"

"Well," said the witness, "there's his nose, you see. I could see that."

"Quite so. You looked upon the nose when it was red."

"I should think it is always red," said Mrs. Bunsbury. "At any rate, it was red then, and it is red now. And then there is his hair."

"Very true. There is his hair. But he is not the only man in the world with a red nose and red hair."

"I don't know anything about that," replied the witness, doggedly. "But I do know that he is the man. I'd swear to him among ten-thousand."

This apparently finished Mr. Lyon for, having again prejudiced his client's case to the best of his ability, he sat down with unimpaired complacency.

The next witness, Miss Doris Gray, gave evidence to the same effect, though with somewhat less emphasis and, when she had been cross-examined and finally vacated the witness-box, Mr. Barnes rose and announced that that was his case. As soon as he sat down, Mr. Lyon rose and made his announcement.

"I call witnesses, my Lord."

397

"Now," Thorndyke said to me in a low tone, "we are going to see whether there is really a case for the defence."

"They haven't made much of it up to the present," I remarked.

"Exactly," he replied. "That is what makes me a little hopeful. They have certainly given the prosecution plenty of rope."

I should have liked to have this observation elucidated somewhat – and so, probably, would Superintendent Miller, who, at this moment, came forth from some inconspicuous corner and took his place at the solicitors' table, for there was more than a shade of anxiety on his face as he looked expectantly at the witness-box. But there was no opportunity for explanations. Even as Miller took his seat, the first witness for the defence was called, and appeared in the person of a pleasant-looking middle-aged lady wearing the uniform of a trained nurse, and bearing, it transpired, the name of Helen Royden. In reply to a question from Mr. Lyon, she deposed that she was the matron of the cottage hospital at Hook Green, near Biddenden in Kent.

"Will you kindly look at the prisoner and tell us if you recognize him?"

The witness turned her head and cast a smiling glance at the accused (whereupon Mr. Dobey's rather saturnine countenance relaxed into a friendly grin), "Yes," she replied, "I recognize him as Mr. Charles Dobey, lately a patient at my hospital."

"When did you last see him?"

"On the first of October, when he was discharged from hospital."

"What were the date and the circumstances of his admission?"

"He was brought to the hospital on the thirtieth of July by Dr. Wale, the medical officer of the hospital, suffering from a compound fracture of the left tibia. I understand that the doctor found him lying in the road."

"Do you remember the exact time at which he was brought in?"

"It was a little before eleven in the forenoon." As the dates were mentioned, I observed the judge and the two prosecuting counsel hurriedly turn over their notes with an expression of astonishment and incredulity, and the jury very visibly "sat up and took notice".

"Did you communicate with any of the patient's relatives?"

"Yes. At the patient's request, I wrote to his wife, who lives at East Malling in Kent, informing her of his admission, and inviting her to come and see him."

"And did she come?"

"Yes. She came the next day, and I allowed her to stay the night at the hospital. After that, she came to see him usually twice a week."

"Have you any doubt that the prisoner is the man whom you have described as your patient, Charles Dobey?"

"No. I couldn't very well be mistaken. He was in the hospital just over two months, and I saw him several times every day, and often had quite long talks with him. Ours is a small hospital, and the patients are rather like a family."

"Did you learn what his occupation was?"

"Yes. He described himself as a plumber and gas-fitter."

"Had you any reason to doubt that that was his real occupation?"

"None whatever. In fact, we had evidence that it was for, when he was convalescent and able to get about, he repaired all the taps in the hospital, and did a number of odd jobs. He seemed to be quite a clever workman."

"Do you keep a record of admissions and discharges?"

"Yes. I have brought the register with me."

Here she produced from a business-like hand-bag a rather chubby quarto volume which she opened at a marked place and handed to the usher, who conveyed it to the counsel. When the latter had examined it and verified the dates, he passed it up to the judge, who scanned it curiously and compared it with his notes. Finally, it was handed to the prosecuting counsel, who appeared to gaze on it with stupefaction, and returned it to Mr. Lyon, who handed it back to the usher for transmission to the witness. This concluded the examination-in-chief, and Mr. Lyon accordingly thanked the witness and sat down. I waited curiously for the cross-examination, but neither of the Crown counsel made any sign. The judge glanced at them enquiringly and, after a short pause, the witness was dismissed and her place taken by her successor. The new witness was a shrewd-looking, clean-shaved man, in whom I seemed to recognize a professional brother. And a doctor he turned out to be, one Egbert Wale by name, and the medical officer of the Hook Green Cottage Hospital. Having given the usual particulars, and been asked the inevitable question, he deposed as follows:

"On the thirtieth of last July, at about twenty minutes to eleven in the forenoon, I was driving down a by-road between Headcorn and Biddenden when I saw a man lying in the road. I stopped my car and got out to examine him, when I found that he had sustained a compound fracture of the left leg below the knee. I accordingly dressed the wound, put on a temporary splint, lifted him into my car, and drove him to the Hook Green Cottage Hospital, of which I am visiting medical officer. He gave the name of Charles Dobey, and explained that he had broken his leg in dropping from a motor-lorry on which he had taken a free lift without the knowledge of the driver. I detained him in the hospital for two months, and discharged him as convalescent on the first of October."

"Did Dobey make a good recovery?"

"Yes, excellent. When he left the hospital, the wound was quite healed, and the broken bone firmly united, but there was a large knob of callus, or new bone, which, I hope, will disappear in time."

"Would you recognize the wound if you were to examine it?"

"Certainly I should. I saw it last only about three weeks ago."

"Then, if his Lordship will grant his permission, I will ask you to make the examination."

His Lordship – bearing in mind, no doubt, the evidence of the finger-print experts – gave his permission readily, whereupon the doctor came out of the witness-box and went over to the dock. There he proceeded dexterously to unwind a length of bandage from the prisoner's leg – which had been exposed by its owner in readiness for the inspection – and examine the member by sight and touch. Then he replaced the bandage and returned to the witness-box.

"What is the result of your examination?" Mr. Lyon asked.

"I find the wound and the fracture in much the same condition as when I saw it last about three weeks ago."

"You have no doubt that it is the same injury?"

"Not the slightest. I recognize every detail of it."

"What is meant by a compound fracture? Is it a very serious injury?"

"A compound fracture is a break in a bone accompanied by a wound of the flesh and skin which communicates with the broken part of the bone and exposes it to the air. It is always a serious injury, even under modern surgical conditions, because the wound and the fracture have both to be treated, and each may interfere with the treatment of the other."

"And you have no doubt that the prisoner is the person whom you treated at the hospital?"

"I identify the prisoner as the man of whom I am speaking. I am quite certain that he is the same person."

On receiving this answer, Mr. Lyon sat down, and the witness looked expectantly at the counsel for the prosecution. But as before, they made no sign and, accordingly, the witness was dismissed. As he retired, the foreman of the jury rose and announced that he and his colleagues did not want to hear any more evidence. "The jury are of opinion," he added, "that this is a case of mistaken identity."

"It is difficult to avoid that conclusion," the judge admitted. Then, turning to the prisoner's counsel, he enquired what further evidence he had proposed to offer. "I had proposed to call the prisoner's wife, my Lord, and then to put the prisoner in the box."

The judge reflected for a few moments and then, addressing the foreman, said, "I think, in fairness to the prisoner, we should hear the rest of the evidence. You will note that the question of the document has not been cleared up. That document was found, you will remember, on premises belonging to the prisoner. We had better hear the evidence, though it may not be necessary for the learned counsel for the defence to address you." The jury having agreed to this eminently sensible suggestion, the prisoner's wife, Elizabeth Dobey, was called and took her place in the witness-box.

"Is the address at East Mailing that you have given your permanent address? Is that your home?" Mr. Lyon asked, when the preliminaries had been disposed of, and the witness had described herself as the wife of Charles Dobey, the prisoner, "Yes. We rent a cottage with a nice bit of garden. My husband is very fond of gardening."

"With regard to the flat in London, 103 Barnard's Buildings? Do you spend much of your time there?"

"Me? I have never been there at all. It isn't a flat. It's just a place where my husband can sleep and cook a meal when he is in Town, looking for a job."

"Do you remember when the prisoner first went up to Barnard's Buildings after he came home from the hospital?"

"He only went up once. That was when the police took him. It was about a week after he came home – on the eighth of October."

"Did he send anyone else up to the flat, before he went himself?"

"No. There wasn't anyone to send, and there wasn't any reason to send them." This concluded the examination-in-chief. But this time, as Mr. Lyon resumed his seat, Mr. Barnes rose with remarkable promptitude. "You have said that your husband kept this flat in London to sleep in when he was looking for a job. What kind of jobs would he be looking for?"

"He is a plumber and gas-fitter by trade. He would be looking for jobs in his own line, of course."

"You have heard the police witnesses state that they found in that flat a number of burglars' tools, a quantity of stolen jewellery, and a stolen document. Do those tools and that stolen property suggest anything to you as to the kind of jobs that your husband went to London to look for?"

"No, they have got nothing to do with his trade."

"Can you account for the presence of burglars' tools and stolen property in the rooms of a plumber and gas-fitter?"

"Yes, I can," Mrs. Dobey replied, viciously, "after all the false swearing that there has been in this court to-day. If you ask me, I should

401

say that the police put them there." At this rather unexpected reply a low rumble of laughter filled the court, including the jury box, and a faint, appreciative smile stole over the judge's face, and was even reflected on the countenance of Mr. Barnes himself.

"I am afraid," he said, good-humouredly, "that you are taking a prejudiced view. But with regard to this flat, have you ever taken any measures to ascertain what your husband does at those rooms?"

"No," she replied. "I don't go spying on my husband. It isn't necessary. I can trust him, if other people can't."

Here it apparently dawned upon Mr. Barnes that he was not going to do his case any good with this witness, Accordingly, he thanked her and resumed his seat and, as Mr. Lyon was not disposed to re-examine, Mrs. Dobey retired in triumph, and her husband was conducted from the dock to the witness-box.

When he had been sworn and had given the usual particulars, his counsel directed him to describe his movements after his escape from the prison, which he did with picturesque conciseness.

"As soon as I was clear of the prison, I scooted round a corner into a by-street, and there I saw a motor wagon piled up with empty baskets. The driver was cranking up the engine and, as there was nobody in sight, I climbed up behind and laid down on the floor among the baskets. Then the driver got up and off she went. When we got out somewhere between Headcorn and Biddenden, the wagon turned down a by-lane, and as I thought that we might be getting near the farm that we seemed to be bound for, I decided to hop off. So I did. But she was going faster than I thought, and I came down a cropper and broke my leg. I laid there in the road for about a quarter-of-an-hour, and then the doctor came along and picked me up, and took me off to the hospital. And there I stayed until I was discharged on the first of October."

"When did you first go up to your London flat?"

"I only went once. That was when I had been at home just over a week – on the eighth of October. The detectives came and collared me just as I was picking the lock to let myself in."

"Why did you have to pick the lock?"

"Because I hadn't got my key. They took all the things out of my pockets at Maidstone police-station. But I had forgotten that I hadn't got my key until I was close to the Buildings, so I had to pop into an ironmonger's shop and get a piece of wire. And I was picking the lock with that piece of wire when the cops nabbed me."

"You have heard about the burglars' tools and the stolen property that the police found in your room. Can you tell us anything about them?"

"No, I don't know anything about them. They were not mine, and I didn't put them there. Somebody must have got into the rooms and planted them there while I was in the hospital."

"Have you any idea who might have planted those things, and for what purpose?"

"I should think anyone could see what they were planted for. It was to put this murder on to me. But, as to who planted them, if the police didn't – and I suppose they didn't, though they do seem to have been working the oracle a bit – it must have been the person who did the murder, seeing that he had got the paper that was taken from the murdered man."

"Do you swear that you never went to the flat after leaving the hospital until the eighth of October?"

"I do. I shouldn't have gone there a second time with a bit of wire to let myself in. I should have got a key."

This was Mr. Lyon's final question and, as he sat down, Mr. Barnes rose to cross-examine, but with no great show of enthusiasm. He began by pressing the witness for a clearer explanation of the purpose for which he kept the rooms in London. But at this point the foreman of the jury again intervened with a protest that the jury were not interested in the prisoner's occupation, and that they did not want to hear any more evidence, whereupon Mr. Barnes sat down with no appearance of reluctance, and the judge enquired of Mr. Lyon if he desired to address the jury.

"If the gentlemen of the jury have come to a decision," was the reply, "it would be useless for me to occupy the time of the court with an address."

Accordingly, the prisoner was led back to the dock, and the judge proceeded to make a few observations.

"I do not pretend to understand this case," said he. "We have been told that it is an impossibility for two different persons to have identically similar finger-prints. Yet here, the impossible seems to have happened. Finger-prints which have been identified as those of the prisoner were made in a house in London on the second of August, at which time the prisoner appears to have been lying, with a broken leg, in a hospital some forty miles away. It would seem that there is some person whose finger-prints are identical with those of the prisoner and, unfortunately for the prisoner, that person appears to be a house-breaker. However, there is no use in trying to resolve this puzzle, for after all, the question is not relevant to the issue that you are trying. What you have to decide is whether you are prepared to accept as true the evidence of the matron of the hospital and Dr. Wale. If their evidence is true, it is

403

physically impossible that the prisoner could have committed the murder with which he is charged. That is for you to decide, and I do not think that I need say anything more."

When the judge had finished speaking, the grey-wigged clerk of the court rose and put the formal question, "Are you all agreed upon your verdict, gentlemen?"

To which the foreman replied, promptly: "We are."

"What do you say, gentlemen? Is the prisoner Guilty or Not Guilty?"

"Not guilty," was the reply, delivered with noticeable emphasis.

The judge briefly expressed his entire concurrence, and then proceeded.

"I understand that the prisoner, having escaped from prison while awaiting his trial, is still in custody, on the original charge. Have you any instructions on the subject?

"Yes, my Lord," replied Mr. Barnes. "It appears that the bill was presented to the Grand Jury at Maidstone on the day on which the prisoner absconded. There would seem to have been some error in presenting the bill, but at any rate, the Grand Jury threw it out."

"I am glad to hear that," said the judge. Then, addressing the prisoner, he continued. "Charles Dobey, you have been tried for the crime on which you were indicted, and have been found not guilty – very properly, as I think – and, as the bill in respect of the original offence has been thrown out by the Grand Jury at Maidstone, there is now no charge against you, and you are accordingly discharged."

He accompanied the rather dry statement with a smile and a kindly nod, which Dobey acknowledged with a low bow and, as the gate of the dock was now thrown open, he descended to meet, with a somewhat stolid grin, the effusive greetings of his wife and the congratulations of his friends from the hospital.

"Well," I said, as we rose to depart, "I hope you find the result of the trial satisfactory."

"I do," Thorndyke replied, "but I don't think Miller does. He looks most uncommonly glum. But I do not feel sympathetic. The police – if they instructed the prosecution – have been hoist with their own petard. They insisted on dragging in these finger-prints and those two women, whose evidence was quite irrelevant and was intended merely to discredit the prisoner, and behold the result. From this time forward, Dobey is practically immune from finger-print evidence and evidence of personal identification. He can prove, from the records of this trial, that there is some person who is engaged in the practice of house-breaking, who is in appearance his exact double, and whose finger-prints are identically similar to his. He can actually quote the judge to that effect."

"Yes," I agreed. "Dobey need not trouble to wear gloves now, if he really is a cracksman, as I have no doubt he is. One cannot help admiring the masterly strategy of the defence in egging on the prosecution to play their trump cards and prove those very facts. But even now, I don't see how you came to be so certain of Dobey's innocence. You knew nothing about the alibi. And apart from that, there was a case against him. Yet apparently you never entertained the possibility of his being guilty."

"I don't think I did," he admitted, "and, if you will reconsider the case in general terms and in detail, I think you will see why. Let me recommend you to do this now, as the completion of the case devolves on us. I must stay and have a few words with Miller, and I suggest that you go on ahead and spend half-an-hour in going over the case with an open mind. You know where to find our notes of the case. Get them out and look them through. Note all the facts that are known to us, consider them separately and as a whole, and see if there does not emerge a perfectly coherent theory of the crime. The evidence that you have heard to-day, inasmuch as it is in agreement with that theory, ought to be helpful to you."

"When you speak of a theory of the crime," said I, "do you mean a general theory, or one capable of a particular application?"

"Our function," he replied, "is to discover the identity of the person who murdered Inspector Badger, and the theory that I refer to is one which is capable of leading us to that discovery."

With this he stepped out into the body of the court to go in search of the Superintendent, and I made my way to the robing-room to divest myself of wig and gown before issuing forth into places of public resort.

Chapter XIV
A Startling Discovery

On my way westward from the Old Bailey to the Temple, I turned over in my mind Thorndyke's last statement. Its exact meaning was not perfectly clear to me, but what I did gather was that he had enough knowledge of the circumstances surrounding Badger's death to make the belief in Dobey's guilt untenable. That implied some positive knowledge pointing to the guilt of some other person, but as to whether that other person was an actual individual to whom a name could be given, or a mere abstraction whom we had yet to convert into a reality, I was unable to decide. What did, however, emerge clearly from his statement was that whatever facts were known to him were also known to me. My problem, therefore, was to examine the facts that I already knew, and try to extract their significance, which I had apparently missed up to the present.

When I arrived at our chambers, I became aware, by certain familiar signs, that Polton had returned from his expedition to Hartsden, and was engaged in some kind of photographic work in the laboratory. Presumably, he was developing the films from the "automatic watcher", and I was tempted to go up and see what luck he had had. But I restrained my curiosity and, having drawn a chair up to the table and procured a note-block and pencil, I went to the cabinet in which the portfolios of current cases were kept and unlocked it. The one labelled "*Inspector Badger, Deceased*", was uppermost, with the finger-print measuring-glass lying on its cover. I lifted them out together and, laying the glass on the table, opened the portfolio and began to glance through its contents, laying the papers out in their order as to the dates.

The first that I picked up I put aside, as it did not appear to belong to the series. It was a rough copy of the entry that Thorndyke had made in his note-book when we were experimenting on the Thumbograph, and had apparently been put in the portfolio out of the way – though it was extremely unlike Thorndyke to put anything in its wrong place. Then I began to go through the various notes, *seriatim*, trying to refresh my memory as to the order of the events and the way in which the case had developed. But as I turned over the notes, I was aware of a growing sense of disappointment. There was nothing new, nothing that I did not remember quite clearly without their aid. I glanced through the brief notes of our expedition to Greenhithe. It was all fresh in my memory. The description of the body, the examination of the tunnel, the finding of

406

the cigar, then the analysis of the cigar, the report of the inquest, and the evidence of the witnesses. I knew it all, and it conveyed nothing to me but a mysterious crime of which we held not a single clue to guide us to the identity of the perpetrator. There was a brief summary of Miller's account of the house-breaking incident, which did now, after the event, point pretty definitely to a personation and the making of false finger-prints. But there was no suggestion as to the identity of the personator. To me, the whole case remained in the air.

At the end of the portfolio was a separate folder labelled "*Finger-prints*", which I took out, doggedly, but with a sense of deep discouragement. Nothing could be much less illuminating than a collection of unidentified finger-prints. Nevertheless, I opened the folder and began to look through the collection. There were Badger's prints, devoid of any meaning to me, and the photograph of Dobey's, taken from the official paper that Miller had shown us, which told me nothing at all. Then I opened a smaller folder, labelled "*Prints from Cigar*". There were two sets of photographs, one the natural size and the other enlarged to about four diameters. Discarding the smaller photographs, I examined the enlargements, and read the inscriptions written below them, with as much attention as I could muster, for, little as they conveyed to me, I realized that they constituted evidence of the highest importance, if only the opportunity should ever come to apply it.

The first was Inspector Badger's left thumb, remarkably clear for a developed print. But though it was, in effect, an indictment of murder, it gave me no help, since I knew already that poor Badger had been murdered. I laid it down and took up the next. "*Right Thumb of Person Unknown*". Having read the inscription, I glanced at the print. This one, too, was admirably clear and distinct. The experts should have no difficulty in identifying it if they could get a known print with which to compare it. Not only was the general pattern – a very distinctive one – perfectly plain, but all the minor "characteristics" were easily legible.

I sat with the print in my hand and my eyes fixed on it musingly, reflecting on all that it meant and all that it did not mean. This thumb-print had been made by the man who had given the poisoned cigar to poor Badger – who had almost certainly murdered him, who had personated Dobey at the sham house-breaking, and who had entered Dobey's flat and there planted the stolen document. It was capable of giving infallible proof of that villain's identity, and yet it offered not the faintest hint as to what manner of man that villain might be. In spite of our possession of this infallible touchstone we might pass this murderer in the street a hundred times without the faintest glimmer of suspicion as

407

to who he was. A finger-print is a poor instrument with which to start the search for an unknown criminal.

As I sat thus, with my eyes fixed only half-consciously on the print, I became aware of a dim sense of familiarity. A finger-print is, to an accustomed eye, much more easy to remember than might be supposed and, as my eye rested on this print, I began to have the feeling that I had seen it before. At first the feeling was not more than vaguely reminiscent, but yet it was enough to arouse my attention. I looked, now, with a critical and purposeful scrutiny and a definite effort of memory. And then, suddenly, in a flash, the revelation came and left me gazing open-mouthed.

It was amazing, incredible – so incredible that I sought instantly for corroboration or disproof. Snatching up the measuring-glass, and picking out the natural-sized print, I placed the central dot of the scale of circles on the summit of the central character of the core and wrote down on the note-block the measurements shown. The pattern was intermediate between a whorl and a twinned loop, but, remembering Thorndyke's rule, I treated it as a whorl. Then, as it was a left-handed, or anti-clockwise, whorl, and as the "core-character" lay entirely within the centre circle ("*Space A*"), the whorl was of the type *A3*. I wrote this down, and then measured the distance to the right delta. The latter was intersected by the circle, *C*, and therefore, by the rule, lay in the space, *D*. The ridge tracing was clearly outside the delta, and I therefore wrote down *O*. The left delta was outside the print, and therefore could not be located. The number of ridges between the centre of the core and the right delta was twelve, while the left ridge-count – since the left delta was outside the print – was unascertainable.

When I had finished, I set out my results in the regular formula, so far as I remembered the method, thus:

> *Right thumb – Unknown.*
> *W (? T.L.). Core, A3, ?, O, D, ?, 12.*

Then I turned back through the portfolio until I found the slip of paper on which Thorndyke had copied the entry in his note-book. The first eager glance at it I showed me that my memory had not deceived me.

The entry ran:

> *Walter Hornby. Right thumb.*
> *W (? T.L.). Core, A3, ? , O, D, ?, 12.*

In addition to the formula, Thorndyke had written down a few of the "ridge characteristics" with their ridge-counts from the centre of the core, and a direction-arrow to show their position, thus:

-}3, Lake, 5, Bif., 8, End, 10, Bif.
{-7, Lake, 9, Bif., 11, Lake.

With intense excitement, I proceeded to verify these characters, not a little surprised at the ease with which they could be recognized and located. Taking first the right direction-arrow, and counting the ridges from the centre of the core, I found in the third ridge one of those little loops, or eyes, known, technically, as "lakes". The fifth ridge divided into a fork, or bifurcation, the eighth ridge terminated abruptly in a free end, and the tenth showed another bifurcation. Then, following the left direction-arrow, the seventh ridge showed a small lake, the ninth a bifurcation, and the eleventh a larger lake. The agreement was complete in every detail.

I laid down the print and reflected on this amazing discovery, still hardly able to credit the evidence of my eyes. For the thing seemed beyond belief. The murderous wretch whose tracks we had been following was none other than Walter Hornby. After all these years, during which I had almost forgotten his very existence, he had suddenly swum into the field of our vision like some strange and horrible apparition. Yet my astonishment was hardly justified, for no detail of his recent villainy was in any way out of character with his past, as it was known to me.

Presently my thoughts took another turn. By what means had Thorndyke been able to identify Badger's murderer as Walter Hornby? It had been no chance shot. The discovery of Hornby's thumb-print in the Thumbograph had been no mere accident. It was now evident to me that Thorndyke had come to our house with the express purpose of seeking that thumb-print, if it was in existence, as was manifest from the fact that he had come equipped with the measuring-glass, and from the anxiety that he had shown as to the fate of the Thumbograph. Clearly, that was the final verification of a theory that was already complete in his mind. Indeed, he had, in effect, said as much this very day in court. He had spoken of "a coherent theory of the crime", an expression that would have been quite inapplicable to the chance discovery of a finger-print. Now, how, from the information that we possessed, had he arrived at this astonishing conclusion?

It is proverbially easy to be wise after the event. "Jobbing back", as this mental exercise is named on the Stock Exchange, is considerably simpler than jobbing forward. So I found it on the present occasion. Now that the conclusion was known to me, I was in a favourable position to consider the processes of reasoning which had led to it. And when I did so, and when I recalled the hints that Thorndyke had dropped from time to time, I was surprised that no inkling of the truth had ever dawned on me. For what Thorndyke had said was perfectly true. When all the facts were considered, separately and as a whole, a consistent theory of the crime emerged, and inevitably brought the figure of Walter Hornby into the picture.

Taking the facts separately, there were those that related to technique and method and those that related to motive. The technique in the present crime included the use of a poisoned cigar and of counterfeit finger-prints. But this was the technique employed, years ago, by Walter Hornby, and it was not only a peculiar and distinctive technique, it was absolutely unique. No other criminal, so far as I had ever heard, had employed it. Then the method of employing it was the same in both cases. In the Hornby case – the case of *The Red Thumb Mark* – an original finger-print (in the Thumbograph) had been obtained from the victim, Reuben Hornby, from which to make, by photo mechanical process, the stamps for the counterfeits. In the Badger case, a sheet of finger-prints had been stolen, evidently for the same purpose. Again, in both cases, the forged finger-prints had been "planted" at the scene of the crime. In short, the technique and method in the Badger case repeated, in the main, those of the Red Thumb Mark case.

Then the motive showed a like similarity in the two cases. When Walter Hornby had tried to murder Thorndyke (by means of a poisoned cigar), his motive was to get rid of the only person who suspected him. As to the motive for the murder of Badger, Miller was almost certainly right, although he had guessed wrong as to the identity of the murderer. Badger's uncanny memory for faces had made him a dangerous enemy. And we had Miller's statement that Badger was the only officer who was able to identify Walter Hornby.

Finally, taking the whole set of facts together, the similarity of the two cases was very striking. In each crime, the criminal act had been preceded by a careful preparation to incriminate an innocent person. There had been a systematic scheme of false evidence, thought out and arranged in advance with remarkable completeness and ingenuity, before the criminal had committed himself. Thus, as a whole and in detail, the murder of Inspector Badger virtually repeated a crime which was known to me, and which was utterly unlike any other crime of which I had ever heard. Reluctantly, I had to admit that I had been distinctly "slow in the uptake".

I had just reached this rather unsatisfactory conclusion when I heard a latchkey inserted in the outer door. A moment later, Thorndyke entered and, as his eye lighted on the open portfolio, be greeted me with the enquiry, "Well, what says my learned friend? Has he reached any conclusion?"

By way of answer, I wrote on a scrap of paper: "*X=Walter Hornby*" and pushed it along the table towards him.

"Yes," he said, when he had glanced at it, "history repeats itself. We had this equation once before, you remember."

"I remember," said I, "and I ought to have remembered sooner. But, tell me, Thorndyke, when did you first suspect Hornby in this case?"

"The word 'suspect'," he replied, "is a little indefinite. But I may say that when we established the fact of a poisoned cigar, the name of Walter Hornby inevitably floated into my mind, especially as the cigar was associated with a stolen sheet of finger-prints which were pretty evidently not those of the person who stole them. In fact, I adopted, provisionally, the hypothesis that the murderer was Walter Hornby, but only as a mere possibility which had to be borne in mind while further developments were being watched for. I argued that if the hypothesis was correct, certain events might be confidently expected to follow. There would be some crime, probably committed in daylight by a man with red hair and a red nose, who would leave Frederick Smith's finger-prints at the scene of the crime, and the stolen paper would be found in some place connected with Frederick Smith.

"As you know, these events occurred exactly according to plan. Thereupon, the mere hypothesis became a very weighty probability. But the *experimentum crucis* was made possible by Juliet. When the Thumbograph had spoken, the hypothesis passed into the domain of established fact."

"Yes," I said. "You have established the murderer's identity beyond any reasonable doubt. The next thing is to ascertain his whereabouts. At present he is no more than a name."

"That," he replied, "is Miller's problem. The police have all the facilities for finding a wanted man. We have none. By the way, have, you seen Polton?"

"No," I replied, "but I expect you will see him before long. He always knows, in some occult way, when you come in. In fact, I think I hear him approaching at this moment."

Almost as I spoke, the door opened and Polton entered, bearing a large vulcanite dish and a long strip of cinematograph film. There was no need to ask for his news, for his face was one large and incredibly crinkly smile of triumph and satisfaction.

411

"We've brought it off, sir," he announced, gleefully, "first shot. I went down to the Manor House this morning, and I waited by the camera until I heard the twelve-o'clock exposure go off. Then I took out the roll-holder and put in a fresh one. But I don't think you will want it. I have developed the strip – nine exposures, altogether, but only two of them matter, and those two I have enlarged to half-plate. They are those made at twelve o'clock on Tuesday and twelve o'clock to-day."

He laid the dish on the table, and watched Thorndyke ecstatically as the latter stooped over it to examine the enlargements.

"The top one is the Tuesday exposure," he explained. "Shows the room just as you saw it, with the box on the table. The bottom one is to-day's. You see there's no box there, and the arm-chair has been moved about a couple of inches, as you can see by the sash of the case behind it."

"Yes," Thorndyke agreed, "it is a true bill, Polton. The box is gone from the table, and boxes don't fly away of themselves. By the way, Polton, what do you make of that box?"

"Well, sir," was the reply, "if it didn't seem so unlikely, I should have said that it looked like a casting-box, one of those biggish flasks that silversmiths use for casting the blanks of things like spoons. It is certainly a metal box, and those things at the side look very much like pin-lugs."

"So I thought," said Thorndyke, "but we shall probably know all about it, before long. At any rate, Polton, you have solved our problem for us, and now we can go ahead with confidence. I shall send Mr. Woodburn a letter and a telegram. He will probably get the letter to-morrow morning, but the telegram will make it safer."

"There's the telephone, sir," Polton suggested.

"Yes, I know," said Thorndyke "but when I whisper secrets, I like to know whose ear they are going into."

"What are you going to say to him?" I asked.

"I shall ask him to meet us to-morrow morning and bring the key of the gallery door. That is what we arranged."

"Then you are going to break the seals and explore the rooms?"

"Certainly. There is now no doubt that someone visits those rooms, and as the next visit seems to be due to-morrow night, we may as well be there to give the visitor a hospitable reception."

"Shall you want me to come with you, sir?" Polton enquired, anxiously.

My impression was that Thorndyke did not particularly want him. But the wistfulness of the little man's face proved irresistible.

"I think you had better come, Polton," he said, "and bring a few tools with you. But it would be as well if you went on ahead of us, so that we don't make too large a party. We mustn't be too noticeable."

"No, sir," Polton agreed, undisguisedly jubilant at being included in the expeditionary party. "I will go down by the early train. Are there any tools in particular that you wish me to bring?"

"Well, Polton," Thorndyke replied, "you know what our problem is. Someone has got into these rooms by some means other than an ordinary door. We may have to pick one or two locks, and they may be rather unusual locks. I would not suggest burglars' tools, because, of course, you haven't any. If you had, they might be useful."

Polton crinkled knowingly as he protested, "There is nothing improper about burglars' tools in themselves. It is the use that is made of them. The tools are quite innocent if they are used for a lawful purpose."

Having delivered himself of this slightly questionable legal dictum, he departed, leaving the photographs for us to examine at our leisure.

Very curious productions they were. I took up the strip of film and examined the tiny negatives through my pocket lens. Small as they were – barely an inch-and-a-half square – they were full of minute detail, and the enlargements, magnified about four diameters, were as clear as if they had been taken with a full-sized camera. The "Automatic Watcher" had turned out, in respect of its efficiency, far beyond my expectations.

"Yes," said Thorndyke, in reply to my admiring comments, "with first-class lenses, you can get surprising results. In fact, the only limit to enlargement is the grain of the film. But we had better put the photographs away for the present, as I am expecting Miller to drop in at any moment. He is dreadfully disgruntled at the result of the trial, though the fiasco is very largely of his own producing. Still, we shall have to try to comfort him, and it had occurred to me that we might take him into this Hartsden adventure. What do you think? We really ought to have a police officer with us."

"Yes, I think it is rather necessary," I agreed. "We don't want a search warrant, as we are acting with Woodburn's authority, but, as we may have to make an arrest, it would be more regular to have a police officer to direct that part of the business. Besides, we don't know how many we may have to deal with. It looks like a one-man job, but we don't know. It may turn out to be a gang. Let us have Miller's beef and experience, by all means."

On this, Thorndyke took the photographs and retired to the laboratory to write and dispatch his letter and telegram. When he returned, he brought in with him the Superintendent, whom he had encountered on the landing.

"Well," growled Miller, as I placed an arm-chair for him, with the usual creature comforts, "we've brought our pigs to a pretty fine market."

Thorndyke chuckled, but refrained from pointing out that the market was of his own choosing.

"What I can't understand," the Superintendent continued, "is why that fool couldn't have trotted out his infernal alibi when we charged him. Then there needn't have been any trial."

Again we refrained from the obvious answer to this question. Instead, Thorndyke proceeded at once to the "comforting" operation.

"Well, Miller," said he, "now that we have cleared Dobey off the stage, we can give our attention to realities. I suppose you will now agree with me that the man who gave Badger that poisoned cigar is the man who murdered him."

"Yes," Miller admitted, "I'll agree to that much. But it doesn't get us a great deal forrarder. The fellow is a mere abstraction. He isn't even a name. He is just a finger-print that we haven't got on our files."

"Not at all," said Thorndyke. "We can tell you *who* he is. It will then be for you to find out *where* he is."

The Superintendent laid down a match that he had just struck, and stared at Thorndyke, open-mouthed.

"You can tell me who he is!" he exclaimed. "Do you mean that you can give him a name?"

"I do," replied Thorndyke. "His name is Walter Hornby."

The Superintendent was thunderstruck. "Walter Hornby!" he gasped in amazement. Then, suddenly, he brought his large hand down heavily on the little table, causing it to rock visibly, to the imminent peril of the whisky decanter. "Now," he exclaimed, "I understand how it happened. Badger told me, himself, that he thought he had seen Walter Hornby, and he was mighty pleased with himself for having spotted him. I gathered that Hornby was either very much changed or else disguised, though Badger didn't actually say so. But I have no doubt that poor old Badger, in his secretive way, kept an eye on him, and probably shadowed him a bit too openly. Then Hornby got alarmed and, in his turn, shadowed Badger, and finally enticed him into that first-class carriage with the cigar all ready in his pocket. But if you knew, Doctor, why on earth didn't you tell me?"

"My dear Miller," protested Thorndyke, "of course I didn't know in time to prevent the prosecution. I have only just completed the case."

"By the way, Doctor," said Miller, "I suppose I can take it that there is no mistake this time? You are quite sure of your man?"

"I am prepared to sign a sworn information," Thorndyke replied, "and I will undertake to present a convincing case for the prosecution. Naturally, I cannot promise a conviction."

"Of course you can't," said Miller. "But a sworn information from you is good enough for me, to start with. We can go into the evidence another time. But I am hanged if I know how to go about looking for the beggar. I suppose you have no idea what he looks like nowadays?"

"I can only guess," replied Thorndyke. "We can safely assume that he has not red hair or a red nose. Probably he has shaved off his beard and moustache and, judging from what Badger told you and from the fact that he has certainly worn a wig when personating Dobey, it is likely that he habitually wears a wig of a colour different from the lightish brown of his own hair. But I must admit that those assumptions are not very helpful. Still, you have the finger-prints that I handed to you, so, if you make an arrest on suspicion you will know, at once, whether you have or have not got the right man. And now let us dismiss this case, and have a few words about another one that we want you to help us to work at."

Here Thorndyke gave the Superintendent a brief outline of the mystery of Hartsden Manor House, dwelling principally on the testimony of the servants and, characteristically, keeping his own counsel about the "Automatic Watcher". Consequently, Miller, though deeply interested, was a little disposed to be sceptical.

"It sounds a tall story," he remarked, "though it is by no means impossible. At any rate, it is worth looking into. Of course, if a party of crooks have managed to get in there, they have got ideal premises for some kinds of jobs. Just think of a bank-note forger, for instance, getting the use of a set of sealed rooms where he could work in perfect safety, and leave all his incriminating stuff about with the certainty that no one would stumble on it by chance! Or a maker of bombs, or any other kind of illicit artisan. Yes, I certainly think it is worth looking into. And you think the sportsmen are likely to turn up to-morrow night?"

"That is merely a matter of probability," said Thorndyke. "Apparently, the visitor or visitors keep to regular days for their calls, and Friday is one of those days. So we shall take the chance and spend the night there. I think you had better come, Miller," he added, persuasively "Even if nobody turns up, it will be worth your while to look over the premises. You may be able to spot something that we might miss."

"I don't think you are likely to miss much, Doctor," said Miller, with a faint grin. "However, I'd like to come with you. In fact, the more I think of the job, the more it takes my fancy. There are all sorts of possibilities in it. But, if you don't mind, I think I will bring a couple of spare men, or let them come on later. You see, we may want to post them in some cover outside, in case our sportsmen should happen to spot us first and nip off. They would know the place better than we should, and they might easily get away while we were trying to find the way out. In that case it would be very handy to have a couple of men outside who could hear the alarm and pounce on them as they came out."

We both agreed heartily to this excellent arrangement and, when we had discussed a few further details and settled the time for starting in the morning, Miller lighted a fresh cigar and took his departure quite revived in spirits by the prospect of the morrow's adventure.

Chapter XV
The Breaking of the Seals

During our journey down to Hartsden on the following morning, Superintendent Miller's state of mind seemed to alternate between a rather extravagant optimism and a haunting fear of an anticlimax that might expose him to the derision of his subordinates. And such was his condition when we introduced him to Mr. Woodburn at Hartsden Station.

"Well, sir," said he, "this is a very remarkable affair – if it isn't a mare's nest. I hope it isn't."

"I rather hope it is," replied Woodburn, "though that is not my expectation. But we shall soon know."

He held open the door of the car and, when we had taken our places, he drove off at a smart pace and soon covered the short distance between the station and the Manor House. There, at the open door, we found Mrs. Gibbins awaiting us, supported by Polton, who seemed to have established himself as the master of ceremonies, and who conveyed to Thorndyke, in a conspiratorial whisper, that the "Automatic Watcher" had been removed and put out of sight. Evidently, he did not intend that his patent should be infringed by the official investigators.

"We may as well go straight to the gallery," said Woodburn. "I've got the key. Shall I show the way?"

Without waiting for an answer, he passed through the narrow doorway that led into the corridor and the rest of the party followed, with the exception of the housekeeper, whose good manners were even greater than her curiosity, and who contented herself with a wistful observation of our departure, following us with her eyes until we were lost in the darkness of the corridor.

"Now," said Woodburn, as we drew up before the massive door of the gallery, "we are going to clear up the mystery, if there is one. And if there isn't, we are going to catch it from Mr. Toke. At any rate, here goes."

He opened his pocket knife and deliberately cut the stout tape that connected the two seals. Then he inserted the little flat key into the modern lock, grasped the handle of the door, and turned them both together. The door moved slightly, far enough to disengage both the latches, but no farther. He gave one or two vigorous pushes and then looked round at us with a somewhat mystified expression.

"This is very odd," said he. "The door is free of the latches, but it won't open. There seems to be something inside preventing it."

The Superintendent laid his large hand on the door and gave a hearty shove. But still the door refused to move more than half an inch.

"Rum," said he. "Doesn't feel like a solid obstruction. There's a distinct give in it. Shall I throw my weight against the door?"

"Better not," said Woodburn. "There's a flight of steps on the inside."

Here Polton's voice was heard enquiring meekly if it wouldn't be better to lever the door open.

"Certainly it would," replied Miller, "if you know where to find a lever."

"I happen to have a case-opener in my pocket," said Polton, in the matter-of-fact tone of one announcing the possession of a lead pencil or a fountain pen. "I think it would answer the purpose."

"I expect it would," Miller agreed, casting an inquisitive glance at our versatile artificer. "At any rate, you may as well try."

Thus encouraged, Polton advanced to the door and unblushingly produced from a long inside pocket a powerful telescopic jemmy of the most undeniably felonious aspect. Quite unmoved by the Superintendent's stare of astonishment, he first felt the door critically to locate the point of resistance, and then, skilfully insinuating the beak of the jemmy into the rebate of the door-jamb, gave a firm wrench at the long handle of the lever. Immediately, there came a bursting sound from within, and the door swung open, disclosing a short flight of steps leading down to the gallery floor.

The Superintendent tripped down the steps and turned to look for the obstruction.

"Well, I'm jiggered!" he exclaimed. "Your Mr. Toke is a cautious man with a vengeance! He isn't taking any risks. Just look at that."

He pointed to the door-post, on which was a large seal and, depending from it, a length of strong tape with a mass of sealing-wax adhering to its free end. We came down the steps and stood gazing at this singular phenomenon while Miller swung the door round and exhibited, near its edge, the broken seal from which the tape had torn out.

"Now, why the deuce," demanded Wilier, "should he have wanted to seal the door on the inside? And when he had done it, how the devil did he get out?"

"Exactly," said Thorndyke, "that is what interests us. This inside seal gives a conclusive answer to our principal question. He couldn't have got out by this door, so there must be some other way out. And a way out is a way in."

"M'yes," Miller agreed in a reflective tone. "That is so. But it seems to raise another question: Is it quite certain that Mr. Toke has really gone abroad? Is it certain, for instance, that he is not just keeping out of sight for some private reasons?"

"Of course," Woodburn replied, a trifle stiffly, "there is no absolute proof that he has gone abroad. But he said that he was going abroad. He locked and sealed his premises, and was seen thereafter to go away from his house. He put his car into storage, and he has not since been seen in any of his usual places of resort. I may say further that he is a gentleman of the highest character and repute, and that I can imagine no reasons that should induce him to keep out of sight."

"Then," said Miller, apologetic – but unconvinced, as I suspected – "that settles it. You must excuse me, Mr. Woodburn, but I did not know Mr. Toke. We shall have to look for some other explanation. Probably we shall find it when we have made our examination of the premises. When we have ascertained, for instance, whether there is anything missing. Shall we take a look round and check the property? I suppose you know roughly what there was in these rooms when Mr. Toke went away?"

"Yes," replied Woodburn. "I think I should know if anything of value had been taken away."

With this, Miller and the solicitor proceeded to make a systematic tour of inspection, passing along the range of wall-cases and rapidly glancing at the objects on the shelves and apparently finding the collection intact.

"It's rather queer, you know," said Miller, when they had made the round, "that none of these things should have been taken. I imagine that they are pretty valuable pieces."

"They are," replied Woodburn, "but they wouldn't be much use to a thief, seeing that they could be so easily identified – at least, that was Mr. Toke's opinion. He always considered the collection quite safe, so far as burglars were concerned."

"To a certain extent he was right," said Miller. "This stuff would be no use to an ordinary burglar if there was a hue and cry and a description of the stolen property. But that doesn't apply to the present conditions. If someone has been entering these rooms, he might have taken the whole boiling away and have offered it quite safely at a common auction, in small lots at a time. Because you see, nobody would have known that it had been taken. And there's plenty of demand for this sort of stuff. What is in this room?" he added, as their peregrinations brought them to a door near the entrance.

"That is where the collection of bronzes is kept," replied Woodburn. "We may as well see if they are all right, too."

Thereupon, he opened the door and entered the room with the Superintendent.

Meanwhile, Thorndyke had been devoting his attention to the seals on the gallery door, making a minute comparison of the outside seal with that on the inside door-post. As Miller and the solicitor disappeared into the adjoining room (closely attended by Polton, who was apparently determined that the Superintendent should not steal a march on his employer), Thorndyke handed me his lens, remarking, "The seals appear to be identical. I should say that they were both made with the same matrix."

"Is there any reason why they should not be?" I asked in some surprise.

"No," he replied, "I don't think there is." I made a somewhat perfunctory comparison – for Thorndyke's opinion was good enough for me – and then remarked, "I am in the same case as Miller. I can't imagine what object Toke can have had in sealing the inside of the door. Do you understand it?"

"Not if the seals were affixed by Toke," he replied. "Seeing that Toke had access to the whole of the house and could examine the sealed door from the outside to satisfy himself that the seals were intact. But it would be quite understandable if the inside seals were fixed by someone who had not access to the house, but who would wish to be assured that the outside seals had not been broken. Supposing, for instance, there had been no inside seals, and supposing that we made our inspection without disturbing anything and went away, locking the door behind us. There would be no trace of our visit, nor any evidence that the rooms had been entered. But now, if we should go away and our friends should return to-night, they would see at a glance that someone had been here and, no doubt, they would discreetly clear off and abandon their tenancy."

"Yes," said I. "That seems to be the explanation. It had not occurred to me, nor apparently to Miller. But there is another point. If the visitors sealed the door on the inside, they must be in possession of the seal."

"Obviously," he agreed. "That is the important point. If it is a fact, it is an extremely significant fact, especially when it is considered in connection with a certain 'Ginger Lushington'."

At this critical stage, our conversation was interrupted by the Superintendent's voice, hailing us from an adjoining room. At once we hurried into the room which we had seen him enter but, finding it empty, passed through into a second room, with which it communicated, and so, by another communicating doorway, into a third. This also was empty, save for a company of bronze statuettes on its shelves, but through the farther doorway, we could see into a fourth, larger room, and thither we made our way.

As we entered, I looked round me with no little surprise. The three small rooms through which we had passed with their glazed wall-cases and rare and curious contents had the trim, well-kept aspect of an art museum. This fourth room presented a startling contrast. Considerably larger than the others, it had the appearance of a goldsmith's or metal-worker's workshop. In one corner was a large, rectangular chemical sink and, adjoining it a fixed wash-hand basin. At one side was a massive crucible-furnace, arranged to burn charcoal and fitted with a foot-bellows. Close by was a massive post, fitted with a flat stake and a jeweller's "sparrowhawk". There were one or two cupboards and enclosed nests of drawers, and a strong bench provided with a serviceable vice. These details my eye took in rapidly, but there was no time for a complete survey, for my attention was instantly riveted on an object on the bench round which our three friends were gathered in a mighty ferment of excitement.

"Here's a discovery, if you like, Doctor!" the Superintendent exclaimed, gleefully. "You remember my telling you about those bogus sovereigns? Well, we've struck the sovereign factory! Just look at this!"

He indicated the object on the bench – which I now recognized as the box that I had seen through the keyhole periscope, resting on the gallery table, and that had been shown in the "Tuesday" photograph.

Polton's diagnosis had been correct. It was a casting box, or "flask" – an iron frame in two halves, held together in position by pins and eyes at the sides. The upper, or pin, half had now been lifted off, and the mould which filled the interior was displayed. And a very remarkable mould it was, and very illuminating as to the kind of industry that was being carried on in this room. In the smooth, flat surface of the matrix were twenty sunk impressions of sovereigns, each beautifully clear and shiny with graphite. The impressions were connected with one another, and with the "pour" or inlet of the mould, by a deep groove, which was one-half of the channel along which the molten metal was conducted to the impressions.

"Quite a workmanlike outfit," chuckled the delighted Superintendent. "Don't you think so, Mr. Polton?"

Polton crinkled approvingly. "Yes, sir," he replied, "and he knows how to use it. He's no amateur. That is a wonderfully good matrix – hard enough to stand brushing with graphite, and to be used over and over again. I should like to know what it is. There's bone-ash in it, but there's something else on the surface."

"Well," said Miller, "that's more interesting to you than to me. Let us have a look at that other flask."

He indicated a second, similar flask that had been pushed to the back of the bench. Reaching out, he drew it forward and passed it to Polton, who tenderly lifted off the top half and turned it over, laying it beside the lower half and thus exhibiting the two halves of the mould. As he laid it down, he bestowed a crinkly leer on the Superintendent.

"Well, I'm jiggered!" the latter exclaimed. "Half-crowns, too! But I always suspected that the half-crowns and the sovereigns were made by the same man. It was the same idea in both cases. But now we have got to find out where the stuff came from – where he kept his bullion, I mean. We had better go through these cupboards and drawers."

He gave a lead by throwing open a deep cupboard and, as the door swung out, he uttered the single word, "Moses!" The relevancy of the exclamation was not obvious, but the cause was extremely so. For the deep shelves were occupied by an assemblage of silver articles – candlesticks, tea-pots, spoons, and the like, mostly a good deal battered, and many of them reduced to small fragments, apparently by means of shears. A second cupboard made a similar sinister display, though the quantity was smaller. But of gold there was no trace.

"He must have kept his gold in the drawers," said Miller. "He couldn't have brought it with him."

"He brought some of it with him, sir," said Polton, who had been pulling out the drawers of a nest and peering in with a school-boy's delight in a treasure-hunt. "Here is a piece of fine gold plate – twenty-four carats – which certainly came from a bullion dealer's."

At this report, Thorndyke, who had hitherto maintained the attitude of a mildly interested observer, suddenly woke up. Taking a pair of pliers from the bench, he went to the drawer which Polton was holding open and carefully lifted out the piece of plate. Having scrutinized it closely on both sides, he held it out for Miller's inspection.

"You had better secure this," said he. "There are some fairly clear finger-prints on it which may be helpful later on, if our friend should fail to keep his appointment to-night."

The Superintendent took the pliers from him and examined the gold plate, but with less enthusiasm than I should have expected. However, he laid it carefully on a shelf of the cupboard, and then returned to the quest in which he appeared to be specially interested. By this time Polton had made some further discoveries that seemed more relevant, one of which he announced by pulling a drawer out bodily and placing it on the bench.

"Sovereigns, by gosh!" exclaimed Miller, as he looked into the drawer. "Now, I wonder whether these are some of the castings, or the originals that he worked from. What do you think, Doctor?"

Thorndyke picked out one of the coins and examined its edge through his lens, turning it round and inspecting the whole circumference.

"I should say that this is certainly genuine," he reported. "There is no trace of the edge tool. The milling is quite perfect, and it seems to show slight traces of wear. Moreover, the number – there are about two-dozen in the drawer – is not more than would be required as models to avoid repetition of a particular coin."

"Yes, I expect you are right," said Miller, "but they will know at the Mint, in any case. Ah!" he exclaimed, as Polton laid another drawer on the bench. "This looks more interesting. No bullion dealer's stuff this time, I fancy."

The drawer contained about a dozen small ingots of gold, each marked by means of a punch with a number – presumably the carats of "fineness." One of these Miller took up and held out for Polton's inspection.

"No, sir," said the latter, "that did not come from a dealer. It was cast in that ingot mould on the shelf, there."

As he spoke, he took the mould down from the shell and slipped the ingot into it, when it was seen to fit with quite convincing accuracy.

The Superintendent regarded it with profound attention for some moments. Suddenly he turned to Polton and asked impressively, "I want you to tell me, Mr. Polton, which of these things might have been brought here by an outsider and which must have been put here by Mr. Toke. There is this gold plate. That must have been brought here. But what was it brought for?"

"To melt down with these ingots," replied Polton, "to bring the gold up to twenty-two-carats. The ingots are all eighteen-carats or less."

"But why couldn't he have used that acid process that you spoke of?"

"Because he would have had to cut up the ingots and hammer the pieces out thin on the stake. But if he had done that at night, they'd have heard him all over the house. Besides, the fine gold plate would be quicker and less trouble, and it would come to the same thing. He would get his money back. As to what you were asking, I should say that the whole outfit of this place must have been put here by Mr. Toke. The furnace certainly was, and the crucibles and ingot moulds seem to belong to it. In fact, it is a regular metal-worker's shop."

"And what do you make of those ingots?"

Polton crinkled knowingly. "I think, sir," he answered, "they are more in your line than mine. They are not trade ingots, but they are about the fineness of good-class jewellery."

At this point, Thorndyke, who had been listening with rather detached interest to this discussion, sauntered out into the gallery, leaving Polton and Miller to their devices.

"I think," said he, as I followed him out, "we had better get on with our own job. This coining business is no concern of ours."

With this, he went along to the entrance door, on the steps of which he had left his research case and, picking it up, carried it back to the table and deposited it thereon.

"We may as well begin with the most obvious probabilities," said he as he opened the case and ran his eye over the contents. "I suppose you noticed this end of the room, as it showed in the photograph?"

I had to admit that I had not taken especial note of it, nor did I now perceive anything particularly striking in its appearance. The end wall was decorated pleasantly enough, by a low elliptical arch of simply moulded oak supported by a pair of oaken pilasters, the surfaces of which were enriched with shallow strap carving in the form of a *guilloche* with small rosettes in the spaces. There was nothing remarkable about it and, to tell the truth, I was not quite clear as to what I was expected to see. And Thorndyke's proceedings enlightened me not at all.

"The police methods are good enough for our present purpose," he remarked, as he took out a wide-mouthed bottle and a large camel-hair brush. "The good old *Hyd. cum-creta.*"

Removing the stopper from the bottle, he picked up the latter and the brush and walked across to the pilaster nearest the window. Dipping the brush into the bottle of powder, he began to paint it lightly over the carved surface. I watched him with slightly bewildered curiosity and, looking through the doorway into the workshop, where I noticed Woodburn listening with an anxious and rather disapproving expression to the comments of our assistant and the Superintendent, I perceived that the two latter had developed a sudden interest in my colleague's activities. Presently Miller came out for a closer inspection.

"I thought you always used a powder-spray," he remarked. "And you needn't worry about finger-prints. Those on the gold plate will tell us all we want to know. And," he added in a lower tone, "let me give you a hint. Your nocturnal stranger is a myth. The name of the chappie who runs the sovereign factory is Toke. Mustn't say so before Woodburn, but it's a fact. It stares you in the face. Mr. Toke is a fence. Dam' clever fence, too. Buys the scrap from the jewel-robbers, sells the stones, and

424

melts down the settings into sovereigns. I take my hat off to him, and I only hope he'll turn up to-night and let me have the pleasure of making his acquaintance."

Thorndyke nodded, but continued to brush the grey powder on to the woodwork in a broad band from near the floor to a little above the eye level. The Superintendent watched him with a slightly anxious expression, and presently resumed, "I don't see why you are so keen on finger-prints, all of a sudden, or why you should expect to find them in this particular and rather unlikely place. At any rate, there don't seem to be any."

"No," said Thorndyke, "we seem to have drawn a blank. Let us try the other side."

He crossed the room and began operations on the second pilaster, watched, not only by Miller, but also by Polton and Woodburn. But this time he did not draw a blank, for, at the first sweep of the brush, the pale-grey of the powder was interrupted by a number of oval shapes, forming an irregular, crowded group close to one side of the pilaster about four feet above the floor. Thorndyke blew away the superfluous powder and examined the group of finger-prints closely. It seemed to be divided into two subgroups, one on the extreme edge of the pilaster and extending round to the side, and the other in the space of one member of the *guilloche*, around and over the enclosed rosette. After another close inspection, Thorndyke grasped the marked rosette between his fingers and thumb, and tried if it were possible to rotate it. Apparently it turned quite easily, but, beyond the rotation, no result followed. After a moment's reflection, Thorndyke took a fresh hold, and gave it another turn in the same direction. Suddenly, from within, came a soft click, and then the whole shaft of the pilaster, from the capital to the plinth, swung out a couple of inches like an absurdly tall and narrow door. Thorndyke grasped it by the edge and drew it fully open, when there came into view a small triangular space of floor and a low, narrow opening at the side, with the beginning of a flight of ladder-like steps, the rest of which was lost to view in the impenetrable darkness of a passage which seemed to burrow into the substance of the wall.

"Well, I'm jiggered!" exclaimed Miller. "Now, I wonder how you guessed that door was there, Doctor?"

"I only guessed that it *might* be there," said Thorndyke. "Hence the search for finger-prints. Without them, we might have spent hours trying to find the secret door, and especially the fastening, which was so cleverly concealed. However, we have solved the most difficult part of our problem. The outside opening of this passage is probably as cleverly hidden as the inside one. But it will be hidden from without, whereas we shall approach it from within, where there is probably no concealment."

"I suppose it is worthwhile to explore that passage," said Miller, looking a little distastefully at the narrow, black chink, "though, really, we want to know who the man is, not how he got in."

"Perhaps," replied Thorndyke, "an exploration of the passage may answer both questions. At any rate, Mr. Woodburn will want to know how the house was entered from the outside."

"Certainly," Woodburn agreed. "That was, in fact, what we came to find out."

As Thorndyke produced from his case a couple of powerful electric inspection lamps, one of which he handed to me, I reflected on his slightly cryptic answer to the Superintendent's question, as also did Miller himself. At least, so I judged from the inquisitive look that he cast at Thorndyke. But he made no remark and, when he had provided himself with an electric lantern from his bag, he announced that he was ready for the exploration.

Thereupon, Thorndyke turned on his lamp and, squeezing through the narrow opening, began to descend the steps, followed, at due intervals, by the rest of the expeditionary party.

Chapter XVI
The Vault

In the course of my descent of that interminable stairway, I found myself speculating curiously on the physical characteristics of the dead and gone Greenlees. They must, I decided, have been a thin family, for surely, no corpulent person, no matter how hard pressed or how deeply embroiled in political machinations, could ever have got down those steps. Vainly did I seek to avoid contact with those slimy, fungus-encrusted walls. They pressed in on me from either side as if I had been sliding down a tube. Not, indeed, that this close contact was without its compensations, for, since there was no hand-rail, and the steps were incredibly steep and narrow and, like the walls, slippery with slime and fungus, it gave some slight feeling of security.

But it was a hideous experience. Soon the faint glimmer of daylight from the doorway above faded out and gave place to the ghostly light of the electric lamps, which glanced off the shiny, unsavoury walls and ceiling in fitful gleams that dazzled rather than illuminated. Moreover, the air, which at first had seemed only musty and close, grew more and more foul, and pervaded by a strange, cadaverous odour unlike the usual earthiness of underground cellars and passages.

At length, the sudden eclipse of Thorndyke's lamp, followed by that of Miller's, and a faint reflection on the wall, told me that they had turned into some other passage. Then I, bringing up the rear, reached the bottom of that apparently endless flight, and found myself on a small paved space from which opened a low tunnel along which my predecessors were creeping in postures more suited to chimpanzees than to representatives of the law. I lowered my head and shoulders and followed, concentrating my attention on avoiding contact with the unclean ceiling. Presently Miller's voice came rumbling unnaturally along the tube-like passage.

"What does your compass say, Doctor? Which way are we travelling?"

"Due west," was the reply. "Towards the church."

I had hardly time to consider the significance of this piece of information when the Superintendent's voice again rang out, this time in a slightly startled tone, "Why, this is a vault!"

A few moments more, and I was able to confirm the statement. The tunnel ended in a narrow, oblong chamber, barely three feet wide, but

427

more than a dozen feet long, and of a height that, at least, allowed one to stand upright. I availed myself of this advantage and looked around me with some curiosity and a strong desire to find the way out. For if the air had been foul on the stairs and in the tunnel, it was here suffocatingly fetid.

The light of the three powerful lamps made it easily possible to see all the details of structure and arrangement. And a strange and gruesome place it looked in that lurid illumination – a long, passage-like chamber, as I have said, paved with stone and enclosed with walls of damp and slimy brick. At the ends, the walls were solid, excepting the arched opening of the tunnel, but the long side walls were each interrupted by a widish arch which opened into a side chamber. Both chambers were fitted with massive stone shelves, something like the bins of a wine-cellar, and on these could be seen the ends of the coffins containing, presumably, mature specimens of the Greenlees vintage. Above, at a height of about ten feet, the long walls supported what looked like a bottomless brickwork box about eight feet long, the rest of the chamber being roofed in with stone slabs. Under the box, towards one end, a thick iron bar – or what would nowadays be called a girder – crossed the chamber and supported at its middle an upright iron post that seemed to be fixed into the top of the box.

But the feature that interested me most was a flight of steep and narrow, but perfectly practicable, brick steps, which started from the mouth of the tunnel and passed up the left-hand wall above the arch to the base of the box near the end opposite to that which was crossed by the iron bar.

"I don't quite understand that contraption up there," said Miller, throwing the light of his lantern on the under-side of the box, "but there's a flight of steps, so I suppose there's a way out, and I propose that we try it without delay. The atmosphere of this place is enough to stifle a pole-cat."

"We mustn't be precipitate, Miller," said Thorndyke. "We want to find the way out, but we don't want to publish it to the world at large. Before we go out, we must send someone up to see that the coast is clear."

"I suppose we shall be able to get out," said Woodburn, "though I don't see very clearly how we are going to do it. But I expect you do, as you nosed out that doorway so readily."

"I think it is pretty obvious," replied Thorndyke. "That coffer-like structure up there I take to be the Greenlees tomb in the churchyard. The top slab seems to rotate on that iron pivot and those curved runners that cross on the under-side. But I will run up and make sure of it before we send out our scouts."

He climbed cautiously up the brick steps, and having reached the top, threw the light of his lamp on the under-side of the slab and examined the simple mechanism.

"Yes," he reported, "I think it is all plain sailing. The runners are clean and smooth, and both they and the pivot have been kept well oiled. It won't do to try it, in case there should be anyone in the churchyard. Now, who is going up as scout? I suggest that you go, Woodburn, as you know the tomb, and the Superintendent had better go with you to learn the lie of the land. Take a stick with you and, if it is all clear, give five distinct taps on the side of the tomb, and be careful not to leave any more tracks than you can help."

Neither of the scouts showed any reluctance. On the contrary, they both assented with a readiness that I attributed to the influence of the deceased Greenlees. At any rate, they waited for no further instructions, but dived forthwith into the tunnel, whence presently came the echoes of their footsteps as they scrambled up the steps towards the fresh air and the light of day.

As they disappeared, Thorndyke began a systematic exploration of the vault, throwing the light of the lamp into all the darker corners and finally extending his researches into the side chambers.

"Isn't it rather odd," said I, "that the air of this place should be so extraordinarily foul? I take it that there have been no recent burials here."

"If the inscriptions are to be accepted," he replied, "the last burial took place more than sixty years ago. I agree with you that the physical conditions do not seem to be quite consistent with the inscriptions. Perhaps we may find some explanation."

He walked slowly round the first chamber that he had entered, throwing the light on the shelves and examining the latter with minute and suspicious scrutiny, reading each of the coffin-plates, and inspecting each coffin critically as to its condition. Having made his round of the first chamber, he crossed to the second, followed by me and Polton – who had developed a profound and ghoulish interest in the investigation. He had passed along nearly the whole length of the first shelf when I saw him stop and look closely, first at the shelf, then at the ground beneath it and, finally, at the two adjacent coffins.

"This wants looking into, Jervis," said he. "These two coffins have been moved quite recently. The thick dust on the shelf has been brushed away – you can see some of it on the floor – but there are clear traces showing that both coffins have been pulled forward. And, if you look closely at the coffins themselves, you will see pretty evident signs of their having been opened at some fairly recent time. This right-hand one has been opened quite roughly, with inadequate tools. The other has been treated more skilfully, but if you look at the screws you can see that they have been withdrawn and replaced quite recently. Parts of the slots have been scraped bright by the screwdriver and the edges of the slots are burred up, particularly on the left side, showing that they were difficult to turn, as you would expect in the case of an old screw that has been in position for years."

"For what purpose do you suppose the coffins were opened?" I asked.

"Why suppose at all?" he replied, "when the coffins are here, and Polton has a whole burglar's outfit on his person? Let us get the lids off and see what is inside. I take it that the damaged coffin is the one that was opened first, so we will begin with the other one. Have you a practicable screwdriver about you, Polton?"

The question was hardly necessary, for Polton had already extracted from some secret and illegal pocket a good-sized ratchet screwdriver with a hollow handle containing several spare blades of different sizes. Having taken a glance at the screws, he fitted in a blade of the appropriate size, and then, as we drew out the coffin to the front of the shelf, he fell to work on it.

"The last operator wasn't much of a hand with the screwdriver," he grumbled. "He's scraped away half the slots."

However, by bearing heavily on the tool, he got the screws started and, as they came out one by one and were put tidily on a clear space on the shelf, we brought the coffin a stage farther forward to bring the next one within reach. When the last of them had been extracted, the "case-opener" was produced, and its beak inserted under the lid. A slight tweak raised the latter, and it was easily lifted off.

As Polton drew it aside and exposed the interior of the coffin, I uttered a cry of astonishment.

"Why, there are two bodies!" I exclaimed.

"Skeletons, I should call 'em, sir," Polton corrected, disparagingly.

"Yes," Thorndyke agreed. "There would hardly have been room for two recent corpses. But they are not so badly preserved, considering that they have been here for close on a century. Now, let us get the other one open, and don't damage the coffin more than you are obliged to, Polton."

"Am I right," I asked, "in supposing that you expected to find two bodies in that coffin?"

"Yes," he replied. "That was what the circumstances seemed to suggest."

"And what do you expect to find in the other one?"

"That question, Jervis," said he, "seems to be answered by the one that we have just opened. Why should a man take a body out of one coffin and cram it into another which is already occupied?"

The answer was certainly pretty obvious. But the discussion came to a premature end, for, in spite of Polton's care, the damaged lid came loose before all the screws had been extracted. As he lifted it off, I threw the light of my lamp into the cavity, and though it disclosed nothing that I had not expected, I stood for a while, silently gazing into the coffin with horrified fascination.

The bright glare of the lamp fell on the figure of a grey-haired man, fully clothed, even to a crumpled soft felt hat. His age, so far as it was possible to judge, appeared to be from fifty to sixty, and his neat worsted clothes and the quality of his linen suggested a man of some means, reasonably careful of his appearance. As to how he had died there was nothing to show, save for the sinister suggestion of a smear of blood on one sleeve. I was just turning to Thorndyke to ask a question when the deathly silence was broken by five sharp taps from above, which reverberated through the vault with quite startling distinctness.

"There is Woodburn," said Thorndyke. "Lay the covers on the coffins."

With this he picked up his lamp and went out into the main vault. Following him, I saw him pick his way carefully up the steep and narrow steps until he reached the little platform at the top. There he paused and threw his light on the under-side of the covering slab. Then, grasping what appeared to be some sort of handle, he gave a pull, first downward and then sideways. Immediately the heavy slab turned on its pivot and runners with a dull grinding sound, and a stream of brilliant daylight poured down into the gruesome interior. A moment or two later it was partially obscured as Miller and Woodburn leaned over the edge and peered down curiously into the vault.

"Is it necessary for us to come down again?" Miller enquired. "The air is a good deal fresher up here."

"I shall want Mr. Woodburn to come down," said Thorndyke. "We have been making some investigations, and I should like to have his opinion on something that we have discovered. Probably you will be interested too."

He was – very decidedly. At the mention of a discovery, his long legs swung, one after the other, over the edge of the sarcophagus, and he followed Thorndyke down the steps as rapidly as was consistent with the necessary caution. Close behind him came Woodburn, all agog with curiosity.

431

"It isn't so bad here," he remarked, "now that we have got that cover open. We had better keep it open, and let a little air in."

"Then," said Thorndyke, "Polton had better go up and keep a look-out. We don't want any other observers. You saw how the slab was moved, Polton. If anyone comes in sight, shut it at once."

I could see that this duty was not at all acceptable to our ingenious coadjutor, who evidently foresaw dramatic developments in the immediate future. Nevertheless, he climbed the steps and thrust his head out of the opening. But I noticed that one eye and both ears were kept focused on the happenings down below.

"Now, Doctor," said Miller, "what is this discovery that you have made?"

"I will show you," said Thorndyke, leading the way into the side chamber. "But I may explain that we found that two of the coffins had been moved, and moved quite recently. But they had not only been moved – they had been opened and reclosed. On observing that, we thought it desirable to open them and ascertain why they had been opened. We did so, with this result: We found in one coffin two bodies – two quite ancient bodies. Mere skeletons, in fact."

"Then," said Woodburn, "you may take it that they are strangers to me, and they are not any concern of mine. So we will take them as read."

"Very well," said Thorndyke. "I will not trouble you with that coffin. But I must ask you to look at the other. This is the one."

He drew the coffin a little farther to the front of the shelf and lifted off the lid, throwing the light of his lamp into the cavity. Mr. Woodburn approached with very evident reluctance, holding his handkerchief to his face, and cast a glance of mingled disgust and apprehension towards the coffin. Suddenly he stopped and then started forward with a half-articulate cry. For a moment he stood staring with incredulous horror. Then, in a voice tremulous with emotion, he exclaimed, "Great God! *It's Mr. Toke!*"

For some moments there was a dead silence. Then Thorndyke replaced the coffin lid, and we went back to the main vault. And still, for a while, no one spoke. On Woodburn this revelation had fallen like a thunderbolt, while Miller, whose theory of the criminal doings at the Manor House was suddenly shattered, was wrapped in the most profound cogitation. At length the latter broke the silence.

"How long do you think Mr. Toke has been in that coffin, Doctor?" he asked.

"I should say," replied Thorndyke, "that he has been there ever since the day on which he was supposed to have gone abroad."

"Yes," said Woodburn, "I think you are right. I have had all along a lurking suspicion that he never really went abroad – that something happened to him on that last day. I didn't at all like the garage man's story of that ginger-haired fellow with the red nose."

"Eh!" exclaimed Miller, all agog in a moment. "What story was that?"

Woodburn gave him a brief summary of the incident of the returned car and the "Ginger Lushington", to which he listened with profound attention, and on which he cogitated for a while when Woodburn had finished. Suddenly he turned to Thorndyke, and regarded him eagerly and almost fiercely.

"Now, look here, Doctor," said he, "you have got to tell us what all this means. It is no use for you to try to put us off. You hold all the clues and you know all about it. You have followed this case as if you were running along rails. You knew that someone had been here. I believe you knew about those sovereigns, and you went for that secret door as if you knew exactly where to look for it. And then you came down into this vault and you went straight for that coffin. I have no doubt that you knew Mr. Toke was there. Now, Doctor, I ask you to tell me who killed Mr. Toke, and who was that red-nosed man."

"You are asking me," replied Thorndyke, "to make a statement, whereas I can only offer an opinion. But you can have that opinion for what it is worth, and I may say that I think it is worth a good deal, as it is based on a mass of evidence. I should say that the red-nosed man at the garage and the murderer of Mr. Toke are one and the same person, and that person is named Walter Hornby."

"What!" exclaimed Miller. "The villain who murdered Badger!"

"That is what I believe," said Thorndyke. "But I hope that we shall have the opportunity to settle the question. At any rate, we may fairly take it that the person who has been frequenting these premises is the person who murdered Mr. Toke."

"And you expect that person to come here to-night?"

"It is only a probability," replied Thorndyke. "You know our reasons for expecting him. It may be to-night, or he may choose some other night. But there is very little doubt that he will come sooner or later to finish up the gold that is left, and take away those sovereigns. But it is quite possible that the next visit will be meant to be the last."

"It will be the last," Miller remarked, grimly. "If I stay here till Doomsday, I am going to have him."

There was a brief pause. Then Woodburn asked, "Where and how do you suppose the murder was committed?"

433

"I should say," answered Thorndyke, "that the deed was done at the top of those steps. There is what looks very much like a blood-stain on the brick there. As to the circumstances, I should say that they were roughly these: I take it that Mr. Toke, when he took the car out of the garage, had for some reason to come down here, unexpectedly, to fetch something from, or deposit something in, the gallery, and he had reasons for not wishing to enter the house and break the seals. I think that the murderer must have come to know of this intended visit, and have come on in advance and waited for him in hiding somewhere. That he saw Toke arrive, followed him into the churchyard, and saw him enter the tomb by the secret opening. I suspect that he waited for him to come out, and then murdered him as he was emerging from the tomb. Then he explored the vault, hurriedly broke open a coffin and, having disposed of the body, made an inspection of the premises, the valuable contents of which may have been known to him. At any rate, he would have found the gold, and known then that it would be worthwhile to come back to take it away. I should think that the sovereigns were probably an afterthought, suggested by the quantity of gold bullion, which would have been rather unsafe to dispose of in the regular way. Moreover, if I am right as to the identity of the man, we must remember that he was an assayist by profession, and would have an expert knowledge of the methods of dealing with gold. But as to that, we shall know more when we have seen him. And now we may as well relieve Polton and get back to the house. I don't think we have left any traces of our visit down here, and we must be careful to leave none in the churchyard as we go out."

"No," Miller agreed fervently, "for the Lord's sake don't let us spoil our chances by giving him any sort of warning. At present, we seem to have him in the hollow of our hand. It would take ten years off my life if we should let him slip."

"I don't think you need have any misgivings, Miller," said Thorndyke. "He is bound to come back, and we are agreed that we are willing to wait for him to come in his own time. We can only hope that he will not keep us waiting too long."

Chapter XVII
The Vigil

We made our way out of the vault, one by one, creeping cautiously up the narrow brick steps, and climbing over the side of the tomb into the green and sunny churchyard. Woodburn was the first to emerge and, as he stepped down on to the grass, he drew a deep breath.

"Lord," he exclaimed, "it is good to be back in the world of living men and to breathe the fresh air. That was a horrible experience!"

I sympathized with him, though naturally my professional training had made me less sensitive to merely physical unpleasantness. For I realized that, whatever misgivings he might have had respecting his client, it must have been a shocking experience to be brought suddenly, without warning, face to face with his murdered corpse. Even Miller was not unaffected by the tragedy that had been so abruptly sprung upon him.

Thorndyke was the last to come up, having lingered to take a final look round and make sure that no tell tale evidence of our visit had been left to arouse the suspicions of the hoped-for visitor. As soon as he had stepped out, he seized the displaced slab and, with a vigorous pull, swung it round into its normal position.

"We may as well make sure, before we go," said he, "that we all understand how this arrangement works from the outside. It seems to be quite a simple device. The slab rocks slightly on its pivot. To release the inside catch, the higher end of the slab has to be pressed down. This raises the other end and so frees the catch. You see that, at present, the slab is quite immovable, but when I throw my weight on this end, I am able to swing it round without difficulty."

As he spoke, he demonstrated the mechanism, and when Miller had satisfied himself by actual trial that he had fully grasped the method, we took our way out of the churchyard and walked across to the house. There we were admitted by Mrs. Gibbins in person, who informed us that two officers had arrived and, further, that lunch would be served in five minutes and, furthermore, that separate arrangements had been made for Mr. Polton and the two officers.

At the latter announcement Miller smiled grimly. "Artful old puss," was his comment, when she had gone. "Made her arrangements to have Mr. Polton all to herself and get the latest news. But it doesn't matter. She's an interested party, and it will save me the trouble of giving my men the particulars."

Nevertheless, he introduced us to the two officers and gave them a few instructions, and then we retired to remove, as far as was possible, the traces of our subterranean activities before sitting down to lunch.

It was a very leisurely meal – almost intentionally so, for there was little more to do in the way of preparation, and a long interval before the next phase of our adventure could be expected to begin. But there was plenty of material for discussion, especially as Woodburn had to be put in possession of the numerous and complicated antecedents of the case. Then the details of the procedure to be adopted in the actual capture had to be considered, and the course that would have to be taken in the event of the quarry failing to appear. As to the former, Miller showed a disposition to simplify the proceedings by making the arrest in the churchyard.

"You see," he explained, "there's a good deal to be said for catching your hare while you have the chance. If we collar him as soon as he has gone up to the tomb, we shall make sure of him, whereas, if we let him go down, he may disappear into some underground passage that we know nothing about."

But Thorndyke shook his head very decidedly. "No, Miller," said he. "That won't do. It is a bad plan in two ways. In the first place, the churchyard is not secure enough. He would have quite a fair chance of escape in that open space, with its various obstructions to dodge among, and possibly a car waiting close by. In the second place, he ought to be arrested, for evidential reasons, in the gallery. Remember that we have got to identify him with the coiner who has used Mr. Toke's gold, and we are going to charge him with the murder of Mr. Toke. Now, if you arrest him in the churchyard, you have got those charges to prove. You will infer, reasonably enough, that he has come into the churchyard for the purpose of entering the house by way of the secret passage. But in a criminal trial, on a capital charge, evidence is sifted very finely. The defence would deny the intention, and you would have to prove it. But if he is taken actually in the gallery, that fact is evidence in itself of his connection with the coining and, by fair inference, with the murder of Mr. Toke."

Miller admitted the force of this contention. "But, still," he urged, "we are not dealing with an unknown man. You say you can prove his identity, which connects him with a previous crime, and you have got substantial evidence in regard to the murder of poor Badger."

Thorndyke, however, was firm. "It won't do, Miller," said he. "We shall want every particle of evidence that we can get. At present, all that we have is circumstantial. But with all respect to the dictum of a certain learned judge, circumstantial evidence is much less satisfactory to a jury than that which is more or less direct."

"Very well," said Miller. "You know more about court work than I do. But what do you suggest – I mean, about planting my men?"

"The best plan, I think," replied Thorndyke, "would be to instruct them to hide behind the yew tree – it must be pitch-dark there at night – and to wait for the man to arrive. They should let him go down into the tomb and, as soon as he has disappeared, they should take up their stations at the side of the tomb nearest the steps. There they would have absolute control of him if he should come up again, as he would be standing on the steps."

"You speak of 'him,'" Miller remarked. "Supposing there should be a gang?"

"That is very unlikely," replied Thorndyke, "but, even so, there are four of us, without counting Polton. I think we can take our chance. Are you and your men armed?"

"No," replied Miller. "We don't much favour firearms in the force. We've brought two or three sets of handcuffs and, for the rest, we've got a pretty serviceable outfit of fists."

"Well, I took the precaution to bring four automatics," said Thorndyke. "You had better have one. A man who has two murders to his account is not likely to boggle at one or two more."

Eventually, the Superintendent accepted Thorndyke's suggestions and, when we had finished lunch, the final preparations were made. Thorndyke showed the two officers the secret door, and demonstrated the working of the catch from outside and from within, and then conducted them down the stairway and through the vault to the opening, at which Polton had been sent to keep a look-out. When they had mastered the working of the movable slab, they were shown the spot behind the yew tree where they were to keep watch later on. Then the whole party returned to the house by way of the vault – to avoid exhibiting themselves to any chance observers in the village.

When the officers had been dismissed to repose and smoke their pipes in Mr. Toke's study, Thorndyke produced a six-inch ordnance map of the district and invited the attention of Woodbury and the Superintendent to a narrow lane that appeared to run close beside the churchyard and, presently to open into a by-road at no great distance.

"It seems probable," said he, "that our friend, or friends, make the journey here by car, unless they should be local persons, which is most unlikely. And if they do, this lane would be an ideal approach, as it would avoid the village street, and be a most convenient place in which to leave the car – quite close to the churchyard and well out of sight. It might be worthwhile to go and inspect that lane."

"I don't think that is necessary," said Woodburn, "because the same idea had occurred to me, and I took the opportunity to walk along it this morning. And I have no doubt that you are right. At any rate, someone has been bringing a car up that lane, for there were clear traces of one – a smallish car it seemed to be – especially at a place near the middle, where it is wide enough to turn round. I could see quite plainly the marks on the grass verge where he had backed in to turn. It appeared that he entered the lane from the by-road and stopped short a couple of hundred yards from the village street. So he must have gone back on the reverse until he came to the wide part, and then have turned round and gone out by the by-road."

"Were these the marks of a single journey," asked Miller, "or were there more than one set?"

"At the wide part," answered Woodburn, "on the soft grass verge, there were a number of tracks on top of one another. I couldn't say how many."

"Then," said Miller, "we needn't trouble to inspect it, which is as well. The less we show ourselves in this neighbourhood the better. I'll tell my men to keep their ears pricked up for the sound of a motor, though if it is occupied by the parties that we are expecting, it isn't likely to be a very noisy one."

"No," Thorndyke agreed, "but in the silence of the country at night it will certainly be audible, especially if the driver should take the precaution – as he probably would – to turn round as soon as he arrived, so as to be ready to drive straight off in the event of an alarm. So we will hope that he comes in style in his car. It would give a very useful warning to your watchers."

"Yes," said Miller, "and it would be rather useful if they could pass the warning on to us in some way. What do you think, Doctor?"

"Of course," replied Thorndyke, "it would be a great help to us. But I think we shall have to do without it. Any kind of signalling would be extremely unsafe. It might easily give a warning in the wrong quarter."

Miller acknowledged the truth of this, and the subject dropped. And then began a somewhat tedious period of waiting, for there were yet several hours of daylight to dispose of before our actual vigil would begin. The Superintendent, being an old hand at this sort of business, retired to the study to smoke and "take forty winks", while Thorndyke, Woodburn, and I whiled away the afternoon by making a complete tour of Mr. Toke's collection.

A very remarkable collection it was. The gallery was filled mainly with Bow, Chelsea, and other porcelain figures, while the three smaller rooms were occupied by bronze busts and statuettes and a small collection of choice pottery and enamels. The entire contents of the rooms must have been of very great value, for all the pieces seemed to have been selected with the most fastidious taste and obviously expert judgment, without regard to cost. As we walked round and admired them one after another, they suggested two rather curious questions.

First, was it credible that the man who had acquired and treasured all these things of beauty, with such obvious enthusiasm and love for them, could be a mere fence – a receiver of stolen property? Those ingots in the workshop had certainly looked suspicious. Yet how could one believe it? The man who had cherished all these beautiful things so lovingly was no common money-grabber. Every one of them seemed to cry out in vindication of Mr. Toke.

The second question was, How came it that Hornby – if he was indeed the mysterious visitor – should have left this treasure-house intact? Many of the pieces were quite portable, especially to a man with a car. And, as Miller had pointed out, they could have been disposed of quite safely, so long as they had not been missed. The first question could not be discussed in Woodburn's presence, but the second I ventured to put to Thorndyke.

"I think the explanation is fairly simple," he replied. "There appears to have been here an accumulation of gold bullion. How much we cannot guess, nor how it came to be accumulated. But here it was, and its presence was probably known to, or suspected by, the murderer, though it may have been discovered after the murder. My impression – though it is nothing more – is that the murder was not committed *ad hoc* – as a means to the carrying out of the robbery, but for some reason that is not known to us, and that the gold robbery was, as it were, a by-product.

"Now, the existence of this gold bullion was, almost certainly, known to no one but Mr. Toke. It follows that if the murderer could have simply taken away the gold and then disappeared, he would have left no trace whatever of his having ever been here. The corpse, you remember, is in a coffin in the vault, to which the only access is by secret openings whose existence was unknown to anybody but Mr. Toke. You see the masterly simplicity of the plan. When Mr. Toke failed to return or give any sign of being alive, and leave had been granted by the court to presume death, these rooms would have been opened and everything found apparently intact. There would have been nothing whatever to suggest any crime. It might have been suspected that Mr. Toke had met

439

with foul play. But not here. The scene of his disappearance would have been placed in some unknown locality abroad.

"But now suppose that this man, in addition to taking away the gold, had rifled the collection. Then, as soon as the rooms were entered, it would have been seen that there had been a robbery. But a robbery in conjunction with a disappearance at once suggests a murder. There would have been a search, with the possible, and even probable, discovery of the body. Obviously, it was worth the murderer's while to abstain from tampering with the collection."

The afternoon wore on and merged into evening. The daylight faded and, as the twilight deepened and the night closed in on the old house, we felt that the time had come to set the watch, for this was a quiet country neighbourhood where people went to rest early and measured time by the sun rather than by the clock. Accordingly, we went forth in search of the Superintendent and found him in the act of mustering his forces, preparatory to placing them at their posts in the churchyard.

"It seems a bit early," said he. "But it won't do to be caught napping. Our friends may turn up earlier than we expect. I'll just go out and see my men posted, and then we will make our arrangements."

With this he departed and we proceeded with the preliminaries that concerned us. First Woodburn instructed Mrs. Gibbins to have all lights out at the usual time – which appeared to be ten o'clock – and advised that the inmates should go to bed when they put out the lights (which I suspected to be a counsel of perfection that was not likely to be followed). Then we made out our programme for the night watch in the gallery. Woodburn not only volunteered, but insisted on joining the party, and Polton, when he was offered the use of a spare bedroom, became, for the first time on record, positively mutinous, absolutely refusing to be driven away from the scene of action. So he had to be put on the roster of the "garrison", and proceeded with us to the gallery to take up our final positions, where we were presently joined by the Superintendent.

"Well," the latter remarked, surveying our party with a grin, "if there is only one man, we ought to be able to manage him. Seven of us, all told. Seems as if we weren't taking many risks. Of course, if there should be more than one, we shan't be too many. And now we've got to settle on our stations, because when once we have taken them, we must keep them. There must be no moving about. Now, we can't lock that door, as there is no keyhole on the inside, so one or two of us had better take post in the first room – the one that is next to the door. The question is, which of us?"

440

"I think you had better take that post, Miller," said Thorndyke, "as that is where he, or they, will probably have to be stopped. They will know that the door is unlocked as soon as they discover that someone is in the room and, as the secret door will be blocked, they will naturally make a burst for the main door."

"Yes," agreed Miller, "I think you are right, Doctor. Then I propose that Mr. Woodburn and I take the end room, and the rest of you take post in the workshop, where you will be close to the secret door."

These arrangements having been agreed to, Thorndyke made a final round to make sure that nothing was visible that might create premature suspicion. First, he inspected the secret door, and set the catch exactly as he had found it, wiping away the last traces of the dusting powder by the light of his lamp (for we had put on no lights in the gallery). Then he went to the main door and, taking the dangling remains of the seal, heated the wax with a lighted match (which he carefully shrouded with his hand), and stuck it in its original place so that, to a casual glance, it appeared to be unbroken.

"Now, I think we are all ready," said he, "and it is about time that we took our places."

The existing arrangements did not make for luxury, or even common comfort. The Superintendent and Woodburn found in their room one chair, and collected another from the adjoining room. But in the workshop there was but one hideously incommodious stool, which we all rejected, preferring to seat ourselves on the bench, when we had removed the flasks and other obstructions. It was far from being a comfortable seat, and the shelves behind it offered but an uneasy support to the back. However, Thorndyke reminded us that many a journeyman tailor spent the greater part of his life seated on just such a bench, and added with undoubted truth that it had the virtue of offering a steady resistance to any tendency to drowsiness.

I look back on that long vigil as one of the strangest experiences of my life. It was like that of a big-game hunter, offering a curious combination of tedium and excitement, of wearisome monotony with the need for incessant alertness and the uncertainty as to what the next moment might bring forth, or whether it might bring forth anything. We took our places, very prematurely, at half-past nine, and thereafter we sat in the dark, conversing little, and then in the softest of whispers, and hardly daring to change our positions. It would have been a relief to smoke, but this was, of course, forbidden, though at intervals, a faint sniff, accompanied by the suspicion of a distinctive scent, informed me that Polton was indulging in the mild dissipation of a pinch of snuff. Once, indeed, the cold touch of a metal snuff-box on my hand was accompanied by a whispered invitation to test the virtues of Brown Rappee – an invitation which I half-reluctantly declined.

The tardy minutes crawled on with incredible slowness. Sitting there in the darkness, encompassed, as it seemed, by the silence of the tomb, I was able to mark their passage by the chimes of a clock, somewhere in the village, which were borne faintly to my ear across the quiet countryside. The clock struck the quarters, but each quarter seemed to have the duration of an hour. I fingered the automatic pistol in my pocket and wondered what degree of urgency would induce me to use it. Like Thorndyke, I had a profound dislike of firearms, and none of our party had seemed to show much enthusiasm when he handed them out. Miller had the typical police officer's contempt for a mere assassin's weapon, and had offered his to Polton. But Polton assured him that he had never fired a pistol in his life and should probably hit the wrong man, upon which Miller hastily took it back.

The distant clock had struck half-past-ten when the dreariness of our vigil was to some extent mitigated by the appearance of the moon. It first came into view through the curtained window of the gallery which was just visible through the half-open door of the workshop, as a misshapen, coppery disc (for it was a few days past the full), just peeping above the window-sill. Then, by slow degrees, it crept up higher and higher and, as its dull copper brightened into a warm, ruddy glow and then to a clear, cold, silvery sheen, the shape of the lofty window became traced on the floor in an elongated, luminous patch, on which the pattern of the lace curtains stood out clearly in forms of delicate shadow.

That shape of patterned moonlight came as a welcome distraction which helped to fill the long intervals between the chimes of the distant clock. Like some solitary prisoner in his cell, I followed its infinitely slow progress across the floor, idly calculating the time that it would take to reach the foot of the pilaster in which was the secret door. At present, the pilaster was enveloped in dense, black shadow, and a wide space of floor separated it from the patch of moonlight. I tried to think of that space in terms of angular distance and time, but failed to reach any intelligible result. Then I fell to thinking about the man for whom we were waiting. Was he now on the road, drawing gradually nearer to his doom – or, perchance, ours? If so, how far away was he now? Was he travelling alone or had he companions with whom we should have to reckon? Or was he, even now, comfortably tucked up in bed in some far-away hiding-place with no intention of sallying forth this night? Or was he lurking in the village, fully warned by the sight of us to keep out of the way, to leave us to our profitless vigil until the coming of daylight should send us away, drowsy and defeated?

The silence of the old house was like the silence of some cavern in the heart of a mountain. Save for the infrequent chime of the far-away clock, there was not a sound. Not a window rattled – for it was a still night – not a joist creaked, no mouse "shrieked in the wainscot" or scuttled through its burrow. None of the ordinary night sounds of an old house were audible. It was as still as the inside of a pyramid.

A few minutes had passed since the hardly audible chime of the distant clock had told out the half-hour after eleven when that deathly silence was, for the first time, disturbed by a sound that seemed to come from within the house. And, even then, it was so faint and indefinite that I doubted whether I had, in fact, heard anything. I listened intently. Then, after the lapse of nearly a minute, it was repeated. It conveyed nothing to me. It was just a sound – infinitely faint and remote, and so devoid of any recognizable character that I was still doubtful. But at this moment Thorndyke silently slid off the bench and was followed – less silently – by Polton. I, too, slipped my legs over the edge and, as I stood upright beside Thorndyke, I asked in a whisper, "Did you think you heard anything?"

"Yes," he replied. "It was the slab turning on its pivot. Listen!"

I strained my ears, but for a few moments I could hear no further sound. Then I became aware of a faint but distinctly audible murmur or rustle as if a number of separate sounds were being confused by echoes. Suddenly it became much more distinct and changed in character, for now I could clearly distinguish footsteps – soft, stealthy footsteps, mingled with their reverberations, but unmistakable.

Nearer and nearer they came, still secret and stealthy, but now recognizable as the tread of feet on the long stairway. Once, the feet slipped or stumbled, and the sound of some hard object striking the steps, followed by a muttered curse, told me that the man was nearer than I had thought. Suddenly on the side of the pilaster, there appeared a bright thread – the light of a lamp from the stairway shining through the crack of the secret door.

With a throbbing heart I watched that thread of light, drawn on the black shadow of the pilaster, as it waxed in brightness from moment to moment. At last plain sounds from within the woodwork told us that our visitor had come. There was a soft scraping like the sound of a groping hand – two successive creaks followed by a sharp click. Then the secret door swung open, and a man stepped out into the room.

At first, he was no more than a dim, dark shape, as he stood in the shadow, but when he moved, I could see that he was hatless, and that he carried a good-sized hand-bag in one hand and in the other what looked like a large electric lamp, the light of which was switched off. From the door he went across to the table and laid his bag on it. Then he walked softly up the room until he came to the door, where he switched on his lamp and threw its light on the seals. Apparently their appearance satisfied him, for he turned away after a brief glance, but then, as if by an after-thought, he turned back and threw the light on again. Evidently he had detected something amiss, for, after a few moments' inspection, he mounted the steps to examine the seals more closely. As be did so, Thorndyke glided like a shadow from the workshop door to the pilaster, where he halted just in front of the secret opening. Almost at the same moment looking out from the workshop, I saw another shadow glide out of the door of the farther room without a sound and slip round behind the stranger as he ascended the steps.

At this point, I crept silently out into the gallery, for the reflection from the moonlit floor enabled me to recognize this second shadow as the Superintendent, and I knew that the critical moment had come. It had seemed to me that Miller had moved quite noiselessly, but apparently I was wrong for, at the very moment when his arm stretched out to seize his prey, the stranger turned sharply and, as the light of his lamp fell on the Superintendent, he uttered a sort of snarl, struck out viciously, and wrenched himself away, springing from the steps and racing down the room, closely pursued by Miller and Woodburn.

As to what followed my recollections are somewhat confused. It all happened so quickly and the light was so imperfect that nothing but a general impression remains. I saw the fugitive adroitly catch up a chair and whirl it back at his pursuers, with the result that Miller staggered heavily sideways, and Woodburn, whose legs it struck, fell sprawling on the floor. The next moment, as the man swerved to pass the workshop door, the light of his lamp fell on Thorndyke. I think that in that instant he must have recognized him, for he uttered a savage cry, checked for a moment, and then threw out his arm. Instantly I realized, though I could not see it, that the hand of that extended arm held a pistol, and I started forward. But at that instant something hurtled past me and struck the stranger in the face with such force that he staggered backward. The report of the pistol rang out sharply, and the missile, whatever it was, clattered heavily on the floor.

It had been a near thing and, indeed it was not yet over, though Miller had now rushed forward and grasped the pistol arm while I sprang at the other. But our prisoner fought and struggled like a maniac, yet with a settled purpose, for the flash and report of the pistol were repeated again and again, not at random, but always when the weapon could be brought to bear in Thorndyke's direction. Now, however, my colleague, having closed and fastened the secret door, came forward to take a hand

444

with the light of his lamp turned full on the struggling, swaying group, which had now been joined by Woodburn.

Suddenly I heard Thorndyke call out sharply, "Keep out of the way, Polton!" At the same moment I caught sight of our artificer, skirmishing round at Miller's side, with his eyes riveted on the pistol. Almost as Thorndyke spoke, a pair of large crucible-tongs came into view, reaching out towards the hand which held the weapon. There was a quick but unhurried movement, and the tongs took firm hold of the pistol by its flat stock. Then the long handles were quietly raised and twisted the weapon irresistibly out of the prisoner's grasp.

The removal of the pistol brought the struggle virtually to an end. I did, indeed, feel the hand which I controlled thrusting towards the waist-belt. But I had already detected the presence there of a sheath-knife of formidable size, and I easily circumvented the movement. And, when Thorndyke seized both the prisoner's wrists and held them together, Miller was able to snap on the handcuffs. Even then, our prisoner continued to struggle violently, and it was not until Thorndyke had encircled his legs and pinioned his arms with a couple of document straps (which he had, apparently, put in his pocket for that purpose) that his resistance ceased. Then we sat him in a chair and, while we recovered our breath, considered the next move.

"I think," said Miller, "I will just run across to the churchyard and relieve my men. They may be able to produce some sort of transport. If not, I shall have to borrow Mr. Woodburn's car. I leave the prisoner in your custody, Doctor."

As soon as he had gone, Woodburn proceeded to light the two hanging lamps which swung by long chains from beams in the gallery ceiling – for there was neither gas nor electric light in the house – when we were able to survey one another and examine our prisoner. Woodburn was the only one of us who had suffered visibly from the encounter, having an undeniable black eye. But the prisoner was a sorry spectacle and, villain as he was, I could not but feel some twinges of compunction as I looked at him. His face was badly bruised and bleeding, at which I was not surprised, when I picked up the missile that had struck him and recognized it as Polton's "case-opener", but what most contributed to his forlorn and wretched aspect was his bald head, from which the wig had been dislodged during the fray. It was not a common, natural, and decent bald head, which would have been normal enough, but the baldness was in large patches with separating areas of stubble – the condition, in fact, known to our profession as *Alopecia areata*.

I picked up the wig and carefully replaced it on his head, disregarding his profane and furious protests. Then I went with

445

Thorndyke to the workshop, where the research case had been deposited, to fetch the little first-aid case that was part of its permanent equipment and, as I was thus engaged, Thorndyke proceeded to moralize.

"That *Alopecia* is interesting," he remarked. "I mean, as an illustration of the incalculability of human affairs. If be had not been compelled to wear a wig, he would probably never have thought of personating Dobey. Probably, too, he would not have murdered Badger – at any rate not in that way, and he might not have murdered Toke. Evidently, the course of his criminal career has been largely influenced by his *Alopecia*. He had to wear a wig, but he could wear any kind of wig that he pleased and change it at any time for any other kind that circumstances seemed to require."

"Yes," I agreed, "a disguise which has to be habitually worn naturally suggests additions and variations."

I took the little emergency case and a basin of water, and we went back to the prisoner. As I was mixing some lotion while Thorndyke prepared a dressing, the patient watched him with a glare of the most concentrated malice.

"Don't you touch me, you devil!" he exclaimed, huskily, "or I'll bite you! I ought to have settled with you years ago."

In different circumstances it might have been permissible to remind him that he had made three pretty determined attempts. Nevertheless, as a matter of policy, he was certainly right. But for Thorndyke, be would have been, at this moment, at large and unsuspected.

I had hardly finished attending to his damaged face when Miller returned.

"We shall be able to manage quite well," he announced. "My men discovered a car in that lane – heard it arrive, in fact. So I shan't want Mr. Woodburn's. We can take him to London in his own car."

Here the two officers entered and, advancing up the gallery, took a long and curious look at the prisoner. Then Miller proceeded to make the formal charge.

"I arrest you, Walter Hornby, for the murder of Mr. Didbury Toke, and I caution you that anything you say will be taken down in writing and may be used against you – "

"Oh, go to blazes!" interrupted Hornby. "Do you think I am a cackling old woman? I am not going to say anything."

Nevertheless, in spite of his bravado, I had the impression that the nature of the charge came as an appalling shock. I think he had expected to be charged only with breaking and entering, for after this outburst he settled down into sullen silence and submitted passively to being carried away by the two officers. Only once, as he was borne out, he turned his head to bestow on Thorndyke a look of the most concentrated malignancy.

When the grim procession, accompanied by the Superintendent, had passed out and the footsteps had died away, Thorndyke turned to his faithful henchman and laid his hand on his shoulder.

"It was fortunate for me, Polton," said he, "that you would not go to bed. But for that remarkable shot of yours, I think Hornby would have settled his account with me, after all."

Polton crinkled apologetically and gave a little embarrassed cough as he replied, "Yes, sir, I thought I might be useful. You see, sir, when I was younger, I used to take a good deal of practice at the coco-nuts on Hampstead Heath. I got to be quite a dab at 'em, and the Aunt Sallies, too."

At this moment, the gallery door opened, and Mrs. Gibbins entered spectrally, bearing a lighted candle in a bedroom candlestick.

"I've come to tell you, sir," she said, addressing Woodburn, "that I have laid supper in the dining-room. Mr. Miller is coming back to join you when he has seen the other officers off in the car."

It was an undeniably welcome announcement and, when Woodburn had extinguished the lamps, we switched on our electric lanterns and followed the housekeeper along the winding corridor.

Chapter XVIII
Postscript

With the arrest of Walter Hornby, this history – which is that of an investigation – naturally comes to an end. In the course of the events that followed, nothing transpired that could be regarded as a new discovery. Certain details were filled in, and certain conclusions which had been arrived at by inference were confirmed by actual demonstration. Thus, at the inquest, it was proved that Mr. Toke had died from a deep knife wound, and the evidence left no doubt that it had been inflicted, as Thorndyke had suggested, just as he was in the act of emerging from the tomb. The wound corresponded exactly with the knife which was on Hornby's person when he was arrested. And though that knife had been carefully washed, when Polton, under Thorndyke's supervision, unriveted and removed the wooden handle, considerable traces of blood were discovered – sufficient, in fact, to admit of a biochemical test which showed it to be human blood.

At the trial, there was practically no defence, nor was there any appeal from the conviction and sentence. The prisoner was indicted for the murder of Mr. Toke, the other crime being held back for a further indictment in the unlikely event of an acquittal. But of an acquittal there was never the remotest chance. For, in addition to the profoundly incriminating fact that Hornby had been captured in actual occupation of the murdered man's premises and in command of the secret passages in which the body was concealed, there was the utterly damning fact that Mr. Toke's signet ring was found in his pocket when he was searched after his arrest.

It was unavoidable that the trial and its dreadful sequel should be a cause of pain to many estimable people, including his cousin Reuben – against whom he had hatched such a dastardly plot in the years gone by. To my wife, who had been almost in the position of a relative, the whole sordidly tragic affair was so harrowing that we tacitly agreed not to speak of it. Even I, who had known the man in the days of his prosperity and respectability, could hardly bring myself to contemplate his present terrible plight, and I was almost disposed to resent Thorndyke's calm, impersonal interest in the trial and his satisfaction at the conviction and the sentence. For a man so kindly by nature, this callousness – as it appeared to me – seemed surprising and hardly natural. I think I must have given expression to some such sentiments on the day, I remember, when the execution had just taken place, and he was calmly collecting the notes and memoranda of the case to put away in the files where the records were kept. His reply was characteristic and, looking back, I am not much disposed to cavil at it.

"I understand, Jervis," said he, "your personal discomfort in contemplating this tragedy, the shipwreck of a life that started with so much promise and had such potentialities of usefulness and success. But it is a mistake to grow sentimental over the Nemesis that awaits the criminal. The most far-reaching mercy that can be exercised in social life is to safeguard the liberties of those who respect the liberties of others. Believe me, Jervis, the great purveyor of human happiness is not philanthropy, which seeks to soften the lot of the unworthy, but justice, which secures to the worthy the power to achieve their own happiness, by protecting them from the wrong-doer and the social parasite."

The End

1933 Hodder & Stoughton, London Cover

Chapter I
Of a Strange Treasure Trove
and a Double Life

The attendant at the cloak room at Fenchurch Street Station glanced at the ticket which had just been handed to him by a tall, hawk-faced, and rather anxious-looking man, and ran an inquiring eye over the assemblage of trunks, bags, and other objects that crowded the floor of the room.

"Wooden, iron-bound case, you said?" he remarked.

"Yes. Name of Dobson on the label. That looks like the one," he added, craning over the barrier and watching eagerly as the attendant threaded his way among the litter of packages.

"Dobson it is," the man confirmed, stooping over the case and, with an obviously puzzled expression, comparing the ticket that had been pasted on it with the counterfoil which he held in his hand. "Rum affair, though," he added. "It seems to be your case but it has got the wrong number on it. Will you come in and have a look at it and see that it is all right?"

The presumptive owner offered no objection. On the contrary, he raised the bar of the barrier with the greatest alacrity and took the shortest route among the trunks and portmanteaux until he arrived at the place where the case was standing. And then his expression became even more puzzled than that of the attendant.

"This is very extraordinary," he exclaimed.

"What is?" demanded the attendant.

"Why!" the other explained, "it is the right name and the same sort of case, but this is not the label that I wrote and I don't believe that it is the same case."

The attendant regarded him with a surprised grin and again remarked that "it was a rum affair," adding, after a reflective pause, "It rather looks as if there had been some mistake, as there easily might be with two cases exactly alike and the same name on both. Were the contents of your case of any particular value?"

"They were, indeed!" the owner exclaimed in an agitated tone. "That case contained property worth several thousand pounds."

The attendant whistled and apparently began to see things in a new light, for he asked a little anxiously, "When do you say you deposited the case?"

452

"Late on Saturday evening."

"Yes, I thought I remembered," said the attendant. "Then the muddle, if there has been one, must have happened yesterday. I wasn't here then. It was my Sunday off. But are you quite sure that this is really not your case?"

"It certainly is not the label that I wrote," was the reply. "But I won't swear that it is a different case, though I don't think that it is the right one. But you see, as the name on the label is my name and the address is my address, it can't be a matter of a simple mistake. It looks like a case of deliberate substitution. And that seems to be borne out by the fact that the change must have been made on a Sunday when the regular attendant was not here."

"Yes," the other agreed, "there's no denying that it does look a bit fishy. But look here, sir, if your name and address is on the label, you are entitled to assume that this is your case. As you say, it is either yours or it is a deliberate substitute and, in either case, you have the right to open it and see if your property is inside. That will settle the question right away. I can lend you a screw-driver."

The presumptive owner caught eagerly at the suggestion and began forthwith to untie the thick cord which surrounded the case. The screw-driver was produced and, while the official turned away to attend to two other clients, it was plied vigorously on the eight long screws by which the lid of the case was secured.

The two newcomers, of whom one appeared to be an American and the other an Englishman, had come to claim a number of trunks and travelling-bags, and as some of these, especially those belonging to the American gentleman, were of imposing dimensions, the attendant prudently admitted them that they might identify their packages and so save unnecessary hauling about. While they were carrying out their search he returned to Mr. Dobson and watched him as he extracted the last of the screws.

"Now we shall see whether there has been any jiggery pokery," he remarked, when the screw had been laid down with the others, and Mr. Dobson prepared to raise the lid. And in fact they did see, and a very singular effect the sight had on them both. Mr. Dobson sprang back with a gasp of horror and the attendant uttered the single word, "Golly!"

After staring into the case incredulously for a couple of amazed seconds, Dobson slammed down the lid and demanded, breathlessly, "Where can I find a policeman?"

"You'll find one somewhere near the barrier or else just outside the station. Or you could get on the phone and – "

Mr. Dobson did not wait to hear the conclusion of the sentence but darted out towards the barrier and disappeared in the direction of the main entrance. Meanwhile, the two strangers, who had apparently overheard Mr. Dobson's question, abandoned for the time being the inspection of their luggage and approached the case, on which the attendant's eyes were still riveted.

"Anything amiss?" the Englishman asked.

The attendant made no reply but silently lifted the lid of the case, held it up for a moment or two and then let it drop.

"Good Lord!" exclaimed the Englishman, "it looks like a man's head!"

"It *is* a man's head," the attendant confirmed. And, in fact, there was no doubt about it, though only a hairy crown was visible, through a packing of clothes or rags.

"Who is the chappie who has just bolted out?" the Englishman inquired. "He seemed mightily taken aback."

"So would you have been," the attendant retorted, "if you had come to claim a package and found this in its place." He followed up this remark with a brief summary of the circumstances.

"Well!" observed the American, "I have heard it said that exchange is no robbery, but I guess that the party who made this exchange got the best of the deal."

The Englishman grinned. "You are right there, Mr. Pippet," said he. "I've heard of a good many artful dodges for disposing of a superfluous corpse, but I have never heard of a murderer swapping it for a case of jewellery or bullion."

The three men stood silently looking at the case and occasionally glancing round in the direction of the entrance. Presently the American inquired, "Is there any particular scarcity of policemen in this city?"

The attendant looked round again anxiously towards the entrance.

"He is a long time finding that policeman," said he in reply to the implied comment.

"Yes," rejoined Mr. Pippet, "and I guess that policeman will be a long time finding him."

The attendant turned on him with a distinctly startled expression.

"You don't think he has done a bunk, do you?" he asked uneasily.

"Well," replied Pippet, "he didn't waste any time in getting outside, and he doesn't seem to have had much luck in what he went for. I reckon one of us had better have a try. You know the place better than I do, Buffham."

454

"Yes, sir, if you would," urged the attendant. "I can't leave the place myself. But I think we ought to have a constable as soon as possible, and it does rather look as if that gent had mizzled."

On this, Mr. Buffham turned and rapidly made his way through the litter of trunks and packages and strode away towards the entrance through which he vanished, while the attendant reluctantly tore himself away from the mysterious case to hand out one or two rugs and suit-cases, and Mr. Pippet resumed his salvage operations on his trunks and portmanteaux. In less than three minutes Mr. Buffham was seen returning with a constable, and the attendant raised the barrier to admit them. Apparently, Mr. Buffham had given the officer a general sketch of the circumstances as they had come along, for the latter remarked, as he eyed the case, "So this is the box of mystery, is it? And you say that there is a person's head inside it?"

"You can see for yourself," said the attendant, and with this he raised the lid and, having peered in, he looked at the constable, who, after an impassive and judicial survey, admitted that it did look like a man's head, and produced from his pocket a portentous, black notebook.

"The first question," said he, "is about this man who has absconded. Can you give me a description of him?"

The three men consulted and between them evolved a description which might have been illuminating to anyone who was intimately acquainted with the absent stranger, but furnished indifferent material for the identification of an unknown individual. They agreed, however, that he was somewhat tall and dark, with a thin face, a Torpedo beard and moustache, and a rather prominent nose, that he was dressed in dark-coloured clothing and wore a soft felt hat. Mr. Pippet further expressed the opinion that the man's hair and beard were dyed.

"Yes," said the constable, closing his notebook, "he seems to have been a good deal like other people. They usually are. That's the worst of it. If people who commit crimes would only be a bit more striking in their appearance and show a little originality in the way they dress, it would make things so much more simple for us. But it's a queer affair. The puzzle is what he came here for, and why, having come, he proceeded to do a bolt. He couldn't have known what was in the case, or he wouldn't have come. And, if the case wasn't his, I don't see why he should have hopped it and put himself under suspicion. I had better take your names and addresses, gentlemen, as you saw him, though you don't seem to have much to tell. Then I think I will get on the phone to headquarters."

He re-opened the notebook and, having taken down the names and addresses of the two gentlemen, went out in search of the telephone.

As he departed, Mr. Pippet, apparently dismissing the mysterious case from his mind as an affair finished and done with, reverted to the practical business of sorting out his luggage, in which occupation he was presently joined by Mr. Buffham.

"I am going to get a taxi," said the former, "to take me to my hotel – the Pendennis in Great Russell Street. Can I put you down anywhere? I see you're travelling pretty light."

Mr. Buffham cast a deprecating eye on the modest portmanteau which contained his entire outfit and a questioning eye on the imposing array of trunks and bags which appertained to his companion, and reflected for a moment.

"The taxi-man will jib at your lot," said he, "without adding mine to it."

"Yes," agreed Pippet, "I shall have to get two taxis in any case, so one of them can't complain of an extra package. Where are you putting up?"

"I am staying for a few days at a boarding house in Woburn Place, not so very far from you. But I was thinking that, when we have disposed of our traps, you might come and have some dinner with me at a restaurant that I know of. What do you say?"

"Why, the fact is," said Pippet, "that I was just about to make the very same proposal, only I was going to suggest that we dine together at my hotel. And, if you don't mind, I think it will be the better plan, as I have got a suite of rooms that we can retire to after dinner for a quiet yarn. Do you mind?"

Mr. Buffham did not mind. On the contrary, he accepted with something approaching eagerness. For his own reasons, he had resolved to cultivate the not-very-intimate acquaintanceship which had been established during the voyage from New York to Tilbury, and he was better pleased to do so at Mr. Pippet's expense than at his own, and the mention of the suite of rooms had strongly confirmed him in his resolution. A man who chartered a suite of rooms at a London hotel must be something more than substantial. But Mr. Pippet's next observation gave him less satisfaction.

"You are wondering, I suppose, what a solitary male like me can want with a suite of rooms all to himself. The explanation is that I am not all by myself. I am expecting my daughter and sister over from Paris tomorrow, and I can't have them hanging about in the public rooms with no corner to call their own. But until they arrive, I am what they call *en garçon* over there."

Having thus made clear his position, Mr. Pippet went forth and shortly returned accompanied by two taxi-men of dour aspect and

456

taciturn habit, who silently collected the baggage and bore it out to their respective vehicles, which, in due course, set forth upon their journey.

Before following them, we may linger awhile to note the results of the constable's mission. They were not very sensational. In the course of a few minutes, an inspector arrived and, having made a brief confirmatory inspection, called for the screws and the screwdriver and proceeded in an impassive but workmanlike manner to replace the former in their holes and drive them home. Then he, in his turn, sent out for a taxi-man, by whom the case with its gruesome contents was borne out unsuspectingly to the waiting vehicle and spirited away to an unknown destination.

When Mr. Buffham's solitary portmanteau had been dumped down in the hall of a somewhat seedy house in Woburn Place, the two taxis moved on to the portals of the quiet but select hotel in Great Russell Street, where the mountainous pile of baggage was handed over to the hotel porter with brief directions as to its disposal. Then the two men, after the necessary ablutions, made their way to the dining room and selected a table in a comparatively retired corner, where Mr. Buffham waited in some anxiety as to the quality of the entertainment. His experience of middle-aged American men had given him the impression that they were not, as a class, enthusiastic feeders, and it was with sensible relief that he discovered in his host the capacity to take a reasonable interest in his food. In fact, the gastronomic arrangements were so much to his satisfaction that, for a time, they engaged his entire attention for, if the whole truth must be told, this dinner was not an entirely unforeseen contingency and, as he had providently modified his diet with that possibility in view, he was now in a condition to do complete justice to the excellent fare provided. Presently, however, when the razor-edge had been taken off his appetite, his attention reverted to larger interests and he began cautiously to throw out feelers. Not that an extreme amount of caution was really necessary, for Mr. Pippet was a simple, straightforward, open-minded man, shrewd enough in the ordinary business of life and gifted with a massive common-sense. But he was quite devoid of cunning, and trustful of his fellow-creatures to an extent that is somewhat unusual in citizens of the United States. He was, in fact, the exact opposite in mental and moral type of the man who faced him across the table.

"Well!" said Buffham, raising his newly-refilled glass, "here's to a successful beano. I suppose you contemplate laying a delicate wash of carmine over the British landscape. Or is it to be a full tint of vermilion?"

"Now you are talking in tropes and metaphors," said Pippet, with an indulgent smile, "but, as I interpret the idiom, you think we are going to make things hum."

"I assume that you are over here to have a good time."

"We always like to have a good time if we can manage it, wherever we may be," said Pippet, "and I hope to pass the time pleasantly while I am in the Old Country. But I have come over with a more definite purpose than that and, if I should tell you what that purpose is, I should make you smile."

"And a very pleasant result, too," said Buffham. "I like to be made to smile. But, of course, I don't want to pry into your private affairs, even for the sake of a smile."

"My private affairs will probably soon be public affairs," said Pippet, "so I need not maintain any particular reticence about them and, in any case, there's nothing to be ashamed or secret about. If it interests you to know, my visit to England is connected with a claim to an English title and the estates that go with it."

Buffham was thunderstruck. But he did not smile. The affair was much too serious for that. Instead, he demanded in a hushed voice, "Do you mean that you are making a claim on your own behalf?"

Mr. Pippet chuckled. "Sounds incredible, doesn't it? But that is the cold-drawn fact. I am setting up a claim to the Earldom of Winsborough and to the lands and other property that appertain to it, all of which I understand to be at present vacant and calling aloud for an owner."

Mr. Buffham pulled himself together. This looked like a good deal bigger affair than he had anticipated. Indeed, he had not anticipated anything in particular. His professional habits – if we may so designate them – led him to cultivate the society of rich men of all kinds, and by preference that of wealthy Americans making an European tour. Not that the globe-trotting American is a peculiarly simple and trustful soul. But he is in a holiday mood, he is in unaccustomed surroundings and usually has money to spend and a strong inclination to spend it. Mr. Buffham's role was to foster that inclination and, as far as possible, to collaborate in the associated activities. He had proposed to fasten upon Mr. Pippet, if he could, in a Micawber-like hope that something profitable might turn up. But the prospect opened up by Mr. Pippet's announcement was beyond his wildest dreams.

"I suppose," Mr. Pippet continued after a brief pause, "you are wondering what in creation a middle-aged American in comfortable circumstances wants with an English title and estates?"

"I am not wondering anything of the kind," replied Buffham. "The position of a great English nobleman is one that might well tempt the

458

ambition of an American if he were twenty times a millionaire. Think of the august dignity of that position! Of the universal deference that it commands! Think of the grand old mansions and the parks planted with immemorial trees, the great town house and the seat in the House of Lords, and – and – "

"Yes, I know," chuckled Pippet, "I've had all that rubbed into me and, to tell the bald truth, I wouldn't give a damn for the whole boiling if I had only myself to consider. I don't want to have people calling me 'My Lord' and making me feel like a fool, and I've no use for baronial mansions or ancestral halls. A good comfortable hotel where they know how to cook answers all my requirements. But I've got to go in for this business whether I like it or not. My womenfolk have got me fairly in tow, especially my sister. She's just mad to be Lady Arminella – in fact, if I hadn't put my foot down she'd have settled the matter in advance and taken the title on account, so to speak."

"I suppose," said Buffham, "you have got your claim pretty well cut-and-dried? Got all your evidence, I mean, and arranged with your lawyer as to the plan of campaign?"

"Well, no!" replied Pippet, "at present things are rather in the air. But if we have finished, perhaps we might take our coffee up in my sitting room. We can talk more freely there. But don't let me bore you. After all, it isn't your funeral."

"My dear sir!" exclaimed Buffham, with genuine sincerity, "you are not boring me. I assure you that I am profoundly interested. If you won't consider me inquisitive, I should like to hear the whole story in as much detail as you care to give."

Mr. Pippet nodded and smiled. "Good!" said he, as they ascended the stairs to the private suite, "you shall have all the detail you want. I shall enjoy giving it to you, as it will help to get the affair into my own head a trifle more clearly. It's a queer story and I must admit that it does not sound any too convincing. The whole claim rests upon a tradition that I heard from my father."

Mr. Buffham was a little disappointed, but only a little. As his host had said, it – the claim – was not his funeral. A wild cat claim might answer his purpose as well as any other, perhaps even better. Nevertheless, he remarked with an assumption of anxiety, "I hope there is something to go on besides the tradition. You'll have to deal with a court of law, you know."

"Yes, I realize that," replied Pippet, "and I may say that there is some corroborative matter. I'll tell you about that presently. But there's this much about the tradition, that it admits of being put to the test, as you'll see when I give you the story. And I will do that right away.

"The tradition, then, as I had it from my father from time to time, in rather disjointed fragments, was that his father was a very remarkable character – in fact, he was two characters rolled into one, for he led a double life. As my father and mother knew him, he was Mr. Josiah Pippet, the landlord of a house of call in the City of London known as The Fox and Grapes. But a persistent tradition had it that the name of Josiah Pippet was an assumed name and that he was really the Earl of Winsborough. It is known that he was in the habit of absenting himself from his London premises from time to time and that when he did so he disappeared completely, leaving no hint of his whereabouts. Now, it seems that the Earl, who was a bachelor, was a somewhat eccentric gentleman of similar habits. He also was accustomed periodically to absent himself from the Castle, and he also used to disappear, leaving no clue to his whereabouts. And rumour had it that these disappearances were, as the scientists would say, correlated, like the little figures in those old-fashioned toy houses that foretold the weather. When the old man came out, the old woman went in, and vice versa. So it was said that when Josiah disappeared from The Fox and Grapes, his Lordship made his appearance at Winsborough Castle, and when his Lordship disappeared from the Castle, Josiah popped up at The Fox and Grapes."

"Is there any record of the movements of the two men?" Buffham asked.

"Well, there is a diary, along with a lot of letters and other stuff. I have just glanced at some of it but I can't I say of my own observation that there is a definite record. However, my sister has gone through the whole lot and she says that it is all as plain as a pike-staff."

Buffham nodded with an air of satisfaction that was by no means assumed. He began to see splendid possibilities in his host's case.

"Yes," said he, "this is much more hopeful. If you can show that these disappearances coincided in time, that will be a very striking piece of evidence. You have got these documents with you?"

"Yes, I have got them in a deed box in my bedroom. I have been intending to make a serious attack on them and to go right through them."

"What would be much more to the point," said Buffham, "would be to hand the box to your lawyer and let him go through them. He will be accustomed to examining documents, and he will see the significance – the legal significance, I mean – of little, inconspicuous facts that might easily escape a non-professional eye. I think you said you had a lawyer?"

"No. That's a matter that I shall have to attend to at once, and I don't quite know how to go about it. I understand that they don't advertise in this country."

"No," said Buffham, "certainly not. But I see your difficulty. You naturally want to get a suitable man, and it is most important. You want to secure the services of a solicitor whose position and character would command the respect and confidence of the court, and who has had experience of cases of a similar kind. That is absolutely vital. I recall a case which illustrates the danger of employing a lawyer of an unsuitable kind. It was, like yours, a case of disputed succession. There were two claimants whom we may call '*A*' and '*B*'. Now Mr. '*A*' had undoubtedly the better case. But unfortunately for him, he employed a solicitor whose sole experience was concerned with commercial law. He was an excellent man, but he knew practically nothing of the intricacies of succession to landed property. Mr. '*B*', on the other hand, had the good fortune to secure a lawyer whose practice had been very largely concerned with these very cases. He knew all the ropes, you see, and the result was that the case was decided in Mr. '*B*'s' favour. But it ought not to have been. I had it, in confidence, from his lawyer (whom I happened to know rather well) that if he had been acting for Mr. '*A*', instead of for Mr. '*B*', the decision would certainly have gone the other way. '*A*' had the better claim, but his lawyer had not realized it and had failed to put it before the court in a sufficiently convincing manner."

Having given this striking instance, Buffham looked anxiously at his host, and was a trifle disappointed at its effect. Still more so was he with that gentleman's comment.

"Seems to me," the latter remarked, "that that court wasn't particularly on the spot if they let your lawyer friend bluff them into giving Mr. '*B*' the property that properly belonged to Mr. '*A*'. And I shouldn't have thought that your friend would have found it a satisfactory deal. At any rate, I am not wanting any lawyer to grab property for me that belongs to somebody else. As long as I believe in this claim myself, I'm going for it for all I am worth. But I am not going to drop my egg into somebody else's rightful nest, like your Mr. '*B*'."

"Of course you are not!" Buffham hastened to reply, considerably disconcerted by his host's unexpected attitude, so difficult is it for a radically dishonest man to realize that his is not the usual and normal state of mind. "But neither do you want to find yourself in the position of Mr. '*A*'."

"No," Pippet admitted, "I don't. I just want a square deal, and I always understood that you could get it in an English court."

"So you can," said Buffham. "But you must realize that a court can only decide on the facts and arguments put before it. It is the business of the lawyers to supply those facts and arguments. And I think you are hardly just to my lawyer friend – his name, by the way, is Gimbler – a

461

most honourable and conscientious man. I must point out that a lawyer's duty is to present his client's case in the most forcible and convincing way that he can. He is not concerned with the other man's case. He assumes – and so does the court – that the opposing lawyer will do the same for his client, and then the court will have both cases completely presented. It is the client's business to employ a lawyer who is competent to put his case properly to the court."

Mr. Pippet nodded. "Yes," he said, reflectively, "I see the idea. But the difficulty in the case of a stranger like myself is to find the particular kind of lawyer who has the special knowledge and experience that is required. Now, as to this friend of yours, Gimbler – you say that he specializes in disputed claims to property."

"I didn't say that he specialized in them, but I know that he has had considerable experience of them."

"Well, now, do you suppose that he would be willing to take up this claim of mine?"

Mr. Buffham did not suppose at all. He knew. Nevertheless he replied warily, "It depends. He wouldn't want to embark on a case that was going to result in a fiasco. He would want to hear an about the claim and what evidence there is to support it. And especially he would want to go very carefully through those documents of yours."

"Yes," said Pippet, "that seems to be the correct line, and that is what I should want him to do. I'd like to have an expert opinion on the whole affair before I begin to get busy. I am not out to exploit a mare's nest and make a public fool of myself. But we didn't finish the story. We only got to the Box and Cox business of Josiah and the Earl. It seems that this went on for a number of years, and nothing seems to have been thought of it at the time. But when Josiah's wife died and his son – my father – was settled, he appears to have wearied of the complications of his double life and made up his mind to put an end to them. And the simplest and most conclusive way to write *Finis* on the affair seemed to him to be to die and get buried. And that is what he did. According to the story, he faked a last illness and engineered a sham death. I don't know how he managed it. Seems to me pretty difficult. But the rumour had it that he managed to get people to believe that he had died, and he had a funeral with a dummy coffin, properly weighted with lumps of lead, and that this was successfully planted in the family vault. I am bound to admit that this part of the story does sound a trifle thin. But it seems to have been firmly believed in the family."

It would have been a relief to Mr. Buffham to snigger aloud. But sniggering was not his role. Still, he felt called on to make some kind of criticism. Accordingly, he remarked judicially, "There do certainly seem to be difficulties, the death certificate, for instance. You would hardly expect a doctor to mistake a live, healthy man for a corpse – unless Josiah made it worth his while. It would be simple enough then."

"I understand," said Mr. Pippet, "that doctors often used to give a certificate without viewing the body. But the lawyer will know that. At any rate, it is obvious that someone must have been in the know, and that is probably how the rumour got started."

"And when did the Earl die?"

"That I can't tell you, off hand. But it was some years after Josiah's funeral."

"And who holds the title and estate now?"

"Nobody. At least, so I understand. The last – or present – Earl went away to Africa or some other uncivilized place, big game shooting, and never came back. As there was never any announcement of the Earl's death, things seem to have drifted on as if he was alive. I have never heard of any claimant."

"There couldn't be until the Earl's death was either proved or presumed by the permission of the court. So the first thing that you will have to do will be to take proceedings to have the death of the Earl presumed."

"Not the first thing," said Pippet. "There is one question that will have to be settled before we definitely make the claim. The tradition says that Josiah's death was a fake and that his coffin was a dummy weighted with lead. Now, that is a statement of fact that admits of proof or disproof. The first thing that we have got to do is to get that coffin open. If we find Josiah inside, that will settle the whole business, and I shan't care a hoot whether the Earl is alive or dead."

Once again Mr. Buffham was sensible of a slight feeling of disappointment. In a man who was prepared to consider seriously such a manifestly preposterous cock-and-bull story as this, he had not looked for so reasonable a state of mind. Of course, Pippet was quite right from his own idiotic point of view. The opening of the coffin was the *experimentum crucis*. And when it was opened, there, of course, would be the body, and the bubble would be most effectively burst. But Mr. Buffham did not want the bubble burst. The plan which was shaping itself vaguely in his mind was concerned with keeping that bubble in a healthy state of inflation. And again, his crooked mind found it hard to understand Pippet's simple, honest, straightforward outlook. If he had been the claimant, his strongest efforts would have been devoted to seeing that nobody meddled with that coffin. And he had a feeling that his friend Gimbler would take the same view.

463

"Of course," he conceded, "you are perfectly correct, but there may be difficulties that you don't quite realize. I don't know how it is in America, but in this country you can't just dig up a coffin and open it if you want to know who is inside. There are all sorts of formalities before you can get permission, and I doubt whether faculty would be granted until you had made out some sort of a case in the courts. So the moral is that you must get as impressive a body of evidence together as you can. Have you got any other facts besides what you have told me? For instance, do you know what these two men – Josiah and the Earl – were like? Do they appear to have resembled each other?"

Mr. Pippet grinned. "If Josiah and the Earl," said he, "were one and the same person, they would naturally be a good deal alike. I understand that they were. That is one of the strong points of the story. Both of them were a bit out-size, well over six feet in height. Both were fair, blue-eyed men with a shaved upper lip and long sandy side-whiskers."

"You can prove that, can you?"

"I can swear that I had information to that effect from my father, who knew one and had seen the other. And there is one other point – only a small one, but every little bit of corroboration helps. My father told me on several occasions that his father – Josiah – had often told him that he was born in Winsborough Castle."

"Ha!" exclaimed Buffham, "that's better. That establishes a definite connexion. It's a pity, though, that he was not more explicit. And now, with regard to these documents that you spoke of – what is the nature of them?"

"To tell you the truth," replied Pippet, "I don't know much about them. I've been used to an active life and I'm not a great reader, so I've not done much more than glance over them. But as I mentioned, my sister has gone through them carefully and she reckons that they as good as prove that Josiah and the Earl were one and the same person. Would you like to have a look at them?"

A mere affirmative would have been inadequate to express Mr. Buffham's ravenous desire to see whether there was or was not the making of a possible legal case. Nevertheless, he replied in a tone of studied indifference, "My opinion is not much to the point, but I should certainly like to see what sort of material you will be able to give your lawyer."

Thereupon Mr. Pippet retired to the bedroom, from which he presently emerged carrying a good-sized deed box. This he placed on the table and, having gone deliberately through a large bunch of keys, eventually selected one and carefully fitted it into the lock while Buffham watched him hungrily. The box being opened, the two men

464

drew their chairs up to the table and peered into its interior, which was occupied by a collection of bundles of papers, neatly tied up with red tape, each bundle being distinguished by means of a label inscribed in an old-fashioned feminine handwriting. In addition, there were seven small, leather-bound volumes.

Buffham picked out the bundles, one after another, and read the labels. "*Letters from J.S. to his wife*", "*Letters from various persons to J.S.*", "*Copies of letters from J.S. to various persons*", "*Various tradesmen's bills and accounts*", and so on. Having asked his host's permission, he untied one or two of the bundles and read samples of the letters and tradesmen's bills with a feeling of stupefaction, mingled with astonished speculations as to the mental peculiarities of his host's sister.

"Yes," he said, gloomily replacing the last of them, "I dare say a careful analysis of these letters may yield some relevant information, but it will need the expert eye of the trained lawyer to detect the relevancy of some of them. There is, for instance, a bill for two pounds of pork sausages and a black pudding, which seems rather beside the mark. But you never know. Important legal points may be involved in the most unexpected matter. What are those little books? Are they the diaries that you spoke of?"

Mr. Pippet nodded and handed one of them to him, which proved to be the diary for the year 1833. He turned over the leaves and scanned the entries with more interest but still with a feeling of bewilderment. After examining a few sample pages, he handed the volume back to Pippet, remarking a little wearily, "The late Josiah didn't go into much detail. The entries are very dry and brief and seem to be concerned chiefly with the trivial happenings of his life from day-to-day and with money paid or received."

"Well, isn't that what diaries are usually filled with?"

Pippet protested, not unreasonably. "And don't you think that those simple, commonplace entries are just the ones to give us the information that we want? My sister said that she learned quite a lot about Josiah's ways of life from those diaries."

"Did she?" said Buffham. "I am glad to hear it, because it suggests that a trained lawyer, going through those diaries with the legal issues in his mind – noting, collating and analyzing the entries – will probably discover significances in the most unexpected places. Which brings us back to the point that you ought to get competent legal assistance without delay."

"Yes, I think you are right," agreed Pippet. "I've got to secure a lawyer sooner or later, so I might as well start right away. Now, to come down to brass tacks, what about this lawyer friend of yours? You say that this case of mine would be in his customary line of business, and you think he would be willing to take it on?"

Mr. Buffham had no doubts whatever, but he did not think it expedient to say so. A retreating tendency on the part of the bait is apt to produce a pursuing tendency on the part of the fish.

"Naturally," said he, "I can't answer for another man's views. He is a busy man, and he might not be prepared to give time to what he might regard as a somewhat speculative case. But we can easily find out. If you like, I will call on him and put the case to him in as favourable a light as possible and, if he doesn't seem eager to take it up, I might use a little gentle pressure. You see, I know him pretty well. Then, if I am successful, I might arrange for you to have an interview, at which, perhaps, it might be advisable for your sister to be present, as she knows more about the affair than you do. Then he could tell you what he thought of your chances and you could let him know what you are prepared to do. What do you think of that plan?"

Mr. Pippet thought that it seemed to meet the case, provided that it could be carried out without delay.

"You understand," said he, "that my sister and daughter will be arriving here tomorrow, and they will be red-hot to get the business started, especially my sister."

"And quite naturally, too," said Buffham. "I sympathize with her impatience and I promise that there shall be no delay on my part. I will call at Gimbler's office tomorrow morning the first thing, before he has had time to begin his morning's work."

"It's very good of you," said Pippet, as his guest rose to take his leave, "to interest yourself in this way in the affairs of a mere stranger."

"Not at all," Buffham rejoined cheerily. "You are forgetting the romance and dramatic interest of your case. Anyone would be delighted to lend you a hand in your adventure. You may depend on hearing from me in the course of tomorrow. Good night and good luck!"

Mr. Pippet, having provided his guest with a fresh cigar, accompanied him down to the entrance and watched him with a meditative eye as he walked away down the street. Apparently, the dwindling figure suggested a train of thought, for he continued to stand looking out even after it had disappeared. At length he turned with a faint sigh and thoughtfully retraced his steps to his own domain.

Chapter II
Mr. Buffham's Legal Friend

No amount of native shrewdness can entirely compensate for deficiency of knowledge. If Mr. Christopher Pippet had been intimately acquainted with English social customs, he would have known that the neighbourhood of Kennington in general, and Kennington Grove in particular, is hardly the place in which to look for the professional premises of a solicitor engaged in important Chancery practice. He did, indeed, survey the rather suburban surroundings with a certain amount of surprise, noting with intelligent interest the contrast between the ways of New York and those of London. He even ventured to comment on the circumstance as he halted at the iron gate of a small garden and read out the inscription on a well-worn brass plate affixed to the gate aforesaid, which set forth the name and professional vocation of *Mr. Horatio Gimbler, Solicitor and Advocate.*

"Buffham didn't tell me that he was an advocate as well as a solicitor," Mr. Pippet remarked, as he pushed the gate open.

"He wouldn't," replied his companion, "but left you to find out for yourself. Of course he knew you would, and then you would give him credit for having understated his friend's merits. It's just vanity."

At the street door, which was closed and bore a duplicate plate, Mr. Pippet pressed an electric bell-push, with the result that there arose from within a sound like the "going off" of an alarm clock and simultaneously the upper half of a face with a pair of beady black eyes appeared for an instant above the wire blind of the adjacent window. Then, after a brief interval, the door opened and revealed an extremely alert youth.

"Is Mr. Gimbler disengaged?" Mr. Pippet inquired.

"Have you got an appointment?" the youth demanded.

"Yes, eleven o'clock, and it's two minutes to the hour now. Shall I go in here?"

He turned towards a door opening out of the hall and marked "*Waiting Room*".

"No," the youth replied, hastily, emphatically and almost in a tone of alarm. "That'th for clienth that haven't got an appointment. What name thall I thay?"

"Mr. and Miss Pippet."

"Oh, yeth, I know. Jutht thtep thith way."

He opened an inner door leading into a small inner hall, which offered to the visitors a prospect of a flight of shabbily carpeted stairs and a strong odour of fried onions. Here he approached a door marked "*Private Office*" and knocked softly, eliciting a responsive but inarticulate roar, whereupon he opened the door and announced, "Mr. and Miss Pippet."

The opened door revealed a large man with a pair of folding pince-nez insecurely balanced on the end of a short, fat nose, apparently writing furiously. As the visitors entered, he looked round with an interrogative frown as if impatient of being interrupted. Then, appearing suddenly to realize who they were, he made a convulsive grimace, which dislodged the eyeglasses and left them dangling free on their broad black ribbon, and was succeeded by a wrinkly but affable smile. Then he rose and, holding out a large, rather fat hand, exclaimed, "Delighted to see you. I had no idea that it was so late. One gets so engrossed in these – er – fascinating – "

"Naturally," said Mr. Pippet, "though I thought it was the documents that got engrossed. However, here we are. Let me introduce you to my sister, Miss Arminella Pippet."

Mr. Gimbler bowed and, for a brief space there was a searching mutual inspection. Miss Pippet saw a physically imposing man, large in all dimensions – tall, broad, deep-chested, and still more deep in the region immediately below the chest, with a large, massive head, rather bald and very closely cropped, a large, rather fat face, marked with wrinkles suggestive of those on the edge of a pair of bellows, and singularly small pale blue eyes, which tended to become still smaller, even to total disappearance, when he smiled. Through those little blue eyes, Mr. Gimbler saw a woman, shortish in stature but majestic in carriage, and conveying an impression of exuberant energy and vivacity. And this impression was reinforced by the strong, mobile face with its firm mouth set above the square, pugnacious chin and below a rather formidable Roman nose, which latter gave to her a certain suggestive resemblance to a bird, a resemblance accentuated by her quick movements. But the bird suggested was not the dove. In short, Miss Arminella Pippet was a somewhat remarkable-looking lady with a most unmistakeable "presence". She might have been a dame of the old French noblesse, and Mr. Gimbler, looking at her through his little blue eyes and bearing in mind the peerage claim, decided that she looked the part. He also decided – comparing her with her mild-faced brother – that the grey mare was the better horse and must claim his chief attention. He was not the first who had undervalued Mr. Christopher Pippet.

468

"I suppose," said the latter, sitting down with some care on a rather infirm cane-bottomed chair (Miss Arminella occupied the only easy chair), "Mr. Buffham has given you some idea of the matter on which we have come to consult you?"

"He has done more than that," said Mr. Gimbler, "and would have done more still if I had not stopped him. He is thrilled by your romantic story and wildly optimistic. If we could only get a jury of Buffhams you would walk into your inheritance without a breath of opposition."

"And what do you think of our chances with the kind of jury that we are likely to get?"

Mr. Gimbler pursed up his lips and shook his massive head.

"We mustn't begin giving opinions at this stage," said he. "Remember that I have only heard the story at second hand from Mr. Buffham – just a sketch of the nature of the case. Let us begin at the beginning and forget Mr. Buffham. You are claiming, I believe, to be the grandson of the late Earl of Winsborough. Now, I should like to hear an outline of the grounds of your claim before we go into any details."

As he spoke, he fixed an inquiring eye on Miss Pippet, who promptly responded by opening her hand-bag and drawing therefrom a folded sheet of foolscap paper.

"This," said she, "is a concise statement of the nature of the claim and the known facts on which it is based. I thought it would save time if I wrote it out, as I could then leave the paper with you for reference. Will you read it or shall I?"

Mr. Gimbler looked at the document and, observing that it was covered with closely-spaced writing in a somewhat crabbed and angular hand, elected to listen to the reading in order that he might make a few notes. Accordingly Miss Pippet proceeded to read aloud from the paper with something of the air of a herald reading a royal proclamation, glancing from time to time at the lawyer to see what kind of impression it was making on him. The result of these inspections must have been a little disappointing, as Mr. Gimbler listened attentively with his eyes shut, rousing only at intervals to scribble a few words on a slip of paper.

When she had come to the end of the statement – which repeated substantially, but in a more connected form, the story that her brother had told to Buffham – she laid the paper on the table and regarded the lawyer with an interrogative stare. Mr. Gimbler, having opened his eyes to their normal extent, directed them to his notes.

"This," said he, "is a very singular and romantic story. Romantic and strange, and yet not really incredible. But the important question is, to what extent is this interesting tradition supported by provable facts? For instance, it is stated that when Josiah Pippet used to disappear from

469

his usual places of resort, the Earl of Winsborough made his appearance at Winsborough Castle. Now, is there any evidence that the disappearance of Josiah coincided in time with the appearance of the Earl at the Castle, and vice versa?"

"There is the diary," said Miss Pippet.

"Ha!" exclaimed Mr. Gimbler, genuinely surprised. "The diary makes that quite plain, does it?"

"Perfectly," the lady replied. "Anyway, it is quite clear to me. Whenever Josiah was about to make one of his disappearances, he noted in his diary quite unmistakably: '*Going away tomorrow for a little spell at the old place*'. Sometimes, instead of '*the old place*', he says plainly '*the Castle*'. Then there is a blank space of more than half-a-page before he records his arrival home at The Fox and Grapes."

"Hmm, yes," said Mr. Gimbler, swinging his folded eyeglass on its ribbon like a pendulum. "And you think that by the expression '*the old place*' or '*the Castle*', he means Winsborough Castle?"

"I don't see how there can be any doubt of it. Obviously, '*the old place*' must have been Winsborough Castle, where he was born."

"It would seem probable," Mr. Gimbler admitted. "By the way, is there any evidence that he was born at the castle?"

"Well," Miss Pippet replied a little sharply, "he said he was, and I suppose he knew."

"Naturally, naturally," the lawyer agreed. "And you can prove that he did say so?"

"My brother and I have heard our father repeat the statement over and over again. We can swear to that."

"And with regard to the Earl? Is there any evidence that, when Josiah returned home to The Fox and Grapes, his Lordship disappeared from the Castle?"

"Evidence!" Miss Pippet exclaimed, slapping her hand-bag impatiently. "What evidence do you want? The man couldn't be in two places at once!"

"Very true," said Mr. Gimbler, fixing a slightly perplexed eye on his dangling glasses, "very true. He couldn't. And with regard to the sham funeral. Naturally there wouldn't be any reference to it in the diary, but is it possible to support the current rumour by any definite facts?"

"Don't you think the fact that my father – Josiah's own son – was convinced of it is definite enough?" Miss Pippet demanded, a trifle acidly.

"It is definite enough," Gimbler admitted, "but in courts of law there is a slight prejudice against hearsay evidence. Direct first-hand evidence, if it is possible to produce it, has a good deal more weight."

"So it may," retorted Miss Pippet, "but you can't expect us to give first-hand evidence of a funeral that took place before we were born. I suppose even a court of law has a little common sense."

"Still," her brother interposed, "Mr. Gimbler has put his finger on the really vital spot. The sham funeral is the kernel of the whole business. If we can prove that, we shall have something solid to go on. And we can prove it – or else disprove it, as the case may be. But it need not be left in the condition of what the late President Wilson would have called a peradventure. If that funeral was a sham, there was nothing in the coffin but some lumps of lead. Now, that coffin is still in existence. It is lying in the family vault, and if we can yank it out and open it, the Winsborough Peerage Claim will be as good as settled. If we find Josiah at home to visitors, we can let the claim drop and go for a holiday. But if we find the lumps of lead, according to our program, we shall hang on to the claim until the courts are tired of us and hand over the keys of the Castle. Mr. Gimbler is quite right. That coffin is the point that we have got to concentrate on."

As Mr. Pippet developed his views, the lawyer's eyeglasses, dangling from their ribbon, swung more and more violently, and their owner's eyes opened to an unprecedented width. He had never had the slightest intention of concentrating on the coffin. On the contrary, that obvious means of exploding the delusion and toppling over the house of cards had seemed to be the rock that had got to be safely circumnavigated at all costs. In his view, the coffin was the fly in the ointment, and the discovery that it was the apple of Mr. Pippet's eye gave him a severe shock. And not this alone. He had assumed that the lady's invincible optimism represented the state of mind of both his clients. Now he realized that the man whom he had written down an amiable ass, and perhaps a dishonest ass at that, combined in his person two qualities most undesirable in the circumstances – hard common sense and transparent honesty.

It was a serious complication, and as he sat with his eyes fixed on the swinging eyeglasses, he endeavoured rapidly to shape a new course. At length he replied, "Of course you are quite right, Mr. Pippet. The obvious course would be to examine the coffin as a preliminary measure. But English law does not always take the obvious course. When once a person is consigned to the tomb, the remains pass out of the control of the relatives and into that of the State, and the State views with very jealous disapproval any attempts to disturb those remains. In order to open a tomb or grave, and especially to open a coffin, it is necessary to obtain a faculty from the Home Secretary authorizing an exhumation.

471

Now, before any such faculty is granted, the Home Secretary requires the applicant to show cause for the making of such an order."

"Well," said Mr. Pippet, "we can show cause. We want to know whether Josiah is in that coffin or not."

"Quite so," said Mr. Gimbler. "A perfectly reasonable motive. But it would not be accepted by the Home Office. They would demand a ruling from a properly constituted court to the effect that the claim had been investigated and a *prima facie* case made out."

"What do you mean by a *prima facie* case?" Miss Pippet inquired.

"The expression means that the claim has been stated in a court of law and that sufficient evidence has been produced to establish a probability that it is a just and reasonable claim."

"You mean to say," said Mr. Pippet, "that a judge and jury have got to sit and examine at great length whether the claim may possibly be a true claim before they will consent to examine a piece of evidence which will settle the question with practical certainty in the course of an hour?"

"Yes," Mr. Gimbler admitted. "That, I am afraid is the rather unreasonable position. We shall have to lay the facts, so far as they are known to us, before the court and make out as good a case as we can. Then, if the court is satisfied that we have a substantial case, it will make an order for the exhumation, which the Home Office will confirm."

"For my part," said Miss Pippet, "I don't see why we need meddle with the coffin at all. It seems a ghoulish proceeding."

"I entirely agree with you, Miss Pippet," said Mr. Gimbler (and there is no possible doubt that he did). "It would be much better to deal with the whole affair in court if that were possible. Perhaps it may be possible to avoid the exhumation, after all. The court may not insist."

"It won't have to insist," said Mr. Pippet. "I make it a condition that we ascertain beyond all doubt whether Josiah is or is not in that coffin. I want to make sure that I am claiming what is my just due, and I shan't be sure of that until that coffin has been opened. Isn't it possible for you to make an application to the Home Secretary without troubling the courts?"

"It would be possible to make the application," Mr. Gimbler replied somewhat dryly, "but a refusal would be a foregone conclusion. Quite properly so, if you consider the conditions. The purpose of the exhumation is to establish the fact of the sham burial. But if that were established, you would be no more forward, or, at least very little. Your claim would still have to be stated and argued in a court of law. Of course, the proof of the sham burial would be material evidence, but still, your claim would stand or fall by the decision of the court. Naturally, the Home Office, since it cannot consider evidence or give a decision, is not

472

going to give a permit until it is informed by the proper authority that an exhumation is necessary for the purposes of justice. Believe me, Mr. Pippet, we should only prejudice our case by trying to go behind the courts, and moreover, we should certainly fail to get a permit."

"Very well," said Mr. Pippet. "You know best. Then I take it that there is not much more to say at present. We have given you the facts, such as they are, and we shall leave my sister's statement with you, and it will be up to you to consider what is to be done next."

"Yes," agreed Gimbler. "But something was said about documents – some letters and a diary. Are they available?"

"They are," replied Mr. Pippet. "I've got the whole boiling of them in this box. My sister has been through them, as she mentioned to you just now."

"And you?" Mr. Gimbler asked with a trace of anxiety, as he watched his client's efforts to untie the parcel. "Have you examined them thoroughly?"

"I can't truly say that I have," was the reply, as Mr. Pippet deliberately opened a pocket knife and applied it to the string. "I had intended to look through them before I handed them to you, but Mr. Buffham assured me that it would be a waste of labour, as you would have to study them in any case, so, as I am not what you would call a studious man, and they look a pretty stodgy collection, I have saved myself the trouble."

"I don't believe," said Miss Pippet, "that my brother cares two cents whether we succeed or not."

The lady's suspicion was not entirely unshared by her legal adviser. But he made no comment, as, at this moment, Mr. Pippet, having detached the coverings of the parcel, and thereby disclosed the deed box which he had shown to Buffham, inserted a key and unlocked it.

"There," said he, as he threw the lid open, "you can see that the things are there. Those bundles of paper are the letters and the little volumes are the diary. There is no need for you to look at them now. I guess you will like to study them at your leisure."

"Quite so," agreed Mr. Gimbler. "It will be necessary for me to examine them exhaustively and systematically and make a very careful *précis* of their contents, with an analysis of those contents from an evidential point of view. I shall have to do that before I can give any opinion on the merits of the case, and certainly before I suggest taking any active measures. You realize that those investigations will take some time?"

"Certainly," said Mr. Pippet, "and you will not find us impatient. We don't want to urge you to act precipitately."

"Not precipitately," agreed Miss Pippet. "Still, you understand that we don't want too much of the law's delay."

Mr. Gimbler understood that perfectly and, to tell the whole truth, looked with much more favour on the lady's hardly-veiled impatience than on her brother's philosophic calm.

"There will be no delay at all," he replied, "but merely a most necessary period of preparation. I need not point out to you, Madam," he continued after a moment's pause, "that we must not enter the lists unready. We must mature our plans in advance, so that when we take the field – if we decide to do so – it will be with our weapons sharpened and our armour bright."

"Certainly," said Miss Pippet. "We must be ready before we start. I realize that – only I hope it won't take too long to get ready."

"That," replied Mr. Gimbler, "we shall be better able to judge when we have made a preliminary inspection of the documentary material, but I can assure you that no time will be wasted."

Here he paused to clear his throat and adjust his eyeglasses. Then he proceeded. "There is just one other little matter that I should like to be clear on. You realize that an action at law is apt to be a somewhat expensive affair. Of course, in the present case, there is a considerable set-off. If you are successful, the mere material gain in valuable property, to say nothing of the title and the great social advantages, will be enough to make the law costs appear a negligible trifle. Still, I must warn you that the outlay will be very considerable. There will be court fees, fees to counsel, costs of the necessary investigations, and of course my own charges, which I shall keep as low as possible. Now, the question is, are you prepared to embark on this undoubtedly costly enterprise?"

He asked the question in a tone as impassive and judicial as he could manage, but he awaited the answer with an anxiety that was difficult to conceal. It was Miss Pippet who instantly dispelled that anxiety.

"We understand all about that," said she. "We never supposed that titles and estates were to be picked up for the asking. You can take it that we shall not complain of any expense in reason. But perhaps you were thinking of our capacity to bear a heavy expense? If you were, I may tell you that my own means would be amply sufficient to meet any likely costs, even without my brother's support."

"That is so," Mr. Pippet confirmed. "But, as I am the actual claimant, the costs will naturally fall on me. Could you give us any idea of our probable liabilities?"

Mr. Gimbler reflected rapidly. He didn't wish to frighten his quarry, but he did very much want to take soundings of the depth of their purse. Eventually, he took his courage in both hands and made the trial cast.

"It is mere guess work," said he, "until we know how much there may be to do. Supposing – to take an outside figure – the costs should mount to ten-thousand pounds. Of course, they won't. But I mention that sum as a sort of basis to reckon from. How would that affect you?"

"Well," said Mr. Pippet, "it sounds a lot of money, but it wouldn't break either of us. Only we look to you to see that the gamble is worthwhile before we drop too much on it."

"You may be quite confident," Gimbler replied in a voice husky with suppressed joy, "that I shall not allow you to embark on any proceedings until I have ascertained beyond a doubt that you have at least a reasonable chance of success. And that," he continued, rising as his visitors rose to depart, "is all that is humanly possible."

He stuck his glasses on his nose to shake hands and to watch Mr. Pippet as he detached the key of the deed box from his bunch. Then he opened the door and escorted his visitors through an atmosphere of fried onions to the street door, where he stood watching them reflectively as they descended the steps and made their way along the flagged path to the gate.

As Mr. Gimbler closed the street door, that of the waiting-room opened softly, disclosing the figure of no less a person than Mr. Buffham. And, naturally, the figure included the countenance, which was wreathed in smiles. Looking cautiously towards the kitchen stairs, Mr. Buffham murmured, "Did I exaggerate, my little Gimblet? I think not. Methought I heard a whisper of ten-thousand pounds. An outside estimate, my dear sir, in fact, a wild overestimate. Hey? What O!"

Mr. Gimbler did not reply. He only smiled. And when Mr. Gimbler smiled – as we have mentioned – his eyes tended to disappear. They did on this occasion. Especially the left one.

Chapter III
Mr. Pippet Gives Evidence

American visitors to London often attain to a quite remarkable familiarity with many of its features. But their accomplishments in this respect do not usually extend to an acquaintance with its intimate geography. The reason is simple enough. He who would know London, or any other great city, in the complete and intimate fashion characteristic of the genuine Town Sparrow, must habituate himself to the use of that old-fashioned conveyance known as "shanks's mare". For the humblest of creatures has some distinctive excellence, even the mere pedestrian, despised of the proud motorist (who classes him with the errant rabbit or the crawling pismire) and ignored by the law, has at least one virtue: He knows his London.

Now, the American visitor is not usually a pedestrian. As his time appears to him more valuable than his money, he tends to cut the Gordian knot of geographical difficulties by hailing a taxi, whereby he makes a swift passage at the sacrifice of everything between his starting-point and his destination.

This is what Mr. Pippet did on the afternoon of the day of his conference with Mr. Gimbler. The hailing was done by the hotel porter and, when the taxi was announced, Mr. Pippet came forth from the hall and delivered to the driver an address in the neighbourhood of Great Saint Helen's, wherever that might be, and held open the cab door to admit the young lady who had followed him out, who thereupon slithered in with the agility born of youthful flexibility, extensive practice, and no clothing to speak of.

"I am not sure, Jenny," said Mr. Pippet, as he took his seat and pulled the door to, "that your aunt was not right. This is likely to be a rather gruesome business, and the place doesn't seem a very suitable one for young ladies."

Miss Jenny smiled a superior smile as she fished a gold cigarette case out of her hand-bag and proceeded to select a cigarette. "That's all bunk, you know, Dad," said she. "Auntie was just bursting to come herself, but she thought she had to set me an example of self-restraint. As if I wanted her examples. I am out to see all that there is to see. Isn't that what we came to Europe for?"

476

"I thought we came to settle this peerage business," replied Mr. Pippet.

"That's part of the entertainment," she admitted, "but we may as well take anything else that happens to be going. And here we have struck a first-class mystery. I wouldn't have missed it for anything. Do you think it will be on view?" she added, holding out the cigarette case.

Mr. Pippet humbly picked out a cigarette and looked at her inquiringly. "Do you mean the head?" he asked.

"Yes. That's what I want to see. You've seen it, you know."

"I don't know much about the ways of inquests in England," he replied, "but I don't fancy that the remains are shown to anyone but the jury."

"That's real mean of them," she said. "I was hoping that it would be on view, or that they would bring it in – on a charger, like John the Baptist's."

Mr. Pippet smiled as he lit his cigarette. "The circumstances are not quite the same, my dear," said he, "but, as I am only a witness, you'll see as much as I shall – though, as you say, I have actually seen the thing, or, at least, a part of it, and I have no wish to see any more."

"Still," persisted Jenny, "you can say that you have really and truly seen it."

Mr. Pippet admitted that he enjoyed this inestimable privilege for what it might be worth, and the conversation dropped for the moment. Miss Jenny leaned back reposefully in her corner, taking occasional "pulls" at the cigarette in its dainty amber holder, while her father regarded her with a mixture of parental pride, affection, and quiet amusement. And it has to be admitted that Mr. Pippet's sentiments with regard to his daughter were by no means unjustified. Miss Jenifer Pippet – to give her her full and unabridged style and title – was a girl of whom any father might have been proud. If – as Mr. Gimbler had very properly decided – the majestic Arminella "looked the part" of an earl's sister (which is not invariably the case with the genuine possessors of that title), Mistress Jenifer would have sustained the character of the earl's daughter with credit even on the stage, where the demands are a good deal more exacting than in real life. In the typically "patrician" style of features, with the fine Roman nose and the level brows and firm chin, she resembled her redoubtable aunt, but she had the advantage of that lady in the matter of stature, being, like her father, well above the average height. And here it may be noted that, if the daughter reflected credit on the father, the latter was well able to hold his position on his own merits. Christopher J. Pippet was fully worthy of his distinguished womenkind, a fine, upstanding gentleman with an undeniable "presence".

It was probably the possession of these personal advantages that made the way smooth for the two strangers on their arrival at the premises in which the inquest was to be held. At any rate, as soon as Mr. Pippet had made known his connexion with the case, the officiating police officer conducted them to a place in the front row and provided them each with a chair directly facing the table and nearly opposite the coroner's seat. At the moment, this and the jurymen's seats were empty and the large room was filled with the hum of conversation, for the sensational nature of the case had attracted a number of spectators greatly in excess of that usually found at an inquest, so much so that the accommodation was somewhat strained, and our two visitors had reason to congratulate themselves on their privileged position.

A few minutes after their arrival, a general stir among the audience and an increase in the murmur of voices seemed to indicate that something was happening. Then the nature of that something became apparent as the jurymen filed into their places and the coroner took his place at the head of the table. There was a brief interval as the jurymen settled into their places and the coroner arranged some papers before him and inspected his fountain pen. Then he looked up, and as the hum of conversation died away and silence settled down on the room, he began his opening address.

"The circumstances, gentlemen," said he, "which form the subject of this inquiry are very unusual. Ordinarily the occasion of a coroner's inquest is the discovery of the dead body of some person, known or unknown, or the death of some person from causes which have not been ascertained or certified, but whose body is available for examination. In the present case, while there is indisputable evidence of the death of some person, and certain evidence which may enable us to form some opinion as to the probable cause of death, the complete body is not available for expert examination. All that has been discovered, up to the present, is the head, whereas it is probable that the physical evidence as to the exact cause of death is to be found in the missing portion of the remains. I need not to occupy your time with any account of the circumstances, all of which will transpire in the evidence. All that I need say now is that the efforts of the police to discover the identity of the deceased have so far proved fruitless. We are accordingly dealing with an entirely unknown individual. The first witness whom I shall call is Thomas Crump."

At the sound of his name, Mr. Crump made his way to the table, piloted thither by the coroner's officer, and took his stand, under the latter's direction, near to the coroner's chair. Having been sworn, he stated that he was an attendant in the cloak room at Fenchurch Street Station.

"Were you on duty in the evening of Saturday the 19th of August?"

"Yes, sir, I was."

"Do you remember receiving a certain wooden case on that evening? A case which there has been some question about since?"

"Yes. It was brought in about nine-twenty, just after the nine-fifteen from Shoeburyness had come in."

"Was there anything on the case to show where it had come from?"

"No, there were no labels on it, excepting one with what I took to be the owner's name and address. I supposed that it had come by the Shoeburyness train, but that was only a guess. If it did, it couldn't have travelled in the luggage van. The guard wouldn't have had it without a label."

"Who brought the case to the cloak room?"

"It was brought in by the gentleman who I took to be the owner. And a rare job he must have had with it, for it weighed close on a hundredweight, as near as I could tell. He staggered in with it, carrying it by a cord that was tied round it."

"Can you give us any description of this man?"

"I didn't notice him very particularly, but I remember that he was rather tall and had a long, thin face and a big, sharp nose. He looked a bit on the thin side, but he must have been pretty strong to judge by the way he handled that case."

"Did you notice how he was dressed?"

"So far as I remember, he had on a dark suit – I fancy it was blue serge but I wouldn't be sure, but I remember that he was wearing a soft felt hat."

"Had he any moustache or was he clean shaved?"

"He had a moustache and a smallish beard, cut to a point, what they call a Torpedo beard. His beard and his hair were both dark."

"About what age would you say he was?"

"He might have been about forty or perhaps a trifle more."

"And with regard to the case, can you give us any description of that?"

"It was a wooden case, about fifteen-inches-square and perhaps eighteen-inches-high. It was made of plain deal strongly put together and strengthened at the corners with iron straps. The top was fitted with hinges and held down by eight screws. The wood was a good deal stained and rubbed, as if it had seen a fair amount of use. It had a label fastened on with tacks, just a plain card with the owner's name on it – at

479

least, somebody's name – and an address. The name was Dobson, but I wouldn't swear to the address."

"Well," the coroner pursued, "you took in the case. What happened next?"

"Nothing on that night. I gave the man his ticket and he took it and said he would probably call for the case on Monday. Then he said 'Good night' and went off."

"When did you see him again?"

"That was on Monday evening, about seven o'clock. It happened to be a slack time and I had more time to attend to him. He came and handed me his ticket and asked for the case. He pointed out one which he thought was his, so I went over to it and looked at the label that had been stuck on it, but it was the wrong number. However, he said that his name was on the case – name of Dobson – and I saw that there was a private label with that name on it, so I said he had better have a look at it and see if it really was his case. So he came into the cloak room and examined the case. And then he got into a rare state of excitement. He said it was certainly his name that was on the case and his address, but the label was not the same one that he wrote. But still he thought that the case was his case.

"Then I asked him if the contents of his case were of any particular value, and he said 'Yes'. They were worth several thousand pounds. Now, when he said that, I began to suspect that there was something wrong, so I suggested that we had better open the case and see if his property was inside.

"He jumped at the offer, so I got a screw-driver, and we took out the screws and lifted the lid. And when we lifted it, the first thing that we saw was the top of a man's head, packed in with a lot of rags. When he saw it, he seemed to be struck all of a heap. Then he slammed down the lid and asked me where he could find a policeman. I told him that he would find one outside the station, and off he went as hard as he could go."

Here the coroner held up a restraining hand as he scribbled furiously to keep up with the witness. When he had finished the paragraph, he looked up and nodded.

"Yes, he went out to look for a policeman. What happened next?"

"While we had been looking at the case, there were two gentlemen who had come to collect their luggage and who heard what was going on. When Mr. Dobson – if that was his name – went out, they came over to have a look at the case, and we all waited for Mr. Dobson to come back. But he didn't come back. So, after a time, one of the gentlemen went out and presently came back with a constable. I showed the constable what was in the case, and he then took possession of it."

"Yes," said the coroner, "that is all quite clear, so far. Do you think you would recognize this man, Dobson, if you were to see him again?"

"Yes," replied Crump. "I feel pretty sure I should. He was the sort of man that you would remember. And I did look at him pretty hard."

"Well," said the coroner, "I hope that you will have an opportunity of identifying him. Does any gentleman wish to ask the witness any questions? I think he has told us all that he has to tell. The other witnesses will be able to fill in the details. No questions? Then we will pass on to the next witness. William Harris."

Mr. Harris came forward with rather more diffidence than had been shown by his colleague, which might have been due to his age – he was little more than a youth – or to the story that he had to tell. But, ill at ease as he obviously was, he gave his evidence in a quite clear and straightforward fashion. When he had been sworn and given the usual particulars, he stood, regarding the coroner with a look of consternation, as he waited for the dread interrogation.

"You say," the coroner began impassively, "that you are an attendant in the cloak room at Fenchurch Street Station. How long have you been employed there?"

"Not quite three munce," the witness faltered.

"So you have not had much experience, I suppose?"

"No, sir, not very much."

"Were you on duty on Sunday, the twentieth of August?"

"Yes, sir."

"Who was on duty with you?"

"No one, sir. It was Mr. Crump's Sunday off and, being a slack day, I took the duty by myself."

"On that day, you received a certain wooden case. Do you remember the circumstances connected with it?"

"Yes, sir. The case was brought in about half-past ten in the morning. The man who brought it said that he would be calling for it about tea-time."

"Did this man bring the case himself?"

"Yes, sir. He carried it by a thick cord that was tied round it, and he brought it right in and put it down not far from another case of the same kind."

"Did you examine these cases or read the labels that were on them?"

"No, sir, I can't say that I did. I just stuck the ticket on the case that the man had brought in, but I didn't examine it. But I remember that there was another case near it that looked like the same sort of case."

"Did this man come back for the case?"

"Yes, sir. He came about four o'clock with another man who looked like a taxi-driver. He handed me the ticket and I went with the two men and found the case. Then the man who had brought it told the other man to take it out and stow it in the taxi. Then he pulled a time-table out of his pocket and asked me to look over it with him and see how the trains ran to Loughton and Epping. So we spread out the time-table on the luggage-counter and went through the list of Sunday trains, and while we were looking at it, the taxi-man took up the case and went out of the station. When we had finished with the time-table and the man had taken one or two notes of the trains, he put the time-table back in his pocket, thanked me for helping him, and went away."

"Did it never occur to you to see whether he had taken the right case?"

"No, sir. My back was towards the taxi-man when he picked the case up. I saw him carrying it out towards the entrance, but it looked just like the right case, and it never occurred to me that he might have taken the wrong one. And the one that was left looked like the right one and it was in the right place."

"Yes," said the coroner, "it was very natural. Evidently, the exchange had been carefully planned in advance, and very skilfully planned, too. Now, with regard to these two cases: Were you able to form any opinion as to the weight of either or both of them?"

"I never felt either of them," the witness replied, "but the one that the man brought in seemed rather heavy, by the way that he carried it. He had hold of it by the cord that was tied round it. The other one seemed a bit heavy, too. But when I saw the taxi-man going out with it, he had got it on his shoulder and he didn't seem to have any difficulty with it."

"And, with regard to these two men. Can you give us any description of them?"

"I hardly saw the taxi-man, and I don't remember what he was like at all, excepting that he was a big, strong-looking man. The other man was rather small, but he looked pretty strong-built, too. When we were looking at the time-tables, I noticed two things about him. One was that he seemed to have a couple of gold teeth."

"Ah!" said the coroner, "presumably gold-filled teeth. Do you remember which teeth they were?"

"They were the two middle front teeth at the top. He showed them a good deal when he talked."

"Yes, and what was the other thing that you noticed?"

"I noticed, when he put his hand on the time-table, that his fingers were stained all browny yellow, as if he was always smoking cigarettes, and his hand was shaking, even when it was laying on the paper. I didn't notice anything else."

"Can you tell us how he was dressed?"

"He had on an ordinary tweed suit – rather a shabby suit it was. And he was wearing a cloth cap."

"Had he any moustache or beard?"

"No, sir, he was clean shaved – or, at least, not very clean, because he had about a couple of days' growth, and as he was a dark man, it showed pretty plainly."

"How did he strike you as to his station in life? Should you describe him as a gentleman?"

"No, sir, I should not," the witness replied with considerable emphasis. "He struck me as quite a common sort of man, and I got the idea that he might have been a seaman or some kind of waterside character. We see a good many of that sort on our line, so we get to recognize them."

"What sort of men are you referring to?" the coroner asked with evident interest, "and where do they come from?"

"I mean sailors of all kinds from the London and the India Docks, and fishermen and longshoremen from Leigh and Benfleet and Southend and the sea-side places up that way."

"Yes," said the coroner, "this is quite interesting and may be important. Fenchurch Street has always been a sailors' station. However, that is for the police rather than for us. I think that is all that we want to ask this witness, unless any of the gentlemen of the jury wish to put any questions."

He glanced interrogatively at the jury, but none of them expressed any curiosity. Accordingly, the witness was allowed to retire, which he did with undisguised relief.

The next witness was the constable who had been called in to take charge of the case and, as his evidence amounted to little more than a statement of that fact, he was soon disposed of and dismissed. Then the coroner pronounced the name of Geoffrey Buffham, and that gentleman rose from the extreme corner of the court and worked his way to the table, casting a leer of recognition on Mr. Pippet as he passed. His evidence, also, was chiefly formal, but, when he had finished his account of his search for the constable, the coroner turned to the subject of identification.

"You saw the man who had come to claim the case. Can you add any particulars to those given by the attendant?"

"I am afraid I can't tell you very much about him. The light was not very good and, of course until he had gone, there was nothing to make one take any special notice of him. And then it was too late. All I can say is that he was a tallish man with a rather dark beard and a prominent nose."

The coroner wrote this down without comment, and then, apparently judging Mr. Buffham to be worth no more powder and shot, glanced at the jury for a moment and dismissed him. Then he pronounced the name of Christopher J. Pippet, and the owner of that name rose and stepped over to the place that had been occupied by the other witnesses. The coroner looked up at the tall, dignified figure, apparently contrasting it with its rather scrubby, raffish predecessor, and when the preliminaries had been disposed of, he asked apologetically. "It is of no particular importance, but would you tell us what the 'J' in your name stands for? It is usual to give the full name."

Mr. Pippet smiled. "As I have just been sworn," said he, "I have got to be careful in my statements. My impression is that the 'J' stands for Josiah, but that is only an opinion. I have always been accustomed to use the initial only."

"Then," said the coroner, "we will accept that as your recognized personal designation. There is no need to be pedantic. Now, Mr. Pippet, I don't think we need trouble you to go into details concerning the discovery of this case, but it would be useful if you could give us some further description of the man who came to claim the property. The descriptions which have been given are very sketchy and indefinite, can you amplify them in any way?"

Mr. Pippet reflected. "I took a pretty careful look at him," said he, "and I have a fairly clear mental picture of the man."

"You say you took a pretty careful look at him," said the coroner. "What made you look at him carefully?"

"Well, sir," Mr. Pippet replied, "the circumstances were rather remarkable. From his conversation with the attendant, it was clear that something quite irregular had been happening, and when he mentioned the value of the case, it began to look like a serious crime. Then when he rushed out pell-mell in search of a policeman, that struck me as a very strange thing to do. What was the hurry about? His own case was gone, and the one that was there wasn't going to run away. But I gathered that there was something in it that oughtn't to have been there. So when he came running out full pelt, I suspected that the cause of the hurry was behind him, not in front and, naturally, my attention was aroused."

"You suspected that he might be making off?"

"It seemed a possibility. Anyway, I have never seen a man look more thoroughly scared."

"Then," said the coroner, "as you seem to have taken more notice of him than anyone else, perhaps you can give us a rather more complete description of him. Do you think you would recognize him if you should see him again?"

"I feel pretty sure that I should," was the reply, "but that is not the same as enabling other people to recognize him. I should describe him as a tall man, about five-feet-eleven, lean but muscular and broad across the shoulders. He had a long, thin face and a long, thin nose, curved on the bridge and pointed at the end. His hair and beard were nearly black, but his skin and eyes didn't seem to match them very well, for his skin was distinctly fair and his eyes were a pale blue. I got the distinct impression that his hair and beard were dyed."

"Was that merely an impression or had you any definite grounds for the suspicion?"

"At first, it was just an impression. But as he was running out he got between me and the electric light for a moment, and the light shone through his beard. Then I caught a glint of that peculiar red that you see in hair that is dyed black when the light shines through it, and that you never see in natural hair – a red with a perceptible tinge of purple in it."

"Yes," said the coroner, "it is very characteristic. But do you feel quite sure that you actually saw this colour? It is a very important point."

"I feel convinced in my own mind," replied Mr. Pippet, "but, of course, I might have been mistaken. I can only say that, to the best of my belief, the hair showed that peculiar colour."

"Well," said the coroner, "that is about as much as anyone could say, under the circumstances. Did you notice anything of interest in regard to the clothing? You heard Mr. Crump's evidence."

"Yes, and I don't think I can add much to it. The man was wearing a well-used dark blue serge suit, a blue cotton shirt with a collar to match, a soft felt hat and dark brown shoes. He had a wrist watch, but he seemed to have a pocket watch as well Anyway, he had what looked like a watch guard, made, apparently, of plaited twine."

"Is that all you can tell us about him, or is there anything else that you are able to recall?"

"I think I have told you all that I noticed. There wasn't much opportunity to examine him closely."

"No, there was not," the coroner agreed. "I can only compliment you on the excellent use that you made of your eyes in the short time that was available. And, if that is all that you have to tell us, I think that we need not trouble you any further."

He glanced at the foreman of the jury, and as that gentleman bowed to indicate that he was satisfied, Mr. Pippet was allowed to return to his seat, where he received the whispered congratulations of his daughter.

"That," said the coroner, addressing the jury, "concludes the evidence relating to the discovery of the remains. We shall now proceed to the evidence afforded by the remains themselves, and we will begin with that of the medical officer to whom the head was handed for expert examination. Dr. Humphrey Smith."

Chapter IV
The Finding of the Jury

The new witness was a man of about thirty with a clean shaved, studious face, garnished with a pair of horn-rimmed spectacles, and a somewhat diffident, uneasy manner. Having advanced to the table and taken his seat on the chair which had been placed for him close to that occupied by the coroner, he produced from his pocket a notebook which he held unopened on his knee throughout the proceedings. In reply to the preliminary questions, he stated that his name was Humphrey Smith, that he was a bachelor of medicine, a member of the Royal College of Surgeons and a Licentiate of the Royal College of Physicians.

"You are the Police Medical Officer of this district, I believe," the coroner suggested.

"Temporarily, I hold that post," was the reply, "during the absence on sick leave of the regular medical officer."

"Quite so," said the coroner. "For the purposes of this inquiry, you are the Police Medical Officer."

The witness admitted that this was so, and the coroner proceeded, "You have had submitted to you for examination a case containing a human head. Will you give us an account of your examination and the conclusions at which you arrived?"

The witness reflected a few moments and then began his statement.

"At ten-fifteen on the morning of the twenty-second of August, Inspector Budge called on me and asked me to come round to the police station to examine the contents of a case, in which he said were certain human remains. I went with him and was shown a wooden case, strengthened by iron straps. It had a hinged lid which was further secured by eight screws, which, however, had been extracted. On raising the lid, I saw what looked like the top of a man's head, surrounded by rags and articles of clothing which had been packed tightly round it. With the inspector's assistance I removed the packing material until it was possible to lift out the head, which I then took to a table by the window where I was able to make a thorough examination.

"The head appeared to be that of a man, although there was hardly any visible beard or moustache and no signs of his having been shaved."

"You say that the head appeared to be that of a man. Do you feel confident that the deceased was a man, or do you think that the head may possibly be that of a woman?"

"I think there is no doubt that the deceased was a man. The general appearance was masculine, and the hair was quite short and arranged like a man's hair."

"That," remarked the coroner, "is not a very safe criterion in these days. I have seen a good many women who would have passed well enough for men excepting for their clothes."

"Yes, that is true," the witness admitted, "but I had the present fashion in mind when I formed my opinion and, although there was extremely little hair on the face, there was more than one usually finds on the face of a woman – a young woman, at any rate."

"Then are we to understand that this head was that of a young person?"

"The exact age was rather difficult to determine, but I should say that the deceased was not much, if any, over thirty."

"What made it difficult to estimate the age of the deceased?"

"There were two circumstances that made it difficult to judge the age. One was the physical condition of the head, and the other was the extraordinary facial character of this person."

"By the physical condition, do you mean that it had undergone considerable putrefactive changes?"

"No, not at all. It was not in the least decomposed. It had been thoroughly embalmed, or, at least, treated with preservative substances – principally formalin, I think. There was quite a distinct odour of formalin vapour."

"Then it would appear that it was in quite a good state of preservation, which ought to have helped rather than hindered your examination."

"Yes, but the effect of the formalin was to produce a certain amount of shrinkage of the tissues, which naturally resulted in some distortion of the features. But it was not easy to be sure how much of the distortion was due to the formalin and how much to the natural deformity."

"Was the shrinkage in any way due to drying of the tissues?"

"No. The tissues were not in the least dry. It appeared to me that the formalin had been mixed with glycerine and, as glycerine does not evaporate, the head has remained perfectly moist, but without any tendency to decompose."

"How long do you consider that the deceased has been dead?"

"That," replied the doctor, "is a question upon which I could form no opinion whatever. The head is so perfectly preserved that it will last in its present condition for an almost indefinite time and, of course, what applies to the future applies equally to the past. One can estimate the time that has elapsed since death only by the changes that have occurred in the interval. But if there are no changes, there is nothing on which to form an opinion."

"Do you mean to say that the deceased might have been dead for a year?"

"Yes, or even longer than that. A year ago the head would have looked exactly as it looks now, and as it will look a year hence. The preservatives have rendered it practically unchangeable."

"That is very remarkable," said the coroner, "and it introduces a formidable difficulty into this inquiry. For we have to discover, if we can, how, when, and where this person met with his death. But it would seem that the 'when' is undiscoverable. You could give no limit to the time that has elapsed since death took place?"

"No. I could make no suggestion as to the time."

The coroner wrote this down and looked at what he had written with an air of profound dissatisfaction. Then he turned to the witness and opened a new subject.

"You spoke just now of the remarkable facial peculiarities of the deceased. Can you describe those peculiarities?"

"I will try. The deceased had a most extraordinary and perfectly hideous face. The peculiar appearance was due principally to the overgrown condition of the lower part, especially the lower jaw. In shape, the face was like an egg with the small end upwards, and the jaw was not only enormously broad, but the chin stuck out beyond the upper lip and the lower teeth were spread out and projected considerably in front of the upper ones. Then the nose was thick and coarse and the ears stood out from the head, but they were not like ordinary outstanding ears, which tend to be thin and membranous. They were thick and lumpy and decidedly misshapen. Altogether, the appearance of the face was quite abnormal."

"Should you regard this abnormality as a deformity, or do you think it was connected with the deceased's state of health?"

"I should hardly like to give an opinion without seeing the rest of the body. There is no doubt about the deformity, but whether it was congenital or due to disease, I should not like to say, There are several rather rare diseases which tend to produce malformations of different parts of the body."

"Well," said the coroner, "medical details of that kind are a little outside the scope of this inquiry. The fact which interests us is that the deceased was a very unusual-looking person, so that there ought not to be much difficulty in identifying him. To come to another question, from your examination of this head, should you say that there is any evidence of special skill or knowledge in the way in which the head has been separated from the trunk?"

"I think that there is a suggestion of some skill and knowledge. Not necessarily very much. But the separation was effected in accordance with the anatomical relations, not in the way in which it would have been done by an entirely ignorant and unskilful person. The head had been separated from the spinal column – that is, from the top of the backbone – by cutting through the ligaments that fasten the backbone to the skull, whereas a quite ignorant person would almost certainly have cut through the neck and through the joint between two of the neck vertebrae."

"You think that it would not require much skill to take the head off in the manner in which it was done?"

"No, it would be quite easy if one knew where to make the cut. But most people do not."

"You think, then, that the person who cut off this head must have had some anatomical knowledge?"

"Yes, but a very little knowledge of anatomy would suffice."

"Do you think that such knowledge as a butcher possesses would be sufficient?"

"Certainly. A butcher doesn't know much anatomy, but he knows where to find the joints."

"And now, to take another question, can you give us any information as to the cause of death?"

"No," was the very definite reply. "I examined the head most carefully with this question in view, but I could find no trace of any wound, bruise, or mark of violence, or even of rough treatment. There was no clue whatever to the cause or mode of death."

There was a brief pause while the coroner glanced through his notes. Then, looking up at the jury, he said, "Well, gentlemen, you have heard what the doctor has to tell us. It doesn't get us on very far, but, of course, that is not the doctor's fault. He can't make evidence. Would any of you like to ask him any further questions? If not, I think we need not occupy any more of his time."

Once more he paused with his eyes on the jury, then, as no one made any sign, he thanked the witness and gave him his dismissal.

The next witness was a smart-looking uniformed inspector of the City Police who stepped up to his post with the brisk, confident air of one familiar with the procedure. He stated that his name was William Budge and, having rattled through the preliminaries, gave a precise and business-like account of the circumstances in which he made the acquaintance of the "remains" in the cloak room. From this he proceeded to the examination of the case in collaboration with the medical officer. His description of the case tallied with that given by Mr. Crump, but he was able to supply a few further details.

"Mr. Crump referred in his evidence," said the coroner, "to a private label on this case. You examined that, of course?"

"Yes. It was a piece of card – half of a stationer's postcard – fastened to the lid of the case with four tacks. It had a name and address written on it in plain block letters with a rather fine pen. The name was *J. Dobson* and the address was *401 Argyle Square, King's Cross, London.*"

"Four-hundred-and-one!" exclaimed the coroner.

The witness smiled. "Yes, sir. Of course, there's no such number, but I went there to make sure."

"You did not extract any other information from the label?"

"I did not make a particular examination of it. I took it off carefully with the proper precautions and handed it to the superintendent."

"You did not test it for finger-prints?"

"No, sir. That would not be in my province."

"Exactly!" said the coroner. "And it is not really in ours." He paused for a few moments and then asked, "Have you any idea, Inspector, where this case might have come from, or what its original contents might have been?"

"I should say," was the reply, "that it originally contained some kind of provisions and that it formed part of a ship's stores. It is very usual for firms who supply provisions to ships to send them out in cases of this kind. The lids are screwed down for security in transit, but furnished with hinges for convenience when they are in use on board. There was no mark on the wood to indicate where the case came from. The issuer's name and address was probably on a label which has been taken off."

"Did you find anything that seemed to confirm your surmise that this case had formed part of a ship's stores?"

"Yes. When the doctor had taken the head out, I took out the clothes and rags that had been used for packing and went over them carefully. Most of them seemed to be connected with a vessel of some sort. I made out a list, which I have with me."

He produced an official-looking notebook and, at the coroner's request, read out the list of items.

"At the top, immediately surrounding the head, was a very old, ragged blue jersey, such as fishermen wear. There was no mark of any kind on it, but there were some ends of thread that looked as if a linen tab had been cut off. Next, there was a pair of brown canvas trousers, a good deal worn and without any marks or any name on the buttons, and an old

491

brown canvas jumper. Then there were several worn-out cotton swabs such as they use on board ship, three longish ends of inch-and-a-half manilla rope and, at the bottom of the case, a ragged oil-skin coat. So the whole contents looked like the throw-outs collected from some ship's fo'c'sle, or from the cabin of a barge or some other small craft."

"Do you associate these cast-off things with any particular kind of vessel?"

"As far as the things themselves are concerned, I do not. But the case rather suggests a deep-water craft. A barge or a coaster can pick up her provisions at the various ports of call, and hardly needs the quantity of stores that this case suggests."

"And what about the other case – the case that was stolen? Do you connect it with the one that contained the head?"

The inspector reflected. "There is not much information available at present," said he, "and what there is you have had in Crump's evidence. It appears that the two cases were exactly alike and, if that is so, they might have come from the same source. Evidently, the man who brought in the case with the head in it knew all about the other case, and what was in it."

"Which, I take it, is more than you do?"

The inspector smiled and admitted that the unknown man had the advantage of the police at present and, with that admission his evidence came to an end and he retired to his seat. There followed a pause, during which the coroner once more looked over his notes and the jury exchanged remarks in an undertone. At length, when he had run his eye over the depositions, the coroner leaned back in his chair and, taking a general survey of the jury, began his summing-up.

"This inquiry, gentlemen," he began, "is a very remarkable one, and as unsatisfactory as it is unusual in character. It is unsatisfactory in several respects. We are inquiring into the circumstances surrounding the death of a deceased person. But we are not in possession of the body of that person but of only a part of it, and that part gives us no information on either of the three headings of our inquiry – the time, the place and the manner. We are seeking to discover: First, when this person died, second, in what place he died, and third, in what manner and by what means he came by his death. But, owing to the incomplete nature of the remains, the strange circumstances in which they were discovered, and the physical condition of the remains themselves, we can answer none of these questions. We do not even know who the deceased is. All that we can do is to consider the whole body of facts which are known to us and draw what reasonable conclusions we can from them.

492

"Let us begin by taking a glance at the succession of events in the order of their occurrence. First, on the Saturday night, comes a man with a heavy case which, according to his subsequent admission, contains property of great value. He leaves this case in the cloak room for the week-end. Then, on the Sunday, comes another man with another case which appears to be identically similar to the first. He very adroitly manages to exchange this case for the one containing the valuable property. Then, on the Monday, comes the first man to claim his property. He sees that some substitution appears to have occurred and, in order to make sure, opens the case. Then he discovers the head of the deceased and is, naturally enough, horrified. Instantly, he rushes out of the station, ostensibly in search of a policeman, but actually to make his escape, as becomes evident when he does not return. That is the series of events which are known to us, and which form, in effect, the whole sum of our knowledge. Let us see what conclusions we can draw from them.

"The first question that we ask ourselves is: Why did that man not come back? The case which had been stolen contained, according to what was probably a hasty, unguarded statement, property worth several thousand pounds. Without committing ourselves to a legal opinion, we may say that he could have made a claim on the railway company for the value of that property. Yet at the sight of that dead man's head, he rushed out and disappeared. What are we to infer from that? There are several inferences that suggest themselves. First, although it is evident that the head in the case came to him as a complete surprise, it is possible that, as soon as he saw it, he recognized it as something with which he had a guilty association. That is one possibility. Then there is the question as to what was in his own case. It was property of great value. But whose property was it? There is in the behaviour of this man a strong suggestion that the valuable contents of that case may have been stolen property, of which he was not in a position to give any account. That appears to be highly probable, but it does not greatly concern us, excepting that it suggests a criminal element in the transaction as a whole – a suggestion that is strengthened by the apparent connexion between the two men.

"When we come to the second man, the criminal element is unmistakable. To say nothing of the theft which he undoubtedly committed, the fact that he was going about with the head of a dead man in a box, definitely puts upon him the responsibility for the mutilation of a human body, to say the least. The question of any further guilt depends on the view that is taken of that mutilation. And that brings us to the question as to the manner in which the deceased came by his death.

"Now, we have to recognize that we have no direct evidence on this point. The doctor's careful and expert examination failed to elicit any information as to the cause of death, which was what might have been expected from the very insufficient means at his disposal. But, if we have no direct evidence as to the actual cause of death, we have very important indirect evidence as to some of the circumstances surrounding his death. We know, for instance, that the body had been mutilated, or at least decapitated, and we know that some person was in possession of the separated head – and, probably, of the mutilated remainder of the corpse.

"But these are very material facts. What does our common sense, aided by experience, suggest in the case of a corpse which has been mutilated and a part packed in a box and planted in a railway cloak room? What is the usual object of dismembering a corpse and of disposing of the dismembered remains in this way? In all the numerous cases which have occurred from time to time, the object has been the same: To get rid of the body of a person who has been murdered, in order to cover up the fact and the circumstances of the crime. No other reason is imaginable. There could be no object in thus making away with the body of a person who had died a natural death.

"That, however, is for you to consider in deciding on your verdict. The other known facts do not seem to be helpful. The singular and rather repulsive appearance of the deceased does not concern us, although it may be important to the police. As to the curious use of a preservative, the object of that seems to be fairly obvious. Mutilated remains have been commonly discovered by the putrefactive odour which they have exhaled. If this head had not been preserved, it would have been impossible for it to have been left in the cloak room for twenty-four hours without arousing suspicion. But, as I have said, the fact, though curious, is not material to our inquiry. The material facts are those which suggest an answer to the question, How did the deceased come by his death? Those facts are in your possession, and I shall now leave you to consider your verdict."

Thereupon, while the hum of conversation once more pervaded the court room, the jury drew together and compared notes. But their conference lasted only a very few minutes, at the end of which the foreman signified to the coroner that they had agreed on their verdict.

"Well, gentlemen," said the latter, "what is your decision?"

"We find," was the reply, "that the deceased was murdered by some person or persons unknown."

"Yes," said the coroner, as he entered the verdict at the foot of the depositions, "that is what common sense suggests. I don't see that you could have arrived at any other decision. It remains only for me to thank you for your attendance and the careful attention which you have given to the evidence, and close the proceedings."

As the court rose, Mr. Buffham emerged hurriedly from the corner in which he had been seated and elbowed his way towards Mr. Pippet and his daughter.

"My dear sir," he exclaimed, effusively, "let me offer my most hearty congratulations on the brilliant way in which you gave your evidence. Your powers of observation positively staggered me."

The latter statement was no exaggeration. Mr. Buffham had been not only staggered but slightly disconcerted by the discovery of his friend's remarkable capacity for "keeping his weather eyelid lifted". In the peculiar circumstances, it was a gift that he was disposed to view with some disfavour, and he found himself wondering, a little uncomfortably, whether Mr. Pippet happened to have observed any other facts which he was not expected or desired to observe. But he did not allow these misgivings to interfere with his suave and ingratiating manner. As Mr. Pippet received his congratulations without obvious emotion, he bestowed on Miss Jenny a leer which was intended to express admiring recognition and then turned with an insinuating smile to her father.

"This charming young lady," said he, "is, I presume, the daughter of whom I have heard you speak."

"You have guessed right the first time," Mr. Pippet replied. "This is Mr. Buffham, my dear, but you know that, as you heard him give his evidence."

Miss Jenny bowed, with a faint suggestion of stiffness. The ingratiating smile did not seem to have produced the expected effect. The "charming young lady" was not, in fact, at all favourably impressed by Mr. Buffham's personality. Nevertheless she exchanged a few observations on the incidents of the inquest, as the audience was clearing off, and the three moved out together when the way was clear. Here, however, Mr. Buffham suffered a slight disappointment, for when the taxi which Mr. Pippet hailed drew up at the curb, the hoped-for invitation was not forthcoming, and the cordial hand-shake and smiling farewell appeared an unsatisfactory substitute.

Chapter V
The Great Platinum Robbery

Thorndyke's rather free and easy custom of receiving professional visitors at unconventional hours tended on certain occasions to result in slightly embarrassing situations. It did, for instance, on an evening in early October when the arrival of our old friend Mr. Brodribb was followed almost immediately by that of Mr. Superintendent Miller. Both were ostensibly making a friendly call, but both, I felt sure, had their particular fish to fry. Brodribb had almost certainly come for a professional consultation, and Miller's informal chats invariably developed a professional background.

I watched with amused curiosity to see what would happen. Each man would probably give the other a chance to retire, and the question was, which would be the first to abdicate? The event would probably be determined by the relative urgency of their respective fish-frying. But the delicate balance of probabilities was upset by Polton, our invaluable laboratory assistant, who happened to be in the room when they arrived, and who instantly proceeded to make the arrangements which immemorial custom had associated with each of our visitors. The two cosiest armchairs were drawn up to the fire and a small table placed by each. On one table appeared, as if by magic, the whisky decanter, siphon, and cigar box which clearly appertained to Miller, and on the other, three port glasses.

"This is your chair, sir," said Polton, shepherding the Superintendent in the way he should go. "The other is for Mr. Brodribb." And with this he vanished, and we all knew whither he had gone.

"Well," said Brodribb with slight indecision, as he subsided into his allotted chair and put his toes on the curb, while Thorndyke and I drew up our chairs, "if I shan't be in the way, I'll just sit down and warm myself for a few minutes."

His "defeatist" tone I judged to be due to the fact that Miller, in ready response to my invitation, had mixed himself a stiff jorum, got a cigar alight, and apparently settled himself comfortably for the evening. I think the old lawyer was disposed to give up the contest and retire in favour of the Superintendent, but at that moment Polton returned, bearing a decanter of port which he deposited on Mr. Brodribb's table, whereupon the balance of probabilities was restored.

"Ha!" said Brodribb, as Thorndyke filled the three glasses, "it's all very well to sentimentalize about the Last Rose of Summer, but the First Fire of Winter makes more appeal to me."

"You can hardly call it winter at the beginning of October," Miller objected.

"Can't you, by Jove!" exclaimed Brodribb. "Perhaps not by the calendar, but when I came through the Carey Street gateway just now, the wind was enough to nip the nose off a brass monkey. But I haven't got a fire yet. It's only you medico-legal sybarites who can afford such luxuries."

He sipped his wine ecstatically, spread out his toes, and blinked at the fire with an air of enjoyment that suggested a particularly magnificent old Tom cat. The superintendent made no rejoinder, and Thorndyke and I filled our pipes and waited curiously for the situation to develop.

"I suppose," said Brodribb, after an interval of silence, "you haven't got any forrarder with that Fenchurch Street mystery – I mean the box with the gentleman's head in it?"

"Gentleman, indeed!" exclaimed Miller. "He was about the ugliest beggar that I ever clapped eyes on. I don't wonder they cut his head off. He must have been a lot better-looking without it."

"Still," said Brodribb, "you've got to admit that the man was murdered."

"No doubt," rejoined Miller, "and if you had seen him, you wouldn't have been surprised. His face was an outrage on humanity."

"So it may have been," retorted Brodribb, "but ugliness is not provocation in a legal sense. You don't mean to say that you have abandoned the case?"

"We never abandon a case at The Yard," replied Miller, "but it's no use fussing about when you've nothing to go on. As a matter of fact, we expect to approach the problem from another direction. For the moment, we are letting that particular box rest while we give a little attention to the other box – the one that was stolen."

"Ha!" said Brodribb. "Yes, very necessary, I should say. But what is your idea about it? You don't think it possible that it contained the body which belonged to the head?"

Miller shook his head. "No," said he. "I think you can rule that out. If the original case had contained a headless corpse, Mr. Dobson would not have been so ready to open the doubtful one in the presence of the attendant. You see, until they got it open, it wasn't certain that it was a different case."

"Then," said Brodribb, "I don't quite see the connexion. You said that you were approaching the problem of the head from another direction – through the stolen box, as I understood."

"That is so," replied Miller, "and you must see that there is evidently some connexion between the two cases. To begin with, the second case, which we may call the head case, was exactly similar to the first one – the stolen case – and we may take it that the similarity was purposely arranged. The head case was prepared as a counterfeit so that it could be exchanged for the other. But from that it follows that the person who prepared the head case must have known exactly what the other case was like, even to what was written on the label, and as he was at a good deal of trouble to steal the first case, we may take it that he knew what that case contained. So there you have a clear connexion on the one side. As to whether the man, Dobson, recognized the head or knew anything about it, we can't be sure."

"The way in which he made himself scarce when he had seen it," said Brodribb, "rather suggests that he did."

"Not necessarily," Miller objected. "The question is: What was in the stolen case? He stated that the contents were worth several thousand pounds, but in spite of that, he made no attempt at recovery or claim for compensation. It looks as if he was not in a position to say what was in the case. But that suggests that the contents were not his lawful property – in fact, that the case contained stolen property – perhaps the loot from some robbery. Now, if that were so, he would have to clear off in any event to avoid inquiries. Naturally, then, when he came on that head, he would have realized that he was fairly in the soup. The fact that he had been in possession of stolen property wouldn't have been a bit helpful if he had been charged with complicity in a murder. I'm not surprised that he bolted."

"Is there any clue to what has become of the stolen case?" Brodribb asked.

"No," replied Miller, "but that is not the question which is interesting us. What we want to know is, not where it went, but where it came from, and what was in it."

"And that, I presume, you don't know at present," said Brodribb.

The Superintendent took a long draw at his cigar, blew out a cloud of smoke and performed the operation that he would have described as "wetting his whistle". Then he set down his glass and replied, cautiously, "As the Doctor is listening, I mustn't use the word 'know'. But we think we've got a pretty good idea."

"Have you?" Brodribb exclaimed. "Now, I wonder what you have discovered. But I suppose it isn't in order for an outsider like me to pry into the secrets of Scotland Yard."

The Superintendent did not reply immediately, but from something in his manner, I suspected that he had come expressly to discuss the matter with us, but was "inhibited" by Brodribb's presence. At length, Thorndyke broke the silence.

"We are all very much interested, Miller, and we are all very discreet."

"Hmm, yes," said Miller. "Three lawyers and a detective officer ought to be able to produce a fair amount of discretion between them. And I don't know that it's such a deadly secret, after all. Still, we are keeping our own counsel, so you will understand that what I may mention mustn't go any farther."

"You are perfectly safe, Miller," Thorndyke assured him. "You know Jervis and me of old, and I can tell you that Mr. Brodribb is as close as an oyster."

Thus reassured, Miller (who was really bursting to give us his news) moistened his whistle afresh and began. "You must understand that we are at present dealing with what the Doctor calls *hypothesis*, though we have got a solid foundation of fact. As to what was in that stolen case, we have no direct evidence, but we have formed a pretty confident opinion. In fact, we think we know what that case contained. What do you suppose it was?"

I ventured to suggest jewellery, or perhaps bullion. "You are not so far out," said Miller. "We say that it was platinum."

"Platinum!" I exclaimed. "But there was a hundredweight of it! Why, at the present price, it must have been worth a king's ransom!"

"I don't know how much that is," said Miller, "but we reckon the value of the contents at between seventeen and eighteen-thousand pounds. That is only a rough estimate, of course. We think that the witness, Crump, was mistaken about the weight, and it was only a guess, in any case. He hadn't tested the weight of the package. At any rate, we can't account for more than about half-a-hundredweight of platinum."

"You have some perfectly definite information, then?" said Thorndyke.

"Definite enough so far as it goes," replied Miller, "but it doesn't go far enough. We are quite clear that a parcel of platinum weighing about twenty-five kilograms – roughly, half-a-hundredweight – was stolen and has disappeared. That is actual fact. The rest is inference, or, as the Doctor would say, hypothesis. But I will give you a sketch of the affair, leaving out the details that don't matter.

"Our information is that, about the end of last June, a quantity of platinum was shipped by a Latvian firm at Riga. It was packed in small wooden cases, each containing twenty-five kilos, and consigned to various dealers in Germany, France, and Italy. Well, the cases were all duly delivered at their respective destinations, and everything seemed to be in order excepting the contents of one of the Italian cases. That happened to be the last one that was delivered and, as the ship had made a good many calls on her voyage, it wasn't delivered until the beginning of August. When it was opened, it was found to contain, instead of the platinum, an equal weight of lead.

"Obviously there had been a robbery somewhere but, owing to the time which had elapsed, it was difficult to trace. One thing, however, was clear: The job had been done by somebody who was in the know. That was evident from the fact that the case was in all respects exactly like the original case and all the other cases."

"Why shouldn't it have been the original case with the contents changed?" I asked.

"That hardly seems possible. It would have been difficult enough to steal the case, but to steal it, empty it, refill it and put it back, looks like an impossibility. No, we can be pretty certain that the thieves had the dummy case ready and just made a quick exchange. That must have been the method, whoever did the job, but the puzzle was to discover the time and place of the robbery. The stuff had made a long journey to the port of delivery and the robbery might have taken place anywhere along the route.

"Eventually, suspicion arose with regard to an English yacht, the *Cormorant*, which had berthed close to the *Kronstadt* – that was the name of the ship which carried the stuff while she was taking in her cargo at Riga. It was recalled that she had occupied the next berth to the *Kronstadt* at the time when the platinum was being shipped, and someone remembered that, at that very time, the *Cormorant* was taking stores on board, including one or two big hampers. Accordingly, the Latvian police made some inquiries on the spot and, though they didn't discover anything very sensational, the little that they did learn seemed to favour the idea that the platinum might have been taken away on the yacht. This is what it amounted to, together with what we have picked up since.

"The *Cormorant* is a sturdy little yawl-rigged vessel – she appears to be a converted fishing lugger from Shoreham – of about thirty tons. She turned up at Riga on the 21st of June and took up her berth alongside the quay where the *Kronstadt* had just berthed. She went out from time to time for a sail in the Gulf but always came back to the same berth. Her crew consisted of four men, of whom three seemed to be regular seamen of the fisherman type, while the fourth, the skipper, whose name was Bassett, was a man of a superior class. The description of Bassett agrees completely with that of the man whom we have called Dobson – the man who deposited the case that was stolen from the cloak room, and the description of one of the crew seems to tally with that of the man who stole the case – the man whom we have called 'the head man'. Perhaps we had better call him Mr. '*X*' for convenience.

"Well, as I have said, at the time the platinum was shipped, the *Cormorant* was taking in stores, and her hampers and cases were on the quay at the same time as the cases of platinum and quite close to them. The platinum was unloaded from a closed van and dumped on the quay, and the *Cormorant*'s stores were unloaded from a wagon and also dumped on the quay. Then, as soon at the *Cormorant* had got her stores on board, she put out for a sail in the bay. But she was back in her berth again in about a couple of hours, and there she remained, on and off, for the next five days. It was not until the 26th of June that she left Riga for good."

"Doesn't the fact that she stayed there so long rather conflict with the idea that she had the stolen platinum on board?" I suggested.

"Well," Miller replied, "on the face of it, it does seem to. But if you bear all the circumstances in mind, I don't think it does. As soon as all the platinum was on board the *Kronstadt*, the danger of discovery was over. Remember, there was the right number of cases. There was nothing missing. It was practically certain that the robbery would not be discovered until the dummy case was opened by the consignees. Bearing that in mind, you see that it would be an excellent tactical plan to stay on at Riga as if nothing had happened, whereas it might have looked suspicious if the yacht had put to sea immediately after the shipment of the platinum.

"The next thing we hear of the yacht is that she arrived at Southend on the 17th of August."

"Have you ascertained where she had been in the interval?" I asked.

"No" he replied, "because, you see, it doesn't particularly concern us, as our theory is that she still had the platinum on board. But I must admit that, apart from the cloak room incident, we can't get any evidence that she had. At Southend she was boarded by the Customs Officer and, as she had just come from Rotterdam and had been cruising up the Baltic and along the German and Dutch coasts, he made a pretty rigorous search, especially for tobacco. He turned out every possible place in which a few cigars or cakes of 'hard' could have been stowed, and he even took up the trap in the cabin floor and squeezed down into the little hold. But he didn't find anything beyond the few trifles that had been declared. So his evidence is negative."

"It is rather more than negative," said I. "It amounts to positive evidence that the platinum wasn't there."

"Well, in a way, it does," Miller admitted. "It certainly doesn't help us. But there was one curious fact that we got from him. It seems that there were still four men on board the yacht, but they were not the same four men. One of them, at least, was different. The Customs man didn't see anybody corresponding to the description of Mr. '*X*'. On the other hand, there was a tall, clean shaved, elderly man who didn't look like a seaman – looked more like a lawyer or a doctor and spoke like a gentleman, or, at least, an educated man, though with a slight foreign accent, and didn't seem very anxious to speak at all, seemed more disposed to keep himself to himself. But the interesting point to us is the disappearance of Mr. '*X*'. That seems to give us something like a complete scheme of the whole affair, including the transaction at the cloak room."

"Were you proposing to let us hear your scheme of the robbery?" I asked.

"Well," said Miller, "I don't see why not, as I have told you so much. Of course, you will understand that it is very largely guess-work, but still, it comes together into a consistent whole. I will just give you an outline of what we believe to have been the course of events.

"We take it that this was a very carefully planned robbery, carried out by a party of experienced criminals who must all have had a fair knowledge of sea-faring. One of them, at least – probably the skipper, Bassett – must have had some pretty exact information as to the time and place at which the platinum was shipped and the size and character of the cases that it was stowed in. They must have arrived at the selected berth with a carefully prepared dummy case ready for use at the psychological moment. Then, when the cases of platinum arrived – and they must have known when to expect them – the dummy was smuggled up to the quay, covered up in some way, and slipped in amongst the genuine cases. Then they must have managed to cover up one of these, and they probably waited until the whole consignment, including the dummy, had been put on board and checked. There would have been the right number, you must remember.

"Well, when all the platinum appeared to have been put on board, there would have been no difficulty in taking the one that they had pinched – still covered up – on to the yacht along with their own stores. As soon as they had got it on board, they cast off and went for a sail in the bay, and during that little trip, they would be able safely to unload the case, break it up and burn it and stow the platinum in the hiding-place that they had got prepared in advance. When they came back to their berth, they had got the loot safely hidden and were ready to submit to a search, if need be. And it must have been an uncommonly cleverly devised hiding-place, for they made no difficulty about letting the Customs officer at Southend rummage the vessel to his heart's content."

"It must, as you say, have been a mighty perfect hiding-place," I remarked, "to have eluded the Customs man. When one of those gentry becomes really inquisitive, there isn't much that escapes him. He knows all the ropes and is up to all the smugglers' dodges."

"You must bear in mind, Jervis," Thorndyke reminded me, "that he was not looking for platinum. He was looking for tobacco. Do you know, Miller, in what form the metal was shipped? Was it in ingots or bars or plates?"

"It was in plates, thin sheets, in fact, about a millimetre in thickness and thirty centimetres – roughly twelve inches – square, a most convenient form for stowing in a hiding-place, for you could roll up the plates or cut them up with shears into little pieces."

"Yes," said Thorndyke, "and the plates themselves would take up very little room. You say the Customs man squeezed down into the hold. Do you know what the ballast was like? In a fishing vessel, it usually consists of rough pigs of iron and square ends of old chain and miscellaneous scrap, in which a few rolled-up plates of metal would not be noticed."

"Ah!" Miller replied. "The *Cormorant*'s ballast wasn't like that. It was proper yacht's ballast, lead weights, properly cast to fit the timbers and set in a neat row on each side of the kelson. So the hold was perfectly clear and the Customs man was able to see all over it from end to end.

"But to return to our scheme. When they had got the platinum safely hidden, our friends decided to stay on in their berth for a few days for the sake of appearances. Then they put to sea and proceeded in a leisurely, yacht-like fashion to make their way home. But during the voyage something seems to have happened. It looks rather as if the rogues had fallen out. At any rate, Mr. 'X' seems to have left the ship, and this stranger to have come on board in his place. I don't understand the stranger at all. I can't fit him into the picture. But Mr. 'X' apparently had a plan for grabbing the loot for himself, and when he went ashore, he must have left a confederate on board to keep him informed as to when the cargo was going to be landed.

"As to the landing, there wouldn't have been any difficulty about that. When the Customs man had made his search and found everything in order, the papers would be made out and the ship would be passed as 'cleared'. After that, the crew would be at liberty to take any of their goods ashore unchallenged. And the arrangements for getting the platinum landed were excellent. The yacht was brought up in Benfleet Creek, quite close to the railway. Evidently, the case was carried up to the station, and Bassett must have taken it into the carriage with him to avoid having a label stuck on it and giving a clue to the cloak room attendant.

"Why Bassett decided to plant it in the cloak room is not very clear. We can only suppose that he hadn't any other place to put it at the moment, and that he left it there while he was making arrangements for its disposal. But it gave Mr. '*X*' his chance. No doubt his pal on board made it his business to find out what became of the case, and gave Mr. '*X*' the tip, which Mr. '*X*' acted on very promptly and efficiently. And he and his pal are at this moment some seventeen-thousand pounds to the good.

"That is the scheme of the affair that we suggest. Of course, it is only a rough sketch, and you will say that it is all hypothesis from beginning to end, and so it is. But it hangs together."

"Yes," I agreed, "it is a consistent story, but it is all absolutely in the air. It is just a string of assumptions without a particle of evidence at any point. You begin by assuming that the case which was stolen from the cloak room contained the missing platinum. Then, from that, you deduce that the case came from the yacht, and therefore the man who deposited it must be Bassett, and the other man must be a member of the crew. And you don't even refer to the trivial circumstance that a box containing a man's head was left in exchange."

"I have already said," Miller rejoined a little impatiently, "that we are letting the problem of the head rest for the moment, as we have nothing to go on. But it is evidently connected in some way with the stolen case, so we are following that up. If we can connect that with the platinum robbery and lay our hands on Bassett and Mr. '*X*', we shall soon know something more about that head. I don't think your criticism is quite fair, Dr. Jervis. What do you say, Doctor?"

"I agree with you," said Thorndyke, "that Jervis's criticism overstates the case. Your scheme is admittedly hypothetical, and there is no direct evidence. So it may or may not be a true account of what happened. But I think the balance of probabilities is in favour of its being substantially true. You don't know anything about any of these men?"

"No, you see they are only names, and probably wrong names."

"You found no finger-prints on the address label of the 'head case'?"

"None that we could identify. Probably only those of chance strangers."

"And what has become of the yacht and the crew?"

"The yacht is still lying in Benfleet Creek. Bassett left her in charge of a local boat builder as there is no one on board, and the crew have gone away. We got a search warrant and rummaged her thoroughly, but we didn't find anything. So we sealed up the hatches and put on special padlocks and left the keys with the local police."

"Do you know whom she belongs to?"

"She belongs to Bassett. He bought her from a man at Shoreham. And she is now supposed to be for sale but, as the owner's whereabouts are not known, of course, she can't be sold. For practical purposes she is abandoned, but we are paying the boat builder for keeping an eye on her, pending the re-appearance of Mr. Bassett. Meanwhile we are keeping a look-out for that gentleman and Mr. '*X*', and for the appearance on the market of any platinum of uncertain origin. And that is about all that we can do until we get some fresh information."

"I suppose it is," said Thorndyke, "and, by the way, to return to the mysterious head, what has been done with it?"

"It has been buried in an air-tight case in Tower Hamlets Cemetery, with a stone to mark the spot in case it should be wanted. But we've got a stock of photographs of it which we have been circulating in the provinces to the various police stations. Perhaps you would like me to send you a set."

"Thank you, Miller," Thorndyke replied. "I should like a set to attach to the report of the inquest, which I have filed for reference."

"On the chance that, sooner or later, the inquiry may come into your hands?"

"Yes. There is always that possibility," Thorndyke replied. And this brought the discussion to an end, at least so far as Miller was concerned.

Chapter VI
Mr. Brodribb's Dilemma

The silence which fell after Thorndyke's last rejoinder lasted for more than a minute. At length it was broken by Brodribb who, after profound meditation, launched a sort of broadcast question, addressed to no one in particular.

"Does anyone know anything about a certain Mr. Horatio Gimbler?"

"Police court solicitor?" inquired Miller.

"That is what I assumed," replied Brodribb, "from his address, which seemed to be an unlikely one for a solicitor in general practice. Then you do, apparently, know him, at least by name."

"Yes," Miller admitted, "I have known him, more-or-less, for a good many years."

"Then," said Brodribb, "you can probably tell me whether you would consider him a particularly likely practitioner to have the conduct of a claim to a peerage."

"A peerage!" gasped Miller, gazing at Brodribb in astonishment. "Holy smoke! No. I – certainly – should – *not*!" He paused for a few moments to recover from his amazement and then asked, "What sort of a claim is it, and who is the claimant?"

"The claimant is an American and, at present, I don't know much about him. I'll give you some of the particulars presently, but first, I should like to hear what you know about Mr. Gimbler."

Miller appeared to reflect rapidly, accompanying the process by the emission of voluminous clouds of smoke. At length he replied, cautiously, "It is understood that what is said here is spoken in strict confidence."

To this reasonable stipulation we all assented with one accord and Miller continued, "This fellow, Gimbler, is a rather remarkable person. He is a good lawyer, in a sense *Cormorant* at any rate, he has criminal law and procedure at his finger-ends. He knows all the ropes – some that he oughtn't to know quite so well. He is up to all the tricks and dodges of the professional crooks, and I should think that his acquaintance includes practically all the crooks that are on the lay. If we could only pump him, he would be a perfect mine of information. But we can't. He's as secret

506

as the grave. The criminal class provide his living, and he makes it his business to study their interests."

"I don't see that you can complain of that," said Brodribb. "It is a lawyer's duty to consider the interests of his clients, no matter who they may be."

"That's perfectly true," replied Miller, "in respect of the individual client, but it is not the duty even of a criminal lawyer to grease the wheels of crime, so to speak. However, we are speaking of the man. Well, I have told you what we know of him, and I may add that he is about the downiest bird that I am acquainted with and as slippery as an eel. That is what we know."

Here Miller paused significantly with the air of a man who expects to be asked a question. Accordingly, Brodribb ventured to offer a suggestion.

"That is what you know. But I take it that you have certain opinions in addition to your actual knowledge?"

Miller nodded. "Yes," said he. "We are very much interested in Mr. Gimbler. Some of us have a feeling that there may possibly be something behind his legal practice. You know, in the practice of crime there is a fine opening for a clever and crooked brain. The professional crook, himself, is usually an unmitigated donkey, who makes all sorts of blunders in planning his jobs and carrying them out, and when you find the perfect ass doing a job that seems right outside his ordinary capabilities, you can't help wondering whether there may not be someone of a different calibre behind the scenes, pulling the strings."

"Ah!" said Brodribb. "Do I understand that you suspect this legal luminary of being the invisible operator of a sort of unlawful puppet show?"

"I would hardly use the word 'suspect'," replied Miller. "But some of us – including myself – have entertained the idea. And not, mind you, without any show of reason. There was a certain occasion on which we really thought we had got our hands on him, but we hadn't. If he was guilty – I don't say that he was, mind you – but if he was, he slipped out of the net uncommonly neatly. It was a case of forgery *Cormorant* at least we thought it was. But if it was, it was so good that the experts wouldn't swear to it, and the case wasn't clear enough to take into Court."

Mr. Brodribb pricked up his ears. "Forgery, you say, and a good forgery at that? You don't remember the particulars, I suppose? Because the question has a rather special interest for me."

"I only remember that it was a will case. The signature of the testator and the two witnesses were disputed, but, as all three were dead,

507

the question had to be decided on the opinions of experts, and none of the experts were certain enough to swear that the signatures might not be genuine. So the will had to be accepted as a genuine document. I suppose I mustn't ask how the question interests you?"

"Well," said Brodribb, "we are speaking in confidence, and I don't know that the matter is one of any great secrecy. It concerns this peerage claim that I was speaking about. I have had a copy of the pleadings, and I see that the claimant relies on certain documents to prove the identity of a very doubtful person. If you would care to hear an outline of the case, I don't think there would be any harm in my giving you a few of the particulars. I really came here to talk the case over with Thorndyke."

"If the pleadings were drawn up by Mr. Gimbler," said Miller, "I should like very much to hear an outline of the case. And you can take it that I shall not breathe a word to any living soul."

"The pleadings," said Brodribb, "were drawn up by counsel, but, of course, on Gimbler's instructions. The facts, or alleged facts, must have been supplied by him. However, before I come to his part in the business, there are certain other matters to consider, so it will be better if I take the case as a whole and in the natural order of events.

"Let me begin by explaining that I am the Earl of Winsborough's man of business. My father and grandfather both acted in the same capacity for former holders of the title, so, naturally, all the relevant documents on the one side are in my keeping. I am also the executor of the present Earl's will, though there is not much in that, as practically everything is left to the heir."

"You speak of the present Earl," said Thorndyke. "But if there is a present Earl, how comes it that a claim is being made to the earldom? Is an attempt being made to oust the present holder of the title?"

"I spoke of the present Earl," replied Brodribb, "because that is the legal position, and I, as his agent, am bound to accept it. But, as a matter of fact, I do not believe that there is a present Earl of Winsborough. I have no doubt that the Earl is dead. He went away on an exploring and big game hunting expedition to South America nearly five years ago, and has not been heard of for over four years. But, of course, in a legal sense, he is still alive and will remain alive until he is either proved or presumed to be dead. Hence these present proceedings, which began with a proposal on the part of the heir presumptive to apply to the Court for permission to presume death. The heir presumptive is a young man, a son of the Earl's first cousin, who has only recently come of age. As I had no doubt that he was the real heir presumptive – there being, in fact, no other possible claimant known to me – and very little doubt that the Earl was dead, I did not propose to contest the application, but, as the Earl's agent, I could not very well act for the applicant. Accordingly, I turned the business over to my friend, Marchmont, and intended only to watch the case in the interests of the estate. Then, suddenly, this new claimant appeared out of the blue, and his appearance has complicated the affair most infernally.

"You see the dilemma. Both claimants wish to apply for permission to presume death. But neither of them is the admitted heir presumptive, and consequently neither of them has the necessary *locus standi* to make the application."

"Couldn't they make a joint application?" Miller asked, "and fight out the claim afterwards?"

"I doubt whether that could be done," replied Brodribb, "or whether they would be prepared to act in concert. Each would probably be afraid of seeming to concede the claim to the other. The alternative plan would be for them to settle the question of heirship before applying for leave to presume death. But there is the difficulty that, until death is presumed, the present Earl is alive in a legal sense, and that being so, the Court might reasonably hold that the question of heirship does not arise. And, as the Earl is a bachelor and there are no near relatives, there is no one else to make the application."

"In any event," said I, "the new claimant's case would have to be dealt with by a Committee of Privileges of the House of Lords. Isn't that so?"

"I don't think it is," replied Brodribb. "This is not a case of reviving a dormant peerage. If the American's case, as stated in the pleadings, is sound, he is unquestionably the heir presumptive."

"What does his case amount to?" Thorndyke asked.

"Put in a nutshell," replied Brodribb, "it amounts to this: The American gentleman, whose name is Christopher Pippet, is the grandson of a certain Josiah Pippet who was the keeper of a tavern somewhere in London. But there is a persistent tradition in the family that the said Josiah was living a double life under an assumed name, and that he was really the Earl of Winsborough. It is stated that he was in the habit of going away from his home and his usual places of resort and leaving no address. It is further stated that during these periodical absences – which often lasted for a month or two – he was actually in residence at Winsborough Castle, that, when Josiah was absent from home, the Earl was in residence at the Castle, and when Josiah was at the tavern, the Earl was absent from the Castle."

"And did Josiah and the Earl die simultaneously and in the same place?" I inquired.

509

"No," said Brodribb. "The double life was brought to an end by Josiah, who is said, after the death of his wife and the marriage of his sons and daughter, to have grown weary of it. He wound up the affair by a simulated death, a mock funeral and the burial of a dummy coffin weighted with lumps of lead, after which he went to the Castle and took up his residence there for good. That is the substance of the story."

The Superintendent snorted contemptuously. "And you tell us, sir," said he, "that this man, Gimbler, is actually going to spin that yarn in a court of law. Why, the thing's grotesque – childish. He'd be howled out of Court."

"I agree," said Brodribb, "that it sounds wild enough. But it is not impossible. Few things are. It is just a question of what they can prove. According to the pleadings, there are certain passages in a diary of the late Josiah which prove incontestably that he and the Earl were one and the same person."

"That diary," said Miller, "will be worth a pretty careful examination, having regard to the circumstances that I mentioned."

"Undoubtedly," Brodribb agreed, "though it seems to me that it would be extremely difficult to interpolate passages in a diary. There is usually no space in which to put them."

"Does the claimant propose to produce the dummy coffin with the lumps of lead in it?" I asked.

"Nothing has been said on that subject up to the present," Brodribb answered. "It would certainly be highly relevant, but, of course, they couldn't produce it without an exhumation order."

"I think you can take it," said Miller, "that they will leave that coffin severely alone – if you let them."

"Probably you are right," said Brodribb. "But the difficulty that confronts us at present is that it may be impossible to proceed with the case. When it comes on for hearing, the Court may refuse to consider the application until one of the applicants has established his *locus standi* as a person competent to make it, and it may refuse to hear evidence as to the claim of either party to be the heir on the grounds that, inasmuch as the Earl has been neither proved nor presumed to be dead, he must be presumed to be alive, and that, therefore, in accordance with the legal maxim, *Nemo est heres viventis*, neither of the applicants can be the heir."

"That," said Thorndyke, "is undoubtedly a possible contingency. But judges are eminently reasonable men and it is not the modern practice to favour legal hair-splittings. We may assume that the Court will not raise any difficulties that are not unavoidable, and this is a case which calls for some elasticity of procedure. For the difficulty which

510

exists today might conceivably still exist fifty years hence, and meanwhile, the title and the estates would be left derelict. What are the proceedings that are actually in contemplation, and who is making the first move?"

"The American claimant, Pippet, is making the first move. Gimbler has briefed Rufus McGonnell, K.C. as his leader with Montague Klein as junior. He is proposing to apply for permission to presume the death of the Earl. I am contesting his application and challenging his claim to be the heir presumptive. That, he thinks, will enable him to produce his evidence and argue his claim as an issue preliminary to and forming part of the main issue. But I doubt very much whether the Court will consent to hear any evidence or any arguments that are not directly relevant to the question of the probability of the Earl's death. It is a very awkward situation. Pippet's claim looks like a rather grotesque affair, and if he is depending on the entries in a diary, I shouldn't think he has the ghost of a chance. Still, it ought to be settled one way or the other for the sake of young Giles Engleheart, the real heir presumptive, as I assume."

"Why shouldn't Engleheart proceed with his application?" said I.

"Because," replied Brodribb, "the same difficulty would arise. The other claimant would challenge his competency to make the application. It is a ridiculous dilemma. There are two issues, and each of them requires the other to be settled before it can be decided. It is very difficult to know what to do."

"The only thing that you can do," said Thorndyke, "is what you seem to be doing, let things take their own course and wait upon events. Pippet is making the first move. Well, let him make it and, if the Court won't hear him, it will be time for you to consider what you will do next. Meanwhile, it would be wise for you to assume that the Court will allow him to produce evidence of his competency to make the application. It is quite possible, and if you are supporting Mr. Engleheart's claim, you ought to be ready to contest the other claim."

"Yes," said Brodribb, "that is really what I came to talk to you about, and the first question is, do you know anything about these two counsel, McGonnell and Klein? I don't seem to remember either of them."

"You wouldn't," 'replied Thorndyke. "They are both almost exclusively criminal practitioners. But in their own line, they are men of first class capabilities. You can take it that they will give you a run for your money if they get the chance, in spite of their being rather off their usual beat. Have you decided on your own counsel?"

"I have decided to secure your services, in any event. Would you be prepared to take the brief?"

"I will take it if you wish me to," replied Thorndyke, "but I think you would be better advised to employ Anstey. For this reason. If the case comes into court, it is possible that certain questions may arise on which you might wish me to give expert evidence. I think you would do well to let me keep an eye on the technical aspects of the case and let Anstey do the actual court work."

Brodribb looked sharply at Thorndyke but made no immediate reply and, in the ensuing silence, a low chuckle was heard to proceed from the Superintendent.

"I like the delicate way the Doctor puts it," said he, by way of explaining the chuckle. "The technical aspects of this case will call for a good deal of watching, and I need not tell you, Mr. Brodribb, that, if the Doctor's eye is on them, there won't be much that will pass unobserved. In fact, I shouldn't be surprised to learn that the Doctor has got one or two of them in his eye already."

"Neither should I," said Brodribb. "Nothing surprises me where Thorndyke is concerned. At any rate, I shall act on your advice, Thorndyke. One couldn't ask for a better counsel than Anstey, and it is not necessary for me to stipulate that you go over the pleadings with him and put him up to any possible dodges on the part of our friend Mr. Gimbler. Remember that I am retaining you, and that you do as you please about pleading in court."

"I understand," said Thorndyke. "You will keep Anstey and me fully instructed, and I shall give the case the most careful consideration in regard to any contingencies that may arise. As Miller has hinted, there are a good many possibilities, especially if Mr. Gimbler should think it necessary to throw a little extra weight into the balance of probabilities."

"Very well," said Brodribb, "then we will leave it at that. If you have the case in hand, I shall feel that I can go ahead in confidence, and I only hope that McGonnell will be able to persuade the Court to hear the evidence on his client's claim. It would be a blessed thing if we could get that question settled so that we could go straight ahead with the other question – the presumption of death. I am getting a little worried by the more or less derelict condition of the Winsborough estates and it would be a relief to see a young man fairly settled in possession."

"You are rather taking it for granted that the American's claim will fall through," I remarked.

"So I am," he admitted. "But you must allow that it does sound like a cock-and-bull story, and none too straightforward at that. However, we shall see. If I get nothing more out of it, I have had an extremely pleasant evening and a devilish good bottle of wine, and now it's about time that I took myself off and let you get to bed."

With this he rose and shook hands, and the Superintendent, taking the rather broad hint conveyed in the concluding sentence, rose too, and the pair took their departure together.

Chapter VII
The Final Preparations

Most of us have wit enough to be wise after the event, and a few of us have enough to be wise before. Thorndyke was one of these few, and I – alas! – was not. I am speaking in generalities, but I am thinking of a particular case – the Winsborough Peerage Claim. That case I could not bring myself to take seriously. The story appeared to me, as it had appeared to Miller, merely grotesque. Its improbabilities were so outrageous that I could not entertain it as a problem for serious consideration. And then, such as it was, it was a purely legal case, completely outside our ordinary line of practice. At least, that is how it appeared to me.

Now Thorndyke made no such mistake. Naturally, he could not foresee developments in detail. But subsequent events showed that he had foreseen, and very carefully considered, all the possible contingencies, so that when they arose they found him prepared. And he also saw clearly that the case might turn out to be very much in our line.

As I was unaware of his views – Thorndyke being the most uncommunicative man whom I have ever known – I looked with some surprise on the obvious interest that he took in the case. So great was that interest that he actually adopted the extraordinary habit of spending week-ends at Winsborough Castle. What he did there I was unable to make out. I heard rumours of his having gone over the butler's accounts and some of the old household books and papers with Brodribb, which seemed a not unreasonable proceeding, though more in Brodribb's line than ours. But most of his time he apparently spent rambling about the country with a notebook, a small camera, and a set of six-inch Ordnance Maps. And he evidently covered a surprising amount of ground, as I could see by the numbers of photographs that he brought home, and which he either developed himself or handed to our invaluable laboratory assistant, Polton, for development. Over those photographs, when they were printed, I pored with a feeling of stupefaction. They included churches, both inside and out, windmills, inns, churchyards, and quaint village streets, all very interesting and many of them charming. But what had they to do with the peerage case? I was completely mystified.

On one occasion I accompanied him, and a very pleasant jaunt it was. The Castle was rather a delusion, though there were some mediaeval ruins of a castellated building, but the mansion was a pleasant, homely brick house of the late seventeenth century in the style of Wren's country houses. But our ramblings about the house and the adjoining gardens and park yielded no information – excepting as to the mental condition of a former proprietor, as suggested by the costly and idiotic additions that he had made to the mansion.

These were, I must admit, perfectly astounding. On a low hill in the park near to the house was a stupendous brick tower – a regular Tower of Babel – from the summit of which we could look across the sea to the white cliffs of the coast of France. It stood quite alone and appeared to have no purpose beyond the view from the top, but the cost of its construction must have been enormous. But "George's Folly", to give the tower its appropriate local name, was not the most astonishing of these works. When we came down from the roof, Thorndyke produced a bunch of large keys, which he had borrowed from the butler, and with one of them opened a door in the basement. Then he switched on a portable electric lamp, by the light of which I perceived a flight of stone steps apparently descending into the bowels of the earth. Picking our way down these, we reached an archway opening into a roomy brick-walled passage, and making our way along this for fully a hundred yards, at length reached another door which, being unlocked, gave entrance to a large room, lighted by a brick shaft that opened on the surface. A moth-eaten carpet still covered the floor and the mouldering furniture remained as it had been left, presumably, by the eccentric builder.

It was a strange and desolate-looking apartment, and the final touch of desolation was given by a multitude of bats which hung, head downwards, from the ceiling ornaments or fluttered silently in circles in the dark corners or in the dim light under the opening of the shaft.

"This is a weird place, Thorndyke," I exclaimed. "What do you think could have been the object of building it?"

"So far as I know," he replied, "there was no particular object. It was the noble lord's hobby to build towers and underground apartments. This is not the only one. The door at the other end of the room opens into another passage which leads to several other large rooms. We may as well inspect them."

We did so. In all, there were five large rooms connected by several hundred yards of passages, and three or four small rooms, all lighted by shafts and all still containing their original furniture and fittings.

"But," I exclaimed, as we threaded our way along the interminable passages back to the tower, "this man must have been a stark lunatic."

"He was certainly highly eccentric," said Thorndyke, "though we must make some allowance for an idle rich man. But you see the significance of this. Supposing that the peerage claim were to be tried by a jury, and supposing that jury were brought here and shown these rooms and passages. Do you think Mr. Pippet's story would appear to them so particularly incredible? Don't you think that they would say that a man who could busy himself in works of this kind would be capable of any folly or eccentricity?"

"I think it very likely," I admitted, "but for my own part, I must say that I cannot imagine his Lordship as landlord of a London pub. Playing the fool in your own park is a slightly different occupation from drawing pints of beer for thirsty labourers. I wonder if the Kenningtonian Gimbler knows about these works of imagination."

"He does," said Thorndyke. "A description of them was included in the 'material facts' set forth in the pleadings. And he has examined them personally. He applied to Brodribb for permission to view the mansion, and naturally Brodribb gave it."

"I don't see why 'naturally'. He was not called on to assist the claim which he was opposing."

"He took the view – correctly, I think – that he ought not to hinder, in any way, the ascertainment of the material facts – facts, you must remember, that he does not dispute. And, really, he can afford to deal with the American claimant in a generous and sporting spirit. Mere evidence of eccentricity on the part of the late Earl will not do more than establish a bare possibility. A positive case has to be made out. The burden of proof is on Cousin Jonathan."

"That is, if the case ever comes into court. I doubt if, it will."

"Then you need doubt no longer," said he. "The case is down for hearing next week."

"The deuce it is!" I exclaimed. "Do you know what form the proceedings will take?"

"It is to be heard in the Probate Court. Ostensibly, it is an application by Christopher Pippet for permission to presume the death of Percy Engleheart, sixth Earl of Winsborough. Brodribb, acting in virtue of a power of attorney, opposes the application and challenges the *locus standi* of the applicant. Of course, we cannot say how far the case will be allowed to proceed, but I take it that it is proposed to allow Pippet to produce evidence establishing his *locus standi* as a person having such an interest in the estate as would entitle him to make the application. That is to say, he will be allowed to present the case on which he bases his claim to be the heir presumptive to the Earl. I certainly hope he will. There are all sorts of interesting possibilities in the case."

516

"Interesting, no doubt, in a legal sense, but I don't see where we come in."

"Perhaps we shan't come in at all," he replied with a faint smile. "But I rather suspect that we shall. The special interest of the case to me lies in the fact that Mr. Pippet's counsel will be instructed by Mr. Horatio Gimbler."

Something in Thorndyke's manner, as he made this last statement, seemed to suggest some special significance. But what that significance might be I was unable to guess, beyond the fact that the said Gimbler, being neither an infant nor a man of irreproachable reputation, might adopt some slightly irregular tactics. But I suspected that there was something more definite than this in my colleague's mind. However, the conversation went no farther on this occasion, and I was left to turn the problem over at my leisure.

Thorndyke's announcement had come to me as a complete surprise, for I had never believed that this fantastic case would actually find its way into the courts. But the case furnished a whole series of surprises, of which the first was administered on the day when the proceedings opened, and was connected with the personality and behaviour of the claimant. I had assumed that Mr. Christopher Pippet was an American adventurer who had come over to tell this cock-and-bull story in the hope of getting possession of a valuable English estate. Probably the idea arose – not quite unreasonably – from the fact that the claimant made his appearance under the guidance of a slightly shady police-court solicitor. In my mind I had written him down an impostor, and formed a picture of a hustling, brazen vulgarian, suitable to the part and appropriate to his company. The reality was surprisingly different.

On the morning of the hearing, Brodribb appeared at our chambers accompanied by his clients, Mr. Giles Engleheart and his mother, to whom he presented us in his old-fashioned, courtly manner.

"I thought it best," he explained, "that you should not meet in court as strangers. I have introduced Anstey already, and I think he is going to join us here. So we shall be able to make our descent on the Halls of Justice in a united body and thereby impress the opposition."

"I suspect," said Mrs. Engleheart, "that the opposition is not so easily impressed. But my boy and I will feel some encouragement if we arrive escorted by our champions. Have we plenty of time?" she added, glancing a little anxiously at her watch.

"We have," replied Brodribb, "if Anstey doesn't keep us waiting. Ah! Here he is!" And as a quick footstep was heard on the stair, he strode over to the door and threw it open, when our leading counsel entered with an exaggerated pretence of haste, holding his watch in his hand.

"Come," he exclaimed, "this won't do. We ought to be starting."

"But," said Mrs. Engleheart, "we have been waiting for you, Mr. Anstey."

"Exactly," he retorted. "That is what I meant." Then, as the lady, unaccustomed to his whimsicalities, looked at him in some perplexity, he continued, briskly, "It is always desirable to be in court early on the opening day. Are we all ready? Then let us go forth and make our way to the scene of conflict. But not too much like a procession. And I want to have a few words with you, Thorndyke, en route."

With this, he took Thorndyke's arm and led the way out. Brodribb followed with Mrs. Engleheart, and I brought up the rear with her son.

As we walked at a leisurely pace – set by Anstey – across the precincts by way of the Cloisters and Pump Court, I took the opportunity to consider my companion as to his appearance and personality in general, and in all respects I was very favourably impressed, as I had been by the gentle dignity of his mother. Giles Engleheart was not only a fine, strapping, handsome young man and very unmistakeably a gentleman, but – like his mother – he conveyed the impression of a kindly, generous and amiable disposition. But unlike his mother, he seemed disposed to regard the legal proceedings as a gigantic joke.

"Well, Mr. Engleheart," I said, by way of making conversation, "I think we shall make pretty short work of your American rival."

"Do you?" said he. "I don't think Mr. Brodribb is so confident, and for my part, I rather hope you won't make it too short. He ought to have a run for his money – and he may give us a run for ours. After all, you know, sir, his statements are pretty definite, and we've no right to assume that he is a liar. And if he isn't, his statements are probably true. And if they are true, we've got to imagine George Augustus, fourth Earl of Winsborough, with his sleeves rolled up and a black linen apron on his tummy, pulling at the handles of the beer engine in a London pub. It's a quaint idea. I'm all agog to hear his counsel tell the story and trot out his evidence."

"For my part," said I, "I can't bring myself to view the claim as anything more than a gross and crude imposture, and I shouldn't be surprised if the case ended in a charge of perjury."

"Do you mean against Mr. Pippet?" he asked.

"I don't know anything about Pippet," I replied, "but I look with considerable suspicion on his solicitor."

Engleheart laughed cheerfully. "You are like Mr. Brodribb," said he. "The very mention of the name of Gimbler makes him spit – metaphorically – whereas I never hear it without thinking of Jabberwocky and the Slithy Toves."

"What is the connexion?" I asked, rather foolishly.

"Don't you remember, sir?" said he. "The Slithy Toves *'did gyre and gimble in the wabe'*. Therefore they were gimblers. *Q.E.D.*"

"Perhaps," said I, laughing at his schoolboy joke, "Mr. Brodribb has noticed the connexion and suspects our friend of an intention to *'gyre and gimble'* in a legal sense. And perhaps he is right. Time will show. But here we are at what Anstey calls *'the scene of conflict'*."

Entering the great doorway, we followed our friends along the rather gloomy passages until Anstey pushed open a heavy swing door and stood, holding it open while Mrs. Engleheart and the rest of us passed through. Then he and Thorndyke and I retired to the robing room and hastily donned our wigs and gowns.

When we returned to the court, the clock showed that there was still a quarter-of-an hour to spare and, with the exception of one or two reporters, a few spectators in the gallery, and a stray barrister, we had the place to ourselves. But not for long. Even as the quarter was chiming, the heavy and noisy swing doors were pushed open and a party of strangers entered.

There was no doubt as to who they were for, though I had not recognized the name of Gimbler, I recognized the man, having seen him on several occasions at the Central Criminal Court – a big, burly man with a large, rather fat face, and small, furtive eyes. A sly-looking fellow, I decided, and forthwith wrote him down a knave. But the other members of the party gave me quite a little surprise. There were three of them – two women and a man, and the out-standing fact which instantly impressed me was their imposing appearance. It was not only that they were all well above the average of good looks, though that was a fact worth noting, but they all had the unmistakeable appearance and bearing of gentlefolk.

Of course, my surprise was quite unreasonable, being due to an entirely gratuitous pre-conceived idea. But still more unreasonable was the instant change in my state of mind in regard to the claim. Looking at the claimant – as I assumed him to be, seeing that there was no other man – I found myself talking a revised view of the case. Clearly, this fine, upstanding gentleman with his clear-cut, strong, reposeful face, was an entirely different creature from the raffish cosmopolitan adventurer of my imagination, who had come over to "tell the tale" and try to snatch a stray fortune.

The two parties – our own and "the opposition" – took an undissembled interest in one another, and Mr. Giles conveyed his sentiments to me in an undertone.

"Good-looking crowd, sir, aren't they? If that young lady is a fair sample of an American girl, I am going to emigrate if we lose the case."

"And if you don't lose the case?" I asked.

"Well, sir," he replied, smilingly evading the question, "I shall be able to pay my lawyer, which will be pleasant for us both."

Here my attention was diverted by what looked like a difference between Mr. Gimbler and his client. The solicitor appeared distinctly annoyed and I heard him say, almost angrily, "I do certainly object. It would be entirely out of order."

"No doubt you are right, as a lawyer," was the calm reply, "but I am not a lawyer". And with this, he turned away from his legal adviser and, to that gentleman's evident dismay, began to move across in our direction. As he was obviously bearing down on us with intent, we all, excepting Mrs. Engleheart, stood up, and I could hear Brodribb muttering under his breath.

Having saluted us with a comprehensive bow, the stranger addressed himself to our old friend.

"I believe you are Mr. Brodribb."

"At your service, sir," was the reply, accompanied by a bow of such extreme stiffness that I seemed to hear him creak.

"I understand," said Mr. Pippet, "that I am committing a gross breach of legal etiquette. But etiquette is made for man, especially for European man, and I am venturing to take an aboriginal view of the matter. Would it appear particularly shocking if I were to ask you to do me the honour of presenting me to your clients?"

"I think," replied Brodribb, recovering himself somewhat, "that I should survive the shock, and my clients, I am sure, will be delighted to make your acquaintance."

With this he proceeded, with the air of a Gold-Stick-in-Waiting approaching a royal personage, to present the American to Mrs. Engleheart.

"This is most kind of you, Mr. Pippet," the lady exclaimed with a gracious smile. "Mr. Brodribb is quite right. I am delighted to make your acquaintance, and so, I am sure, will my son be. May I introduce him?"

Here Giles stepped forward and the two men shook hands heartily.

"It is very good of you, sir, to make this friendly move," said he, "seeing that our presence here is not exactly helpful to you."

"But," said Mr. Pippet, "that is just my point. All this talk of fights and battles and contests that I have been hearing from my solicitor makes me tired. I am not here to fight anybody, and neither, I take it, are you. There are certain matters of alleged fact that I am submitting for the consideration and judgment of the court. I don't know whether they are

520

true or not. That is for the court to find out. My lawyers will argue that they are, and yours will argue that they are not. Let us leave it to them. There's no need for us to have any unfriendly feeling about it. Isn't that so, Mr. Brodribb?"

"There is no reason," Brodribb replied cautiously, "why opposing litigants should not be personally friendly – without prejudice, of course. But you are not forgetting that these proceedings involve certain consequences. If the decision is in your favour, you obtain possession of a title of nobility and property of great value, which Mr. Engleheart thereby loses, and vice versa."

"Not quite vice-versa, Mr. Brodribb," Mr. Pippet corrected. "The cases are not identical. If the court decides that my respected grandfather was not the Earl of Winsborough, Mr. Engleheart steps into the late Earl's shoes as soon as the death has been presumed, and I retire out of the picture. But if it is decided that my grandfather was the Earl, then, as I have no male descendants, Mr. Engleheart has only to wait for those shoes until I step out of them."

I could see that this statement made a considerable impression on both Mr. Brodribb and Mrs. Engleheart, and it did certainly ease the situation materially from their point of view. Brodribb, however, made no comment, and it fell to Mrs. Engleheart to make the acknowledgments.

"Thank you, Mr. Pippet," said she, "for letting us know the position. I won't pretend that I am not very much relieved to know that it is only a question of postponement for my son. But whichever way the decision goes, I hope it will be a long time before a vacancy is declared in those shoes. But you haven't completed the introductions. Is that very charming girl your daughter?"

"She is, Madam," was the reply. "My only child and, with the exception of my sister, who is with her, my only kin in the world – unless it should transpire that I have the honour to be related to you and your son."

"Well," said Mrs. Engleheart, "if your kinsfolk are not very numerous, you have reason to be proud of them, as I dare say you are. Do you think they would care to know us?"

"I have their assurance that they would like very much to make your acquaintance," Mr. Pippet replied, on which Mrs. Engleheart rose and was requesting to be taken to them when they were seen to be moving in our direction, apparently in response to some subtle telegraphic signals on the part of Mr. Pippet. As they approached, I looked them over critically and had to admit that their appearance was at least equal to their pretensions. The elder lady – like the late Queen Victoria –

521

combined a markedly short stature with a most unmistakeable "presence", aided not a little by the strong, resolute face and a somewhat out-size Roman nose, while the younger was a tall, handsome girl, noticeably like her father and her aunt both in features and in the impression of dignity and character which she conveyed. And both ladies had that un-selfconscious ease of manner that is usually associated with the word "breeding".

The introductions were necessarily hurried, for the time for the opening of the proceedings was drawing nigh. The clerk had taken his seat at his desk, the reporters were in their places, the ushers had taken up their posts, a few more spectators were drifting into the seats in the public gallery and the counsel had established themselves in their respective places and were now turning over the pages of their briefs – excepting Thorndyke and myself, who had no briefs but were present merely in a watching capacity. Mr. Pippet returned to the place where his solicitor sat glumly by the solicitor's table, but the two ladies remained with our party, Miss Pippet sitting by Mrs. Engleheart and the young lady (who, I gathered, bore the picturesque old English name of Jenifer) by Mr. Giles.

They had hardly settled themselves when the judge entered and took his seat on the bench. Having laid some papers on his desk, he leaned back in his seat and ran his eye with undissembled interest over the parties to the proceedings.

"Now," Miss Jenifer remarked in a low tone to her companion, "we are going to hear whether we are cousins or only friends."

"Or both," added Giles.

"Of course," said she. "That was what I meant. But we mustn't talk. The play is going to begin, and that nice-looking old gentleman in that quaint wig has got his eye on us."

Thereupon she subsided into silence, and Mr. McGonnell proceeded to open the case.

Chapter VIII
The Opening of the Case

"This, my Lord," said Mr. McGonnell, rising and turning an ingratiating eye on the bench, "is an application by Mr. Christopher Josiah Pippet, a citizen of the United States, for permission to presume the death of Percy Engleheart, sixth Earl of Winsborough, but there are certain peculiar and unusual features in the case. The application is opposed by the representatives of the Earl, who challenge the *locus standi* of the applicant on the ground that he is, as they allege, a stranger having no legitimate interest or concern in the estate of the said Earl. The applicant, on the other hand, affirms, and is prepared to prove, that he is the direct descendant of the fourth Earl of Winsborough, and that he is, in effect, the heir presumptive to the earldom and the settled estate.

"Accordingly, the applicant petitions to be allowed to produce evidence of his title to the estate and to obtain a decision on that issue as an issue antecedent to the application for permission to presume death."

The judge looked keenly at the counsel during the making of this statement and then he turned a slightly curious glance on Mr. Pippet and from him to his solicitor.

"I must be perfectly clear," said he, "as to the scope of this further application. There appears to be a claim to a title and to the settled property associated with it. Now, I need not remind you that claims in respect of titles of honour lie within the jurisdiction of the House of Lords through a Committee of Privileges."

"We realize that, my Lord," said Mr. McGonnell. "But we are not seeking a final and conclusive decision in this court on the question whether the applicant, Christopher Pippet, is or is not entitled to succeed the present tenant, Earl Percy, but merely whether he has such an interest in the estate as will give him the *locus standi* necessary to entitle him to make an application to presume the death of the said Earl Percy."

"That application," said the judge, "implies certain further proceedings, including, perhaps, a petition to the House of Lords."

"That is so, my Lord," counsel agreed. "But we are in a difficulty, and we ask your Lordship to exercise a discretion in the matter of procedure. Our difficulty is this: There is reason to believe that Earl Percy is dead, but no direct evidence of his death exists. Consequently, he is, in a legal sense, a living person and, since no one can be the heir of a living person, it is not possible for Mr. Pippet to initiate proceedings in the House of Lords. Before any such proceedings could become possible, it would be necessary for the death of Earl Percy to be either proved or presumed.

"Therefore, the applicant applies for the permission of the court to presume the death. But his right to make this application is contested on the grounds that I have mentioned. Thus he is in this dilemma: He cannot prove his claim until death is presumed, and he cannot apply for permission to presume death until he has proved his claim. But this dilemma, it is submitted, is contrary to the interests of justice, and we accordingly ask your Lordship to hear such evidence as shall establish the applicant's position as a person having such an interest in the estate as renders him competent to make the application."

"It is not perfectly clear," said the judge, "that the fact of his having this belief in his title to succeed does not constitute him an interested party to that extent. But we need not go into that, as the issue is not raised. What is the position of the Earl's representatives in regard to the heir presumptive?"

"Our position, my Lord," said Anstey, rising as the other counsel sat down, "is that the heir presumptive is Mr. Giles Engleheart, the only son of the late Charles Engleheart, Esquire, who was the Earl's first cousin. Apart from Mr. Pippet's claim, there is no doubt whatever about Mr. Engleheart's position. It is not contested. And I may say, if it is permissible, that we are in full agreement with what my learned friend has just said with regard to the applicant's claim. Since the question has been raised, we submit that it is desirable that the applicant be permitted to produce such evidence as may establish the existence or non-existence of a *prima facie* case. We agree with my learned friend that the present impasse is against the interests of justice."

"Yes," said the judge, "there ought certainly to be some escape from the dilemma which the learned counsel for the applicant has mentioned. The actual claim will, no doubt, have to be decided in another place, but there is no objection to such provisional proof as may be necessary for the purposes of the present application. I am therefore prepared to hear the evidence in support of the applicant's claim."

He looked at Mr. McGonnell, who thereupon rose and proceeded to open the preliminary case, by a recital of the alleged facts in much the same terms as the sketch which I had heard from Mr. Brodribb, but in somewhat greater detail and, as I listened, with my eyes on the judge's face, to the unfolding of that incredible and ridiculous story, I was once more astonished that anyone should have the confidence to tell it seriously in a court of law. How it impressed the judge it was impossible to tell. Judges, as a class, are not easily surprised, nor are they addicted to giving facial expression to their emotions, and the present specimen was a particularly wooden-faced old gentleman. All that I could gather from my observations of his countenance was that he appeared to be listening with close attention and placid interest

"That, my Lord," said Mr. McGonnell, when he came to the end of the "story" with a description of the sham funeral, "is an outline of what are alleged to be the facts of the applicant's case, and it would be useless to deny that, taken at its face value, the whole story appears wildly incredible. If it rested only on the family tradition, no one would entertain it for a moment. But it does not rest only on that tradition. It is supported by a considerable body of evidence, including certain very significant entries in a diary kept by Josiah Pippet and certain facts relating to the Earl, George Augustus, who, it is claimed, was the alter ego of the said Josiah. Perhaps it will be well to glance at the latter first.

"The thesis on which Mr. Christopher Pippet's claim is based is that the said Earl, George Augustus, was in the habit of leaving his mansion from time to time and going to The Fox and Grapes Inn, where he assumed the name and style of Josiah Pippet and lived the life and carried out the activities of an inn-keeper. Now, it will naturally be asked, 'Is it credible that any man in the possession of his senses would conduct himself in this manner?' And the answer obviously is that it is not. But here the question arises, 'Was the said Earl in the possession of his senses?' And the answer to that is that, apparently, he was not. At any rate, his conduct in general was so strange, so unusual and erratic, that it would be difficult to name any eccentricity of which he might not have been capable. Let us see what manner of man this was.

"In the first place, he appears to have been a man who had no fixed habits of life. He would live for months at his mansion, busying himself in certain works which we shall consider presently, and then, apparently without notice, he would disappear, leaving no clue to his whereabouts. He would stay away from home for months – in some cases for more than a year – and then would suddenly make his appearance at the mansion, unannounced and unexpected, giving no account of himself or his doings during his absence. And it is worth notice that his alleged double, Josiah Pippet, had similar peculiarities of behaviour. He also was in the habit of making mysterious disappearances and leaving no clue to his whereabouts."

"Is it ascertained," the judge asked, "that the disappearances of the two men coincided in time?"

"That is what is alleged, my Lord," was the reply. "Naturally, after the many years that have elapsed, it is difficult to recover the dates as exactly as might be desired."

"No doubt," his Lordship agreed, "but the point is highly material."

"Certainly, my Lord," counsel admitted. "Its importance has been fully realized and the point has been carefully examined. Such evidence as has been available goes to prove that the disappearances synchronized.

"But these strange disappearances are not the only, or even the most, striking evidences of the Earl's eccentricity. Still more suggestive of an unbalanced mind is the way in which he occupied himself in the intervals of those disappearances, when he was in residence at the mansion. Nothing in the traditional story which I have recited is more incredible than the history of his doings when he was at home. For then, it appears, he was in the habit of assembling an army of workmen and, at enormous expense, employing them in carrying out works on the most gigantic scale and of the most preposterous character. In one part of his grounds, he set up an immense and lofty tower, with no ascertainable purpose except the view from the summit. From the base of this tower, a flight of steps was constructed leading down into the bowels of the earth, and communicating with a great range of subterranean passages of an aggregate length of close upon a mile. Connected with these passages were several large subterranean rooms, lighted from the surface by shafts and elaborately furnished. No reason is known for the construction of these rooms, though it appears that the Earl was accustomed, from time to time, to retire to them with a stock of provisions and pass a few days underground, hidden from the sight of men. These strange burrows and the great tower are still in existence and will be described in detail by a witness who, by the courtesy of the Earl's representatives, was enabled to make a thorough examination of them. But the slight description of them which I have given is sufficient to demonstrate that the Earl George Augustus was a man who, if not actually insane, was so strange and erratic in his behaviour that there is hardly any eccentricity of which he might not have been capable. The objection, therefore, to the traditional story, that it postulates an unbelievable degree of eccentricity in the Earl George Augustus, has no weight, since the said Earl did, in fact, give evidence of an unbelievable degree of eccentricity.

"I will say no more on the subject of this strange man's personality, though further details of his peculiarities will be given in evidence. But, before finishing with him, it will be material to note the salient facts of his life. George Augustus, fourth Earl of Winsborough, was born on the 9th of August in the year 1794 and he died unmarried in 1871, aged 77. He had no brothers. He was succeeded by his cousin, Francis Engleheart, who died in 1893 and was succeeded by his only son – and only child – then twenty-six years of age, the present Earl Percy.

"We now pass to the alleged double of the Earl George Augustus, Josiah Pippet. Of his personal character we have less direct information, but, on the other hand, we have an invaluable and unimpeachable source of evidence in a diary which he kept for many years, and up to the date of his death. From this, we, at least, gather one highly suggestive fact that he, like the Earl, was in the habit of disappearing at intervals from his home and from his usual places of resort, of staying away for months at a time, and on two occasions for over a year and, so far as we are able to discover, leaving no clue as to the place to which he had gone or where he was living.

"When I say that he left no clue to his whereabouts, I mean that he gave no information to his wife or family. Actually, the diary furnishes quite a considerable number of clues, and it is a very striking fact that these clues all refer to the same locality, and that the locality referred to happens to be the very one in which Winsborough Castle is situated. But not only is the locality referred to – there are actual references to the Castle itself, and in such terms as to leave no doubt that the writer was, at the time, in residence there. As the diary will be put in evidence, I need not occupy the time of the court with quotations at this stage, but will proceed to the few but important facts that are known respecting Josiah Pippet.

"The first fact that I shall mention – and a very striking and suggestive fact it is – is that, although the date of Josiah's birth is known, no entry recording it appears in any known register. Exhaustive search has been made at Somerset House and elsewhere, but, so far as can be discovered, no record whatever exists of this man's birth. He seems to have dropped from the skies.

"But, as I have said, the date of his birth is known, for it is stated with great exactness on the vault in which his coffin was deposited. Above the entrance to that vault is a marble tablet on which is carved this brief but significant inscription: '*Josiah Pippet, died the 12th day of October 1843. Aged 49 years, 2 months and 3 days*'.

"Now here is a very exact, though rather roundabout statement, from which we can compute the very day of his birth. And what was that day? A simple calculation shows that it was the 9th of August 1794 – the very same day on which George Augustus, Fourth Earl of Winsborough, was born!

"If this is a coincidence, it is a most amazing one. The Earl and his alleged double were born on the same day. And not only that. The birth of the double is unrecorded. There is no evidence that it ever took place.

Which is precisely what we might expect in the case of a double. The birth of the Earl duly appears in the register at Somerset House, and I submit that it is a reasonable inference that that entry records the birth, not only of George Augustus Engleheart, but also of Josiah Pippet. That those two men were, in fact, one and the same person, or, in other words, that Josiah Pippet was a purely imaginary and fictitious person.

"But the mysterious circumstances connected with the birth of these two persons – or these two aspects of the same person – are repeated in connexion with their deaths. Just as only one of them is known, and can be proved, to have been born, so only one of them can be proved to have died. It is true that, in the case of Josiah, there was a funeral and a coffin which was solemnly interred. But there was a current belief that the funeral was a sham and that the coffin contained no human remains. And that belief is supported by the fact that there was no medical certificate. The death certificate was signed only by 'Walter Pippet', the son of the alleged deceased, as was possible in those days, before the passing of the Medical Act of 1858. There is nothing to show that the alleged deceased was attended by any medical practitioner or that there was anything to prevent the sham funeral from taking place with the collusion of the said Walter Pippet. The circumstances of the death, I repeat, like those of the birth, are fully compatible with the belief that there were not two persons at all, but only one person enacting two alternating parts. In other words, that Josiah Pippet was a mythical personage, like John Doe, created for a specific purpose.

"Nevertheless, when we come to the matter of the applicant's ancestry and descent, we must treat the said Josiah as a real person, since he is the applicant's visible ancestor. And he has undeniably the qualities of a real person inasmuch as, in the character of Josiah Pippet, he married and had children. In the year 1822, in the church of St. Helen's, Bishopsgate, he was married to Martha Bagshaw, spinster, he being then twenty-eight years of age and, according to the register, following the occupation of a ship's steward. The exact date at which he became landlord of The Fox and Grapes is not certain, but he is so described in the register where the birth of his eldest child is recorded.

"There were three children of this marriage: Walter, the eldest, born in 1824, Frederick William, born in 1826, and Susan, born in 1832. Susan married and died in 1897. Walter carried on The Fox and Grapes after his father's real or fictitious death, and died unmarried in 1865. Frederick William took to a sea-faring life and eventually settled, in the year 1853, at the age of twenty-seven, in the United States, in the city of Philadelphia, Pennsylvania. There he began business by opening a small shop, which grew by degrees into a large and important department store.

528

In 1868, he married Miss Elizabeth Watson, the daughter of a well-to-do merchant of Philadelphia, by whom he had two children: A son, Christopher Josiah, the present applicant, and a daughter Arminella. He lost his wife in 1891, and he died in 1905, leaving the bulk of his large fortune to his daughter and the residue together with the business to his son, who carried on the concern until 1921, when, having made a further considerable fortune, he sold out and retired. It was then that, for the first time, he began seriously to consider raising the claim to what he believes – justly, as I submit – to be his legitimate heritage.

"Before proceeding to call witnesses, I venture, my Lord, to recapitulate briefly the points of the case which favour the belief that Josiah Pippet and the Earl George Augustus, Fourth Earl of Winsborough, were one and the same person.

"First: That the said Earl was a man of such wildly eccentric habits and conduct that he might credibly have behaved in the manner alleged.

"That his habit of absenting himself from home for long periods and disappearing from his known places of resort would have rendered the alleged impersonation easily possible.

"That the man called Josiah Pippet was in the same way addicted to absences and disappearances.

"That the said Josiah is reported to have claimed to be the Earl.

"That, whereas both these persons were born on the same day, there is evidence of the birth of one only.

"That, in like manner, there is evidence of the death of only one of them, the circumstances being such as to support the rumour which was current that the coffin which was interred contained no corpse.

"Those, my Lord, are the facts on which the applicant's claim is based, and I submit that if they can be proved – as they will be by the testimony of the witnesses whom I shall call – they constitute a case sufficiently convincing for the purpose of this application."

Here Mr. McGonnell paused and inspected his brief while the judge shifted his position in his chair and the usher pronounced the name of Christopher Josiah Pippet. Thereupon Mr. Pippet moved across to the witness-box and, having been sworn, gave his name and the usual particulars. Then his counsel proceeded to open the examination in chief.

Chapter IX
The Evidence of
Christopher J. Pippet

"Can you remember, Mr. Pippet," the counsel asked, "when you first became aware that you were possibly the direct descendant of the Earl of Winsborough?"

"No, sir, I cannot," was the reply. "It must have been when I was quite a small boy."

"From whom did you receive the information?"

"From my father, Frederick William Pippet."

"Did he refer to the matter on more than one occasion?"

"Yes, on a great many occasions. It was rather a favourite subject with him."

"Did you gather that he believed in the truth of the tradition?"

"I didn't have to gather," replied the witness, with a dry smile. "He said in perfectly unmistakable terms that he regarded it as pure bunkum."

"Do you know what reasons he had for taking that view?"

"There were several reasons. In the first place, he didn't care a dime whether it was true or not. He was a prosperous American citizen, and that was good enough for him. But I think his beliefs were influenced by the character and personality of his father, Josiah Pippet. Josiah was a very peculiar man, very erratic in his behaviour and, my father thought, not particularly reliable in his statements. Then he was an inveterate joker and much addicted to what is now called 'leg-pulling'. I gathered that my father regarded the whole story as a leg-pull. But he did express surprise that Josiah should have kept the joke up so long and that so many people seemed to have been taken in by it."

"What people was he referring to?"

"The people who were connected with The Fox and Grapes and those who frequented the place. He made a trip to England soon after the death of his brother Walter to see to the disposal of the family property. He had to go to The Fox and Grapes' to arrange about the sale of the good-will and effects, and there he found a general belief among the staff and the regular frequenters of the house that there was some mystery about Josiah. It was then, too, that he heard the rumour of the bogus funeral."

"Did he tell you what, exactly, it was that the staff and the other people believed?"

"A good deal of it seemed to be rather vague, though they all agreed that Josiah was not what he appeared to be – just an inn-keeper – but that he was a member of some noble house, masquerading as a publican for some unknown reasons. And they all appeared to believe that he was not really dead, but that he had arranged a sham funeral in order to bring the masquerade to an end without disclosing his real personality."

"But apart from these vague rumours, was there anything more definite?"

"Yes, there were some very definite statements, particularly those made by Walter's manager, who succeeded him. He professed to have been on terms of close intimacy with Josiah and to have received confidences from him which were made to no one else. Among these was the categorical statement that he, Josiah Pippet, was actually the Earl of Winsborough, that he had been born in the Castle at Winsborough and that he intended, if possible, to die there. And he, the manager, expressed himself as quite certain that Josiah was not dead, giving as his reason a number of reports which had reached him from time to time. One man, he stated, who was a frequenter of The Fox and Grapes, had seen Josiah coming out of the town mansion in Cavendish Square and stepping into a carriage. Another customer, a Channel pilot, had met Josiah riding along the road across the sand-hills from Sandwich to Deal. He was perfectly certain that the man was Josiah Pippet, having often been served by him with liquor at the bar of The Fox and Grapes. Another customer, who occasionally had business at Sandwich in Kent, happened to walk out from that town to Winsborough, and there he saw Josiah Pippet riding out of the main gate of the Castle grounds, followed by a mounted groom. He also was quite certain that the man he saw was really Josiah. And there were several other instances of persons who had seen Josiah since his alleged death which were mentioned by the manager, but my father could not remember the particulars."

"And did not all these circumstantial statements make any impression on your father?"

"No, none whatever. His opinion was that Josiah had amused himself by throwing out mysterious hints and that these had been repeated over and over again, growing with each repetition, until this story had taken definite shape."

"And as to the reports that Josiah had actually been seen in the flesh?"

"His explanation of that was that Josiah and the Earl were probably a good deal alike, and he suspected that Josiah's hints arose from that

531

circumstance. He remarked that Josiah certainly came from that part of the country, and that he probably knew the Earl by sight."

"You do not, I presume," said the counsel, slightly disconcerted, I thought, by the witness's tone, "take quite the same view as your father."

"I am trying to keep an open mind," the witness replied, calmly, "but I am telling you what my father thought, if his opinions have any bearings on the case."

"It is not clear that they have," said the judge. "We are, I believe, endeavouring to elicit facts."

"I would submit, my Lord," the counsel replied, "that they have this bearing: That the statements being those of an entirely unconvinced man, they may be assumed to be quite free from any suspicion of exaggeration. The speaker's bias was clearly against the truth of the reports and his testimony has, accordingly, an added value."

The judge acknowledged this "submission" with a grave nod but made no further comment, and the counsel resumed his examination.

"When your father used to speak to you about Josiah's story, did he give you any particulars as to what Josiah had told him?"

"He did occasionally. But most of Josiah's talk on the subject took the form of vague boastings to the effect that his real station was very different from what it appeared. But now and again he let himself go with a straight statement. For instance, on one occasion he said quite definitely that Pippet was not his real name, that he had assumed it because it seemed to be a good name for an inn-keeper. I don't know what he meant by that."

"He gave no hint as to what his real name was?"

"No. The nearest approach to a disclosure of an identity other than that of Josiah Pippet was in his parting words to my father when the latter was starting on a long voyage a few months before Josiah's death. He then said – I am quoting my father as well as I can remember his words – 'When you come back, you may not find me here. If you don't, you can look for me down at Winsborough, near Sandwich in Kent, and you will probably find me living at the Castle'. That was the last time that my father saw him."

"You have referred to the alleged bogus funeral of your grandfather, Josiah Pippet, and to a dummy coffin weighted with lead. In the accounts which you received, was any mention made of the kind of lead used – whether, for instance, it was lead pipe, or bars, or lead pig?"

"Most of the accounts referred simply to lead, but one – I forgot who gave it – mentioned a roll of roofing-lead and some plumber's oddments, left after some repairs. But I am not very clear about it. I can't quote any particular account."

"Are there any other facts or statements known to you tending to prove that the man known as Josiah Pippet was in fact the Earl of Winsborough?"

"No. I think you have got them, all except those contained in the diary."

"Then," said the counsel, "in that case, we will proceed to consider the entries in the diary which seem relevant." With this, he produced seven small, antique-looking, leather-bound volumes and passed them across to the witness.

"What do you say these volumes are?" he asked.

"To the best of my belief," was the reply, "they are the diary kept by my grandfather, Josiah Pippet."

"How did they come into your possession?"

"They were among the effects of my late father, Frederick William Pippet. They were obtained by him, as he informed me, when he was disposing of the effects of his deceased brother, Walter. He found them in a deed box with a large number of letters, the whole being tied together and docketed *'Diary and letters of Josiah Pippet, Deceased'*. As the surviving son, he took possession of them and the letters."

"You have no doubt that these volumes are the authentic diary of Josiah Pippet?"

"No, I have not. His name is written in each volume and my father always referred to them as his father's diary, and I have no reason to doubt that that is what they are."

"Are they, in all respects, in the same condition as when they came into your possession?"

"They were up to the time that I handed them to my solicitor, and I have no doubt that they are still. They were always kept in the deed box in which my father found them, together with the letters. I handed the whole collection in the deed box to my solicitor for him to examine."

"Would it be correct to say that it was the study of this diary that led you seriously to entertain the possibility that Josiah Pippet was really the Earl of Winsborough?"

"It would – with the proviso that the studying was not done by me. It was my sister who used to study the diary, and she communicated her discoveries to me."

"Since you have been in England, have you made any attempts to check the accuracy of the entries in the diary?"

"I have, in the few cases in which it has been possible after all these years."

"There is an entry dated the 3rd of September, 1839: '*Home on the brig Harmony. Got aground on the Dyke, but off next tide*'. Have you been able to check that? As to the locality, I mean."

"Yes, I find that the Dyke is the name of a shoal by the side of a navigation channel called The Old Cudd Channel, leading to Ramsgate Harbour. I find that it is used almost exclusively by vessels entering or leaving Ramsgate Harbour or Sandwich Haven. At Sandwich, I was allowed to examine the old books kept by the Port authorities and, in the register of shipping using the port I found, under the date 1st September, 1839, a note that the brig *Harmony* sailed out of the Haven in ballast, bound for London."

"What significance do you attach to that entry?"

"As Sandwich is only a mile-and-a-half from Winsborough, and is the nearest port, the fact of his embarking there is consistent with the supposition that Winsborough was the place in which he had been staying."

"There is a previous entry dated the 12th of June, 1837: '*Broached an anker of prime Dutch gin that I bought from the skipper of the* Vriendschap'."

"I checked that at the same time in the same register. There was an entry relating to a Dutch galliot named the *Vriendschap* which discharged a general cargo, including a quantity of gin. She arrived at Sandwich on the 10th of April and cleared outward on the 25th of the same month. At that time, the diary shows that Josiah was absent from home."

"Is there anything to show where he was at that time?"

"There is an entry made just after he arrived home. I am not sure of the date."

"Are you referring to the entry of the 6th of May, 1837: '*Home again. Feel a little strange after the life at the Castle*'?"

"Yes. Taking the two entries together, it seems clear that the castle referred to was Winsborough Castle and that he was in residence there."

"I will take only one more passage from the diary – that of the 8th of October, 1842: '*Back to the Fox. Exit G. A. and enter J. P., but not for long*'. What does that convey to you?"

"The meaning of it seems to me to be obvious. The initials are those of the Earl, George Augustus, and himself, Josiah Pippet. It appears plainly to indicate that George Augustus now retires from the stage and gives place to Josiah Pippet. And, as the entry was made within ten months of his alleged death, or final disappearance, the expression, '*not for long*', seems to refer to that final disappearance."

On receiving this answer, counsel paused and glanced over his brief. Apparently finding no further matter for examination, he said, "I need not ask you anything about the passages from the diary which I quoted in my opening address. The diary is put in evidence and the passages speak for themselves."

With this he sat down and Anstey rose to cross-examine.

"You have told us, Mr. Pippet," he began, "that you were led to entertain the belief in the dual personality of your grandfather, Josiah Pippet, by your study of certain passages in his diary."

"Not my study," was the reply. "I said that my sister studied the diary and communicated her discoveries to me."

"Yes. Now, which of these passages was it that first led you to abandon the scepticism which, I understand, you formerly felt in regard to the story of the double life and the sham funeral?"

"I cannot remember distinctly, but my impression is that my sister was strongly influenced by those passages which imply, or definitely state, that Josiah, when absent from his London home, was living at the Castle."

"But what caused you to identify 'the Castle' as Winsborough Castle? There is nothing in the diary to indicate any castle in particular. The words used are simply 'The Castle'. How did you come to decide that, of all the castles in England, the reference was to this particular castle?"

"I take it that we were influenced by what we had both heard from our father. The stories that he had been told referred explicitly to Winsborough Castle. And the inquiries which I have made since I have been in England – "

"Pardon me," interrupted Anstey, "but those inquiries are not relevant to my question. We are speaking of your study of the diary when you were at your home in America. I suggest that you then had very little knowledge of the geography of the county of Kent."

"We had practically none."

"Then I suggest that, apart from what you had heard from your father, there was nothing to indicate that the words '*The Castle*' referred to Winsborough Castle."

"That is so. We applied what my father had told us to the entries in the diary."

"Then, since the connexion was simply guess-work, is it not rather singular that the mere reference to '*The Castle*' should have made so deep an impression on you?"

"Perhaps," the witness replied, with a faint smile, "my sister may have been prepared to be impressed, and may have communicated her enthusiasm to me."

To this answer Anstey made no rejoinder but, after a short pause and a glance at his brief, resumed. "There is this entry of the 8th of October, 1842: '*Back to the Fox. Exit G. A. and enter J. P., but not for long*'. Did that passage influence you strongly in your opinion of the truth of the story of Josiah's double life?"

The witness did not answer immediately, and it seemed to me that he looked a little worried. At length he replied, "It is a remarkable fact, but I have no recollection of our ever having discussed that entry. It would almost seem as if my sister had overlooked it."

"Do you remember when your attention was first drawn to that entry?"

"Yes. It was at a consultation with my solicitor, Mr. Gimbler, when he showed me a number of passages which he had extracted from the diary, which he considered relevant to the case, and which he wished me to try to verify if possible."

"Have you, since then, discussed this passage with your sister?"

"Yes, and she is as much surprised as I am that it did not attract her attention when she was reading the diary."

"So far as you know, did she read the entire diary?"

"I understood that she read the whole seven volumes from cover to cover."

"Has she ever made a definite statement to you to that effect?"

"Yes. A short time ago, I put the question to her explicitly and she assured me that, to the best of her belief, she had read every word of the diary."

"And you say that she had no recollection of having noticed this particular entry?"

"That is what she told me."

Here the judge interposed with a question.

"I don't understand why we are taking this hearsay testimony from the witness as to what his sister read or noticed. Is not the lady in court?"

"Yes, my Lord," replied Anstey, "but I understand that it is not proposed to call Miss Pippet."

The judge turned and looked inquiringly at Mr. McGonnell, who rose and explained, "It was not considered necessary to call Miss Pippet as she is not in possession of any facts other than those known to her brother."

With this he sat down, but for some seconds, the judge continued to look at him fixedly as if about to ask some further question, a

536

circumstance that seemed to occasion the learned counsel some discomfort. But if his Lordship had intended to make any further observations, he thought better of it, for he suddenly turned away and, leaning back in his chair, glanced at Anstey, who thereupon resumed his cross-examination.

"Now, Mr. Pippet," said he, taking up the last volume of the diary – (The seven volumes had been passed to him at the conclusion of the examination in chief.) – and opening it at a place near the end, "I will ask you to look at this entry, dated the 8th of October, 1842." (Here the open book was passed across to the witness.) "You will see that there is a blank space between the last entry made before the writer went away from home and this, the first entry made after his return. Is that so?"

"It is," replied Mr. Pippet.

"And does it not appear to you that this entry is in a very conspicuous position – in a position likely to catch the eye of any person glancing over the page?"

"It does," the witness agreed.

"Then I put it to you, Mr. Pippet: Here is a diary which is being searched by an intelligent and attentive reader for corroboration of the story of Josiah's alleged double life. Here is an entry which seems to afford such corroboration. It is in a conspicuous position, and not only that, for, being the first entry after Josiah's return from his mysterious absence, it is in the very position in which an intelligent searcher would expect to find it. Now, I ask you, is it not an astounding and almost incredible circumstance that this entry should have been overlooked?"

"I have already said so," Mr. Pippet replied, a little wearily, delivering the open diary to the usher, who handed it up to the judge. There was a short pause while Anstey turned over the leaves of his brief and the judge examined the diary, which he did with undissembled interest and at considerable length. When he had finished with it, he returned it to the usher, who brought it over to Anstey, by whom it was forthwith delivered into the hands of Thorndyke.

I watched my colleague's proceedings with grim amusement. If, in Anstey's cross-examination, certain hints were to be read between the lines, there was no such reticence on Thorndyke's part. Openly and undisguisedly, he scrutinized the entry in the diary, with the naked eye, with his pocket-lens, and finally with a queer little squat, double-barrelled microscope which he produced from a case at his side. Nor was I the only observer. The proceeding was watched by his Lordship, with a sphinx-like face but a twinkling eye, by the two opposing counsel, and especially Mr. Gimbler, who seemed to view it with considerable

537

disfavour. But my attention was diverted from Thorndyke's activities by Anstey, who now resumed his cross examination.

"You have referred to the alleged bogus funeral of your grandfather, Josiah Pippet, and to a dummy coffin weighted with lead. Now, so far as you know, is that coffin still in existence?"

"I have no doubt that it is. I visited the cemetery, which is at a place near Stratford in the east end of London, and examined the vault from the outside. It appeared to be quite intact."

"Is the cemetery still in use?"

"No. It was closed many years ago by Act of Parliament and is now disused and deserted."

"Had you any difficulty in obtaining admission?"

The witness smiled. "I can hardly say that I was admitted," said he. "The place was locked up and there was nobody in charge, but the wall was only about six feet high. I had no difficulty in getting over."

"Then," said Anstey, "we may assume that the coffin is still there. And if it is, it contains either the body of Josiah Pippet or a roll of sheet lead and some plumber's oddments. Has it never occurred to you that it would be desirable to examine that coffin and see what it does contain?"

"It has," the witness replied, emphatically. "When I came to England, my intention was to get that coffin open right away and see whether Josiah was in it or not. If I had found him there, I should have known that my father was right and that the story was all bunk, and if I had found the lead, I should have known that there was something solid to go on."

"What made you abandon that intention?"

"I was advised that, in England, it is impossible to open a coffin without a special faculty from the Home Secretary, and that no such faculty would be granted until the case had been heard in a Court of Law."

"Then we may take it that it was your desire to have this coffin examined as to its contents?"

"It was, and is," the witness replied, energetically. "I want to get at the truth of this business, and it seems to me, being ignorant of law, that it is against common sense to spend all this time arguing and inferring when a few turns of a screw-driver would settle the whole question in a matter of minutes."

The judge smiled approvingly. "A very sensible view," said he, "and not such particularly bad law."

"So far as you know, Mr. Pippet," said Anstey, "have any measures been taken to obtain authority to open the vault and examine the coffin?"

"I am not aware of any. I understood that, until the court had given some decision on the case, any such measures would be premature."

"Are you aware that it is within the competency of this court to make an order for the exhumation of this coffin and its examination as to its contents?"

"I certainly was not," the witness answered.

Here the judge interposed with some signs of impatience.

"It seems necessary that this point should be cleared up. We are trying a case involving a number of issues, all of which are subject to one main issue. That issue is: Did Josiah Pippet die in the year 1843 and was he buried in a normal manner? Or was his alleged death a fictitious death and the funeral a sham funeral conducted with a dummy coffin weighted with lead? Now, as Mr. Pippet has most reasonably remarked, it seems a strange thing that we should be listening to a mass of evidence of the most indirect kind – principally hearsay evidence at third or fourth hand – when we actually have within our grasp the means of settling this issue conclusively by evidence of the most direct and convincing character. Has the learned counsel for the applicant any instructions on this point?"

While the judge had been speaking, a hurried and anxious consultation had been taking place between Mr. Gimbler and his leading counsel. The latter now rose and replied, "It was considered, my Lord, that, as these proceedings were, in a sense, preliminary to certain other proceedings possibly to be taken in another place, it might be desirable to postpone the question of the exhumation, especially as it seemed doubtful whether your Lordship would be willing to make the necessary order."

"That," said the judge, "could have been ascertained by making the application, and I may say that I should certainly have complied with the request."

"Then in that case," said Mr. McGonnell, "we gratefully adopt your Lordship's suggestion and make the application now."

"Very well," the judge rejoined, "then the order will be made, subject to the consent of the Home Secretary, which we may assume will be given."

As he concluded, he glanced at Anstey but, as the latter remained seated, and no re-examination followed, Mr. Pippet was released from the witness-box.

Of the rest of the evidence I have but a dim recollection. The sudden entry, like a whiff of fresh air, into this fog of surmise and rumour, of a promise of real, undeniable evidence, made the testimony of the remaining witnesses appear like mere trifling. There was an architect and surveyor who described and produced plans of the old Earl's

539

underground chambers, and there was an aged woman whose grandfather had been a potman at The Fox and Grapes and who gave a vague account of the strange rumours of which she had heard him speak, but it was all very shadowy and unreal. It merely left us speculating as to whether the story of the bogus funeral might or might not possibly be true. And the speculation was not worthwhile when we should presently be looking into the open coffin and able to settle the question definitely, yes or no.

I think everyone was relieved when the sitting came to an end and the further hearing was adjourned until the result of the exhumation should be made known.

Chapter X
Josiah?

The last resting-place – real or fictitious – of the late Josiah Pippet was a somewhat dismal spot. Not that it mattered. The landscape qualities of a burial ground cannot be of much concern to the inmates. And in Josiah's day, when he came here prospecting for an eligible freehold, the aspect of the place was doubtless very different. Then it must have been a rural burial ground adjoining some vanished hamlet (it was designated on the Ordnance Map "*Garwell Burial Ground*") hard by the Romford Turnpike Road. Now, it was a little grimy wilderness, fronting on a narrow street, flanked by decaying stable-yards and cart sheds, and apparently utterly neglected and forgotten of men. The only means of access was a rusty iron gate, set in the six-foot enclosing wall, and at that gate Thorndyke and I arrived a full half-hour before the appointed time, having walked thither from the nearest station – Maryland Point on the Great Eastern. But early as we were, we were not early enough from Thorndyke's point of view for, not only did we find the rusty gate unlocked (with a brand-new key sticking out of the corroded lock), but, when we lifted the decayed latch and entered, we discovered two men in the very act of wrenching open the door of a vault.

"This," said Thorndyke, regarding the two men with a disapproving eye, "ought not to have been done until everyone was present and the unopened door had been inspected."

"Well," I said, consolingly, "it will save time."

"No doubt," he admitted. "But that is not what we are here for." We approached the operators, one of whom appeared to be a locksmith and the other an official of some kind, to whom, at his request, we gave our names and explained our business.

"I expect," said Thorndyke, "you had your work cut out, getting that door unlocked."

"It was a bit of a job, sir," the locksmith replied. "Locks is like men. Gets a bit stiff in the joints after eighty years. But it wasn't as bad as I'd expected. I'd got a good strong skeleton key filed up and a tommy to turn it with, and when I'd run in a drop of paraffin and oil, she twisted round all right."

As he was speaking, I looked around me. The burial ground was roughly square in shape, enclosed on three sides by a six-foot brick wall, while the fourth side was occupied by a range of the so-called vaults, which were not, strictly speaking, vaults at all, but sepulchral chambers above ground. There were six of them, each provided with its own door, and over each door was a stone tablet on which was inscribed brief particulars of the inmates. Josiah alone had a chamber all to himself and, running my eye along the row of tablets and reading the dates, I noted that he appeared to be the last of the tenants. At this moment, the sound of a motor car in the street outside caused us to step back to bring the gate within view, when, to my surprise – but not, apparently, to Thorndyke's – our old friend, Mr. Superintendent Miller, was seen entering. As he approached and greeted us, I exclaimed, "This is an unexpected pleasure, Miller. What brings you here? I didn't know that the police were interested in this case."

"They are not," he replied. "I am here on instructions from the Home Office just to see that the formalities are complied with. That is all. But it is a quaint business. What are we going to find in that coffin, Doctor?"

"That," replied Thorndyke, "is an open question, at present."

"I know," said Miller. "But I expect you have considered the probabilities. What do you say? Bones or lead?"

"Well, as a mere estimate of probabilities," replied Thorndyke, "I should say lead."

"Should you really!" I exclaimed in astonishment. "I would have wagered fifty-to-one on a body. The whole story of the bogus funeral sounded to me like 'sheer bunk', as Pippet would express it."

"That would certainly have been my view," said Miller, "but I expect we are both wrong. We usually are when we disagree with the Doctor. And there does seem to be a hint of something queer about that inscription. '*Josiah Pippet, died on the 12th day of October, 1843. Aged 49 years, 2 months and 3 days*'. If he was so blooming particular to a day, why couldn't he have just given the date of his birth and have done with it?"

While we had been talking, the official and his assistant had produced two pairs of coffin trestles, which they set up side by side opposite the open door of the vault, and they had hardly been placed in position when the sound of two cars drawing up almost at the same moment announced the arrival of the rest of the party.

"My eye!" exclaimed Miller, as the visitors filed in and the official – beadle, or whatever he was – advanced to meet them and lock the gate after them, "it's a regular congregation."

It did look a large party. First there was Mr. Pippet with his sister and daughter and his solicitor and Mr. McGonnell, and then followed Mrs. Engleheart and her son with Mr. Brodribb. But, once inside the burial ground, the two groups tended to coalesce while mutual greetings were exchanged, and then to sort themselves out. The two elder ladies decided to wait at a distance while "the horrid business" was in progress, and the rest of us gathered round the half-open door, the two young people drawing together and seeming, as I thought, to be on uncommonly amicable terms.

"I leave the conduct of this affair in your hands, Thorndyke," said Mr. Brodribb, casting a wistful glance at the two ladies, who had retired to the farther side of the enclosure. "Is there anything that you want to do before the coffin is removed?"

"I should like, as a mere formality, to inspect the interior of the vault," was the reply, "and perhaps the Superintendent, as a disinterested witness, might also take a glance at it."

As he spoke, he looked inquiringly at Mr. Gimbler, and the latter, accepting the suggestion, advanced with him and Miller and threw the door wide open. There was nothing very sensational to see. The little chamber was crossed by a thick stone shelf on which rested the coffin. The latter had a very unattractive appearance, the dark, damp oak – from which every vestige of varnish had disappeared – being covered with patches of thick, green mildew and greasy-looking stains, over which was a mantle of impalpably fine grey dust. A layer of similar dust covered the shelf, the floor, and every horizontal surface, but nowhere was there the faintest sign of its having been disturbed. On coffin and shelf and floor it presented a perfectly smooth, unbroken surface.

"Well, Doctor," said Miller, when he had cast a quick, searching glance round the chamber, "are you satisfied? Looks all right."

"Yes," replied Thorndyke. "But we will just take a sample or two of the dust for reference, if necessary."

As he spoke, he produced from his pockets a penknife and two of the inevitable seed-envelopes which he always carried about him. With the former he scraped up a little heap of dust on the coffin lid and shovelled it into one envelope, and then took another sample from the shelf, a proceeding which was observed with a sour smile by Mr. Gimbler and with delighted amusement by the Superintendent.

"Nothing left to chance, you notice," chuckled the latter. "Thomas Didymus was a credulous man compared with the Doctor. Shall we have the coffin out now?"

As Thorndyke assented, the beadle and his assistant approached and drew the coffin forward on the shelf. Then they lifted the projecting end, but forthwith set it down again and stood gazing at it blankly.

"Moses!" exclaimed the locksmith. "He don't seem to have lost much weight in eighty years! This is a four-man job."

Thereupon, Miller and I stepped forward and, as the two men lifted the foot-end of the coffin, we took the weight of the other end, and as we staggered to the trestles with our ponderous burden, Miller whispered to me, "What's the betting now, Dr. Jervis?"

"There may be a lead shell," I suggested, but without much conviction. However, there was no use in speculating, seeing that the locksmith had already produced a screw-driver from his tool-bag and was preparing to set to work. As he began, I watched him with some interest, expecting that the screw would be rusted in immovably. But he was a skilful workman and managed the extraction with very little difficulty, though the screw, when at last he got it out and laid it on the coffin lid, was thickly encrusted with rust. Thorndyke picked it up and, having looked it over, handed it to Miller with the whispered injunction, "Take charge of the screws, Miller. They may have to be put in evidence."

The Superintendent made no comment, though I could see that he was a little puzzled, as also was I, for there appeared to be nothing unusual or significant in the appearance of the screw. And I think the transaction was observed – with some disfavour – by Mr. Gimbler, though he took no notice, but kept a watchful and suspicious eye on Thorndyke, who, during the extraction of the other screws, occupied himself with an exhaustive examination of the exterior of the coffin, including the blackened brass name-plate (the fastening-screws of which he inspected through a lens) and the brass handles and their fastenings.

At length the last of the eight screws was extracted – and pocketed by Miller – and the locksmith, inserting his screw-driver between the lid and the side, looked 'round as if waiting for the word. We all gathered around, making space, however, for Mr. Pippet, his daughter, and Mr. Giles.

"Now," said Mr. Pippet, "we are going to get the answer to the riddle. Up with her."

The locksmith gave a single wrench and the lid rose. He lifted it clear and laid it on the other trestles, and we all craned forward and peered into the coffin. And then, at the first glance, we had the answer. For what we saw was an untidy bundle of mouldy sacking. We could not see what the bundle contained, but it certainly did not contain the late Josiah Pippet.

The excitement now reached its climax and found expression in low-toned, inarticulate murmurs, in the midst of which Mr. Pippet's calm, matter-of-fact voice was heard directing the locksmith to "get that bundle open and let's see what's inside." Accordingly, with much tugging at the unsavoury sacking, the bundle was laid open and its contents exposed to the light of day – a small roll of whitened sheet lead and four hemispherical lumps of the same metal, apparently the remainders from a plumber's melting-pot.

For some moments there was a complete silence as nine pairs of fascinated eyes remained riveted on the objects that reposed on the bottom of the coffin. It was broken, not quite harmoniously, by the voice of Mr. Gimbler.

"A roll of sheet lead and some plumber's oddments."

As he spoke, he turned, with a fat, wrinkly and rather offensive smile to Mr. Giles Engleheart.

"Yes," the latter agreed, "it fits the description to a *T*." He held out his hand to Mr. Pippet and continued, "It's heads up for you, sir. I congratulate you on a fair win, and I wish you a long life to enjoy what you have won."

"Thank you, Giles," said Mr. Pippet, shaking his hand warmly. "I am glad to have your congratulations first – even if they should turn out premature. We mustn't be too previous, you know."

He spoke in a singularly calm, unemotional tone, without a trace of triumph or even satisfaction. Indeed, I could not but be impressed (and considerably surprised) by the total absence of any sign of elation on the part either of the claimant or his daughter. It might have been simply good manners and regard for the defeated rival. But it looked uncommonly like indifference. Moreover, I could not but notice that, in the midst of the congratulations, Mr. Pippet was keeping an attentive eye on Thorndyke, and indeed, my colleague's proceedings soon began to attract more general notice.

When the leaden objects were first disclosed, he had viewed them impassively with what had almost looked like a glance of recognition. They were, in fact, as I knew, exactly what he had expected to see. But after a general, searching glance, he proceeded to a closer inspection. First, he lifted out the roll of sheet lead and, having looked it over, critically, laid it on the coffin-lid. Then he turned his attention to the "oddments", of which there was one appreciably larger than the other three, having apparently come from a bigger melting-pot. This mass, which looked like the half of a metallic Dutch cheese, he lifted out first and, in spite of its great weight, he seemed to handle it without any difficulty as he turned it about to examine its various parts. When he had inspected it all over, he laid it on the coffin-lid beside the roll of sheet lead, and then, dipping into the coffin once more, took up one of the smaller "remainders".

And it was at this moment that I became aware that "something had happened". How I knew it, I can hardly say, for Thorndyke was a perfectly impossible subject for a thought-reader. But my long association with him enabled me to detect subtle shades of expression that were perceptible to no one else. And something of the kind I had seen now. As he lifted the lump of lead, he had checked for a moment and seemed to stiffen, and a sudden intensity of attention had flashed into his eyes, to vanish in an instant, leaving his face as immobile and impassive as a mask of stone.

What could it be? I could only watch and wait for developments. As he turned the mass of lead over in his hands and pored over every inch of its surface, I caught the twinkling eye of Superintendent Miller and a low chuckle of appreciative amusement.

"Nothing taken for granted, you observe," he murmured.

But the others were less indulgent. As Thorndyke laid the last of the leaden pot-leavings on the coffin-lid, Mr. McGonnell interposed, a little stiffly.

"Is there anything more, Dr. Thorndyke? Because if not, as we seem to have done what we came here to do, I suggest that we may consider the business as finished."

"That is," said Mr. Pippet, "if Dr. Thorndyke is satisfied. Are you satisfied, Doctor?"

"No," replied Thorndyke. "I am not satisfied with this lead. It purports to have been placed here in 1843, and part of it – the sheet lead – was then old. It was said to have been old roofing-sheet. Now, I am not satisfied that this lead is of that age. This sheet lead looks to me like modern milled lead."

"And how do you propose to settle that question?" McGonnell asked.

"I propose that an assay of the lead should be made to determine, if possible, its age."

McGonnell snorted. "This is Thomas Didymus, with a vengeance," he exclaimed. "But I submit that it is mere hair-splitting, and I don't believe that any assayist could give an opinion as to the age of the lead, or that the court would pay any attention to him if he did. What do you say, Gimbler?"

Mr. Gimbler smiled his queer, fat, wrinkled smile, to the entire extinction of his little blue eyes, and swung his eye-glasses on their ribbon like a pendulum.

"I say," he replied, oracularly, "that the proposal is inadmissible for several reasons. First, the objection is frivolous. We came here to find out whether this coffin contained a body or some lumps of lead. We find that it contained lead. Now Dr. Thorndyke doubts whether it is the original lead. He thinks it may be some other lead of a later vintage. But if it is, how came it here? What does he suggest?"

"I suggest nothing," said Thorndyke. "My function in this case is the purely scientific one of ascertaining facts."

"Still," persisted Gimbler, "there is a suggestion implied in the objection. But I let that pass. Next, I assert that an assay would not produce any evidence that the court would take seriously. The proposed proceeding is merely vexatious and obstructive. It would occasion delay and increase the costs to no useful purpose. And, finally, the order of the court does not authorize us to make an assay of the lead. It merely authorizes us to open the coffin and ascertain whether it contains a body. We have done that and we find that it does not contain a body."

Here Mr. Brodribb, who had been showing signs of increasing discomfort, intervened in the discussion.

"I am inclined, Thorndyke," said he, "to agree with Mr. Gimbler. Your proposal to make an assay of the lead does seem to go beyond the powers conferred by the judge's order. Of course, if it is necessary, we could make a special application. But is it necessary? Do you say definitely that this lead is not of the age that it is assumed to be?"

"No," replied Thorndyke, "I do not. I merely say that I am not satisfied that it is."

"Then," said Brodribb, "I suggest that we waive the question of the assay, at least for the present. I should much prefer to do so, especially as there is no denying that your proposal does imply certain suggestions which should not be lightly made."

Thorndyke reflected for a few moments, and I waited curiously for his decision. Finally, he rejoined, "Very well, Brodribb, I will not press the matter against your sense of the legal proprieties. We will waive the assay – at any rate, for the present."

"I think you are wise," said McGonnell. "It would have seemed an extravagant piece of scepticism and couldn't have led to any result. And now," he added, looking anxiously at his watch, "I suppose we have finished our business. I hope so. Have we got to see to the re-placing of the coffin?"

"No, sir," replied Miller. "That is my business, as official master of the ceremonies. There is nothing to detain you."

"Thank goodness for that," said McGonnell, and began forthwith to move towards the gate, while Mr. Pippet, the two solicitors, and the two young people advanced up the path to meet the two elder ladies and give them the latest news of the discoveries. Then the beadle unlocked the gate and, as the procession moved towards it, we joined the party to exchange polite greetings and see them into their cars (in which the opposing litigants got mixed up in the most singular and amicable manner).

"Can I give you two a lift?" inquired Brodribb, as he held the door of his car open.

"No, thank you," replied Thorndyke. "We have a little business to transact with Miller."

Thereupon Brodribb wriggled with some difficulty into his car, and we re-entered the gate, which the beadle locked after us, and rejoined the Superintendent.

Chapter XI
Plumber's Oddments and
Other Matters

As Thorndyke and I returned from the gate, the Superintendent met us with a peculiarly knowing expression on his countenance.

"Well, Doctor," said he, "what about it?" And, as this slightly ambiguous question elicited no reply beyond an indulgent smile, he continued, "When I hear a gentleman of your intellect propose to assay a lump of old lead to ascertain the exact vintage year, experience tells me that that gentleman has got something up his sleeve. Now, Doctor, let's hear what it is."

"To tell you the truth, Miller," Thorndyke replied, "I don't quite know, myself. But you are wrong about the lead. The age of a piece of lead can be judged fairly accurately by the silver content. If you find a piece of sheet lead with a silver content of, say, ten ounces to the ton, you can be pretty sure that it was made before Pattinson's process for the desilverization of lead was invented. Still, you are right to the extent that the question of age was not the only issue that I had in my mind. There were other reasons why the assay should be made."

"But you have abandoned the assay," objected Miller, "and very surprised I was to hear you give way so easily."

"I gave way in your favour," said Thorndyke, with a cryptic smile. "You are going to have the assay carried out."

"Oh, am I?" exclaimed the Superintendent. "It's as well to know these things in advance." We turned into a side path to get a little farther from the beadle and his mate, and Miller continued, "Now, look here, Doctor, I want to be clear about this business. This is a civil case, and it is no concern of mine as a police officer. What's the game? You seem to be dumping this blooming lead on me, and then there are these screws. Why did you want me to take charge of them?" He drew out of his pocket the rusty handful and looked at them disparagingly. "I don't see anything special about them. They look to me like ordinary screws such as you could buy at any ironmonger's."

Thorndyke chuckled. "They are common-looking screws, I must admit," said he. "But don't despise them. Like many other common-looking things, they have their value. I want you to put them into an envelope and seal it with your official seal, and write on the envelope, '*Screws extracted in my presence from the coffin of Josiah Pippet*', and sign it. Will you do that?"

"Yes," replied Miller, "I don't see any objection to that, though I am hanged if I can guess what you want them for. But with regard to this lead – you want me to have it assayed on my own initiative, as a police officer. But I must have something to go on. The judge's order doesn't cover me. Now, I know quite well that you have got something perfectly definite in your mind and, knowing you as I do, I am pretty sure that it is not a delusion Can't you tell me what it is?"

Thorndyke reflected for a few moments. "The fact is," he said at length, "I am in a difficulty. My position in this case is that of a counsel instructed by Brodribb." Here Miller indulged in a broad grin, but made no comment, beyond something like a wink directed towards me, and Thorndyke continued, "You saw that Brodribb disliked the idea of the assay. He is a very acute lawyer, but he is a most scrupulously courteous old gentleman, and he was obviously unwilling to seem to throw the slightest doubt on the good faith of the other side, even Gimbler. Now, I could not act against Brodribb's wishes, and there was no need. I had given the other side their chance, and they didn't choose to take it."

"So now," said Miller, "you want, in effect, to run with the hare and hunt with the hounds. And I am the hounds. Isn't that the position?"

Thorndyke regarded the Superintendent with an appreciative smile. "Very neatly put, Miller," said he, "and I won't deny that it does seem to state the position. Nevertheless, I am going to ask you to help me, and to take on trust my assurance that, if you act on what I will call my suggestions, you will, in your official capacity, 'learn something to your advantage', as the solicitors express it."

"Still," urged Miller, "if you don't care to let the cat out of the bag, you might at least show us her head, or even her tail, so that we may see what sort of animal is in the bag."

Once more, Thorndyke reflected for a few moments before replying. At length he said, "I fully appreciate your difficulty, Miller. You can't, as a detective officer, start an investigation in the air. But you have known me long enough to feel certain that I should not send you off in search of a mare's nest."

"I am quite clear on that point," Miller agreed, warmly. "I only want reasonable cover."

"Very well," rejoined Thorndyke, "I can give you that, if you will take my information on trust without the production of evidence."

"Let's hear the information," said Miller, cautiously.

"It is this," said Thorndyke, "and I am prepared to give you the information in writing, if you want it."

"I don't," said Miller. "I only want a definite statement."

"Then," said Thorndyke, "I will give you one. I declare, positively, that, if this is the original coffin, it has, at some time after the date of the burial, as set forth on the tomb and on the coffin, been opened and reclosed, and that the objects which we have found in it are not its original contents. But I am of opinion that this is not the original coffin, but a new coffin substituted with the intent to commit a fraud. Will that do for you?"

"Yes," replied Miller. "That is good enough for a start, and not a bad start, either. If there has been a fraudulent substitution for the purpose of obtaining possession of valuable property, that brings the matter fairly within my province. And, what is more, it seems to bring Mr. Horatio Gimbler within reach of my claws. But I have a sort of feeling that this faked coffin is not the whole of the business. How's that for a guess?"

"I will say, as the children say in the game of Hot Boiled Beans, that you are 'getting warm'. And I would rather not say any more. I want to start you on an independent investigation and keep out of it, myself, as counsel in this case. But I shall expect that, if you bring any facts to light that have a bearing on that case, you will bring them to my notice."

At this, Miller turned to me with a chuckle of delight.

"Just listen to him, Dr. Jervis!" he exclaimed, waggishly. "Isn't it as good as a play? He stipulates that I shall bring the facts to his notice, when you and I know perfectly well that he has got the whole pack of cards up his sleeve at this very moment. I wouldn't use the word 'humbug' in connexion with a gentleman for whom I have such a profound respect. But – well, what do you want me to do, Doctor?"

"The first thing," said Thorndyke, "is to get rid of those two men. We don't want any witnesses. As this ground is closed for burials and is not open to the public, there is no reason why you should not take possession of the keys. You will want to seal the vault and to have access to it in case any further inspection is necessary. The beadle won't make any difficulty."

He did not. On the contrary, he accepted his release gratefully and gave up the keys without a word. But, before dismissing the men, we replaced the coffin on the shelf and, for the sake of appearances, we returned the lead to its interior and laid the lid on top.

"There is no need to screw it down," the Superintendent explained. "It may have to be re-examined, and I am going to seal up the vault."

With this he sent the two men off with a small donation for the provision of refreshments, accompanying them to the gate and watching their disappearance down the street. Then they were out of sight, he signalled to the driver of his car – a big, roomy, official vehicle – and, when it had drawn up at the gate, he returned, and we began operations.

"I understand," said he, as we lifted off the coffin lid, "that we have got to shift this stuff to some assayist's."

"I don't think we need take the sheet lead," said Thorndyke, "though that would furnish the best evidence on the question of age."

"Then let's take the whole boiling," said Miller. "May as well do the thing thoroughly."

Accordingly, he seized the roll of lead and carried it to the gate, where he deposited it on the rear seat of the car. I followed with the biggest of the pot-leavings. The driver of the car came back with Miller, and he, Miller, and Thorndyke took the other three leavings. The whole collection took up a good deal of the accommodation, but Thorndyke occupied the seat next to the driver, in order to give directions, and Miller and I packed ourselves in amongst the lead as well as we could.

"I wish the Doctor wasn't so deuced secretive," Miller remarked, as the car trundled away westward with a misleading leisurely air. "Of course, it doesn't really matter as we shall know all about it presently, but I am on tenterhooks of curiosity."

"So am I, for that matter," said I, "but I am used to it. To work with Thorndyke is a fine training in restraint."

After what seemed an incredibly short journey, we drew up at a large building in Bishopsgate. Here Thorndyke alighted and disappeared into the entry, and the Superintendent's patience was subjected to a further trial. At length, our friend re-appeared, accompanied by an alert-looking elderly gentleman, while three workmen in white aprons emerged from the doorway and lurked in the background. The elderly gentleman, whom I recognized as a Mr. Daniels, a very eminent assayist and metallurgist, approached and, when he had been introduced to Miller, stuck his head in at the window of the car and surveyed our collection.

"So that's the stuff you want an opinion on," said he. "Queer-looking lot. However, the first thing to do is to get it moved up to the laboratory."

He made a sign to his three myrmidons, who forthwith came forward and, grabbing up the ponderous samples, tucked them under their arms as if they had been lumps of cork and strolled off into the building. We followed them through the weighing rooms on the ground floor to a staircase and up to one of the great laboratories, flanked on one side by a row of tall windows, and on the other by a long range of cupel furnaces. Here, on a bench under the windows, our treasures had been dumped down and, once more, Mr. Daniels ran his eye over them.

"What's the problem with regard to this?" he asked, indicating the roll of lead.

"It is merely a question of age," replied Thorndyke. "We can leave that for the present."

"And what is this?" asked Daniels, lifting the large pot-remainder and turning it over in his hands.

"It is supposed to be lead, eighty years old," said Thorndyke.

"Well, it may be," said Daniels, laying it down and giving it a tap with a hammer and eliciting the dull sound characteristic of lead. "And what are these other lumps supposed to be?"

"They are supposed to be lead, too," replied Thorndyke.

"Well, they are not," said Daniels. "Anyone can see that." He gave one of them a tap with the hammer, and the peculiar sharp chink spoke at once of a hard, brittle metal. On this, he laid down the hammer and took the lump of metal in his hands. And then there came over him the very change that I had noticed in the case of Thorndyke, though there was now no disguise. As he lifted the mass of metal, he suddenly paused and stood quite still with his eyes fixed on Thorndyke and his mouth slightly open. Then he said, "You knew that this was not lead, Doctor."

"Yes," Thorndyke admitted.

"What do you suppose it is?"

"I don't suppose," said Thorndyke. "I have brought the Superintendent to you in order that you may ascertain what it is and give him a confidential report on the subject."

"What do you suppose it is?" asked Miller.

"I don't suppose either," replied Daniels with a faint grin. "I am an assayist, and it is my business to find out."

The Superintendent smiled sourly and looked at me. "These men of science don't mean to give themselves away," he remarked.

"Well," said Daniels, "what is the use of guessing, and perhaps guessing wrong, when you are going to make a test? We have our reputations to consider. Now, what do you want me to do about this stuff?"

"The Superintendent," said Thorndyke, "wants you to make a trial assay, just to let him know what the material is. You will report to him what you find – and remember, this is a confidential matter, and the Superintendent, acting for the Criminal Investigation Department, is your employer."

"And what about you?" Daniels asked.

"If the matter concerns me in any way," Thorndyke replied, "I have no doubt that the Superintendent will communicate the substance of your report to me."

"Ah!" exclaimed Daniels, with a broad smile, "and what a surprise it will be to you. Ha! Ha!"

"Yes," growled Miller, "the Doctor is a regular impostor. Of course, he knows all about it, without either of us telling him. How long will this job take?"

"It will take some little time," replied Daniels, "as you will want some sort of rough estimate of quantities besides the mere qualitative test. Will five o'clock do? And shall I report to you on the phone?"

Miller considered the question. "I am not fond of telephone messages on confidential business," said he. "You never know who is at the other end, or in the middle. I think I had better run across in the car. Then we can go into the affair in more detail, and safe from eavesdroppers. If I am here at five o'clock, I can depend on getting your report?"

"Yes, I shall have everything cut and dried by then," Daniels assured him and, the arrangements being thus concluded, we shook hands and took our departure.

As we emerged into Bishopsgate, I noticed that Miller seemed to look a little disparagingly at the big car that was drawn up at the curb and, instead of entering at once, he turned to Thorndyke and asked, "What do you say, Doctor, to walking home? There are one or two matters connected with this case that I should like to talk over with you, and the car isn't very convenient, and then there is the driver. We could talk more freely if we walked."

Naturally, Thorndyke, who was an inveterate pedestrian, agreed readily and, when Miller had informed the driver of our decision, we set forth, shortening the distance and securing more quiet by striking "across country" through the by-streets. As soon as we were clear of the main thoroughfare with its bustle and din, Miller proceeded to open the discussion.

"I suppose, Doctor, you are quite clear that there has been some faking of that coffin? You've got something solid to go on?"

"Yes," was the reply, "I have no doubt on the subject, and I am prepared to say so in the witness-box."

"That seems to settle it," said Miller. "But there are some queer features in the case. You saw the dust in the vault? But I know you did, for I spotted you taking samples of it. But it really did look as if it had not been disturbed for the best part of a century. Was there anything in that dust that looked to you suspicious, or did you take those samples just as a routine precaution?"

"I should have taken a sample in any case," replied Thorndyke. "But in this case, it was not merely a routine precaution. That dust did not appear to me to agree with the conditions in which it was found. The dust that would accumulate in the course of eighty years in a vault above ground would be very miscellaneous in its origin. It would consist of particles of all sorts of materials which were light enough to float in the air, and in still air at that. They would be mostly minute fragments of fibres derived from textiles, and these would naturally be of all sorts of different colours. The result of such a miscellaneous mixture of different-coloured particles, aided by the fading effect of time, would be a dust of a completely neutral grey. But this dust was not of a completely neutral grey. It had a recognizable colour, very faint and very nearly neutral, but yet there was just a shadowy trace of red. And this subtle, almost indistinguishable, tint of red pervaded the whole mass. It was all alike. To what the colour may have been due, I cannot judge until I have examined the sample under the microscope, but the suggestion – the very strong suggestion – is that this dust was all derived from the same source, which, as I have said, is irreconcilable with the ostensible conditions."

Thorndyke's explanation seemed to furnish the Superintendent with considerable food for thought, for he made no immediate answer, but appeared to be wrapped in profound cogitation. At length, he remarked, "You are a wonderful man, Doctor. Nothing seems to escape you, and you let nothing pass without consideration and a confirmatory test. I wish, now, that we had put you on that damned head – you know the one I mean – the human head that was found in a case at Fenchurch Street Station."

"I remember," said Thorndyke. "It was an odd affair, but I fancy that the head was only a by-product. The purpose of the man who left it was to get possession of the case containing property worth several thousand pounds. He happened to have a human head on his hands, and he, very wisely, took the opportunity to get rid of it and so kill two birds with one stone."

"That may be," said Miller, "but I am not taking that head so calmly as you are. It has been the bane of our lives at the Yard, with all the newspaper men shouting 'unsolved mystery' and 'another undetected murder' and asking perpetually what the police are doing. And it really was a mysterious affair. I have been surprised to notice how little interest you have taken in that head. I should have thought it would have been a problem exactly in your line. But you medical jurists are a cold-blooded lot. You were speaking just now of this man 'having a human head on his hands' as if it were a worn-out umbrella or an old pair of boots."

Thorndyke smiled indulgently. "I am not disparaging the head, Miller," said he. "It presented quite an interesting problem. But it was not *my* problem. I was a mere disinterested onlooker."

"You don't usually take that sordid view," grumbled Miller. "I have generally found you ready to take an interest in a curious problem for its own sake."

To this Thorndyke made no rejoinder, and for some time we walked on in silence. Suddenly, the Superintendent stopped short and stood gazing across the road.

"By the immortal Jingo!" he exclaimed. "Talk of the Devil – !"

He broke off and started to run across the road and, following his movements with my eyes, I saw, on the opposite pavement, a newspaper boy bearing a poster on which was printed in enormous type:

Horrible Discovery – Headless Corpse by Roadside

It was certainly curiously apropos of the subject of our conversation, and I so far shared the Superintendent's excitement that I was about to follow him when I saw that he had secured three copies of the paper and was coming back to us with them in his hand. He distributed his gifts rapidly, and then, backing into the wide entry of a draper's shop, proceeded eagerly to devour the paragraph indicated by the "scare" headlines. Following him into his retreat, I opened the paper and read:

> *Some months ago the public was horrified by the discovery in the cloak room at Fenchurch Street Station of a human head packed in a wooden case. No solution of the mystery surrounding this terrible relic was forthcoming at the inquest, nor were the police ever able to discover any clue to its origin or the identity of the murderer. The matter was allowed to lapse into oblivion, to be added to the long list of undiscovered murders. But questions relating to this tragedy have been revived by a strange and shocking discovery which was made this morning by the side of the arterial road known as the Watling Street, which passes from London through Dartford to Rochester. Between three and four miles on the Rochester side of Dartford, the road passes through a deep cutting, which was made to reduce the gradient of the hill, the sides of which are in two stages, there being, about half-way up, a shelf several feet wide. As*

this shelf is some thirty feet above the road, its surface is entirely invisible to anyone passing along the latter, though it is, of course, visible from above. But the hill through which the road is cut is covered with dense woodland, seldom trodden by the foot of man. Thus, for months at a time, this shelf remains unseen by any human eye.

But this morning Fate guided the footsteps of an observer to this spot, so remote and yet so near. A local archaeologist, a Mr. Elmhurst of Gravesend, happened to be making a sketch-map of the features of the wood when his wanderings took him to the edge of the cutting. Looking down the cliff-like descent, he was horrified to observe, lying on the shelf immediately below him, the headless and perfectly nude body of a man. Its huddled attitude suggested that it had rolled down the steep slope and been arrested by the shelf, and even from the distance at which he stood, it was evident that it had been lying exposed for a considerable time.

Mr. Elmhurst did not stay to make any further observations, but, taking the shortest way to the road, hailed an approaching motorist, who very obligingly conveyed him to Gravesend, where he notified the police of his discovery. An ambulance was at once procured and, guided by the discoverer, proceeded to the spot, whence – after a careful examination by the police – the body was conveyed to Dartford, where it now lies in the mortuary awaiting an inquest.

The body appears to be that of a youngish man, rather short and exceptionally muscular, and the condition of the strong and well-shaped hands suggests that the deceased was a skilled workman of some kind. The inquest will be opened tomorrow.

As I reached the end of the account, I glanced at the Superintendent and remarked, "A very creditable piece of journalism. The reporter hasn't wasted much time. What do you think of it, Miller?"

"Well, I'm very relieved," he replied. "I've been waiting for this for months. I'm fairly sick of all the talk about the unsolved mystery, and the undiscovered murder. Now, we may be able to get a move on, though I must admit that it doesn't look like a very promising case. It's a long time since the man was murdered, and there doesn't seem much to go on.

Still, it's better than a head in a box with no clue to the owner. What do you think of it, Doctor? I suppose you've been expecting it, too?"

"I wouldn't say 'expecting'," Thorndyke replied. "The possibility of something of this kind had occurred to me. But you must bear in mind that the head, being preserved and packed in a case, offered no suggestions as to the time or place of death. As this body was apparently not preserved, it will be possible to arrive at an approximate date of death and, as it was found in a particular place, some idea of locality may be formed. But any conclusions as to the locality in which the murder took place will have to be very cautiously considered, having regard to the ease with which, in these days, bodies can be carried away long distances from the scene of the crime. And, again, the body is nude, so that there will be no help from the clothing towards identification and, as it appears to have been exposed in the open for months, its own condition will make identification difficult. I agree with you, Miller. It does not look a very promising case."

The Superintendent nodded and growled an inarticulate assent. But in spite of Thorndyke's rather cold comfort, he still seemed disposed to be optimistic, and when we parted at the Inner Temple gate, he walked away with a springy step and an almost jaunty air.

Chapter XII
Thorndyke Becomes Interested

$\mathbf{M}$iller's intense interest in the "horrible discovery" did not surprise me at all. But Thorndyke's did. For what the Superintendent had said was perfectly true. The mysterious "head in a box" had aroused in him only the most languid curiosity – which, again to quote Miller, was entirely unlike him. It is true that he liked, if possible, to be officially appointed to investigate an interesting case. But appointment or no appointment, from sheer professional enthusiasm, he always kept himself informed on, and followed with the closest interest, any criminal case that presented unusual or obscure features.

Now the "head in the box" case had appeared to me eminently unusual and obscure. It had seemed to imply an atrocious crime which combined with its atrocity a remarkable degree of callous ingenuity. And the mystery surrounding it was undeniable. Excepting some vague connexion with the great platinum robbery (itself an unsolved mystery) it offered not a single clue. Yet Thorndyke had seemed to dismiss it as a mere oddity. He could not have been less moved if it had been a wax-work head – which it certainly was not.

His own explanation did not seem to me to be entirely satisfactory. It was true, as he had said, that there was a total lack of data, and "a mere mystery, without a single leading fact is not, to a medical jurist, worth powder and shot." The fact that the head was preserved and practically imperishable excluded any inferences as to time or place. It might, for any evidence to the contrary, have been the head of a person who had died in Australia twenty years ago.

So he had dismissed it into the region of the unknowable – at least, so I had understood, though I had never felt quite sure that he had not, in his queer, secret fashion, just docketed it and packed it away in some pigeon-hole of his inexhaustible memory, there to repose until such time as the "leading fact" should come into view, unrecognized by anyone but himself.

This faint suspicion now tended to revive. For though the headless body looked as hopeless a mystery as the bodyless head, there was clearly no question of dismissing it as "not worth powder and shot". That powder and shot were already being expended, I ascertained that very evening, when, returning to our chambers after a lengthy consultation, I found on the table a six-inch Ordnance Map, a boxwood scale, a pair of dividers, and a motor road-map.

The purpose of the latter was obvious on inspection. The Ordnance Map was dated 1910 and did not show the arterial road. The motor map showed the new road – and mighty little else, but as much, no doubt, as interested the average motorist. From the road-map, the new road had been transferred in pencil to the Ordnance Map, which was thus brought up to date while retaining all the original topographical features, and the locality shown left no doubt as to the nature of the investigation.

I was still looking at the maps and reflecting as above when the door opened and my colleague entered.

"I thought you were out, Thorndyke," said I.

"No," he replied, "I have been up in the laboratory, having a chat with Polton about a job that I want him to do. I see you have been inspecting what the reporters will call 'the scene of the tragedy'."

"I see that you have," I retorted, "and have been speculating on your change of front. The 'head in the box' apparently left you cold, but you seem to be developing quite a keen interest in this problem. Why this inconsistency?"

"My dear fellow," he replied, "there is no inconsistency. The case is entirely altered. We have now a number of facts from which to start an inquiry. From the state of the body, we can form an approximate judgment as to the date about which death occurred. Perhaps the cause of death many transpire at the inquest. We knew where the body was found, and even if it may have been conveyed thither from a distance, the selection of the place where it was deposited suggests some local knowledge. The spot was extremely well-chosen, as events have proved."

"Yes, but it was a queer idea to dump it there. A sort of ghastly practical joke. Just think of it, Thorndyke. Think of that great procession of traffic of all kinds – cars, motor coaches, lorries, cyclists – streaming along that road by the thousand, day after day, month after month, and all the time, within a biscuit-toss of them, that gruesome thing lying there open to the sky."

"Yes," he agreed, "there is certainly an element of the macabre in the setting of this crime, though I don't suppose it was intentional."

"Neither do I. Nor do I suppose that the horrible picturesqueness of the setting is what is attracting you. I wonder what is."

Thorndyke did not reply immediately, but sat regarding me with a sort of appraising expression (which I recognized, and had come by experience, to associate with some special exhibition of thick-headedness on my part). At length he replied, "I don't see why you should. The problem of this headless body abounds in elements of interest. All sorts of questions arise out of it. There is that embalmed head for instance. That seems to have an obvious connexion with this body."

"Very obvious indeed," said I, with a grin, "and the connexion was still closer when the head was on the body."

He smiled indulgently and continued, "Disregarding the suggested anatomical connexion, there is the connexion of action and motive. What, for instance, is the connexion of the man who deposited the head in the cloak room with this body? We don't know how he came by that head. The fact that he had it in his possession is an incriminating fact, but it is not evidence of murder. It is not even certain that he knew what was in the case. But whether he did or not, he is obviously involved in a complex of circumstances which includes this body. However, it is premature to discuss the case until we have the additional facts that will probably transpire at the inquest. Meanwhile," he concluded, with an exasperating smile, "I recommend my learned friend to go carefully over all the facts in his possession, relating both to the embalmed head and the headless body. Let him consider those facts critically as to their separate value and in relation to one another. If he does this, I think he will find that some extremely interesting conclusions will emerge."

It is unnecessary to say his opinion was not justified by results. I did, indeed, chew the cud of the few, unilluminating facts that were known to me, but the only conclusion that emerged was that, in some obscure way of which I could make nothing, this headless corpse was connected with the mystery of the stolen platinum. But this, I felt sure, was not the conclusion that was in Thorndyke's mind. And at that, I had to leave it.

On the following morning, Thorndyke went forth to attend at the inquest. I was not able to go with him, nor did I particularly wish to, as I knew that I should get full information from him as to the facts elicited. He started, as I thought, unnecessarily early and he came back unexpectedly late. But this latter circumstance was presently explained by the appearance on the Ordnance Map of a pencilled cross at the roadside, indicating the spot on which the body had been lying when it was first seen. Later in the evening, when giving me particulars of the inquest, he mentioned that he had visited the site of the discovery and "gone over the ground, roughly", having taken his bicycle down by train for that purpose.

"Did you pick up anything of interest at the inquest?" I asked.

"Yes," he replied, "it was quite a good inquest. The coroner was a careful man who knew his business and kept to it, and the medical witness had made a thorough examination and gave his evidence clearly and concisely. As to the facts, they were simple enough, though important. The body was, of course, a good deal the worse for exposure to the weather. As to the date of death, the doctor wisely declined to make a definite statement, but he estimated it at not less than three months ago. The body appeared to be that of a man between thirty and forty years of age, five feet, six inches in height, broad-shouldered and muscular, with rather small, well-shaped hands, which showed a definite, but not considerable, thickening of the skin on the palms, from which, and from the dirty and ill-kept finger-nails, the doctor inferred that the deceased was a workman of some kind, but not a labourer.

"The head had been separated from the spinal column with a knife, leaving the atlas intact and, to this extent, the separation had been effected skilfully."

"Yes," said I. "That point was made, I remember, at the inquest on the head. It would require some skill and the knowledge as to where the joint was to be found. By the way, was the question of the head raised?"

"Yes. Naturally a juryman wanted to question the doctor on the subject, but the witness very properly replied that his evidence dealt only with facts observed by himself, and the coroner supported him. Then the question was raised whether the head should not be produced for comparison with the body, but the doctor refused to go into the matter, and the coroner pointed out that the head had already been examined medically and that all the facts were available in the depositions of the witnesses. He did, however, read out some of the depositions from the previous inquest and asked the doctor whether the facts set forth in them were consistent with the belief that the head and the headless body were parts of one and the same person, to which the doctor replied that the mode of separation was the same in both and that the parts which were missing in the one were present in the other, but beyond that he would give no opinion."

"Did he give any opinion as to the cause of death?" I asked.

"Oh, yes," replied Thorndyke. "There was no mystery about that. There was a knife-wound in the back, near the angle of the left scapula, penetrating deeply and transfixing the heart. It appeared to have been inflicted with a large, single-edged knife of the 'Green River' type, and obviously with great force. The witness stated, confidently, that it could not have been self-inflicted."

"That seems to be pretty obvious, too," said I. "At any rate, the man could not have cut his own head off."

"A very capable detective-sergeant gave evidence," Thorndyke resumed, dismissing – to my secret amusement – the trivial and uninteresting detail of the manner in which this unfortunate creature had been done to death. "He stated that the wood had been searched for the dead man's clothing, but I suspect that it was a very perfunctory search, as he was evidently convinced that it was not there, remarking, plausibly enough, that, since the clothing must have been stripped off to prevent identification, it would not be reasonable to expect to find it in the vicinity. He was of opinion that the body had been brought from a distance in a car or van, and that, probably, two or more persons were concerned in the affair."

"It seems likely," I said, "having regard to the remoteness of the place. But it is only a guess."

"Exactly," Thorndyke agreed. "There was a good deal of guessing and not many facts, and the few facts that were really significant do not seem to have been understood."

"What are the facts that you regard as really significant?" I asked – not that I had the slightest expectation that he would tell me. And he did not. His inevitable reply was, "You know what the known facts are, Jervis, and you will see for yourself, if you consider them critically, which are the significant ones. But, to return to the inquest: The coroner's summing-up was excellent, having regard to the evidence that had been given. I took shorthand notes of some of it, and I will read them to you. With reference to the embalmed head he remarked:

> It has been suggested that the head which was found at Fenchurch Street Station ought to have been brought here for comparison. But to what purpose? What kind of comparison is possible? If the head is broken off a china figure and the two parts are lost and subsequently found in different places, the question as to whether they are parts of the same figure can be settled by putting them together and seeing whether the fractured surfaces fit each other. But with a detached human head – especially after the lapse of months – this is not possible. If the preserved head had been exhumed and brought here, we could have learned nothing more from it than we can learn from the depositions of the medical witness, which I have read to you. Accordingly, we must fall back on our common sense, and I think we shall find that enough for our purpose.

> Let us look at the facts. A headless body has been found in one place, and a body-less head in another. The doctor has told us that they might be – though he doesn't say that they are – the head and body of one and the same person.

They agree in the peculiar and unusual mode of separation. The parts which are absent in the one are present in the other. There is no part missing, and no part redundant. If that head had been cut off this body, the appearances would be exactly what they are.

Now, gentlemen, if headless human bodies and bodyless human heads were quite common objects, we might have to search further. But fortunately, they are so rare and unusual that we may almost regard these remains as unique. And if they are not parts of the same person, then there must be, somewhere, an undiscovered body belonging to the head and, somewhere else, an undiscovered head belonging to this body. But, I submit, gentlemen, that common sense rejects such enormous improbabilities and compels us to adopt the obvious and simple explanation that the head and the body are those of one and the same person.

As to the cause of death, you have heard the doctor's evidence. The deceased was killed by a knife-wound, which he could not have inflicted himself, and which was therefore inflicted by some other person. And with that I leave you to consider your verdict.

"An excellent summing-up," said I, "and very well argued. The verdict was Wilful Murder, of course?"

"Yes. 'By some person or persons unknown'. And the jury could hardly have come to any other conclusion. But as you see, the case is, from the police point of view, left in the air."

"Yes," I agreed. "If Miller is taking up the case, as I assume that he is, he has got his work cut out. I don't see that this body was such a wind-fall as he seemed to think. Scotland Yard may catch some more trouble from the Press if something fresh does not turn up."

"Well," Thorndyke rejoined, by way of winding up the conversation, "we must hope, like medico-legal Micawbers, that something will turn up."

For the next few days, however, the case remained "in the air", but it was not alone in this respect. Presently I began to be conscious that there were other matters in the air. For instance, our invaluable assistant, Polton, suddenly developed a curious, stealthy, conspiratorial manner of going about, or locking himself in the laboratory, which experience had taught me to associate with secret activities foreshadowing some important and dramatic "move" on Thorndyke's part. Then, on the fourth day after the inquest, I detected my colleague in the suspicious act of pacing the pavement at the lower, and more secluded, end of King's Bench Walk, in earnest conversation with Mr. Superintendent Miller. And the *prima facie* suspiciousness of the proceeding was confirmed by the eagerness and excitement that were evident in the face and manner of our friend, and even more by the way in which he suddenly shut up, like a snapped snuff-box, as I approached.

And that very evening, Thorndyke exploded the mine.

"We have got an expedition on, tomorrow," he announced.

"Who are we?" I asked.

"You and I, Miller, and Polton. I know you have got the day free."

"Where are we going to?" I demanded.

"To Swanscombe Wood," was the reply.

"What for?"

"To collect some further facts relating to the headless body," he replied.

As a mere statement, it did not sound very sensational. But to one who knew Thorndyke as I knew him, it had certain implications that gave it a special significance. In the first place, Thorndyke tended habitually to under-statement and, in the second, he took no one into his confidence while his investigations were at the tentative stage. As Miller expressed it, "The Doctor would never show a card until he was ready to take the trick." Whence there naturally arose in my mind a strong suspicion that the "further facts" which we were to collect were already in Thorndyke's possession.

And events proved that I was not so very far wrong.

Chapter XIII
The Dene Hole

The products of Polton's labours impressed me as disappointing and hardly worthy of his mechanical ingenuity, consisting of nothing more subtle than an immense coil of rope, rove through two double blocks and forming a long and powerful tackle, a tripod formed of three very stout iron-shod seven-foot poles, and a strong basket such as builders use, furnished with strong rope slings. There was one further item, which was more worthy of its producer: A large electric lamp, fitted with adjustable lenses and, to judge by the suspension arrangements, designed to throw a powerful beam of parallel rays vertically downwards.

But if Polton's productions were of an unexpected kind, the vehicle in which the Superintendent drove up to our entry was even more so. For though it bore no outward distinguishing marks, it was an undeniable motor ambulance. However, if less dignified and imposing than the official car, it was a good deal more convenient. The unwieldy tripod, tackle, and basket were easily disposed of in its roomy interior, still leaving ample accommodation for me and Polton and the detective-sergeant whom Miller had brought as an additional assistant. The Superintendent, himself, was at the steering wheel, and Thorndyke took the seat beside him to give directions as we approached our destination.

I asked no questions. The character of our outfit told me pretty plainly what kind of job we had in hand, and I felt a malicious satisfaction in tantalizing Polton, who was, so to speak, bursting with silence and secrecy and the desire to be questioned. So little was said – and nothing to the point – while the ambulance trundled out at the Tudor Street gate, crossed Blackfriars Bridge, threaded its way through the traffic of the South London streets, and presently came out upon the Dover Road. A few minutes later, as we mounted a steep rise, the sergeant, who hitherto had uttered not a word, removed his pipe from his mouth, remarked "Shooter's Hill", and replaced it as if it were a stopper.

The ambulance bowled smoothly along the straight line of the old Roman road. Welling, Crayford, and Dartford were entered and left behind. A few minutes after leaving Dartford, the road began a long ascent and then, after a short run on the level, fell away somewhat steeply. At this point, the sergeant once more removed his pipe, nodded at the side window and, having affirmed, stolidly, "That's the place," reinserted the stopper.

The ambulance now began to slow down and, a minute or two later, drew in by the side of the road and halted. Then, as Thorndyke and the Superintendent alighted, we also got out, and the sergeant proceeded to occupy the driver's seat.

"You and Polton had better stay here for the present," said Thorndyke. "The Superintendent and I are going to locate the spot. When we have found it, he will remain there while I come back and help you to carry the gear."

He produced from his pocket a marching-compass and a card, on one side of which a sketch-plan had been drawn while a number of bearings were written on the other. After a glance at the latter, he set the direction line of the compass and started off along a rough foot-path, followed by the Superintendent. We watched their receding figures as they ascended the hill and approached the wood by which it was covered. At the margin of the latter, Thorndyke paused and "turned to take a last, fond look" at his starting-point and check his compass bearings. Then he faced about and, in a few seconds, he and the Superintendent disappeared into the wood.

Waiting is usually a tedious business, and is still more so when the waiter is on the tip-toe of expectation and curiosity. Vainly, I endeavoured to repress a tendency to useless and futile speculation as to what Thorndyke was seeking (or, more probably, had already found and was now about to disclose). As for Polton, if he could have been furnished with an emotional pressure-gauge, it would certainly have burst. Even the stolid sergeant was fain to come off his perch and pace up and down by the roadside, and once he actually went so far as to take out the stopper and remark that, "It seems as if the Doctor has made some sort of discovery."

Anon, our sufferings were somewhat alleviated by the arrival of a police patrol, who came free-wheeling down the hill from the direction of Dartford. As he approached us, he slowed down more and more and eventually dismounted to make a circuit of our vehicle, with the manner of a dog sniffing at a suspicious stranger. Apparently it appearance did not satisfy him, and he proceeded to interrogate.

"What's going on?" he asked, not uncivilly. "This looks like an ambulance, but I see you have got some lifting gear inside."

Here the sergeant interposed with a brief and unlucid explanation of our business, at the same time producing his credentials, at the sight whereof the patrol officer was visibly impressed, and showed an unmistakeable tendency to linger, which the sergeant by no means sought to discourage.

"Can I give any assistance?" the patrolman asked, a little wistfully.

"Well," the sergeant replied, promptly, "if you could spare the time to give an eye to this car, that would release me to lend the Superintendent a hand."

It was obvious that the patrol man would have preferred to transpose these functions, but nevertheless, he agreed readily, and at this moment Thorndyke reappeared from the wood and came striding swiftly towards us along the foot-path. As he came up, the sergeant explained the new arrangements with some anxiety as to whether they would be approved. To his evident relief, Thorndyke accepted them readily.

"We shall be none the worse for an extra hand," said he. "Now we shall be able to carry the whole kit up in one journey."

Accordingly, we proceeded to get the gear out of the ambulance and distribute the items among the party. Thorndyke and I took the tripod on our shoulders – and a deuce of a weight it was. The sergeant got the great coil of rope on to his back with the aid of a spare sling, and Polton brought up the rear with the basket, in which was stowed the lamp, while the patrolman kept a look-out with a view to heading off any inquisitive strangers who might be attracted by the queer aspect of our procession.

Appreciation of the beauties of the countryside is not favoured by the presence on one's shoulder of three massive ash poles with heavy iron fittings. The character of the ground was what chiefly occupied my attention, particularly after we had entered the wood, where I got the impression that some ingenious sylvan devil had collected all the brambles from miles around and arranged them in an interminable series of entanglements, compared with which the barbed-wire defences of a German trench were but feeble and amateurish imitations. But we tramped on, crashing through the yellow and russet leafage, Thorndyke leading with his compass in his unoccupied hand and trudging forward in silence, save for an occasional soft chuckle at my lurid comments on the landscape.

Suddenly I heard Miller's voice informing us that "here we were", and we nearly collided with him at the edge of a small opening. Here we set down the tripod, opening it enough to enable it to stand upright.

"You didn't have to blow your whistle," said Thorndyke. "I suppose you heard us coming?"

"Heard you coming!" exclaimed Miller. "It was like a troop of blooming elephants – to say nothing of Dr. Jervis's language. Hallo, Sergeant! I thought I told you to stay with the car."

The sergeant hastily explained the arrangements, adding that "The Doctor" had concurred, on which the Superintendent, having also approved, set him to work at getting the gear ready.

A glance around the little opening in which we were gathered showed me that my diagnosis of the purpose of the expedition had been correct. Near the middle of the opening, half concealed by the rank undergrowth, yawned the mouth of one of those mysterious pits known as *dene holes* which are scattered in such numbers over this part of Kent. Cautiously, I approached the brink and peered down into the black depths.

"Horrible, dangerous things, these dene holes are," said Miller. "Ought to be fenced in. How deep do you say this pit is, Doctor?"

"This one is just about sixty feet, but many of them are deeper. Seventy feet is about the average."

"Sixty feet!" exclaimed Polton, with a fascinated eye on the yawning hole. "And anyone coming along here in the dark might step into it without a moment's warning. Horrible! Did I understand you, sir, to say that it was dug a very long time ago?"

"It has been there as you see it," replied Thorndyke, "for thousands of years. How many thousands we can't say. But there seems to be no doubt that these dene holes were excavated by the men of the Old Stone Age."

"Dear me!" exclaimed Polton. "Thousands of years! I should have thought that, by this time, they would have been full to the brim of the people who had tumbled into them."

While these exclamations and comments were passing, the preparations were in progress for the exploration. The tripod was set up over the hole (which was some three feet in diameter and roughly circular, like the mouth of a well), the tackle securely hooked on, and the lamp suspended in position. The Superintendent switched on the light by means of a push at the end of a cord and, grasping the tripod, leaned over the hole and peered down the well-like shaft.

"I can't make out very much," he remarked. "I seem to see what looks like a boot, and that's about all."

"It is a long way down," said Thorndyke, "and it doesn't matter much what we can see from above. We shall soon know exactly what there is down there."

As he spoke, he switched off the lamp and hooked the basket on to the tackle by means of a pair of clip-hooks, provided with a safety catch. Then he produced a candle from his pocket and proceeded to light it.

"I don't like the idea of your going down, Doctor," said the Superintendent. "It's really our job."

"Not at all," replied Thorndyke, drawing the basket to the edge of the hole and stepping into it. "I proposed the exploration and undertook to carry it out. Besides, I want to see what the bottom of this dene hole is like."

"Don't you think, sir," Polton interposed, earnestly, "that it would be better for me to go down? I am so much lighter and should put less strain on the tackle."

"My dear Polton," said Thorndyke, regarding his devoted henchman with an appreciative smile, "this tackle would bear a couple of tons, easily. There isn't any strain. But I will ask you to pay out the rope as steadily as you can, and keep an eye on this candle. If it goes out, you had better haul up at once without waiting for a signal, as you will know that I have dropped into foul air. Now, I am ready if you are."

He steadied himself by lightly grasping two of the tackle-ropes and I took a turn round the trunk of a birch tree with the "fall" by passing the big coil round. Then Miller and the sergeant hauled on the rope while I gathered in the slack, the tackle grew taut, the basket began to rise from the ground and swung directly over the black hole.

"Now, pay out steadily and not too fast," said Thorndyke, and as we began to ease out the rope, he slowly sank, like a stage demon, and disappeared into the bowels of the earth, while Polton, grasping the tripod and leaning over the hole, watched his descent with starting eyes and an expression of horror.

Owing to the great power of the tackle, the weight on the fall was quite trifling. I could, alone, have paid it out easily with the aid of the turn round the tree. So we were able, in turn, to leave it to satisfy our curiosity and relieve our anxiety by a glance down the shaft, which now looked even more alarming than when we had looked into the mere, impenetrable blackness of the hole. For now, as we peered down the well-like shaft at our friend – already grown small in the distance-faintly illuminated by the glimmer of the candle – we were able to realize the horrible depth to which this strange memorial of a forgotten race sank into the earth.

But the unfailing glimmer of the candle-light – though it had now dwindled to a mere distant spark – reassured us, for, apart from the possibility of "choke damp", there was really no appreciable danger. Notwithstanding which, Polton was fain, from time to time, to relieve his overwrought feelings by hailing the now invisible explorer with the inquiry, "All right, sir?" to which a strange, sepulchral, but surprisingly loud voice replied, "All right, Polton."

After an almost interminable paying-out, the diminishing remainder of rope warned us that Thorndyke must have nearly reached the bottom, and then a sudden relaxation of the tension informed us that he had already done so. Immediately afterwards, that uncanny, megaphonic voice announced the fact and directed us to switch on the light and throw down the spare sling. I at once complied with the first order and was about to carry out the other when it occurred to me that a stout rope sling might fall with unpleasant force after a drop of sixty feet. Accordingly, I coiled it loosely round the tackle-ropes and, securing the ends with a hitch, let go, when I saw it slide smoothly down the ropes to the bottom.

"I wonder what he wants with that sling," Miller speculated, grasping the tripod and leaning over to peer down. But as the only result was to obscure the light of the lamp and throw the shaft into shadow, he withdrew and waited for events to enlighten him. Then the voice came reverberating up the shaft, commanding us to hoist.

If the paying-out had been a long business, the hauling up was longer. There seemed to be no end to that rope, and as I hauled and hauled, I found myself wishing that Thorndyke had been a little less cautious and contented himself with a less powerful but quicker tackle. From time to time, Miller was impelled by the intensity of his curiosity to thrust his head over the hole to see what was coming up, but as his head cut off the light of the lamp and rendered the ascending object invisible, he retired each time, defeated and muttering. At length, as the accumulating coils of rope told us that our freight must be nearing the surface, he succeeded in catching a glimpse of the object. But so far was that glimpse from allaying his curiosity that it reduced him to a frenzy of excitement.

"It looks like a body!" he exclaimed. "A man's body. But it can't be!"

It was, however. As we hauled in the last few feet of the rope and made fast to the tree, there arose out of the hole the body of a tall, well-dressed man which had been suspended from the hook of the tackle by the sling, passed round the chest under the arms. Miller helped me to haul it away from the hole, when we unfastened the sling and let the body fall on the ground.

"Well," said the Superintendent, surveying it gloomily, "this is a disappointment. We have come all this way and taken all this trouble just to salve the body of a poor devil who has stumbled into this infernal pit by accident and who is no concern of ours at all. Of course, it is not the Doctor's fault. He discovered that there was something down there and he drew the very natural conclusion, though it happened to be the wrong one. Let the damn tackle down again as fast as you can and get the Doctor up. I expect he is as sick as I am."

The lowering of the tackle was a slow and tedious business, for, as there was now no weight to pull it down, it had to be "overhauled." Fortunately, Polton had oiled the sheaves so that they turned smoothly and easily, but it was a long time before the voice from below notified us that the lower block had reached the bottom. Its reverberations had hardly died away when the order came up to hoist, and we straightway began to haul, while Polton coiled down the rope as it was gathered in. Presently I noticed a puzzled expression on the Superintendant's face and, as I looked at him inquiringly, he exclaimed, "This can't be the Doctor. He's a bigger man than that poor beggar, but there doesn't seem to be any weight on the rope at all."

I had noticed this, myself, and now suggested that we might take advantage of the light weight by hauling up more quickly, which we did with such a will that Miller's opinion was presently confirmed by the appearance of the basket at the mouth of the pit. As it came into view, the Superintendent gazed at it in astonishment.

"Why, it's the clothes, after all!" he exclaimed, seizing the basket and turning its contents out on to the ground, "and the right ones, too, by the look of them. A complete outfit: Suit, shirt, underclothing, socks, boots – everything but the hat. He must have had a hat, and so must the other fellow. Perhaps the Doctor will bring them up with him."

Having emptied the basket, we sent it down again, and now being able to judge the distance, we let it run down by its own weight, only checking it as it neared the bottom. After a very brief interval, the hollow voice from below directed us to haul up, and once again we began to gather in the rope and coil it down.

"This is queer," said Miller, as he took his turn at the rope. "It is no heavier than it was last time. I wonder what he is sending up now."

In his impatience to solve this new mystery, he hauled with such energy that beads of sweat began to appear on his forehead. But it is difficult to hurry a four-fold tackle and it was a long time before the basket came into view. When, at last, it became visible a few feet down, its appearance evidently disappointed him, for he exclaimed in a tone of disgust, "Hats. Two hats. I should have thought he might have brought them up with him and saved a journey."

"There is something in it besides the hats," said I as the basket rose out of the mouth of the pit and I drew it aside on to the ground, while the others gathered round. I seized the two hats and lifted them out, and then I stood as if petrified, with the hats in my hands, too astounded to utter a sound.

"My God!" Miller exclaimed, huskily. "A man's head! Now what the blazes can be the meaning of this?"

He stood, staring in amazement – as, indeed, we all did – at the horrible relic that lay at the bottom of the basket. Suddenly he seized the latter and turned it upside down, when the head rolled out on the ground. Then he flung the basket into the hole and gruffly ordered us to "Let go!"

There was no interval this time, for almost as the rope slackened, informing us that the basket had settled on the bottom, the hollow voice from below commanded us to haul up. And as soon as we had taken in the slack, we knew by the weight that Thorndyke was at the other end of the tackle. Accordingly, I once more took a turn round the tree to prevent the chance of a slip or jerk and the others hauled steadily and evenly. Even now, the weight seemed comparatively trifling, but what we gained from the tackle in lifting power we lost in speed. In mechanics as in other things you can't have it both ways. However, at long last, Polton, grasping the tripod and craning over the hole, was able to announce that "The Doctor" was nearly up, and after another couple of minutes he appeared rising slowly above ground, when Polton carefully drew the basket on to the solid earth and helped him to step out.

"Well, Doctor," said Miller, "you've given us a bit of a surprise, as you generally do. But," he added, pointing to the head, which lay with its shrunken, discoloured face turned up to the sky, "what are we to make of that? We've got a head too many."

"Too many for what?" asked Thorndyke.

"For what we were inquiring into," Miller replied testily. "See what you have done for us. We find a head in a box at Fenchurch Street Station. Then we keep a look-out for the body belonging to it, and at last it turns up. Then you bring us here and produce another head, which puts us back where we started. We've still got a spare head that we can't account for."

Thorndyke smiled grimly. "I am not under a contract," said he, "to supply facts that will fit your theory of a crime. We must take the facts as they come, and I think there can be no doubt that this head belongs to the body that was found on the shelf a few yards from here."

"Then what about the other head?" demanded Miller. "Where is the body belonging to that?"

Thorndyke shook his head. "That is another story," said he. "But the immediate problem is how these remains are to be disposed of. We can't carry them and the gear down to the ambulance without assistance."

Here the sergeant interposed with a suggestion.

"There is a big electric station a little farther down the road. If I were to run the patrolman down there, he could get on the phone to his headquarters, and perhaps, meanwhile, they could lend us one or two men from the works. We've got a folding stretcher in the car."

"Good," said Miller. "That will do to a *T*, Sergeant. You cut along as fast as you can, and perhaps Mr. Polton might go with you to take charge of the patrolman's bicycle."

As Polton and the sergeant retired along the now plainly visible track, Miller turned to Thorndyke with a puzzled and questioning air.

"I can't quite make this out, Doctor," said he. "You brought us here, as I understood, in the expectation of probably finding that poor devil's clothes. Had you any expectation of finding anything else?"

"I thought it probable," replied Thorndyke, "that if we found the clothes, we should probably find the head with them. But I certainly did not expect to find that body. That came as quite a surprise."

"Naturally," said Miller. "A queer coincidence that he should have happened to tumble in, just about the same time. Still, he isn't in the picture."

"There," said Thorndyke, "I think you are mistaken. I should say that he is very much in the picture. My very strong impression is that he is none other than the murderer."

"The murderer!" exclaimed Miller. "What makes you think that? Or are you just guessing?"

"I am considering the obvious probabilities," Thorndyke replied. As he spoke, he stooped over the dead man and drew up first the jacket and then the waistcoat. As the latter garment rose, there came into view, projecting up from within the waist-band of the trousers, the haft of an undeniable Green River knife. Thorndyke drew the weapon out of its leather sheath, glanced at it, and silently held it out for our inspection. No expert eye was needed to read its message. The streaks of blackened rust on the blade were distinctive enough, but much more so was the shiny black deposit at the junction of the steel and the wooden handle.

"Yes," said Miller, as Thorndyke replaced the knife in its sheath, "that tells the tale pretty well. And exactly the kind of knife that the doctor described at the inquest." He cogitated profoundly for a few moments and then asked, "How do you suppose this fellow came to fall into the pit?"

"I should say," Thorndyke replied, "that the affair happened somewhat in this way: The murderer either enticed his victim into this wood, or he murdered him elsewhere and brought his body here. We shall probably never know which, and it really doesn't matter. Obviously, the murderer knew this place pretty well, as we can judge by his acquaintance with the dene hole. Having committed the murder, or deposited the body, near the edge of the wood close to the road, he stripped the corpse and carried the clothes through the wood to the hole and dropped them down. And when we bear in mind that this must, almost certainly, have been done at night, we must conclude that, not only must the murderer have been familiar with the locality, but he had probably planned the crime in advance and reconnoitred the ground.

"Having dropped the clothes down the pit, he returned to the corpse. And now he had the most difficult part of his task to do. He had to detach the head, and he had to detach it in a particular way – and in the dark, too."

"Why did he have to?" Miller asked.

"Let us leave that question for the moment. It was part of the plan, as the case presents itself to me. Well, having detached the head, he dragged the nude and headless corpse the short distance to the edge of the cutting and pushed it over, knowing that it would roll down only as far as the shelf. Then he carried the head to the dene hole.

"Now, we may assume that he was a man of pretty strong nerves, but, by the time he had murdered this man, stripped the corpse, and cut off the head – in a public place, mind you, in which discovery was possible at any moment – he must have been considerably shaken. He was walking in the dark with the dead man's head in his hands, over ground which, as Jervis can testify, is a mass of traps and entanglements. In his terror and agitation he probably hurried to get rid of his dreadful burden and, just as he approached the hole, he must have caught his foot in a bramble and fallen, sprawling, right into the pit. That is how I picture the course of events."

"Yes," said I, "it sounds pretty convincing as to what probably did happen, though I am in the same difficulty as Miller. I don't quite see why he did it. Why, for instance, he didn't throw the body, itself, down the pit."

"We must go into that question on another occasion," said Thorndyke, "but you will notice that – but for this investigation of ours – he did actually secure a false identification of the body."

"Yes," agreed Miller, "he had us there. We had fairly fixed the body on to that Fenchurch Street head."

Once more the Superintendent fell into a train of cogitation, with a speculative eye on the body that lay on the ground at his feet. Suddenly he roused and turning to Thorndyke, asked, "Have you any idea, Doctor, who these two people are?"

"I have formed an opinion," was the reply, "and I think it is probably a correct opinion. I should say that this," indicating the dead man, "is the person known as Bassett, or Dobson, the man who deposited the case of stolen platinum at the cloak room, and this man," pointing to the head, "is the one who stole the case and left the embalmed head in exchange."

Thorndyke's answer, delivered in calm, matter-of-fact tones, fairly took my breath away. I was too astonished to make any comment. And the Superintendent was equally taken by surprise, for he, too, stood for a while gazing at my colleague without speaking. At length he said – voicing my sentiments as well as his own – "This is a knock-out, Doctor! I wasn't aware that you knew anything about this case, or were taking any interest in it. Yet you seem to have it all cut and dried. Knowing you, I assume that this isn't just a guess. You've got something to go on?"

"In respect of the identification? Certainly. Without going into any other matters, there is the appearance of these remains. In both cases it corresponds exactly with the description given at the inquest. The man who stole the case – "

"And left the box with the human head in it," interpolated Miller. "You are ignoring that trivial detail."

"Yes," Thorndyke admitted. "We are dealing with the robbery, in which they were both concerned. Well, that man was described by the attendant as dark, clean-shaved, and having conspicuous gold fillings in both central incisors. If you look at that head, you can see the gold fillings plainly enough, as well as the other, less distinctive characteristics.

"In the case of this other man, the correspondence is much more striking. Here is the long, thin face with the long, thin, pointed nose, curved on the bridge, and the dark, nearly black hair. The fair complexion and pale blue eye colour are not now clearly distinguishable. But there is one very impressive correspondence. You remember that the witness, Mr. Pippet, was strongly of opinion that the hair and beard were dyed. Now, if you take my lens and examine the roots of the hair and beard, you will see plainly that it is light brown hair dyed black."

Miller and I took the lens in turn and made the examination, with the result that the condition was established beyond any possible doubt.

"Yes," Miller agreed handing back the lens, "that is dyed hair, right enough, and it seems to settle the identification."

"But we needn't leave it at that," pursued Thorndyke. "The very clothing agrees perfectly. There is the blue serge suit, the brown shoes, the wrist watch, and the additional pocket watch with its guard of plaited twine."

He took hold of the latter and drew out of the pocket a large silver watch of the kind used by navigators as a "hack watch".

"Yes," said Miller. "It's a true bill. You are right, Doctor, as you always are. These are the two men to a moral certainty."

"Isn't it rather strange," said I, "that this man should have gone about with his dyed hair and beard and the very clothes that had been

576

described at the inquest? He must have known that there would be a hue-and-cry raised after him."

"I think," said Thorndyke, "that the explanation is that this affair must have taken place within a day or two of the discovery at the station."

Miller nodded, emphatically. "I'm pretty certain you are right, Doctor," said he. "And that would account for the fact that no trace of these men was ever found. We had their descriptions circulated and the police looking for them everywhere, but nobody ever got a single glimpse of either of them. Naturally enough, as we can see now. They were lying at the bottom of this pit."

At this moment, sounds of trampling through the wood became audible and rapidly grew more distinct. At length, the sergeant and Polton emerged into the opening, followed by the patrol man and four athletic figures in blue dungaree suits, of whom two carried a folded stretcher.

"I've made all the arrangements, sir," said the sergeant, saluting as he addressed the Superintendent. "We can take the remains and the clothing in the ambulance and hand them over to the police at Dartford, and the manager of the works has kindly lent us a car to take you and the doctors to Dartford Station."

"As to me," said Miller, "I shall go on to Dartford with the ambulance. There are two suits of clothes to be examined. I want to go through them thoroughly before I return to town. What do you say, Doctor? Are you interested in the clothes?"

"I am interested," Thorndyke replied, "but I don't think I want to take part in the examination. I dare say you will let me know if anything of importance comes to light."

"You can trust me for that," said Miller. "Then I take it that you will go on to Dartford Station."

With this, we parted, Miller remaining to superintend the removal of the remains and the gear, while Thorndyke, Polton, and I retraced our way along the well-trodden track down to the road where the manager's car was waiting.

Chapter XIV
Dr. Thorndyke's Evidence

The adjourned hearing in the Probate Court opened in an atmosphere which the reporters would have described as "tense". The judge had not yet learned the result of the exhumation (or he pretended that he hadn't), and when Mr. Gimbler took his place in the witness-box, his Lordship regarded him with very evident interest and curiosity. The examination in chief was conducted by Mr. McGonnell's junior, this being the first chance that he had got of displaying his forensic skill – and a mighty small chance at that. For Gimbler's evidence amounted to no more than a recital of facts which were known to us all (excepting, perhaps, the judge) with certain inevitable inferences.

"You were present at the opening of the vault containing the coffin of Josiah Pippet, Deceased?"

"I was."

"What other persons were present?"

Mr. Gimbler enumerated the persons present and glanced at a list to make sure that he had omitted none.

"When the vault was opened, what was the appearance of the interior?"

"The whole interior and everything in it was covered with a thick coating of dust."

"Was there any sign indicating that that dust had ever been disturbed?"

"No. The surface of the dust was perfectly smooth and even, without any mark or trace of disturbance."

"What happened when the vault had been opened?"

"The coffin was brought out and placed upon trestles. Then the screws were extracted and the lid was removed in the presence of the persons whom I have named."

"Was the body of the deceased in the coffin?"

"No. There was no body in the coffin."

"What did the coffin contain?"

"It contained a roll of sheet lead and certain plumber's oddments, to wit, four lumps of lead of a hemispherical shape, such as are formed when molten lead sets in a plumber's melting-pot."

"Do those contents correspond with the traditional description of this coffin?"

"Yes. It was stated in evidence by Mr. Christopher Pippet that the traditional story told to him by his father was to the effect that the coffin was weighted with a roll of sheet lead and some plumber's oddments."

Having elicited this convincing statement, Mr. Klein sat down and, as Anstey made no sign of a wish to cross-examine the witness, Mr. Gimbler stepped down from the witness-box with a hardly-disguised smirk, and McGonnell rose.

"That is our case, my Lord," said he, and forthwith resumed his seat. There was a brief pause. Then Anstey rose and announced, "I call witnesses, my Lord," a statement that was almost immediately followed by the usher's voice, pronouncing the name, "Dr. John Thorndyke."

As my colleague stepped into the witness-box with a small portfolio under his arm, I noticed that his appearance was viewed with obvious interest by more than one person. The judge seemed to settle himself into a position of increased attention, and Mr. McGonnell regarded the new witness critically and, I thought, with slight uneasiness, while Mr. Gimbler, swinging his eyeglass pendulum-wise, made a show of being unaware of the witness's existence. But I had observed that he had taken in, with one swift glance, the fact that the usher had deposited the seven volumes of Josiah's diary, at Anstey's request, on the latter's desk. Remembering the double-barrelled microscope, I viewed those volumes with sudden interest, which was heightened when Anstey picked up one of them and, opening it, sought a particular page and handed the open volume to Thorndyke.

"This," said he, "is a volume of the diary which has been identified in evidence as the diary of Josiah Pippet. Will you kindly examine the entry dated the 8th of October, 1842."

"Yes. It reads: '*Back to the Fox. Exit G. A. and enter J. P., but not for long*'."

"Have you previously examined that entry?"

"Yes. I examined it at the last hearing very carefully with the naked eye and also with the Comparison Microscope invented by Albert S. Osborn of New York."

"Had you any reason for making so critical an examination of this passage in the diary?"

"Yes. As this is the only passage in the diary in which the identity of the Earl, George Augustus, with Josiah Pippet is explicitly stated, it seemed necessary to make sure that it was really a genuine entry."

"Had you any further reason?"

"Yes. The position of this entry, after a blank space, made it physically possible that it might have been interpolated."

"And what opinion did you form as a result of your examination?"

"I formed the opinion that this entry is not part of the original diary, but has been interpolated at some later date."

"Can you give us your reasons for forming that opinion?"

"My principal reason is that there is a slight difference in colour between this entry and the rest of the writing on this page, either preceding it or following it. The difference is hardly perceptible to the naked eye. It is more perceptible when the writing is looked at through a magnifying lens, and it is fairly distinct when examined with the differential microscope."

"Can you explain, quite briefly, the action of the differential, or Comparison Microscope?"

"In effect, this instrument is a pair of microscopes with a single eyepiece which is common to both. The two microscopes can be brought to bear on two different letters or words on different parts of a page and the two magnified images will appear in the field of the eyepiece side by side and can be so compared that very delicate differences of form and colour can be distinguished."

"Was your opinion based exclusively on the Comparison Microscope?"

"No. On observing this difference in colour, I applied for, and received, the permission of the court to have a photograph of this page made by the official photographer. This was done, and I have here two sets of the photographs, one set being direct prints from the negative, and the other enlargements. In both, but especially in the enlargements, the difference in colour is perfectly obvious."

Here Thorndyke produced from his portfolio two sets of photographs which he delivered to the usher, who passed one pair up to the judge and handed the remainder to Mr. McGonnell and the other interested parties, including myself. The judge examined the two photographs for some moments with profound attention. Then he turned to Thorndyke and asked, "Can you explain to us why differences of colour which are hardly distinguishable by the eye appear quite distinct in a photograph?"

"The reason, my Lord," replied Thorndyke, "is that the eye and the photographic plate are affected by different rays, the eye by the luminous rays and the plate by the chemical rays. But these two kinds of rays do not vary in the same proportions in different colours. Yellow, for instance, which is very luminous, gives off only feeble chemical rays, while blue, which is less luminous, gives off very powerful chemical rays. So that a yellow device on a rather deep blue ground appears to the eye light upon dark, whereas, in a photograph, it appears dark upon light."

The judge nodded. "Yes," said he, "that makes the matter quite clear."

"In what way," Anstey resumed, "does this difference in colour support your opinion that this passage has been interpolated?"

"It shows that this passage was written with a different ink from the rest of the page."

"Is there any reason why Josiah Pippet should not have used a different ink in writing this particular passage?"

"Yes. In 1842, the date of this entry, there was only one kind of black ink in use, excepting the Chinese, or Indian, ink used by draughtsmen, which this is obviously not. The common writing ink was made with galls and copperas – sulphate of iron – without any of the blue colouring which is used in modern blue-black ink. This iron-gall ink may have varied slightly in colour according to whether it was freshly made or had been exposed to the air in an ink-pot. But these differences would disappear in the course of years, as the black tannate and gallate of iron changed into the reddish-brown oxide and, there being no difference in composition, there would be no difference in the photographic reaction. In my opinion, the difference shown in the photographs indicates a difference in composition in the two inks. But a difference in composition is irreconcilable with identity in the date of this passage and the rest of the page."

"Would the difference of composition be demonstrable by a chemical test?"

"Probably, but not certainly."

"You do not question the character of the handwriting?"

"I prefer to offer no opinion on that. I detected no discrepancy that I could demonstrate."

"And now, coming from matters of opinion to demonstrable fact, what are you prepared to swear to concerning this entry in the diary?"

"That it was written with a different ink from that used in writing the rest of the page."

Having received and noted down this answer, Anstey turned over a leaf of his brief and resumed his examination.

"We will now," said he, "pass on to an entirely different subject. I believe that you have made certain investigations in the neighbourhood of Winsborough. Is that so?"

"It is."

"Perhaps, before giving us your results, it might be well if you were to tell us, in a general way, what was the object of those investigations and what led you to undertake them."

"It appeared to me," Thorndyke replied, "when I considered the story of the double life of Josiah Pippet and the Earl, George Augustus, that, although it was not impossible that it might be true, it was highly improbable. But it also seemed highly improbable that this story should have been invented by Josiah out of his inner consciousness with nothing to suggest it or give it a start. It seemed more probable that the story had its origin in some peculiar set of circumstances, the nature of which might, at some later time, be entirely misunderstood. On further consideration, I found it possible to imagine a set of circumstances such as might have given rise to this kind of misunderstanding. Thereupon, I decided to go down to Winsborough and see if I could ascertain, by investigation on the spot, whether such circumstances had, in fact, existed."

"When you went to Winsborough, you had certain specific objects in view?"

"Yes. I sought to ascertain whether there existed any evidence of the birth of Josiah Pippet, as a separate individual, and whether he was, in fact, born at the Castle, as alleged. Further, as subsidiary question, I proposed to find out, if possible, whether there was, in the neighbourhood, any ancient inn of which the sign had been changed within the last eighty years."

As Thorndyke gave this last answer, the judge looked at him with a slightly puzzled expression. Then a slow smile spread over his face and he settled himself comfortably in his chair to listen with renewed attention.

"Did your investigations lead to any discoveries?" Anstey asked.

"They did," Thorndyke replied. "First, with regard to the inns. There are two inns in the village, both of considerable age. One has the sign of The Rose and Crown, which is probably the original sign. The other has the sign of The Earl of Beaconsfield, but, as this house bears the date, 1602, and was evidently built for an inn and, as Benjamin Disraeli was created Earl of Beaconsfield only in 1876, it follows that the sign must have been altered since that date. But I could find nobody who knew what the sign had formerly been.

"I next turned my attention to the church register, and first I looked up the entry of the 9th of August 1794. On that day there were born in this small village no less than three persons. One was George Augustus, the son of the Earl of Winsborough, born at Winsborough Castle. The second was Elizabeth Blunt, daughter of Thomas Blunt, carpenter, and third was Josiah Bird, son of Isabella Bird, spinster, serving-maid to Mr. Nathaniel Pippet of this parish, and there was a note to the effect that the said Josiah was born in the house of the said Nathaniel Pippet.

"I followed the entries in the register in search of further information concerning these persons. Three years later, on the 6th of June, 1797, there was a record of the marriage of Nathaniel Pippet, widower, and Isabella Bird, spinster. Two months later, on the 14th of August, 1797, there was recorded the death of Nathaniel Pippet of this parish, inn-keeper, and three months after this, on the 8th of November, 1797, was an entry recording the birth of Susan Pippet, the posthumous daughter of Nathaniel Pippet, Deceased. This child lived only four days, as her death is recorded in an entry dated the 12th of November, 1797.

"As none of these entries gave any particulars as to the residence of Nathaniel Pippet, I proceeded to explore the churchyard. There I found a tombstone the inscription on which set forth that '*Here lieth the body of Nathaniel Pippet, late keeper of the Castle Inn in this parish, who departed this life the 14th day of August, 1797*'. As there was no other entry in the register, this must have been the Nathaniel Pippet referred to in the entry which I have mentioned. I took a photograph of this tombstone and I produced enlarged copies of that photograph."

As he spoke, Thorndyke opened his portfolio and took out a number of mounted enlargements which he delivered to the usher, who handed one to the judge and passed the others round to the various interested parties. Looking round the court, I was amused to note the expressions with which the different parties regarded the photograph. The judge inspected it with deep interest and an obvious effort to maintain a becoming gravity. So also with Brodribb, whose struggles to suppress his feelings produced a conspicuous heightening of his naturally florid complexion. Mrs. Engleheart viewed the photograph with polite and unsmiling indifference. The young people, Mr. Giles and Miss Jenifer (who, for some reason, known only to the usher, had a single copy between them), giggled frankly. Mr. Gimbler and his two counsel examined the exhibit with wooden-faced attention. The only person who made no attempt to "conceal or cloak" his amusement was Mr. Christopher Pippet, who inspected the photograph through horn-rimmed spectacles and laughed joyously.

When the photograph reached me the cause of his hilarity became apparent. It happens often enough that the designs on ancient rural tombstones are such as tend "to produce in the sinful a smile". But it was not the work of the artless village mason that was the cause of Mr. Pippet's amusement. The joke was in the inscription, which ran thus:

Here lyeth ye Bodey
of NATHANIEL PIPPET late Keeper of The
CASTLE INN in this Parish who Departed this
Life ye 14th Day of August in ye Year of Our Lord
1797 Aged 58 years. He was an Honest Man and a
good Inn Keeper who sold no Ale but the Best.

He that buys Land buys Stones
He that buys Meate buys Bones
He that buys Egges buys Many Shelles
But He that buys Good Beer buys Nothing Elles.

584

The verses were certainly unconventional and tended to engender the suspicion that the jovial Nathaniel might have embodied them in certain testamentary dispositions. But however that may have been, the inscription was profoundly significant.

Having given time for the inspection of the photographs, Anstey resumed his examination.

"What inferences do you deduce from these facts which you have discovered?" he asked. But, at this point, Mr. McGonnell rose and objected that the witness's inferences were not evidence.

"The learned counsel is technically correct," said the judge, "and I must allow his objection if he insists, though, in the case of an expert witness, where an investigation has been made *ad hoc*, it is customary to allow the witness to explain the bearing of the facts which he has elicited."

The learned counsel was, however, disposed to insist and the question was accordingly ruled out.

"Apart from any inferences," said Anstey, "what facts have your investigations disclosed?"

"They have disclosed the fact," replied Thorndyke, "that on the 9th of August, 1794, the day on which the Earl, George Augustus, was born at Winsborough Castle, there was born at The Castle at Winsborough an individual named Josiah whose mother subsequently married Nathaniel Pippet."

"That fact is the sum of what you discovered?"

"Yes."

"And what relation does that bear to the imaginary set of circumstances of which you have told us?"

"The circumstances that thus came to light were substantially identical with those which I had postulated theoretically."

Anstey noted down this answer and then proceeded. "You were present at the exhumation of the coffin of Josiah Pippet with the other persons who have been mentioned?"

"I was."

"Did the appearances which you observed seem to you to agree with the conditions which were assumed to exist – that this coffin had lain undisturbed in this vault for eighty years?"

"No. In my opinion, the appearances were not reconcilable with that assumption."

"In what respect did the appearances disagree with the ostensible conditions?"

"There were three respects in which the appearances disagreed with the conditions which were assumed to exist. The disagreements were concerned with the dust in the vault, the coffin, and the contents of the coffin."

"Let us take those disagreements in order. First, as to the dust. Do you say that there were signs that it had been disturbed?"

"No. The dust that was there had not been disturbed since it was deposited. But it had not the characteristics of ancient dust, or of any dust which might have become deposited in a vault above ground which was situated in an open burial ground, remote from any dwelling house."

"What are the distinguishing peculiarities of such ancient dust?"

"The dust which would be deposited in a vault over a period of eighty years would consist of very light and minute particles of matter, such as would be capable of floating in still air. There would be no mineral particles, excepting excessively minute particles of the lighter minerals, and very few of these. Practically the whole of the dust would consist of tiny fragments of organic matter, of which a large part would be derived from textiles. As these fragments would be of all sorts of colours, the resulting dust would be of no colour at all – that is to say, of a perfectly neutral grey. But this dust was not of a perfectly neutral grey. It had a very faint tinge of red, and this extremely faint tinge of colour was distinguishable in the whole of the dust, not only in one part. I accordingly took two samples for examination, one from the coffin and one from the shelf on which it rested, and I have since made a microscopical examination of each of these samples separately."

"And what conclusion did you arrive at as a result of your examination?"

"I came to the conclusion that the whole of this dust had been derived from a single room. That room was covered with a carpet which had a red ground with a pattern principally of green and blue with a little black. There was also in this room a cotton drapery of some kind – either a table-cloth or curtains – dyed a darkish blue."

"Those are your conclusions. Can you give us the actual facts which you observed?"

"On examining the dust through the microscope, I observed that it consisted chiefly of woollen fibres dyed a bright red. There were also woollen fibres dyed green and blue, but smaller in number than the red, and a still smaller number of woollen fibres dyed black, together with a few cotton fibres dyed a darkish blue. In addition to the fibres, there were rather numerous particles of coal and some other minerals, very small in size, but much too large to float in still air. I have here two samples of the dust mounted and arranged in small hand microscopes. On holding the microscopes up to the light, it is quite easy to see the fibres which I have described and also one or two particles of coal."

He handed the two little instruments (in which I recognized the handiwork of the ingenious and indefatigable Polton) to the usher, who passed them up to the judge. His Lordship examined each of them with deep interest and then returned them to the usher, by whom they were handed, first to McGonnell and then to the other parties to the case. Eventually, they came to me, and I was surprised to see how efficiently these little instruments served their purpose. On turning them towards the window, the coloured fibres were visible with brilliant distinctness, in spite of the low magnification. And their appearance, corresponding exactly with Thorndyke's description, was absolutely convincing, as I gathered from the decidedly glum expression that began to spread over Mr. McGonnell's countenance.

When the dust had been inspected, Anstey resumed his examination.

"Can you account for the presence of this dust in the vault?"

"Only in general terms. Since it was obviously not derived from anything in the vault itself, or the immediate neighbourhood of the vault, it must have been brought there from some other place."

"Can you suggest a method of procedure which would have produced the appearances which you observed?"

"A possible method, and the one which I have no doubt was employed, would be this: First, the sweepings from the room, or more probably the accumulations from the receiver of a vacuum-cleaner, would be collected and conveyed to the vault. There, the dust could be blown into the air of the upper part of the vault by means of a vacuum-cleaner with the valve reversed, or more conveniently by means of a common pair of bellows, the dust being fed into the valve-hole. If it were blown up towards the roof, it would float in the air and settle down slowly, falling eventually in a perfectly even manner on the coffin, the shelf, and the floor, producing exactly the appearance that was seen."

"You are not prepared to swear that this was the method actually employed?"

"No, but it would be *a* possible method, and I cannot think of any other."

"Well," said Anstey, "the method is not important. We will let it go and come to another matter. You referred to three discrepancies in the appearances, the dust, the coffin, and the contents of the latter. In what way did the coffin disagree with the ostensible conditions?"

"The coffin was assumed to have been lying undisturbed in the vault for eighty years. That was not the case. If this was the original coffin, it had certainly been opened and re-closed since the year 1854."

"How are you able to fix the date so exactly?"

"By the screws with which the lid was fastened down. These screws are in the possession of Detective-Superintendent Miller, who is now in court."

Here the Superintendent rose and, producing an envelope, handed it to the usher, who passed it up to the judge. He then evicted Thorndyke from the witness-box and, taking his place, was duly sworn and, in reply to a question from Anstey, declared that the screws in the envelope were the screws which had been extracted in his presence from the coffin of Josiah Pippet.

The judge opened the envelope and tipped the screws out into the palm of his hand. Then he remarked – in almost the very words that I had heard the Superintendent use – that he did not see anything at all unusual about them. "To my unsophisticated eye," he concluded, "they look like the kind of screws that one could buy at any ironmonger's."

"That, my Lord," said Thorndyke – who had, in his turn, evicted the Superintendent and resumed his place in the witness-box – "is exactly what they are, and that is the fact which gives them their evidential importance. This coffin was supposed to have been screwed down in the year 1843. But in that year, you could not have bought screws like these at any ironmonger's. There were no such screws in existence. At that time, wood screws were like metal screws, excepting as to their threads. They were flat-ended, so that, in order to drive them in, it was necessary to bore a hole as deep as the screw was long. But about 1850, an American inventor devised and patented a sharp-pointed, or gimlet-ended screw, which would find its own way through wood, regardless of the depth of the hole. Later, he came to England to dispose of his patent rights, and in 1854 he sold them to Chamberlain and Nettlefolds, who thereupon acquired the virtual monopoly of the manufacture of wood screws, for, owing to the great superiority of the sharp-pointed screw, the old, blunt-ended screw went completely out of use. I am able, by the kindness of the Master of the Worshipful Company of Ironmongers, to show a set of the old type of screws, the date of manufacture being 1845."

Here he produced a wooden tablet to which were secured six screws of various sizes with blunt, flattened ends like the screws still used by metal workers. The tablet was passed up to the judge, who inspected it curiously and compared the screws on it with those from the envelope.

"It is always easy," he moralized, "to be wise after the event, but it does really seem astonishing that mankind should have had to wait until 1854 for so obvious an improvement."

With this he returned the coffin screws to the envelope and handed the latter and the museum tablet to the usher, who proceeded to pass them round for inspection. I watched their progress with considerable interest, noting their effect on the different parties to the case. Particularly interested was I to observe the expression on Mr. McGonnell's face as he compared the two exhibits. There was no question as to his recognition of their significance and, by the flush that rose to his face, and the unmistakable expression of anger, I judged that Mr. Gimbler had not taken him into his confidence and that these revelations were coming to him as a very disagreeable surprise.

When the screws had been inspected by the principal parties, Anstey resumed his examination.

"When you stated the latest date at which this coffin could have been screwed down, you used the qualification, 'If this was the original coffin'. Did you mean to express a doubt that this was the original coffin?"

"Yes. My opinion is that it is not the original coffin, but a new one to which the brass name plate and other metal 'furniture' from the original coffin have been screwed. The plate and handles appeared to me to be the original ones, and they appeared to be fastened on with the original brass screws. The slots of those screws showed clear indications of their having been unscrewed quite recently."

"What were your reasons for believing that this was a new coffin rather than the old one, opened and reclosed?"

"There were several reasons. First, there were the screws. These were modern screws, apparently artificially rusted. At any rate, they were rusty. But if the original coffin had been opened and re-closed, it would be natural for the screws which had been extracted to be used to fasten down the lid. There would be no object in obtaining rusty screws to use in their place. Then the coffin did not look old. It was much discoloured, but the discolouration did not look like the effect of age but rather like that of staining. Further, the coffin was covered, both inside and out, with a thick coating of mildew. But there was nothing to account for this mildew. The wood was not damp, and it had the character of new wood. The mildew had the appearance of having been produced artificially by coating the surface with some substance such as size, mixed with sugar or glycerine. Moreover, on the assumption that some substitution had been made – which all the appearances indicated – it would obviously be more convenient to use a new coffin than to open and remove the contents of the old, particularly if the old one should have happened to contain a body. But that is a matter of inference. Taking only the appearances observed, I consider that they indicated that this was a new coffin."

"Then," said Anstey, "we now come to the third set of disagreements, the contents of the coffin. What have you to tell us about those?"

"The contents of the coffin," Thorndyke replied, "were, according to the traditional account, a roll of sheet lead and some plumber's oddments, which had been left over from some repairs. Now, sheet lead, removed in 1843, or earlier, from the roof of a house, would, even then, be old lead. It would certainly be cast sheet – cast upon a sand casting table, and it would certainly contain a considerable proportion of silver. But the sheet of lead which was found in the coffin was the ordinary milled sheet which has, in recent times, replaced the old cast sheet. As to the amount of silver that it contained, I could form no opinion. I therefore suggested that an assay should be made to ascertain the silver content. This proposal was contested by Mr. Gimbler on the ground that we had no authority to make an assay, and by Mr. McGonnell on the ground that the evidence was of a kind that would not be taken seriously by the court. And Mr. Brodribb objected, apparently on the ground that the proceeding would seem to throw doubt on the good faith of the applicant. Accordingly, I did not press my proposal, but I made a careful examination of the contents of the coffin, with very surprising results. in addition to the sheet lead, the coffin contained four hemispherical lumps of metal which had apparently solidified in a plumber's melting pot, which we may call pot-leavings. There were four of these, one large and three smaller. The large one had the appearance and all the visible and palpable properties of lead, and I had no doubt that it was lead. The other three were evidently not lead, but had the appearance and properties of an alloy of lead and some other metal."

"Bid you form any opinion as to the nature of the other metal?"

"I did, but with the reservation that the inference seemed so incredible that I was doubtful about accepting it."

"What was the opinion that you formed as to the nature of these lumps of lead alloy?"

"I was forced to the conclusion that they were composed of an alloy of lead and platinum."

"Platinum!" exclaimed the judge. "But is not platinum a very rare and precious metal?"

"It is always a precious metal," Thorndyke replied, "and since the war it has become extremely scarce and its value has gone up to an extravagant extent. At present, it is several times more valuable than gold."

"And how much platinum did you consider to be present in these lumps of alloy?" the judge asked.

"I estimated the weight of the three lumps together at about a hundredweight and, about half that weight appeared to be platinum."

"Half-a-hundredweight of platinum!" exclaimed the judge. "It does indeed seem incredible. Why, it is a fortune. What do you suppose the value of that amount would be?"

"At the present inflated prices," replied Thorndyke, "I should put it at anything from fifteen- to seventeen-thousand pounds."

"It is beyond belief," said the judge. "However, we shall see." And with this he sat back in his chair and glanced at Anstey.

"As this opinion seems to be so utterly incredible, even to yourself," said Anstey, resuming his examination, "perhaps you might explain to us how you arrived at it."

"It was principally a question of weight," Thorndyke replied.

"But," said Anstey, "have you had sufficient experience to be able to detect platinum in an alloy by the sense of weight to the hand?"

"No," Thorndyke answered, "but it was not a case of absolute weight, or I should have been still less confident. There was a term of comparison. When I picked up the big lump, it felt just as I should expect a lump of lead of that size to feel. But when I then picked up the first of the smaller ones, I received a shock, for, though it was little more than half the size of the big one, it was nearly as heavy. Now, there are not many metals that are much heavier than lead. For practical purposes, ignoring the rare metals, there are only two – gold and platinum. This did not look like gold, but it might have been, a mass of gold, for instance, with a lead casing. On the other hand, its colour – a faint, purplish grey – was exactly that of a lead-platinum alloy. So there seemed to be no escape from the conclusion that that was what it was."

While this evidence was being given, I kept my eyes on Mr. Gimbler and his leading counsel. The latter listened in undisguised astonishment and little less disguised displeasure. Obviously, he had begun to smell a rat and, as it was not his rat, he naturally resented its presence. But even Gimbler failed to maintain the aspect of wooden indifference that he had preserved hitherto. This disclosure had evidently sprung on him a complete surprise and, as I looked at him and noted the dismay which he struggled in vain to conceal, I found myself wondering whether, by any chance, the expression of consternation on his face might have some significance other than mere surprise. But my speculations were cut short by Anstey, who was continuing his examination.

591

"Have you anything more to tell us about the contents of this coffin?"

"No," was the reply. "That is all the information that I have to give."

On receiving this reply, Anstey sat down and McGonnell was rising to cross-examine when the judge interposed.

"Before we pass on to other matters," said he, "we ought to be a little more clear about the nature of this metal which was found in the coffin. That is a question which is highly relevant to the issues which are before the court. But it is also relevant to certain other issues concerned with public policy. Dr. Thorndyke is not prepared to say definitely that this is actually platinum, but he is evidently convinced – and on apparently sufficient grounds – that it is. But the question cannot be left at that. It can be settled with certainty, and it should be. Do I understand that this metal, worth possibly many thousands of pounds, is still lying in that coffin?"

This question was addressed to Thorndyke, who accordingly replied, "No, my Lord. As my proposal of an assay was rejected, and in view of the questions of public policy to which your Lordship has referred, I informed Mr. Superintendent Miller that, in my opinion, an examination of the pot-leavings would yield information of great importance to the police. The Superintendent thereupon took possession of the whole of the contents of the coffin and conveyed them to the premises of Mr. Daniels, the eminent assayist, and left them there for an assay to be made."

"And has an assay been made?" the judge asked.

"I believe it has, my Lord, but I have no information as to the result. Mr. Superintendent Miller is now in court."

Here the Superintendent rose and approached the solicitor's table carrying a small but obviously heavy box, which he laid on the table.

"I think," said the judge, "that what the Superintendent has to tell us should go in evidence."

Accordingly, Miller once more evicted Thorndyke from the witness-box, and the judge continued, "You have already been sworn, Superintendent. Will you now give the facts, so far as they are known to you, concerning the contents of this coffin?"

The Superintendent stood at "attention" and delivered himself of his evidence with a readiness born of long practice.

"In consequence of certain information communicated by Dr. Thorndyke, I took possession of the contents of the coffin alleged to be that of Josiah Pippet, Deceased, and conveyed them forthwith to the premises of Mr. Daniels in Bishopsgate and delivered them to him with instructions to make a trial assay and report to me what he found. On the

592

same evening, I received a report from him in which he informed me that he had ascertained the following facts: The roll of sheet lead was practically pure lead, almost completely free from silver, and was probably of recent manufacture. The large pot-leaving was also pure lead of the modern silver-free type. The three smaller pot-leavings were composed of a lead-platinum alloy, of which about half by weight was platinum. On receiving this report, I directed Mr. Daniels to recover the whole of the platinum in a pure state and deliver it to me. He did this, and I have here, in the box on the table, the platinum which I received from him and which he assured me is practically the whole of the platinum which was contained in the pot-leavings. It amounts, roughly, to just under half-a-hundredweight."

As he concluded, he stepped down from the witness-box and, approaching the table, unlocked a small padlock of the Yale type by which the hasp of the box was secured and opened the lid. Then, from the interior, he lifted out, one after another, eight little bright, silvery-looking bars, or ingots, and laid them in a row on the table. Picking up the end one, he handed it up to the judge, who weighed it in the palm of his hand, looking at it with a faint smile of amusement. When he received it back from the judge, Miller carried it round the court and allowed each of the interested parties to take it in his hand and, when it came to my turn, and the Superintendent handed it to me (with something exceedingly like a wink, and a sly glance at Thorndyke), I understood the judge's smile. There was something ridiculous in the monstrous disproportion between the size of the little bar and its weight, for, small as it was, it had the weight of a good-sized iron dumb-bell.

When Miller had returned the bars to the box and locked the padlock, he went back to the witness-box to await further questions or cross-examination, but, as neither of the counsel made any sign, the judge dismissed him and then announced the adjournment of the hearing. "I regret," he added, "that, in consequence of other and more urgent business, it will have to be adjourned for a week. The delay is unfortunate, but," here he glanced at McGonnell with a faint smile, "it will have the advantage that learned counsel will have time to consider their cross-examination of Dr. Thorndyke."

Hereupon the court rose and we all prepared to take our departure. Glancing at "the other side", I observed Mr. Pippet looking a little wistfully in our direction as if he would have liked to come and speak to us. But apparently his native wisdom and good sense told him that the occasion was inopportune and, after a momentary hesitation, he turned away with a somewhat troubled face and followed his legal representatives out of the court.

Chapter XV
A Journey and
a Discussion

"This adjournment," remarked the Superintendent as he attached a strong leather rug-strap to his precious box, "is a piece of luck for me – at least I am hoping that it is. You'll have tomorrow free I suppose, Doctor?

"I have got plenty to do tomorrow," Thorndyke answered, "but I haven't any appointments, as I expected to be here. Why do you ask?"

"Because," replied Miller, "I have had a bit of luck of another sort. I told you that the suspected yacht was laid up in Benfleet Creek with her hatches sealed and a local boat-builder told off to keep an eye on her. Well, it seems that this man – his name is Jaff – spotted some Johnnie trying to break into her in the cool of the evening, about eleven p.m. So Mr. Jaff collared the said Johnnie after a bit of a tussle and handed him over to the local police.

"Then the police had a brain-wave – quite a good one too. They phoned down to Southend for the Customs officers who had rummaged the yacht when she arrived from her voyage. So the Preventive men – there were two of them – hopped into the train and came over to have a look at the chappie who had been nabbed, and they both recognized him, at once, as one of the three men they had seen on board the yacht when they rummaged her. And one of them remembered his name – Bunter – and when it was mentioned, he didn't deny it, though he had given a false name, as the police had already assumed, when he said it was John Smith. Of course, there are people in the world named John Smith. Plenty of them. But the crook is apt to exaggerate the number.

"Well, when we got notice of the capture, we thought at first of having him sent up to the Yard to see if we could get a statement from him. But then I thought it would be better for me to go down and have a talk with him on the spot and just have a look at the yacht at the same time. And that's where you come in – at least I hope you do, as you seem to be like one of those blooming spiders that I've heard about that have got eyes all over them. What do you say? I think you would find it an interesting little jaunt."

594

Thorndyke appeared to think so too, for he accepted the invitation at once and included me in the acceptance, as I also had the day at my disposal. Accordingly, we settled the program, much to the Superintendent's satisfaction and, having arranged to meet on the following morning at Fenchurch Street Station, we escorted Miller, with his precious burden, to his car and bade him *au revoir*.

"I agree with Miller," said I, as, having achieved the perilous crossing of the Strand, we strolled towards the Temple Gate. "This is a bit of luck. A nice little trip to the seaside instead of a day in that stuffy court. And it will probably be quite amusing."

"I hope it will be more than amusing," said Thorndyke. "We ought to be able to pick up some useful facts. We want them badly enough, for there are a lot of gaps that we have to fill up."

"What gaps are you referring to?" I asked.

"Well," he replied, "look at our case as it stands. It is a mere collection of disconnected facts. And yet we know that those facts must be connected, and that we have got to establish the connexion. Take this platinum, for instance. It disappears from the cloak room and is lost to view utterly. Then it reappears in the coffin, and the problem is, how did it get there, where has it been in the interval, and what is Gimbler's connexion with it?"

"Aren't we rather guessing about that platinum?" I objected. "We all seem to be assuming that this platinum is the platinum that was stolen."

"And reasonably so, I think," said Thorndyke. "Consider the probabilities, Jervis. If it had been a case of an ounce, or even a pound, there might have been room for doubt. But half-a-hundredweight, at a time when every grain of platinum is precious and worth many times its weight of gold, and at a time when that very weight of platinum has been stolen and is still missing – well, we may be mistaken, but we are justified in accepting the overwhelming probabilities. And, after all, it is only a working hypothesis."

"Yes," I admitted, "I suppose you are right, and we shall soon know if you are on the wrong track. But you are also assuming that Gimbler has some connexion with it. You haven't much to go on."

Thorndyke laughed. "You are a regular Devil's advocate, Jervis," said he. "But you are right, so far. We haven't much to go on. Still, I suppose you will agree that we have fair grounds for assuming that Gimbler has some connexion with that bogus coffin."

"Yes," I was forced to admit, "I will concede that much, as the coffin appears to have been planted there to furnish evidence in support of his case. But I am not so clear as to the connexion between Gimbler and that platinum. He seemed mighty surprised when you mentioned it."

"He did," Thorndyke agreed, "and there is certainly something extremely odd about the whole affair. But you see the position. Gimbler arranges for a dummy coffin to be planted, and that dummy coffin is found to contain the proceeds of a robbery. There is thus established a connexion of some sort between Gimbler and this stolen property. We cannot guess the nature of the connexion. It may be of the most indirect kind. Apparently Gimbler had no suspicion of the nature of the metal in the coffin. But some kind of connexion between that loot and Mr. Gimbler there must be. And it is not impossible that the platinum may eventually be the means of pointing the way to some unguarded spot in Gimbler's defences, for I take it that there will be considerable difficulty in getting direct evidence of his part in the planting of the coffin."

His conclusion brought us to our doorstep, at which point the discussion lapsed. But I felt that it was only an adjournment, for something in the Superintendent's manner had suggested to me that he, also, had certain questions to propound.

And so it turned out. On our arrival on the platform at Fenchurch Street, I perceived the Superintendent doing "sentry-go" before the door of an empty first-class smoking compartment, and I suspected that he had made certain private arrangements with the guard. At any rate, we had the compartment to ourselves, and when we had passed the first few stations in safety, he proceeded to fire his first shot.

"I've been puzzling my brains, Doctor, about those pot-leavings."

"Indeed?" said Thorndyke. "What is the difficulty?"

"The difficulty is how the deuce they became pot-leavings. I have always understood that platinum was almost impossible to melt. Isn't that so?"

"Platinum is very difficult to melt," Thorndyke agreed. "It has the highest melting-point of all metals, excepting one or two of the rare metals. The melting-point is 1,710 Centigrade."

"And what is the melting-point of cast iron?"

"1,505 Centigrade," Thorndyke answered.

"Then," exclaimed Miller, "if it takes about two-hundred degrees more to melt platinum than it does to melt iron, how the devil was it possible to melt the platinum in a common plumber's melting-pot which is made of cast iron? It would seem as if the pot should melt before the platinum."

"So it would, of course, if the metal had been pure," Thorndyke replied with a smile that suggested to me that he had been expecting the question, and that something of importance turned on it. "But it was not

596

pure. It was an alloy, and alloys exhibit all kinds of queer anomalies in respect to their melting-points. However, with your permission, we will postpone the discussion of this point, as we shall have to consider it in connexion with certain other matters that we have to discuss. You have not told us whether those clothes from the two dead men yielded any information."

"They gave us the means of identifying the two men, as you will have learned from the reports of the inquest, and the names were apparently their real names, or at least their usual aliases. The murderer, Bassett, the skipper of the yacht, was a local man, as you guessed. He lived at Swanscombe, and seems to have been a Swanscombe man, which accounts, as you suggested, for his knowledge of the dene hole. The man he killed, Wicks, was living at Woolwich at the time, but he seemed to be a bird of passage. That is all that I got out of the clothes excepting the name and address of a man called Samuels, who describes himself as a gold refiner and bullion dealer, but who may be a fence. We know him by name, but we haven't anything against him, though we bear him in mind. These small bullion dealers have to be kept in view, as they have so many facilities for getting rid of stolen jewellery and plate."

"Yes," Thorndyke agreed, "and in the special circumstances, any refiner and bullion dealer is of interest to us. It seems likely that Bassett intended to approach this man, Samuels, on the object of the disposal of the platinum, if he hadn't already made some arrangements with him. You'll have to continue to keep Mr. Samuels in view. But now tell us a little more about this present business."

"There isn't much more to tell you," said Miller. "It seems that Mr. Jaff, the boat-builder gent, was cruising about Benfleet Creek in his dinghy – he lives afloat, himself – when he saw our friend, Bunter, trying to prise open the yacht's fore scuttle, whereupon, having a natural prejudice against people who break into yachts, he pulled alongside, stepped on board and, creeping silently along the deck in his rubber mud-boots, grabbed Bunter and hauled him into his dinghy, where they seem to have had a mighty scrap until another mariner came along and lent a hand. Then they got him ashore and handed him over to the local police as I have told you."

"What do you suppose could have been his object in trying to break into the vessel?" I asked. "There wasn't anything of value left on board, was there?"

"There was not supposed to be," said Miller, with a knowing look, "but I have an idea that there may have been. My notion is that there may have been more platinum than we thought, and that he had come to snap up what was left. What do you say, Doctor?"

Thorndyke shook his head. "I don't think so, Miller," he replied. "You have recovered practically all the platinum that was said to have been stolen. My impression is that, as our friend Mr. Pippet might express it, you are barking up the wrong tree."

"Am I?" said Miller. "Then if you will point out the right tree, I'll bark up that. What do you think was his object in trying to break in?"

"My idea is," Thorndyke replied, "that he supposed that the whole of the platinum was still on board."

"But," protested Miller, "how could he? He knew that Bassett had carted the bulk of it away."

Thorndyke chuckled. "My impression is, Miller," said he, "that it was at this point that the chapter of accidents began, and it is here that the answer to the question that you raised just now comes in."

"About the melting-pot?" demanded Miller.

"Yes. I have a theory that the whole mystery of the murder and the appearance of the platinum in the coffin hinges on that question. Perhaps, as we have some time at our disposal, there would be no harm in my giving the reins to my fancy and sketching out my hypothetical scheme of the events as I believe they occurred."

"Do, by all means," Miller exclaimed, eagerly, "for, if your imaginary scheme satisfies you, it is likely to satisfy me."

"Then," said Thorndyke, "I will begin with what I believe to have been the hiding-place in which the platinum was concealed on the yacht."

"But, good Lord, Doctor" Miller exclaimed, "you've never seen the yacht!"

"It wasn't necessary," Thorndyke replied. "I had your description of the yacht and of the search made by the Customs officer, and they seemed to me to indicate an excellent hiding-place. When you described how that officer crept down into the hold and found it all perfectly clear and empty with the exception of the lead ballast-weights, it occurred to me that it was quite possible that the platinum was staring him in the face all the time. Remember that he was not looking for platinum but for tobacco."

"Do you suggest that the platinum was hidden in the ballast-weights?" Miller demanded.

"That is exactly what I do suggest," replied Thorndyke, "and I will describe to you what I believe to have been the method used in concealing it. You will remember that these weights were proper yacht's ballast, lead weights cast to a correct shape to fit the timbers and sits comfortably along the kelson. Each would probably weight about half-a-hundredweight, that being the usual and most convenient weight. Now, my theory is that our friends took with them a mould of the ballast-weights – an ordinary sand-flask would do, though a fireclay mould would be more convenient – so that they could cast new weights whenever they might want them. Possibly they also took some spare lead with them.

"Now, as soon as they had got possession of the platinum – which, you will remember, was in thin sheets – they cut it up into suitably sized pieces, or rolled or folded it up to a size that would go easily into the mould. They put the pieces into the mould, probably propping them up a little with some pieces of lead to keep them off the bottom, so that the platinum should not be visible on the surface. Then they melted some spare lead, or one of the ballast-weights and poured the molten lead into the mould. When the lead set solid, there would be a quite ordinary-looking ballast-weight. Then they did the same with the rest of the platinum, producing a second ballast-weight, and the two could be laid down with the rest of the weights alongside the keel. If there was any lead left over, that would be thrown overboard together with the mould."

"Yes," said Miller, "that sounds quite convincing. Deuced ingenious, too. Uncommonly neat. That's how they were able to walk past the customs in the way they did. But where does the chapter of accidents come in?"

"It came in at that point," said Thorndyke. "Somebody had made a trifling miscalculation. I don't say that Bassett made the mistake, though I suspect that he did. But someone did. You know, Miller, as well as I do that people who embark on a fake of any kind need to have a good deal of knowledge. And usually they haven't. Our friend, Gimbler, didn't know enough about dust, and the craftsman who made the bogus coffin didn't know enough about screws. And I suspect that the downy bird who invented the ballast-weight dodge didn't know enough about platinum.

"The rock, I think, on which these gentry split was this: Most people know, as you know, that platinum is one of the most infusible of metals. It cannot be melted in any ordinary furnace. Only a very special furnace, or the most powerful type of blowpipe, will melt it. Now, to a person who knew that, and no more, it would naturally seem that platinum, put into a mould and then covered up with melted lead, would simply be imbedded in lead. And, since lead is very easily fusible – it melts at the comparatively low temperature of three-hundred-twenty-five degrees Centigrade – it would naturally seem that, when it was required to recover the platinum, all that would be necessary would be to melt the lead weight and pick out the platinum."

"Yes," agreed Miller, "that seems perfectly feasible. What's the snag?"

"The snag is," replied Thorndyke, "that platinum has one most singular property. Everyone knows that you can melt lead in an iron ladle or pot, and it would be quite natural to infer that, since platinum is more difficult to melt than iron, it would be equally easy to melt lead in a platinum ladle or pot. But the inference would be quite wrong. If you were to try to melt lead in a platinum pot, the bottom of the pot would drop out. In spite of its enormously high melting-point, platinum dissolves freely in melted lead."

"The deuce it does!" exclaimed Miller. "That is most extraordinary."

"It is," Thorndyke agreed, "and it is a property of the metal that would be totally unexpected by anyone who did not happen to know it. And now you will see how this curious fact affects our problem. Supposing the platinum to have been put into the mould as I have described, and the melted lead poured in on top of it, and supposing the thieves – or some of them – to be unacquainted with this property of the metal. They would expect, as I have said, that when they wanted to recover the platinum, all they would have to do would be to melt the lead weight and pick out the platinum with tongs.

"Now our friend Wicks, who made the exchange at the cloak room was evidently 'in the know'. He knew what was in the case that he stole, and he had come to get that case. The relic that he left in exchange was, I feel sure, merely a by-product. It may even have furnished the means or the suggestion for the exchange. Obviously, he had the thing on his hands, and it was the kind of thing that he would naturally wish to get rid of and, if he was able to get a suitable case, as he evidently was, the exchange was a quite masterly tactical plan. But I think we may take it that it was the case – worth fifteen-thousand pounds – that he had come for.

"We will assume that he knew the platinum to be concealed in the lead weights. It is practically certain that he did. He was one of the yacht's crew, or gang, and the thing must have been known to all of them. Probably he had seen the job carried out, but, at any rate, he knew what had been done. Accordingly, as soon as he had got his booty into a safe place, he proceeded to melt down the lead weights to get at the platinum.

"And then it was, I suggest, that the fatal mistake occurred. As the weights melted, he looked for the platinum to appear. Apparently, he fished for it with a ladle and then transferred the molten metal by degrees to some empty pots. But when he had ladled the whole of it into the other pots, there was still no sign of the platinum. To his eye, the pots contained nothing but melted lead.

"Now, what would he be likely to think, under the circumstances? He might have thought that Bassett had made a mistake and put the wrong weights into the case, but more probably (seeing that he had tried to rob the gang and snatch the whole of the booty for himself and the confederate who had helped him to carry off the case) he would think that he had been suspected and that 'the boss' had deliberately laid a booby-trap for him by planting a couple of the plain lead weights in the case. At any rate, he had, apparently, got nothing but a quantity of lead. What did he do with that lead? We have no means of judging. He may have thrown it away in disgust or he may have sold it to a plumber for a few pence. But, if we accept this hypothetical construction of the course of events, we can see how these lumps of lead-platinum alloy came into being."

"Yes," Miller agreed, "it all fits the facts perfectly, even to the murder of Wicks. For, of course, each of these two rascals, Wicks and Bassett, thought the other had nobbled the whole of the swag. My eye! What a lark it is!" He laughed grimly and then added, "But I begin to have an inkling of the way you dropped on that dene hole so readily. You'd been keeping an account of the case all along. I wonder if you can make any suggestion as to how that stuff got into the coffin, and who put it there."

"I am afraid not, Miller," Thorndyke replied. "You see that the hypothetical sketch that I have given you is based on known facts and fair probabilities. But the facts that we have do not carry us much farther. Still, there is one fact that we must not overlook."

"What is that?" Miller demanded, eagerly.

"You will admit, I think," said Thorndyke, "that the faking of that coffin must have been carried out on the initiative and under the direction of Gimbler. There is really no reasonable alternative."

"Unless Mr. Pippet did the job himself, which doesn't seem at all likely, though he may have been a party to it. But I agree with you. Gimbler must have been the moving spirit, and probably Pippet knows nothing about it."

"That is my own view," said Thorndyke. "Tippet impresses me as a perfectly honest man, and I have no doubt that the planting of the coffin was exclusively Gimbler's scheme, carried out by certain agents. But one of these agents must have had these lumps of alloy in his possession – unconscious, of course, of their nature. But that agent must have been in touch, directly or indirectly, with Wicks. Now, it ought not to be impossible to discover who that agent was. There are several ways of approach to the problem. One of them, perhaps, is Mr. Bunter. Since Wicks was not on board the yacht when Bassett took away the case of platinum, he must have had a confederate who was. Now, there were only two men left when Bassett had gone – not counting the man whom the Customs officer saw, who seems to have been a stranger who had probably taken a passage on the yacht and is not really in the picture at all. As Bunter was one of those two, there is, at least, an even chance that he was Wicks's confederate and, when you come to have a talk with him, you must bear in mind that he, also, may be assumed to be unaware of the change that the platinum would undergo when the melted lead was poured on to it."

"Yes, by Jove!" Miller agreed. "I begin to hope that we may get something really useful out of Mr. Bunter, if we deal with him tactfully. But Lord! What a stroke of luck it was for me that you were able to come with me on this jaunt. If it hadn't been for what you have just told us, I might have missed the whole point of his story, even if he was prepared to tell one. I shouldn't have known any more about it than he did."

As Miller concluded this frank and generous acknowledgment, the train began to slow down and presently drew up at Benfleet Station. A sergeant of the local police was waiting on the platform and, when we had introduced ourselves, he took us in charge and conducted us out of the station. A few steps took us to the waterside, where we halted to survey the interminable levels of Canvey Island and the winding creek, now full of water, with its amazing assemblage of house boats and floating shacks of all kinds.

"That's the *Cormorant*," said the sergeant, pointing to a sturdy-looking, yawl-rigged yacht that was moored some distance down the creek. "I suppose you will not be wanting to go on board her?"

"Not at present," replied Miller, "and probably not at all. But we will hear what Bunter has to say."

"I'm afraid, sir," said the sergeant, "you'll find that he hasn't very much to say. We haven't found him particularly ready to talk. But perhaps he'll let himself go a bit more with you."

We turned away from the water and, under the sergeant's guidance, entered the little town, or village, and headed towards the police station.

Chapter XVI
The Statement of
Frederick Bunter

"Well, Bunter," the Superintendent remarked, cheerfully, as the prisoner was brought into the little office and given a seat at the table, "here you are."

"Yes," Bunter agreed, gloomily, "here I am. But I don't see why they wanted to run me in. I wasn't doing no harm."

"You were trying to break into a yacht," Miller ventured to remind him. "That isn't quite according to Cocker, you know."

"I was trying to get on board," said Bunter, "and I'm not denying it. But you seem to be forgetting that I was a member of the crew of that yacht. All I wanted was to get some of my kit what I had left behind. I've told the sergeant so."

"That's right, sir," the sergeant confirmed. "He said he had left his pocket-knife behind, and we did find a pocket-knife on board – a big knife with a cork-screw and a marlin-spike in it, such as he had described. But he could have got it from us without breaking into the vessel."

"Yes," said Miller, "that's so. Still, it's a point in his favour. However, it isn't the burglary that we are interested in. If everything else was satisfactory we might let that pass, as he didn't actually break in and he has some sort of explanation. But you know, Bunter, what the real business is, and what we want to ask you about. It's that platinum job."

"What platinum job?" demanded Bunter. "I don't know nothing about any platinum."

"Now, Bunter," the Superintendent remonstrated, "don't be silly. We know all about that job, and we know that you were in it with Bassett and Wicks and the other man."

As he spoke, he drew a packet of cigarettes from his pocket and, taking one out, pushed it across the table with a box of matches. Bunter accepted the gift with a grunt of acknowledgment but maintained his unaccommodating attitude.

"If you know all about it," said he, "there ain't no need for you to ask me no questions."

"Oh, yes, there is," said Miller. "We know enough for the purpose of the prosecution. But there are certain matters that we should like to clear up for other reasons. Still, you are not obliged to say anything if you don't want to. I suppose you have been cautioned. If you haven't, I caution you now that anything you say will be taken down in writing and may be used in evidence at the trial. But I don't want you to say anything that might make the case any worse against you. I want some particulars, as I told you, for other reasons. What you may tell us won't do your two pals any harm, as they are both dead. And I think I may say that we are not inclined to be vindictive to you as no very great harm has been done to anybody, seeing that we have recovered the swag."

At the moment when Miller made this last statement, the prisoner was in the act of striking a match to light his cigarette. But, as the words were spoken, the action became arrested and he sat with his mouth open and the unheeded match burning – until the flame reached his finger, when he dropped it with an appropriate observation. "Did you say," he demanded, speaking slowly and in a tone of the utmost amazement, "that you had recovered the swag?"

"I did," Miller replied, calmly, proceeding to fill his pipe.

"Do you mean the platinum?" Bunter persisted, gazing at the Superintendent with the same expression of amazed incredulity.

"I do," replied Miller. "Pass the matches when you have lit up."

Bunter lit his cigarette perfunctorily and pushed the match-box across the table.

"How did you get hold of it?" he asked.

"We got it," Miller replied, with a twinkle of enjoyment, "from someone who had it from Wicks."

"Get out!" exclaimed Bunter. "You couldn't. Wicks never had it. You are fooling me. I don't believe you've got it at all."

"Look here, Bunter," the Superintendent said, stiffly, "I am not bound to tell you anything. But if I do tell you anything, you can take it that it's the truth. I'm not in the habit of making false statements to prisoners, nor is any other police officer. I tell you that we have got all that platinum back, so you can take that as a fact and steer your course accordingly."

"But," persisted Bunter, "you couldn't have got it from Wicks. I tell you he never had it."

"Nonsense, Bunter," said Miller. "Didn't he pinch that case from the cloak room at Fenchurch Street? You know he did."

"Yes, I know all about that," rejoined Bunter, "and I know that he thought the stuff was in that case. But it wasn't."

"That's what he told you," said Miller, hardly able to conceal his enjoyment of this contest of wits, and the consciousness that he had the trumps securely up his sleeve. "But it was he that was doing the fooling. He meant to keep the whole of the swag for himself."

"Now that's where you're mistaken," said Bunter. "You think I am going on what he told me. But I ain't. I know the stuff wasn't in that case."

"How do you know?" demanded Miller.

"That's my business, that is," was the reply.

"Well," said Miller, "I don't know that it matters so very much. We have got the stuff back, which is the important thing. But of course, we like to fill in the details if we can."

Bunter re-lit his cigarette and reflected. No one likes a misunderstanding or cross-purposes, and Bunter evidently felt that he was being misunderstood. Furthermore, he was intensely curious as to how the platinum could possibly have been recovered. At length, he said. "Supposing I was to tell you the whole story – would you let the prosecution drop?"

The Superintendent shook his head, "No, Bunter," he replied promptly. "I can't make any promises. The man who makes a promise which he doesn't mean to keep is a liar, which is what no police officer ought to be, and the man who keeps a promise that he oughtn't to have made, in a case like this, is guilty of bribery. The English law is dead against compounding felonies or any other crimes. But you know quite well that, if you choose to help us, you won't do yourself any harm."

Bunter took a little more time for reflection, and eventually reached a conclusion.

"Very well," he said, "I will tell you the whole blooming story, so far as it is known to me, and I look to you not to take advantage of me from what I have told you."

"I think you are wise, Bunter," said the Superintendent, obviously much relieved at the prisoner's decision. "By the way, Sergeant, what time did Bunter have his breakfast?"

"About seven o'clock, sir," was the reply.

"Then," said Miller, "if he is going to make a longish statement, he won't be the worse for a little refreshment. What do you say, Bunter?"

Mr. Bunter grinned and admitted that "he could do with a beaver".

"Very well," said Miller, "perhaps we could all do with a beaver – say, a snack of bread and cheese and a glass of beer. Can you manage that, Sergeant?"

The sergeant could and, being provided with the wherewith in the form of a ten-shilling note, went forth to dispatch an underling in search of the materials for the said "beaver". Meanwhile, Bunter, having been furnished with a fresh cigarette, lighted it and began his narrative.

"You must understand," said he, "that this job was run by Bassett. The rest of us carried out orders, and we didn't know much more about the job than what he told us, and he didn't tell us any more than we was bound to find out for ourselves. We didn't even know that the stuff was platinum until Wicks spotted it by its weight. All that we knew was that we were going to lift some stuff that was pretty valuable, and I doubt if the fourth man, Park, knew even that."

"How did you come to know Bassett?" the Superintendent asked.

"He came to my house – leastways my brother-in-law's house at Walworth – and said he had been recommended to me by a gentleman, but he wouldn't say who the gentleman was. Whoever he was, he must have known something about me, because he knew that I had been to sea on a sailing barge, and he knew about a little trouble that I had got into over some snide money that some fool gave me for a joke."

"Ah!" said Miller, "and how did that trouble end?"

"Charge dismissed," Bunter replied, triumphantly. "No evidence of any dishonest intent. Of course there wasn't."

"Certainly not," Miller agreed. "Of course, you explained about the practical joke?"

"Rather – at least my lawyer did. He talked to the beak like a father, I can tell you."

"Yes," said Miller, "I can imagine it. These advocates are uncommonly persuasive."

"He wasn't," Bunter exclaimed, indignantly. "He was an English gentleman."

"Oh!" said Miller. "What was this gentleman's name?"

"His name," Bunter replied, haughtily, "was Gimbler, and a first-class man at his business he was. Knew all the ropes like an A.B."

"Yes," said Miller. "But to return to Bassett: Had Wicks known him previously?"

"No. Bassett called on him, too. Got his address from a gentleman who knew him. Same gentleman, I expect, as Bassett wouldn't say who he was. But he knew that Wicks had been brought up as a waterman, and I think he knew a bit more about him – more than I did, for Wicks was a stranger to me – and he didn't let on much as to what he did for a living. So there was four of us on the yacht: Bassett, Wicks, me, and a bloke named Park, but he wasn't really in the swim. He was a bawleyman out of Leigh, a simple sort of cove, but a rare good seaman. He wasn't told nothing about the job, and I fancy he thought it was some sort of smuggling racket – nothing for a honest man to mind."

"And what was the arrangement as to pay, or shares?"

"We all got monthly pay at the ordinary yachtman's rate, and there was to be a bonus at the end of the voyage. Park was to have fifty pounds, and me and Wicks was to have two-hundred each if we brought the job off and landed the swag."

Here the "beaver" arrived, and Bunter was allowed to refresh himself with a glass of beer, which he did with uncommon gusto. But the narrative proceeded without interruption, excepting such as was due to slight impairment of articulation when the narrator took an extra liberal mouthful, which we shall venture to ignore.

"I can't tell you exactly how the actual job was done at Riga, as I was down below at the time. Bassett and Wicks did the sleight of hand on the quay, but I think it was done something like this: We had been in the habit of getting our provisions on board in a big hamper, and this used to be left about on the quay so as to get the people there used to seeing it. Now, on the day when the job was done, Bassett put into the hamper the little dummy case that he had got ready with half-a-hundredweight of lead in it. I don't know how he got the particulars for making up the case, but I reckon he must have had a pal on the spot who gave him the tip. Anyway, he made up the dummy case and put it in the hamper wrapped up in a waterproof sheet. Then it was took up and dumped down on the quay close to where the cases of platinum was being dumped down by the men who brought them out of the van. Then, I understand, someone gave an alarm of fire and, while everyone was looking at the place where the fire was supposed to be, the dummy was put out on the quay and the waterproof sheet flicked off the dummy and over one of the real cases, and the dummy was shoved nearer to the other cases. Then Bassett sat down on the case that he had covered with the sheet and lit his pipe. Then they waited until all the cases, dummy and all, had been put on board the ship. Then they lifted the case, still covered with the waterproof sheet, into the hamper and brought it on board the yacht.

"As soon as it was on board, Park and me was told to cast off the shore ropes and get the yacht out of her berth and put out into the bay, which we did, though, as it was nearly a dead calm, she crept out mighty slowly. When we had got the sails set, I left Park at the helm and went below to lend a hand, and then it was that I found out how the swag was to be disposed of – and a mighty clever wheeze it was, and it worked out to a *T*.

"You must know that our inside ballast was a lot of lead weights, all cast to the same size – about half-a-hundredweight each and forty of them, all told. Now, as soon as we was fairly under way, Bassett and

607

Wicks lighted a big Primus stove and set a large melting-pot on it, and into the pot they put one of the lead weights from the hold. Then Bassett brought out of the lazarette a fireclay mould like the one that the weights had been cast in. It was an open mould what you just poured the lead in, and when it had set, you turned it over and the weight dropped out with the top surface rough as it had set.

"While the lead was melting, me and Bassett and Wicks opened the case and took out the platinum, which was in thin sheets about a foot square. We cut the sheets up with tinman's snips into narrow strips what would go snugly into the mould. Then Bassett put a bit of cold lead into the mould for the strips of platinum to rest on, and then we laid the strips in the mould, fitting them in carefully so as to get as many in as possible. Then, when we had got them in and the lead in the pot was melted, Bassett takes a ladle, dips it into the pot, and pours it into the mould. He had made the lead a bit extra hot, so that it should not be cooled by the cold platinum. Well, when we had filled up the mould and covered up the platinum, we had to wait while it was setting, and Bassett put another ballast-weight in the pot to melt. When the lead in the mould was set, we turned it out, and there was an ordinary-looking ballast weight what you wouldn't have known from any other ballast-weight.

"We did the same with the rest of the platinum, and that just made up another weight. Then we marked the numbers on them with punches – all the ballast-weights were numbered and laid in their regular order, one to forty. These two weights were numbered twenty-two and twenty-five, and when we had marked them, we laid them down in their proper places in the hold. Then we cleaned up. The lead what was left over we chucked overboard, and the fireclay mould went after it. The case what the platinum had come in, we broke up and shoved the pieces in the galley fire, so now there was no trace left of this little job, and we didn't mind if the police came on board and rummaged the ship. There wasn't nothing for them to find. So we sailed back to our berth and made fast, and there we stayed for five days to give them a chance to come on board and rummage if they wanted to. But they never came. Naturally. Because nothing had been found out. So, on the sixth day, we put to sea for the voyage home.

"But we didn't come straight home. We kept up the appearances of a cruising yacht. You won't want particulars of the voyage, but there is one little incident that I must mention. It was at Rotterdam, our last port of call, on the morning when we started for home. We had got the sails loosed and was just about to cast off, when a cove appeared on the quay and hailed Bassett, who was on deck giving orders. Bassett replied as if he had expected this bloke, and reached up and took the man's luggage –

a small suit-case and a brown-paper parcel with a rug-strap fastened to it – and helped the covey down the ladder. Then we cast off and put out to sea, so we could see that this stranger had arranged with Bassett for a passage to England.

"Shortly after we had started, Bassett sends me to the forepeak for one of the empty cases what our provisions had been stowed it. I took it to the cabin, but I didn't know what it was wanted for until I saw the passenger stowing it in the locker what belonged to his berth. Later, I found the brown paper from the parcel and a big bit of oiled silk which seemed a bit damp and had a nasty smell, so I chucked it overboard. I don't know whether Bassett knew what was in that parcel, but none of us ever guessed.

"Now, when we was about abreast of the Swin Middle Light-ship, we met a stumpy barge what was bound, as it turned out, from London to Colchester. Bassett hailed her and, when we was near enough, he asked the skipper if he would take a passenger. The skipper wanted further particulars, so Wicks and Park went off to the barge in the boat, taking the passenger's case with them. Apparently it was all right, for Wicks waved his hand and Park started to row back to the yacht."

"Had Wicks or Bassett told you anything about this business?" the Superintendent asked.

"No. Not a word was said at the time, but Wicks told me all about it afterwards, and I may as well tell you now. It seems that the passenger – his name was Sanders – had got Bassett's permission to make an arrangement with Wicks to smuggle the case ashore and take it to Fenchurch Street Station and leave it in the cloak room. He gave Wicks ten pounds for the job and a pound for the barge skipper, and a rare mug he must have been to pay Wicks in advance. Well, the skipper took Wicks with him up the Colne and put him ashore, after dark, somewhere between Rowhedge and Colchester, and Wicks took a walk inland with his case and picked up a motor bus that took him into Colchester. He stayed there a day or two, having a bit of a beano, because he wasn't due to dump the case in the cloak room until the following Monday, so that it shouldn't be waiting there too long. But on Saturday evening he took the train to London and went straight to the house of my brother-in-law, Bert Wallis, where I was in the habit of living."

"Why did he go there?" asked Miller.

"Ah!" said Bunter, "that's another story, and I may as well tell you that now. You must know that, after Wicks found out about the platinum, he got very discontented. He reckoned that the swag might be worth anything from ten- to twenty-thousand pounds, and he said we'd been done in the eye. Two-hundred pounds apiece, he said, wasn't anything like a fair share, seeing that we'd taken a equal share of the risk. And he was very suspicious of Bassett. He doubted whether he was a perfectly honest man."

"What a horrible suspicion!" Miller exclaimed with a grin.

"Yes," agreed Bunter. "But I believe he was right. He suspected that Bassett meant to clear off with the whole of the swag and not pay us anything. And so did I, so we arranged that I should keep an eye on Bassett and see that he didn't get away with it.

"Now, when we had done with the Customs at Southend – of course they didn't twig nothing – we ran up into Benfleet Creek and took up moorings. Then on Saturday, Bassett said he was going to take the stuff up to a dealer what he knew of and wouldn't be back for a day or two. So, in the evening, I helped him to carry the case, with the two doctored weights in it, up to the station and saw him into a first-class carriage and shut him in. But I didn't go back to the yacht. I'd taken the precaution to get a ticket in advance, and given Park the tip that I mightn't be back that night so, when I left Bassett, I went to the rear of the train and got in. I travelled up to town in that train, and I followed Bassett and saw him stow the case in the cloak room. Then, when I had seen him out of the station, I nipped straight off home to Bert Wallis's place at Walworth.

"It happened that I got there only a few minutes after Wicks had turned up. I told him what had happened, and we talked over what we should do to keep our eyes on the case of platinum. But at the moment, Wicks was all agog to know what was in Mr. Sanders's case. I pointed out to him that it was no business of his, but he said if it was worth all the money and trouble that had been spent on it, there must be something of value inside, and he was going to see what that something was, and whether it was worthwhile to take it to the cloak room at all.

"Well, I got him a screwdriver and he had the screws out in a twinkling and pulled up the lid. And then he fairly hollered with surprise and I was a bit took aback, myself. You know what was inside – a man's head, packed in some of our old duds. I tell you, Wicks slammed the lid down and ran the screws in faster than he took them out. Then I asks him what he was going to do about it. 'Do?' says he. 'I'm going to plant the damn thing in the cloak room tomorrow morning and get clear of it, and I'll send the ticket on to Sanders at Benfleet Post Office as I promised. I've been paid, and I'm going to carry out my contract like a honest man'.

"But the sight of that man's head seemed to have given him something to think about, for he was mighty thoughtful for a while. Then, all of a sudden, something seemed to strike him, for he turns to me and asks, 'What sort of case did Bassett pack them two weights in?'

'Why', I says, 'one of the provision cases, same sort as that head is packed in'. 'Then, by gum', says he, 'we are going to steal a march on that dishonest blighter, Bassett, if we can manage it. Do you know what marks there were on that case?' Now, it happened that I did, for I had taken the precaution to make a copy of the label. I showed it to Wicks and he got a card like the one I had seen on Bassett's case and wrote the name and address on it from my copy and tacked it on to Sanders's case.

"'And now', says he, 'the question is how we are going to get that case here from the station. We might take a taxi, but that wouldn't be very safe. We don't want to leave no tracks.' Then I thought of Joe Wallis, Bert Wallis's brother, what had a shop a couple of doors off and kept a motor van for carting timber about."

"What is his trade?" Miller asked.

"He is a carpenter what does work for some small builders. He served his time as a undertaker, but he give that up. Said it wasn't cheerful enough. He didn't mind the coffins, but he couldn't stick the corpses. Well, the end of it was that Wicks persuaded Joe to take on the job. I don't know what story he told him, Of course, Joe didn't know what was in either of the cases, but he is a big, strong chap and Wicks made it worth his while. Being Sunday, he put on a leather coat and a cap like a taxi-driver, for the sake of appearances.

"Well, Wicks got rid of Sanders's case all right and posted the ticket off to Benfleet, and then, in the afternoon, he set off to do the more ticklish job of swapping Sanders's case for Bassett's. But he brought it off all right and got the right case safely to Bert's crib. Being Sunday, Bert wasn't doing nothing, so we had the run of his workshop to do our little job in."

"What is Bert's trade?" the Superintendent asked.

"He is a plumber," replied Bunter. "That's what he is."

"Oh!" said Miller, with a sly look. "Doesn't do anything in the pewter and plaster mould line, I suppose?"

"I said he was a plumber," Bunter replied, haughtily, "and, consequentially, he'd got a workshop with a big gas ring and some melting-pots, which was just what we wanted.

"Well, we opened Bassett's case and there, sure enough, was the two lead weights. And they seemed to be the right ones, by the punch marks on them – twenty-two and twenty-five. So we took the biggest melting-pot, which was half full of lead and, when we had tipped the lump of lead out on the floor, we put the pot on the ring and lighted up, and then we shoved one of the lead weights in it.

"'Now', says Wicks, 'we are going to make our fortunes. But we shall have some difficulty in getting rid of this stuff. We shall have to go slow'. So he sat on a chair by the gas ring and watched the weight and made all sorts of plans for getting rid of the platinum. The weight was a long time before it showed any signs of melting, but, at last it began to slip down the pot, and me and Wicks leaned over the pot and watched for the bits of platinum to stick out. But we couldn't see no sign of them. We watched the weight as it slipped down further and further until it had crumpled up and was all melted. But still we couldn't see nothing of the platinum. Then Wicks got a iron rod and raked about in the melted lead to see if he could feel the bits of platinum. But he couldn't. Then he got a ladle and tried to fish out the bits that he couldn't see, and I tell you, he was fair sweating with anxiety, and so was I for that matter. For nothing came up in the ladle but melted lead.

"Then I suggested that we should ladle out the whole of the lead, a little at a time, into another pot, and I got three small empty pots and set them alongside the big one, and Wicks ladled out the lead from the big one into the little ones. But still we didn't come to the platinum. And at last we come to the bottom of the pot, and then we could see that there wasn't no platinum there.

"By this time Wicks was nearly blue with rage and disappointment, and I was pretty sick, myself. However, we emptied the last drop of lead out of the big pot and started to melt the other weight. But it was the same story with that one. We ladled the lead out into the small pots, and by way of doing the thing thoroughly, took the big pot up by its handle and drained the very last drop of lead out of it into the small pots. And there wasn't a grain of platinum to be seen anywhere.

"My eye! You ought to have seen Wicks's face when he had done with the second weight and tried it right out. His language was something awful, And no wonder. For you see it wasn't no mistake. The numbers on the weights was all right. It was a fair do. Bassett had deliberately sold us a pup. He'd got a pair of the plain lead weights, hammered the numbers out, and punched fresh numbers on them. It was a dirty trick, but I suppose he must have suspected Wicks and got this plant ready for him. At any rate, Wicks saw red, and he swore he would do Bassett in. We'd got Bassett's address at Swanscombe, because we had got to go there for the money that was owing to us when the swag should have been disposed of and, on the Tuesday, Wicks went off to see if Bassett was at home and, if he was, to have a few words with him. And that was the last I ever saw of Wicks. When he didn't come home, I supposed he had made himself scarce on account of the hue-and-cry about the head in the case. Now I know that he must have tried to do Bassett in, and Bassett must have got his whack in first. And that's all I know about the business."

"Good," said Miller. "You've made a very straightforward statement, and I can tell you that you have not done yourself any harm and what you have told us will probably be quite helpful to us. I'll write it out presently from my notes and you can read it and, if you are satisfied with it, I'll get you to sign it. In the meantime, I want to ask you one or two questions. First of all, about this man Sanders, can you give us any description of him?"

"He was a tall man," replied Bunter, "a good six foot if he had stood up straight – which he didn't, having a stoop at the shoulders. I should put his age at about fifty. He had dark hair and beard and he wore spectacles."

"What kind of spectacles?" Thorndyke asked.

"I dunno," replied Bunter. "Spectacles is spectacles. I ain't a optician."

"Some spectacles are large," said Thorndyke, "and some are small. Some are round and some are oval, and some have a line across as if they had been cracked. Would his fit any of those descriptions?"

"Why, yes, now you come to mention it. They was big, round spectacles with a sort of crack across them. But it couldn't have been a crack because it was the same in both eyes. I'd forgotten them until you spoke."

I noticed that Miller had cast a quick look at Thorndyke and was now eagerly writing down the description. Evidently, he "smelt a fox", and so did I. For, though Thorndyke had not really put a "leading question", he had mentioned a very uncommon kind of spectacles – the old-fashioned type of bi-focal, which is hardly ever made now, having been superseded by the cemented or ground lunette. I had no doubt, nor, I think, had Miller, that he was describing a particular pair of spectacles, and this suspicion was strengthened by his next questions.

"Did you notice anything peculiar in his voice or manner of speaking?"

"Nothing extraordinary," replied Bunter. "He'd got a squeaky voice, and there's no denying it. And he didn't speak quite proper English, like you and me. Seemed to speak a bit like a Dutchman."

I surmised that Mr. Bunter used the word "Dutchman" in a nautical sense, meaning any sort of foreigner who was not a "Dago", and so, apparently, Thorndyke interpreted it, for he said, "He spoke with a foreign accent? Was it a strong accent, or only slight?"

"Oh, it was nothing to notice. You'd hardly have taken him for a foreigner."

"Did you notice his nose?"

613

"You couldn't help noticing it. Lord! It reminded me of a parrot. And it had got a pretty strong list to starboard."

"You would say that he had a large, curved, or hook nose, which was bent towards the right. Is that so?"

"That's what I said."

"Then, Superintendent," said Thorndyke, "I think we have a working description of Mr. Sanders. Shall we take a note of Mr. Bert Wallis's address?"

"I don't see what you want with that," Bunter objected. "He didn't have nothing to do with the job. We used his work-shop, but he didn't know what we wanted it for."

"We realize that," said Thorndyke, "and we have nothing whatever against him. But he may be able to give us some information on some other matters. By the way, speaking of that lead that you ladled out of the pot, what did you do with it?"

"Nothing. It wasn't no good to us. We just left it in the pots for Bert, in case he had any use for it."

"And Bert's address is – ?"

"Sixty-four Little Bolter Street, Walworth. But don't you go worrying him. He don't know nothing what he didn't ought to."

"You needn't be afraid of our giving him any trouble," said Miller. "We may not have to call on him at all, but, in any case it will only be a matter of a few questions which he won't mind answering. And now, perhaps you'd like another cigarette to smoke while I am writing up your statement."

Mr. Bunter accepted the cigarette readily and even hinted that the making of statements was dry work, on which Miller directed the sergeant to provide him with a further half-pint. Meanwhile, Thorndyke and I, having no concern with the formalities of the statement, went forth to stretch our legs and take a more detailed survey of the waterside. When we returned, the statement had been transcribed and duly signed by Mr. Frederick Bunter. And this brought to an end a very satisfactory day's work.

Chapter XVII
The Unconscious Receivers

During the return journey, the Superintendent showed a natural disposition to discuss the bearings of what we had learned from Bunter and reckon up his gains in the matter of evidence.

"It was a pleasant surprise to me," said he, "to hear Bunter let himself go in the way he did. I was afraid, from what the sergeant said, that we shouldn't get much out of him."

"Yes," said I, "he was rather unexpectedly expansive. I think what started him was your insistence that Wicks had got possession of the platinum, when he knew, as he supposed, that Bassett had planted the wrong weights. He was mightily staggered when you told him that the swag had been recovered. Still, we've a good deal more to learn yet before we shall know exactly what did happen."

"That is true," agreed Miller. "We've learned a lot from Bunter, but there is a lot more that we don't know, and that Bunter doesn't know. The question is, how much do we know? What do you say, Doctor? I should like to hear you sum up what we have gained by this statement, and tell us exactly how you think we stand."

"My feeling," said Thorndyke, "is that we have advanced our knowledge considerably. We have shortened the gap between the two parts of the problem which are known to us. When we came down, our knowledge of the platinum ceased with its disappearance from the cloak room and began again with its reappearance in the coffin. That was a big gap. But, as I have said, that gap is now to a great extent filled up. The problem that remains is to trace those lumps of alloy from Bert Wallis's workshop to the false coffin, and I don't think that we shall have much difficulty in doing it. But before we proceed to count up our gains, we had better consider what it is that we want to know.

"Now, I remind you that there are two distinct problems, which we had better keep quite separate – the platinum robbery and the substituted coffin. Bunter's statement bears on both, but we must not get them confused. Let us take the robbery first. My impression is that we now know all that we are likely to know about it. We all have probably formed certain suspicions, but suspicions are of no use unless there is some prospect of confirming them. And I do not think that there is. But, after all, is there any object in pursuing the matter? The two visible principals in the robbery are dead. As to poor Bunter, he was a mere spectator. He never knew any of the details."

"He was, at least, an accessory after the fact," said Miller.

"True. But is he worth powder and shot? Remember, this robbery was committed outside British jurisdiction. It will be an extradition case, unless you charge Bunter with complicity in the theft from the cloak room. It will be for the Latvian police to make the first move, which they probably will not, as the property has been recovered and the principal offenders are dead."

Miller reluctantly admitted the cogency of this argument.

"Still," he insisted, "there is more in it than that. Didn't it strike you that certain parts of Bunter's statement seemed to suggest the possibility that the robbery had been planned and engineered by our friend, Gimbler?"

"It did," Thorndyke admitted. "That was what I meant when I spoke of certain suspicions that we have formed. It would be possible, from Bunter's statement, to build up quite a plausible argument to prove that Gimbler was probably the moving spirit in that robbery. But it would be a mere academic exercise, very entertaining, but quite unprofitable, since the principals are dead and Bunter knows less than we do. There are no means by which our suspicions could be put to the proof or our knowledge enlarged."

"I expect you are right," Miller agreed, gloomily, "but I should like to hear the argument, all the same."

"It will be a waste of time," said Thorndyke. "However, our time is not very valuable just now, and there will be no harm in assembling the relevant facts. Let us take them in order.

"1. Bunter had been defended on a criminal charge by Gimbler.

"2. Bunter was introduced to Bassett by 'a gentleman', who must have, therefore, known them both.

"3. A gentleman – apparently the same gentleman – introduced Wicks to Bassett and, therefore, knew Wicks.

"4. The said gentleman – assuming him to be the same in both cases – was therefore acquainted with three persons who are known to us as having been engaged in crime.

"5. One of these three persons – Bunter – was acquainted with Gimbler.

"6. The unknown 'gentleman', who was acquainted with three criminals, took an active and helpful part in the robbery inasmuch as he introduced Bassett to persons who would be likely to agree to assist in the carrying out of a criminal enterprise.

"Those are the principal facts, and now as to their application. The appearance of this mysterious 'gentleman', acquainted with criminals and apparently acting, at least as an accessory, strongly suggests someone in the background directing, and possibly planning, this robbery. This suggestion is reinforced by the fact that someone connected with the robbery must have had a substantial amount of capital available. The yacht, even if bought quite cheap, must have cost not less than a hundred pounds, and then there were the considerable out-goings in respect of the provisioning and fitting-out for the cruise, and the payments of wages which seem to have been made, apart from the final 'bonus', which might have been paid out of the proceeds of the robbery. Of course, Bassett may have had the money, but it is not probable. Persons who get their livelihood by crime are not usually capitalists. There is a strong suggestion that the 'gentleman' was behind the robbery in a financial sense as well as furnishing the brains and management. This is all reasonable inference – though of no evidential value. But when we try to give a name to this mysterious 'gentleman', our inferences become highly speculative. However, let us speculate. Let us propose the hypothesis that the hidden hand behind this robbery was the hand of Mr. Horatio Gimbler. What is there to support that hypothesis?

"First, there is the coffin. It contained the proceeds of this robbery. Gimbler was not aware of the fact, but the circumstance that it was there establishes the fact of some sort of contact between Gimbler and the persons who were concerned in the robbery. The persons whom he dealt with in the preparation of the coffin had dealings with the persons who carried out the robbery."

"There isn't much in that," I objected. "It might have been pure chance."

"So it might," he agreed, "and there is very little in it, as you say. But circumstantial evidence is made up of little things. I merely assert that some sort of connexion is established.

"The next point is that, of the three criminals engaged in this robbery, the only one known to us – Bunter – was acquainted with Gimbler. But Bunter was also acquainted with the unknown gentleman. There isn't much in that, taken alone, but it points in the same direction as the other facts.

"And now let us consider how Gimbler fits the character of the hypothetical person who may have directed and financed the robbery.

"First, this hypothetical person must have had a somewhat extensive acquaintance with members of the criminal class in order to be able to select suitable persons to carry out this rather peculiar and specialized piece of work. Criminals with a practical knowledge of seamanship cannot be very common. But Gimbler has a very extensive acquaintance with the criminal class.

"The next point is that this hypothetical person must have had a modest amount of capital at his disposal, say two- or three-hundred pounds. We do not know much of Gimbler's circumstances, but it would be very remarkable if he were not able to produce that amount to finance a scheme which was likely to yield a profit of thousands. But, as there must be innumerable persons in the same financial position, this argument has no significance. It is merely an argument.

"Finally, our hypothetical person must have combined considerable ingenuity with extreme dishonesty. Here there is undoubted agreement, but unfortunately, Gimbler is in this respect far from unique.

"That is the argument and as you see, though it is enough to allow of our entertaining a suspicion of Gimbler, it is not enough to establish the most flimsy *prima facie* case. If Gimbler was the hidden director of this crime, he was extremely well hidden, and I think he will remain hidden. Probably, Bassett was the only person who knew the whole of the facts."

"Yes," Miller agreed, glumly, "I'm afraid you are right. Unless the Latvian police raise an outcry, it will probably be best to let the matter drop. After all, the robbery failed and we have got the stuff back. Still, I feel in my bones that Gimbler engineered the job, and I should have liked to lay my hands on him. But, as you say, he kept out of sight and is out of sight still. He always does keep out of sight, damn him!"

"Not always," said Thorndyke. "You are forgetting the other case – the counterfeit coffin. That is an entirely different matter. There he is already in full view. A manifest fraud has been committed, and there are only two persons who could possibly be suspected of having committed it – Gimbler and Pippet. Actually, I suppose, no one suspects Pippet. But he is the claimant in whose interest – ostensibly – the fraud was perpetrated, and it is certain that Gimbler will try to put it on him, If it were not for Pippet, you could arrest Gimbler tomorrow and be confident of a conviction. As it is, direct evidence against Gimbler is a necessity, and it is for you, Miller, to secure that evidence. I think you will not have much difficulty, with the facts now in our possession."

"No," said Miller, "we seem to have got a pretty good lead from Bunter, but all the same, I should like to hear your views on the evidence that we have."

"Well," said Thorndyke, "let us approach the problem from both ends. At one end we have four lumps of metal, one lead and three alloy, in the workshop of a plumber, Bert Wallis. At the other we have the same four lumps of metal in a coffin, and the problem is to bridge the interval between the two appearances.

"Now, the fact that those four lumps appeared together in the coffin is evidence that the interval was quite short. There were no intermediate wanderings during which they might have become separated. We may be sure that the passage from the workshop to the coffin was pretty direct, in effect, we may assume that the man who prepared the coffin got his lead from Bert Wallis. The next inference is very obvious, though it may be erroneous. But when we consider that a couple of doors from Bert Wallis's premises were those of a man who had served his time as an undertaker, and who was, therefore, capable of making a perfectly correct and workmanlike coffin, who had a motor van and who was Bert Wallis's brother, it is impossible to ignore the probability that the coffin was made by Joe Wallis. He had all the means of carrying out the substitution – you will remember that there was a cart shed adjoining the wall of the burial ground, in which a van could be conveniently hidden, and from which the coffin could be easily passed over the wall – and, if he had done the job, he would presumably have got his lead from his brother whose premises were close by. The only weak place in the argument is that we are accusing a man who may be a perfectly honest and reputable tradesman of being concerned in a crime."

"I don't think you need worry yourself about that," said Miller. "You heard what I said to Bunter on the subject of pewter and plaster moulds. He knew what I meant. There had been some suspicion that Mr. Bert Wallis occasionally turned his hand to the manufacture of counterfeit coin. It was never brought home to him, but the fact that Bunter – who lives with him when he is at home – had been charged with issuing counterfeit money (which I had not heard of before) gives colour to the suspicion. And Bunter, himself, as we know, is a decidedly shady customer. I don't think we need have any scruples of delicacy in giving Mr. Joseph Wallis a little attention. I'll call and have a friendly talk with him."

"I shouldn't do that," said Thorndyke, "at least, not in the first place. It would be much better to make the initial attack on Bert. There, you have something definite to go on. You know that the metal was in his workshop. And, if he has not heard of the facts disclosed in the Probate Court, or has not connected them with the metal that he had, you will have a good opening for an inquiry as to what has become of certain valuable property which is known to have been in his possession. When he learns what the value of that metal was, I fancy you may look for an explosion which may give you the leading facts before he has realized the position. Besides, there is the possibility that he gave away or sold the metal without any knowledge of its origin."

"So there is," agreed Miller, leaning back to laugh with more comfort. "In fact, it is quite probable. My eye! What a lark it will be! I shall go straight on from Fenchurch Street. Couldn't I persuade you to come with me and do some of the talking?"

Thorndyke required no persuading, nor did I, for the interview promised to be highly entertaining. Accordingly, the arrangement was made and the plan of campaign settled and, on our arrival at the terminus, after a brief halt at the buffet for a sandwich and a glass of beer, we made our way to the tube railway, by which we were conveyed to The Elephant and Castle.

"By the way," said I, as Miller struck out towards the Walworth Road, "I suppose you have got the address?"

"Yes," was the reply, "I got it from Bunter when he signed the statement. It's in East Street. I made a note of the number."

He brought out his note-book and glanced at it as we threaded our way through the multitude that thronged the pavement. Presently he turned to the left down a side street and walked on with his eyes on the numbers of the houses.

"This is the show," he said, at length, halting before a seedy-looking plumber's shop, the façade of which bore the inscription, "*A. Wallis*". "Shop looks as if it was open."

It was, technically, although the door was closed, but it yielded to a push, announcing the fact by the jangling of a bell, which brought a man out of the parlour at the back. Apparently we had disturbed him at a meal, for his jaws were working as he came out, and he looked at us inquiringly without speaking. Perhaps "inquiringly" hardly expresses the kind of look that he gave us. It was a mere coincidence, but it happened that we were, all three, over six feet in height, and Miller, at least, looked a good deal like what he was.

The Superintendent opened the ball. "You are Mr. Bert Wallis, I think?"

Mr. Wallis nodded, chewing frantically. Finally, he bolted his mouthful and replied, "Yes, that's who I am. What about it?

"My friend here, Dr. Thorndyke, who is a lawyer, wants to make a few inquiries of you."

Mr. Wallis turned to Thorndyke but made no comment, having, apparently, some slight arrears to dispose of in the matter of chewing.

"My inquiries," said Thorndyke, "have reference to certain valuable property which came into your possession some time ago."

"Valuable property in my possession?" said Wallis. "It's the first I have heard of it. What property are you talking about?"

"It is a quantity of metal," replied Thorndyke. "You had it from two men named Wicks and Bunter."

Wallis stared at Thorndyke for a few seconds and gradually the look of apprehension faded from his countenance and gave place to one of amusement. His mouth extended laterally until it exhibited an undeniable grin.

"I know what you are talking about, now," he chuckled, "but you've got hold of the wrong end of the stick altogether. I'll tell you how it happened. Them two silly fools, Wicks and Bunter, thought they had got hold of some valuable stuff. I don't know what they thought it was, but they asked me to let them melt it down in my workshop. I didn't much like the idea of it, because I didn't know what stuff it was or how they had got it, but, as Bunter is my wife's brother and I knew Wicks, I didn't quite like to refuse. So I let them have the run of my workshop on a Sunday night when I was out, and they did the job. They melted down this here valuable stuff, and what do you suppose it turned out to be, after all?"

Thorndyke shook his head and waited for the answer.

"It was lead!" Wallis exclaimed with a triumphant giggle. "Just think of it! These two silly asses had put theirselves to no end of trouble and expense to get hold of this stuff – I don't know how they did get hold of it – and when they come to melt it down, it was just lead, worth about twopence a pound! But, my aunt! Wasn't they blooming sick! You ought to have heard the language that Wicks used!"

The recollection of this anticlimax amused him so much that he laughed aloud and had perforce to wipe his eyes with a handkerchief which might once have been clean.

"And what became of this lead?" asked Thorndyke. "Did they take it away with them?"

"No," replied Wallis. "It wasn't no good to them. They just left it in the pots."

"And is it in your workshop still?" asked Thorndyke.

"No, it ain't. I sold it to a builder for five bob, which paid for the gas that they had used and left a bit over."

"Do you know what the builder wanted it for?"

"Said he wanted some lead for to fix some iron railings in their sockets."

"Did he take the whole of it?"

"Yes, he took the whole boiling of it, and a small roll of sheet lead as well. But the sheet wasn't included in the five bob."

"Do you mind telling us the name of this builder?" Thorndyke asked.

Wallis looked rather hard at Thorndyke, and the slightly apprehensive expression reappeared on his face.

"I don't see as his name is neither here nor there," said he. "What's all the fuss about? You was speaking of valuable property. Lead ain't valuable property."

"For legal reasons," said Thorndyke, "I wish to trace that lead and see where it went to. And there is no reason for you to be secret about it. The transaction between you and the builder was a perfectly lawful transaction, but I should like to ascertain from the builder exactly what he did with the lead."

The plumber was evidently still a little uneasy, but the question was so simple and straightforward that he could hardly refuse to answer.

"Well," he replied, grudgingly, "if you must know, the builder what I sold the lead to was my brother, Joe Wallis, what lives a couple of doors further up the street."

"Thank you," said Thorndyke. Then, turning to Miller, he said, "That is all I wanted to know. Probably Mr. Joe Wallis will be able to help us a stage further. Is there anything that you want to ask?"

"No," replied Miller, "that seems to be all plain sailing. I don't think we need trouble Mr. Wallis any further."

With this, Thorndyke thanked the plumber for the assistance that he had given and we took our departure. As soon as we were outside, the Superintendent broke out into low-voiced self-congratulations – low-voiced – by reason of the fact that Mr. Wallis had taken his post at the shop door to observe our further movements.

"It was just as well," said Miller, "that you were able to get the information without letting the cat out of the bag. It has saved a lot of chin-wagging. But I expect we shan't have such an easy job with our friend Joseph. Bert had nothing to conceal, but Joseph must have been in the swim to some extent. This is his house."

The premises, which bore the superscription, "*J. Wallis, Builder and Decorator*", were divided into two parts, a carpenter's shop and an office. We entered the latter and, as it was at the moment unoccupied, the Superintendent thumped on the counter with his stick, which brought out from some inner lair a very large youth of about eighteen who saluted us with an amiable grin.

"Dad in?" inquired Miller, making a chance shot, which was justified by the result, as the youth replied, "Yes. What's it about?"

"This gentleman, Dr. Thorndyke, wants to see him on important legal business," Miller replied, whereupon the youth grinned again and retired. In about a minute he returned and requested us to "walk this way", indicating the direction by walking in advance. We followed him across a hail and up a flight of stairs to a door, which he opened and, having seen us enter, once more departed.

The room was quite an interesting survival – a typical example of a Victorian tradesman's drawing room, with the typical close, musty smell. As we entered, I noticed that Thorndyke cast his eyes down and then took a quick glance at the window. But there was no time for detailed observation, for we were almost immediately followed by a man whom I judged from his stature and a certain family resemblance to be "Dad." But the resemblance did not extend to the amiable grin, On the contrary, the newcomer viewed us with an expression compounded of a sort of foxy curiosity and a perceptible tinge of hostility.

"Which of you is Dr. Thorndyke?" he inquired.

My colleague introduced himself, and the inevitable question followed.

"And who are these other two gentlemen?"

"This," replied Miller, indicating me, "is Dr. Jervis, also a lawyer, and – " Here he produced a professional card and pushed it across an occasional table. " – that's who I am."

Mr. Wallis studied the card for a few moments, and the hostility of his expression became more pronounced. Nevertheless, he said with gruff civility, "Well, you may as well sit down," and gave us a lead by sitting down, himself, in an arm-chair.

"Now," said he, "what's this important legal business?"

"It is concerned," said Thorndyke, "with certain property which came into your hands and which you had from your brother, Albert Wallis."

"Property what I had from my brother Albert Wallis!" our friend repeated in obviously genuine surprise. "I haven't had no property from him. What do you mean?"

"I am referring to certain pieces of metal which you bought from him about three months ago."

Mr. Joseph continued to stare at Thorndyke for some seconds.

"Pieces of metal!" he repeated, at length. "I haven't bought no pieces of metal from him, You've made a mistake."

"The metal that I am referring to," said Thorndyke, "consisted of a roll of sheet lead and some remainders from melting-pots."

"Gawd!" exclaimed Joseph, contemptuously, "you don't call that property, do you? I gave him five bob for the lot, and that was more than it was worth."

"So I understood," said Thorndyke. "But we have reasons for wishing to trace that metal. We have managed to trace it to you, and we should be greatly obliged if you would tell us what has become of it, supposing it not to be still in your possession."

At this persistence on Thorndyke's part, the hostility expressed in Joseph's countenance became tinged with unmistakeable uneasiness. Nevertheless, he answered truculently enough. "I don't see what business it is of yours what I do with the material that I buy. But if you must know, I used that sheet lead for making a damp-course, and the other stuff for fixing some iron railings in a stone kerb."

"Then," said Miller, "somebody has got some pretty valuable iron railings."

Wallis looked at him inquiringly, and from him to Thorndyke.

"Perhaps," said the latter, "I had better explain. Some time ago, two men, one of whom was named Wicks, stole a case containing a quantity of platinum from the cloak room at Fenchurch Street. They took it to the house of your brother Albert, who, not knowing what it was, or anything about it, allowed them to melt it down in his workshop. But, when they had melted it down, they did not recognize it. They thought it was lead, and that they had taken the wrong case. So they left the lumps in the melting-pots for your brother to do what he pleased with. But he, also, did not recognize the metal. He, also, thought that it was lead, and he sold the whole consignment to you for five shillings. And I take it that you, like the others, mistook it for lead."

Mr. Wallis had suddenly become attentive and interested.

"Certainly, I took it for lead," said he. "And you say it was platinum. That's rather expensive stuff, isn't it?"

"The little lot," said Miller, "that you bought for five shillings has been valued at just under eighteen-thousand pounds."

That "knocked him", as they say in the Old Kent Road, For some seconds he sat speechless, clutching the arms of his chair and staring at Miller as if he had been some dreadful apparition.

"Eighteen-thousand pounds!" he exclaimed, at length, in something approaching a screech. "Eighteen – thousand – pounds! And to think – "

"Yes," said Miller, "to think of those iron railings. We shall have to see that you don't go rooting them up."

Mr. Wallis made no reply. As with the dying gladiator, "his thoughts were far away," and I had little doubt whither they had strayed. I do not profess to be a thought-reader, but the expression on Joseph's face conveyed clearly to me that he had, in that moment, decided, as soon as the night fell, to make a bee-line for Josiah Pippet's vault. His reverie was interrupted by Thorndyke.

"So, Mr. Wallis," said he, "you will understand our natural anxiety to find out where this metal went to."

"But I've told you," said Wallis, rousing himself from dreams of sudden opulence, "so far as I can recollect, that I used the stuff to plant some iron railings."

As we seemed to have got into a blind alley, the Superintendent abruptly changed his tone.

"Never mind about those iron railings," he said, sharply. "We want to know what you did with that stuff. Are you going to tell us?"

"I have told you," Wallis replied doggedly. "You can't expect me to remember what I did with every bit of lead that I bought."

"Very well," said Miller, "then perhaps it might help your memory if we were to do a bit of supposing. What do you say?"

"You can if you like," Joseph replied, sulkily, "so long as you don't ask me to help you."

"Now, Wallis," said Miller, "you've got to bear this in mind. Those two fools didn't know this stuff when they had got it in their hands, and neither did you or Bert. But there were other people who knew what was in that case. Bassett, the man who murdered Wicks, knew, because he put the stuff in the Case. And there was another man, a very artful gentleman, who kept out of sight but who knew all about it. We mustn't mention names, so we will just call him Mr. Rumbler, because he rumbled what had happened.

"Now, supposing this Mr. Rumbler, knowing where the stuff had been left by those two gabeys, had a bright idea for getting hold of it without showing his hand. Supposing he went to a certain undertaker whose place was close to Bert's and pitched him a yarn about wanting a dummy coffin weighted with lead. Supposing he employed him to make that coffin, knowing that he would be certain to get his lead from Bert, and plant it in a nice convenient vault in a disused burial ground – say, somewhere out Stratford way – where he could get at it easily with a big skeleton key and a tommy to turn it with. How's that? Mind you, I am only supposing."

As Miller recited his fable, a cloud fell on Mr. Wallis's countenance. The dream of sudden opulence was dissipated. The resurrection job was obviously "off". But, glum as the expression of Joseph's face became, the effect produced was not quite the one on which Miller had based his calculations.

"If you know where the coffin is," was the natural comment, "why don't you go and open it and take the stuff out?"

"Because," Miller replied, impressively, "the stuff isn't there. Somebody has had the coffin open and taken it out."

Even this did not answer. Wallis looked sulky enough, but he had not gorged the bait.

"I don't believe there is any coffin," said he. "You've just invented it to try to get me to say something."

I detected an expression of grim amusement on Thorndyke's face. Perhaps he was contrasting – as I was – Miller's present proceedings with the lofty standard of veracity among police officers that he had presented to Bunter. But I was also aware of some signs of impatience. As a matter of fact, all these artful probings on Miller's part were getting us nowhere. Moreover, we had really ascertained nearly all that we wanted to know.

"Perhaps," said Thorndyke, "as I am not a police officer, I may venture to be a little more explicit with Mr. Wallis. We are not interested in the present whereabouts of this platinum. We know where it is, but we want to know exactly how it got there. As to the coffin, we have evidence that it was made by you, Mr. Wallis, and planted by you in the vault. But this coffin was made to some person's order, and we want to know with certainty who that person is. At present, our information is to the effect that it was made to the order of a Mr. Gimbler, a solicitor who resides in the neighbourhood of Kennington. But Mr. Gimbler has managed to keep, to some extent, out of sight and put the whole responsibility on you. Even the dust that was found in the vault was your dust. It came from this very room."

At this latter statement, Wallis started visibly, and so did Miller.

"Yes, by Jove!" the latter exclaimed, after a glance at the floor and another at the window, "here is the identical carpet that you described in court, and there are the blue cotton curtains."

"So you see, Mr. Wallis," Thorndyke continued, "you have nothing to conceal respecting the coffin. The facts are known to us. The question is, are you prepared to tell us the name of the person to whose order this coffin was made?"

"If you know his name," was the reply, "you don't want me to tell you."

"Your evidence," said Thorndyke, "would save us a good deal of trouble, and perhaps it might save you some trouble, too. Are you prepared to tell us who this person was?"

"No," was the dogged reply. "I'm not going to tell you nothing. The least said the soonest mended. I don't know nothing about any coffin, and I don't believe there ever was any coffin."

At this reply Miller's face hardened, and I think he was about to pursue the matter farther, but Thorndyke calmly and civilly brought the interview to a close.

"Well, Mr. Wallis," said he, "you must do as you think best. I feel that you would have been wiser to have been more open with us, but we cannot compel you to give us information which you choose to withhold."

With this, he rose, and Miller reluctantly followed suit, looking distinctly sulky. But nothing further was said until, shepherded by our host, we had descended to the office and had been thence launched into the street. Then Miller made his protest.

"I think, Doctor," said he, "that it is a pity you didn't let me play him a little longer. I believe he would have let on if we had kept rubbing into him that he had been used as a cat's paw by Gimbler to get hold of that platinum."

"I don't think he would," said Thorndyke. "He is an obstinate man, and he evidently doesn't like the idea of turning upon his employer, and we can hardly blame him for that. But after all, Miller, what would have been the use of going on with him? We have got a complete train of evidence. We have got Bunter's written and signed statement that he left the platinum in Bert Wallis's workshop. We have got Bert Wallis's statement, made before witnesses, that he sold the stuff to his brother Joe Wallis. We have got Joe Wallis's statement, made before witnesses, that he bought the stuff from Bert. We know that Joe is a coffin maker, and that the stuff was found in a coffin, together with certain dust which came from a room which was identical in character with Joe Wallis's drawing room. The agreement is complete, even without the dust."

"So it is," Miller agreed, "but it proves the wrong thing. We can fix this job on Joseph all right. But it isn't Joseph that we want. He is only the jackal, but we want the lion – Gimbler. And if Joseph won't talk, we've got no direct evidence against Gimbler."

Thorndyke shook his head. "You are magnifying the difficulties, Miller," said he. "I don't know what you, or the Public Prosecutor, may propose to do, but I can tell you what I am going to do, if you don't. I am going to lay a sworn information charging Gimbler with having conspired with Joseph Wallis to commit certain fraudulent acts including the manufacture of false evidence, calculated and intended to defeat the ends of justice. We have enough evidence to convict him without any assistance from Wallis, but I think you will find that Joseph, when he discovers that he is involved in a fraud of which he knew nothing, will be far from willing to share the burden of that fraud with Gimbler. I think you can take it that Joseph will tell all that he knows (and perhaps a little more) when we begin to turn the screw. At any rate, I am quite satisfied with my case against Gimbler."

"Well, Doctor," said Miller in a less gloomy tone, "if you see your way to a conviction, I have nothing more to say. It's all I want."

Here the subject dropped, and the effect of the sandwiches having by this time worn off, we agreed with one accord to seek some reputable place of entertainment to make up the arrears in the matter of nourishment. As those arrears were somewhat considerable, the settling of them occupied our whole attention for a time, and it was not until our cravings had been satisfied and the stage of coffee and pipes had been reached that Miller suddenly raised a question which I had been expecting, and which I had secretly decided to raise, myself, at the first opportunity.

"By the way, Doctor," said he, "what about that head in the box? All these alarums and excursions in chase of that blooming platinum had driven it out of my head. But, now that we have done with the metal, at least for the present, supposing we have a word about the box. From the questions that you put to Bunter, it is clear to me that you have given the matter more attention than I had supposed, and it is obvious that you know something. I wonder how much you know."

"Not very much," replied Thorndyke, "but I shall probably know more when I have made a few inquiries. You are so far right that I have given the affair some attention, though not a great deal. But when I heard of the discovery in the cloak room, and afterwards read the account of the inquest, I formed certain opinions – quite speculatively, of course – as to what the incident probably meant, and I even formed a still-more speculative opinion as to the identity of one, at least, of the persons who might be concerned in the affair. Bunter's account of the passenger with the parcel seemed to agree with my hypothesis, and his answers to my questions seemed to support my identification of the person. That is all. Of actual, definite knowledge I have none."

"And your opinions," said Miller, a trifle sourly, "I suppose you are going to keep to yourself."

"For the present, I propose to," Thorndyke replied, suavely. "You can see, from what Bunter said, that the affair is of no importance to you. If a crime has been committed, it has not been committed within your jurisdiction. But leave the matter in my hands for a little longer. I believe that I shall be able to elucidate it, and you know that you can depend on me to keep nothing from you that ought, as a matter of public policy, to be communicated to you."

"Yes, I know that," Miller admitted, grudgingly, "and I see that the case is not what we supposed it to be. Very well, Doctor. Have it your own way, but let us have the information as soon as it is available."

Thorndyke made the required promise and, if the Superintendent was not as satisfied as he professed to be, it was only because, like me, he was devoured with curiosity as to what the solution of the mystery might be.

Chapter XVIII
The End of the Case and
Other Matters

The proceedings in the Probate Court at the third hearing of the Winsborough Peerage Case were brief but somewhat dramatic. As soon as the judge had taken his seat, Mr. McGonnell rose and addressed him to the following effect: "I have, this morning, my Lord, to bring to your Lordship's notice certain facts which would seem to make it unnecessary to proceed with the case which has been before the court. That case was an application by Mr. Christopher Pippet for permission to presume the death of Percy Engleheart, Sixth Earl of Winsborough. Now, in the interval since the last hearing, information has reached the Earl's representatives that the said Earl Percy died about three years ago."

"You say 'about' three years ago," said the judge.

"The exact date, my Lord, has not been ascertained, and is not, apparently, ascertainable, but it is believed that the Earl's death took place sometime in March 1918. The uncertainty, however, relates only to the time when the death occurred, of the fact that it did occur there appears to be no doubt at all. I understand that the body has been recovered and identified and is being sent to England. These facts were communicated to me by Mr. Brodribb, and perhaps the Earl's representatives might more properly inform your Lordship as to the exact circumstances in which the Earl's death occurred."

Here McGonnell sat down and Anstey took up the tale.

"The tidings of the Earl's death, my Lord, were conveyed to us in a letter written by a certain Major Pitt at Pará and dated the 13th of last October. The facts set forth in that letter were briefly these:

"In the latter part of 1917 and the beginning of 1918, Major Pitt and the Earl were travelling together in the neighbourhood of the River Amazon, shooting, collecting, and exploring. About the middle of January 1918, the Earl announced his intention to explore the tract of country inhabited by the Munderucu Indians and, as Major Pitt had planned a journey along the main stream of the Amazon, they separated and went their respective ways. That was the last time that Major Pitt saw the Earl alive, and for three years he had no knowledge of the Earl's whereabouts or what he was doing. The Major, himself, made a long journey and was several times laid up for long periods with severe attacks of fever. It was not until the spring of the present year that he, at last, got tidings as to what had befallen his friend. Then, taking the Munderucu country on his way back to the coast, he learned from some natives that a white man had come to the country some three years previously and had died from fever soon after his arrival, which would be about March 1918.

"On this, Major Pitt made more particular inquiries, the result of which was to leave no doubt that the man who had died could be none other than the Earl Percy. However, the Major, realizing the importance of accurate information, not only assembled the dead man's effects – a considerable part of which he was able to recover, and which he was, of course, able to identify – but he went so far as to cause the body to be disinterred. Naturally, it was, in the ordinary sense, unrecognizable, but by the stature and by certain characters, particularly the teeth, some of which had been filled with gold, he was able to identify it with certainty as the body of Earl Percy.

"But, to make assurance doubly sure, he commissioned the natives – who have great skill in preserving bodies – to preserve this corpse, in so far as there was anything to preserve, so that it could be sent to England for further examination if such examination should seem necessary or expedient. But the Major's description of the body, the clothing, the weapons, scientific instruments and other effects, together with the natives' description of the man, the time of his arrival, and all the other circumstances, leave no doubt whatever that this man was really the Earl Percy."

"In that case," said the judge, "if the fact of the Earl's death is to be accepted as proved, the application for permission to presume death necessarily lapses, automatically. And the applicant's claim to be the heir presumptive also lapses. He will now claim to be the heir, and that claim will have to be preferred in another place."

"I understand, my Lord," said McGonnell, "that it is not proposed to proceed with the claim. That is what I am informed by Mr. Pippet."

The judge glanced at the vacant solicitors' table and then asked, "Was that decision reached on the advice of his solicitor?"

"No, my Lord. Mr. Gimbler is not in court and, I believe, is absent from his residence. I understand that he has been unexpectedly called away from home."

The judge received this piece of information with an inscrutable face.

"It is not for me to express an opinion," he remarked, "as to whether Mr. Pippet is well- or ill-advised to abandon his claim, but I may point out that the crucial question is still in suspense. According to the evidence which we have heard, the coffin which was examined was not the coffin of Josiah Pippet and, consequently, the question whether the funeral was a real or a sham funeral has not been settled, It is unfortunate that that important issue should have been confused by what look like highly irregular proceedings, concerning which I may say that they will call for further investigation and that I shall consider it my duty to hand the papers in this case to the Director of Public Prosecutions."

This rather ominous observation brought the proceedings to an end and, as we were no longer litigants, the whole party trooped out of the court to gather in the great hall for more or less friendly, unofficial discussion. Mr. Pippet was the first to speak.

"His Lordship," he remarked, "was extremely delicate in his language. I should call the proceedings in regard to that coffin something more than irregular."

"His Lordship," McGonnell remarked, "was probably bearing in mind that all the facts are not known. He, no doubt, has his suspicions as to what has happened and who is responsible but, until the suspicions have been verified, it is as well not to be too explicit in assigning responsibility to individuals."

Mr. Pippet smiled grimly. "It is well for you to say that, Mr. McGonnell," said he, "seeing that both you and I are involved in those suspicions. But I am not inclined to take this business lying down, if you are. Gimbler was acting as my agent and I suppose I am responsible for whatever he chose to do, ostensibly in my interests. But I presume I have some remedy. Is it possible for me to prosecute him? You are my legal adviser. I put the question to you. What remedy have I for being involved in this discreditable affair?"

Mr. McGonnell looked uncomfortable, as well he might, for he was in an unpleasant position in more than one respect. After a few moments' reflection, he replied, "I have as little reason as you have to be pleased with the turn of events. If a fraud has been committed in this case, that will not enhance my professional reputation. But I must again remind you that we have not got all the facts. It does certainly appear as if that coffin had been tampered with, and if it had, the responsibility lies between you and me and Mr. Gimbler. Evidently, the suspicion lies principally on Gimbler. But having regard to the fact that a quantity of stolen property – which was certainly not his – was found in the coffin, there is a clear possibility that the coffin may have been tampered with by some persons for their own purposes and without his knowledge. We have to bear that in mind before we make any direct accusations."

"That is a very ingenious suggestion," said Mr. Pippet, "but it doesn't seem to commend itself to me. I should leave it to him to prove, if he can."

McGonnell shook his head. "That is not the position, at all, Mr. Pippet," said he. "If you assert that Gimbler planted a sham coffin in the vault, it will be for you to prove that he did, not for him to prove that he did not. But I think that you had better take the advice of a solicitor on the subject, or at any rate, of some lawyer other than me. You will understand that I shall naturally be reluctant to be the first to set up a hue-and-cry after a man who has been my colleague in this case. If he has committed a fraud, I hope that he will receive the punishment that he will have deserved, but I should rather that some hand other than mine delivered the blow."

"I understand and respect your point of view," said Pippet, "but it leaves me high and dry without any legal guidance."

Here Thorndyke interposed. "If I might venture to offer you a word of advice, Mr. Pippet," said he, "it would be that you do nothing at all. If any offence against the law has been committed, you may rely on the proper authorities to take the necessary measures."

"But suppose they regard me as the offender?"

"When you are accused, it will be time to take measures of defence. At present, no one is accusing you – at least, I think I may say so. Am I right, Superintendent?" he asked, turning to Miller, who had been unostentatiously listening to the conversation.

The Superintendent was guarded in his reply. "Speaking personally," said he, "I am certainly not accusing Mr. Pippet of any complicity in this fraud, if there has really been a fraud. Later, I may have to apply to him for some information as to his relations with Mr. Gimbler, but that is in the future. For the present, your advice to him is the best. Just wait and see what happens."

"And meanwhile," said Thorndyke, "if it appears that Mr. Gimbler has withdrawn himself from among us permanently, I am sure that Mr. Brodribb will consent to take charge of your affairs so far as recovery of documents and other winding up details are concerned."

To this, Brodribb agreed readily, to Mr. Pippet's evident relief.

"Then," said the latter, "as we have disposed of business matters, I am going to propose that we make up a little luncheon party to celebrate the end of the Winsborough Peerage Case. I'd like to have the whole crowd, but I suspect that there are one or two who will cry off."

His suspicions were confirmed on particular inquiry. McGonnell had business at the Central Criminal Court, Mrs. Engleheart and Miss

Pippet had some secret mission, the nature of which they refused to divulge, and Anstey had other legal fish to fry.

"Am I to have the pleasure of your Lordship's company at lunch?" Pippet inquired, fixing a twinkling eye on Mr. Giles, and obviously convinced that he was not.

Giles laughed, knowingly. "I should have been delighted," said he, "to lunch with my noble cousin, or uncle, or whatever he is, but I have an engagement with another noble cousin. I am taking Jenny to the Zoo to show her the new chimpanzee, and we shall get our lunch on the way."

Mr. Pippet shook his head resignedly and turned to the faithful few, consisting of Thorndyke, Brodribbm Miller, and myself, and suggested an immediate adjournment. Thorndyke and I retired to the robing room to divest ourselves of our legal war-paint and, on emerging, rejoined the party at the main gate, where two taxis were already waiting, and were forthwith conveyed to Mr. Pippet's hotel.

Throughout these proceedings and those of the subsequent luncheon, I was aware of a rather curious feeling of pleased surprise at our host's attitude and apparent state of mind. Especially did I admire the sporting spirit in which he accepted his defeat. He was not in the least cast down and, apart from the discreditable incidents in the conduct of the case, he appeared perfectly satisfied with the result. But the oddest thing to me was his friendly and even deferential attitude towards Thorndyke. A stranger, unacquainted with the circumstances, might have supposed my colleague to be the leading counsel who had achieved a notable victory for Mr. Pippet, instead of an expert witness who had, vulgarly speaking, "put the kybosh" on Mr. Pippet's case. Any pique that he might, quite naturally, have felt seemed to be swallowed up by a keen sporting interest in the manner in which he had been defeated, and I was not surprised when, as the luncheon approached the coffee and cigar stage, he began to put out feelers for more detailed information.

"This trial," said he, "has been to me an education and an entertainment. I've enjoyed every bit of it, and I'm only sorry that we missed the judge's summing-up and reasoned decision. But the real tit-bit of the entertainment was Dr. Thorndyke's evidence. What delighted me was the instantaneous way in which every move in the game was spotted and countered. Those screws, now – it was all obvious enough when it was explained. But the astonishing thing was that, not only was the character of those screws observed, but the significance of that character appreciated in a moment. I want you to tell me, Doctor, how you manage to keep your eyes perpetually skinned, and your brain skinned at the same time."

Thorndyke smiled appreciatively as he thoughtfully filled his pipe.

"You are giving me more credit than is due, Mr. Pippet," said he. "You are assuming that certain reactions were instantaneous which were, in fact, quite deliberate, and that certain deceptive appearances were exhibited to unprepared eyes, whereas they had been carefully considered in advance. I have no doubt that the person who prepared the evidence made a similar mistake."

"But," objected Mr. Pippet, "I don't see how you could consider in advance things that you didn't know were going to happen."

"It is possible to consider in advance," Thorndyke replied, "those circumstances which may conceivably arise as well as those which will certainly arise. You seem to think that the little surprise packets which the manipulator of evidence devised for our undoing found us all unprepared. That was certainly the intention of the manipulator, but it was very far from what actually happened."

"Why call him 'the manipulator'?" Mr. Pippet protested. "His name is Horatio Gimbler, and we all know it."

"Very well," said Thorndyke, "then we will throw legal caution to the winds and call him Gimbler. Now, as I said, Gimbler made his little arrangements, expecting that they would come on us with all the charm of novelty and find us unprepared to give them that exhaustive consideration which would be necessary to ascertain their real nature, but which would be impossible in the course of proceedings in court. He would assume that, whatever vague suspicions we might have, there would be neither the time nor the opportunity to test the visible facts presented. What he had overlooked was the possibility that the other players might try the moves over in advance. But this is exactly what I did. Would it interest you to have some details of my procedure?"

"It would interest me very much," Brodribb interposed, "for, as you know, I sat on the bird-lime like a lamb – if you will pardon the mixed metaphor. Perhaps I might say 'like a fool' and be nearer the mark."

"I hope you won't, Mr. Brodribb," said Pippet, "because the description would include the lot of us, except the Doctor. But I am sure we should all like to hear how that rascal, Gimbler, was unmasked."

"Then," said Thorndyke, "let us begin by noting what our position was. This was a claim advanced by an unknown person to a title and some extremely valuable property. The claimant was an American, but there was nothing significant in that. All Americans of English origin have, of course, English ancestors. What was significant was the fact that this stranger had elected to employ a police court solicitor to conduct his case. Taking all the circumstances together, there was quite a fair probability that the claim was a false claim, and if that were so, we should have to be on the look-out for false evidence.

635

"That was my function in the case: To watch the evidence, particularly in regard to the physical characteristics of any objects produced as 'exhibits' or put in evidence. The purely legal business was in the hands of Mr. Brodribb and Mr. Anstey, whereas I was a sort of Devil's Advocate, in an inverted sense, concerned, not with the legal issues, but with illegal attempts to tamper with the evidence. Now, in the criminal department of my practice, I have been in the habit, from the first, of using what I may call a synthetic method. In investigating a known or suspected crime, my custom has been to put myself in the criminal's place and ask myself what are the possible methods of committing that crime and, of the possible methods, which would be the best – How, in fact, I should go about committing that crime, myself. Having worked out in detail the most suitable procedure, I then change over from the synthetic to the analytic method and consider all the inherent weaknesses and defects of the method, and the means by which it would be possible to detect the crime.

"That is what I did in the present case. I began by assuming that wherever the evidence was insufficient or adverse, that evidence would be falsified."

"Sounds a bit uncharitable," Mr. Pippet remarked, with a smile.

"Not at all," retorted Thorndyke. "There was no accusation. It was merely a working hypothesis which I communicated to nobody. If there had been no falsification, nothing would ever have been said and nobody would ever have known that the possibility had been entertained. But supposing falsification to be attempted – what form would it take? Apart from mere oral tradition and rumour, the value of which the judge would be able to assess, there was very little evidence. Of real, demonstrable evidence there were only two items – the diary and the coffin. Let us take the diary first. In what respects was falsification of the diary possible?

"There were two possibilities. The entire diary might be a fabrication. This was extremely unlikely. There were seven volumes, extending over a great number of years. The fabrication of such a diary would be a gigantic and very difficult task. Still, it was possible, but if the diary was in fact a fabrication from beginning to end, the falsification would almost certainly have been the work of the claimant, himself. But when one considers that the latest volume of this dairy was alleged to have been written eighty years ago, it is obvious that the difficulties surrounding the production of a new work which could possibly be passed off as genuine would be practically insurmountable. I need not consider those difficulties or the means by which the fraud could be detected, since the case did not arise. On inspection, it was obvious that the diary was a genuine document.

"The second possibility was the insertion of a false entry, and this was not only quite practicable but, in the known circumstances, not very improbable. The question was, therefore, supposing a false entry to be inserted, would that entry have any special characteristics for which one could be on the look-out? And the answer was that it almost certainly would.

"As to the forgery itself, it would certainly be a good forgery. For, if it had been executed by the claimant, it would have to be good enough to satisfy Mr. Gimbler. That gentleman was too-experienced a lawyer to attempt to pass off an indifferent forgery in a court of law. But if it were not the work of the claimant, it would have to be produced either by Gimbler, himself, or under his superintendence. In either case it would certainly be a first-class forgery and, as the passage would probably be quite short – possibly only a few words – it would be almost impossible to detect by mere examination of the written characters. In a short passage, the forger's attention need never flag, and no effects of fatigue would become apparent. The forger could try it over and over again until he could execute it perfectly. But in such a case, even the greatest experts – such as Osborn in America, or Mitchell or Lucas in this country – could give no more than a guarded opinion. For however eminent an expert may be, he cannot detect differences that do not exist.

"But if the imitation of the hand-writing were too good for detection to be possible, were there any other, extrinsic, characters that we could be on the look-out for? Evidently, by the nature of the case, there must be three. First, if a passage were inserted, it would have to be inserted where insertion was possible – that is to say, in a blank space. Accordingly, we should have to keep a look-out for blank spaces. And, if those blank spaces were of any considerable size, we should look for the interpolated passage or passages either at the beginning or end of the blank space or spaces.

"The second character of an interpolated passage would be the matter contained in it. It would contain some matter of high evidential value which was not contained in any of the genuine entries, for, if it did not, there would be no object in inserting it. As to the nature of this matter, since the crucial issue in this case was whether the two persons, Josiah and the Earl, were one and the same person, an interpolated passage would almost certainly contain matter supporting the belief that they were.

"The third character would be an unavoidable difference between the ink used for the forgery and that used by the writer of the genuine entries. They could not be the same unless the writer of the diary had elected to use carbon ink, which was infinitely improbable and, in fact, was not the case. If he used ordinary writing ink – the iron-gall ink of the period – that ink would have become changed in the course of over eighty years. The original black tannate or gallate of iron would have become converted into the faint reddish-brown of the oxide of iron. Now, the forged writing would have to imitate the colour of this old writing. But a new ink of the same colour as the old would necessarily be of a different chemical composition. Probably it would contain no iron, but would be one of the modern brown drawing inks, treated to match the colour exactly.

"In this difference of chemical composition would lie the means of detecting and exposing the forgery. A chemical test would probably be objected to, though it could be insisted on if the forgery were definitely challenged. But, for the reasons that I gave in my evidence, a photograph would be nearly certain to demonstrate the difference in the chemical composition of the ink. And to a photograph there could be no objection.

"Thus, you see, the whole matter had been examined in advance, so that, if a forgery should be offered in evidence, we knew exactly what it would be like. And when it did appear, it corresponded perfectly with the hypothetical forgery. We heard McGonnell read out, in his opening statement, a number of quotations from the diary, all very vague and unconvincing, and then, at the end, a single short entry of an entirely different character, explicitly implying the identity of the two persons, Josiah and the Earl. Here was one of the characters of the possible forgery, and when Anstey had elicited in cross-examination that neither you nor your sister had seen it before the book went into the hands of Mr. Gimbler, it became a probable forgery. Then, on inspection, it was seen to have another of the postulated characters: It was at the end of a blank space. Finally, on closer examination, it was found to have the third character: It was written in an ink which was different from that used in the rest of the diary.

"So much for the forgery. In the case of the coffin a similar method was used. I put myself in Gimbler's place and considered the best way in which to carry out the substitution."

"But," objected Mr. Pippet, "Gimbler had never suggested any examination of the coffin. On the contrary, he had decided to avoid any reference to an examination until the case went to the House of Lords. I thought he was giving that coffin as wide a berth as he could."

"Exactly," said Thorndyke. "That was the impression that he managed to convey to us all. And it was that which made me suspect strongly that a substitution was intended. It looked to me like a very subtle and admirable tactical manoeuvre. For, you see, the examination could not be avoided. It was impossible to burke the coffin, and Gimbler knew it. Not only was it the one piece of definite and undeniable evidence in the case, it contained the means of settling conclusively the whole issue that was before the court. If Gimbler did not produce the coffin himself, it would certainly be demanded by the other side or by the judge.

"But now observe the subtlety of Gimbler's tactics. The crude thing to do would have been to make the substitution and then apply for an order of the court to have the coffin examined. But in that case, the coffin would have been approached by the other side with a certain amount of suspicion, and minutely scrutinized. But when Gimbler seemed to have been taken by surprise, and to agree reluctantly to the examination of the coffin, the suspicion that he had got it all ready and prepared for the examination would be unlikely to arise. 'The other side' would be caught off their guard."

"Yes, by Jove!" chuckled Brodribb, "and so they were. I was quite shocked and embarrassed when I saw you sniffing round that coffin and openly showing that you suspected a fraud, and McGonnell was really and genuinely indignant."

"Yes," said Pippet, "he very much resented the implied doubt as to his good faith, and I must admit that I thought the Doctor a trifle over-sceptical. But don't let me interrupt. I want to hear how you anticipated so exactly what Gimbler would do."

"As I said," Thorndyke resumed, "it was by putting myself in Gimbler's place and considering how I should go about making this substitution. There were two possible methods. One was to open the old coffin and take out the body, if there was one there, the other was to prepare a new coffin to look like an old one. The first method was much the better if it could have been properly carried out. But there were one or two serious difficulties. In the first place, there would, presumably, have been a corpse to dispose of, and the operators might have objected to handling it. But the most serious objection was the possibility of a mishap in opening the coffin. It was an old coffin, and the wood might be extensively decayed. If, in the process of opening it, the lid should have broken or some other damage should have been done, the fraud would have been hopelessly exposed. For no repair would be possible. But in any case, an ancient coffin could not have been opened without leaving some plainly visible traces.

"The second plan had several advantages. The new coffin could be prepared at leisure and thoroughly examined, and the proceedings on the spot could be quite short. You remember that there is, adjoining the burial ground, a stable yard with an empty cart shed in which a van could be housed while the substitution was being made. There would be little more to do than drive into the yard, exchange the coffins and drive away again. I considered both plans in detail and eventually decided that the second one was the one that would be more probably adopted.

"Now suppose that it was. What would the exact procedure be, and what pit-falls lay in wait for the operators? What would they have to do, and what mistakes would they probably make in doing it? In the first place, the coffin would pretty certainly be made by a regular coffin-maker, and the chances were a hundred to one, or more, that he would use modern screws and try to produce the appearance of age by rusting them. If he did, the coffin would be definitely labelled as a fabrication beyond any possible dispute.

"Then there was the sheet-lead. What he would put in would most probably be modern, silver-free milled lead, whereas the original would almost certainly have been cast sheet. Still, he might have got some old sheet lead, and in any case the discrepancy would not have been conclusive or very convincing to the judge. We could not have given a definite date, as in the case of the screws.

"The next pit-fall would be the dust. In that vault, everything would be covered with a mantle of dust of eighty years' growth. But if once that dust were disturbed – as it necessarily would be in moving the coffin – there would be no possibility of obliterating the marks of disturbance. There would be nothing for it but to sweep the vault out clean and blow in a fresh supply of dust which would settle down in a smooth and even layer. And there one could confidently expect that a serious mistake would be made. To most persons, dust is just simply dust, a material quite devoid of individual character. Few people realize consciously that dust is merely a collection of particles detached from larger bodies, and that when those particles are magnified by the microscope, they reveal themselves as recognizable fragments of those bodies. If our friends blew dust into the vault, it would be dust that had been collected *ad hoc* and would be demonstrably the wrong sort of dust.

"That was how I reasoned the matter out in advance, and you will see that, when I came to the vault, all that I had to do was to note whether the appearances were normal or whether they corresponded to the false appearances which were already in my mind. As soon as I saw the screws, the question was answered. It remained only to look for additional details of evidence such as the dust and anything that might be distinctive in the character of the lead."

"The platinum, I take it," said Pippet, "had not been included in your forecast?"

"No," replied Thorndyke. "That was a free gift of Providence. It came as a complete surprise, and I might easily have missed it but for the rule that I have made to let nothing pass without examination. In accordance with this routine procedure, I took up each piece of lead and inspected it to see if it showed any peculiarities by which it would be possible to date it. As soon as I lifted the first lump of platinum alloy, I realized that Providence had delivered the gay deceiver into our hands."

"Yes," said Pippet, "that was a stroke of pure luck. But it wasn't necessary. I can see that your method of playing a trial game over in advance – of ascertaining what your adversary may do, instead of waiting to see what he does do – brings you to the table with all the trumps up your sleeve, ready to be produced if the chance occurs."

He reflected awhile, stirring his coffee thoughtfully and, apparently turning something over in his mind. At length, he looked up at Thorndyke and disclosed the subject of his cogitations.

"You have told us, Doctor," said he, "that you got this vanishing coffin stunt worked out in advance in all its details. But there is one little matter that you have not referred to, and it happens to be one which interests me a good deal. I am wondering what has become of Josiah. It may seem only a matter of sentiment, but he was my grandfather, and I feel that it is up to me to see him put back in his proper residence in accordance with his wishes and the arrangements which he made during his life. Now, did the advance scheme that you drew up include any plans for disposing of Josiah?"

"Certainly," replied Thorndyke, "Assuming a new coffin to be used, the disposal of the old one was an important part of the problem – important to those who had to carry out the proceedings, and to us who had to prove that they had been carried out. The recovery and production of the old coffin would be conclusive evidence for the prosecution."

"Well, now," said Pippet, "tell us how you proposed to dispose of Josiah and how you intend to go about getting him back."

"There were two possible methods," said Thorndyke, "of getting rid of the old coffin. First, since a van or cart must have been used to bring the new coffin to the vault, it would have been available to take the old one away. This would have been a bad method, both for the plotters and for us, for it would have left them with the coffin on their hands, and us with the task of finding out where it had been hidden. So we will leave it until we have dealt with the more obvious and reasonable plan. I did not propose to bring the coffin away at all."

"You don't mean that you proposed to bury it?" said Pippet.

"No," replied Thorndyke. "There was no need to. You have forgotten the arrangement of the place. There were six vaults, each secured only by a large, simple lock. Now, our friends must have had a big, strong skeleton key to open Josiah's vault. With the same key they could have opened any of the other vaults, and there was a perfectly excellent and convenient hiding-place."

"Gee!" chuckled Mr. Pippet. "That's a quaint idea! To think that, while we were poring over that dummy coffin, Josiah, himself, was quietly reposing next door! But I guess you are right, Doctor, and the question is, what are you going to do about it?"

Thorndyke looked at the Superintendent.

"It is your move, Miller," said he. "You have got the skeleton key, and you have the Home Office authority."

"That is all very well," Miller replied, cautiously, "but the judge's order doesn't authorize us to break into any of the other vaults."

"The judge's order," said Thorndyke, "doesn't say anything about a particular vault. It authorizes and directs you to open and examine the coffin of Josiah Pippet. But you haven't done anything of the sort. You opened the wrong coffin. You have not complied with the judge's order, and it is your duty to do so without delay."

Miller grinned and glanced knowingly at Mr. Pippet.

"That's the sort of hair-pin the Doctor is," he said, admiringly. "Thomas Didymus combined with a casuist of the deepest dye. He could argue the hind leg off a donkey, and that donkey would have nothing for it but to get a wooden leg."

Here Mr. Brodribb intervened with some warmth. "You are doing Dr. Thorndyke an injustice, Superintendent," said he. "There is nothing casuistical in his argument. He has stated the legal position quite correctly, not only in the letter but in the spirit. The judge made an order for the examination of the coffin of Josiah Pippet for the declared purpose of ascertaining the nature of its contents. But we have not examined that coffin, and we still do not know the nature of its contents. You will remember that the judge, himself, pointed that out at this morning's proceedings."

Miller was visibly impressed by these observations from the very correct and experienced old lawyer, and I could see that he was quite willing to be impressed, for he was as keen on the examination as any of us. But he was a police officer and, as such, Josiah Pippet was not his pigeon. Civil cases were not in his province.

Thorndyke evidently saw the difficulty, and proceeded adroitly to turn his flank.

"Besides, Miller," he said, "you seem to be overlooking the importance of this matter in relation to a possible prosecution. A police officer of your experience is lawyer enough to realize the great difference in value between positive and negative evidence. Now, at present, all that we can do is to show cause for the belief that the coffin that we found in the vault was not Josiah's coffin. But suppose that we are able to produce the actual coffin of Josiah Pippet. That would leave the defence nothing to say. And, in any case, for the sake of your own reputation and that of the C.I.D., that coffin has got to be found, and common sense suggests that we begin the search in the most likely place."

This argument disposed effectually of Miller's difficulties.

"You are quite right, Doctor," he agreed. "We shall be expected to produce that coffin, or at least, to prove its existence and its whereabouts, and I certainly agree with you that the vault is the most likely place in which to look for it. I hope we are both right, for, if it isn't there, we may be let in for a mighty long chase before we get hold of it."

Agreement on the principle having been reached, it remained only to settle the details. Mr. Pippet, with characteristic American eagerness to "get on with it", would have started forthwith for the burial ground, but, as Miller naturally had not got the keys about him, and as Thorndyke had certain preparations to make, it was arranged that the parties to the expedition should meet at the latter's chambers at ten o'clock on the following morning.

Chapter XIX
Josiah?

There was something distinctly furtive and conspiratorial in the appearance and bearing of the party of six which filed into the burial ground under the guidance of Superintendent Miller. At least, so it seemed to me, though the impression may have been due to Polton, who carried a small suit-case with a secretive and burglarious air, persisted in walking on tip-toe, and generally surrounded himself with the atmosphere of a veritable Guy Fawkes.

As soon as we were all in, the Superintendent closed the gate and locked it from the inside, putting the key in his pocket. Then he followed us to the neighbourhood of the vaults, where we were screened from the gaze of possible onlookers.

"Well," he remarked, stating an undeniable truth, "here we are, and here are the vaults. We've got five to choose from, and the chances are that we shall open four wrong ones before we come to the right one – if there is a right one. What do you say, Doctor? Any choice?"

"On general grounds," said Thorndyke, "it would seem that one is as likely as another, but on psychological grounds, I should say that there is a slight probability in favour of the sixth vault."

"Why?" demanded Miller.

"Because," replied Thorndyke, "although, as a hiding-place, any one vault would be as good as any other, I think there would be a tendency to get as far as possible from the vault in which the dummy coffin had been planted. It is merely a guess, but, as we have nothing else to guide us, I would suggest that we begin with Number Six."

"While the brief discussion had been taking place, Polton had been peering into the keyholes with the aid of a small electric lamp and inspecting the edges of the respective doors. He now reported the results of his observations. "I think you are right, sir," said he. "There seems to be a trace of grease in the inside of the lock of the last door, and there is something that looks rather like the mark of a jemmy on the jamb of the door. Perhaps Mr. Miller might take a look at it."

Mr. Miller, as an expert on jemmy-marks, accordingly did take a look at it, and was inclined to confirm our artificer's opinion, on which it was decided to begin operations on Number Six. The big skeleton key

644

was produced from the Superintendent's pocket and handed to Polton, by whom it was tenderly anointed with oil. Then a dressing of oil was applied to the rusty wards of the lock by means of a feather poked in through the keyhole, and the key inserted. As it refused to turn, in spite of the oil, Polton produced from his case a "tommy" – a steel bar about a foot long – which he passed through the bow of the key and worked gently backwards and forwards to distribute the oil and avoid the risk of wrenching off the bow. After a few trials, the key made a complete turn, and we heard the rusty bolt grate back into the lock.

"I expect we shall have to prise the door open," said Polton, after one or two vigorous tugs at the key, using the tommy as a handle. He threw back the lid of his suit-case, which was lying on the ground at his side, and looked into it – as, also, did the Superintendent.

"Well, I'm sure, Mr. Polton!" the latter exclaimed. "Are you aware that it is a misdemeanour to go abroad with housebreaking implements in your possession?"

Polton regarded him with a cunning and crinkly smile.

"May I ask, Mr. Miller," he demanded, "what you would use to force open a jammed door? Would you use a corkscrew or a sardine opener?"

Miller chuckled, appreciatively. "Well," he said, as Polton selected a powerful telescopic jemmy from his outfit, "I suppose the end justifies the means."

"You can take it, sir," said Polton, sententiously, "that people whose business it is to open doors have found out the best tools to do it with."

Having delivered himself of this profound truth, he inserted the beak of the jemmy between the door and the jamb, gave it one or two tweaks at different levels, and then, grasping the key and the tommy, pulled the complaining door wide open.

The first glance into the mouldy and dusty interior showed that Thorndyke's selection had been correct. There were two names on the stone slab above the vault, but there were three coffins, two lying in orderly fashion on the stone shelf, and a third flung untidily across them. That the latter was the coffin which we were seeking was at once suggested by the fact that the handles and name-plate were missing, though the spaces which they had occupied and the holes for the screws were conspicuously visible.

"That is Josiah's coffin right enough," said Mr. Pippet, pointing to these marks. "There can't be a shadow of doubt."

"No," agreed Thorndyke, "but we mustn't leave it at that. We must put the two coffins side by side and make an exact comparison which can be described in evidence in terms of actual measurement. I noticed that

645

the beadle had not taken away the trestles. We had better set them up and put this coffin on them. The other one can be put on the ground alongside."

We fetched the trestles and, having set them up, the four tallest of us proceeded to hoist out the coffin.

"He's a mighty weight," Mr. Pippet remarked, as he lowered his end carefully to the trestles.

"Probably there is a lead shell," said Miller. "There usually was in the better class coffins. I'm surprised they didn't put one in the dummy to make it a bit more convincing."

While the removal was being effected, Polton, armed with the skeleton key – the jemmy was not required – had got the door of the other vault open. Thither we now proceeded and, lifting out the empty and comparatively light dummy, carried it across and laid it on the ground beside the trestles.

"The first thing," said Thorndyke, "will be to take off the name-plate and try it on the old coffin. An actual trial will be more convincing to a judge or jury than the most careful measurements."

"Is it of any great importance," Mr. Pippet asked, "to prove that the dummy was faked by using the old coffin furniture?"

"It is absolutely vital," Thorndyke replied. "How else are we to prove that this is the coffin of Josiah Pippet? There is no mark on it by which it could be identified, and we find it in a vault which is not Josiah's. Moreover, in the vault which is his, there is a coffin bearing his name-plate which is alleged to be his coffin, and which we are trying to prove is not his coffin."

"I thought you had done that pretty effectually already," said Pippet.

"We can't have too much evidence," Thorndyke rejoined, "and in any case, we have got to produce positive evidence of the identity of this coffin. At present we are only guessing, though I have no doubt that we are guessing right. But if we can prove that the nameplate on that coffin was removed from and belonged to this one, we shall have proved the identity of this one and the fraudulent character of the other."

While Thorndyke had been arguing this rather obvious point, Polton had been engaged in carefully and methodically extracting, with a clock-maker's screw-driver, the six screws with which the name-plate was attached to the dummy coffin-lid. He now held one of them up for his employer's inspection, remarking, "You see, sir, that they used the original brass screws – the old, flat-ended sort, which will be better for testing purposes, as they won't go into a hole that wasn't properly bored for them."

While the screw was being passed round and examined, he proceeded with the testing operations. First, he lifted the plate from its bed, whereupon there was disclosed an oblong patch of new, unstained wood, which he regarded with a contemptuous crinkle.

"Well!" he exclaimed, "if I had been faking a coffin, I'd at least have finished the faking before I screwed on the plate and not have given the show away like this."

With this, he picked up the plate and laid it on the old coffin-lid in the vacant space, which it fitted exactly. Then, with a fine awl, he felt through one of the corner holes of the plate for the corresponding hole in the wood and, having found it, dropped in one of the screws and ran it lightly home. Next, in the same manner, he probed the hole in the opposite corner of the plate, dropped in the screw and drove it home. Then, discarding the awl, he dropped in the other four screws, all of which ran in quite smoothly.

"There, Mr. Pippet," said Thorndyke, "that establishes the identity of the coffin. The six holes in the brass plate coincide exactly with the six holes in the wood, for, as Polton points out, the screws, being blunt-ended, would not enter the wood if the holes were not precisely in the right place. So you can now take it as an established fact that this is really the coffin of your grandfather, Josiah Pippet. Does that satisfy you? Or is there anything else that you wish to have done?"

Pippet looked at him in surprise. "Why!" he exclaimed, "we've only just begun! I thought we came here to find out exactly what is in that coffin. That is what I came for. I had made up my mind before I came to England that the first thing that I would do would be to find out whether Josiah was or was not in that coffin. Then I should have known whether to haul off or go ahead."

"Exactly," said Thorndyke, "but are you sure that you still want to know?"

I looked quickly at Thorndyke, and so did Mr. Pippet. The question was asked in the quietest and most matter-of-fact tone, and yet I had the feeling that it carried a significance beyond either the tone or the words. And this, I think, was noticed also by our American friend, for he paused a few moments with his eyes fixed on Thorndyke before he replied, "It doesn't matter so much now, as I've dropped the claim. But, still, if it doesn't seem irreverent, I think I should like to have a look at Josiah. I hate to leave a job unfinished."

"Very well," said Thorndyke, "it's your funeral in a literal as well as allegorical sense. You would like to have the coffin opened?"

"I should, though I don't quite see how you are going to manage it. There don't seem to be any screws."

"The screws are plugged," Thorndyke explained, "as they usually are in well-finished coffins. They are sunk in little pits and the pits are filled up with plugs of wood, which are planed off clean so as to show an uninterrupted surface. Possibly those plugs were the deciding factor in the question as to whether the old coffin should be opened and faked, or a new one made. You can see that it would be impossible to get those plugs out and replace them without leaving very visible traces."

This statement was illustrated by Polton's proceedings. From the inexhaustible suit-case he produced a cabinet-maker's scraper, with which he set to work at the edge of the lid, scraping off the old surface, thereby bringing into view the little circular inlays which marked the position of the screws, of which there were eight. When they were all visible, he attacked them with a nose bit set in a brace, and quickly exposed the heads of the screws. But then came the tug of war. For the rust of eighty years seemed to have fixed the screws immovably, and by the time that he had managed, with the aid of a driver bit in his brace, to get them out, his crinkly countenance was streaming with perspiration.

"All right this time," said Mr. Pippet, picking up one of the screws and inspecting its blunt end. "I guess I'll take these screws to keep as a memento. Ah! You were right, Doctor," he added, as Polton prised up the lid and lifted it clear. "It was the lead shell that made it so blamed ponderous."

Here Mr. Brodribb, casting a slightly apprehensive glance at the leaden inner coffin, announced, as he selected a cigar from his case,

"If you are going to open the shell, Thorndyke, I think I will take a little stroll and survey the landscape. I haven't got a medical jurist's stomach."

Thorndyke smiled, unsympathetically, but nevertheless, offered him a light and, as he moved away, exhaling fragrant clouds, Polton approached the coffin with a formidable hooked knife and a pair of tinman's shears.

"Do you want to see the whole of him, sir?" he asked, bestowing a crinkly smile on Mr. Pippet, "or do you think his head will be enough?"

"Well, Mr. Polton," was the guarded reply, "perhaps his head will be enough – to begin with, anyway."

Thereupon, Polton, with a few gentle taps of a hammer, drove the point of the knife through the soft lead and began to cut a line in a U shape round the head end of the shell. When he had extended it sufficiently, he prised up the end of the tongue-shaped piece enclosed by the incision and turned it back like a flap. We stood aside respectfully to allow Mr. Pippet to be the first to look upon the long-forgotten face of his ancestor, and he accordingly advanced and bent down over the dark

648

opening. For an appreciable time he remained looking silently into the cavity, apparently overcome by the emotions natural to the occasion. But I must confess that I was somewhat startled when he gave expression to those emotions. For what he said – and he said it slowly and with the strongest emphasis – was, "Well – I'm – damned!"

Now, when a gentleman so scrupulously correct in speech as was Mr. Pippet, makes use of such an expression, it is reasonable to assume that something unusual has occurred. As he withdrew his head from the opening, mine and Thorndyke's met over it (and I am afraid mine was the harder). But in spite of the collision, I saw enough in a single glance to account for Mr. Pip pet's exclamation. For what met that glance was no shrivelled, mummified human face, but the end of a slender roll of canvas embedded in time-discoloured sawdust.

"Now," commented Miller, when he had made his inspection, "isn't that just like a blinking crook! They are all fools, no matter how artful they may be. And they can't imagine the possibility of anyone else being honest. Of course, Gimbler thought that the coffin story was all bunkum, so he pitched the old coffin away without troubling to open it and see what was really in it. If he had only left it alone, Mr. Pippet's claim would have been as good as established."

"It would certainly have been important evidence," said I. "But, for that matter, it is still. The story of the bogus funeral is now proved beyond any possible doubt to be true. And, though the claim has lapsed for the moment, it lapsed only on a technical point. What do you say, Brodribb?" I asked as that gentleman, in the course of his perambulations, passed the vault at a respectful distance.

"What do I say to what?" he demanded, reasonably enough.

"We have opened the shell and we find that it does not contain a body."

"What does it contain?" he asked.

"Something wrapped in canvas and packed in sawdust," I replied.

"That is not a very complete account," he objected, approaching cautiously to take a peep into the interior of the shell. "It certainly does not look like a body," he admitted after a very brief inspection, "but it might be. A very small one."

"It would be a very small one, indeed," said Thorndyke. "But I agree with you Brodribb. We ought to ascertain exactly what the contents of the coffin are."

On this, Polton re-inserted the hooked knife and prolonged the incision on one side to the foot of the shell and carried it across. Then he raised the long flap and turned it back, exposing the whole of the mass of sawdust and the long roll of canvas which was embedded in it. The latter,

649

being lifted out and laid on the coffin-lid, was seen to be secured with three strands of twine or spun-yarn. These Polton carefully untied – they were fastened with reef-knots – and, having thus released the canvas, unrolled it and displayed its contents, which consisted of a small roll of sheet lead, a portion of a battered rain head and a flattened section of leaden stack-pipe.

"This is interesting," said Brodribb. "It corresponds with the description more closely than I should have expected."

"And you notice, sir," Polton pointed out, "that the sheet lead is proper cast sheet, as The Doctor said it would be."

"I take your word for it, Polton," said Brodribb. "And that is a further agreement, which, I may add – since we are all friends – is not without its evidential significance."

"That is the point that we were discussing," said I. "The bearing of this discovery on Mr. Pippet's claim."

"I beg your pardon, Dr. Jervis," Mr. Pippet interposed, "but there isn't any claim. My sister and I agreed some time ago to drop the claim if we got a chance. And Dr. Thorndyke gave us a very fair chance, and we are very much obliged to him."

"I am glad to hear that," said Brodribb, "because this discovery does really confuse the issues rather badly. On this new evidence it would be possible to start a long and complicated law-suit."

"That," said Mr. Pippet, "is, I guess, what the Doctor meant when he asked me if I still wanted to know what was in the coffin. But a nod is as good as a wink to a blind horse, and I was that blind horse. I rather wish I had left that durned coffin alone and taken it for granted that Josiah was inside. Still, we have got the monopoly of the information. is there any reason why we should not keep it to ourselves? What do you say, Superintendent?"

"The fact," replied Miller, "that there was no body in the coffin is of no importance to the prosecution, but I don't see how it can be burked. We shall have to produce the original coffin – or prove its existence. We needn't say that we have opened it, but the question might be asked in cross-examination, and we should have to answer it. But what is the objection to the fact being known? You have dropped the claim, and you don't intend to re-open it. Nobody will be any the worse."

"But I am afraid somebody may be," Mr. Pippet rejoined. He reflected a few moments and then continued, "We are all friends, as Mr. Brodribb has remarked, so I needn't mind letting you see how the land lies – from my point of view. You see, I embarked on this claim under the impression that the estates were going begging. I knew nothing of any other claimant. But when my sister and I saw Mr. Giles and his mother, we were a little sorry that we had started the ball. However, we had started it, and after all, there was my girl to consider. So we went on. But very soon it became evident that our two young people were uncommonly taken with each other, and then my sister and I were still more sorry, and we began to hope that our case might fall through. While matters were in suspense, however, Giles made no formal advances, though there was no concealment of his feelings towards my girl. But in the evening of the day when the Doctor obligingly knocked the bottom right out of my case, and showed us who the genuine heir-presumptive was, Giles asked my daughter to marry him, and naturally she said 'Yes'.

"And now you will see my point. Giles, with proper, manly pride, waited until he had something to offer besides his own very desirable person. He didn't want to come as a suitor with empty hands. When the prize was practically his, he asked Jenifer to share it with him. And I should have liked to leave it at that. And that was why I wanted that coffin opened. I had taken it as a cinch that Josiah was inside, and if he had been, that would have settled the question for good. Instead of which I have only confused the issues, as Mr. Brodribb says.

"Now, see here. I want this affair kept dark if it possibly can be. I want Giles to feel that the title and estates that he asked Jenny to share with him are his own by right, and not by anyone's favour. But that would be all spoiled if he got to know about this damned lead. For then he might reasonably suspect that I had voluntarily surrendered this claim for his benefit when I could, if I had pleased, have carried it to a successful issue. Of course, I couldn't have done anything of the kind. But that is what he might think. And he mustn't. There must be no fly in his ointment, and I look to you all to keep it out."

It is needless to say that we all listened with the greatest sympathy to Mr. Pippet's explanation, and we promised, so far as was possible, to suppress the fact that the coffin had been opened, which we were able to do with a clear conscience, since that fact was neither material nor even relevant to the charge of fraud against Gimbler.

"Naturally," said Mr. Pippet, when he had thanked us, "you will say that I ought to have thought of all this before I asked to have the coffin opened, but I am not so long-sighted as the Doctor. If you would like to call me a fool, I shan't contradict you."

"Thank you," laughed Thorndyke, "but I don't think I will avail myself of the permission. Still, I will remark that you allowed yourself to entertain a complete fallacy. You have spoken of my having knocked the bottom out of your case by my exposure of Gimbler's fraud. But that was not the position at all. The coffin which Gimbler produced as Josiah's coffin was not Josiah's coffin. Therefore it had no relevance to the issue.

651

It proved nothing, one way or the other, as to the condition of the real coffin. The effect of my evidence was purely negative. It simply rebutted Gimbler's evidence and thus restored the *status quo ante*. The judge, if you remember, drew your attention to this fact when he reminded you that Josiah's coffin had not been examined, and that the bogus funeral had been neither proved nor disproved."

"Well," said Mr. Pippet, "it has been proved now, and what I should like to know, just as a matter of curiosity, is what it really and truly means. Is it possible that the whole story was true, or was this just one of Josiah's little jokes?"

"I am afraid you will never know now," said Thorndyke.

"No," Pippet agreed. "Josiah has got us guessing. Of course, it doesn't matter now whether he was an earl or an inn-keeper, but if you have any opinion on the subject, I should like to hear it."

"Mere speculative opinions," said Thorndyke, "formed in the absence of real evidence, are not of much value. I really have nothing that one could call an opinion. All I can say is that, though the balance of probabilities for and against the truth of the story is nearly even, there seems to be a slight preponderance against, since, added to the general improbability of the story, is the very striking coincidence of Nathaniel Pippet of The Castle at Winsborough. But I am afraid we shall have to return an open verdict."

"And keep it to ourselves," added Pippet. "And now the practical question arises: What are we to do with this coffin?"

"I suggest," said Thorndyke, "that Polton closes it up as neatly as possible and that we then put it, with Gimbler's masterpiece, in the vault to which it properly belongs. We may hope that it may not be necessary to disturb that vault again, in which case no one need ever know that the coffin has been opened."

This suggestion being generally approved, was duly carried out. The two coffins were placed, side by side, on the shelf, and then Miller locked the door and dropped the key into his pocket. This done, the procession moved out of the burial ground, and the incident was formally closed when Miller slammed the outer gate and turned the key in the rusty lock.

We went back in the same order as that in which we had come. Mr. Pippet and Brodribb travelled in the former's car, and the rest of us occupied the roomy police car, Polton, at his own request, occupying the seat next to the driver where he could observe the mechanical arrangements and the operator's methods.

Chapter XX
Thorndyke Resolves a Mystery

Modern transport appliances have certain undeniable advantages, particularly to those who are principally concerned with rapidity of transit. But these advantages, like most of the gifts of "progress", have to be purchased by the sacrifice of certain other advantages. The Superintendent's car was, in respect of speed, incomparably superior to a horse carriage, but in the opportunity that it afforded for sustained conversation it compared very unfavourably with that obsolete type of vehicle. Thorndyke, however, not yet, perhaps, emancipated from the hansom cab habit, chose to disregard the inevitable interruption and, as the car trundled smoothly westward, remarked to Miller, "The subject of coffins, with which our minds are at present occupied, suggests, by an obvious analogy, that of a head in a box. I promised, a little while ago, to pass on to you any facts that I might unearth respecting the history of that head. I have looked into the matter and I think I now have all the material facts, and I may say that the affair turns out to be, in effect, what I had, almost from the first, supposed it to be."

"I didn't know," said Miller, "that you supposed it to be anything. I thought you were quite uninterested in the incident."

"Then," said Thorndyke, "you were mistaken. I watched the developments with the keenest interest. At first, when the head was discovered in the cloak room, I naturally assumed, as everyone did, that it was a case of murder and mutilation. But when I read the account of the inquest I began to suspect strongly that it was something quite different, and when I saw that photograph that you were so kind as to send me, I had very little doubt of it. You remember that photograph, Jervis?"

"Indeed I do," I replied. "A most extraordinary and abnormal mug that fellow had. There seemed to me to be a suggestion of acromegaly."

"A suggestion!" Thorndyke exclaimed. "It was a perfect type. That photograph might have been used as the frontispiece of a monograph of acromegaly. Its appearance, together with the physical and anatomical facts disclosed at the inquest, seemed to me quite distinctive. I came to the conclusion that this head was no relic of a crime, but simply a museum specimen which had gone astray."

"Good Lord!" exclaimed Miller, gazing at Thorndyke in amazement. I did not share his surprise, but merely felt an urgent desire to kick myself. For the thing was so ridiculously obvious – as soon as it was stated. But that was always the way with Thorndyke. He had the uncanny gift of seeing all the obvious things that everyone else overlooked.

"But," Miller continued, after a pause, "you might have given us the tip."

"My dear Miller," Thorndyke protested, "I had no tip to give. It was merely an opinion, and it might have been a wrong opinion. However, as I said, I watched developments most attentively, for there were at least two possibilities which might be foreseen, one by no means unlikely, the other almost fantastically improbable. The first was that some person might be accused of a murder which had never been committed, the other was that some real murderer might take advantage of the extraordinary opportunity that the circumstances offered. Curiously enough, it was the wildly improbable possibility that was actually realized."

"What was the opportunity that was offered?" Miller asked.

"It was the opportunity to commit a murder with almost perfect security from detection, with a whole set of false clues ready made, with the equivalent in time of a nearly watertight alibi."

"A murderer's chief difficulty," said Miller, "is usually in getting rid of the body. I don't see that the circumstances helped him in that."

"They helped him to the extent that he had no need to get rid of the body," Thorndyke replied. "Why does a murderer have to conceal the body? Because if it is found it will be recognized as the body of a particular person. Then the relations of the murderer to that person will be examined, with possibly fatal results. But supposing that a murderer could render the body of his victim totally unrecognizable. Then it would be the body of an unknown person, and all the persons related to it would be equally unknown. If he could go a step further and not only render the body unrecognizable but give it a false identity, he would be absolutely secure, for the body would now be related to a set of circumstances with which he had no connexion.

"This is the kind of opportunity that was offered by the discovery of this head. Let us study the conditions in the light of what actually happened. On a certain day in August, Wicks deposited in the cloak room a human head. Now, obviously, since it was brought there by Wicks, it could not be Wicks's head. Equally obviously, it must have been the head of some person who had died while Wicks was still alive.

654

Thus the death of that person was clearly dated in one direction, and since the head had been treated with preservatives, the date of death must have been some time anterior to that of its deposition in the cloak room. Again, obviously, there must be somewhere a headless body corresponding to this body-less head.

"Now, Bassett evidently intended to murder Wicks, for, as we saw, the murder was clearly premeditated. See, then, what a perfect opportunity was presented to him. If he could contrive to murder Wicks, to strip and decapitate the body and deposit it in a place where it would probably remain undiscovered for some time, when it was discovered, it would, quite naturally, be assumed to be the body belonging to the embalmed head. In other words, it would be assumed to be the body of some person who could not possibly be Wicks, and who had been murdered at some time when he, Bassett, was on the high seas. No slightest breath of suspicion could possibly fall on Bassett.

"But, as so constantly happens in the case of carefully planned crimes, one little point had been overlooked – or, rather, was unknown to the intending murderer. Strangely enough, it seems also to have been overlooked by everyone else, with the result that Bassett's scheme was within a hair's-breadth of working out exactly according to plan."

"As he was at the bottom of the dene hole," remarked Miller, "it didn't matter much to him whether it did or not."

"Very true," Thorndyke agreed. "But we are considering the plan of the crime. Now, when I read the report of the finding of the headless body, I realized that the fantastic possibility that I had hardly ventured to entertain had actually come to pass."

"You assumed that the headless body was a fake," said Miller, "and not the body belonging to the cloak room head. Now, I wonder why you assumed that."

"I did not," replied Thorndyke. "There was no assumption. The excellent newspaper report made it perfectly clear that the body found by the Watling Street could not possibly be the body belonging to the embalmed head. That head, let me remind you, was the head of a person who suffered from acromegaly. The body of that person would have been distinguished by atrophied muscles and enormous, mis-shapen hands and feet. But our admirable reporter specially noted that the body was that of a muscular man with strong, well-shaped hands. Then he certainly was not suffering from acromegaly.

"You see what followed from this. If this body did not belong to the cloak room head, it must belong to some other head. And that head was probably not far away. For, as no one suspected its existence, there was no need for any elaborate measures to hide it. As I happened to be aware of the existence of a number of dene holes in the immediate neighbourhood, it occurred to me that one of them probably contained the head and the clothes. Accordingly, I examined the six-inch map of the district, on which the dene holes are shown, and there I found that one of them was within four-hundred yards of the place where the body was discovered. To that dene hole I paid a visit after attending the inquest, having provided myself with a compass, a suitable lamp and a pair of night-glasses. I was not able to see very much, but I saw enough to justify our expedition. You know the rest of that story."

"Yes," replied Miller, "and a very interesting story it is. And now I should like to hear about these new facts that you have unearthed."

"You shall have them all," said Thorndyke, "though it is only a case of filling in details. I have told you what I decided – correctly, as it turns out – as to the nature of the mysterious head, that it was simply a pathological specimen illustrating the rare disease known as acromegaly, which had got into the wrong hands.

"Now, when one thinks of acromegaly, the name of Septimus Bernstein almost inevitably comes into one's mind. Dr. Bernstein is a world-famous authority on giantism, dwarfism, acromegaly, and other affections and anomalies of growth connected with disorder of the pituitary body. He is an enthusiast in his subject and gives his whole time and energy to its study. But what was still more important to me was the fact that he has a private museum devoted to the illustration of these diseases and anomalies. I have seen that museum, and a very remarkable collection it is, but, when I visited it, although it contained several gigantic and acromegalous skulls, there was no specimen of a head in its complete state.

"Naturally, then, I was disposed to suspect some connexion between this stray specimen and Dr. Bernstein. But this was pure hypothesis until I heard Bunter's statement. That brought my hypothesis concerning the head into the region of fact. For Bunter's description of the passenger on the yacht was a fairly exact description of Dr. Bernstein and, on the strength of it I was in a position to take the necessary measures to clear the matter up.

"Accordingly I called on Bernstein. I did not, in the first place, ask him any questions. I simply informed him that a preserved human head which he had imported, apparently from Holland, had been causing the police a good deal of trouble, and that it was for him to give a full and candid explanation of all the circumstances connected with it. The alternative was for the police to charge him with being in unlawful possession of certain human remains.

"My statement seemed to give him a severe shock – he is a nervous and rather timid man – but, though greatly alarmed, he seemed, in a way, relieved to have an opportunity to explain matters. Evidently, the affair had kept him in a state of constant apprehension and expectation of some new and horrible development, and he consented almost eagerly to make a full statement as to what had really happened. This is what his story amounts to:

"He had for years been trying to get possession of the head of some person who had suffered from acromegaly, partly for the purpose of studying the pituitary body more thoroughly and partly for the enrichment of his museum with a specimen which completely illustrated the effects of the disease. What he especially wanted to do was to remove the pituitary body without injuring the head and mount it in a specimen jar to accompany the jar containing the head, so that the abnormal condition of the pituitary and its effects on the structure of the face could be studied together."

"By the way," Miller asked, "what is the pituitary body?"

"It is a small body," Thorndyke explained, "situated at the base of the brain and lodged in a cavity in the base of the skull. Its interest – for our present purpose – lies in the fact that it is one of the so-called ductless glands and produces certain internal secretions which contain substances called hormones which are absorbed into the blood and seem to control the processes of growth. If the pituitary – or, at least, its anterior part – becomes overgrown, it appears that it produces an excess of secretion, with the result that either the whole body becomes overgrown and the sufferer develops into a giant, or certain parts only of the body, particularly the face and the extremities, become gigantic while the rest of the body remains of its normal size. That is a very rough account of it, just enough to make the matter intelligible."

"I think I have taken in the idea," said Miller, "and I'm glad you explained it. Now, I am able to feel a bit more sympathetic towards Dr. Bernstein. He isn't such an unmitigated cannibal as I thought he was. But let us hear the rest of the story."

"Well," Thorndyke resumed, "a short time ago, Bernstein heard from a Dutch doctor of a set of specimens, the very description of which made his mouth water. It appeared that an unclaimed body had been delivered for dissection at a medical school in a certain town in Holland. Bernstein asked to be excused from giving the name of the town, and I did not press him. But, of course, if it is essential, he is prepared to disclose the further particulars. On examining this body, it was found to present the typical characters of acromegaly, whereupon the pathologist decided to annex the head and extremities for the hospital museum and

657

return the remainder in the coffin. At the time when the information reached Bernstein, the specimens had not been put in the museum but were in the curator's laboratory in course of preparation.

"Thereupon, Bernstein started off, hot-foot, to see if he could persuade the pathologist to let him have the head. And his mission was obviously successful. What methods of persuasion he used, and what was the nature of the deal, he preferred not to say, and I did not insist, as it is no particular concern of ours. It would seem as if it must have been slightly irregular. However, he obtained the head, and having got it, embarked on the series of foolish proceedings about which Bunter told us. A bolder and more self-confident man would probably have had no serious difficulty. He would have travelled by an ordinary passenger ship and simply declared the head at the Customs as a pathological specimen. The Customs people might have communicated with the police, and there might have been some inquiries. But if there had been no secrecy there would have been no trouble."

"No," Miller agreed. "Secrecy was the stupidest thing possible under the circumstances, Why the deuce didn't he notify us, when the thing was found in the cloak room? It would have saved us a world of trouble."

"Of course that is what he ought to have done," said Thorndyke, "but the discovery took him unawares and, when he suddenly found himself involved in a murder mystery, he got in a panic and made things worse by trying to keep out of sight. He is in a mighty twitter now, I can assure you."

"I expect he is," said Miller, "and the question is, what is to be done? It's a queer case, in a legal sense. Have you any suggestion to make?"

"Well," said Thorndyke, "I think you should first consider what the legal position really is. You will admit that no crime has been committed."

"Apparently not," Miller agreed. "At any rate, not in British jurisdiction."

"Furthermore," pursued Thorndyke, "it is not clear to me that any offence against the law has been committed. Admittedly, Bernstein evaded the Customs, but, as a human head is not a customable commodity, there was no offence against the Revenue. And so with the rest of his proceedings, they were very improper, but they do not appear to amount to any definite legal offence."

"So I take it," said Miller, "that you think we might as well let the matter drop. I don't quite like that, after all the fuss and outcry there has been."

"I was hardly suggesting that," said Thorndyke. "I certainly think that, for the credit of the Force, the mystery ought to be cleared up in a more or less public manner. But, since you invite me to make a suggestion, I will make one. Perhaps it may surprise you a little. But what I think would be the best way to bring the case to a satisfactory conclusion would be for you to disinter the specimen – which I believe was buried temporarily, in the case in which it was found, in the Tower Hamlets Cemetery – have it examined and reported on by some authorized persons, verify Bernstein's statements so far as may be necessary and, if you find everything correct, hand the specimen back to Bernstein."

"My eye!" exclaimed Miller, "that's a pretty large order! But how could we? The head is not lawfully his property. No one is entitled to the possession of human remains."

"I am not sure that I can agree to that," Thorndyke dissented. "Not, at any rate, without certain reservations. The legal status of anatomical and pathological specimens in museums is rather obscure, and perhaps it has been wisely kept obscure. It is not covered by the Anatomy Act, which merely legalizes the temporary possession of a human body for the purpose of dissection. As you say, no one can establish a title to the possession of a human body, or part of one, as an ordinary chattel. But you know as well as I do, Miller, that sensible people turn a blind eye to this question on suitable occasions. Take the case of the Hunterian Museum of the Royal College of Surgeons. There, the anatomical and pathological collections are filled with human remains, all of which must have been acquired by methods which are not strictly legal. There are even the remains of entire individuals, some of whom are actually known by name. Now, if they were challenged, what title to the possession of those remains could the Council of the College establish? In practice, they are not challenged. Reasonable people tacitly assume a title.

"And that is what you would do, yourself. Supposing that someone was to steal the skeleton of the late Corporal Byrne, or O'Brian, the Irish Giant, which is in that museum, and supposing you were able to recover it, what would you do? Why, of course, you would hand it back to the museum, title or no title."

"Yes," Miller admitted, "that is so. But Bernstein's case is not quite the same. His is a private museum, and he wants this head as a personal chattel."

"The principle is the same," Thorndyke rejoined. "Bernstein is a proper person to possess this head, and he wants it for a legitimate purpose – for the advancement of medical knowledge, which is for the benefit of all. I insist, Miller, that, as a matter of public policy, this specimen ought to be given back to Bernstein."

Miller looked at me with an undissembled grin. "The Doctor can be mighty persuasive on occasion," he remarked.

"Still," I urged, "it is a perfectly reasonable proposition. You are concerned, primarily, with crime, but ultimately with the public welfare. Now, there hasn't been any crime, or any criminal intent, and it is against the public welfare to put obstacles in the way of legitimate and useful medical research."

"Well," Miller rejoined, "the decision doesn't rest with me. I must see what the Commissioner has to say. I will give him the facts, and you can depend on me to tell him what you say and to put your case as strongly as I can. He is not out to make unnecessary trouble any more than I am. So we must leave it at that. I will let you know what he says. If he falls in with your view, he will probably want your assistance in fixing up the details of the examination and the inspection of the specimen. You may as well give me Bernstein's address."

Thorndyke wrote the name and address down on one of his own cards and handed it to the Superintendent. And this brought the business to an end. The latter part of the conversation had been carried on in the stationary car, which had been drawn up in King's Bench Walk opposite our chambers. We now shook hands with Miller and got out and, as the car turned away towards Crown Office Row, we entered the wide doorway and ascended the stairs to our own domain.

Chapter XXI
Jervis Completes
the Story

The time has come for us to gather up the threads of this somewhat discursive history. They are but ends, and short ones at that, for, in effect, my tale is told. But even as the weaver's work is judged by the quality of the selvedge, so the historian's is apt to be judged by its freedom from loose ends and uncompleted episodes.

But since the mere bald narration of the few outstanding incidents would be but a dull affair, I shall venture (on the principle that the greater includes the less) to present an account of them all under cover of that which most definitely marked the completion of our labours: The establishment of the young Earl and his Countess in firm possession of the ancestral domain. For however thrilling may have been the alarums and excursions that befell by the way, they were but by-products and side issues of the Winsborough Peerage Case. With the settlement of that case we could fairly say that our work was done and, if disposed to tags or aphorisms, could take our choice between *Nunc dimittis* and *Finis coronat opus*.

It was a brilliant morning in that most joyous season of the year when late spring is merging into early summer, and the place was the spot upon the earth's surface where that season develops its most perfect loveliness – the south-east corner of Kent, or, to be more precise, the great lawn at the rear of the unpretentious mansion "known as and being" Winsborough Castle. Thither Thorndyke and my wife and I, together with Brodribb (who came also in his official capacity) had been invited to the house-warming on the return of the young Earl and Countess from their prolonged honeymoon. But we had not come as mere visitors, or even friends. The warm-hearted Jenifer had formally adopted us as members of the family, and as no one could ask for more delightful relatives, we had accepted the position gratefully.

As we strolled together across the sun-lit lawn, I glanced from time to time at the young couple with that sober pleasure which a middle-aged man feels in contemplating the too-rare spectacle of a pair of entirely satisfactory human beings. They were both far beyond the average in good looks, of splendid physique, gay and sprightly in temperament, and

661

gifted with the faultless manners that spring from natural kindliness and generosity coupled with quick intelligence. Looking at them, one could not but reflect pensively on the might-have-been, and think what a pleasant place the world would be if it could be peopled with their like.

"I wonder," said Jenny, "what has become of Pap and Uncle John." ("Uncle John" was Thorndyke)

"I don't," said Giles, "because I know, I saw them sneaking off together towards the churchyard. My impression is that they are trying to make a complete and exhaustive collection of ancestral Pippets."

Jenny laughed delightedly. "Inquisitive old things!" she exclaimed. "But I don't see why they need fuss themselves. There are no particular points about the ancestral Pippets. They never did anything worth speaking of excepting that they sold good beer – and, incidentally, they produced me."

"Not incidentally," Giles objected. "It was their crowning achievement. And I don't know what more you would have. I call it a deuced good effort."

The girl glanced at me with sparkling eyes. "Conceited young feller, isn't he, Uncle Kit? He will persist in thinking that his goose is a swan."

"He knows that she is," retorted Giles. "But, I say, Jenny. You'll have to keep an eye on Dad. What do you think he has done?"

She looked at him in mock alarm. "Break it gently," she pleaded.

"To my certain knowledge," said Giles, "he has taken over the lease of The Earl of Beaconsfield and he is having the sign changed back to The Castle Arms. What do you make of that?"

"My prophetic soul!" she exclaimed. "I see it all. He's going to have '*by C. Pippet*' written underneath the sign. If we don't mind our eyes, we shall have him behind the bar before we can say 'knife'. 'What's bred in the bone', you know."

Giles laughed in his delightful school-boy fashion.

"My word, yes!" he agreed. "We shall have to take a strong hand. We are not going to spend our lives under the Upas shadow of The Fox and Grapes. But I must hook off. Mr. Brodribb has got the bailiff chappie here – Mr. Solly – and they are going to rub my nose on all the things that they say a land-owner ought to understand. Brodribb insists that there is no eye like the master's eye, and I expect he is right, though I fancy I know an eye that is better still – to wit, the eye that adorns the countenance of the master's Pa-in-law. What are you going to do?"

"I," replied Jenny, "am going to extract a statement from Uncle Kit on the subject of the various happenings since we had Mr. Brodribb's summary. I want to know how it all ended."

"Good!" said Giles, "and when you have wormed all the facts out of him, you can pass them on to me. Now I'm off."

With a flourish of his hat and a mock-ceremonial bow, he turned and strode away across the turf towards the old brick porch, the very type and embodiment of healthy, virile youth. Jenny followed him with her eyes until he disappeared into the porch, then she opened her cross-examination.

"Now, Uncle K., you've got to tell me all you know about everything."

"Yes," I agreed, "that seems to offer some scope for conversation. Would you like to begin anywhere in particular?"

"I want, first of all, to know just exactly what has happened to poor Mr. Gimbler."

"Poor Mr. Gimbler!" I exclaimed. "You needn't waste your sympathy on a rascal like that."

"I know," said she. "Of course he is a rascal. But he did manage things so bee-yutifully."

Her tone jarred upon me slightly, and I think she must have observed something in my expression, for she continued, "You think I am taking a purely selfish view of the case, and I must admit that, as events have turned out, I am the greatest gainer by what Giles calls 'Mr. Gimbler's gimblings'. But I assure you, Uncle Kit, that Mr. Gimbler did the very best for us all. Pap loves him. He says he is going to give him a pension when he comes out of chokee – if that is where he is. I suppose it is."

"Yes," I replied. "Chokee is his present address,"

"I was afraid it was," said she. "The benefactor of humanity is languishing in a dungeon, and you don't care a hoot. You seem even to feel a callous satisfaction in his misfortunes. But see here, now, Uncle K., I want you to understand the benefits that he has showered on us. And, first of all, you've got to understand my father's position. You have got to realize that he never wanted the earldom at all. Pap is a thorough-bred American. He had no use for titles of nobility, and he was very clear that he didn't want to stand in the way of anyone else who had.

"But Auntie Arminella and I didn't take that view at all. We were as keen as mustard on an English title and a beautiful English estate, and Auntie started to stir my father up. He didn't take much stirring up. As soon as he realized that I wanted 'this toy', as he called it, and had ascertained, as he thought, that the title and estates were lying derelict and unclaimed, he decided to go for them all out. And when Pap makes a decision, he usually gets a move on, right away.

663

"Now, the first shock that he got was when he discovered that there was another claimant. Then he met Giles and his mother, and he fell in love with them both at first sight, as Auntie and I did. He didn't know how poor Giles was – he was actually working in a stockbroker's office, if you will believe me – but he realized that the decision of the court meant a lot more to Giles than it did to him, and he would have liked to back out of the claim."

"Why didn't he?" I asked.

"He couldn't. When once the claim had been raised, it had got to be settled. Giles didn't want the earldom as a gift, and Mr. Brodribb wouldn't have let the case drop, with the chance of its being re-opened in the future. So it had to go on. And now see what Mr. Gimbler did for us. Supposing he hadn't changed the coffins, and supposing the real one had been found to be stuffed with lead. It might have been. That would have gone a long way towards establishing my father's claim. Supposing the decision had gone in his favour. Then he would have been the Earl of Winsborough. And he would have hated it. Supposing I had married Giles – and I guess I should have had to ask him, myself, as he was a poor man and as proud as Lucifer – what would Pap's position have been? He would have defeated his own plans. He would have got the title for himself, and he would have kept his daughter and her husband out of it during his lifetime. But now, thanks to Mr. Gimbler, we have all got what we wanted. Pap has escaped the title, and he has the satisfaction of seeing his girl Countess of Winsborough."

I smiled at her quaint and somewhat wrong-headed way of looking at the case. But I refrained from pointing out that "Mr. Gimbler's gimblings" might easily have produced the undesired results but for Thorndyke's intervention. It was a dangerous topic, with my secret knowledge of what was in the real coffin, So I held my peace – or rather, led the conversation away from possible shoals and quicksands.

"By the way," I said, "if Giles had no money, who was going to pay his costs if he had lost the case?"

"I don't know," she replied. "We suspect dear old Brodribb. He told Giles and his mother that 'there were funds available', but he wouldn't say what they were. Of course, it is all right now. But you haven't told me what happened to Mr. Gimbler."

"You will be relieved to hear that he was let off quite lightly. Three years. It might easily have been seven, or even fourteen. Probably it would have been if we had included the forgery in the charges against him."

"I suppose it really was a forgery?"

"Yes, it was undoubtedly. For your father's satisfaction, we tested it chemically – but not until after the conviction. The ink was a modern synthetic drawing-ink. But it was a wonderfully skilful forgery."

"Pity," Jenny commented. "He is a really clever and ingenious man. Why couldn't he have run straight? But now tell me about the other people. There was an undertaker man, who made the coffin. What happened to him?"

"Joseph Wallis was his name. He also had better luck than he deserved, for he got only three months. It was originally proposed to charge him and Gimbler together with conspiracy. But there is this awkward peculiarity about an indictment for conspiracy in which only two persons are involved: If one of them is acquitted, the other is acquitted automatically. For a conspiracy is like a quarrel – it can't be a single-handed job. A man can't conspire with himself. So if, of two alleged conspirators, one is found innocent, it follows that there was no conspiracy, and the other man must be innocent, too.

"Now, Joseph pleaded that he had no knowledge of the purpose for which the coffin was required – thought it was a practical joke or a wager. And this plea was supported by Gimbler, who, in a statement to the police, declared that he never told Joseph what the coffin was really wanted for. Which seems likely enough. So the conspiracy charge against Joseph was dropped and, of course, it had also to be dropped in respect to Gimbler."

"I am glad," said Jenny, "that The Slithy Tove, as Giles calls him, was man enough to clear his confederate."

"Yes, it is something in his favour, though we must bear in mind that the Tove was a criminal lawyer – in more senses than one – and knew all about the law of conspiracy. Is there anything else that you want to know?"

"There was a man named Bunter, but I don't think he was much concern of ours, was he?"

"He was an invaluable link in the chain of evidence," I replied, "though he seems rather outside the picture. However, I can report favourably on his case, for he got off altogether. Nobody wanted his blood. The police accepted his explanation of his attempt to break into the yacht, *Cormorant*, for, though it was probably untrue, it was quite plausible. There remained only his complicity in the platinum robbery. But that had been committed outside British jurisdiction and, as the platinum had been recovered and restored to its lawful owners, and as the principal robbers were dead, no one was inclined to move in the matter. Accordingly, Mr. Frederick Bunter was released and went on his way rejoicing, with only one or two slight stains on his otherwise spotless character. And I think that completes the list, unless you can think of anything more."

"No," she answered, "I think that finishes up the history of the Winsborough Peerage Case. A queer story it is, looking back on it, with its ups and downs, its hopes and anxieties, to say nothing of one or two ugly passages."

"Yes," I agreed, "there have been some anxious moments. But all's well that ends well."

"Very true," said she. "And it has ended very well indeed, for me and for Giles, for our parents, and for Arminella. We have all got what we wanted most, we are all happy and contented, and we are all tremendously pleased with one another. It couldn't have ended better. And to think that we owe it all to poor Mr. Gimbler!"

I smiled, but I didn't contradict her. It was a harmless delusion. Perhaps it was not a delusion at all. At any rate, one might fairly say of Mr. Horatio Gimbler that he builded better than he knew.

The End

About the Author

Richard Austin Freeman was born on April 11th, 1862 in the Soho district of London. He was the son of a skilled tailor and the youngest of five children. As he grew, it was expected that he would become a tailor as well, but instead he had an interest in natural history and medicine, and so he obtained employment in a pharmacist's shop. While there, he qualified as an apothecary and could have gone on to manage the shop, but instead he began to study medicine at Middlesex Hospital.

Austin Freeman qualified as a physician in 1887, and in that same year he married. Faced with the twin facts of his new marital responsibilities and his very limited resources as a young doctor, he made the unusual decision to join the Colonial Service, spending the next seven years in Africa as an Assistant Colonial Surgeon. This continued until the early 1890's, when he contracted Blackwater Fever, an illness that eventually forced him to leave the service and return permanently to England.

For several years, he served as a *locum tenens* for various physicians, a bleak time in his life as he moved from job to job, his income low, and his health never quite recovered. However, he supplemented his meager income and exercised his creativity during these years by beginning to write. His early publications included *Travels and Live in Ashanti and Jaman* (1898), recounting some of his African sojourns.

In 1900, Freeman obtained work as an assistant to Dr. John James Pitcairn (1860-1936) at Holloway Prison. Although he wasn't there for very long, the association between the two men was enough to turn Freeman's attention toward writing mysteries. Over the next few years, they co-wrote several under the pseudonym *Clifford Ashdown*, including *The Adventures of Romney Pringle* (1902), *The Further Adventures of Romney Pringle* (1903), *From a Surgeon's Diary* (1904-1905), and *The Queen's Treasure* (written around 1905-1906, and published posthumously in 1975.)

In approximately 1904, Freeman began developing a mystery novella based on a short job that he had held at the Western Ophthalmic Hospital. This effort, "31 New Inn", was published in 1905, and it is the true first Dr. Thorndyke story. In 1907, the first Thorndyke novel, *The Red Thumb Mark*, was published.

From Thorndyke's creation until 1914, Freeman wrote four novels and two volumes of short stories. Then, with the commencement of the

First World War, he entered military service. In February 1915, at the age of fifty-two, he joined the Royal Army Medical Corps. Due to his health, which had never entirely recovered from his time in Africa, he spent the duration of the war involved with various aspects of the ambulance corps, having been promoted very early to the rank of Captain. He wrote nothing about Thorndyke during this period, but he did publish one book concerning the adventures of a scoundrel, *The Exploits of Danby Croker* (1916).

Following the war, he resumed his previous life, writing approximately one Thorndyke novel per year, as well as three more volumes of Thorndyke short stories and a number of other unrelated items, until his death on September 28th, 1943 – likely related to Parkinson's Disease, which had plagued him in later years. He is buried in Gravesend.

If you enjoy Dr. Thorndyke, then you'll love
The MX Book of New Sherlock Holmes Stories
Edited by David Marcum
(MX Publishing, 2015-   )

"This is the finest volume of Sherlockian fiction I have ever read, and I have read, literally, thousands." – Philip K. Jones

"Beyond Impressive . . . This is a splendid venture for a great cause!
– Roger Johnson, Editor, *The Sherlock Holmes Journal,*
The Sherlock Holmes Society of London

In Preparation
Part XXV – 2021 Annual

. . . and more to come!

The MX Book of New Sherlock Holmes Stories
Edited by David Marcum
(MX Publishing, 2015-   )

Publishers Weekly says:

Part VI: *The traditional pastiche is alive and well . . . .*

Part VII: *Sherlockians eager for faithful-to-the-canon plots and characters will be delighted.*

Part VIII: *The imagination of the contributors in coming up with variations on the volume's theme is matched by their ingenious resolutions.*

Part IX: *The 18 stories . . . will satisfy fans of Conan Doyle's originals. Sherlockians will rejoice that more volumes are on the way.*

Part X: *. . . new Sherlock Holmes adventures of consistently high quality.*

Part XI: *. . . an essential volume for Sherlock Holmes fans.*

Part XII: *. . . continues to amaze with the number of high-quality pastiches . . .*

Part XIII: *. . . Amazingly, Marcum has found 22 superb pastiches . . . This is more catnip for fans of stories faithful to Conan Doyle's original*

Part XIV: *. . . this standout anthology of 21 short stories written in the spirit of Conan Doyle's originals.*

Part XV: *Stories pitting Sherlock Holmes against seemingly supernatural phenomena highlight Marcum's 15th anthology of superior short pastiches.*

Part XVI: *Marcum has once again done fans of Conan Doyle's originals a service.*

Part XVII: *This is yet another impressive array of new but traditional Holmes stories.*

Part XVIII: *Sherlockians will again be grateful to Marcum and MX for high-quality new Holmes tales.*

Part XIX: *Inventive plots and intriguing explorations of aspects of Dr. Watson's life and beliefs lift the 24 pastiches in Marcum's impressive 19th Sherlock Holmes anthology*

Part XX: *Marcum's reserve of high-quality new Holmes exploits seems endless.*

Part XXI: *This is another must-have for Sherlockians.*

The MX Book of New Sherlock Holmes Stories
Edited by David Marcum
(MX Publishing, 2015-   )

 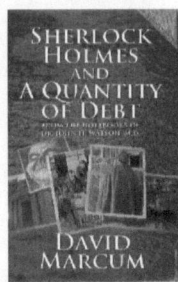 

Sherlock Holmes in Montague Street
by Arthur Morrison
Edited, Holmes-ed, and with Original Material
by David Marcum

Separate Paperback Editions

Combined Hardcover Edition

*"It's been suggested that Hewitt was the young Mycroft Holmes,
but David Marcum has a more plausible and attractive theory
– that he was Sherlock, early in his career as an investigator
. . . these are remarkably convincing in their new guise."*
– Roger Johnson, Editor, *The Sherlock Holmes Journal*,
The Sherlock Holmes Society of London

MX Publishing

MX Publishing is the world's largest specialist Sherlock Holmes publisher, with several hundred titles and over a hundred authors creating the latest in Sherlock Holmes fiction and non-fiction.

From traditional short stories and novels to travel guides and quiz books, MX Publishing caters to all Holmes fans.

The collection includes leading titles such as *Benedict Cumberbatch In Transition* and *The Norwood Author*, which won the 2011 *Tony Howlett Award* (Sherlock Holmes Book of the Year).

MX Publishing also has one of the largest communities of Holmes fans on *Facebook*, with regular contributions from dozens of authors.

www.mxpublishing.co.uk (UK) and *www.mxpublishing.com* (USA)

www.ingramcontent.com/pod-product-compliance
Lightning Source LLC
Chambersburg PA
CBHW030737030726
47497CB00001B/22